Lost Lyrebird

THE HARBINGERS OF CHAOS SERIES

DARBY BRIAR

Published by Darby Briar 2025

CREDITS

HOC Insignia: Andrea Macedo

Editing: Roz Kelly & Book Bunny Editing

Formatting: Dream Echo Designs

Audiobook produced by Blue Nose Productions

Voice Actors: Heather Firth and Joe Arden

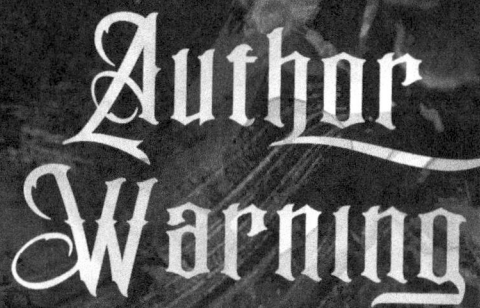

Author
Warning

This book is a walk-in-the-sunshine-holding-hands romance story, but it also contains depravity, dark matter, and heartbreak. There is a wealth of villainy and love.

Pieces of my own puzzle are littered throughout these pages. I hope you can identify with the symbolism I weaved through this story. These symbols hold significant meaning for me, and I hope you carry them forward with you.

These TRICKS are not for kids, folks. Intended for adults and those over the age of 18. Please also mind your mental health and read through the triggers to make sure this book is suitable for you. The **trigger warnings** will be listed at the back of the book, so feel free to check them out if you prefer to know what you're getting into.

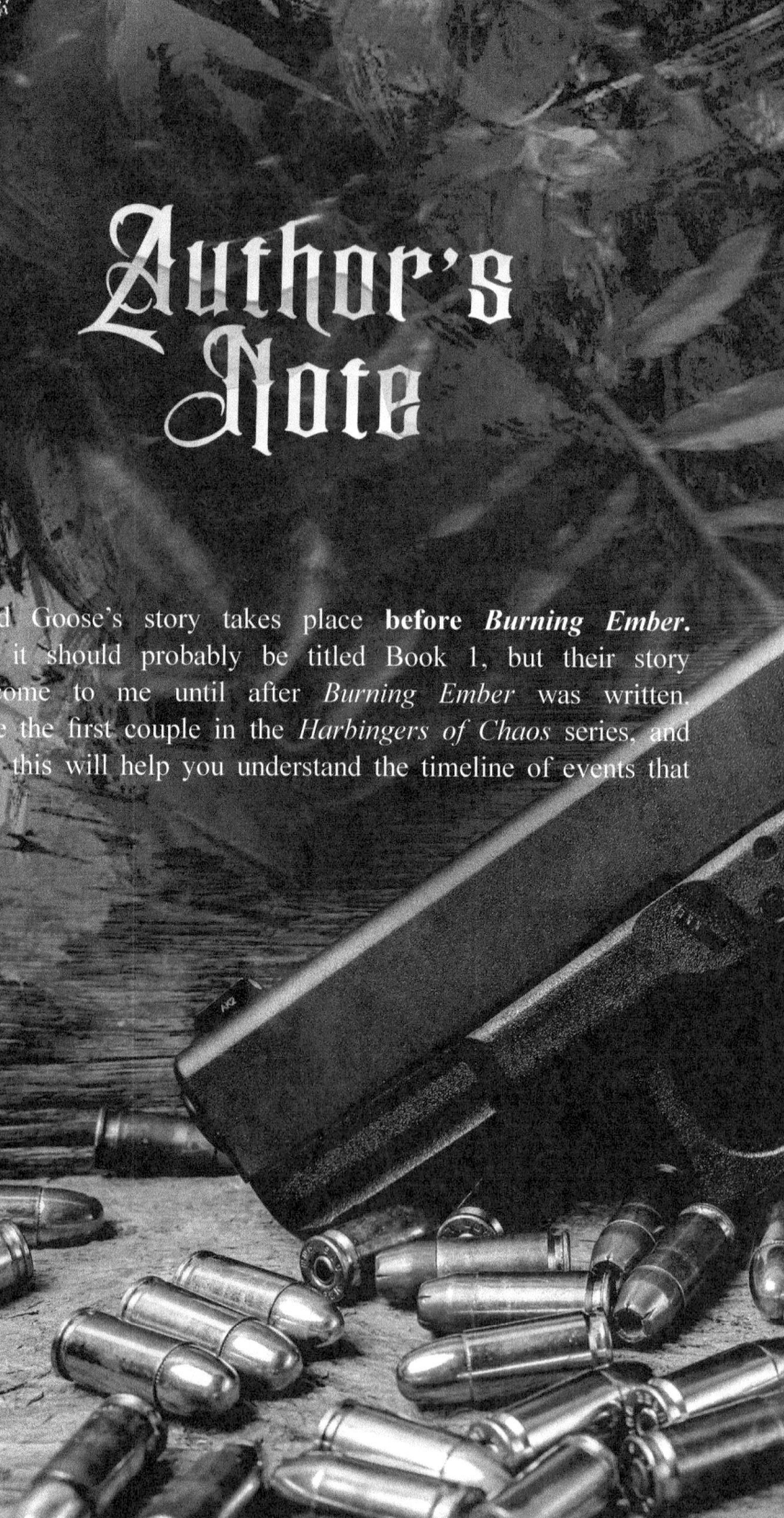

Author's Note

Lily and Goose's story takes place **before** *Burning Ember*. In fact, it should probably be titled Book 1, but their story didn't come to me until after *Burning Ember* was written. They are the first couple in the *Harbingers of Chaos* series, and knowing this will help you understand the timeline of events that follow.

Playlist

This is meant to be more than a book.
The book, audiobook, and playlist will all give you the full
Lost Lyrebird experience.
I recommend listening to *Outlaws & Outsiders*
by Cory Marks, Travis Tritt, Ivan Moody & Mick Mars
and
Lost Birds
by Zeds Dead & Elliot Moss,
before starting this story.

https://open.spotify.com/
playlist/5onkzxhW4CMh7YfkGvd1vj?si=61d990101a374c50

TO MY FREE BIRD.

OUR STORY WASN'T SOMETHING

ANYONE COULD CALL PERFECT,

BUT THERE WAS A LIFETIME OF LOVE.

THANK YOU FOR HOLDING MY HAND

THROUGH THIS JOURNEY.

No matter how long the journey or
how harsh the weather, birds will brave
many dangers to find their way home

Part one

Finn

Prologue

Some things in life are worth turning your back on heaven for.

NOVEMBER 1997

The air is thick with the stench of sulfur, gasoline, and copper. It's choking my lungs as an eerie stillness hangs inside the transport. The kind that presses in on you, forcing you to acknowledge your worst nightmare. We're a twisted pile of limbs, weapons, smoke, fire, and body parts. Blood—dark and vivid—coats everything, the aftermath of being tossed around like ragdolls in an exploding metal coffin.

Beyond the utter despair and fear riding me, I also feel relief. I'm alive, and by the sounds I'm hearing, I'm not the only one.

A rustle of fabric. A moan. A cough. The gasping for breath. Tell-tale signs that someone else survived.

But from where I lie crumpled in the footwell, I can't see shit. No idea who it is. Gritting my teeth, I shove the agony aside. There's no time for it. Men are missing. Seats torn out. The driver's side is just... fucking gone. Flames lick at the edges of where the door used to be. The heat sears my skin the closer I crawl toward the backseat.

Moving sends searing pain hammering down my lower back, but

I fight through it. When I finally see into the backseat, the sight of what I see guts me, and I swallow hard to force down bile rising in my stomach.

A black pit of grief rolls through me. I shake my head over and over, my knuckles turning white as I fight off the useless tears.

These men… they were good men. They have families. And some will never return to them.

I reach out, grabbing a hand. My eyes trace it to a face—Brady. That broad smile of his flashes in my mind. Twenty-nine, and a newlywed. The kind of guy who had a bright future. I grip his blood-slicked hand, wishing with everything I am that I could turn back time.

"Fuck, man. Just fuck."

I sit with him a moment and send up a prayer, then I let go of his hand and focus on the sounds. The living. That's who needs me right now.

A low groan, followed by a hand slapping over the top of the seat, sends my heartbeat into overdrive. Ignoring the pain, I drag myself over the middle console.

A bloody blond head pops up. Blue eyes meet mine. "My own gun, man," Rivers gasps, voice ragged. "Nearly fucking impaled me. And the damn seatbelt… almost cut me in half." He dips his chin to indicate the wound to his shoulder, which is bad. Then his eyes flick past me, to the wreckage. His usual grin is gone, dimples inverted into a deep frown. His jaw flexes, nostrils flaring as he sucks in a slow, shaky breath. When he hauls himself over the seat, I examine the severity of the gash across his eyebrow. Blood is streaming down his face, mixing with the dirt and sweat. But it's the way his eyes widen once he gets a better look at me that has a rock forming in the pit of my stomach.

"Fuck, Sarg," he mutters, voice low, head tilted. "You're bleeding like hell."

Yeah, I figured. My skull feels like it's been split wide, wedged open by a fucking crowbar. It's everything I can do not to let the agony riddling my body drag me under. "Just a scratch," I lie, even though blood is pouring down my neck in a steady flow.

"Scratch?" He shakes his head. "You've got a damn crater in your skull."

"I'm still breathing," I say.

"Yeah, but—"

"And I'd like to stay that way, so let's focus on getting the fuck out of here."

His camo is soaked, the right side of his body painted red. Blood spreads from his jacket down to his pant leg. I can't help but think that if he's the most mobile of us, we're fucked.

I nod toward the massive gash in his shoulder. "We're gonna need to patch that."

"I'm still breathing," Rivers replies, as if mocking me.

A barrage of bullets pings against the metal exterior in rapid succession. Glass shatters. We both duck to avoid being hit. Thankfully, the onslaught ends without either of us taking a bullet.

It lights a fire under us, sparks a sense of urgency. We need to get the fuck out of here.

"We've got minutes—maybe—before they come to finish the job."

He nods. "Let's med up and get ready to move."

Fighting the fog clouding my vision, I say, "Find the med kit if you can. I'll patch you up first—don't want you passing out from blood loss on me."

We both freeze at the sound of movement.

"Jesus! Ahh… my leg! My fucking leg!"

Our heads snap to the back of the Humvee. Larsen is sitting upright. He's covered in blood and soot.

"Damn, Lars. I thought you were a goner," Rivers says, crawling into the back so he can reach him. "Hey—calm down. Don't touch it," he scolds.

"My fuckin' leg, Riv."

Rivers digs through the supplies and gets to work, trying to stabilize what's left of Larsen's leg. It's a goddamn mess—barely held together. This is just a stopgap, and we all know it.

At one point, Larsen hisses, "Just leave me."

"Shut up," Rivers snaps, not looking up from his work. "None of that shit."

"I'm seriou—"

"We're all getting out of here," I cut him off. When that doesn't stave off Larsen's panic, I add,

"Nico and Sasha. They need you, man. You give up now, you're giving up on them. Don't you want to see their faces again?"

Larsen's eyes meet mine and hold. He sucks in a long breath, then nods rapidly to Rivers. His nostrils flare as his pain-fueled despair slowly subsides. "Okay, do what you need to do."

Seeing the will to live come back into his eyes floods me with relief. And though it hurts like hell to move, I do. I push through the pain to get closer to him and clasp his hand with mine, and pour every ounce of my strength into him. He squeezes my hand in a death grip to make it through the worst of it.

Rivers works fast as Larsen curses him out, all the while muttering, "Push through, Lars. We'll get you back to your wife and kid."

When Rivers finishes, he patches me up, and then we address the next problem. He can't carry both of us, and neither of us can stand, much less walk. I tell him to take Larsen first and come back for me. He doesn't like it, but he follows my orders.

Rivers gears up, loading himself with weapons and ammo, then drags Larsen to the doorway and prepares to make a run for it. Before they disappear, he looks back over his shoulder, and his blue eyes lock with mine. "Hang tight, Sarg. I'll be back for you before you know it."

I nod and say, "Go. Get him out."

To Larsen, River says, "On three. I'll be your legs. You fire every round you've got at those motherfuckers."

The second they're gone, I start praying—hard—that some guardian angel is watching over them, helping them dodge the bullets I know are coming. Then I sit alone in what feels like a metal coffin surrounded by the dead, and hope like my life depends on it that I don't become one of them.

I wake to a fog—real or in my head, I can't tell.

Did Rivers get us out?

I force myself to sit up fully, testing my body for damage. Pain ripples through me—sharp but also distant, like a knife buried too deep for too long. My legs tingle, my muscles still scream in protest. But it's duller, as if I'm numbed from it.

Off-balance and trembling, I manage to get to my feet.

"Finn."

I shiver at the sound of the voice. I tell myself it has to be off due to the echo. But why is he talking so low, so quiet? And why is he using my given name?

"I'm here, man. Where you at?"

"Finn."

"Yeah, man. Right here," I call out again.

The more I focus on the voice, the clearer it becomes. The deep, raspy baritone strikes an old chord, triggering memories. This isn't Rivers. And I have no business hearing this voice, because the man it belongs to I buried only a few short months ago.

My senses scramble to make sense of the thick fog around me, searching for movement, something to orient myself. I try clearing the mist with a sweep of my arm, but each time, more haze fills the space.

I step forward cautiously, and eventually, the sand beneath my boots stops shifting. It turns solid, like wood or stone. The stillness stirs unease deep in my gut. Then it hits me—the oppressive, stifling heat of the Iraqi desert has vanished. The air no longer tastes of copper, sulfur, and gasoline. My fatigues aren't clinging to my sweat-soaked skin.

The voice calls out again, as if nowhere and everywhere all at once. No matter which direction I turn, I get no closer.

The fog thins, and the scent around me changes. It's teakwood and pine. Home.

My chest aches, not from the pain—though the pain is there, a fuck-ton of it, especially at the back of my head—but from loss. It dawns on me then that when I turn around, I'll see something that will hit me square in the chest.

But I have to look.

When my father finally steps into view, the sadness in his eyes shakes me to my core.

"No," I say, shaking my head.

I sense it too. The wrongness of it. I don't belong here. But how can I deny what I'm seeing? My father's face is the same but different— more youthful. His onyx hair is full and thick, just a slight wave, like my own.

The thought would be comforting if it weren't for what it means to see him again.

He strides toward me, and as he closes in, I start forward to meet him.

When we collide, it's like two boulders crashing together. I melt into the embrace I thought I'd never feel again. His hug is the kind only a bear of a man can give to his grown son. The peace in that moment is everything. It fills the cracks in my heart that have been there since the day he died. The day I held his fragile hand as he slipped away.

The fights. The harsh words. Everything I never said. In that hug, it's all forgiven and forgotten. It's the best thing I've felt in months.

"You're not supposed to be here," he says gruffly, pulling me even tighter. I don't mind one bit.

"Honestly, I don't understand what's happening."

He grunts, a sound that carries so much weight.

"Is this… it, then?" I ask.

I feel more than see him shake his head. "No."

"Then what? I don't understand."

He pulls back, one hand gripping the back of my neck as our eyes meet. His stare drinks me in, his jaw tight with something like pain.

I try to finish my thought, but the words won't come. "Am I…?"

His eyes narrow, grief lining his face. He touches my cheek, my jaw, then lets his hand drop to my shoulder, gripping it tightly. "I'm sorry."

"It's not your fault."

He stands two inches taller than me, and I remember how, as a kid, he seemed like a giant.

He shakes his head again, his voice thick. "Not for this. For the time we never had. The time we don't have now. For the time we wasted."

"Dad… what time? I don't understand. Am I… dead? Because I can't… I can't be. There's someone… someone I made a promise to. I told her… nothing would stop me from making it home."

He smiles, just barely, one corner of his mouth lifting as he nods, but the grief never leaves his eyes. "I know. Your little bird."

Choked up now, I say, "Yeah, Dad. My little bird. She's waiting for me."

"Go to her, son."

I stare at him, trying to make sense of it all.

"I love you. You know that?" His voice cracks. My throat tightens as he turns his head, nodding toward the misty horizon to his right. "You need to fight, Finn. It won't be easy, but you can make it back. If we had more time, I'd tell you everything, but we don't. Just know I love you, and I'm so fucking proud of the man you've become. Keep helping the people who need it most. Keep pushing for what's right."

I place my hand over his on my shoulder, squeezing. When I finally nod, he grabs me in another fierce hug. I relish it. He pats my back, and I swear his touch lingers like a brand after we part.

"Go, son. I'm good here. I'll see you again when it's time."

So I do. I take one step. Then another. When I glance back, he's watching me with steely blue eyes, arms folded over his chest. His expression holds so much emotion, but his shoulders are drawn back, a stubborn stance I'd known as a kid—a sign there's no point in arguing further.

"Keep your promise to her."

I nod, and focus on what lies ahead, not what I'm leaving behind. Step after step, I move toward the promise I never intended to break.

A promise to a little bird, a woman who needs me more than he ever did.

Lily

CHAPTER 1

If our mind tells us what's real, who are we to judge?

JULY 2002

Spreading his thighs, I bend my knees, bringing my face level with Deeds's jean-clad erection. The position no doubt gives half the room a glimpse of my G-string. Not that it deters me—in fact, it spurs me on.

There's something about seducing a lethal man that makes me feel powerful. Seducing a clubhouse full of them? That's like a hit of crack for my ego, unlike anything you could imagine, and addicting as hell.

The flare of lust in his hazel eyes pinned on me tells me he feels it too. The sexual tension between us fuels the energy in this smoke-filled room. Envy of him coils in the air, silent but palpable.

It's intoxicating, this unique little gift I have. For so long, I saw my beauty as a curse.

I wasted years hiding it. Denying it. Deeds made me realize it didn't have to be that way. I could mold a man's lust and reshape it into something that benefits me instead of letting it be the thing that brings about my downfall.

He showed me how to wield it—and have a whole lot of fun doing so. And that's precisely what I do now: perform for the mass of people gathered inside the clubhouse, and give this man a lap dance worthy of an audience.

Nearly everyone here is fucked up in some way or another—if not on the drugs being passed around, then on the liquor flowing freely at the bar. Exhaustion clings to them, but they're far too happy to be home to care about sleep.

Some old ladies remain. The rest are women who exist here for one reason—to relieve the men's tension. I came tonight to do the same and help Deeds unwind. Except, as always, my nature got the best of me.

As the song shifts, I straddle his lap, my skirt riding up in the process. His hands grip my ass, yanking me forward so my core rubs over his hard-on.

Grabbing his wrists, I push his hands away, tutting. "Uh-uh-uh."

He growls in response, the drugs making him impatient. Usually, he loves our games as much as I do, but tonight, he's worked up, horny as hell, and ready to get between my thighs. I'm not necessarily opposed to that. But I'm the kind of person who plays with the frosting of a decadent cake before eating a slice. I play with my food and my men, taking as much pleasure as I can before devouring my meal.

Swiveling my hips, I ride him hard enough to leave a trace of my arousal on his jeans. My fingers find their way into his hair, gripping tight as I tilt his head back.

A deep groan rumbles out of his chest. "Fuck… Gypsy Girl. You're a menace when you get like this." His words are raspy, dripping with lust.

I bring my face closer to his, breathing out a wicked laugh. I bite his bottom lip and let it pop free of my teeth. "You know you like it."

He sits up, twists my long hair around his fist, and yanks. Tit for tat. "You're damn right I do. Now, are you gonna ride my dick or dick me around all night?"

Scraping my teeth across my bottom lip, I think it over.

"Sweet girl," Cecil drawls, pulling my gaze towards him. "You plannin' to rub up on our prince all night, or share the love?" Half-turning, I pause. My gaze travels over him. He's a striking male, masculine as all get-out, with long, dirty-blond hair pulled back into a ponytail.

"That depends." I grin. "What do you have in mind?"

"Not tonight, man. Been a long week, and I need a little one-on-one time with our little Gypsy here, if you know what I mean." Deeds emphasizes his point by planting his hands firmly on my thighs. He trails kisses up my neck, leaving a bit of beard burn in his wake.

Cecil clicks his tongue. "That's too bad. Another time?"

I give him a playful wink. "You can bet on it."

Deeds bites down on my earlobe. "Nope. Not happening," he mutters against my skin.

I pull back, scowling. "Why not?"

"Because."

"Because?"

He gives me a pointed look. "Because I said so."

I roll my eyes in irritation. Technically, I'm what the Greenbacks consider a clubpiece—meant to be shared. I open my mouth to say this, but it will instigate a fight, and the fallout isn't worth it. Deeds temper, once triggered, is unpredictable.

On the flip side, he is a potent drug when relaxed or happy, one I love to indulge in from time to time. If we get into it over this petty shit, then I can kiss tonight's fun goodbye.

Deeds—*Decker* to his mama, *Sonny Boy* to a few of the old-timer Greenbacks he grew up both fearing and idolizing—is more than just nice to look at. He has a wealth of muscle, tight abs, freckled shoulders, and porn-worthy biceps, riddled with colorful tattoos. He doesn't share the full lilt of his father's Irish accent, but speaks Gaelic on occasion. He uses it to seduce me, which is like wildfire to my pussy.

A definite perk to our friends-with-benefits situation.

He's like an Irish James Dean, if James Dean were taller, more built, and had long, dark-auburn hair.

"You gonna take me out, Gypsy Girl, and wrap those sweet lips around me, or let me fuck you?"

I let an evil grin slip onto my lips. Because fuck him if he thinks I'll go down that easily tonight. Instead, I run my fingers through his hair, massaging his scalp, using his weakness against him. He groans, and his body goes boneless under my ministrations. He melts back into the couch, his head kicking back in pleasure.

He pierces me with a smoldering stare as he murmurs, "I swear to God, you're a witch."

I close the distance between our mouths. The scent of Jameson on his lips amps up my need to taste him. "You love it, so don't play like you don't. You want a villain at night and an angel in the morning."

His cock jumps beneath me at my taunt, and in the next instant, he grips my jaw and pulls me into a kiss that's damn near abusive, stealing all thoughts from my head.

A chorus of shouts pulls me out of the force of nature that is Decker Pierce. The noise comes from a dozen or so bikers funneling in from the lobby.

The newcomers are a mixed bag—men of all shapes and sizes. They blend in with the Greenbacks easily, but their jackets, their "colors," tell me they're not another chapter—they're another club entirely.

A few head toward the Greenbacks at the bar. Half a dozen break off to join the party in the main lounge area. Hugs are exchanged, backs slapped, and some kisses given by the old-timers.

Something about the man-on-man action sends small tingles through my body, making me question if I'm a big voyeur or just turned on by anything taboo. Maybe a little of both.

Pappy, aka Dean Pierce, leader and President of the Greenbacks and Deeds's father, is one of them. He grabs an older blond man, smushes his cheeks, and plants a big kiss straight on his lips. The other man sputters, laughs, and pushes him off, before they throw their arms around each other and sidle up to the bar.

Honestly, it's the most I've ever seen Pappy smile. Usually, he's all doom and gloom and murderous deadpan stares.

A guy breaks off from the group, one with bright-red hair speckled with grays, and a long, wiry beard. He heads straight for us. When he arrives, he addresses Deeds with no fanfare. "You gonna kindly remove the scorchin' hot bunny from your lap and greet your uncle properly?" He flashes me a sexy smile. "Sorry, darlin', but I need a hug from this here little shit."

Deeds laughs heartily. He quickly removes me from his lap and gets to his feet. "Who you callin' a little shit, old man? I'm twenty-nine, or is that old brain of yours already losin' time?"

"Hardy-har-har, little fucker. I see your old man hasn't beatin' that smart mouth outta ya."

Deeds hugs him and slaps his uncle's shoulder as he draws back. "Lord knows he tried. But no. Got plenty of it for when your old ass finally shows up and when Mom tries to set me up with a"—he uses air quotes as he says—"nice girl." This has me sharing a conspirator's grin with Deeds because his mother's matchmaking schemes are legendary.

When the man turns, I get a good look at the club's insignia on the back of his jacket. It reads, "Harbingers of Chaos" across the top rocker and "New Mexico" across the bottom.

I vaguely recall Deeds mentioning the HOCs, but in my mind, it had been *Hawks,* not an abbreviated name for the club. And, if I'm remembering correctly, Deeds's uncle was a founding member of the Greenbacks. Due to some kind of rift, he and another founder split, and they started their own club.

It's surprising because most MCs don't have an exit door. Not unless you count the one that leads six feet under. Men like these don't fuck around when it comes to protecting their secrets.

The insignia, the larger patch on the back of his leather cut, depicts a demented skull sitting between ragged wings, with arrows shooting out in all directions.

Wings and arrows.

I love both.

My body is tattooed with several of them. They all have different sayings and meanings. Like the one on my forearm, an arrow with a small dreamcatcher tied to the end with two feathers trailing behind it as if caught in the wind.

A little reminder that *when life is dragging you back to launch yourself forward.*

I contemplate that as the two men chat. I've always seen moments like this as signs, not just random coincidences. Like with tarot readings, I search for hidden meanings in small things and symbols. Then I try to figure out how they connect to my life or circumstances.

So, using my knuckles, I count the months that have gone by since Deeds convinced me to move here. I'm taken aback when I realize it's been over a year.

I met him when I'd been working in Vegas, dancing my ass off, trying to make my way up the ranks to bigger and better things. Deeds had been setting up a new chapter in the area. We hooked up a few times, and he eventually discovered I had a few men giving me trouble. Some guys I'd dated or met while dancing there. Men who didn't want to take no for an answer when I turned them down or broke things off. He handled them, and we'd been on and off ever since until he convinced me to move here to San Diego and work for the club.

I'd hesitated for a while, not wanting to get sucked into the madness this lifestyle entails, but trouble followed me no matter where I went, I thought it might be good to have men like him at my back, just in case.

The redheaded HOC slaps Deeds's chest. "You gonna be the gentleman your mama raised you to be and introduce me?"

Smiling, I scoot to the end of the couch to get up. Before I can, Deeds's uncle assists me. He immediately brings my hand to his mouth and kisses my knuckles.

"Hello, darlin'." The drawl in those words nearly sets my panties aflame. It's that fucking sexy.

"None of that." Deeds snatches my hand away. "I've been on the road for days. No way am I lettin' you haul her off or sweet talk her with that sweet southern-boy thing you do."

His uncle grins wickedly at me, and I grin right back. He winks, and right away, I know I've found a kindred spirit. So I saddle up to his side, curl my arm around his, and lay my head on his shoulder. I blink up at Deeds innocently, and his uncle plays along, placing his large hand over mine and patting it.

Deeds pinches the bridge of his nose. Under his breath, he mutters,

"Fuck. Should've known you two would get along. Both pains in my ass."

We laugh, and he joins in.

Deeds motions to me. "Uncle Griz, this is Gypsy. Gypsy, meet my mean—"

Reaching forward, Griz slaps the back of Deeds's head. He's probably the only person in the world who could get away with it. "Boy, I will take you over my knee."

"Please don't," I say. "He'd like that too much." Deeds eyes the two of us and groans.

We spend the next few minutes laughing and bullshiting until Griz politely asks to steal his nephew for a bit. After they walk away, I make my way to the bar and order a drink.

It doesn't take long before my gaze returns to the HOC insignia, which is kind of badass and fascinating. It's filled with a variety of different symbols. There's a skull with a third eye and bird-like clawed feet that grip a pirate banner. The banner reads, "Revel in Chaos, Regret Nothing."

It's more pleasant to look at than the Greenback colors—a demented, demon-like leprechaun with missing teeth standing over a pile of skulls and bones. According to Deeds, Pappy designed it to lay claim to their Irish roots, instill fear in the "squares" who judged their lifestyle, and as a "fuck you" to those who openly opposed the war the founders nearly died in.

I'm just finishing my drink when hands wrap around my waist. A warm body presses against my back. Hot breath ghosts over my neck, sending a rush of goosebumps down my arms. "See somethin' you like?"

Looking over my shoulder, I study Deeds's expression and the curiosity written all over his features.

"I thought you weren't in the mood to share?"

He shrugs. "I'm not, but if that's what you need…"

It's times like these when I get frustrated with him. One day, he's possessive, and the next, he's setting me free to explore to my heart's content. Always a contradiction. Which is it? Does he even know?

Because it's confusing as fuck and leaves me with mental whiplash.

He's the opposite of Finn in every way.

God, *Finn.*

He was always brutally honest, steadfast, and had clear intentions. I see his face in my mind and feel an instant ache in my chest. His name lives in my heart, under an invisible scar that didn't heal right, and even thinking about his name hurts. It reopens that old wound.

Deeds turns me around, hands gripping my hips tightly. He brings our lower bodies together and stares at me in a way that would have most women swooning. He slowly draws me back to the couch. After lighting up a joint, we pass it back and forth, and resume our playful foreplay. I eventually end up in a reverse cowgirl position with his mouth running up the length of my neck.

I work him up, slowly rolling my hips above him. He takes matters into his own hands, pushes down his pants to mid-thigh, and frees himself from his jeans. My skirt is pushed up, and his fingers tease my clit in lazy circles. As the song hits the chorus, he pushes one, then two fingers inside me.

In no time at all, he's teasing the tip of his cock back and forth over my entrance. It's a punishment for what I did to him earlier. As my need grows, I sink my nails into his thigh and reach around to grab a handful of his hair. He plays with the tension, taking his time, before notching himself in place, then pulls me down onto his cock.

He lets the hard beat of the song set the pace. On each downward thrust, I tighten my inner walls around him.

A sound of both pleasure and pain leaves him. "Jesus Christ, this fuckin' body."

I get lost in the sensations of it all, the desire his strokes ignite, the pulsing song, the scent of sex, the thrill of being watched. It's pure adrenaline, and it has me spiraling.

"Yeah, keep moving just like that. Just. Like. That. Fuck, yes. I love watching this ass bounce over me. Cuireann tú mo mheabhair as, a ghrá!"

You drive me out of my mind, love.

One side of my shirt is pushed aside, baring my breast. He fondles and squeezes my nipple between his fingers, bringing the pain he knows I need. He keeps me open and exposed to the entire room. And though it shouldn't, it has me flying on a high only rough sex can bring.

When he bites down on my earlobe, I let out a desperate whimper and draw every biker's gaze in the vicinity to me.

"Fuck. Yes, harder."

And yet, in the back of my mind, a little voice scolds me and says I must be mad to want this.

A little insane.

To prove my point, my mind spins a familiar daydream. I picture Finn standing among them—black hair, shiny with a few premature gray streaks that he once said ran in his family. He'd look so fucking sexy in leather, like that guy at the bar with a wallet chain, studded belt, ripped jeans, and tattoos.

God, yes. Black-as-night tattoos.

The vision pushes me closer to release, and it only takes a few seconds to have me on the brink.

I hold the image of Finn in my mind, savoring the daydream behind my eyelids. I think about that one night we shared, and it sends me into orbit, a space where pleasure meets euphoria.

Deeds, oblivious, gives me exactly what I crave—he rams himself inside of me, collars my throat with his large hand, and cuts off a little of my air. I fuck him so hard there's pain. Maybe because my heart is hurting, and I want to hurt everywhere else too.

"Uh-uh… right… there." Nothing but hoarse words leave my lips, hardly audible over the loud music. "Fucking hell, Deeds."

He slams home. His powerful drives are fueled by the strength in his arms and the vice-like grip he has on my hip.

"Fuck. Sea, sin í mo chailín salach dána."

Yes, that's my dirty girl.

"Ride this fuckin' cock."

Those words do it for me, and I ignite. My orgasm crashes into me so violently that it blots out the world around me. A cry leaves my mouth as ripples of pleasure roll through me. For an endless moment…

I'm weightless, floating there as waves pulse through me. I try to hold on for as long as possible, but all too soon, I'm free-falling from it.

Falling.

Falling.

Falling.

Slowly, I come down from the clouds, back to the land of the living.

It happens gradually, like it always does. I slide quietly back into awareness. As I open my eyes and take in my surroundings, the emotions come. Guilt. Shame. Regret. They flood through me like a river spilling into a lake, a lake with a dam and a faulty foundation full of cracks bursting at the seams.

I take a moment to imagine what I must look like. I picture myself from above. From *his* vantage point. Half-naked. Eyes dilated. The blue washed-out by my blown-out pupils. My hair a disheveled mess.

Unworthy of him.

Not that I ever was.

The riot of emotions sobers me quickly. The rush quickly turns sour as a cyclone of shame I can't seem to escape weighs heavily on me.

Each time this happens, I swear I won't let myself think of Finn in these moments. My brain is fully on board but it's my fucking heart that can't keep that promise.

I blink open my eyes, expecting the mirage to fade. But for the first time, blue eyes stay blue. Long, ink-black hair speckled with gray doesn't fade. The jaw. The chin. The broad chest and corded arms— they stay.

I blink. One. Two. Three times. I even bite my lip to wake from this hallucination.

The hand I see, with the thumb hooked in his pocket, moves. His fingers drum on his jeans.

Chills spread over every inch of my skin, and an indescribable pain pierces my chest.

No. That's… not possible.

This reaction is not just from seeing the familiar *tap tap tap* gesture that Finn used to do. There's also a bird tattoo on his left hand—a finely crafted hummingbird that matches the one on my right hand.

Only where mine is pink, his is black.

Tears pool behind my eyes, and I fucking hate myself for it.

The body behind me sits up and brushes against my back. I jerk from the sensation and stand. I hastily fix my clothes and put everything rapidly back into place.

Deeds, ever perceptive of my moods, catches the shift. He stands, tucking himself back into his jeans. "What's wrong?" His brows crease with concern.

"Nothing," I lie. Crossing my arms over my chest, I internally pinch myself. It must be the weed we've smoked. Maybe it was laced with something, because this isn't real. It can't be. I look anywhere but at the man at the bar. I just need to give it time and sober the fuck up. After I've pushed down the storm of emotions raging inside of me, he'll be gone.

"You're crying?" Deeds' voice is sharp with alarm.

"What?"

He closes the space between us. "Jesus, Gypsy, you're crying. What's going on?"

I quickly swipe at my face. "Nothing. It's stupid. I'm fine."

"Talk to me." He lifts my chin, forcing me to meet his gaze.

I step back, needing space. When he tries to grab me again, I turn and freeze. My breath escapes me in a rush. A familiar burn begins to build, spreading pressure through my ribs like a vise. It's slow at first, but it builds the longer I look at him.

Because yes, he's still there.

The man's face hasn't morphed back into that of a stranger.

I gasp, and he must hear it. Because the man at the bar, the one who looks like Finn, turns his head and looks directly at me.

That's when I know I'm not imagining it. Finn and this HOC are one and the same.

How? Why? I don't know.

I stare, disbelieving. The sight of him is a jagged blade being driven straight through my chest.

I stumble back. Deeds catches me, grabs my hand. He attempts to stall my escape by grabbing my arm.

"Let me go," I plead.

He tries to turn me toward him. "No, talk to me."

"I said, let me fucking go!" The force behind my words, the wild panic in my eyes, makes him release me at last, more out of shock than anything else. I quickly navigate my way through a sea of people and don't stop until I hit the parking lot. My heels catch on the gravel, and I crash hard onto the pavement.

It's there that I completely lose it.

On the ground, with scratched-up palms and knees, a sob tears from me. My body locks up. My lungs seem to collapse.

I've experienced it before, but it doesn't make it any less scary. Each time, I'm filled with the fear that the air won't come. That this time, I won't survive it. That I'll never be able to take another breath, and I'll die here just like this.

Then Deeds is there. He pulls me up to my knees. Lifting my hands, he inspects the damage. "What the fuck, Lily? What happened?"

"I can't breathe," I rasp.

He grabs my chin, gently turning my face up to his. When his eyes meet mine, alarm floods his features. "You can't breathe?"

Grabbing his shirt, I shake my head frantically. For a minute or two, he just holds me, his grip firm and reassuring, as I suck in what little air I can find. But my chest burns with white-hot agony.

I hear a thud and glance behind us toward the club's front door. I freeze when I see the figure in black standing there, watching us.

I'm not crazy. This is real. He's fucking real.

Deeds's gaze follows mine. Something flickers in his eyes, and a dark understanding passes over his face.

"It's him, isn't it?" His voice drops low, the realization sinking in.

I can't answer. But I don't need to. My silence, my tears, my inability to breathe—all of it speaks volumes.

Deeds's jaw clenches. His fingers twitch as if he's barely holding himself in check.

"I thought he was dead," he mutters, the venom in his voice palpable.

The words tear from me, brittle and shaky. "He's supposed to be."

LOST LYREBIRD

CHAPTER 2

A scorned woman is a beautifully dangerous thing.

APRIL 2007

From the parking lot across the street, I have a clear view of the two-lane road leading up to the strip club. I've been sitting here for hours, waiting for the moment when the past comes riding back into my life.

But Finn is once again missing in action, and once again, I'm left wondering where in the hell he could be. As I wait, it's all too easy to let my mind drift back to the days upon days where I did this exact same thing—paused my life for Finn.

I was three weeks from turning eighteen, full of hopes and dreams, when he went off to play hero.

For months after he left, I worried myself sick. Held out hope he would show up or send a letter, a fucking email—anything.

It took months of silence before I'd had enough and started searching for answers.

I'd been led to believe that, like so many other soldiers, he died while serving our country. The news had crushed me. Made my life barely worth living. Until I saw him alive and well with my own two eyes nearly five years ago, and realized the joke was on me.

At some point over the years, he'd traded his fatigues for leather and one brotherhood for another. And while I'd been doing anything I could to survive and forget the love I found and lost, he'd been partying, banging a slew of women, and drinking as much alcohol as his body would let him consume.

See, I'd had it all wrong. I wasn't the girlfriend of a dead soldier. There wasn't some remarkable man up in Heaven watching me, waiting for me. I was just someone he cared for once, and left in the dust of New Mexico.

He'd made it out alive... and me, well... I'd been abandoned.

The knowledge hurt, and it also hardened me. Made me critical of all my faults. If I couldn't be loved, I'd be wanted. Desired. Envied. Feared. A weapon dressed in satin, lace, and perfume—perfect in every conceivable way. Talented. Beautiful. Fierce.

Turns out, men will pay dearly for the attention of a woman who doesn't flinch at her own reflection, who owns her sexuality, and keeps them guessing. And nothing pays better than rich and powerful men with dirty secrets, which is where I found my niche. A short game, and a dangerous one. But backed by the most notorious motorcycle club in the country, I didn't just survive—I carved out power and profit on my own terms.

This job, though, isn't about that. It's not about the money. It's about paying back a debt no amount of money can repay.

Years ago, Deeds had helped me rescue my sister and kill the monster who'd invaded my childhood home. My Stepfather. A man who'd made my teenage years a living hell, to the point I'd run away at sixteen. Together, Deeds and I made sure he'd never lay his hands on another child. Then we found a lovely family to take in Lacy, and over the years, with the money I earned working for the GBs, I ensured she not only recovered but thrived.

Now, Deeds needs me to repay the favor. To do that, I have to sneak back into the life of the man who left me. Use my skills and my old connection with Finn to infiltrate the HOCs, discover how deeply their ties run with the Thirteen Devils, and figure out who among them might not be as loyal as they seem.

Because war is coming. The Greenbacks are preparing to face the Escarra Cartel, and figuring out how far the arm of the Cartel extends is paramount.

The Thirteen Devils aren't all they appear to be. We suspect some of them are cartel men—or in bed with them. One in particular is another Monster from my past I plan to take care of while I'm here. Veneno, Veno for short. He is back to his old ways, trafficking women after being released from prison when his case was overturned.

But his payback will come later.

It'll be my last job before I take a sort of retirement and revel in the splendor my hard work has provided. It's something I'm looking forward to, the closure of this chapter of my life, an opportunity to finally put the past behind me and do all the things I'd dreamed of, once I was free of this debt, my past, and the remaining questions I had for Finn.

I want to travel around the world unburdened, with a new identity and a clean slate.

After another hour and another handful of roasted sunflower seeds, I decide to circle the building to see if I somehow missed him. As a fresh wave of salt floods my mouth, I reach forward to start up my 1998 Honda Civic, which is part of my cover. But that's when I hear the sound I've been waiting for—the unmistakable rumble of a Harley.

I shut off the car and inch further down into my seat. My glasses shield my eyes, but I still make sure the brim of my baseball cap shades my face.

All too soon, I see him driving up a small incline a quarter mile south of me. As I take him in, my brain sort of short-circuits.

He's now a personified vision of everything that makes a woman weak in the knees.

Long, dark hair.

Leather. Ink. Goatee.

Not the G.I. Joe I remember. More like an aged version of the biker I thought I'd willed back into existence five years ago.

He has the kind of facial hair that separates the men from the boys. Like his hair, it's speckled with gray; a harsh silver and black combo that you rarely see on a man who still has the face and body of a thirty-nine-year-old. It's a premature gray that runs in his family, something his father had too.

Even though he's wearing mirrored shades, I can make out a few familiar features—straight brows, a perfectly proportioned nose, and the kind of jaw that would give Brad Pitt a run for his money.

He's wearing a gray Henley and well-worn jeans, along with his cut—a leather vest with his club colors. One gloved hand hangs loosely on the handlebar, the other rests on his thigh, giving off the impression that the death machine beneath him is practically driving itself.

It's a softail with ape hangers, painted deep green, teeming with custom parts and finished with chrome and gold highlights. The details speak of a love for the open road and loyalty to the brotherhood he's now part of. I hate to admit it, but the bike's beautiful. The sight of him on it is a pretty picture I may never be able to scrub from my brain.

What's odd, though, is there's no seat beyond the one he's sitting in. No sissy bar. The seat is small and made of brown leather. To the average person, it wouldn't say anything. To a biker or someone versed in their world, it says a whole hell of a lot.

It's symbolic.

It clearly states that company is not needed or welcome. I mentally throw a brick wall in front of that thought before it goes anywhere. I don't give a shit.

He's my way in, a means to an end. I remind myself.

Meanwhile, Finn McCown, known to his HOC friends as Goose, aka the abandoning bastard whose heart I'd like to impale with my six-inch heel, parks the bike in the lot across from mine. He backs in close to the building, facing me. When he finally stands, he reveals his lean but strong body and height, six feet to the mark.

As I watch from across the street, he bites the fingertips of his leather gloves and pulls them off before shoving them into his pocket. Lifting his corded arms, he rakes his fingers through his hair, slicking it away from his face.

It's sexy as hell, and I flinch from the pinch it ignites in my chest.

Fuck. This man. Fuck him.

He has no damn right to look this good.

In a fair world, he'd have a mangled face, marred and mutilated, to match the vital organ he shredded years ago. But no. Instead, men who go around breaking hearts age to perfection, while the women they leave behind walk around with ice in their veins, impenetrable walls surrounding their hearts, for fear of being made the fool a second time.

For a moment, he looks up into the cloudless sky. There's nothing but a few birds. Then he warily scans his surroundings, giving me a glimpse of the man I remember and all his rough edges, the tension held in his thick shoulders, the hard set to his strong jaw, like he doesn't trust the world around him, or is worried about an attack he can't see coming.

It shouldn't please me, but it does until he pulls off the aviators.

I can't see their color from here, but I know it well. Blue. Sometimes azure. Other times navy.

They bewitched me the first time I saw them. Shattered my resolve when I was seventeen, when I tried to put some distance between me and what I knew I couldn't handle. A man who was way out of my league.

Meeting them eye to eye again may just be one of the hardest things I'll ever do.

Then maybe you should've looked at the pictures.

Yes, inner devil, thank you very much. Maybe I should've. But I didn't, couldn't, and now I have to suffer the consequences.

I did my research. I know more details about the HOCs than probably any of their brothers do. I saw picture after picture of each patch member, read their files. Except him. Goose. *Finn.* I couldn't. Not only because I wanted to put it off as long as possible, but also because if I had to look at him, then I wanted to do it for the first time with my own two eyes. No picture. No video. He was never a ghost or a figment of my imagination. He was real, and what he did to me did indeed happen. He'd made me fall in love with him and then left me behind with no word.

I fight the reaction my body has to the sight of him. My heart

27

beating out of rhythm, stuttering one moment, and racing the next, as if it can't decide whether to curl into a ball or make a run for it. Both sound appealing as hell. But I can't hide. I've done that for too long. It's time I finally face him and get some answers.

I shut down all the feelings. I flip the switch off with a *click*. It's what I do, what I had to learn to do—to turn off my feelings when they become too much.

When he disappears inside the club, I glance at the clock on my dashboard. In less than two hours, I'll face him, strip off my clothes, and convince him to give me a job.

I pick up my phone and text Deeds, the one person who is always on my side and somehow knows what to say to help me set my mind right.

Remind me why I agreed to do this.

He replies:

For the greater good.

A smile pulls at the corner of my mouth.

What did the greater good ever do for me?

He shoots back:

For world domination then.

I chuckle. Only he could pull that out of me when I'm feeling so unsteady.

I don't want to dominate the world. We're talking about me. Not you.

Hmmm... Right. Let me think.

A few seconds later, he texts again.

For me, baby. Because I saved you when it should've been him, and I can't save this club without your help.

He sends another quicker than I can reply.

And this is your chance. To make him regret giving you up.

Those words cement every bit of what's softened inside me. My resolve strengthens. My jaw sets. I take a few moments and relive the months I waited for Finn. The danger I put myself in by sticking around, and how, in the end, I barely made it out of New Mexico alive.

Veno nearly saw to it that I didn't, and eventually he's going to pay for that.

Deeds may be a little evil, but at least he's honest about it. Yes, he uses me. But I use him just as much. It's an equal relationship of give and take, take, take.

You highly motivated now?

Yes.

That's my girl. Make him sorry, baby.

I plan to.

All right, Gypsy Girl. You do just that and call me tonight.

He quickly sends another.

You got this.

Taking a Goliath-sized breath, I repeat aloud, "I've got this."

I'm not the girl Finn left behind. I'm the woman I've made myself into. One that can make a grown-ass man beg, heel, cry, and come on command if I choose.

My determination firmly in place, I grab my makeup bag from the passenger seat. My armor. When I'm made up, it feels like I'm inhabiting another body. Which is exactly what I need. To be someone else. Someone likeable. Someone sweet. Not the person I see when I look in the mirror.

I'm good at this, I remind myself. I can play any role to fit the needs or wants of my clients. Finn isn't a client, though; he's a target, but the same rules apply.

The first place I use the cover-up is over the tattoo on my forearm. It's not much, but enough to push down the real me and that old pain hiding just under my skin. When I'm done, I get out of the car, ready to be a different person.

Once again, it's time to put all those dancing and acting classes to good use.

CHAPTER 3

Some things once lost disappear from our lives entirely, while others reappear when we least expect to find them.

APRIL 2007

I hate days like this, when pain is my steady companion upon waking. It makes spending the day surrounded by bright lights and loud music a cacophony of torture, and in those moments, I want nothing more than to sell my share of the club and be done with the alcohol, women, and pasties.

It wasn't always this way. There was a time when the migraines were few and far between, when I used to feel like what I was doing here mattered. The women reminded me of Elle. They were at risk in the same way she was. Protecting them gave me a purpose. One I couldn't easily walk away from.

After all, if I didn't look after these ladies, who would?

But this? This right here, is bullshit. It makes me want to pull every silver hair from my head. The bass is a sharp knife splitting my skull apart. The song choice and the sight of another girl without the necessary skills to do the job—it's a fucking medley of torment.

I used to have more patience for this shit. After five years, I'm worn the fuck out. Running a strip club means many moving parts and a ton of drama. I've done what I can to minimize it, but it's still too much sometimes.

I rub my forehead. "Seriously... what is this? What in the fuck is she doin'?"

Bodie, my HOC brother and best friend, tilts his head to the side. Maybe he thinks a different angle will give him deeper insight. "Uh-mmm... walkin' like an Egyptian is my guess? Or it could be that modern dance shit Blaire likes."

A frustrated groan rumbles out of me. *How is this my life?*

Raven, the best assistant manager in the world, stands off to the side of the stage waiting for my signal. I give her a slight shake of my head. That's all it takes for her to stop the music, thank the girl, and lead her off the stage.

A short-haired, dark-skinned woman with more than a few handfuls of curves is up next. Her best move is a dolphin dive where she belly flops on the stage, then proceeds to hump it to the beat.

Bodie rewards her with a standing ovation. Only when she's escorted offstage does he plop back into his seat beside me and laughs like an idiot. "Oh my God! Please hire her. I need that girl in my life."

I glare at him and massage my temples. As the auditions progress, I pop half a dozen aspirin.

The potential is here to make this place a goldmine. However, the locale and the available talent have hindered its success.

Another dancer takes the stage, and it's another no.

"But I haven't even taken off my bra yet," the busty brunette whines.

Bodie smacks my chest. "Yeah, man, let her at least take off her bra first." The girl hears him and frowns. Her gaze darts between us, like Bodie has a say, and maybe if she can convince him, she'll get the job. I elbow his side hard enough that he'll feel it tomorrow. The grunt followed by a curse is music to my ears. The man has been a pain in my ass for longer than I can remember. *Literally.*

"You ready for the next one?" Raven calls out.

No, but fuck, it has to be done. "How many left?"

"Two."

My woeful groan is all in my head. I nod grimly, then look up to curse the man upstairs. *Am I really asking for too much here? C'mon.*

Bodie grins and rubs his hands together. "This shit is just gettin' good."

I hear Raven kindly say, "You're on, honey. Knock 'em dead." Then the music kicks in, and 'Bawitdaba' by Kid Rock blasts through the speakers.

A young, fresh-looking blonde steps onto the stage wearing a red two-piece, fishnets, and clunky heels. She doesn't appear comfortable in the shoes. If anything, she's unsteady. She has little curves to speak of, but some men love that sort of thing.

If I had to guess, she's a college student looking for a way to pay that hefty tuition bill. You do this long enough, it's easier to spot what category the girls fall into: single mom, college student, lifers—girls who get addicted to the attention and never want to give it up, and the Annies—the girls searching in the wrong place for their version of Daddy Warbucks.

She spins around the pole with some skill, and for a spare second, I think maybe I judged her too quickly. There's some raw talent there.

As soon as the thought hits me, the girl slips. She falls, and I swear to God, the sound of her head cracking on the stage echoes.

"Shit!" I'm not sure who shouts it—maybe both of us at once—as Bodie and I jump up and race toward her. We swiftly assess the damage, much like we used to do in the field back in our Ranger days, when he was just Rivers to me, a West Coast beach bum turned soldier.

The girl moans as she comes to. She reaches for the back of her head, but Bodie pulls her hand away and holds her arm down. He begins asking her questions to gauge her awareness. I get a quick flash of memory of him doing the same to me after the Humvee incident we nearly died in. It's one of the memories I haven't lost track of, and this moment brings it to the surface.

While he takes care of the girl, I call for an ambulance, and Bodie's baby blue eyes meet mine as soon as I end the call. They say *she seems fine, but fuck, she landed hard. Hope you have good insurance, man.*

Bodie tells her to relax until they get here.

Staring at the girl, all I can think is… this is a sign, right? Because it sure as fuck feels like one.

For a moment, I let myself think about what that would look like—more time to work in my woodshop, more time helping the women in Veno's circle get back to their families. However, if I push any harder, it might draw too much attention, and that means blowback for the club.

"What can I do to help?"

The voice cuts through my morbid thoughts. It washes over me like aged bourbon. There's a sultry elegance to each word. A divinely feminine lyrical quality to it. My focus snaps away from the girl and up. For a moment, the overhead lights momentarily blind me. An outline of a shapely form stands over me, her face in shadow. Her curves, though, are insane. The golden glow hitting her skin and hair makes her appear otherworldly. I know it's merely a trick of the light, but it feels as if someone upstairs is telling me to pay fucking attention. So, I do. I eat up the vision before me.

The word angel pings in my mind, but no, there are no wings attached to this beauty.

"Is she okay?" Her voice stirs up an image of a meadow filled with wildflowers in my mind. I'm not sure why, maybe it's her scent that triggers the memory, but the connection to that visceral image is instant, and it leaves behind a feeling of lingering warmth.

She drops to her knees beside me, face pinched with concern. I take note of her long, French-tipped nails and olive skin as she reaches out and asks her directly if she's all right. When her gaze slowly pans to me, I'm struck stupid.

I see women, beautiful women, all the time. But this woman is next-level stunning. Her most prominent features are her angular cheekbones and plush lips, until her eyes steal the show. They're a captivating blue, with an inner ring of a honey hue around the pupil.

Time—*whatever the fuck it is*—sort of shifts to a halt as our gazes tangle together. Me… I'm over here trying to understand how this exotic creature practically landed in my lap. Like, where the fuck did she come from?

A blush blooms over her cheeks, and she shyly looks away. Her hair is long as hell, rich brown with lighter strands, the ends curling over her ample chest. As I take in the rest of her, I see that my assessment of her is correct. She's unreal. Every bit of her is pleasing to the eye.

Too perfect. Almost suspiciously so. I continue to stare until her lips twist as she fights a smirk.

"She's gonna be fine, but damn, gorgeous, where'd you come from?" Bodie's voice snaps me out of the trance I've fallen into.

She folds her hands in her lap. "Backstage. I was supposed to go on next."

Her sultry voice is infused with Southern charm. The accent has a lyrical quality, making her words flow seamlessly into one another and sound sweeter than they are.

When we both continue to eye-fuck her, she becomes visibly nervous and runs her fingers through her hair, sweeping from left to right. Her scent works like a fucking defibrillator, burrowing deeply into my chest. It's alluring and seductive, but also soft. A gentle floral scent with hints of raspberry. It wakes my dormant libido and kickstarts it into overdrive instantly. Because yeah, my dick perked right the fuck up.

I'm so caught off guard by it, I sway in my crouched position, dropping to a knee and planting my fingertips on the floor to steady myself, so I don't, you know, eat shit and end up on my ass over this woman.

A familiar blast of pain hits behind my eyes. Pressing my palm to my temple, I apply pressure and bear it.

Bodie speaks, but it's a murmur to me as picture-like images flash behind my eyes. *A cholo, Veno Chavez, wearing a black folded bandana over his forehead and eyebrows. An adversary I know well. The three blue teardrop tattoos below the corner of his eye and the scorpion neck tattoo are his most distinguishable features.*

His face is pinched in pure rage. He's shouting and pushing a nine-millimeter into a girl's mouth, a teenager with bleached hair. Wild strands cover half her beat-to-shit face. One of her eyes is swollen to the point it's completely shut.

I catalogue the details as the memories begin to fracture. *A torn black dress. Matching ballet flats with pink flowers on the toes. The arrow tattoo with script, and a pink hummingbird inked on her hand. A full garbage bag at her feet. We're all standing in a dirty alley.*

And then there's the fact she's warning me to stay back with one hand, while seeming to beg Veno for her life with her wide and tear-filled eyes.

My little bird.

Some memories, like this one, make me so sick it's all I can do not to lose the contents of my stomach.

The tattoos I know well. One old-fashioned arrow, a dream catcher under the head, with feathers, and cursive script below. The bird matches mine; it's pink, and mine's black.

The garbage bag, though… without a double check in my journal, I don't know if it's a new feather or a lost detail I've recovered.

These rapid flashes are a short glimpse into the past. They rarely make any sense. I call them feathers because they're feathers to follow like puzzle pieces or breadcrumbs, each leading me further down the trail my little bird left behind.

But why these? Why now?

After the Humvee incident, followed by surgery, it'd taken months before the doctor deemed me healthy enough to get discharged from the VA hospital. Rehabilitation followed. When I returned to my life in New Mexico, nothing seemed right. I knew I was missing memories, but how many had taken some time to determine. I discovered I'd sold my home and relocated to a leased apartment on the other side of town. The apartment I tracked through cashed checks. When I got there, it was trashed, as if it'd been searched, and the utter lack of girlish belongings sent me reeling.

Most likely, she'd taken off to avoid the evil son of a bitch in this exact memory. Veno was still hounding me about her whereabouts, still looking to get payback for whatever she'd done, so this, at least, gave me hope that she'd made it out of New Mexico alive.

She's a ghost, and one I've been searching for since.

Distantly, I hear the woman ask if I'm okay. Bodie assures her I am and to just give me a moment.

When the pain dissipates, my gaze returns to the too-sexy, angelic face and those striking eyes. Fierce kitten eyes. At first glance, they seem bright and clear, but as I look a bit deeper, they show a wariness, an edge of uncertainty, and maybe even a speck of vulnerability. I can't help but ask myself, are they *"love me"* eyes? I think so. They're the same color as a forget-me-not, but I've jumped to conclusions before, and it's bitten me in the ass.

Could this be my *little bird*? I'm scared to hope when it's only ever made me look fucking mad. And I hate that I'm handicapped by my inability to remember.

But I have fuck all to go off to find her. And I'm starting to lose the plot. Not only do the flashbacks make my migraines worse, but the aftermath drains me. And that makes me irritable and incapable of suffering through my worst days without needing something to take the edge off.

I hear Bodie ask, "You got a name?"

"Lily."

Lily. Just as beautiful, but not the name I'm aching to hear.

"I'm Reese Rivers. Everybody calls me Bodie, and this is Finn. He goes by Goose." He bobs his chin in my direction.

She reaches out very businesslike and offers her slim hand to him first and then to me. It catches me off guard initially, but I finally extend my own and shake hers. I note how her hand is half the size of mine, her skin like satin and warm to the touch.

"Have we ah… maybe met before?" I ask. There is a palpable energy as we clasp hands. It builds the longer we hold.

Out of my peripheral vision, I see Bodie palm his face and shake his head. His blond waves bounce with the motion.

Yeah, fuck him. If there's a slight chance it's her, I'm gonna ask. You'd think, with as long as we've been friends, he'd have gotten over his second-hand embarrassment issues, but no. He tries to hide my disability, shield me from the fallout, or at least other people's reaction to it.

Me? I don't have time, nor the patience, for shitty people. So I don't give a fuck.

Lily's eyes hold my gaze for an exceptionally long time. She very slowly shakes her head, then looks away. "No, uh, not that I know of. I think I'd remember something like that." Nothing in her body language belies her words, so I take them at face value. It's another letdown, but it is what it is.

Bodie gestures to me. "I keep telling him he needs some new lines, but he refuses to listen. He thinks he has to go old school so chicks'll think he's as old as the hair makes him look."

"Oh yeah?" Lily laughs.

Fuck you, Rivers. I glare at him. He makes a face back at me like he's ten goddamn years old. Another aspect of our friendship. He's doing his thing. The thing he does where he thinks he needs to speak for me. Most women assume it's because I'm shy or some shit. This couldn't be further from the truth. I talk when I *need* to. I say what I *need* to. I speak to those important to me. My circle is small and filled with the people I trust. Which is the way I like it.

My deadpan glare tells him he'll pay for this shit later.

When my attention moves back to Lily, I find that she's checking me out. My tattoos. A steady heat spreads through my chest. I try to tamp it down, even though I secretly like how she's eyeing me. Like I'm a mystery she's trying to solve.

Ironic, since I feel the same about her.

"I can come back another day, that is… if you're still hiring."

"Oh, he's definitely hiring. And if he wasn't, I would be. Hell, girl, I'd open up another club just so you could grace the stage."

She laughs. It's airy and bright, as if it carries a touch of sunlight. Her eyes travel appreciatively over Bodie. A desire to kick him the fuck out of my club hits me out of nowhere.

He motions for me to respond to Lily. "Tell her." And shoots me a look that says, *Man the fuck up. Talk. To. The. Beautiful. Woman.*

Clearing my throat does nothing to diminish the husky tone in my voice. "Could you come back tomorrow?"

A huge grin stretches across her sinfully luscious mouth. "Sure. When?"

Oh shit, that's a full smile. It's fucking devastating. Like heart-attack inducing. I nearly say noon and decide against it. I don't want to appear eager as fuck.

"Would two p.m. work?"

She gets to her feet and *fuuuck*. Her legs are damn sexy, tanned, toned, and the sight I'm getting of her thighs due to her skirt having ridden up sends a surge of heat south. My dick's feeling confined as fuck now. The seam of my briefs is probably imprinted on the fucker.

"Great. I'll come then."

Bodie chokes on his spit and has to pound his chest.

What the fuck did she just say?

When Bodie recovers, he rasps, "Is that a promise, sweetheart? Because I gotta say, I'm down for that." He grins like a mad bastard, throwing his dimples into the mix.

Her smile falters. A flush creeps up her chest, contrasting against her blue blouse. Do my eyes stay on the swell of her cleavage longer than appropriate? Yes, they do. Can't be helped, because Jesus Christ, her body is insane.

"Oh, Jeez." She chuckles. "I mean… I'll see you tomorrow at two."

"Looking forward to it," Bodie says. "Don't want to miss the sight of you shakin' that ass." He leans back a bit for a better look. She grins and turns, giving him a better view and a saucy grin. Her ass is high, tight, and plump as hell, uncommon on such a thin frame. It's like every inch of her was made with a man's pleasure in mind. Every. Single. Fucking. Inch.

It makes a man imagine all sorts of dirty, sweat-filled, raw, and animalistic sex. Which is what fills my head as I stare up at her.

When she gives us one last sexy smile over her shoulder, Bodie flashes her his own killer grin. "You sure you want to work here, sweetheart? Say the word and I'll open up an extra receptionist position at my auto body shop just for you."

His offer, his blatant lust, and lecherous grin, have something rearing up inside me that I've never felt before, and it fucking tugs at my baser instincts, bringing them forward.

I can't stand the thought of her being just another one of his used and discarded toys. One look, and I know she's worth a whole hell of a lot more than that.

She doesn't deign to reply to that comment, as she already gets that he's full of shit and a jokester at heart. Instead, she tells him, "Put in a good word for me, will ya?"

"You got it."

She gives us both a slight wave. "See ya tomorrow." Then she's sauntering off backstage. And yeah, the enthralling swing of her hips is a sight neither of us looks away from.

The second she's out of sight, I curse under my breath and rub a hand over my mouth.

"She just jacked up your blood pressure, didn't she?" Bodie laughs.

Fuck yeah, she did.

Bodie's eyes stay on me for a moment, probably to make sure I'm solid, then he checks back in with the girl. The one lying on the floor that I've practically forgotten about.

I mentally scroll through my journals, cataloguing everything I know about Elle. It wouldn't hurt to double-check some details.

Bodie shakes his head. "Don't even go there. I see that look."

Bodie, Dozer, and Cap—our president—are the only people who know about Elle, and why I'm not able to remember. Bodie, because he was there before, when she was my world, and after, when I had no fucking clue she existed. He'd never met her, but I'd talked about her on that last tour. Dozer, because one night over a bottle of Jack, we were commiserating over the women we'd lost while overseas. And I told Cap when I prospected into the club, so he knew my weaknesses and the drawbacks.

"You gonna tell me if that girl isn't her, you're not interested?"

"I didn't say that," I grumble. I'm interested, but do I really have anything to offer a girl like that? And what about Elle?

"That's what I thought." He sighs. "Look, man, I get it. Elle was pretty amazing. But there are a ton of other fish in the sea. If you haven't noticed, they keep swimming around you like sharks waiting for a piece. Pretty fish. Fun fish. Exotic fish. Slippery-when-wet fish. Fish that will let you—"

My head begins to pound again. "I swear to God, you should come with a warning label and a gag." I pinch the bridge of my nose, though it does little to relieve the ache building there.

"You should hitch a ride with this chick to the hospital. Have Alister check you out."

I've been checked out by Alister many, many times. "Nah, I'm good."

"They seem worse."

They are, but I didn't know it was obvious.

"You takin' the meds he gives you?"

The drugs. "Which ones? The ones that make me nauseous, the ones that turn me into a walking zombie, or the ones that make me a temperamental asshole like Rick the Dick? Or how about the ones that cause me to sleepwalk?" Barrels of fun when you wake up in the dead of the night, standing in the middle of your yard in nothing but your briefs—pills which also have the side effect of making me sleep so deep that I don't dream, and if I do, I don't remember shit upon waking. And I can't afford not to dream. I need my dreams to find her. They're windows into the past.

Either way, it's a no-win situation, and I'm sick of trying shit that doesn't work. So, I ignore his question and stand up.

"Brother…"

"I've got it under control."

No more drugs. No more surgeries. I'm done with trying shit that only fucks me up more.

He mutters, "By that, you mean you'll ignore them until they fuckin' kill you. Good plan, man. Let me know how that fuckin' works out for you." He holds up a hand. "Oh wait, I forgot, you won't be able to, because when your fuckin' brain explodes, you'll be lyin' in a pine box. Genius. Why the fuck didn't I think of it?" He glares up at me, and the righteous anger is so unlike him that I pause in my retort.

Looking down at the girl, he mutters, "I'll make sure they put 'Died because my stupid ass wouldn't listen to the doctor' on your headstone."

"You should really go see a doctor if they're that bad," the girl chimes in. "My aunt had headaches like that, and she ended up having a tumor."

Great! Just fucking great.

Uncomfortable with a stranger calling me out on my shit, I thread my hands through my hair, pushing it away from my face. "I'm fine. He's exaggerating. It's what he does."

Bodie glares so hard his dimples invert. He opens his big mouth again, but light spills into the room, distracting him. Raven guides the EMTs inside. They stabilize and load the girl into the ambulance.

I hop on my bike to follow them, make sure she gets checked out, and give the hospital my info for the bill.

I don't see Alister, the club-designated doctor on call for our drama. I don't need to. I'm already certain no doctor can fix what's broken inside my head.

LOST LYREBIRD

CHAPTER 4

How does one let go of the need to do unto others as they've done unto you?

I dig through my bag for the hotel room key, my fingers clumsy, unsteady. When I finally get a hold of it, it slips from my grasp and clatters to the floor. My hands are shaking as I bend down to snatch it up. It takes three tries before I manage to jam the key card into the lock. I push the door open and stumble inside, slamming it shut behind me.

I lean my forehead against the door, eyes squeezed tight, and let go of all the emotion I've caged in. I clench my fists until my nails dig painfully into my palms.

His voice—*his motherfucking voice*—a low tenor like a slow whirl of smoke, a velvety caress to the ear. The husky edge to each word and how it sent a kindling of warmth through me, like a finely aged Cognac after the most brutal day.

My memory of his voice didn't do it justice.

And yet, his first words to me stabbed brutally and twisted a knife deeper, splitting old wounds wider. The poison they carry spreads like venom through my bloodstream.

"Have we met before?"

That fucking asshole.

I force down the sickening churn of nausea, trying to purge the toxic animosity clawing its way up my throat.

I need to get myself under control.

But God... I didn't think he could hurt me more than he already had. Turns out, I was so fucking wrong.

I kick off my heels, sending them skittering across the room, and make my way to the bathroom. My palms press into the cold marble as I lean over the sink, staring hard at my reflection in the mirror. The lovesick teenager stares back—older now, her edges sharpened by time, yet still haunted by that same face and those old scars. Nose. Lips. Cheeks. Chin. The beautiful shell, nothing but a winning DNA lottery ticket. Maturity has reshaped me, but not enough to erase the girl I used to be.

The lovesick teenager who grew the hell up.

I remind myself that he'd just lost his father. He needed comfort, someone to bear the weight of his grief with him. And then he'd stumbled upon me, in my own dire straits—a damsel that a soldier like him probably felt compelled to help. Sure, we'd connected. We were both going through heavy shit, probably some of the darkest moments of our lives. But I'd always been too young for him, something he'd insisted over and over, keeping me at a safe distance for as long as his willpower held out.

Still, none of those reasons explained why he hadn't taken the time to write a letter, why he couldn't spare a few measly minutes to make a phone call. Why make promises and ask me to wait, tell me we'd run together as soon as his service date ended, only to cut off all contact? Why leave me in that dangerous situation, the one *he'd* stirred up, and then completely disappear?

The Finn I knew could never be that callous. That heartless.

I used to tell myself there had to be a reason. But the more I learned about him through Deeds, the more my mind ran wild with the possibilities.

Our last days together flutter through my mind. Finn standing in front of me, his thumb brushing the soft skin just under my ear, his gaze intense and unwavering. The look in his eyes—I'll never forget it. Like he ached to kiss me, but his morals wouldn't let him.

At first, I couldn't stand to be touched. I flinched at even the slightest brush of his skin against mine, recoiled from any physical contact. But months later, when I wanted his hands on me—after he'd earned my trust and every part of me craved him—he kept holding himself back.

He blamed it on the age gap. Said it was *wrong* for him to want someone so young.

Most people would see it that way, but I didn't.

To me, age had nothing to do with love. The way he watched over me, protected me at the risk of his own life, made me feel safe in a way I'd never known before. He loved me without words. Loved me in the face of death.

Or so I'd thought.

In the end, none of it mattered. Time dwindled, and the end of his leave loomed on the horizon. The pull between us grew stronger with each passing day. The clock *tick, tick, ticking*, and hanging over our heads. The uncertainty, the danger we were both facing, and the fact that I might never see him again, drove everything higher.

So, if he wouldn't cross that line, then I would.

I knew he only had so much control, and I admit, I pushed him over that line. I wanted him. His love. His hands on my body. I wanted to touch him, kiss him, to know how good we could be together. I wanted his skin imprinted on mine. I wanted the memory of it to carry me forward into the unknown days ahead.

So, in the dead of night, I went to him when I knew his willpower would be at its lowest.

I tore down his walls, threw his objections aside, and told him, point blank, that I wanted him to make love to me. That I needed him to love me in a way that would wash away the bad memories.

"Please touch me. I never feel more real, more alive, than when you do. Please, Finn. Show me what real love looks like, help me replace these bad memories with good ones."

He crumpled like a pyramid of stacked poker cards.

What followed was the most magical moment of my life. Transcendent. Fucking life-altering. He'd cherished and devoured me in equal measure, with such intensity that I'd nearly glimpsed white lights and pearly gates. I'd died a small death at the peak of the orgasm he'd wrung from me, my lungs momentarily incapable of drawing air from the pleasure of it all.

A panic attack in reverse. Something I was all too familiar with. Instead of terror starving my body of air, it was bliss.

When it was over, I thought we'd spend his last two days in New Mexico tangled in his bed, losing ourselves in each other until reality tore us apart. But Finn had done a one-eighty. He'd acted like he'd committed some unforgivable sin, a grievous crime, like what we'd shared had been a mistake. He bore the weight of that guilt and used it to build a wall between us that I couldn't breach.

He'd hold my hand like it meant everything, but look at me with an expression riddled with love and shame.

Like I was his entire world and his biggest regret.

I can't help but wonder if pushing his boundaries was what ultimately drove him away. I'd feared as much, but I had no way of knowing for sure.

I'd come here wanting answers. But the fact that he doesn't even know who I am? Yeah, that changes things.

Unable to cope with this fresh wave of rejection, I push off the counter, fill the sink with cold water, and splash it on my face. I take out my makeup remover and get to work. I scrub the make-up off a little too aggressively, then strip and toss my clothes into the corner. I crank on the hot water in the shower and step inside, hoping it's hot enough to melt these ridiculous, weak feelings from my skin.

Later, after I've picked at the pasta that room service delivered, I consider the subtle differences between the old Finn and the biker he's become. The prominent scar on his temple cutting into his hairline. The slight crookedness of his nose, broken at some point. The way his dark-blue eyes carry a haunted look, shadows of trials I know nothing about.

There's a wealth of new ink, winding over thick biceps, down his forearms, traveling onto his hands. Hands that once moved over my body like a sculpture he'd brought to life.

He was still the same man, but somehow completely changed.

More serious. His voice deeper, and his words more censored, like he thinks carefully about them before he utters them.

I eventually crawl beneath the covers, switch on the bedside lamp, and grab the magazine I'd left on the table. I continue the article about forgiveness. The gist of it being, if we seek absolution and learn from our mistakes, then we're worthy of forgiveness and should grant it to ourselves even if other people refuse to grant it in return.

I know I shouldn't, but I try to foresee a day when I'll learn Finn's truths and tell him mine.

Could I ever forgive him for the way he left me?

The man doesn't even know who the fuck you are.

I toss the magazine across the floor in a huff. Reaching up, I flick off the lamp.

He's a job, nothing more.

"Fuck him."

My fingers dig desperately into the damp, gritty soil. Nails break as I claw at the unyielding earth. My voice cracks as the scream rips from me. It's followed by hoarse sobs interspersed with hiccupping gasps. All are audible in the cold, eerie stillness of this grey, dreary dawn. He can't be dead. I won't allow it.

Shadows lengthen, stretching toward the unmarked grave in front of me, as if trying to pull him down even further.

"No!" I keep clawing with frantic hands, dirt caking my skin as I try to reach him because I can't let him go.

The very earth begins to shake, as if I'm willing it to give him back.

My eyes pry themselves open as I register the vibrations, not of the earth quaking beneath my hands and knees, but of the phone buzzing on the nightstand.

I'm drenched in sweat, chest heaving, hands clutching the sheets. They ache with stiffness as I open them and draw them up to cover the burning sensation in my chest. I struggle to swallow the tightness in my throat, forcing my mind to catch up with reality.

It was just a dream. Just another fucked-up dream.

The screen from my phone casts a ghostly glow from where it rests on the nightstand, buzzing in steady pulses. I flip it over. Deeds's name is split down the middle by a crack on the screen. I close my eyes for a moment and forcibly pull myself together. After three deep, cleansing breaths, I answer, bracing for the difficult conversation ahead.

"Hey." My voice is ragged and hollow, tinged with remnants of the nightmare.

Heavy rock music thumps in the background on his end, bass rattling through the speaker like a pulse. His voice cuts through, low and clear. "Hey, baby. How did it go?" There's a scrape and a heavy thud, the sound of a door slamming, making the song a steady hum in the background.

I picture Deeds sitting in his room at the clubhouse, sprawled out on the old black suede couch—the leather worn to gray patches— boots kicked up on the coffee table, waiting to hear my answer.

I plop back into my pillow and stare up at the ceiling, wishing it would open up and swallow me whole. "Not well."

"What happened?"

I push my hair out of my face, exhaling a deep breath as I let the words fall. "He didn't recognize me."

Silence stretches between us, tense and heavy. "Come again?"

"He looked me straight in the eye and asked me if we'd met before. Like I looked familiar, but he couldn't place me." My stomach is a void filled with snakes; it writhes, as this truth gnaws at me.

"Bullshit." Deeds's voice is sharp, clipped.

A bitter laugh escapes me, rough and raw. "It's true."

A pause, then softer, "It's gotta be the head injury."

I blink and pop up on an elbow. I tap the screen, put it on speaker, and stare down at it. "What head injury?" Then I remember the scar, that jagged line across his temple.

There's a long pause that makes me want to reach through the phone and shake him. "Didn't you read his file?"

"No, I couldn't." It's a confession that when it comes to Finn, I'm not handling shit like I should.

"Jesus, Gypsy." There's a sound like sandpaper being brushed against brick. He's scratching at his beard. Then the heavy clop of his boots as he begins to pace. "It's the reason he left the Army. Medically discharged. Courtesy of his time overseas."

"How bad could it be? He's walking, talking… seems fine. I mean, he's their Road Captain, for hell's sake, and runs a successful business." I try to keep my voice steady, but the words sound defensive even to my own ears.

"I don't know. I could have Bones hack into his records and send you a copy. The file we have on him is pretty thin. Guy's low-key, off the grid mostly. Doesn't use credit much, limited trackable spending except for utilities and small shit. Has a few rental properties that he reports on his taxes, as well as the strip club. Cell phone and bank account data, but there's nothin' much goin' on there. He's pullin' cash from the club, splittin' it with the HOCs."

I grit my teeth, frustration prickling up my spine. "So what do I do? Because I'm not about to latch on to him and go down memory lane if he doesn't know who the hell I am."

"No man forgets a girl like you, Gypsy," he says, his voice almost reverent. "He's just fucked in the head—like Taz. Could be the injury. PTSD. Hell, from what I hear, all the HOCs are fucked up."

It's not lost on me that the man other bikers have dubbed "Sonny Psycho" is calling other bikers crazy.

I let out a snort, a grim smile tugging at my lips. "Pot, kettle."

His laugh is rough, amused. "Touché."

The pacing stops, fabric rustles, and the sound of papers being flipped comes through the line. He curses under his breath, and then the sound of footsteps resumes. A tiger in a cage, full of restless energy, until his mind works through whatever problem is stressing him out. "I didn't think—Jesus. Shit always goes sideways, and it's never how you can predict."

"I guess I made less of an impression on him than I thought. Maybe I was just some girl crushing on an older guy out of my league." I let out a sigh as I flop back onto the bed. "Maybe it was all in my head."

"Don't do that," he growls. "Don't let this guy's inability to remember you drag you back to that place, baby. Self-doubt is the fuckin' enemy. You know that."

"I'm trying, but holy shit, Deeds, hearing him ask me like that was a fucking punch to the chest."

"So flip it off. Shut it down. Remain in control. They're your emotions. You can either let them run wild or get a handle on them and try to understand the why of it."

"Fuck! I'm trying to. But sometimes you can't see past it, you know?"

"Yeah, I do. But you need to."

Grinding my teeth, I take a few deep inhales. I force the darkness from my thoughts—the frustration and pain out of my body, pushing it away with a metaphysical forcefield.

"That's it. Just breathe," he says.

I roll my eyes and start over.

When my breath steadies, he asks, "So you didn't say anything to contradict him?" The rock in my stomach solidifies at his words. At his complete lack of interest in my feelings.

"No."

The rigidness of my tone must go unnoticed because he says, "Good, that's good."

"What was I supposed to say? That I was the girl he asked to wait for him, and then disappeared on? That we nearly—" My voice catches, and I stop myself before I say too much. "Hell no. I wasn't about to lay my heart out on a platter and watch him toss it to the floor and stomp on it."

"We pivot, then." His tone is pure business—cold and calculating. "Use another HOC to pull you in. But there's a risk he'll figure it out later."

I grab the phone so tightly that the ache from the dream comes to fruition. "I thought you might say that and figured it was the best way to move forward."

The flick of a lighter, then a deep inhale comes through the line. "I thought I'd be killing two birds with one stone," he murmurs.

"I regret ever telling you that."

He chuckles darkly. "What? It's cute."

"Shut up. Maybe it was once, but I'm not that girl anymore. And he's definitely not that guy."

"No? But you still care for him. He's always been *The Man*..." He emphasizes this with sarcasm.

"Deeds," I growl.

Another stretch of silence. I hear the *click, click, click* of his lighter as he flips it open and shut. He takes another deep drag on his cigarette. "He's always been between us."

My chest tightens. "What are you talking about?"

Click, click, click.

I expel a lengthy sigh and grit out, "Just say it."

"It's why you'd never let me in. Never let me be someone you could trust and lean on fully. And I get why—"

My pulse quickens. "You don't think I trust you—"

"In a way, yeah. Mostly, but not fully."

Twisting my fingers in the sheet, I clench the fabric tightly. "That's insane. How can you honestly think that?"

"You never really gave us... fuck... you know, a shot. A real shot. We fucked. Became fuck buddies or whatever, but you shied away from anything more—acted like you didn't notice when shit changed on my end—played dumb. Like you didn't see the way I wanted you." There's a curtness he's trying—and failing—to hide.

"Are you kidding me right now? Because the way I remember it, there was me, and there were all the other women you could never say no to. Every time I needed a break, you had some other girl in your lap or in your bed. That's the reason we never became more."

Silence hangs heavy on the line. Finally, his voice drops, almost too soft to hear. "Maybe at first, yeah. But not later. Not when we got close."

"What?"

"At first, you were just out of a fucked-up situation. You wanted freedom and space, so I gave you that. I wanted you, but you didn't want any man except for him. Fuck, it's like you were looking over your shoulder every chance you got. Looking for him. I figured I'd never measure up unless I allowed you time to get over him. You were a flight risk, and I didn't want to get attached until you weren't."

"Stop with the fucking bird references. You know I hate that." A fresh wave of bitterness claws its way up my chest. Of all days to hash this out, of course, he wants to do this today.

He goes quiet. Finally, he sighs. "I figured time would change things. But all it did was let you close yourself off more. You hardened up. Like caring about anyone made you vulnerable, and you weren't gonna let that happen."

"Don't act like you didn't play a part in that. You crafted me into a chess piece—to turn the tides for the club and connect you to powerful people."

"Maybe. But I wanted you strong. Strong enough to decide who was worthy of you. Strong enough to never need anyone. Powerful in your own right. Able to defend yourself and be self-sufficient. It wasn't all about the club." He pauses. "The other women were just to see if you'd care. To see if you'd react. I thought you'd speak up, but you didn't. Because the real you was locked away, and the performer stepped forward."

I close my eyes, the memories of some of my darkest days spiraling through my mind. "How can you say that? You act like I've been some emotionless doll."

"No, not a doll. There were times I almost felt it. But it's been years now, Lily, since I felt anything from behind that caged heart of yours. And I needed to know."

"I care. I cared then. It bugged the fuck out of me, seeing you with those women who used you for status."

He exhales on a long sigh, then chuckles, flicks his lighter again. The long pull he takes on his cigarette speaks volumes. Voice strained, he says, "But not because you wanted to be in their place? Or jealous they were trying to steal your man?"

"I was. At times."

"You could've put an end to it, you know? Any word from you would've done it."

"Deck."

"Fuck. Just… when this needed to be done, I thought I'd know."

"Know wh—"

He cuts me off. "If you were his, or mine. I don't want to dance to this tune anymore, Lily. I need to know. One way or the other. If he's not the one, then maybe you come back to me. Maybe you finally come back whole."

"After the job, though, first, right? Fix things for the club first? You think he's still going to give a fuck about me when he finds out why I'm here?" A heavy pause follows, each of us clinging to our piece of the past.

"If he's the man you thought he was…"

"He doesn't remember me, Deck! Looked me right in the face and didn't know who I was. So, what the fuck ever. It's a moot point."

I hear a thump. Then another. He's smacking his chest like he does, his *off* switch. "Like I said. Two birds, one stone."

"You're a real asshole."

It's a long time before either of us speaks again, although I know he's still there, just breathing and thinking on the other end of the line.

"You don't have to get close to him now. No messy past, no emotions."

I'd have to act like we never happened. He'd be my boss, so there was no escaping him entirely unless I scrapped the idea of working at the strip club altogether, since I don't need the job to get close to the club.

"If shit goes sour, we'll pull you out. Just say the word."

"Your faith in me is astounding," I say, with all the sarcasm I can muster.

"You can do this, Gypsy. We need you to do this."

"I know. I will. It's just a mind fuck. Don't worry, I'll handle it like always."

"I'll have Bones sweep your background and replace it with the Vegas job cover."

"Okay."

"Watch yourself. And call me if shit goes south."

55

"I will."

We're both silent until he adds, "I care more about you makin' it out whole than anythin' else. I hope you believe that."

Picking at some lint on the comforter, I nod. "I do." Do I sound bitter? Yes, I fucking do. But I do know this.

"Good." More quietly, he says, "Take your time. There's plenty of it before we make our move. Focus on dancin', gettin' yourself set up. Let them warm up to you."

Deeds doesn't know this, but I love him as much as someone like me can. He's the older brother I never had. The lover I miss. A little fucked up, yes, but that's us in a nutshell.

"Remember why you're there, Gypsy. Not only to pay back the favor you owe me, but to cripple every piece of shit who wronged you."

His words coil through me. Bolstering me, helping me replace my mental walls. I can't forget why I'm here. It's not just about the debt. Or about righting the past and paying back the Thirteen Devils for what they did to me. This is about war, and the innocents caught between many forces.

Before he drops off the line, I say, "So, this is it then. I'm on my own. And I'm one of them."

He pauses. His voice goes tight and hoarse. "You'll always be one of us. But yeah, you're one of them now, too. So be the best stripper, clubpiece, or old lady—if it comes to that—you can be. It's the only way this works." His tone softens, like when he's whispering into my ear. "But fuck, I miss you already."

Through the melancholy, a small smile stretches across my lips. At the same time, a familiar ache starts between my thighs. "Me too."

"When it's done, maybe…"

"What?"

"Maybe we talk about us, yeah?"

A weighty silence is my answer. Because I don't know what to say. In the end, I speak his name softly. "Decker."

It's like he doesn't hear me at all when he says, "'Kay, baby, then I best let you go. Go do what you gotta do."

Something shifts in my chest. The words "let you go" feel final, though I know he doesn't mean them that way. But maybe it's time to let go. Clinging to Deeds isn't going to help me now.

This is more than just another job. This is something I've trained years for, and the outcome will affect many lives, including mine. Whether my heart survives it… that's anyone's guess.

CHAPTER 5

Our subconscious is smarter than we are. It recognizes a kindred soul when it sees it.

As the hours bleed into one another, sleep evades me. There's something about Lily—some shadow that lingers at the edges of my memory. It gnaws at me like an itch just under my skin.

My mind and body are too wired to rest, so I spend the better part of the night rifling through journals, sifting through scraps of notes, chasing the ghost of a connection that, at times, seems to only live inside my mind.

If it weren't for the strings tying clues together on my wall and giving me evidence of Elle's existence, I would think I'd gone insane. Maybe I have a little.

What was once a clean, organized assortment of feathers, breadcrumbs, and puzzle pieces has turned into total chaos. Like a man living on his last nickel, desperately searching for gold, I've scoured through all my notes in a frenzy.

There has to be an explanation for why this niggling unease hasn't left me, even after smoking as much dope as I have to help numb the pain.

Around two thirty in the morning, I find it. A long-forgotten note I scrawled years ago, written while I'd been in medical rehab, spending half my days in physical therapy, the other half popping opioids to dull the knife, constantly driving into my skull.

Her hand in mine as she leads me through a forest. She's constantly sweeping her hair out of her face. The blonde ends with dark-brown roots. The bruises marring her olive skin are fading. Dandelion seeds floating into the sky.

Is this it? What's been driving me fucking insane? A few matching details? The swept hair, olive skin, and brown roots.

I caution myself not to read too much into those feathers. Hope can be deadly. And yet, those words give the longing for her that has refused to die, new life.

I crash for four hours and wake with the sun.

When my morning trickles by like motor oil through a corroded engine and I still have hours to kill, I head out back to my workshop. There, I work on my latest side project—reshaping a storm-felled tree into a piece of furniture. Something with purpose. With longevity. Something that, hopefully, will see many days to come.

It's a gift for a man who helped me in my search for Elle—my old landlord.

First, I had to strip out the rot and damage. Then prepare and cure the wood, cutting it down into usable boards for the legs, seat, back, arms, and rockers.

The base rockers were the hardest to get right. Matching the curves took time and patience. Breathing life into each piece is how I spend my morning. I finish carving in the small details and sand down the rough edges, smoothing every curve and contour. The stain I apply last pulls out the grain and knots as if the tree's memories are rising to the surface.

Watching it soak in and seeing it transform is deeply satisfying.

The scent of the sawdust and oil grounds me. Earthy, sharp, and familiar. But getting it off my skin and the sawdust out of my hair is another matter, so I head back inside to clean up thoroughly.

When I finally arrive at Wet Tips, it's nearly noon. With the kinetic energy still riding high, I immediately start on my to-do list. Maintenance shit. Things that have needed my attention for months: a broken shelf in the storage area, dead or flickering bulbs, a loose railing, and a few wobbly or broken tables and chairs. I fix what I can and jot down a list of replacements for the rest.

By the time I finish, I still have an hour to kill. So I sit back and drum my fingers on the desk, considering a nap on the couch in my office. I should sleep. Going without is bound to bring on a migraine. I know this, but with whatever's coursing through my veins, I'm sure it'll be for nought.

Instead, I pull the blueprints for the club's renovation from the bottom drawer. Mav sketched them up for me a while back, the original plans to turn this place into something classy, upscale. At first, I put it on hold to offer some stability to the staff after the hell they'd been through with the previous owners. Later, the plans got shoved to the back burner as the day-to-day grind—and my responsibilities to the HOCs—took over. And for the past two years, as my migraines grew worse, I started to accept that I might not be around long enough to see the project through.

So these have been all but forgotten.

As I spread them across my desk, I can't help but imagine the changes I'd make. The possibilities. With deliberate care, I jot down updates in neat script, knowing Mav will have to decipher my handwriting later. It might not be anytime soon—he's got more than enough on his plate—but at least I can pass them on and see if additional changes are doable.

Checking my watch, I see it's 2:03 p.m. My pulse speeds up as I make my way to the back entrance.

I'm leaning against the building, smoking a cigarette, when I hear the guttural rumble of a Harley in the distance.

Bodie rolls in. His blue shop shirt, with his name embroidered on it, is oil-stained, open over a wrinkled white tee, as if he just rolled out of bed and threw on whatever was on the floor.

"Why the fuck didn't you call?" he asks as he dismounts.

Squinting against the sunshine, I give it to him straight. "Was hoping you forgot."

He arches a brow over the rim of his sunglasses and spins his hat backward over his messy blond hair. "You think I'd forget a smokin' hot chick that can turn you catatonic? Hell no, I gotta see this."

Still leaning against the back of the club, boot heel against the stucco, arms crossed over my chest, I shoot him a dark look. Which only makes him laugh harder.

He removes his glasses and tucks them into his collar. "Be honest. How long's it been since a chick with her clothes on made your dick stand up and take notice?"

I say nothing and look away. Apparently, that's answer enough. Because he bursts into laughter. "Seriously?"

Sex is a daily offer, here, at the clubhouse, women walking around all but naked like it's nothing, coming on to me, even though I haven't shown them a lick of interest because none of it appeals to me. My body's been numb for a while. Shut down in a way I can't describe or make sense of. Except to say it feels like I'm older than I am.

"You realize how fucked up that is, right? What? You switchin' sides on me?"

"Oh, shut the fuck up with that shit. I'm not gay, and you know I've got no problem with it. Just not for me, nor am I interested in anything on offer."

"How long's it been since you—" He swivels his hips and mimes fucking.

I rub my forehead, my irritation doubling. "Is nothing sacred to you?"

He shrugs. "Sex is sex. Ain't nothin' sacred 'bout it, unless it's so good you see stars. Don't know why people gotta act like it's more than that."

"This is why your sex life with Blaire has gone down the rabbit hole," I shoot back.

He laughs, unapologetic. "Nah, man. I didn't start that; she did. I'm just a horny bastard, and my wife's got kinks I've tried to tell you about but—"

"Yeah, no. Keep that shit to yourself."

Throwing his hands up, he says, "That. That's exactly what you do."

"What? Fuck. I don't want to know."

His fists curl at his sides, and his shoulders tense up. "Then don't throw shade, man."

I study him for a moment and read his body language, because I can't see his eyes. Exhaling, I say, "Fine, I'm listening. But no details. Give me the gist of it."

His built-up tension deflates, and the corner of his mouth kicks up. "Blaire knows exactly what I'm doing when I'm not with her. She acts all high and mighty in front of you all, but she goes off like a fuckin' Roman candle when I whisper in her ear all the seedy shit I've been up to with other chicks. It's our thing. Don't gotta make sense to anyone but us."

I give him a look because, in my opinion, that's fucked up. But their relationship's always been toxic, and I don't think he sees it for what it is—or would know what a good relationship looks like if it bit him in the ass. Not that I'm the expert. But you can be sure I wouldn't stick around if my woman wanted to stray. I wouldn't expect her to if I did either. And you can be damn sure I wouldn't want a woman who was okay with me going to another woman's bed. It's just not how I'm built.

"So, where is she? You said two, right? Thought I'd be late and miss the show."

It's nearly 2:35. I shrug as anxiety hits me. I hate this feeling of not knowing where she is or what happened. It messes with my head, pulling at old threads that are barely holding me together.

We both fall silent, waiting, leaning against the building. Bodie attempts to start a conversation several times, but when I don't bite, he gives up and calls me an ornery ass.

Finally, a little Honda whips into the lot. A second later, she jumps out of the car, flustered and breathless. "I'm so sorry… I'm never late. I swear." She's distracted, reaching into her purse. "A cop stopped me for speeding." She produces an inhaler and takes a quick pull on it. After taking a few steadying breaths, her gaze finally meets mine.

Bodie mutters, "Fucking Davis."

"Do you have asthma?" My question catches her off guard, she looks down at the inhaler, then back to me. She hurries to stuff the inhaler back into her purse.

"Yeah, it's no big deal. It won't hinder me in any way."

"That's not why I was asking." It's another feather, and a big one at that. The way she's studying my expression sets off little alarm bells pinging in my mind.

"Oh, yeah. I've had it my whole life. It's manageable if I don't get too worked up. But I keep one of these on me at all times."

I nod, tucking these details away. "Good to know."

She's a little disheveled. Her hair is pinned up in a messy bun, a few loose strands blow in the breeze across her face. There's a light sheen of sweat on her skin and the sight has my hand twitching with the urge to reach out, touch her, and calm her nerves. To feel that rapid beating pulse beneath my fingers.

Bodie bumps my shoulder. "Dude, she asked you a question."

I blink and meet her stare. "What?"

Her eyebrows are drawn together. "Can I still audition?" There's a touch of desperation in her question. She adjusts the bag on her shoulder, eyes flicking between me and Bodie. "Look, I promise I won't ever be late again. I'm a good dancer—a good employee. If you give me a shot, you won't regret it." She's still out of breath. Something about the way she's looking at me makes me think this isn't just nerves. She needs this, which has me wondering and worrying about why. Like, is she low on cash, desperate, and behind on bills?

Fuck. I care about the people I hire, but the degree at which I care about this chick, in like a day, is bordering on levels that sound crazy even to me.

I tuck my hair, which has fallen forward, behind my ear. Her gaze follows the movement, roaming over my tattoos. A spark of something flitters across her eyes, and for a second, I think it's lust. But it's there one second and gone the next, leaving me questioning if I saw it.

"Have you danced anywhere before?" Bodie asks, granting mercy on my dumb ass.

"Yeah, I uh—danced at the Pink Melon in Vegas for a little over a year and at a small joint in Fresno for a year and a half. But to be honest, it's been a while since I've been on stage. My brother got into some trouble… with drugs… and well, he needed me. So I've spent the last few months making sure he stayed clean and out of prison."

I feel an instant kinship with her. I know what it's like to put your life on hold to take care of a family member.

"And what brings you to Albuquerque?" I ask. It's one of the million questions I have for her queued up in my head.

Bodie throws his hands up. "Finally! He speaks!"

I stifle the urge to knock him on his ass.

"The city that never sleeps isn't the best place for my brother to stay clean, if you know what I mean. I thought moving somewhere a little slower-paced and getting him away from his friends would be what he needed to start over. There's also a great outpatient rehab center here that his mentor referred him to." She shrugs. "So here I am."

"And your brother?" I ask.

Lily smiles warmly, and her eyes light up. "Doing better. Thanks for asking. He's staying with family for a while until I find my feet, but once I get set up here, he'll follow me down. Maybe get a job and a place of his own. Or at least, that's the plan."

I nod as respect for her ignites in my chest. What she's had to live through couldn't have been easy, and yet she still stood by her brother. She's got her shit together and is raising up those around her, something I believe in wholeheartedly.

"No, you didn't miss your chance. The audition's still on if you feel up to it." I head toward the back door and hold it open for her.

Relief floods her face. She smiles full wattage, and *oh fuck*, the sight sends a ripple of chills down my spine.

I eye her layered silver jewelry and the many rings on her fingers. Her shirt is white, thin, and dips low enough that it gives me a mouthwatering view of her cleavage, her ample tits barely contained in a white lace bra that's visible underneath. The shirt itself reads, "Wild Beauty," which suits her to a T—a little wild, a whole lot beautiful, and I love that she's confident enough to flaunt it.

For a moment, she meets my stare head-on. Her brow lifts as if calling me out on my ogling. Her expression pulls a smirk from me, something I haven't done in ages.

I don't understand it, but she seems as fascinated with me as I am with her.

Bodie clears his throat, ruining the moment.

I gesture toward the door. "Come on. I'll show you around."

She walks ahead, and I can't help but watch the figure-eight sway of her hips.

She might not be Elle, but my curiosity to know more about her is definitely piqued.

The frightened teen I've seen in my dreams is miles apart from this strong, independent woman who is hell on wheels. Linking them in any way is just wishful thinking. People change, but do they change this much? No, not in my opinion.

My gaze falls to her ass in those faded jean cutoffs. They're tight and hug her bubble butt. It's all too easy to imagine the biteable ass I'd find underneath. But would it be covered in lace or cotton? What color?

Fuck. Where the fuck is my mind today?

On sex. Yes, that's fucking obvious. My libido, like a separate entity, is suddenly awake and demanding I sate myself with every inch of her, like a starved fucker.

Bodie and I almost collide as we try to enter the door. We jockey for position behind her like two kids. He reaches out, faking a grab. I shove his hand away and slam him against the doorframe, my forearm across his chest.

This only delights him, if the wide dimple smile is anything to go by. After I deliver a warning, I let him go. He wastes no time in catching up with me.

"Did he give you a ticket?" Bodie asks.

She casts a glance back at us over her shoulder. "Yeah."

Curious, I ask, "For what?"

She pauses and waits for me to fall just a step behind her. Her smirk is a little wicked. "For going twenty over."

A grunt escapes me. My mouth twitches as I fight my amusement. "Speed demon."

"Yeah. I love the wind in my hair. Feels like…" She trails off,

66

something flickering behind her eyes.

A memory surfaces, a hand surfing in the breeze out of a car window. It's there and gone in a heartbeat. "What were you gonna say?" I press, hoping against hope for a tie to this breadcrumb, even if it's not at all possible she's Elle.

She waves me off. "Nothing, just… like it, is all. Feels like being on the run. Like I'm getting away with something."

Her words have a dull edge, and the emotion behind them lacks substance.

"Which way to the dressing room?"

"I'll show her," Bodie jumps in.

The fuck he will.

I turn with a scowl. My glare says it all. I will beat his ass if he says another word. I point towards the bar. *Go.* And like a good fucking boy, he does. His hands come up in defeat as he backs away, grinning like a fiend.

Once Lily and I get to the dressing room, I apologize for Raven not being here and explain she had plans, a music festival with her girlfriend. She tells me it's fine and then watches intently as I peel the name Jules off the top of the mirror.

"Do you have music you want me to play?"

"Oh, yeah." She reaches into her bag and pulls out an iPod. "Let me just prep the song." After a moment of scrolling, she hands it to me. I note the song, an old rock song—one I love. Fate? Coincidence? Because *fuck* does this one bring back memories.

She gestures toward my hand and asks, "Why'd she leave?"

I stare at the crumpled tape. "Oh, uh-mmm. She didn't. I had to let her go."

When she continues to stare at me, I explain. I'm not sure why I do so, but maybe I don't want her to think poorly of me. "A customer made a pass at her. I didn't know she was seeing Jaxson, my bartender, and shit went down." She furrows her brow, so I keep going. "Had I known they were dating, I could've kept Jaxson off the same shift or had security keeping a closer eye on them."

"What happened?"

"Jaxson lost it when the guy touched her. Shouldn't have happened, but the bouncer didn't catch the creep in time. Guy was too slick."

"And?"

"Jaxson broke his nose and put him in the hospital."

Her eyes go wide. "And you fired her for that?"

"Both of them," I say, my tone resolute.

"But why? The customer was the one out of line."

"Because they kept it from me. I let my employees get away with a lot, but something like this… a lie by omission that puts people at risk? No."

She considers it momentarily. After dropping her bag in the chair, she crosses her arms over her chest. "Maybe it was new. Maybe they hadn't gotten around to telling you yet."

There's something about her stance, her attitude, her backbone, that stirs my blood.

"I found out it had been going on for months. I'm not unreasonable."

"They probably just wanted to work the same shifts."

I shake my head. "Nah. They knew it would cause problems, and they still kept it quiet. Had coworkers lie for them. My life's complicated enough without having to guess who I can and can't trust."

Her gaze is scrutinizing, like she's evaluating the stubborn man living under my skin and taking his measure.

Finally, she says, "I won't be but a few minutes."

It hits me then—that I'm standing in the dressing room and she needs to change. I turn to leave but hesitate at the door and peer at her over my shoulder.

"I'm not… I don't…"

She tilts her head, confused. "What?"

"I'm not that guy." It comes out rougher than intended. "The strip club manager who expects, you know, favors. Just… in case you were worried about that." And yet, in my mind, I'm tempted to pick her up, sit her pretty ass on the vanity, and wedge my hips between those thighs, maybe even steal my first taste of her bee-stung lips.

She faces the vanity and begins to pull items from her bag, and surprises me by saying, "I know. I checked you out a little before I decided to try for the job."

"Smart girl." The words are coated with pride.

"I try to be. Although I make stupid decisions sometimes, or my heart does. But I stopped listening to that years ago."

When her head lifts, she meets my gaze through the mirror. There's a cold, detached expression now covering her features. Whatever memory she visited just now shut her down.

I'm dying to know what it was. Instead, I force myself to say what I should. "Let me know if you need anything."

"I'm good," she says. "I'll be out there soon."

I hope to God she is *good*, because I don't think I have it in me to turn her away. Seeing her again, learning more about her, is the only thing on my mind.

The dilemma sticks with me as I reenter the main room and take a seat next to Bodie, who immediately hands me a cold beer.

I've lived by a certain moral code all my life. And now I'm what, going to suddenly throw it out the window? Not to mention, there's my staff to consider. I'd look like the worst fucking hypocrite if I started anything with Lily after letting Jules and Jaxson go.

My undeniable attraction to her should stop me from bringing her on board. Will it, though? No. But it should. It fucking should.

CHAPTER 6

The best dancers lose and find themselves on the stage.

When Lily calls out that she's ready, I kill the overhead lights and flip the switch for the neon in one motion. The club's logo, a spilled cocktail with the name Wet Tips in bright teal and pink, duplicates itself across every glossy black surface—the bar top, upholstery, and polished tables.

As I return to the table, one row back from the stage, I spin my chair around and hook my arms over the back. It's mainly foresight on my part to use it as a shield. If Lily can get me semi-hard in nothing but shorts, my dick has no chance when she reveals more of her tawny skin.

I hit Play on the remote, and the music cues up immediately. The first notes of Whitesnake's "Here I Go Again" stream through the speakers, starting as a melancholy ballad of synthesized keyboard tones. The song sends a rush of nostalgia through me. My dad loved this song. He'd tell Joey and me to crank it up whenever it came on the radio while we worked endlessly together to rebuild my old 1969 Charger.

Fuck, I miss them. Wish they were still here. The memories fade as Lily steps out onto the stage, pulling me firmly back to the present.

I'm prepared for some type of sexy outfit. What I'm not prepared for is a homely person—no, make that a homeless person—with layers of baggy clothes and dirt on her face. So much dirt that she's almost unrecognizable. The most distinguishable piece is a huge old Army jacket, and she's hidden her beautiful hair under a beanie to give her the full effect of a homeless vet.

Something about it tugs at my heart. What is this? Because she might as well have cast a line, sunk a damn hook into the tender walls of my chest, and reeled me right in, ripping out chunks of me in the process.

I look over at Bodie. He looks over at me. Somehow, both sadness and amusement light up in his eyes. He sits up a little straighter and grins.

She said she looked into me, but how deeply? Does she know I was Army? The questions fire off rapidly inside my mind, and at the same time, I watch this multifaceted woman come closer.

She swaggers, almost drunkenly, to the middle of the stage with her head down and hands at her sides. When she reaches her destination, she falls to her knees. Her palms open in front of her. She stares at her hands, as if she's puzzling out all the world's problems, and the answers sit there in the palms of her hands. Then she looks up and meets my gaze. Not Bodie's. She looks directly into my eyes as her hands slide forward.

Like she's asking for help. Begging.

A flashback crashed into me like the one I had yesterday. A guy in an alleyway. He's holding an old red coffee can up to me. I can't place it—this memory. And the tether to it breaks as the chorus explodes.

Lily's fingers curl. She brings clenched fists to her forehead, and she begins to sway. In the next instant, she curls over herself and pounds her fists on the stage. In anger, in frustration, I don't know. But she's telling me something, and my entire body is triggered by it. My chest tight, my gut hollow, every muscle tense as if ready to go to her. An eerie feeling of familiarity floods over me.

The beanie falls off. Snatching it up, she cleans her face and spins on one knee around the floor. In profile, she falls back, her hips lifting and rotating in a circle. She stops, her pelvis raised, her arms dropping beside her. Silently, she cries out and rises as if shouting her pleas to the ceiling or sky above her. The move reeks of desperation.

But what is it she's desperate for?

Fuck.

It sinks in that this isn't an audition to see how much experience she has, nor is it a test to see if she has what it takes to make men adore her. This is an act. A story. It's art she's performing on that stage, not a hustle.

Bodie whispers, "Is it wrong that she's dressed like a dude and I'm hard as fuck right now?"

I ignore him, and the chorus begins. Drums start to pound. In quick, harsh movements, she divests herself of her jacket, and her hair fans out as she gracefully rolls to her feet. A plaid shirt is now revealed, buttoned at the neck and open below, showing a white ribbed tank top. For a moment, I'm taken back to the flashback yesterday with Veno.

It can't be a fucking coincidence, can it?

Lily's knees bend as her hips rock. Her hands rise above her and cross. When they come back down slowly over her chest, she rips her shirt open and flings it away. The movement reveals more of her perfect skin, a pair of tits straining the fabric of the thin wife-beater tank, a black bra evident underneath.

When the tank eventually comes off, I drag my hand over the bottom half of my face because *God damn...* the bra is sheer and hides nothing.

My cock hardens further, kissing my zipper and attempting a jailbreak.

Out of the corner of my eye, I see Bodie shift in his chair and adjust himself. He grates out, "If you don't hire her, I'll have you committed. Tell Prez you've gone full mental and have your ass locked up."

He won't need to.

She kicks off her shoes and pulls off her belt and jeans while dancing across the stage. The rest comes off as she moves toward the pole. Then she's circling it once, playfully spinning around it.

This is when I see the massive black wings tattooed down her back. From here, they look like eagle feathers, and one wing is bent at an odd angle, as if broken.

She turns, holding the pole from above as she grinds her ass against it, using it as a tool to taunt us before letting go and bending over to touch the floor. She runs her hands slowly up her body as she rolls back up. The way the light touches her skin, the way it reflects off the silkiness of it, has me entranced. She certainly takes care of the gifts God has given her.

"Jesus," I groan.

Bodie nods. "What I wouldn't give to be that thong right now. Snug as a b—."

"Shut up." I backhand his chest before he can finish that sentence. Thankfully, he doesn't.

As the guitar solo of the song riffs, she jumps and straddles the pole. When she gains some height, she becomes a wingless angel in flight, doing moves that I've only seen at conventions. Moves no other girl working here can pull off, spinning around the pole like she's mastered the art, the muscles in her arms flexing.

It seems unreal that she can hold her body weight in these positions with her arms alone. Her toned muscles pop as she grips and releases her hold, even the ones in her legs, which work in concert to keep her airborne and spinning.

To say she's experienced is an understatement. Lily works the pole with class, making it look like magic. A balance of ballet, acrobatics, and dance working perfectly as one, as she spins and tips upside down, like gravity doesn't apply to her, toes pointed, hands poised.

This isn't just something she's good at. She must have practiced this for years.

She's flawless.

The final chorus repeats, layering harmonies, and her movements slow and become reverent. She walks on air and uses it to spin in an unbelievably seamless flow. As the song winds down, she comes to a gradual stop, and her eyes flicker up to mine.

Defiance and some intense emotion stare out at me from her irises. Her breaths are deep. Her lips parted. Hair wild and untamed, her skin slick with sweat. I shift in my chair and blatantly make my dick more comfortable, letting her know that I more than loved everything she did up there. It's inappropriate as fuck. But at the moment, I don't feel like the boss. I'm just a man. A man who wants the woman up on that stage staring back at him, like I'm all she sees.

Another song starts. One that automatically makes you think of down-and-dirty sex. I doubt a priest could listen to it without getting hard. It's "Closer" by Nine Inch Nails.

Lily scoops up the plaid shirt and puts it on, but leaves it open. She turns and stops. The sight of her about to walk away has my muscles coiling, wanting nothing more than to follow her.

My father used to say, "There's no justice and no fairness in this life. Get over it and find the sparks of hope and peace that remain." I feel like this is one of those times. I may not find what I've lost. I may not ever fully recover from my head trauma. But does that mean I should deny myself every good thing that comes along?

Lily studies me as if she knows I'm warring with myself.

My gaze blatantly trails down her body, taking in every silken inch, all the way from her wickedly sinful, rock-hard nipples to her bare toes. Before I can blink, she's moving straight towards me. She reaches the end of the stage and then begins to descend the steps. Her hips swing wide with each step.

Oh fuck!

I comb both hands through my hair, trying to calm myself down. But with the look in her eyes and the lyrics hinting at all the naughty things we could do to each other, it's a losing game.

She circles me slowly, her fingers barely touching my shoulders and the tips of my hair, sending a shudder down my spine.

She places a finger under my chin, lifting my face. Her gaze travels over my features. Then her hands are in my hair. The sensation of her hands tenderly combing through my hair has a half-growl, half-groan rumbling out of my chest. *It feels so fucking good. So right.*

There's something there, something precious in her eyes, and desire sitting alongside whatever it is.

Before I can demand she never stop, her hands trail to my shoulders, and she begins to dance.

Gradually, she lets one side of the shirt fall off her shoulder, then the other. With her legs parted, her knees move languidly, the long waves of hair swaying in opposition. She turns and eases the hem of the shirt down, teasing and torturing me as she hides and reveals the luscious globes of her ass from sight. She bends forward over her legs but turns her head to keep eye contact with me.

This close-up view, the unquenchable need to touch, almost unravels every bit of my control. While studying my expression, she reaches behind her and unlatches her bra.

I'm not at all prepared when the sheer material drops to the floor.

Because fuck the Grand Canyon. Fuck Niagara Falls. Fuck Yellowstone and the Grand Tetons. This—right fucking here— is the best view I've seen in all thirty-nine of my years.

A sight I could never get enough of.

She motions for me to turn in my chair, and I do.

Somewhere in the back of my mind, my subconscious screams, *You shouldn't be doing this*! But that part of my brain is drowned out by the pure, unfiltered cravings for this woman who currently has my cock's fealty.

I'm goddamn desperate for a taste of everything she's offering.

Before I can get my bearings, she's on me, straddling my thighs and sitting on my stiff cock, her nipples brushing over my pecs.

Testing the waters, I skim my hand down her spine. Soft to the touch, and I'll be damned if she doesn't arch like a cat. Hungry as hell for more, I hold onto her hip, tentatively, then more aggressively as if to show her that I'm committing to stepping over this line with her. We both crossed it ages ago, might as well revel in it now.

I grind up as she presses down, and a moan simultaneously escapes both our mouths. Her light-blue eyes hold mine captive. Then she's snaking her hands through my hair as her mouth nears mine. She stops a millimeter away from making contact. Our heavy breaths dance for what seems like an eternity.

Before we can fall into a kiss, she pulls back, bending away from me, laying her body out like a banquet on my lap, until she's bent over my legs and her hair is spilling over the floor. Though disappointment pierces my chest, I feast on what's before me. My eyes raking over her flat stomach, her sinfully gorgeous round tits, the tight little buds of her nipples, the miles of beautiful skin, every bit so divine I feel fucking unworthy.

She grabs my right hand and runs it roughly between the valley of her breasts and down over her stomach. I let her hand be my guide until it gets a mind of its own.

Lily palms her tit and squeezes one nipple. My other hand travels south, teasing the top edge of her panties. My thumb lightly plays there, tentatively sweeps underneath. An inch, then three. And I watch, mesmerized, as her entire body shivers.

She comes back up to face me. Her hand moves up my chest, up my neck, and in no time, her fingers softly caress my bottom lip. She moves forward as if to kiss me, veering off at the last second to press her cheek to mine. Her breaths tickle the shell of my ear.

"Open," she demands. She draws back, then slowly slides her thumb into my mouth. As I stare into her seductive crystal eyes, my tongue studies her taste, her sugary taste. It's sweet and addictive.

She bites her lip and her eyes close. I swear to God, I come a little at the sight.

The song ends, and silence descends.

Lily and I both blink, as if coming out of a mental fog. We sit, stare, and suck in air as if we just fucked each other raw.

"Tell me you've got a box of tissues lying around here somewhere," Bodie mutters. "My boxers are wet as fuck."

It's like we forgot we weren't alone. In the seconds that follow, her finger comes out of my mouth. She dips her face and then takes a moment to look around. At Bodie, at me, at our positions as if to ensure that yep... I'm still here and she's still on my lap, riding my happy and hard-as-fuck dick. She scrambles off. Her eyes won't meet mine as she gathers her shirt and bra.

"I'm sorry—I didn't mean—I don't usually take it that far. I sometimes get a little lost in the music," she explains.

No shit! Only... she's not the only one, apparently.

"You're sorry?" Bodie asks. "What the hell is there to be sorry for?

That was pure fucking porn."

Lily's skin flushes a pretty pink as she hastily buttons the shirt and covers herself. She stuffs the bra into the front pocket. When she does finally dare to look me in the face again, she's hesitant and flustered. "So... uh... did I get the job?"

"Fuck yeah, you got the job!" Bodie responds.

I throw him a I-swear-to-God-I-will-put-you-to-ground look.

All the reasons why I shouldn't hire her swirl around in my head with all the reasons I should. Which is mainly, I want her. Undeniably. I want her. For the first time in my life that I can remember, I want more. I want something like this girl to help me fill the void that lives inside me. Maybe then, I can find a bit of hope and a reason to press on and stop losing my mind trying to chase a ghost.

But that's a double-edged knife, because giving in to these feelings doesn't come with complications and issues.

Lily bites her lip, most likely reading my quiet thoughtfulness as me weighing whether or not I'll let her into my life and this club. Which I am, just probably not for the reasons she thinks. Her pleading blue eyes burrow right through me, and hell... I thought I was putty a moment ago. That look melts away my ability to say no. She could own me with that look.

Maybe she already does.

Two songs, one lap dance, and one heart-stopping look, and she's fucking turning me into something beyond what I've been. All but dead and heartless.

"Yeah, you got it. The job's yours."

Her smile blooms so bright, then turns impish, and it's the cutest thing I've ever seen. "Really?"

She clasps her hands together.

"We'll need to figure out your pay and schedule and see what we can work out." I nod toward the dressing room. "Go get changed and meet me in the room at the end of the hall when you're done. My office is just down from the dressing room."

She agrees, and after picking up the last of her clothes, she heads to the back of the club.

"Goose, c'mon, man. Help a brother out. Throw me a towel or somethin'. I made a mess of myself." Bodie has his belt off. He's pulled open his jeans to peek into his pants. The evil grin he's sporting is ridiculous.

"Fuck off, Rivers."

I give him shit, but truth be told, my briefs aren't exactly dry either.

CHAPTER 7

The answers are simple, yet we twist them until they're unrecognizable.

I tentatively enter the doorway of Finn's office. The space is larger than I expected. The right half is set up like an office, with his desk in the corner, a filing cabinet, and two credenzas. The other half is more of a lounge area, with a couch, two sofa chairs, and a coffee table. The walls are a subtle gray, complemented by newer, modern black furniture, all done in a minimalist style.

The click of my heels must have alerted him to my arrival, because the computer screen shuts down, as if he put it in sleep mode. Spinning in his chair, he faces me, gestures to a chair in front of his desk. "Come in. Take a seat." His expression is difficult to read, and I wonder if he's finally figured it out—who I am.

The thump of my pulse overrides all sound.

I drop my purse beside the chair and sit, crossing my legs as I do.

Finn leans back and laces his fingers over his flat stomach. The motion stretches his distressed black tee between the width of his shoulders, prominently displaying his upper body strength. The amount of ink he's sporting tells a story, so does the scar and the amount of silver in his coarse, wavy hair. It speaks of a life lived, one I know nothing about.

And like me, he likes his jewelry. There's a bulky ring on every finger, beaded and leather bracelets, and a long chain rests between his pecs, holding a HOC pendant at the end.

My awareness of the mistake I've made unfolds as I examine my emotions.

I'm a fucking liar.

But believing my own bullshit is a new one.

It's not anger riding me right now. It's hope. It's a desperate ache for what once was—to hear his voice in my ear, to know his mind again, to feel his touch on my skin, even though his hands were all over me less than fifteen minutes ago. I still want him in a way I shouldn't. Sure, I got lost in the music, but it was more than that. I got lost in him, in the heady sensation of him finally touching me again. He touched me like a woman he wanted to take to his bed and couldn't get enough of.

This need is like faulty wiring I haven't fixed yet, sparking just under my skin. It's a weakness and something I can't afford to let loose, or it'll wreak nothing but havoc and ruin everything I'm attempting to do.

Under his stare, time stretches, making me self-conscious of every movement I make. I break the stare and take in his office.

It's clean and organized, with zero clutter. Everything is in its proper place, even the papers on his desk. The only personal item is a picture frame facing him, and I burn to see it.

His cut hangs from a tree-like coat rack in one corner. There are some black-and-white pictures on the walls, scenic views, a lake, a forest, and a close-up of a tree. Similar to the one at what I think of as "our place".

My gaze slowly returns to him, and I find him watching me. He has one arm propped up now, his chin resting on his fist.

The words in bold black tattooed lettering mock me from his forearm.

RESPECT

Give it to those worthy

HONOR

Bleed it

HONESTY
Demand it
LOYALTY
Above all else

I fight not to grind my teeth. *Really? Loyalty*? To whom? Certainly not to me.

"Why stripping?" he asks, still studying me.

I shrug. "Why not? I love to dance. I've done it my whole life, and the money's great. Plus, I'm not too proud to say I like material things."

His mouth twitches with amusement or disappointment—I don't know. "You said you've been dancing for a long time?" He tilts his head, analyzing my response. "Ever had any classical training?"

I fight the urge to shift. "Yes." I offer nothing more. *What is this?* Is this a game or does he really still not remember me? Needing to steer this conversation before I give too much away, I ask, "How long have you owned the club?"

"Five years."

"I've been wondering," he says, his voice low, controlled. "Why that costume? The Army jacket, the plaid shirt?"

"I wanted to stand out. Tell a tragic story," I say, my heart pounding. *Our story.*

"You know I served?"

"Oh, uh-mmm, yeah." I gesture to his left bicep. "I saw the tattoo."

Maybe he has an inkling of what's really going on here, but it doesn't look like he's going to come right out and ask. Before I can put it out there, he hammers another nail home in my chest.

"You know, you remind me of a girl," he says, and breaks eye contact as he looks directly at the picture I was eyeing a moment ago.

Not a woman. A girl.

"What, like an old girlfriend?"

"In a way, yeah." Well, if that doesn't feel like shit, I'm not sure what does.

"Somebody you went to school with?" I ask, knowing the answer but needing to hear more truths spill from his lips, the whole of it.

"No. Someone I met after. In Albuquerque."

"Someone special?"

He hesitates. "Someone I lost… a girl I lost track of."

Not special then. Just… lost.

When he turns back to me, I struggle to hold his gaze, instead studying the new ink on his other fist—a red swallow. Like he took something that was "ours" and made it into a "theirs". Possibly to represent whoever's heart he stole after mine?

I swallow the toxic urges bubbling up inside me and fight to steady my resolve. I've come this far. I won't crumble now and fuck everything up. And fuck him for his lost girl comment. He lost track of me? I was right fucking here. I waited so long for him that I nearly died trying to escape the chaos he stirred up before he left. Veno finally tracked me down, and where the fuck was he? Not here protecting me, that's for damn sure.

"How much did you check into me?" He asks with a sharper-than-normal tone.

"Enough to know you don't usually let things go that far with an employee," I say, keeping my tone light, but there's an edge to it. I think he catches on as the muscle in his jaw jumps. He swipes his hand slowly down his mouth, palming his goatee as he licks his bottom lip. The muscles in his arm flex with the movement, his tattoos transforming into arm porn.

Bastard, I think, as wetness coats my panties, although my eyes eat up every detail.

"The girls who audition don't usually sit on my lap, grind on my dick, and stick their sweet little fingers in my mouth for me to suck on." His dark-blue eyes penetrate with each word. The room shrinks, the air sucked away by his comment and the heat in his gaze. "Not sure if that's a regular thing for you, but it was definitely a first for me."

Mentally, I'm walking over and slapping him across the face. It's a struggle, but I maintain my composure. "It won't happen again," I say, projecting sincerity. "I'm here for the job. Nothing more."

He watches me for a long moment, then nods, jaw tight. "Good.

Because that can't happen again if I hire you. Whatever this is"—he motions between us—"would be something we'd both need to ignore."

I hold his gaze, trying to act as if I'm on the fence, though I'm solidly on one side of it. Using another HOC will be safer and easier. And once I'm working here, I'll have better access to other members of the MC, since they supposedly visit the establishment quite often.

Nodding, he says, "We have a deal then. I'll have my assistant, Raven, contact you." He hands me the paperwork from the corner of his desk. "If you'll just fill out the first two now, we'll know how to contact you, what kind of shifts you're looking for, and what you're okay with. Raven likes to review those details before putting you on the schedule. She'll give you a call to confirm everything, get you set up with the person who handles costumes, and answer any questions you might have."

"Okay, no problem."

The tension between us is palpable as I fill out the forms, his presence like a malignant storm cloud, hovering over me and studying my every move. His mood charges the air, the intensity building with every second I sit in front of him.

When I'm done, I stand and hand over the papers while slinging my bag over my shoulder. "Thank you for the job. It'll help me get my brother back on his feet so we can make a go of it here."

He nods and takes them from my hands. I turn to go.

"Lil'," he says suddenly, stopping me in my tracks. I freeze, stomach tightening.

Masking my surprise, I ask, "Lil'?"

"It's a good name for the stage. Or would you prefer something else?" His gaze is inquisitive as if he's daring me to react.

I swallow the lump in my throat. "As long as it's not Angel, I'm good with whatever."

He doesn't pry, but the curiosity has a wrinkle forming between his brows. "I already told you what went down with the employees I let go, but it still needs to be said. I expect honesty and that the other girls are treated with courtesy and respect. I don't tolerate drama or lies."

"I understand."

For a long beat, he says nothing, then nods once. "Good. As far as private dances go, it's your body, your choice. You decide when and what you're willing to do. Raven will review it with you and fill the staff in so they know what to tell clients when they ask. If there's ever a problem with a client, another employee, or something outside of the club that gets too big for you to handle, I hope you'll come to me. If not me, go to Raven. Raven handles most of the day-to-day stuff, but if it's bigger than that, I expect you to come see me."

"I can do that."

Something passes between us—an unspoken truth, a shared acknowledgment of our attraction that we're both going to ignore. But I push it aside and head for the door.

"You know, you already had the job, Lily. Before the lap dance."

I pause, a grin tugging at my lips. "I know."

I walk away, ready to put some much-needed distance between me and the man who has the power to turn me back into the woman who was too weak to survive on her own. I'm not that girl anymore. And if being around him brings her to the surface, then distance is exactly what I need to keep her at bay.

LOST LYREBIRD

CHAPTER 8

*When our inner compass keeps spinning,
we're left without a direction to move forward.*

I fight like the damned to hold on to the dream. I want nothing more than to sink deeper, to pull more details into focus, to see her face clearly—the girl who haunts most of my nights. But it's no use. She's a wisp of smoke, slipping away when I reach for her.

I'm tugged into consciousness, chest heaving, sweat coating my skin. I cling to what remains. Nonsensical pieces. Riddles with no rhyme or reason, as if surrendered from a fractured kaleidoscope. There are too many potholes to navigate in my waking hours, too many dead ends.

I'm fucking lost.

A Road Captain with no map.

Unable to move forward for fear of what I'm leaving behind.

Like always, the dream leaves me devastated, filled with longing and regret, as my heart rate begins to regulate.

I sit up and swing my legs over the side of the bed, pushing my fingers through my hair. For a good while, I sit there and try to hold on to the details. Then I reach into my nightstand for my journal and pen out everything I can remember. More puzzle pieces. Breadcrumbs. And feathers to follow.

I attempt to make sense of the fragments, these small windows into moments from the past, twisted with fantasy, mixed with flashes from my tours of duty and childhood. Sometimes I don't know what's real and what shit my brain has made up. However, one thing stands firm, she's there in some way, hiding in the details, a ghost at the edge of my consciousness.

When I finish jotting it all down, I pull out my highlighters. Green for the Army shit. Purple for the fantasy crap that doesn't seem real. Like *Puff the Magic Dragon* shit. Blue for my dad, since it was his favorite color, and pale pink for her. Always pink for her. Because when I think of her, I see a sea of pink details, her bird tattoo, flowers, heels, and pink lemonade in her glass. Even her lips, as plush as they were, were a pretty petal pink, which is the only part of her face I ever get a good glimpse of.

Line by line, I highlight it all. It's a ritual, and my way of navigating the madness inside my head.

When I'm finished, I drop the journal into the bottom drawer of my nightstand and send up another prayer to the man upstairs. Not God, but my father. Because God may have given up on me long ago, but I know for damn sure my old man hasn't. He's throwing me guidance. I just have to be smart enough to pay attention and recognize it when it comes.

I check the time on my phone and see it's a little after eight. I don't hear any movement outside my door, so I quickly tug on some jeans and head to the window, buttoning them as I go. As expected, my '70 Roadrunner and two bikes sit in the driveway.

After crossing the loft, I bang on Mateo's door. When there's no response, I swing his door open. I'm greeted by the rank smell of teenage boy, gym socks, with the recent addition of sex. His mom is going to have a field day when I tell her, but fuck, it's not like I can judge him when I was doing the very same thing at his age—sneaking girls through my bedroom window at night to get my rocks off, all under the parental radar.

However, with the number of hours I spend at Wet Tips and the clubhouse, it's not like I can put him on lockdown or monitor his goings-on.

As suspected, Mateo is sprawled facedown on his bed, his head under a pillow. He's so tall now that one foot hangs off the end of the twin bed.

But in my defense, when he first moved in, it was supposed to be for a few weeks. Now it appears as if he's here for the foreseeable future, instead of moving back in with his mom.

With no clear path to the bed, I toe shit out of the way—discarded clothes, and crumpled sheets of paper. My gaze drops to the sketchpad lying open on the floor. There are lines of text in chicken-scratch penmanship, but most of the page is covered in a drawing of a skeletal face screaming. Its mouth gapes open as if it's using every fiber of its being to yell to the heavens. There's also black smoke and debris shooting out from its body.

Dark shit, but I'm honestly happy he's getting it out in some way. This exact thing worked for me. I'm hoping it does the same for him.

I jostle the bed with my foot. "Mateo!"

A groan and a grumbled "Stop" come from under the pillow. He grips it tighter, pressing it down over his head.

"You're late."

"I'm already failing my Chem class. What does it matter?"

"You're failing because you keep missing the first hour and don't make up the work. Your mom's not gonna let you stay here if your grades keep dropping."

He mutters something that I don't catch and continues to lie there.

"Get moving, or you'll be taking a bath in ice water again."

He curses under his breath, knowing I don't make idle threats. In the next instant, he flings the pillow at the floor. The glare he hits me with is lethal. His irises are brown and deep pits of anger. But I've dealt with far scarier men, so his attempt to stare me down has the opposite effect and causes me to chuckle under my breath.

He throws the duvet off, revealing long, hairy legs and black briefs. Thank fuck he doesn't sleep nude, or it would be awkward as fuck. Though yeah, with his morning predicament, there's still that. So I turn and walk out.

In the kitchen, I start the coffee. I pour a cup for myself and fill a thermos for him.

I settle on the couch, resting my mug on the coaster on the far side of the coffee table as I consider where to start on the jigsaw puzzle spread out before me. The remaining pieces are systematically organized by color. A little over a hundred pieces to go before it's finished. That'll take me about a day, maybe two, then I'll glue the pieces together and add it to the pile of puzzles leaning against the wall, which is about a foot deep.

I'm running out of space for them.

The attic is full of boxes with things I salvaged from my childhood home after the meth lab incident. A good portion of the space is taken up by puzzles I've finished over the years.

My shop in the garage isn't an option because of the sawdust, so at some point, I'll need to either start giving them away or find another place to store them.

I like seeing them around, though. They're a reminder that if I can collect all the pieces and put them in the proper order, even if a few go missing, I'll have a clearer view of the image as a whole. Maybe even solve one of the biggest mysteries of my life, if I can do the same with holes in my memories.

Mateo finally appears, broody as ever. He's sporting stubble and wet hair that's haphazardly styled. Grabbing some bread, he slathers it with peanut butter and honey, then tosses it into a baggie. Spying the thermos, he holds it up. "For me?"

I take a sip from my mug and glance at him over the rim. "Looks that way."

A grunt and words follow. Either a "Thank you" or a "Fuck you." Hard to tell. He snatches up his backpack by the door.

"You still meeting your mom after school?"

After scoffing, he murmurs, "If she bothers to show." Then he heads out, slamming the door behind him. I grit my teeth because Jesus, the frame is gonna fall on his head one of these days.

A few seconds go by before I hear him fire up his bike. The engine revs three times, and I'm in the process of shaking my head when his tires screech in protest as he peels out of the driveway.

I take a few deep breaths and roll my shoulders to relieve some tension. When that doesn't work, I grab the remote and hit Play. I spend a good part of my morning drinking coffee and getting lost in the small connections I can make on the puzzle.

As soon as my mind is completely at ease, it begins to drift where it shouldn't—to Lily and her audition.

Not sure I can even call it an audition at this point. It was more of a potent mindfuck, certain moments of it hinting at Lily's complex mind, leaving me with more unanswered questions. Others were so sensual and seemingly intentional, they've driven deep into my psyche and left a permanent impression.

She lingers in my mind. The vision of her nearly naked body is vividly imprinted there in ways I won't be able to unsee. And not having it is going to bring more torment than pleasure.

Same with the sensation of her fingers running through my hair. They left behind a sense of rightness. And it's like my hands remember the feel of her skin. I flex a fist, trying to shake the feeling, but the sweet glide of my palms against her silky skin is right fucking there, as if on instant recall.

Eventually, I stop fighting it. Because I know what this is—biology warring with my years of mastered control. Hormones firing synapses, chemical signals screaming through my veins, urging me to act on instincts as old as the first man who craved the first woman. Oxytocin, dopamine, testosterone—an orchestra of need and want crashing through me in a symphony I can't silence. My body doesn't care about morality, propriety, or the vow I made to keep our relationship on a professional level.

You can't go without sex with another person for years and not acquire the knowledge of your body's basic biological needs.

So after grabbing the stereo remote and changing the playlist to an '80s hit list, I sit back against the couch, close my eyes, and spread my thighs, letting my mind wander where it will. The ease it takes to conjure her to life, the realness of this fantasy, should be unsettling.

Simple Minds' "Don't You" is the first song to come on, and like a siren off the bow of a sinking ship, she's right there waiting, appearing in front of me in my apartment.

I change the babydoll-pink color of her bra and panties, because it reminds me of Elle and makes me feel like a bastard. So baby-blue it is, a set just as sheer, if not more so, than what she wore during her audition. Only this time, it's better, because it's my fantasy she's wielding as she moves, my music she's swaying her hips to, and my gaze the only one she's performing for.

I rub my chest, massaging my pecs before letting my hand fall and cup the bulge in my jeans.

There are times, like in the shower, when I'm limited on hot water supply when I just get right to it, but this isn't one of them. Alone, with nothing but time on my hands today, I edge myself, taking my time and letting the dance build as she moves.

The music shifts U2's "With or Without You" as I rub my cock over my jeans and focus on her hands skimming over her body as she gets lost in song after song.

When "In the Air Tonight" by Phil Collins kicks in, my jeans are open, my dick is in my hand being teased and taunted with strokes and pulls as my other hand plays across my chest. The heat in the loft and on my skin rises as her performance becomes more sensual. A deliberate, sinful tease.

The light blue pops against Lily's golden skin. She comes closer, and the sight of her small nipples on display through the fabric elicits a deep moan from my lips. She places her hands on the coffee table in front of me and bends forward, her tits nearly spilling out of the bra. In the fantasy, she swipes the puzzle to the floor and crawls toward me. She kneels there in front of me and spreads her thighs wide, giving me a close-up view of her gorgeous body as she undulates to the music. Her hands slowly travel up her body, palming her breasts, then reaching behind her to release the clasp of her bra.

Slowly, and with a sly smile, she drops it to the floor.

Her panties come off seconds later, and I melt them away. She sweeps her beautiful hair from one side to the other and gazes straight at me. Reaching out, she takes my hand and moves over me, straddling my lap. The fantasy builds from there. Her hands roaming over my body, mine doing the same to hers.

I pump my cock harder and faster as I imagine what it would be like to sink into her pussy for the first time. That first moment. The wet glide as I buried myself inch by inch. The tight grip of her around me. What her breathy moans would sound like. And fuck, her sultry voice in my ear.

The daydream spins a little darker as I envision a different scenario, her beneath me, fucking her in a way that's not sweet or soft. Giving her all of me and watching her fall apart.

My balls fucking tingle. My mind runs wild with this part of the fantasy. I thrust and fuck into her, as deep as I can get, over and over again until she comes undone and cries my name.

I'm jerking myself hard and fast. An avalanche shifts, and a rumble of pleasure vibrates through me. Like a genie escaping a bottle, my orgasm erupts. It's liquid bliss as far as I'm concerned, ribbons of cum shoot out from my tip, landing across my chest and funneling over the head of my cock. I keep pumping as it goes on and on, an endless fountain because it's been too fucking long since I've felt anything like it. I ride those waves of pleasure until they slowly recede, leaving me a blissed-out state.

I'm not sure how the daydream wielded itself into a motion picture inside my head, but it did, and sure as fuck took on a life of its own.

Two abrupt knocks at the door startle the shit out of me. I scramble off the couch as muttered curses spill from my lips.

Fuck. "Be right there. Just, uh… give me a sec." In the kitchen, I wash my hands and grab a towel, quickly wetting it to wipe myself down. I button up my jeans with hurried fingers as I head to the front door.

Deidre, one of my tenants, stands on the other side of the door, sporting an all-too-knowing smirk when I open it.

"Did I catch you at a bad time?" she asks, peering over my shoulder for a split second, even standing a little on her tiptoes to see around me.

I comb my hair away from my face as concern floods me. "Hey, Deidre. What's up? Something broken at your place?" There's always something breaking in one of the units, and since I don't trust property management companies anymore, not after what happened with Dad's place, I'm left holding the bag when shit goes awry.

But being a landlord has its perks too—a steady stream of income, neighbors I handpick, and helping people like Deidre.

When I pull the door shut somewhat behind me, it forces her to focus on me instead of her search for the woman she thinks is in my apartment. Honestly, it makes me a little uncomfortable as her eyes travel over the expanse of my chest and my tattoos, something I usually keep hidden from the world. Not just due to the scars, but because I hate the questions my tattoos inevitably bring.

"Sorry, let me just grab a shirt, and I'll be right back."

"I don't mind," she calls after me, but I'm already moving through my place. Finding what I need in my middle drawer, I grab the navy shirt at the top and yank it on. When I reenter the doorway, I cross my arms over my chest and lean against the frame. "What's going on?"

Deidre looks good, healthy. She has facial scars from her years of drug use, but her brown skin is clear now. Her hair is freshly styled in thick, colorful braids. She's even wearing a decently modest outfit, and she's put on a good amount of weight. I didn't notice in passing, but it's obvious now, as she stands in front of me, that she's kept her promise to me and stayed clean.

Reaching behind her, she pulls an envelope from her back pocket and holds it out for me to take. "I wanted to give you this in person. It's my notice." I open it and thumb through the contents. Inside is a check for two months' rent and a letter. She shakes her head when she sees my confusion. "It's not what you think. I got a new gig, a job in New Orleans—my auntie owns a restaurant and she's been lookin' for help. My mom told her how I turned my life around, and she's offered it to me. She's giving me a chance to study under her and become a chef."

The corner of my mouth twitches. I clamp down hard on the emotion burning in my chest. "Damn, Deidre—I'm happy for you."

She shrugs, but I can see she's proud of herself too. Her mouth spreads in a wide smile. "I thought you would be. I know I owe you so much more than—"

I cut her off by pulling out the check and ripping it up. Her jaw drops. "You don't owe me anything. Seeing you turn your life around is enough for me."

"Goose…"

"I mean it."

She flushes, then rushes forward and wraps her arms around me. I stand there, arms bent and held out, until I awkwardly pat her back. She pulls away, pointing at me. "You're the bee's knees, pappi, you know? I hope you find a woman who can see that someday."

I brush off the comment and ask her more about the move and her new position. Eventually, I wish her my best and she leaves. When I reenter my loft, I lean back against the door and feel the emotions rise. Thoughts of the day I offered Diedre a second chance flood through me; thankfully, it's a memory I don't have to reach for or that has fallen into a pothole in my mind. She didn't trust me at first, didn't trust herself, but damn… what a difference a year makes.

Raising my hand, I hold up my pointer finger, acknowledging my father and the request he made of me. *"Keep helping those who need it the most."*

Well, old man, I'm doing my part. Another person off the streets. Think you can start pulling some strings for me with the man upstairs? Because I could use a little help here, and I'm feeling a little lost in the weeds.

As I head to my room, guilt surges again. The shame of what I was doing before Deidre knocked rushes over me. Did she hear me? Wait for me to finish before knocking?

Nice, Finn. Real fucking nice.

I jump into the shower, scrubbing off the evidence of my sins. Cold water, sharp and biting, is just what I need to clear the last hour from my mind. When I'm done, I tie a towel around my waist and start on my morning routine, trimming up my goatee and shaving my jaw. Afterward, I stare at myself in the mirror, letting my gaze roam over my chest, over the tattoo of the bird I can't let go of. It represents the way she disappeared from my life. From a girl to a flight of birds, to nothing but smoke.

Lily's face flashes in my mind—the way she looked at me in my office. The way she stared at the picture that means so much to me. The way she felt in my arms.

Not to mention that fucking lap dance.

For the first time in a long time, I hadn't been thinking, just giving in to my body's demands. I wanted something besides this life I've allowed myself to have. A spark of hope for something more. Yeah, lust was the key player, sure, but that hope—it did something to me. Had she come into my office and given even a slight hint that she'd felt a certain way about me, I would have possibly found a different way to bring her on board while still giving me a chance to get to know her on another level.

She hadn't. She'd walked in like any other applicant, as if not a damn thing had happened between us. It threw me for a fucking loop.

Because fuck, was that how she'd won other gigs in the past? Was that just part of her audition routine? Pretty aggressive, but it put me in a position where I either had to hire her or worry about her suing my ass for sexual harassment.

The whole fucking thing made me feel like a tool for thinking it meant more.

Shaking the thoughts from my head, I drop my towel and get dressed. When I go to pull socks from the top drawer, the bottles of pills inside rattle and taunt me. The temptation hits like a punch.

Take me, they all but whisper. No more pain. No more headaches. *Just one little pill. Just for today.*

I know it's all bullshit. But I still hear them. Every damn day. And like yesterday, and the day before, I tell them to fuck right the hell off, and slam the drawer shut.

They tug at me, though. Like there's a string tied from my gut to the actual fucking pill bottle, one I have to work daily to *snip,* until I'm either far enough away that their effect wavers, or my mind's occupied enough to forget their pull.

I've found facing the temptation each day helps lessen the lure. I'm stronger at fighting my addiction because I don't shy away from it. I face it head-the-fuck-on.

The pain makes it a fucking relentless fight. Most of it's triggered by thoughts of my little bird at the edge of my mind. An inner voice screams at me about my promise. Flashes of memory come too, set off by everything and nothing. And that fucking woodpecker pecks. Peck. Peck. PECKS! Saying… you're forgetting something, something important. Fight harder. Dig deeper. Remember. Find her.

I want to. God, I want to with everything in me. It's why I stretch my mind with the puzzles, why I log all my dreams, why I run the fucking strip club. Why I do almost every goddamn thing in my life to fill the gaps in my memories—the time right before my tour of duty. It's all for one purpose: to find the girl who meant so much to me that I cheated death to get another chance with her. To keep my promise to her that I wouldn't abandon her in this world alone. That I'd live through that tour and come back to her.

I just wish searching for any trace of her wasn't fucking killing me. Because it feels as if I'm nowhere close and that I'm running out of time.

Days without pain are addictive as hell. And I want them all to be, but it's not in the cards for me. A pill sure as hell isn't going to do it. One pill leads to two, then four. I've been down that road—chasing numbness, never quite finding it as my body adapts, needing more, needing stronger doses. And therein lies the problem. Hardcore drugs, being off my fucking rocker from them, that's a no-go for Harbingers of Chaos members, part of the code we live by. It's one of the reasons I joined them. A life insurance policy, if you will.

As Road Captain, it's my job to keep them safe. I can't do that if I'm chasing the Sandman. Which means I have to keep going, deal with the pain, and stay the course. Keep trying to find her while clean and hope that one day I can figure it all out—this mess in my head—before it's too late.

If I fall down that rabbit hole again, I'll lose everything—the respect of my brothers, the cut, the club tattoo on my back that shows my service and dedication. I'd lose pretty much everything remaining in my life that gives me purpose, besides the people I help on the side when I can.

I'm pretty sure I know where my path leads when all is said and done, but I'll claw and scrape my way through each day because if there's a slim chance that unraveling the mess my life has become will mean finding her at the end of it, it'll be worth it.

It's like my dad used to say, *"Only through great sacrifice are we given life's greatest rewards. Earn it, son, and God will reward you."*

LOST LYREBIRD

CHAPTER 9

*Is there anything a good cocktail and good
company can't fix?*

T he moment I've been waiting for comes, and damn, does she bring the sunshine with her. The thought hits me the moment Lily walks into Wet Tips, sporting a wide smile like she's ready to get this night started.

She strolls across the club, weaving through tables toward me, and I'll be damned if I can blink. She's even more stunning than I remember. Her hair falls in loose waves over her shoulders, a few strands out of place. Her lips glisten with pink gloss, and her eyes are lined with kohl, giving her a kitten-like edge. She's wearing nothing special, just cutoffs and a loose gray cotton tank, with layered necklaces and a few rings on her fingers.

The black-and-white rattlesnake-print heels with small ankle straps draw my focus. My mind instantly rockets off into a daydream where I'm getting an up-close view of them while caressing her slender legs.

So not the visual I need in my head. I clench my fist, trying to control the direction of my thoughts.

"Hey there," she calls out. There's a bit of swagger and confidence in her steps. She reaches the bar and places her purse along with the garment bags on the next stool over before resting her arms on the bar top. Her cornflower-blue eyes catch in the low light when she stares up at me.

I lean my hip against the bar, giving her my full attention. "Hey. You getting settled in okay?"

"Yeah. Sorta. I'm holed up at a hotel for now, until I find a place, but it's nice."

Her words catch me off guard because I hadn't realized she'd been that new to town. "You haven't found a place yet?"

Her long hair sways as she shakes her head. "Nah, but I'm in no rush." Pulling out the stool, she takes a seat. "I want to take my time and get to know the area a little before I agree to a lease."

My thoughts immediately go to the apartment Deidre's moving out of. Would Lily take it if I offered it to her, or is that weird? Something tells me to wait. So I push down the notion.

I raise an eyebrow and voice my next thoughts. "You don't look nervous. Most of the new girls are a wreck on their first night, nerves getting the best of them." Lily? She's upbeat and looks raring to go. If anything, she's beaming. A sort of frenetic energy is radiating off her. "I've seen some be a little green around the gills on day one."

She flips her hair. "I am a little. Just trying to hide it." As she tilts her head, her smile softens to something almost shy. "How am I doing?"

"Hiding it like a pro." I gesture to the liquor behind me. "Can I get you something?"

She grins widely. "Sure, why not?"

Leaning down on my elbow, I close some of the distance between us. "What'll it be?"

She clasps her hands together, holding them to her mouth as she thinks it over. "Hmm, so many options."

Fuck. The way she hums goes straight to my cock.

"How about you surprise me. Something original, but with a classic twist."

I'm curious as hell about her. Every detail she reveals feels like a little gold nugget, worthy of collecting and hoarding. I was hoping she'd give me something, but it looks like I'm going to have to learn the hard way.

"Anything you don't particularly like?"

"Anything but tequila. Very bad things happen on tequila nights, and I can't be held responsible. So, for the sake of my ability to stay employed and pay bills, promise never to give me tequila."

I stifle the grin building at the edge of my mouth and nod. "You got it." Secretly, I love that she gives me boundaries but opens the door for me to have fun with it and show her a little of myself in return. It tells me two things—she's willing to give me a small dose of her trust, and she doesn't mind letting someone else take control.

She's independent and fierce, but also soft and pliable—like there's more than one side to her.

I have a feeling I'm going to fucking love discovering all the facets of her.

Turning, I run my hand over my goatee, pondering what to make for her. Whiskey or bourbon is my gut instinct. If I had to guess, it would be something with a kick and a heady flavor. When I glance back, her grin turns wicked. "If it helps narrow down your choices, I'm not really a fufu drink kind of girl. All the sweetness turns my stomach, so I don't mind the strong stuff."

That makes me chuckle. Yeah, I knew it. Bourbon it is. But not bottom shelf. The good stuff.

She rests her chin in her hand, her gaze never leaving me. When I meet her stare, there are questions in her eyes, but ones she doesn't voice, allowing for this quiet moment of silent connection between us.

After I set the drink in front of her, she stares at it for a moment. When her soft blue eyes flick back up to lock on mine, they're bright and filled with curiosity. "What's it called?"

"A Silver Fizz."

A mischievous grin, then her teeth capture her bottom lip and hold it hostage. She gives me one sexy-as-fuck, knowing look as she brings the glass to her lips.

The fact that she closes her eyes and seems to hold her breath on that first sip pleases me. She's shutting off some of her senses to fully take it in. I love that. I watch her neck muscles work as she swallows, followed by a small, breathy moan that sends a good deal of my blood rushing south. Seeing her little tongue dart out to lick across her bottom lip, chasing the flavor, doesn't help matters at all.

When those blue eyes open, surprise and delight flash across them. I note all these tiny tells as I wait. "You like?"

"God, that's… really damn good." She gives a deep laugh, the sound rolling over me like a cool breeze.

Christ, she's gorgeous. A low chuckle slips out, and I fight the urge to pound my chest. Clearing my throat, I ask, "So your file said you're from Georgia… that's where you grew up, or just born there?"

Her cheeky grin over the rim of the glass is almost too much. "You didn't do a background check on me? I'm surprised."

I did. Took the info from her application, her references, and her driver's license. Hell, I even hired a hacker Dozer knows to dig deeper, a guy he calls Whiz Kid, who D's considering sponsoring as a prospect.

She sees my guilty expression and laughs. "Don't feel bad. I figured you would."

There were enough details to finally put my doubts about her being Elle to bed. Lily was halfway across the country when I met Elle. I saw her grades and her high school attendance. I saw the number of speeding and parking tickets she'd accumulated over the years, and I knew one thing for a fact. Lily was not a law-abiding citizen. She had a rap sheet for theft when she was younger and a few drunk and disorderly charges.

No angel. At least not in the biblical sense.

"Ah… back to being the silent, thoughtful type, huh?" She teases.

Her words snap me back to the present and shake the thoughts circling in my head. "I zone out from time to time. Got a lot on my mind."

"Mmmm. I see that."

I put the bottles away. Over my shoulder, I tell her, "I've already let the staff know you'll be doing a different kind of show. Raven liked all your ideas, so I'll give you some room to make some changes and mix things up. Just let her know what you need, and she'll take care of it. When you go on, the other girls will take a break, except for the waitstaff."

She chuckles nervously. "You didn't have to do that. I mean… I'm flattered, but I was kind of just bouncing around ideas with her when we had lunch. I'm like that. Full of a million ideas with no real plan or outline for implementing them."

"Yeah, but that's Raven's specialty. She's the kind of person who takes grand plans and turns them into reality." I laugh darkly under my breath. "Believe me. If it's a stupid idea, she'll shut you down cold. No tact, that one. But if she sees potential, she'll find a way to make it work."

"What if my ideas fall flat? Maybe the people here aren't ready for a Vegas style of stripping."

Her audition pops into my head, and from the way her gaze holds mine and the quirk of her mouth, I'm guessing she's thinking about it too.

"Oh, they may not be ready for it, but the clients will love it."

"All right. You're the boss." She sassily salutes me.

Clearing my throat roughly, I say, "If Raven's on board, then I'm sure it'll be the shake-up this place needs. Plus, it'll give the other girls a chance to get off their feet."

"Okay, but don't say I didn't warn you."

"Noted."

We don't talk about her audition. But it's right there in the back of my mind. My body hums like a damn tuning fork. What makes it worse is that while I work, her eyes track my every movement. I also notice how she moves slightly to the music playing low in the background, and taps her nails on the counter to the beat.

Not sure if I'm successful, but I'm trying to play it off like she hasn't got every bit of my attention. Like I'm not losing the battle to hide how much being near her affects me.

Thankfully, I can manage the bar on autopilot.

My staff slowly trickles in. I introduce them one by one to Lily and study their interactions.

When we're alone again, I ask if she's good.

"Yeah, I've been the new girl enough times that I get how it is. There's always a bit of genuine welcome mixed with some judgment and suspicion." She shrugs. "It's just how it is."

"Doesn't make it right."

"Doesn't matter. That's just life. Unfair as shit."

I huff in agreement. Because fuck yeah, it is. "Just let me know if any of them give you a hard time. A few might see you as easy prey, thinking you don't know how shit works around here. Don't let anyone steer you wrong. In fact, check with Raven on anything they tell you."

Lily gives me a no-nonsense look. "I can handle myself."

I feel her words more than I hear them. I hate that I can't protect her from it. But I love that she's strong enough to want to handle it herself.

I nod once in understanding. Silently proud of her fortitude.

When I glance at the clock and see how little time is left before our doors open, I broach the subject from earlier.

"I own a few apartments not too far from here. One of my tenants just gave notice. You can come look at it and see if you're interested. It's nothing special, but it's yours if you want it." She opens her mouth immediately, and I can already see the refusal coming, so I hold up my hand. "The rent's affordable, and you could go month-to-month. No strings attached, no pressure."

She shuts her mouth, sits back in her chair, and considers me. Her blue eyes search my face. There's something deeper there, more than just hesitation.

"I'm not sure that's a good idea." Her voice is softer somehow, and her conflicting emotions are evident. "There's already this." She waves a hand between us. "Whatever this is. Being that close… that's just asking for trouble."

"Maybe," I admit, holding her gaze. "But it also means I'm right there if you need anything. Or if your brother does. Another shoulder to lean on when you need one. It's a two-bedroom, one-and-a-half bath. Nice, but not fancy."

"It sounds great, really. I just don't know if it's wise. Can I think about—"

"Of course," I say, cutting in gently. "There's no rush. I'll hold it for a week or two. And it's no big deal if you don't take it. I have it coming available and didn't want to be an asshole for not putting it out there."

She smirks, her lips twitching. "So, you're only offering it because you don't want to be an asshole?"

I chuckle, "God, woman. There's no winning with you, is there?"

"Nope. Not even a little bit." She laughs. "You should just get used to it now." She shrugs at my deadpan stare. The smoky, sexy laugh that follows has my cock thickening further. "What? I'm just sayin'."

"Yeah, yeah." And fuck if I know why I do it, but I wink and say, "I see you." Which has her smile widening.

"I see you too, boss man." Annnddd I'm fully hard now. Up for whatever, whenever, with this woman. *Goddamn, does she do it for me.*

Her face is a work of art—achingly beautiful. I want nothing more than to grip her dainty chin and hold it steady as I explore her soft lips with mine.

She bites her lip as if she can read my damn mind. "I promise. I'll think about it. But this is already fucking torture."

It sure the fuck is.

"Yeah," I say gruffly and nod. We're in a goddamn pickle here.

My security staff starts to arrive. They react the same—a brief moment of stunned silence when they first see her. The new bartender, Bryan, nearly trips over himself. His eyes land on Lily, and his feet stop working while the rest of him doesn't get the memo. The males I employ gravitate towards her, smiling like idiots at everything she says. I shake my head as I watch it go down.

They look at her like she's a goddamn myth come to life. A fucking unicorn.

Fuck my thoughts right now.

I wave Bryan over to join me behind the bar to start his training. All the while, I keep Lily in my peripheral vision.

Lily greets Raven like they've known each other forever. Within minutes, she also has Jinx and Alex laughing at something she said. She's sociable, handing out compliments and asking questions like she genuinely wants to get to know each of them.

Meanwhile, Bryan begins to get on my nerves because he's distracted. I try to cut him some slack since neither of us can focus while Lily weaves her threads, flashing that blinding smile, and filling the lounge area with her southern accent and that breathy laugh of hers.

Andre, my head of security, a big guy with linebacker bulk, relays the rules for the clientele and what to do if she needs help.

"If anyone crosses the line, we'll be watching. We've got you, but flag one of us down if someone gives you the wrong vibes or does something on the sly. We got no problem throwin' someone out on their ass if they touch you inappropriately."

"I would hope so." Lily squeezes his bicep. "My God, look at these jacked muscles." I've never seen Andre blush before, but damn if he doesn't at her compliment.

I'm hit by unexpected pain, a nail hammering straight into my temple. It doesn't just strike home. It spirals outward through my skull.

"Motherfuck." I grip the bar, fighting to stay upright. My knuckles hit something, and a second later, I hear a glass tumble across the bar top. My vision blurs. I wince against what feels like my brain being pried open and brace for what I know is coming.

It funnels through without warning—*half movie reel, half rapid-fire images. A burly man yanking open the door of a blue classic car—a Chevelle, maybe—a girl's arm gripped tightly as she exits. Her dress, hair, and side profile. She stumbles, nearly tripping. Bleached-blond hair. Pink heels. I strain to see more of her face, but just as I'm about to make out her features, the image dissolves like smoke.*

When I pull myself back together, the silence around me is unnerving. Fucking awkward, like always.

People are staring—Raven's one of the few who knows not to.

I'm fully aware of the halt in conversation, along with the concern and curiosity, and the discomfort that follows my episodes. Which is what I call them.

"You all right, boss?" Bryan asks. I wave him off and clean up the spilled drink.

The pain doesn't leave entirely. It only dims a bit, enough for me to breathe steadily again. But knowing I need a minute to pull myself together, I mumble that I'll be right back and make my escape.

Whispers follow me. They're probably explaining my episodes to Bryan and Lily. My gut clenches at the idea, but maybe it's better if she knows now. It's not like it'll be the last one she'll see.

What matters is what I saw. A new piece of the puzzle. That blue car.

I hurry to my office, jotting down the details before they slip away. I send my notes to myself in a text so I can think on it later, when Bryan's not waiting on me. After swallowing a few aspirin, I splash some cool water on my face, clear my head, and then head back to the bar.

What I hear when I reenter halts me in my tracks. Honey interrupts Raven and Lily's conversation with a snide comment. "So, you're here to show us how it's done."

Lily catches my gaze for a mere moment. Her look tells me to stand down. With a raised brow, I silently say, *let me see it then.*

"I'm just trying to be me," Lily says calmly, tapping her fingers on the bar. "Maybe the customers will like it, maybe they won't. But from what I've heard, you're already killing it here. I just want to add to that, if I can."

"You ever danced before, honey?" Roxy asks, her tone all fake sweetness and condescension.

"Yep, sure have." Lily's reply is no-nonsense, full of quiet confidence.

Honey shares a whispered retort with Roxy before they head to the dressing room. They burst into laughter the second they're out of the main bar area.

Anger and frustration roll through me, because I knew they'd be a problem. Honey's desperate to be the favorite and isn't, and Roxy's the reigning queen and doesn't like the look of her competition.

Raven claps her hands and signals that we're about to open our doors, so everyone needs to get to work. Lily finishes her drink, thanks me, and stands. But before she can get far, I call out to her and meet her halfway.

"If they give you any—"

"It's okay," she interrupts, her voice steady. She pats my fucking chest. My muscles jump, and something inside me ignites. "I expected it. I'll let you know if it gets out of hand."

I don't know why I fucking do it, but I cover her hand with mine. Her eyes flare. I pull her hand away from my chest and give her fingers a quick squeeze. The temptation to bring them to my lips rides me hard, but I ignore it and slowly release her.

We're almost eye to eye, her heels making up some of the height difference. My hands itch to hold her. But I can't. She's my employee, and that's how it has to stay.

She gives me a grim smile. "I'll handle it. You just manage"—she gestures behind me—"this place."

"That includes you," I reply, watching as her eyes flare wide with shock. I step closer, unable to help myself. Her gaze falls to my mouth for a beat, then rises again.

This close, her beauty is devastating. My fingers twitch, aching to slide into her hair, to pull her close and kiss her senseless.

"Bryan's the one who needs your help," she says breathlessly.

"You're the one I wanna worry about, not fucking Bryan."

She laughs softly. "Fucking Bryan." We share a conspirator's smile for a second before she steps back. Our fingers brush, and a jolt runs up my arm.

"Promise me you'll come to me if it gets out of hand."

Something flashes in her eyes. Emotion drains from her face, like a veil falling between us. The smile she gives me next is fake and throws me for a loop. "Promise."

Without another word, she turns and walks away. I'm left wondering what the fuck just happened, what triggered it, and how the hell do I fix it?

LOST LYREBIRD

CHAPTER 10

Some women simply can't hide how bright the light of life shines inside them, and others are drawn to it without necessarily knowing why.

"**D**amn. You hire a rockstar or what?" Dozer, our VP, takes a seat next to Bodie. "The place is packed." He's a big guy, blond hair, clean-cut, eyes as steely as his father's, who happens to be the club president. His knuckles are bruised up, but I let my questions about that slide for now, handing him a beer.

"Yeah, thanks to this asshole." I chin-lift toward Bodie.

A loud cheer erupts as Roxy hits the stage in a lime-green bikini and sky-high platforms. Her long blonde hair is pin-straight and pulled into a high ponytail. Like always, she heads straight for the high rollers and flashes them a large smile.

Bodie laughs, ignoring my scowl. "Isn't a packed house a good thing?"

"She didn't need the extra pressure."

I asked him and Dozer to be here tonight so I had a few extra men watching things while I trained Bryan. I did not tell them to invite every member of our MC, which is what Bodie did, turning Lily's debut into a spectacle.

"Or maybe you just wanted to keep her to yourself a little longer."

I don't respond. Just wipe my towel across the bartop and drill him with a glare that would have smart men ducking for cover. He remains unaffected because he's been on the receiving end of it far too many times.

Bryan moves behind me, and I groan when I hear glass shatter. Bodie leans over the bar to inspect the mess. "Clean-up on aisle seven!"

I toss some towels to the kid. "I'll grab the broom and mop. Just pick up the larger pieces and be careful. Don't cut yourself."

"Shit, Finn. I'm sorry, man." Frazzled, Bryan moves quickly to clean it up.

"Don't sweat it. Happens all the time."

The slight headache I had earlier builds along with the tension in my shoulders as the boys get rowdier and Lily's first performance draws nearer. The over-the-counter pain meds have done nothing to dull the edge. My body's adapted to them. But at this point, I'll take any relief I can get.

The loud music and flashing lights make matters worse. Usually, I'd take a break and spend an hour in my office with the lights off to get some relief—it's soundproof for this very reason—but I can't hide in the back tonight.

Not only do I want to see her perform, but now I need to play babysitter to these fools, and train fucking Bryan. He's not a bad kid, but definitely not my best hire. This is evident when he doubts every drink he makes and checks with me before passing it to the customer.

That and the club is buzzing. Some of the dancers not on stage are socializing, while the waitresses make their rounds wearing their usual work attire: tight, hot-pink metallic skirts and white crop tops with the club's logo across the chest.

Two of my guys are posted at the door checking IDs. Andre and Ken are here in the main area, keeping their eyes on the dancers as they mingle. Stone—another HOC brother with long black hair and a wealth of muscle—is upstairs with my bouncer, TJ, monitoring the private rooms and those giving privates in the lounge area up there. Dozer is my floater. He's watching everything and working with different members of my security crew to cover breaks and check in.

Thankfully, only a few low-scale issues have popped up.

Doesn't stop my anxiety from rising, though, and there's fuck all I can do about it except manage the bar and pass out drink after drink to the waitresses who seem to be a little overwhelmed by the unexpected increase in patrons.

I switch the channel on the two-way radio on my hip and lift it to my mouth as I ask, "How many?"

It takes Raven a moment to get back to me. Her laugh is the first thing I hear in my earpiece. "She's up next." She's been giving me shit all night, because apparently, Bodie also filled her in about what went down during Lily's audition.

"Good, it's a fuckin' circus out here. I hope she's ready for that."

The confidence in her tone when she gets back to me is a relief. "She's ready. More than, I'd say. She's super excited to get out there."

And here I thought she'd be nervous as hell.

"You're head over nuts for this girl, aren't you?" Bodie taunts, inspecting me like he's reading a book.

I give him a two-finger salute. "Fuck. Off. Rivers."

His grin widens. "Why so serious, bro?"

Dozer comes by in time to catch the conversation. He chuckles and lifts an eyebrow at me. I point to each of them. "Not another word, or you're both cut off."

Time ticks on. My head pulses, but I stay behind the bar, keeping busy. Then the music cuts out, and Sasha exits the stage, collecting all the dollars littering its edge.

Alex, our emcee, takes the mic. "Who's ready for something special?" He plays to the crowd and builds up the moment. Finally, he announces, "We got a new girl, and let me tell you… this stage is about to become lit the fuck up. She's something to see."

Whistles and raunchy comments erupt. The noise and spinning spotlight are the equivalent of a knife being wedged into my brain. A combination that hurts like a motherfucker, but I grin and bear it.

The lights dim, plunging the club into total darkness, except for the LED lights that run in lines along the aisles on the floor. Then a pink light flicks on. It highlights the black stage backdrop for a beat before smoke begins to pour out and crawl across the stage floor, swirling outward. It stirs anticipation throughout the club as people wait for the act to start.

"Give it up for our little flower… Lily!"

The crowd erupts and keep the cheers going as they wait. For a long moment, nothing happens. The overhead light leaves the stage and circles in a wide figure of eight around the club until it stops. When it does, every gaze locks on her like goddamn heat-seeking missiles.

She's in the far corner, an opalescent diamond in the dark.

Her feet are kicked up on the table in front of her, crossed at the ankles, one leg draped lazily over the other, the toes of her silver heels bounce to the beat as the song begins. Her dress is skin-tight, sheer, and studded more heavily with crystals in certain areas. The spotlight glints off of them, sending fragments of neon dancing throughout the room.

With a slow, sultry smile, she kicks her legs high, extending them straight and holding for a moment before circling them in the air and then swinging them to the floor. In one fluid motion, she's on her feet, bending over the table, leaning on her elbow. She playfully taps her nails on her teeth and sticks her ass out and gives a blinding smile to the crowd, all the while shaking her ass in a hypnotic rhythm that builds. The song is "Maneater" by Nelly Furtado, but it's mixed with another song I can't name.

Her makeup is darker now, with silver on her eyes and long, thick lashes. Pink blush and pink lipstick highlight her insane cheekbones and lips. She's teased her hair a bit, and it lies in messy curls around her shoulders.

She's a sight. One I'm having a hard time looking away from.

Her body moves like molten gold—smooth, controlled—as she slowly gets up and crawls across the table. She makes her way to the other side with her back in a perfect arch. Less than a foot from one of the customers, she straightens and begins dancing while kneeling, letting her hands roam over her body. She draws one finger over her lips and trails it slowly down her chest to the V of her low-cut dress.

Each man there is given some special attention before she gets down and seductively walks across the room, all the while maintaining that confident, sexy smile.

Mid-fucking-walk, she locks eyes with me and fucking winks. Her grin also kicks up another notch.

It jacks up my heart rate like it just got a jumpstart.

On her way to the stage, she pauses at a table. She zeros in on the oldest gentleman of the three sitting there. She spends a little time seducing him, trailing her nails down his tie, tugging the end until his head snaps back up. She leans close to his ear, never touching, but he stiffens from whatever he heard.

His gaze is full of an intense, fiery lust when she backs away.

I'm no better. I'm trapped by the movements of her divine hourglass figure—the toned muscles in her legs, the infinitesimal swaying motion of her hips. The skirt on the dress is revealing and molded to her ass, long enough to cover it, but just barely.

She continues to work the room as she goes. It's as if she's fully aware of her effect and confident in her ability to make every man here fall in love with her.

It bothers me. But with the pain thumping behind my eyes, it's impossible to fully grasp the thought before it's gone.

When she finally makes her way to the stage, the walls vibrate with the volume of the cheers.

At this point, her performance transforms and becomes more erotic. It's evident in her movements, the constant flow of her body, that she's not just a stripper, but a trained dancer.

Her hands hike up the already short hem of her dress as she sinks to her bent knees. She parts her thighs and runs her hands over her body. She performs a more intimate dance, playing up to the group surrounding the stage. And by the looks of it, they're enjoying the hell out of it.

When she's back on her feet, she pushes down the shoulders of her dress. With teasing, sultry taunts, she peels it off, slow and deliberate, until, inch by inch, every sinful curve is on display.

What's left—white sheer crystal panties and silver pasties—draws every eye to the parts of her body that are pure eye candy to a man's soul.

Her long walk to the pole has mouths gaping open. The sight of her bare ass framed by the stark white strip of thong even has a few men fumbling for their wallets.

She grips the golden pole and starts with a lazy swing around it. Then, turns and goes around in the opposite direction. She rests her back against it and bends forward. As she rises, her pink nails sweep up her leg from ankle to ass cheek. But there's also the sight of her breasts to contend with, and my gaze pings between the two.

Seconds later, she spins and kicks up, catching the pole between her thigh and calf. Like her dancing before on the front of the stage, the build-up starts. She begins with a few small, easy tricks that increase in difficulty and intensity.

She moves from one position to the next, adding a sultry grind against the pole. The movements and pauses are purposeful, as if to highlight her best assets and skills. Her body arcs in a slow, deliberate spin, an elegant tease that promises more. She bends and flexes as she swings herself into the air, wrapping her legs or arms around it at times to stabilize herself.

The muscle definition in her arms, thighs, and calves is more evident than ever. They ripple beneath skin and glow under the stage lights.

And still she climbs higher, spinning this way and that, twisting upside down, and showing her experience by letting go and catching herself at the last moment.

I'm a fucking ball of anxiety as I watch. The image of that other girl falling is right there in the back of my mind, haunting me. Fear of Lily doing the same has me on a knife's edge the entire time.

My worry seems to be unfounded, though, as she proves to have absolute control over each movement.

From the looks of it, the crowd is just as fascinated as I am.

As the song winds down, she comes off the pole and performs a more sexual routine on the floor, dominating in that area too. The finish is big and dramatic, and leaves her sucking in air as her chest heaves.

The entire act leaves us all a little stunned.

It's like one of those once-in-a-lifetime things. Not something you'd see in a place like this, and yet here she is, appearing out of nowhere and pulling off shit I guarantee no man in here has seen. It's like seeing an exotic animal in the wild. You know instantly that you're a lucky son of a bitch to have been in the right place at the right time to experience it.

When she finishes, the applause can probably be heard down the block. Half the crowd gets to their feet. Lily smiles and takes a cute little bow, soaking it all in.

She grabs her dress and walks back into the audience, approaching a table of women, a bachelorette party. Sweat glistens on her body. Her hair, a tangle of curls, is damp with it.

The group gets louder as Lily closes in on them.

Even from afar, her laugh is the most beautiful thing I've ever heard.

Lily offers the bride-to-be her dress. The girls freak right the fuck out, giddy with excitement. The bride immediately starts bawling and throws her arms around Lily's neck.

Dozer moves to stop the physical contact, but I wave him off. Let the bride have her moment.

The girls scream in delight when the bride turns and holds up the dress like a trophy. The rest of the crowd cheers. Lily seems to delight in their happiness a moment before she waves goodbye to them. She blows the rest of the room a kiss and even does a cute little princess curtsy, gaining herself one last round of applause and high-pitched whistles.

Jesus.

This fucking woman.

Where in the fuck did she come from?

And how in the ever-loving hell did she learn to do everything she just did? Also, she left every single bill thrown her way on the stage. What is that about?

I radio Raven and tell her to send someone out there to collect it. She tells me she's already on it, because apparently, she already knew this was going to happen. I'm the only one left in the dark.

Story of my fucking life.

CHAPTER 11

*Most women will only trust a man to protect
and shelter her once.
Then she'll shelter and protect herself.*

Sliding into my car after another long night at the club, I scroll through my playlist as I pull out of Wet Tips' parking lot. I flip through song after song until I find the one that'll drown out my doubts about who I've chosen to pull me into the HOCs instead of Finn—because that beautiful bastard is making it damn near impossible to ignore him.

Finn is a complication I don't need and can't afford. Stone's the easy mark. Attractive enough, but that's not the point. He's weak to persuasion, especially the kind wrapped in sex and whispered promises. He's a man ruled by his dick. And I can use that.

When "Numb" by Linkin Park hits my speakers, I crank the volume and roll down the windows.

Once I'm on the highway, I check my mirrors. Once, twice. Old habits die hard. Sure, it's to check that I'm not being followed—but it's a small reminder that my history with Finn needs to stay exactly where it belongs: in the rearview.

Earlier tonight, after my routine, he asked to see me. Said he'd been getting questions from waitresses and staff—clients sniffing around for private dances. He wanted to know if I was ready for that.

The conversation was awkward as hell. His eyes said he hated every second of it. His body language screamed he was forcing himself to go through the motions.

What kills me is how being around him shreds my calm. Every look he gives me slides under my skin and splits me wide open. I hate it—how his eyes wreck me, how my body hums when he's close. *Fuck.* I'm barely days into this job and already questioning everything. How I'm supposed to survive months of this, I have no goddamn idea. And seeing that same storm of emotion in his eyes? Doesn't bode well for either of us.

Are you the desperate girl who lets a man turn her inside out? No. You're stronger. Wiser. Fucking act like it.

Honestly, I don't know this woman. She's not whose skin I've lived in these last few years.

The end game is what matters now, and there's too damn much riding on my success to fuck this up.

I force myself to shut down these feelings and focus on what's important.

With my weak self firmly tucked away, I drive. Knowing I'm too wired to sleep, I pass the exit for my hotel and continue on. I re-familiarize myself with the city. It's changed so much since I've been away, yet some things remain the same. I stop at a gas station, fill up, and grab some snacks. Eventually, I park so I can watch the sunrise. It's mid-morning when the first few raindrops begin to hit my windshield.

I take this as a sign to call it a night—or morning, whatever—and head back to the hotel. I get about five hours of sleep before my phone rings, jolting me awake.

The five-zero-five area code takes me by surprise. Because yeah, *it's him*, Finn, and suddenly all those feelings I'd successfully buried hours ago resurface.

I slowly hit accept and bring the phone to my ear. "Hello."

"Lily?

The way he says my name. There should be fucking laws against it. I close my eyes and have a moment, because *goddamn him.* His voice is whiskey-rough and addictive.

"Yeah."

"I'm sorry, did I wake you?"

I try to pull myself together and shake the sleep from my voice. "Yeah, but only because I stayed up way later than I should have. I have a minute, though. What's up?"

"I just wanted to see if you'd thought anymore about the apartment I have for rent."

I clear my throat, a ball of anxiety is hindering me from talking like a normal person. "Uh-mmm, I don't know. I guess I figured it was a bad idea, with you being my boss and all."

"I can keep my hands to myself if you can."

Damn you, Finn.

"Can I think about it when I'm more awake and call you back?"

"Sure. No problem."

"Great."

I press to end the call much harder than necessary, then toss my phone. Burying my head back into the pillow, I scream. I lie there, fighting to control the emotions his offer stirs up.

It's all too easy to picture him, the way he looked last night. The way he fucking looked at me last night. He always looks at me like I'm the most beautiful thing he's ever seen. Like I'm a mirage that might vanish if he looks away.

Even when I dance, I'm constantly aware of his gaze, which is always on me when I perform, and it's like a living, breathing thing. My body lights up even now just thinking about it. *Okay, fuck, don't do that,* because now I'm having sexual thoughts and I'm warm all over.

Turning, I stare at the tattoo on my forearm that I cover up whenever I'm on the job. It's an Australian lyrebird scavenging through the brush. The words beneath it read:

Her heart heavy. Her wings broken. It was no wonder she never learned to fly.

The memory comes unbidden.

The driver curses and takes the turn three times faster than necessary. I'm thrown from one side of the car to the other. Pain ricochets outward and spreads through my limbs. I push out every molecule of oxygen from my lungs in an eardrum-shattering shriek.

The pain is unbearable. I don't blame the driver, though. I think I'd do the same if I had a girl dying in my backseat, too.

"Oh, God. It hurts." I suck in a shaky breath. Every inch of my body trembles, gripped by a truckload of agony. I force my fingers to stay on the wound in my stomach even though the blood and the rocking motion of the car make it damn near impossible.

The knife wound is deep, and my blood is flowing like a river out of me, through my fingers and down my leggings.

The driver takes another sharp turn. I thrust my hand out to steady myself, but it slips on the leather seat, smearing a crimson handprint across it. "There's so much blood." It's all I see. It's pooling around me, covering my skin. Just red. Red on my clothes. Red on the door.

The driver's gaze swings sharply from the road to mine in the rearview mirror. "Just hold on, okay? We're almost there. I can see the hospital just ahead." His panicked brown eyes are wide and shifting, from me to the road, from me and back to the road.

"Two blocks. You can make it."

I lay my head back and look up at the car's roof. Then past it to the night sky. I stare at the stars and try to picture Finn up there, looking down on me. Watching my life come to an end. Is he sad for me? Or is he happy because now I'll be able to join him in heaven... if that's even where I'll go... or even where he is...

Fuck.

I hadn't thought of that. What if I don't end up wherever he is? What if I'm headed in the opposite direction?

I thought I had more time to become a better person and change. Time to prove I was someone he could be proud of. Someone worthy of him.

The last memory of that night is of the driver screaming, *"Dammit! Don't close your eyes. We're almost there. Oh, God... don't... don't you dare fucking die on me!"* Panic bled from his voice. Even now, I can recall his accent and the tone of his voice.

I push the memory to the back of my mind, so far back that I won't reach for it again anytime soon.

I don't need saving. I can take care of myself. Yes, I may have trusted him once, but I'll be damned if I let myself be that vulnerable a second time. I wait until later in the day to text him back. When I finally bring up Finn's number, I type:

Thanks for the offer, but I think it's best to find somewhere else.

It takes him a minute to reply:

You sure?

Yes.

Ten minutes go by before he replies again:

Okay. Let me know if you change your mind.

CHAPTER 12

Pick your moments with care.

I'm almost finished adding all the recent expenses in the club's ledger, when another text pops up on my phone from Bodie. Before reading the thread, I massage my temples and pop some aspirin, attempting to fight off today's migraine that's been gnawing at the front of my skull.

Yo, the boys and I are headed over. We're bringing the party to your place tonight.

We're here. Where you at?

Are you dead or ignoring me?

The only voicemail is from Dozer. "Hey, brother. A couple of the boys wanted to head your way. See you in a few."

I shove the phone in my pocket, lock my office, and head to the main floor. It doesn't take long to find Raven and check in. It's a pretty slow weekday night, so I don't expect anything out of the ordinary. After giving me a rundown, she says, "You know, I am quite capable of handling everything in your absence." Before I can respond, she adds, "You look like shit. Rough day on the books?"

"Migraine."

Her lips press into a line. "I'd say head home and get some sleep, but I know you won't."

She's right. If I left, I'd just spend my time worrying about shit going wrong.

"Why don't you take the rest of the night off? I can handle things 'til close," she offers, her tone soft, almost sympathetic.

My first instinct is to tell her no—that I'm fine and can handle it—but putting up a front for the rest of the night and staying on my feet? I don't have the energy. My body feels like it's been hit by a truck.

Raven pats my chest lightly. "Don't worry. If something big comes up, I'll come get you."

I nod, grateful for once to let someone else take the reins.

I find my brothers at their usual table

"Where the fuck you been, man?" Bodie hollers the moment he sees me.

"Here. Workin'. Where else?" I slap hands with Dozer. Griz stands to clap me on the back, and Mav and Stone give me chin nods from across the table. Taz tips his beer in my direction before his eyes flick back to the stage. Stone follows suit with a nod.

Bodie's stare lingers on me. The smile he had a second ago fades as he takes me in. He shares a look with Dozer.

"What?" I ask gruffly.

He simply shakes his head and takes a long pull of his beer.

I hike my thumb over my shoulder. "Gonna go out for a smoke. Ya'll good? Need anything?" I flag down Gina, one of the waitresses. I ask her to take good care of them before I head out for fresh air and a break from the music and lights.

Out the back door, I light up a joint, which seems to be the only thing lately that will grant me any relief from the pain. Being in the dark helps too.

By the time I make it back inside, the party has kicked into high gear. Most of the customers have cleared out. Only the die-hards remain. Some of the dancers who've finished for the night have stayed to hang out with the guys. Usually, I wouldn't mind an impromptu get-together, but tonight I'm done in.

I tell myself I'll have one beer and call it a night.

I even drag it out, though it takes a lot out of me to do so. But I figure if I can prove I'm fine, maybe Bodie will get off my ass about the headaches and quit acting like my fucking babysitter.

Lily walking into the main bar area, wearing a tight red lace top, skinny jeans that look painted the fuck on, and snake-skin heels, has second-guessing that idea.

She and Raven talk for a bit. When they close the group at the table, Bodie reaches out to grab Raven's hand. She's too fast for him, though, and swats at him. Then she proceeds to back away while making the sign of the cross with her fingers.

"One day, Raven," he says. "You're gonna regret not gettin' a piece of this."

"Yes, that day is called when pigs fly with rainbow wings, and the world is ass up and backwards. Plus, we'd have to be the only two people on Earth, which means I'd be desperate as hell. Until then, my friend, I'll happily keep a ten-foot pole between us."

Bodie palms his crotch. "It's not ten feet, but it's big enough to make even you beg for mercy."

She shakes her head. "It's not the size of the dick, or haven't you heard. You gotta know how to use it." She shrugs one shoulder and smirks.

Bodie purses his lips in a pout. "Come on. Teach me. I'm all for lessons if you wanna show a brother how it's done."

She scrunches up her nose in disgust and turns to me. "Can we not house-train him before letting him out in public? Surely there's gotta be a collar we can buy, a zapper or something we can use anytime he misbehaves."

Taz takes the toothpick from between his lips and points it at Raven. "That's not a bad fuckin' idea."

"Seconded," Griz adds.

Bodie throws up the bird and flashes it around the room. "Fuck you all. I'm not wearin' no damn collar." He tilts his head, and something wicked flashes in his blue eyes. "Unless Raven's holdin' the end of my leash and ridin' my cock, while callin' me a good boy. I'm down for that."

Raven laughs full out. "You're incorrigible."

The banter continues as more dancers join us. Raven drags a chair over to our table. Before Lily can grab one, Stone pipes up, "Got a seat right here for ya, babygirl," patting his lap with a lecherous grin.

"That right?" She gifts him with a coy smile.

The interaction makes my blood boil. It's been going on for weeks now—the flirting. *Weeks.* As in, she's been all but ignoring me and acting weird as fuck, and yet anytime my brothers visit the club, there's massive flirting going on. Stone's her most recent conquest. Hell, he probably instigated tonight's impromptu party so he could get another crack at trying to get under her skirt.

I don't realize how tense I've become until Dozer glances at me. Stone catches on too, turning with a raised brow.

"What?" he asks, his tone has an edge. "You got a problem with this?"

Every eye at the table shifts toward me. I grunt, which is about all I can manage. I can't voice shit, because I don't know how to speak about what the fuck I'm feeling. Frustration. Anger. And the magnitude of jealousy shocks the shit out of me.

Being tongue-tied is new.

Lily answers that question. "I'm my own woman, thank you very much."

"Whoa. Easy there, killer. Just checkin' in with the boss man," Stone says.

Bodie watches me. When I don't say shit, he huffs. A moment later, he pulls one of the other dancers into his lap with a dramatic flourish and ravages her mouth without asking. She swats at him at first, but within seconds, she completely falls under his spell and melts into him.

"Jesus, man," Taz scolds.

When the kiss finally breaks, the girl's breathless. Bodie gives her a wicked smile, palming her tit, and wiggling his eyebrows at her. I roll my eyes at her giggle.

Griz laughs. "How the fuck he gets away with that shit, I'll never know."

"You and me both," I mutter.

Taz is standing, arms crossed just behind Griz, and glares down at Bodie.

My focus shifts to Lily as she speaks to Stone. Her hand is on his shoulder as she circles him. He grabs her waist, pulling her onto his lap.

It's a straight punch to the chest. The more I watch, the hotter my blood runs. It takes everything I have to sit here and watch. I try to reengage in the conversation around me, but it's a lost cause. The way he chats her up, the way she flirts sweetly back, and plays up his ego—yeah, both annoy the fuck out of me. But worse is the way she smiles at him.

Fucking Christ. That does something to me, twists my insides into a tight knot.

I want nothing more than to yank her off his lap and slam my fist into his smarmy face. Every word he says is ridiculous, and she eats it up like he's waxing poetic. Swear to fuck, it's acid to my goddamn ears.

I grind my jaw and hunch forward over the table.

Fuck.

The music is cranked and shit gets out of hand. Clothes come off, people pair off, and dancers get extra friendly in a way that regular customers pay top dollar for. As long as it's consensual, I don't care—except where Lily's concerned.

The sight of her grinding against Stone a few feet away makes me want to rip out my eyeballs. It's that fucking painful to watch. His hand freely roams over her ass, and her arm is around his neck, their faces close. Fucking inches apart.

Dozer leans over and nudges me. "Why the fuck didn't you say somethin'?"

"Say what?" My voice is hoarse, pure gravel.

"Don't play stupid with me, Goose. We both know how smart you are."

"She's my employee."

He tugs his chair closer and places his large, crossed arms on the table to keep the convo private. "Just 'cause you haven't gone there, doesn't mean you can't. Shit happens."

"After what went down with Jules and Jaxson?" I shake my head. "How would that look? Plus, it's not like she's interested. I mean, look at her, man."

The displeasure on his face says that answer's bullshit. "Don't let a good thing pass you by. Club be damned."

"That's rich." The insinuation about him and Bethany and the history there is left unsaid.

Two frown lines crease his forehead. "Yeah, don't I fuckin' know it. There was a time, before she married Hodge, that I didn't take my shot. I let bullshit get in the way. I regret that. Wish I'd stepped up, and worked to figure our shit out."

"You still could."

He shakes his head and looks down at the table. Then he grabs his beer and chugs the rest of it. "It's about picking the right moment, though. You step up at the wrong time, you're gonna fuck up a lot of people's lives, or risk another rejection. Just waitin' for my next moment."

I openly stare at Stone and Lily now. They're so lost in each other, they're none the wiser.

"This is your fuckin' moment," Dozer says, tilting his beer in Lily's direction. It's the same moment Stone pulls her face close to his and kisses her.

The jealousy rioting through my body is unlike anything I've ever known. It's a new kind of pain. It stretches and digs deep under my skin. I exhale a pent-up breath and feel the loss of something vital down to my bones. "Nah, man. Think it already fuckin' passed me by and that shits on me."

Dozer slaps his large hand on my shoulder. "Welcome to the club inside the club, man. The dumb fuckers who revel in chaos and are full of regrets."

We both chuckle, and Dozer gets up to grab liquor bottles from behind the bar. He fills our glasses, then clinks his against mine before we each take a large swallow. We get blitzed, and within an hour, I'm too fucked up to care about anything or anyone.

Raven becomes our babysitter and DD. My last memories of the night are of her cursing out my name as her and Dozer help my drunk ass up the stairs to my apartment. That and her asking me, as I tug my shirt off, if I'm solid.

"Fuckin' peachy," I grumble, plopping down onto the end of my bed and struggling to take off my boots. The world blacks out after that.

CHAPTER 13

When a person reveals their limits, it is with respect that you acknowledge them, and with love, you cross them when warranted.

JULY 2007

"**G**oose! Hey, man."

Fuck off. I hold up my hand, eyes fixed on Lily's performance. She weaves seduction through her movements like it's a magical ability. The song is "After Dark" by Tito & Tarantula, and it delivers a slow, thumping beat—a beat she hits with each seductive sway of her hips. It's a combination of belly dancing intoned with the luring call of a siren.

In no time at all, she's got all the males here under her spell and has become the main attraction at the club.

Great for the club. But hell on me and my security team.

The more the clientele watch her, the bolder they get.

If I look to the right, I can easily find a man palming his crotch and laughing off his blatant arousal with friends. If I look to the left, I'll find the same fucking suit from her first night here, sitting in his regular spot, staring up at her like she's some goddess come to life.

She's reeled them all in.

And day by day, week by week, I've had to witness every single man pant after her like some dog in heat.

I hate seeing it in their eyes—the sick gleam of their obsession. The lust for more with her. It triggers dark thoughts in my own mind of murder and dismemberment. Because so help me God, if they touch her or cross those fucking boundaries in any way, I won't be above putting one of them down.

Thoughts like these have spiraled a bit out of my control. But I blame it on the unrequited desires she's stirred up in my blood, and the maelstrom of need I can't get a handle on. Not to mention that, for weeks, I've also had to watch Stone put his hands all fucking over her bod, and watch them lip-lock nearly every fucking night that he visits the Wet Tips, which has increased from one or two nights a week to a bare minimum of four.

The more time that passes, the darker these thoughts become. And God forbid she pays any of the clients special attention.

Because the woodpecker in my brain doesn't like that one fucking bit. He goes into goddamn frenzy when she does, driving his sharp fucking beak repeatedly into my temple like he's wielding a goddamn sledgehammer.

Bam, bam, bam. Like there's not fucking brain matter and important shit I'm trying to store up there.

Like now, as she crawls forward and motions to the man in front of her, sitting at the edge of the stage. She draws him in with the crook of her finger, then seductively dances just for him, palming her breasts, bucking her hips, mimicking riding his cock like she's at some fucking rodeo. One hand travels up her thigh. The other tunnels into her hair, lifting her curls to frame her face. It's sex—or what she'd look like getting fucked. And it's enticing as hell.

And it doesn't stop there. She covers her mound with her hand when it travels back down her body, and she kicks her head back the moment she touches herself, letting out a gasp as if in the throes of pleasure.

My vision blurs a bit. The woodpecker throws a hissy fit and jabs at my skull. It hurts the way I imagine getting stabbed in the eyeball with a pen would.

I cover my right eye and brace against it. Sometimes it helps. Today, not so much.

My hands start to shake. I hold on to the bar with my left hand, trying to stay steady.

Memories—fleeting but intense—hit me in a rush. I grunt and pinch the bridge of my nose to stave off the blinding pain that crashes next into my head.

I get a flash of a woman walking in front of me. *Her hand behind her, her fingers locked with mine as she pulls me through some trees. The sunset is cresting just above the treeline. Dandelion seeds float on the breeze. A heightened view of the city I know so well, Albuquerque. A girl is lying on her stomach on a mattress, watching a movie on a small TV. Her legs are bent and crossed at the ankle. She's popping candy into her mouth. Then I'm standing in the doorway, looking at the words scrawled in black Sharpie on a bathroom mirror, "SMILE MORE", written in big, bold letters, with a squiggly line underneath.*

The visions are vivid one moment and break apart like smoke the next.

I try to force them back. But my knees buckle as another spike of pain drives home inside my skull.

"Goose!" Bodie's voice is suddenly at my side. It's so loud. His voice. The music. And these fucking lights. They're too much.

I press both fists into my eye sockets, pushing back against the pain. I groan out my frustration because I'm so done. So fucking done with this shit. This fucking pain. Some days, it's all there is.

Another flash of memory: *a single pink flower in a vase on the table next to a fashion magazine. There and gone. Then another. A dreamcatcher. They come too fast. Too fucking fast to grasp them all.*

"Goose! Goddammit, G, look at me!" It's Bodie.

I brace against the spikes and work hard to stay upright. "Jesus fucking Christ!" The words are a low, vicious snarl. They rip from my chest like an animal has taken over to fight back against this onslaught. I rage back at my own mind. "Fuck you. Fuck you. Fuck you."

I decide my own fucking fate.

Not you!

139

Someone grabs me and spins me around. "Goose!"

"What?" I snarl, tearing the hand away from my shoulder and opening my eyes.

Bodie draws back at the fury lacing my tone. His expression shifts from shock to apprehension. "You're fucking bleeding everywhere, man."

His words don't make sense at first. "What?"

"Bloody nose," he says, motioning to me.

As soon as he says it, I smell it. Taste it. The metallic tang sits right on my tongue. I feel the warmth of it on my lips. I swipe my hand under my nose, and it comes away smeared with crimson. Looking down, I see a fuck ton of blood. "What the fuck!"

My chest is covered with it, enough to look like I've slit my own throat. Apt, since I feel like I barely survived a battle with my own fucking mind.

Grabbing a bar towel, I press it against my nose. I need to get the fuck out of here and pull myself together.

Dozer comes to stand beside Bodie. Maverick steps behind them.

Griz comes up behind me and lays his hand gently on my back. "You okay, brother?"

More brothers are on their feet and staring at me, ready to do something to help.

Like I'm weak. Like I need looking after. Like, I can't handle my own shit.

"You all right, man?" Dozer asks. "What can we do?"

"Nothin'. Just give me a minute." It comes out garbled with the towel covering my nose and mouth.

Their concerned eyes track my every move as I leave the bar.

Dozer hollers, "Okay, just tell us how we can help."

I don't know what the fuck is happening. This hasn't happened before. I shake my head as I stride toward my office, because fuck, I don't think anyone can do a damn thing to help. All I know is Lily's performances make it worse. Something about watching her perform like that, for these men, is affecting me on another level.

It's sparking an intense physical reaction in me. And it might just be the thing that kills me.

As I make my way down the hallway, my vision narrows and blurs a bit. A few more steps and the world tilts sideways. The walls close in like a tunnel in an Indiana Jones movie.

"Goose, hold up!"

I do, only because I'm afraid I'm going to drop. I lean against the cool wall, one hand braced on its surface as I take a few deep breaths.

"What?" My voice is rough, but I force it out.

Bodie is the one who responds. "Do you need to take one of your pills?" His hand lands on my shoulder. It feels heavy as hell, like its weight alone will send me to my knees.

"No, I'm fine."

"What pills?" Dozer's voice joins in, his tone low and edged with worry.

I laugh bitterly, a wet, rasping sound. "They don't work. Nothing does." I don't have time for this. Don't have time to explain my relationship with all the fucking pills.

I pull the towel away. My nose hasn't stopped bleeding. Blood immediately leaks into my mouth, warm and thick. My body is betraying me. It's faltering. Giving up the fight.

"Tilt your head back."

I roll my eyes, but do it. I lean against the wall and stare at the ceiling. When the lights bring more pain, I close my eyes and groan against the agony spearing inside my skull.

"Shit! We need to get you horizontal." Bodie's arm hooks under mine. "Lean on me. Dozer, get his other side, man."

"I can walk."

"Just lean the fuck on me and stop your bitchin'," he snarls back.

"Fuck. All right."

The thought that I can't walk to my own goddamn office without assistance makes me want to lash out. But it's not Bodie I want to fight. It's my mind and whatever is going on up there.

How the fuck do you fight an opponent you can't see and don't know shit about? It feels like a battle I can't win, no matter how hard I try.

Inside my office, they lay me on the couch.

"Hit the lights," Bodie says.

Any sound, even the thud of what I assume is Dozer's boots, hurt my brain. Darkness wraps around me as the lights go out. It helps, if only a little.

Bodie's voice breaks through the haze. He's squatting beside the couch. "Where the fuck are your pills, Finn?"

Turning my head, I squint at him. "No pills."

"What pills?" Dozer asks.

"Pills for his migraines. He's been getting them more often," Bodie says, his voice almost a whisper because he knows what I'm like when they hit hard.

"I didn't know it was this bad. I knew he got headaches, but not like this. Why haven't you said anything, man?"

"Not the time to have this conversation," I grate out.

Bodie tells me to shut up, and I hear him tell Dozer, "He won't listen to reason. Alister prescribed him some new meds. Gave him a few options for surgery, but he says the pills fuck him up one way or another, and the surgeries in the past haven't fixed the problem so he doesn't want to go under the knife again."

"There's gotta be something that'll help." Dozer's voice is closer now. I can feel the weight of his stare. "What kind of pills has Alister recommended?"

I pull the towel away, but blood streams from my nose again. "Ones that don't fix me. Make me a goddamn zombie or fuck me up even more than I already am. I can't protect the club like that."

I hear drawers rattling as Bodie's voice cuts through the fog. "I'm callin' Allister. You need somethin'. What the fuck have you done with the meds?"

I squeeze my eyes shut. "I'm not taking them." As I lie there, I think back on all the faces that were staring at me like I'm a freak or like I'm broken and in need of help. It guts me—them all seeing me this way.

Something about Lily is triggering the flashbacks, and I don't know why.

The answers I can't for the life of me grasp, because I don't have the brain power to think through any of it. All that exists for me is this motherfucking pain and scattered memories.

Fuck!

Is this all there is to look forward to? More of this until it kills me?

CHAPTER 14

The truth can stare us in the face, but we're too blinded by what we think we know to see it for what it really is.

I linger in the dressing room until closing time, doing my best to blend in. Figuring out who could be a friend or foe takes time, and a keen eye. So for now, I sit back and watch, waiting to see which girls are genuine and have a good heart.

Roxy and Honey do not fit that category. They've been talking shit about me from the moment I arrived. They don't like my costumes. I have a fat ass. My boobs have to be fake. This or that. They always have something demeaning to say about me or the work I do here.

Honestly, it's nothing new.

I've experienced more than my fair share of this kind of behavior. It comes with the territory of the dance industry. I spent my youth circuiting pageants and dance competitions. Then, I graduated to the high-octane version working the Vegas dance scene. My tough-as-nails skin has been hardened by thousands of brush-offs, rejections, other women working to erode my self-confidence, and ruthless judges or people in power passing judgment on me or my skills.

So yeah, they can throw all the shade they want. It'll roll right off.

Raven feels more like a kindred spirit. I gravitated to her right away. She's a boss babe if I ever saw one: intelligent, with a phenomenal work ethic, skills in costume creation, and delivers her criticism in a straightforward, no-nonsense way I can appreciate. It's meant to push me to look at things differently, not to slam the choreography or my outfit choices.

She genuinely wants to help every woman here.

So when I spot her leaning against the wall down the hallway, fidgeting and staring hard at Finn's closed office door, I move toward her. The fact that she doesn't look over at the raucous laughter from the girls leaving the dressroom is telling, because Raven catches everything.

"Hey. Are you okay?"

She glances my way, forcing a smile. "Yeah. Everything's good."

"You sure?"

"You did great tonight, Lily. Really." Her voice sounds flat, though, like she's distracted.

A low rumble of male voices filters through Finn's door and draws my attention. A lightbulb flicks on in my brain and slowly, I connect the dots. Anxiety flutters in my chest. The memory of what the girls in the dressing room discussed earlier resurfaces.

Nose bleed.

So much blood.

Did you see his shirt?

A headache.

Yeah, but that looked like a pretty bad one.

At the time, I thought they were discussing a patron. It didn't click until now. It should have, but I'd been riding the high of my routine.

"Is Finn okay? I heard the girls talking about what happened, but I thought they were talking about a client."

Finn's medical details, which Deeds shared, are sitting in my inbox. My persistent avoidance of knowing more about his past, because it would be like tearing duct tape off a festering wound, is biting me in the ass right now.

Before she can answer me, Andre calls from the back door. "Raven, he just pulled in." Raven's shoulders sag with relief.

Andre holds the back door open, and a young guy rushes in a

146

second later. A few ladies in the hallway, and he veers left to avoid them. When they're out the door, he strides to Raven.

He breezes past me as if I don't exist.

He's a handsome kid, late teens, with olive skin, dark hair, and a few freckles on his nose. Judging by his style—black gauges in his ears, beaded wrist bands, and a charcoal graphic tee—I get the sense he has a rebellious soul. That, and the half dozen tattoos he's sporting. There's a large one on his forearm of a reaper standing over a black coffin. Another prominent one on his neck is of a finely drawn skull with laurel leaves curling up one side of its head and down the other. An hourglass spilling sand, and the image of two hands reaching from opposite ends toward each other, rests beside it. The words "Tempus Fugit" and "Memento Mori" are inked around the design.

He's flustered and asks, "Is he alright?" There's a slight Hispanic lilt to his words.

"Yeah. Did you find them?" Raven asks.

He pulls out a bottle of pills from his jeans and places them in Raven's hand.

"Thanks, Mattie. You're a lifesaver."

He nods and shoves his hands back into his pockets. His shoulders rise and tilt forward.

"You should probably get home before he finds out I let you inside the club."

The kid hesitates, eyes flicking toward Finn's door with trepidation.

"He's okay. I promise. Just a bad one. We'll get him fixed up."

He stares at her for a long moment, then sighs in defeat, and his shoulders fall. "Just text me and let me know if they work, alright?"

She lightly pats his arm. "I will."

His gaze falls on me for a moment as he turns to leave. No greeting whatsoever. If anything, he drills those deep brown irises into me as if daring me to utter a word. I don't, but I do meet his stare head-on. We keep eye contact until he's past my line of vision, and it's weird, because for some odd reason, I get the feeling I just had a duel of wills with this kid. I might not have won, but I didn't let him win either.

Raven knocks on Finn's door softly.

Dozer opens it a moment later. "You got 'em?"

Raven hands them over. Dozer turns and calls, "Heads up," before tossing the bottle to someone inside the room.

Most of what I know about Dozer I've read from his file. Deeds also shared what he could. His legal name is Ethan Coleson, and he's the HOC's Vice President. One of the club's two pseudo-princes. The other being Ty Folsom, or Edge, who's in prison for using lethal force defending a woman who was being raped.

Supposedly, Deeds and both men had once been pretty close. They'd been brought up in *the life* together, but had grown apart when Edge's father died of a drug overdose, and Cap and Griz decided to split from the GBs to start this club.

Now, Dozer and Deeds couldn't be more different. Dozer's an ex-SEAL who turned down football scholarships to three decent colleges so he could serve his country and follow in his father's footsteps, and Deeds is going to find his way onto the FBI's most wanted list if he's not more careful.

They're like yin and yang.

Dozer is the poster boy for Mr. All-American Biker. Good-looking, clean-cut, with dirty-blond hair and blueish-gray eyes. He runs a successful gym in Albuquerque, has a decent income, money in the bank, and received multiple impressive medals during his time as a SEAL.

On paper, he's the total package.

He'd been my first choice when I was considering which HOC to latch onto to pull me into the club. Deeds quickly crossed him off the list. He said not to underestimate Dozer, but I think it had more to do with the fact that Deeds saw him as one of the good guys, and still considered him a friend since they'd spent the better part of their youth in San Diego raising hell.

Dozer turns back to us, and his steely gaze immediately lands on me. "Hey, Lily, right?" He says, offering his hand. I step closer and shake it, giving him my best smile. His grin turns flirty. "You had us all squirmin' in our seats tonight."

Laughing, I say, "Uh-mmm thanks, I think."

He winks and motions for me and Raven to come inside. "Come on in."

I peek into Finn's office, hesitating for a second, not quite sure what I'm walking into. Bodie perks up when he spots me and slides off Finn's desk. "Well, well, well. If it isn't my two favorite girls."

A creak sounds as the door across the room opens. Finn steps out. It appears to be a bathroom based on the fogged-up mirror behind him. There's a towel slung over his broad bare shoulders, and he walks forward, gaze down. The only other things he's wearing are black jeans and a metalcore belt. His wet hair is slicked away from his face.

As he moves across the room, he picks up one end of the towel, drying the water droplets on his tattooed chest. The sparse lighting in the room illuminates the sharp angles of his face. I see a side view of the massive back piece, his HOC colors tattooed in black ink.

He's not tan, per se, but not pale either. There's a light dusting of chest hair over his pecs. Not the solid and rock-hard body of a young soldier, but fitness is something he's maintained since his time in the military. The battle scars littering his torso, though, those are new, so are the abstract tattoos.

The scars are hard to look at. They speak of the battles he's endured. A piece of his history I was not a part of. The thought cuts like a razor blade when I think on it.

I shut it off, the emotion it brings, and tell myself to dwell on it later, or never. Never's good.

Finn moves through the room with purpose, not acknowledging a soul. He's preoccupied. His thoughts miles away. Irritated too—if the pulsing of his jaw is any sign.

I know this mood. It's been years since I've witnessed it, but I recognize it.

He's a storm waiting to break, charged with dark clouds. He's stewing. This silence is the buildup before he unleashes. His laugh lines, which I used to adore, seem etched with grim thoughts. And the three lines that crease his forehead are more prominent at the moment.

I swallow hard, because... *damn it,* I can't look away.

My gaze tumbles over the black leafless tree covering the left side of his torso. The branches stretch like wicked fingers across his pecs. A dead tree, by the looks of it. There's a black figure standing close to the trunk and—oh fuck! Are those birds?

Please tell me those aren't fucking birds… as in plural.

They fly outward from the shadowed figure. Some are half-bird, half-wisps of smoke as they drift up his chest.

The bird thing was our thing. But this looks like he's taken our once beautiful story and turned it into something dark and twisted. Or maybe it was never what I imagined in the first place.

I force my mask of indifference to remain steady, even though there's a war being waged inside me.

Before I can decipher the scripted words scrawled above the tattoo, he turns, opens a large cabinet door, and pulls out a shirt. He's quick to stretch it over his head. When he turns, his eyes are slightly shut, tension tightening in his features. He grips his forehead momentarily, takes a couple of deep breaths, and then drops his hand.

Crossing the room, he drops onto the couch and begins to pull on his socks and boots.

Bodie throws the bottle of pills. They land beside Finn on the couch. Finn shakes his head.

"Yes." Bodie and Dozer say in unison.

When Finn doesn't respond, Bodie says, "Look, man. I know a shit ton of these have side effects. But you're not going to find one that works if you don't at least give them a try. Alister says these are the best out there. He's not going to steer you wrong on purpose."

"We're not doin' this," is Finn's response. He picks up the pills and throws them back at Bodie.

"We are," Dozer says, crossing his massive arms over his chest. He stands like a sentinel a few feet away, all business.

Finn's dark blue gaze, glare and all, shifts from Dozer to Bodie. He sees me and Raven and freezes. Then he does a chin lift in my direction and says, "What the fuck? Is this like some kind of intervention?"

Bodie chuckles. "No, but only because I didn't think of it."

Under his breath, Finn hisses, "Then why is she here?"

"I don't know. Maybe it's like a divine intervention, bro."

The hurt I feel is like an arrow to the gut, a fucking bull's-eye. It's like he's saying anything to do with his life is none of my goddamn business.

I fortify my emotional walls to protect my heart, and point my thumb over my shoulder. "I'm gonna get going. I just wanted to check that you were all right."

Raven scolds him. "Don't be an ass to us just because we care about you." I appreciate her words, but that doesn't make me feel any less like an unwanted outsider.

Bodie rolls his eyes. "It's not what you think, so calm the fuck down. She was just in the right place at the right time."

Finn palms his head and closes his eyes. "Fuck, Lily. I didn't mean for it to come out like that. It's just been one hell of a night."

"It's okay. I was headed out anyway." I don't need this bullshit.

Bodie's hand snakes out to grab my wrist. I nearly yank it away, but force myself to calm down and not react.

Finn is up in a heartbeat, shoving Bodie's arm off me. "Don't fucking grab her."

Bodie's grins wide at this. Why? I have no idea. But his next move shocks me. He goes for the pills and comes back to me. Plops them into my hand. "Do me a solid, babe… get him to take one of these."

Finn curses and paces away from us. He grips the back of his head and mutters under his breath, frustration and anger palpable. When he stops, his gaze is fierce as he stares at his friends. "I mean this with all the love and respect in the world. Everyone but Lily, please get the fuck outta my office."

Raising an eyebrow, Bodie hesitates. "I'm not leaving until I know you've taken one."

Dozer slaps Bodie's chest. "Fuck, Rivers. Stop eggin' him on. We've done what we can. It's time to go."

Turning the bottle over, I read the label. When I look up to meet Finn's eyes, I study his features, the pain he's trying and failing to hide. Worry for him tightens a knot in my stomach.

"Are these for migraines?" I ask.

It's Bodie who responds. "Yeah, and he'll be stubborn about taking one, but believe me when I say, he's gotta do it, or he's gonna land his ass in a pine box."

Finn takes a step forward as if to harm him. His fists balled up at his sides. Dozer plants his meaty hand on Bodie's shoulder and forces him toward the door, seeing the deadly threat on Finn's face. "Come on, let's get outta here before he puts *you* in a pine box for meddling."

Raven follows the guys out of Finn's office without another word.

At the last second, Bodie peeks his head back in before the door can shut. "Just wanted to say… you were sexy as fuck tonight, Lily. Wet Dreams-R-Us cummin' to town." The door shuts with a *thunk*.

I blink, then let out an abrupt, short laugh. "I'm not sure if I want to know."

Finn grumbles as he walks back into the bathroom, "I assure you. You don't. It's best if you ignore anything that comes outta his mouth."

He opens a drawer, removes a comb, and fixes his hair back in place. When finished, he leans against the counter and stares at himself in the mirror. The toll this pain has taken on him is at a level he can't mask, and that alone is telling.

I don't know what drives me forward, maybe the gravitational pull of his pain, but resisting it feels as if it takes more effort than giving in. I take cautious steps forward and stoop at the bathroom doorway.

His gaze moves to me, and I experience a moment of *déjà vu*. We once stood like this, only our roles were reversed. I was the one hurting, weighed down by the hell I'd endured with Veno. Being trafficked by a man who saw me as nothing more than a payday and a punching bag. Finn pulled me out. He'd been my anchor, constantly letting me know that he'd watch over me, be a listening ear if I ever wanted to talk about what had happened. He'd been the one person in the world who cared if I came out the other side of the darkness in my head and heart.

His hair was mostly black then. Cut into a military crew cut. No goatee, which I'm partial to now. His body had been a thing of beauty, hardened and war-ready, but almost too perfect, you know? It was intimidating its flawlessness.

Because mine was anything but perfect.

Now his body tells a similar story to mine, scars and all. There's a certain beauty to be found in the story it tells, mysteries waiting to be discovered.

We stare at each other. The quiet settles in around us. It's not uncomfortable, but profound.

I remember how it was always like this. His presence calmed and centered me, making me feel safe for the first time in a long time. When I was close to him–inside his small bubble—I felt like he could shield me from anything. He had this quiet control about him, like he somehow mastered the space he occupied. My body recognized this, and still, it reacts, orbits around it, like Saturn's rings around its center mass, me around *him*.

I roll the bottle in my hands and reread the label, memorizing the name so I can research it later. I place the pills on the counter beside his hand. His eyes stay fixed on me, intense. I'm tempted to back away. I never thought those eyes could be anything but honest. Anything but kind. Anything but true.

I turn to walk back into his office, heart sick at what we've become, but Finn catches my hand and stops me. He pulls me closer.

"What was that look?"

I shake my head, an emotionless mask over my face now. "Nothing. Look, I should be going." I try to pull away. Finn holds tight.

"You were thinking something just now. Tell me." He pulls my arm up and runs his fingers over my inner forearm, inspecting it.

I yank it away, knowing what he's looking for. "Nothing important."

"Will you tell me anyway?"I meet his gaze head-on and lie. "No, it was nothing worth mentioning."

LILY

CHAPTER 15

Our deepest fears have the power to expose us in ways our words do not.

I motion to the bathroom, or more accurately, to the pill bottle he left on the counter in the bathroom. "You're not going to take one, are you? Even if I ask you to?"

His silence is his answer as he strides to the couch and grabs his cut. He slides his colors on smoothly like it's second nature. And I hate to admit it, but the vest looks sinfully delicious on him. It adds to that bad boy factor, hitting buttons I never thought he could tap into, the ones that bring dirty daydreams to mind and make me want to spend the night inhaling him like a four-course meal.

This new Finn is harmful to my poor heart, though.

"Will it help?" My mask slips, just for a second. I don't know his whole story or why he's refusing the pills. Even if I deny it to myself, try and fail to remain angry, I do care. The truth is, I don't want to see him suffer.

"For a while."

"Then why not take them?"

He reaches into the front pocket of his jeans and pulls out a set of keys. His gaze draws up to meet mine. It's intense and earnest, but his jaw muscle pops as if my questions agitate him.

He sighs and grabs the back of his neck, massaging the base as if trying to relieve some tension. "Because I don't know what they'll fuck with. My head, my sleep, my mood, my blood pressure, my heart." He pauses, considering me, and his arm drops. "And there's the fact that my body figures out pretty quickly now that there's this easy magic trick to switch off the pain, so my brain shouts for another pill and another, because what the fuck if it's just one more little pill, right? It's a slippery slope, one I've battled my way up a few times too many."

Lord. This man.

This is the brutal honesty I remember. The vulnerability Finn never shied from, as if he'd written the chapters himself into the meaning of an "open book"—always delivering raw, honest truths when pried for personal details. He's a guy who never saw the point in white lies or omissions.

"Have you had them long? The migraines?"

He nods. "Too long. And believe me, no one wants them gone more than I do. But a little pill isn't the answer."

"Then what is?"

He mutters, "Breadcrumbs, puzzle pieces, and feathers."

I look up at him with a bewildered expression. "That doesn't make any sense."

"Not to you, but it does to me."

At my intense stare, he says, "No offense, but that's shit I'm not comfortable handing out like candy. It means a great deal to me, and though I like you, we just don't know each other that well, yet." His forced smile is just that: forced. Half-smile, half-grimace.

We've been apart for years. There's a minefield filled with all the things we don't know about each other and what happened in our lives in the time in between.

"Is there maybe another option, like surgery?"

"Already been through the wringer on that front. Did more damage than good, and this is the aftermath." He motions to his head.

When I take my next step, I stumble. Finn immediately grabs my arm to steady me. Heat rushes up my chest and neck. I'm goddamn deadly in heels, have been for years. I can't remember the last time I tripped over my own feet. That I did it in front of him—of all people—makes me feel like a fool.

"What? Like, for real?" I ask.

He nods sadly and knowingly. It's almost as if he's had this same conversation with everyone he's ever known and is sick of slicing himself open for show and tell.

Motioning forward with his hand, he says, "Come on. I'll walk you to your car." I move to walk ahead of him. When I do, his hand comes to the center of my back.

It's a simple touch, yet I feel a profound ache for it to be more. I hate myself for it, too.

"Was this… you know, from your last tour?"

"Yeah."

It's all he gives as he follows me to the back door. He locks up before we continue through the lot.

I fucked up by not looking at his file. Now I desperately want to know what happened on that tour. What he's been through since. The ache to help in some way builds, battling against the fortified wall I've been shielding my feelings behind. It was stupid of me to walk into this blindly, with nothing but assumptions.

I make a mental note to do some research when I get back to my hotel and look into what else might help. Maybe there are some natural remedies he hasn't tried.

As we make our way across the parking lot, I take extra care to walk steadily because the pavement isn't the greatest, and the last thing I need is to get my heel caught in one of the cracks.

He asks, "Where are you parked?"

I point to the right. "Just there." He scans the lot. More than one car remains, so I clarify, "The blue Dull Dory over there." I point it out and hear his barely audible chuckle.

"Dull Dory?"

"Yeah, it's like a reminder that if I just keep dancing instead of swimming, I can trade it in for something nicer. And also because that movie fucking rocks."

"What movie would that be?"

"Surely you're kidding?"

He shakes his head slowly, as if he doesn't know what I'm talking about.

"Just keep swimming, swimming, swimming? Clown Fish?" He shakes his head. "The ocean? Sharks? One little fish's journey to find his way home?"

The corner of his mouth lifts at this, and he gives a subtle shake of his head. "No, I don't think I've seen it."

"Nemo?"

When he continues to say no, I stare at him like he's an alien. "You're not serious?" It's half a question, half a joke. "God, that's a tragedy."

"That good, huh?"

"*Finding Nemo*. Watch it." I point at him. "And that's not a recommendation."

"Yes, ma'am." He does a half-assed salute.

I want to go on and on about why it's an epic tale, but I'm sure he'd look at me like I'm a loon. It's one of my all-time favorites. I love that it's not about romance. It's not about a girl pining for some guy. It's about finding the person and place that represents home for that damn cute little fish.

He's quiet for only a moment before muttering, "If I had to count, I'd say I've probably seen less than a handful of those kinds of films."

"What? No Way."

He nods.

"That's like un-American."

He chuckles at this. "We had one TV, and usually my dad commandeered it. He always had it turned to an action movie or true crime. If not that, then a ball game. He also loved old reruns of *M*A*S*H*. If I wanted to watch anything, I had to wake up early on the weekends to get the TV to myself."

We've moved closer to one another without realizing it, and our arms brush. His gaze meets mine when they do, and we share a moment. One, I'm quick to shut down.

We're nearly past the large dumpster, and a small scream escapes me when a black shadow darts out. I jump back, clutching my chest. Finn is in front of me before I can blink.

I peek from behind him to see the shadow, a small black cat with light eyes. It stands on the dumpster lid, meeting Finn's gaze head-on. It hisses at him. I clutch the back of his cut and try to pull him back.

The next hiss is followed by a growled warning. The sound has chills spreading down my arms. Memories from the year I lived with my grandma flood into my mind. The junk, the smell, and how she not only allowed those mini-devils to treat her home like a litter box and cat motel, but how some of the more diabolical ones would attack even when not provoked. It comes back to me like it was yesterday. Yes, her home was a safer place for me than my own home once my stepfather moved in, but it left me with a lifelong fear of cats.

Finn coos at the thing and reaches out to pet it, even though it looks feral.

I screech, "Don't touch it!"

He arches an eyebrow at me over his shoulder. "It's just a cat." He says it as if I'm crazy. Like he's simply dealing with a cute, cuddly pet. Rabbits are cute. Cats are not. They're little schemers. It's a universal truth that even cat owners can't deny. They love that they're unpredictable and independent.

Finn isn't successful. In exchange for his kind treatment, he curses and recoils when it nearly bites him. But instead of being reasonable, he rationalizes the beast's behavior. "Damn, guess she must have some babies nearby."

I nearly roll my eyes at this, but ask, "How do you know?"

He tilts his head and crouches a bit, as if inspecting her. "Her belly."

I'm tempted to check for myself, but the thought of getting any closer sends a shudder rolling through me. "I'll take your word for it."

He rises and turns, giving me a perplexed look again. I thread my arm through his and guide him to keep walking, using him as a shield until we're a safe distance away.

He studies my expression. "Not a cat person, I take it?" The corner of his mouth pulls to the side. It's not a full smile, but still, it draws my focus to his kissable lips outlined by his trimmed goatee. His sharp jawline is highlighted by contrast alone.

Really, he's aged beautifully—I can't deny it—but my attraction to him goes deeper than his looks, and it always has. His quiet, calm demeanor is a balm, his strength a comfort, and his nature to protect an enticing lure to a girl who has spent her entire life looking over her shoulder.

I scold myself for letting these thoughts take up residence in my mind.

This is precisely why being this close to him is dangerous. His ability to sneak so easily into my heart goes unnoticed until it's too late. He just slips right the fuck in and makes me feel things I shouldn't.

I let go of his arm as we get to my car. "Thanks for walking me out. I appreciate it."

I don't realize Finn's stopped until I turn around. His eyes are closed. His hand is pressed to his head. My worry for him returns.

"Hey, are you all right?"

He doesn't seem to hear me. So I move closer, placing a hand on his arm. When he comes out of it, he shakes his head. The way he looks at me when his eyes finally open… melts me on the spot. He's scanning my face, my features, and then my eyes intently. His gaze falls to my lips. Heat travels down my body.

"Yeah," he whispers gruffly. "Just another feather."

"A what?"

"Feather."

"I don't understand."

"I'm getting more of them lately."

I shake my head in confusion. My hand drops. His large hand catches my arm, holding it gently. Questions linger in his face, and his blue eyes look at me with the kind of knowledge that, not gonna lie, scares me.

"You're afraid of cats."

"What?" I search his face.

This time, it comes out more as a question. "Are you afraid of cats?"

Shit!

Deflect. Lie.

Shrugging, I say, "Normally, no. But that one looked feral." I don't have to fake the creeped-out shiver that runs over me.

"Your pulse is going crazy right now." Not sure how or when his hand circled my wrist, but his thumb is over my pulse.

I pull away.

"I've had some bad experiences in dark parking lots in the past." Which isn't a lie.

I move away, open my door, and toss my purse onto the passenger seat. When I turn back, I sound exasperated. "Look, I'm not weak. I can handle myself. I'm used to this." I motion to the club and the parking lot. "But, you know, sometimes, something like that takes me back. PTSD, you know?"

"Someone attacked you?" He seems taken aback by this.

I nod. "Yeah, and I've worked through it. Mostly, I'm fine. It's just shit like that, and I have a moment. That's all."

He looks off to the side, lips pressing together. When his gaze reconnects with mine, he says, "I'm sorry." The words are hoarse, and I hear the apology in his tone. He runs his hand over his mouth, the other through his long hair. "It's just… a lot of people lie, Lily. And because my memory's fucked, I don't have space for people in my life who can't tell it to me straight. It's a deal-breaker for me."

I rush to say, "I'm not—"

He holds up his hand, cutting me off gently but firmly. "I just wanted to explain why I questioned you. The way you reacted… it triggered something. A memory." His words hang in the air between us, thick with an unspoken weight.

"Is that a good or bad thing?"

His lips twist, not into a smile but something troubling and bitter. "I used to think it was a good thing. But the pain that comes with each memory—I'm not so sure anymore." His voice drops lower, almost resigned. "I get these flashes. Snippets of memories that help fill in the gaps of time I don't remember, but piecing them together is another matter."

His words twist inside me. I want to reach for something, anything, to ground myself. But all I feel is the cold night air and the creeping

161

chill of uncertainty. The truth slowly trickles in, and I rush to say, "Don't remember? What do you mean?" It comes out uneven, because I'm afraid of the answer.

"It's not like in those TV shows," he says, his voice gravelly with exhaustion. "My doctors call it traumatic amnesia. Or, more accurately, dissociative amnesia. Courtesy of my last tour. It didn't wipe my slate clean, but it did punch holes through it."

"Wait… what? Like for real?"

He nods, and the expression covering his features is filled with utter honesty. The reality of the situation sinks in slowly as I realize what it means.

He. Doesn't. Remember.

He doesn't fucking remember me.

Holy shit!

"How? What happened?"

"Our Humvee hit a roadside bomb. We were ragdolls inside, and I ended up with massive head trauma. But I'm lucky. I got out alive. Some of my team—men I fucking cared about—didn't get that chance. Still, parts of me, parts of my life after that day, are just gone. And not all new memories stick around. Some fall into what I think of as a black pit inside my head and get swallowed up. On good days, some memories come back. There's no rhyme or reason to it. Things just get lost and found."

The word *amnesia* bounces around inside my mind like a loose wrecking ball. My thoughts ping until I can pull together all the details I've missed that could have explained so much. As they tie together, my stomach twists into knots. I can't even voice it out loud. It feels absurd, like something that can't be real, and yet, according to Finn, it is.

He watches me closely, his dark-blue eyes searching mine, waiting to see how I react.

I don't know how to react or what to say.

What to feel.

There are too many thoughts and emotions rioting for attention inside my head and my heart. I turn away on shaking legs. A vice grips my chest in a stranglehold. The telltale signs of a panic attack. I press my fist to my chest, trying to push back the sharp ache building there.

He didn't choose to leave. He didn't just disappear. He...

Oh my god.

Sucking in a long breath, I count to three and then let it out in a long exhale. Suck in another and hold for five. *Breathe, Lily. Just breathe.*

I repeat this mantra a few times until Finn draws near.

"Lily, what's wrong?"

I scarcely manage to get the words out. "I'm okay. Just need a minute."

He stays by my side. His hand is on the small of my back. It somehow staves off the panic and centers me.

Finn watches me intently. There's some distance in his gaze. He seems almost wounded by my reaction. And I realize he's waiting. Waiting to see how this truth lands. If it changes anything.

"I knew... knew something was wrong," I say, cautiously. "But I didn't—" My words don't seem like enough. Don't cover the enormity of how messed up this all is, and they don't say what it is I want to say. "No one explained. I didn't know... so I just let it go. It doesn't bother me. I don't want to throw pity at you, because that's probably the last thing you want. There's empathy, though, for what you've been through." I very nearly say, "All these years... I thought you abandoned me." But the words don't come, and he doesn't ask. He waits.

And I hate that, after all this time, a part of me still feels that dangerous flicker of hope. Am I a memory he's lost? I mean, is that the reason he never came back or made contact? Is there even the slightest chance he's retained some of our past and thought about me? Missed me, even?

"Does it bother you?"

My eyes widen. "Bother me?"

The way he's watching me makes me feel like he's cataloguing every nuance of my facial expression. "Or worry you, maybe?" He says gruffly.

I squint, trying to understand his meaning. "What?"

"Are you worried about your job security because your boss doesn't have his shit together? Or …" he trails off, not voicing what he was going to say next, though I can see how intensely interested he is in my opinion.

That is the last goddamn thing on my mind. Holy hell. No digging for dirty details—he just opened up and told me everything I've been dying to know for years.

"No, absolutely not. How could you think that?"

"Then why are you so upset?"

I throw my hands up. "Who wouldn't be?"

"Then what are you doing?" My voice pitches on the last word, my nervous excitement obvious. I back up a step and lean against my car. He follows my retreat. He flashes between the man he used to be and who he is now. I see both versions as I stare up at him. It's like watching two people exist in one body. He's the same, yet so different. More confident. More bold. And undeniably just as tempting. Even thinking it makes me feel like I'm the one who's a little mentally unstable right now. His ability to reel me in like this is alarming.

"Just considering some… things. One of them being how to navigate this while not crossing any lines. At least until you know me better, and I get the chance to see who you really are."

When he moves even closer, I place my hand on his chest to stop him. He picks it up, bringing my fingers to his mouth, and places a barely-there kiss on my knuckles. His eyes never, not for one second, leave mine.

"Such a gentleman."

"For you, maybe I will be."

Breathlessly, I say, "Just for me?"

"Mmmm… I guess time will tell." His smirk stretches, the lines around his mouth bracketing as his smile deepens. "But don't for one second think that part of me doesn't want to say fuck it and break the rules. Ask you to kick Stone to the curb. Shit like that. Not the acts of a rational man who's usually front and center, but the one who rises to the surface when you step into a room."

For a solid minute, I consider my response. Because damn. And yep, I know exactly what he means. The smart girl I've had to become wants to turn and walk away. This other part of me, the one I've stashed away that he brings to the surface when near, wants to give in completely and come out to play.

As long as he keeps his distance, I have control. But I swear to God, if he comes any closer to me, my resolve will begin to fray.

Because he's him. Gorgeous eyes, his slanted dark eyebrows, and that plumper top lip. He has that damn smirk I love so much, and even his aged wrinkles are getting to me. Don't even get me started on the waves of his silver hair and the way my hands ache to run through it.

I've imagined it nearly as often as I've imagined kissing the hell out of his mouth. And fucking him so well that he'll never recover from the memory of it.

Payback for the memories he left me with.

The heat in his gaze has the she-devil inside of me waking. She's a hungry, needy creature who has gone without sex for way too long. Now she's cracking open one eye, licking her lips, and turning my every thought into something more lurid and inappropriate. *Dirty. Dirty. Dirty.* In the best of ways.

Sexy fantasies pinwheel inside my head, each one begging to be fully fleshed out in bright, unbridled color. Me, gripping his hair, clutching it as he goes down on me as if he's longed for nothing else. It's quickly followed by me riding his cock like I'm going for gold in the goddamn rodeo finals, giving him all the pleasure I'm capable of and taking the years of pleasure I've missed out on.

My fingers twitch with the need to reach for him. I curl my hands into fists and let my nails sink deep into my palms. I use the pain to stave off the desperation clawing through me.

Because giving in before I think this through means I could once again become nothing more than a weak girl seeking his attention every dawning day. I'm so tempted, but all the reasons I came here war with this want for him. The truth of what I'm here to do—what I've committed to—is ultimately what drags me back to reality. A reality that's cold and sobering.

I think of Lacy and the debt I owe Deeds.

It helps.

There are things I need to do here for the GBs—payback to be delivered to Veno and his crew. But my decision to walk back into New Mexico and face my past was because I couldn't let go of Finn without knowing why he disappeared on me. I had to know if there was a minuscule chance that I'd gotten it all wrong.

Eventually, I say, "But us getting involved is a really bad idea, right? With everything that just went down with your last employees. And I'm not in the best place right now to start a relationship, especially not with my new boss."

He nods. "Yeah, not at the moment. I'd rather not be a hypocrite. That's exactly how everyone would see this." He motions between us. We stare at each other as inevitability and regret fill the air.

The finality of this conversation is apparent, but we linger as if we're both wondering if this chemistry will ever reach its true destination—the one we see in each other's eyes.

I force myself to say what I should. What will douse this spark like a bucket of cold water. "So we agree. This has 'bad idea' written all over it. We keep it like we agreed… professional. I already have enough drama going on in my life right now with my brother. I don't need to add to it. I need simple and easy right now. And I think we both know this would be anything but."

He looks away, a scowl transforming his face. He nods a few times and slaps his hand on the top of my car. "Yeah, wrong time, wrong place. Bad circumstances. Plus, with the memory loss, it's not always easy to deal with. I get it."

"That's not what I meant."

"Maybe not, but I saw you shut down. Saw you talk yourself fully outta this. So we can drop it."

He motions for me to get into the car. When I do, he places his hand on the door frame. He gives me another forced smile before saying, "Drive safe. I'll see you tomorrow." He closes it, and I'm left reeling as he walks away.

A moment later, his bike fires up, and he walks it forward. Then he waits. I curse his name as I start my car because there's this hollow pit in my stomach opening and flooding me with the worst feeling imaginable.

I want to take back what I said. But I also know it was the smartest decision to make. I can't do what I need to do while also diving into something with Finn.

However, inside, it feels like it was a huge fucking mistake.

He gestures for me to leave before him. I do. Then he revs his motor and takes off in the opposite direction.

Every single part of me screams… this is wrong. But I don't turn back.

On the drive home, as I gun it down the two-lane road, my mind runs a million miles an hour. Getting back to my hotel room so I can go through Finn's file is a need, not a want, at this point.

It's an invasion of his privacy. I know that. And yeah, it feels fucking wrong. But the desperation to know *everything*—right now— is louder than my conscience. That old fear, the one that's lived inside me for years and kept me frozen when it comes to him, is starting to shift. There's a spark of hope in my chest. And it's burning through the paralysis.

I'm afraid of what I'll find. Of what it might mean. Of how it could rewrite my perceptions of who we were, and why he left me. And that's the part I don't think I'm ready for.

Because I'm still here to do a job, that hasn't changed.

But what if he's not okay—never was?

If so… what the fuck does that make me?

The villain in this story?

CHAPTER 16

Dancing around attraction is an art few people have the skills for.

Damaged goods. "Additional drama," as she saw it. Knowing it and having it confirmed is like running full out and getting clotheslined.

That shit fucking hurt.

Sitting on the window nook on the east side of the studio, I lean towards the open window and exhale. The joint between my fingers burns slowly, the smoke curling up and dancing in front of me as if trying to comfort me in my hour of need.

I'm a few pills away from being just like her brother. Or at least Lily's reaction said as much. I'm too much for her to take on. I get that. Some days it's too fucking much for me to take on.

So do I blame her?

No.

Does it suck?

Yep.

Fuck me up a bit?

Hell yeah, there's that too.

Am I going to hold it against her?

Fuck no.

I get it.

She doesn't need another addict in her life, another broken man to fix, and I've got no right to add to her burdens. I've carried my own weight, and it's what I'll continue to do.

The joint's end flares brighter as I take another deep drag, holding the smoke in my lungs until it burns. Not healthy. Not smart. But better than taking pills, which has been more fucking tempting as the minutes tick by. I cough as the exhale bursts from me. The high kicks into another gear a few minutes later, and I sit in silence, watching the smoke drift and swirl, taking my deep thoughts and scattering them into meaningless, hazy wisps.

The first few years after Iraq were hell. I've done my best to put my deeds behind me. But my inability to manage the pain after the incident that ended my career with the Army isn't pretty. The initial torture of months in the hospital, followed by months of rehabilitation. I'm not too proud to admit, I ate up the meds when they were offered.

They were hand-fed to me at first, passed out like treats to a toddler, but then, prescription after prescription, and pill by pill, that shit was on me.

They were the only mercy available to me in a world of agony.

I had trust then. In doctors, in the promise of a fix.

I didn't know then what I know now—that prescription pain management is best left in check because it's a slippery slope to addiction. Some medical professionals are all too happy to push as much of that shit into your hands as you ask for, sometimes beyond what you ask for.

That kind of pain… chronic, absolute, debilitating—the endlessness of it calls darkness and death to the mind like nothing else. Any small measure of relief seems so out of reach. There's no timeline to it, no speck of hope on the horizon, and no way to make it stop.

This is why pain, opioids, and depression go hand and hand. Peace is the goal; death is then dressed up to look like the greatest gift. And sometimes, it still does. Some days, ending it all seems like the only answer. The only measure of relief that is within my control.

Everything in life bows to the pain. Even man.

I close my eyes, the cool night air seeping through the window, grounding me just enough to keep me from spiraling. My mind drifts back to the past and the last time I felt this low.

I'm roused from the couch by a banging on my door. It's loud enough to shatter my skull. I'm ready to tear someone apart, because noises like this are like fucking bolts of lightning spearing into my brain.

When I rip open the door, I find Larsen and Bodie. Kyle Larsen is the only other surviving member of our team. He's standing there in a blue T-shirt and black shorts. My gaze immediately drops to his prosthetic leg.

He shrugs. "It may not win me a modeling contest, but it works, and that's all I need."

The words burst out of me, because fuck he's a welcome sight. "Holy shit, man, it's been a minute. It's good to see you."

Before I know it, we're hugging, slapping each other on the back, like no time has passed.

"Two legs and all," Larsen laughs.

"Does your dick count as the other half, or are we counting the prosthetic?" Bodie, holding the screen door open, walks in behind Larsen. He's attempting to flash that grin of his, but his eyes tell a different story altogether. They hold a quiet worry beneath the surface, as if he wasn't sure I'd be open to their visit.

I mean, for a moment there, it crossed my mind, but seeing them together… it takes me back. Makes me see how far we've come. Makes me see Bodie as Rivers again, the guy who pulled me through so much shit, who never gave up on me, even when I gave up on myself.

Larsen looks good. Healthy. The last time I saw him, he'd been just as much of a mess as me, fighting through physical therapy and hating life. But now? He's that same golden, cheerful force that had been the gravity of our team.

We'd spent the entire night drinking beers and telling old stories. The memories had us either cracking up or choking up. When they left, I hugged Larsen and promised to call more often. Then Bodie stepped toward me, and I gave him a man-hug, too. It lasted longer than it needed to, and in those few seconds, I realized something.

I realized what I'd put him through during those past few months.

When we pulled back, I really fucking looked at him, and I knew—if he didn't have me, who would he have?

No one.

His family life was shit. His wife—fuck, I hate calling women bitches, but she was. She beat him down with words, twisted his insecurities into chains. His kids loved him fiercely, and that's why he stayed. But being married to Blaire was killing him. Slowly, piece by piece, it turned the man with the heart of pure gold into something dull, extinguishing the flame that made him shine.

I stub out the joint, watching the last smoke curl and fade into the air. The ache in my head hasn't gone, but it's duller. Dark thoughts swirl, telling me that no one but him would miss me. That he'd get over losing me eventually. That I'm a burden. They also whisper the promise of oblivion if I just let go and give in to temptation.

I pull my phone from the bedside table. My thumb hovers over Bodie's contact. The seconds feel like hours as I battle the need riding me. In the end, I search for Larsen's number. I'm not sure why, but maybe because he's also been through hell and back—lost a leg, finished rehab, downed the pills, and came out the other side still shining. I press the call button, unsure what to say, but knowing I'm losing the war inside my mind again.

Maybe I won't say anything. Maybe just hearing his voice will be enough.

The phone rings once, twice, and then his voice comes through, groggy but familiar. "Finn?"

I swallow hard, my throat tight. For a second, I consider hanging up.

I don't. I can't.

"Yeah. It's me."

There's a pause on the other end, and I hear him shuffle, probably sitting up in bed. "You good?"

I close my eyes, the weight in my chest easing for a brief moment, only for it to come crashing back down, heavier. "No, man," I rasp, my throat tight with the truth I've been trying to ignore. "I'm not good. I'm losing the battle here, and I don't know how much longer I can keep fighting through this."

Silence stretches between us, and for a second, I wonder if he can hear the crack in my voice—the sound of a man standing at the edge, staring into the abyss.

"Every day's a fucking war," I say. "The pain, the need for the pills, all of it. I'm fucking losing my mind here."

I hear Larsen breathe out on the other end, the sound heavy, like he's been here before and gets it. "You're the strongest and smartest man I know. Doesn't mean you need to fight this alone, though. You hear me?"

"Yeah, man. But fuck, it's hard."

"I know it is. I know, man."

I swallow hard, my hand trembling as I rub my face. "Tell me how you made it out. How you kept going and came out the other side."

The words hang there, raw and jagged, like a confession of how far I've fallen from the man he used to know.

"You just… keep waking up, keep getting up, and find the shit that lights you up. Gotta take a step forward and another until it's not so hard anymore. Let the shadows go. That's part of it too."

I'm silent as his words roll around in my head.

Larsen's voice comes back, low and steady, like he's holding on for both of us. "I'm coming over. Don't do anything stupid, Finn. Just hold on a little longer. I'll be there. I'll call in Rivers. We'll both be there for you. It's why we made it out together."

"He's gonna be all butthurt that I rang you instead of him."

"Nah, man. He's just gonna want to be there for you. All he wants is to see you through this and make sure you don't leave him behind. Whatever we need to do to make that happen, that's all we care about. You'd do the same for him, wouldn't you?"

"Course."

"Just hold on, man. We're on our way."

CHAPTER 17

*When your path becomes blurry, remap out
how to get to your final destination.*

Invisible lines are drawn, and we both stay on our sides, making the following weeks after Finn's confession trudge by like we're both walking through quicksand. We've agreed to keep things professional, but the tension between us is impossible to ignore, seeing that our worlds collide constantly.

The decision doesn't sit well with Finn, or at least that's how it appears. His mood plummets, and it isn't just me noticing. Raven's gaze follows him like a hawk, concern etched into her face. And I can tell she's putting the pieces together, sensing I have something to do with it. The way she looks at me says it all. She's gearing up to talk to me about it.

I'm not sure what I'll say. I'm still warring with my own decision to keep Finn at a distance. I can see he's hurting. It's obvious now that I know about his injury. He struggles through pain each day. Maybe even searching for answers about his past—memories he can't access.

I have a lot of those answers, ones I could share. However, doing so would reveal who I am to him and open more than a can of worms. It would burn the fake identity I've used to get the job, and rip the past wide open for him to sift through.

I'm not ready for that.

It would ruin everything I've been sent here to do.

I know where his old notebooks are, though, and those might help. The ones he journaled in after his dad passed, all the way up until he left for that last tour of duty. He wrote in one daily, pouring his thoughts onto paper, all the things he would never say out loud. They were a window into his soul after he left, giving me a deeper understanding of how his mind worked.

Before running from New Mexico, I re-read and memorized each word. Then I found a hiding spot for them, somewhere his shitty landlord wouldn't think to check.

Over the years, the words have faded from memory. But I've thought about those notebooks more times than I can count. I've berated myself many times over the years for forgetting the words and for not taking them with me somehow. I've even considered flying out here to retrieve them, but seeing them again would've reopened the old wounds I'd fought so hard to close. Not to mention, returning here had once been my greatest fear.

Facing Veno and his crew wasn't something I could do on a whim. It needed proper preparation. I needed a solid plan and to know how to protect myself. I'd also spent years in therapy dealing with the trauma he'd put me through. That had all taken time, which was what I'd needed so that when I came for him, I'd be doing it with a clear head and not be ruled by emotion.

Now that I'm here, it's not as scary. There's also a good possibility, given how different I look, that I could look him in the eye and he wouldn't recognize me.

Or at least that's my hope.

I've been keeping tabs on him when I can, and the shock of seeing him again has worn off. But facing him is a different matter, and it's one I've been mentally preparing myself for because I know that day is just around the corner.

LOST LYREBIRD

CHAPTER 18

A silent observer says the least but sees the most. Remember that.

Joining Dozer's gym, Coal & Iron Fitness, is a strategic move on my part for multiple reasons. It gives me a place to keep an eye on the HOCs in an environment where they feel at ease, somewhere where I can observe their dynamics, and interact with them outside the strip club.

I need them to see me as more than a dancer, in a way that's organic, earned, not forced.

Dozer carries weight in the club. Getting him to not only like me but trust me could mean a great deal when shit inevitably hits the fan.

He wasn't a member I wanted to fuck with, but rather one I'd want on my side in the days to come.

The second I step inside, I find him exactly where I expect—front and center, a towering presence. His gaze cuts to me the moment I enter, even before I've fully crossed the threshold. No makeup, and out of my usual environment, yet he instantly recognizes me.

He straightens from where he'd been leaning over the front desk, seemingly in the middle of reviewing something with the receptionist, but I have his full attention now. His sharp, gray-blue eyes flick over me, taking in the plum-colored sports bra, matching leggings, and white sneakers.

A slow grin spreads over his lips, one that carries just the right edge of amusement. "New recruit?" His voice is rough silk, laced with interest. "I'm guessing I have Raven to thank for the business?"

I drop my small gym bag at my feet, meeting his gaze without hesitation. "That's right. Asked for the best gym around. She pointed me here."

His grin deepens. "Smart woman."

"You wanna check it out for the day or—"

I shake my head before he can finish. "Full membership, please. I'm a sucker for pasta, and if I don't get at least a few solid workouts in a week, on top of dance practice, this body will rebel and pack all those calories into my ass."

He lets out a deep, easy laugh and crosses his arms over his chest. This move draws my eyes to the arm porn that is his extremely large biceps. "Not necessarily a bad thing."

I smirk. "Maybe not for you."

His eyes glint, but he doesn't push it. Instead, he nods toward the receptionist. "Megan here will go over membership options and get you set up in our system. After that, if you want, I can give you the tour."

Smooth. Direct.

And exactly what I was hoping for.

I smile graciously up at him. "I don't want to put you out. I'm sure you've got better things to do."

He waves me off. "Don't mind at all. And I'd do it for you regardless, bein' a friend of Raven's and all."

"He does a tour for pretty much everyone," Megan pipes up. "Especially the pretty newbies." Her eyes dance with amusement.

"Shut it, you," Dozer growls playfully at her. The two banter back and forth. Megan seems like more than an employee. She appears to be a friend. She's around the same age as me, mid-twenties, and wears a sizable sparkly rock on her ring finger. Based on the amount of flirting between them, which is nil, my guess is she's either happily married or doesn't swing that way. Because with Dozer's looks, his contagious smile, and the body of a God, any woman with a working libido would fall over themselves around him. And the various tattoos representing his time as a SEAL only add to his attractiveness.

It's not just his all-American fallen hero vibe, though—it's his posture, his confidence, his boldness, and all the head-on fucking eye contact.

He's not shy and doesn't mince words.

Knowing what I know about him—his military record and prior to that, his stellar football history in this town, not to mention the fact he'll be the one running the club when his old man, Cap, steps down—I imagine he's got quite a slew of females falling over themselves to get his attention.

Thankfully, I'm not one of them, but that has more to do with me than him.

Megan does her thing and gets me all set up. Within ten minutes, Dozer takes over and leads me around the club, pointing out the various areas and exercise rooms. He explains certain equipment and their hygiene practices in the main workout room.

We pass one Grinder, but Dozer doesn't interrupt him. Probably because he's in the zone. Where Dozer is clean cut with Viking-like features, Grinder has short, somewhat curly brown hair, and half of his face is covered in burn scars. He's curling weights in each hand and staring intently at himself in a large floor-to-ceiling mirror, singularly focused on his reflection in the mirror and whatever is playing in the earbuds he's got in his ears.

We move along quickly, and Dozer introduces me to two of his personal trainers—one male and one female. He shows me the new addition to the gym, a boxing area with eight different spaces, hanging bags, and a boxing ring in the corner.

It's here where a few other HOCs have gathered. Taz, the club's enforcer, a guy with short dark-brown hair styled in a mohawk, is battling a speed bag with such rapid movements that the bag blurs.

His body is a work of dark art, completely covered in intricate ink, mechanical, machine-like designs. They crawl up his neck and the side of his face, which is dripping with perspiration. His dark brows are pulled together in concentration, and his mouth is set in a firm line.

When we get within a few feet of him, he stops punching and stills the bag with one hand before giving me a critical once-over.

Dozer kicks his chin. "Lily, Taz. Taz, Lily. She's the new dancer at Tips."

Taz smirks sardonically. His eyes are so brown they're almost black, and they're a bit disturbing as he levels me with his stare. "Yeah, I know. The new girl with the nice rack," he says, before resuming his workout on the bag.

Dozer exhales through his nose, a half-laugh, half-grunt, as he grabs the sides of his waist and drops his head. He shakes it back and forth. "Don't mind him. He's an acquired taste. One I'm still trying to get used to."

"Same, Frogman," Taz fires back.

"Better a frogman than a conman."

"Acquitted."

Dozer chuckles. "Ah, well. The system doesn't always get it right."

Taz grumbles under his breath and puts more force into his next dozen hits.

Maverick Gunn is a few feet over and is a vision in nothing but gray sweats and a silver chain necklace that holds the club's winged-skull pendant at the end. He's not as massive as Dozer or Taz, but he still stands close to six feet. His hair's shaved short, jet-black against his darker skin, and a thick layer of scruff shadows his sharp jaw. Across his back, a huge HOC tattoo stretches from shoulder to shoulder. One of his arms is covered in colorful tattoos, while the other has an angel and a cross.

He drops one gloved hand at our approach and hits me with his intense amber stare, barely acknowledging me when Dozer introduces us. I get a simple "Hey," before he raises his hand and returns to pummeling the heavy bag in front of him with powerful jabs, one right after the other, as if he's trying to knock out some unseen enemy.

I don't say it lightly, because I've seen my fair share, but Mav is by far one of the sexiest bikers I've come across. The girls at the club overlook his attitude and fall all over him. They also refer to him as "Ricky Boy," where most of the guys refer to him as "Rick the Dick."

And he is that. From what I've witnessed, he's as broody as the day is long, and not someone you can easily approach. He's less outspoken, has a standoffish air about him, and often wears a dismissive scowl.

I know from his file—and what Deed's has relayed—that he's the club's SAA, and Cap's right hand. He supposedly took over the role of the sergeant-at-arms when Edge, Dozer's cousin, got locked away a few years back.

Mav's file also told me he has a degree from Cornell, healthy financials, and various business dealings. He's successful, educated, and has a heavy religious background.

Then there's Bodie. His workout, if I'm not mistaken, includes either watching the ceiling or it's quite possible he's sleeping. He's shirtless, wearing ripped jeans and nothing else, lying on his back in the middle of the boxing ring.

Above all the others, he's the most unpredictable guy out of all the HOCs. Not necessarily dangerous, because he's kind of a sweetheart and charmer. But you never quite know what will fly out of his mouth or what he'll do next. Like right now. He's barefoot and lying starfished in the ring.

In a way, he reminds me of myself. He struts to his own beat, colors outside the lines of normality, and goes full out on life. He's not everyone's cup of tea, yet he doesn't let criticism dull his shine. His loud and crazy nature drives some of the other guys bat-shit crazy, Finn especially, but I kind of think Finn needs that. Maybe they all do, so they don't take life too seriously.

Bodie stirs as Dozer calls out to him, groaning loudly and miserably before lifting his head to look at Dozer, who hangs his arms on the ropes. "Did it help?"

Bodie lays his head back on the mat with a thud. "While I was getting my ass beat, sure, but now. Not so much. What the fuck am I going to do? Three days!"

I'm a little lost about what they're discussing until Dozer fills me in. He peers down at me and explains. "His wife is taking off to her mom's place for a few days and leaving him with the kids."

"How old are the kids?" I ask.

Bodie leans up on his elbows. Both of his eyebrows pop up. "Well, look who it is. My favorite flower. You wouldn't by chance know anything about wee ones, would you? Like, say, feedin' them bottles and shit? Changin' diapers?"

I laugh outright. Surely he's not serious. Dozer chuckles, and they both stare at me. "No, sorry. I'm definitely not your girl for that. Clothes, fashion, music, and women, I can give advice on. Kids… that's a no."

"Beth still not answering?" Dozer asks him.

"Nah, man. And Kendra's visiting her family in Mexico."

"You could call my mom."

Bodie shakes his head, and his blond locks, which rest in waves around his face, bounce. His dimples wrinkle as he frowns. "No offense, man, but I'd rather get a swift kick in the balls than have your mom invading my space."

Dozer doesn't look offended. "Bet she'd take them off your hands until Blaire's back in town."

Bodie rolls over and peels himself off the floor. He strides over and sits by us, threads his arms over the rope. "But that's the test, right? Blaire will be even more pissed off at me if Locks throws this shit in her face, which will happen if I pass them off to someone else. And she'll use this shit against me forever. The point is that I'm supposed to manage and show her I'm capable of takin' care of my own damn kids, man."

"Did you try Raven?" I ask.

He scowls. "That girl stopped answerin' my calls ages ago."

Dozer bursts into a laugh that he fails to cover with a cough. "Probably because you all but stalked her and called her non-stop for like a year straight."

"To be fair, she never told me to lose her number." Bodie moans and rubs his forehead in frustration. "Anyone else you can think of?"

"I can send Taffy over after school, if that will help," Dozer offers.

"Anything, man. I'm desperate here."

Dozer pulls out his phone from his pocket and starts typing a text. When finished, he crosses his arms over his chest and levels a downright scary expression at Bodie. "This should go without saying, but I'll say it anyway."

"I know… I know." Bodie holds up one hand.

Dozer talks over him. "Touch her in any way, and I'll rearrange your fucking insides. You got me?"

"I know, man."

"Nah, I fuckin' mean it, brother. My baby sister is not just off-limits, she's a no-go, like ever, or I'll bury you."

"I mean, now that you told me not to, it's like waving a pirate flag at a born rebel."

Dozer goes to slap the back of his head, but Bodie dodges and sinks back and out of the way. He's laughing now, but hollers, "Just a fuckin' joke. Swear on my life, bro. I won't touch her."

Dozer pulls out his phone again and curses.

"What?" Bodie asks, the smile falling away rapidly as he studies Dozer's expression.

"She's got cheer practice. Forgot about that. And she's got a shift at the gas station that starts at six."

Bodie throws his head back while groaning, "Fuucccck, really?"

Shaking his head and getting a kick out of Bodie's situation, Dozer smirks. "Sorry, man. She said tomorrow she can help, but not today."

After rubbing his face vigorously, Bodie's gaze falls back on me, the silent observer to this animated conversation. When his head tilts to the side and he keeps staring, a spark of trepidation flutters in my chest.

"What?"

"Please!" He whines.

I laugh. "Please, what?"

"Help me?"

"Bodie, I—"

He cuts me off. "I know, but surely you know more than me. Or you can at least even the odds. One child, I can handle no problem. It's the two together running around like fuckin' maniacs that stresses me the hell out."

"Why have kids if they stress you out?"

"Because they're cute little fuckers and I love 'em. But this is my first one-on-one, and it's freakin' me the fuck out. At least with some backup, I'd be less anxious."

I eye him suspiciously. "And this isn't just a ploy to get me to your house alone?"

He crosses his fingers over his chest in an *X*. "Swear to fuckin' God, no. Wouldn't do Finn over like that."

Dozer snaps his head to me at that. My eyebrows rise, and I study Bodie's face. His words take me by surprise. He must have taken Dozer by surprise, too, because now the big man analyzes me as if he's seeing me in a new light.

"He's my boss, nothing more."

Bodie grins widely, his dimples making an appearance. "Sure. Sure."

"I'm serious."

"Well, that may be, but doesn't change the fact that you two sure throw a lot of sexual chemistry around when you're within a few fuckin' feet of each other."

"We don't—"

"You do," they both say at the same fucking time.

I roll my eyes in response and bite my bottom lip so I won't give voice to all the thoughts running through my mind. *If only they knew how much history Finn and I share. Knew who I really am and what my angle is here.* If they did, there would be none of this banter. No welcome. And neither of them would be as accepting of me as they are now. Bodie wouldn't be inviting me into his home to meet his kids.

Sure, he's doing it purely for help with his kids. But still.

I agree to help him, which might be a mistake. However, there's a part of me that wants this. This is an opportunity to get to know Finn's best friend. To learn more about the man who is on record as being the one who pulled Finn out of the firefight after the roadside bomb incident. Had Bodie not made it out, had he not saved Finn, then Finn would be what I'd imagined him to be for so long.

Dead.

Just a memory.

For this alone, I commit to helping him as much as I'm capable. He gives me his address, and I promise to show up after I head back to my hotel and change into something more appropriate for the domestic insanity I just signed up for.

I can do this.

Right?

Oh, God. The shit I get myself into.

Bodie's children are cute but a handful. Hallie is a month away from turning one, and she's a small bundle of feistiness who toddles around as she figures out how to use her little legs. She falls quite often but merely picks herself back up and tries again.

Tanner's three and totally gives off Dennis the Menace vibes: looks like an angel, acts like a gremlin. Blond hair, big baby-blue eyes like his dad's, and a grin that says he knows *exactly* what he's getting away with.

From an outsider looking in, I'd say Tanner's behavior is mainly an attempt to get his dad's attention.

But I'm no expert. Any parenting knowledge I have is primarily derived from literature and my studies in psychology and sociology. I particularly loved the discussions on these topics in my college courses. Like how nature and the world around someone can change them, versus the different ways nurturing or not nurturing, in a sense, can impact who a person becomes.

Schooling had always been a sore subject for me. It had been a barrier for steady employment and something I had to work around in my teens, which sort of led me down my path. So later, when Deeds told me he could get me a fake identity and I could go back if I wanted to, I jumped at the opportunity.

The fact that my degree is in a fake name doesn't matter to me. I didn't do it to put it on a resumé or to mount some plaque on a wall. I did it because I loved learning. I spent my free time in local libraries, devouring editorial pieces in various magazines, whether they were about other parts of the world, fashion, cultures, music, history, art, or mental development. I consumed it all. I'd developed a voracious appetite for learning that seemed to have no end.

So yeah, as I watch Bodie rock out with Tanner after he yanked out every pan from the cupboard so that he could beat them with a stick, I have to hold in these truths, or any wisdom I can glean from their personalities and Bodie's parenting style, because these are parts of myself I don't share with another soul—the pieces of me I hide away from the world so I can appear to be who I need to be on any given job.

I can see how playing with Tanner, encouraging art in any form, even if it's drumming on pots and pans, might change something fundamental about him. It just might plant a seed for his love of music, or show an early talent that he could develop as he grows. Had his dad shut it down immediately, what might that have done?

These are the things my own mother didn't consider. And maybe Bodie doesn't either, but he's not discouraging Tanner because it's loud and annoying, he's diving right in, and it's doing the trick. It's wearing them both out, and they're laughing like lunatics.

Tanner might not remember it, but Bodie will, and another seed is planted from the bond this little moment created, which is kind of beautiful if you think about it.

It's not like the neighbors can hear, and it's still daylight, so even if they could, so what?

Let the kid rock out if he wants to. I'm not sure if that's sound parenting, but it's what I would do in this situation.

I'm sitting at the kitchen table, trying and failing to feed Hallie the gloppy orange baby food in a jar that Bodie handed over with a tiny rubber spoon. It's everywhere. The bib caught some of the mess. The rest, though, is smeared over the lower half of her face. It's in her hair, since she grabbed the spoon at one point before I could move it away fast enough.

Bodie assured me it's nothing a bath won't fix, but the lack of control over this situation has thrown me for a loop. It's an entirely new experience. I call it a win, since I've managed to get at least half the jar of food into her small mouth.

From there, we don't even attempt to make dinner. I call for a pizza delivery. While we wait, Bodie bathes his kids. He ends up calling me in to help wrangle Hallie into a towel, so that he could do the same with Tanner.

I'm not entirely sure where everything is, but after searching the yellow dresser in Tanner and Hallie's shared room, I find a set of PJs that look as if they'll fit, and hold them up to Bodie for inspection.

"Yeah, but diaper first." He points at the changing table in the corner.

It's not until this moment that anxiety hits. Carefully, I lay Hallie out on the small mattress resting on top. She greets me with a soft smile and lets out a nonsensical word. Then she proceeds to wiggle out of the towel she's wrapped in. I stand close so she can't fall off and reach for one of the diapers from the pile off to the side.

I stare at it for longer than necessary. I'm not dumb. I know how this works. But putting a diaper on a real, live, wiggling child makes it somehow like an experiment I'm trying to navigate without any actual instructions as to how to go about it.

I turn back and plead with Bodie, "A little help." He's running his hands over Tanner's wet curls as Tanner proceeds to yank toys out of his wooden, ornate toybox and toss them to the floor. The box is dark wood and stained. It looks like something you'd see on a pirate ship. It's beautiful.

Bodie stands next to me. He smiles at Hallie and tickles her. This does not help my anxiety at all because, if anything, she becomes more wriggly. When the tickling stops, Bodie looks at me. His blue-eyed gaze pings from me to the diaper, to Hallie, back to the diaper, and then back to me.

Amusement dances over his face. Those damn dimples make an appearance, though he tries to stifle his grin.

"Shut up," I snap.

He meshes his lips together, but he can't hide that he's getting a kick out of this. I try to pass him the diaper. He holds up his hands and takes a step back.

"She's your baby," I insist.

"Yes, but you're my helper."

"Bodie."

Tanner climbs up on top of a chair beside the changing table. "Mama calls him Weese."

I force a smile at Bodie—or Reese, or Weese, or whatever this asshole's name is—while he grins at me like a fool. I open the tabs of the diaper, lift Hallie's legs, and slide one side underneath.

Bodie laughs. "Other side down."

I spin the diaper and work it up and over her little tummy, attaching the tabs. She kicks her feet, and the gaps on the sides make it obvious it's too loose.

Bodie is about to say something, but I hold up a finger. "Not a word."

He chokes on another laugh.

I tighten the straps a few times until they look to fit just right.

Bodie hands me the PJs.

Fuck. I don't know how to do this. Like any of it. I honestly thought I might never get the chance to. I push that thought down when emotions rise rapidly to the surface.

Come on, Lily, it's not hard. And it's stupid that it stresses me out or has these weird, uncomfortable feelings fluttering in my chest. I don't even know what the feelings are. They're simply there and unexpected, maybe even a bit unwelcome.

When I think about it, I realize there's a burn behind my eyes and nose. I fight it. Of course I do. I do not, under any circumstances, let people see me cry. So I do what comes naturally and click *off* my feelings until I can psychoanalyze them at another time or forget about this entirely.

Because I don't even know what's happening to me right now.

After the pizza arrives, Bodie lays a blanket on the front room floor, and Tanner, Bodie, and I guard our plates from Hallie when she comes close. I lean against the couch, watch her toddle from one place to the next, and put various toys inside her mouth. Eventually, Bodie places her in her bouncer.

Tanner sits on the blanket scarfing down a breadstick as he watches an animated movie on the TV. Bodie falls asleep on the couch while I watch the kids do their thing.

I'm not going to lie. I get a tad overwhelmed by the normality of it all. When Tanner wakes his dad, because there's a question he needs answered and does not care one iota whether Bodie is resting or not, I ask, "You good if I head out?"

He groans as he sits up and combs his hands through his unruly waves. He doesn't seem entirely with it, but looks around at the kids and then at me with glazed eyes. "Yeah. Sorry, I was beat. Didn't mean to pass out on you."

"It's fine."

I peel myself off the floor and get to my feet. He pushes off his thighs and stands. After I've collected my Coach purse, he walks me to the door.

"Ah, domestic bliss. Am I right?" He laughs at this like it's a joke. But I can tell, in a way, it isn't, and in a way, it is. He loves it, but it's also hard. He loves his kids. But it's as if some part of it doesn't work for him, and maybe that's okay. I don't know what it is. Maybe he doesn't either.

It could be his free spirit that longs for family, but feels hindered by it at times.

I let it go because I don't know him or this type of life well enough to judge.

I tell Tanner goodbye and smile down at Hallie one last time before I follow him to the door. He thanks me profusely as I step past him and onto the porch.

"Same time tomorrow?"

I laugh and shake my head. "Tomorrow, Taffy's coming."

"Thursday then?"

I stop in the middle of the yard and think about it. Turning, I meet his hopeful and desperate expression, which is kind of adorable. I exhale in exasperation, and a blinding smile splits over his face. I hike my purse up over my shoulder and spin my keys around a finger.

"I'll owe you big time," he says.

I point at him. "You better."

I'm just about to slip into my car when he hollers in jest, "This could be you one day."

The temptation to flip him off comes over me. I give in and hear his deep laugh. I shut my door and let the words I feel spill over my lips. "I'm not so sure about that."

LOST LYREBIRD

CHAPTER 19

*Religion is what we make it. If you believe in
something enough to dedicate most of your
life to it, that's faith.*

People around the world enter their churches, sit in their chapels, and saturate themselves in their beliefs. For us, this room serves the same purpose. The scent of leather and aged wood fills the air. The low hum of the overhead fan has a calming effect. It's a sacred place to many of us, more than walls filled with memories and a meeting room. It's a space that reminds us of who we are and what we stand for.

Outsiders would call it blasphemy—what we believe in. Hell, even some of the brothers' old ladies don't get it. Not that we give a damn. Judgment rolls off us the second we trade our prospect patches for the real deal. Like a shedding of skin.

Every time we step inside, we do it again. Leave our drama at the door, and baptize ourselves in the code of the club as we cross the threshold. What we do in here? We do for each other. For the club. For the code.

We don't need approval, and we sure as hell don't need anyone else to understand. In this room, every man has a vote. Every voice holds weight. It's where we hash out problems and hold each other accountable. It's where we make decisions that shape the future of the club and everyone tied to it. It's where we come to when we need a reminder of why we do what we do.

This is our house of God. The only God most of us believe in. Our temple.

Hung high on the wall, our colors loom—the insignia dreamed up by Cap and drawn by Griz. The very same design we wear on our backs and have tattooed on our skin.

From where I sit at the table, the sign hangs directly behind my chair. Having arrived early to church and alone, I turn around and become engrossed in the meaning of the details. The wicked arrows spanned out in every direction, symbolizing the chaos of the world we live in. The skull with eyes that see right through you—through the bullshit bred into each one of us. Blood pools from the mouth—a promise that we're willing to spill blood to protect what we hold dear. Curled devil horns with a halo above signify we're not without a conscience to guide us, but we often straddle the line of right and wrong. The jagged wings echo the danger we're guaranteed to meet on the road when we ride. The eye of chaos reminds us to have one eye open for threats against the club, ourselves, and those we love. The banner is broken into two parts: REVEL IN CHAOS—enjoy the chaos, take advantage of the opportunities it presents. REGRET NOTHING—let nothing done in the name of the club darken our soul to the point of no return. And lastly, the claws wrapped around those words to remind us to cling to our code, our brotherhood, our beliefs.

Cap had it hung here so it was the first thing every brother saw upon entering Church, and it's become a ritual for me and some of the other brothers to touch it with respect before sitting at the table.

As I wait for the others, I think about how the elements represent our strongest patch holders. Cap, with his all-seeing eyes. Mav, the halo and horns. Taz, the arrows of chaos. Edge, the wings torn by risk. Bodie, the top banner, because he's always reveling in what this life has on offer. Griz and the old timers—clinging to the code as their years dwindle by because it's their legacy. And me? I'd be the base of the wings, where they should bind and keep the club whole, be a solid foundation, except like me, they're riddled with holes, clearly flawed.

Which leaves the blood dripping from the mouth and Dozer. His hands might have blood on them, but that blood was spilled in the name of the US Navy and for the good of our country, so it somehow doesn't fit because he's also not alone in that aspect. Many of us who served have blood on our hands. So yeah, those two puzzle pieces don't fit.

Having them not fit throws everything off. It makes me question if I've put the right person with the right symbol. But each time I come to the same conclusion.

When I can't fit it neatly into the box inside my mind, I feel ill at ease, like I'm missing something. Maybe that time will come when Dozer takes up the Pres patch and his father steps down. But that also makes me feel like an asshole. Like I'm wishing that kind of fate and a whole hell of a lot of bloodshed on him.

Footsteps echo across the hardwood as Dozer steps into the doorway. His eyes flick to the symbol behind me, and for a moment, there's nothing but the weight of unspoken respect. His boots thud with each step as he makes his way towards it. He touches his lips with two fingers before planting them lightly on the sign, and then takes his seat. The quiet before the others arrive amplifies the reverence.

Five minutes later, the table is full. Rank dictates where everyone sits. We get typical business out of the way first before discussing important matters. I don't speak for the sake of speaking, like Taz, just when I have something to add of importance. Instead, I use this time to study my brothers. You can tell a lot about a person if you shut up and watch. Body language and silence are just as telling. Like, who cares about this issue, who's distracted, who's got money trouble, family drama. Who's lying. Who's genuine and invested.

I log it all mentally as I watch and listen.

It's not until Cap mentions the Greenbacks that I turn down the dial in my brain that analyzes everything.

"I still can't believe the Greenbacks have gotten so deep with them. Pappy's gotta know it'll end only one way." This from Dozer. He's talking about Pappy's business dealings with the Escarra Cartel in Mexico.

Cap nods. "No doubt he does. Probably why he's patching over smaller clubs and spreading his hold over the neighboring states along the coast. Chess pieces. I expect he's put many in place for this very reason. For now, things with the cartel are highly profitable, stable, and serving his purpose, but yeah, you can bet his end game isn't far from his mind."

I jump in to help some newer members get up to speed. "You said before you think it was a temporary fix, his dealings with them, when he had that big fallout with the IRA?"

Cap meets my eyes momentarily and nods in acknowledgment, an unspoken look passing between us, then relays the rest. "Yeah. But even I didn't anticipate the IRA holdin' out this long. For a while now, I've been thinkin' the deal that went south wasn't the only reason for the rift."

Dozer knocks his knuckles on the table. "One bad deal doesn't warrant this kind of freeze-out. Not when there's big money up for grabs."

Brothers around the table nod.

Mav adds his two cents. "The Nevada chapters he's got are flush, and now he's spreadin' his web over Arizona. In no time, he'll be comin' this way, and lookin' to push the Thirteen Devils out." I'm not opposed, but I'm the minority on this, so I keep my opinion close to my chest. "Not a good time when we got Edge on the inside. They fuck up the truce for us, and Edge will be the one facing the fallout on our side."

This has grumbles and discontent stirring around the room.

"So what do we do?" This from Dozer. His fist is clenched so tightly that his knuckles are turning bone white.

Cap turns to his son. "Unofficially and between us sittin' at this table, Pappy's already approached me about putting a chapter here." At the grumbles heard around the table, he holds up his hand. "I held him off, for now. We need time. We need this truce to keep Edge safe on the inside. Letting the Greenbacks set down roots here will jeopardize that. I told him I'm not opposed to a chapter here down the road and with clear lines laid out, but now's not the time."

The tension in the room thickens. The quiet, muffled breathing of everyone tells me how on edge they all are.

Dozer grinds his jaw. The muscle there pulses as he works through whatever is going on in his head. "We can't let the Thirteens get word of this. They won't protect Edge on the inside if they catch wind of it, no matter how much we pay them. The threat of the GBs taking over their business and pushing them out of New Mexico will have them doing something stupid."

"I know," Cap agrees. "So for now, we keep this quiet, stretch time, and buy ourselves as much as we can afford."

Griz chimes in, his deep voice rumbling, "Pappy's askin' out of respect." Meaning, Pappy doesn't have to ask for shit. If he didn't give a fuck about the business we share or the longtime friendship he has with Cap and Griz, and the club as a whole, he'd have already moved his boys here.

I rap my knuckles on the table, the dull thud echoing in the thick silence. "You think we can hold them off until Edge is out?"

"Not sure, but we're sure the fuck gonna try. It feels like our only play here," Cap reasons.

"Wait. Hold up." Mav jumps in as he scrubs a hand over his short black hair. His amber glare lands on each of us for a moment. "I don't know about you, but letting the GBs into our territory seems like a bad fuckin' idea. Maybe it's one chapter at first, but we've seen how fast Pappy's growin' that club. He's gonna lose control, and their chapters will get sloppy. If they bring that kind of heat down on themselves, it's also gonna fall on the rest of us. We don't want the Feds all over our shit, digging through our businesses or the ways we pull in green." He stabs his finger on the table to get his point across. "They move here, we're guaranteed a ticket to a shitshow we didn't sign up for."

"I'm with Mav. You invite a giant into your home, he's gonna fuck everything up," Septic grits out from down the table.

Taz sneers. "They wanna grow. They can spread north. Why the fuck they gotta come here?"

"Everything is runnin' smooth as is. I vote we don't rock the boat. Maybe Pappy is just trying to throw his weight around to see if we're open to it. If we let him know we're not, then maybe he'll back off." This comes from Stone, who's also our newest patched-in member.

I lean forward. Usually, I'd keep my cool and hold this all in. Maybe even maneuver brothers one by one to see how wrong they are about this decision, but after the shit I've seen and experienced over the last year, I know staying silent right now would be a great detriment to not just the club but a lot of fucking innocent people who need someone to be their fucking voice. "I get what you're sayin'. All of you," I say as I work to push down the venom boiling in my blood. "But you also haven't seen the shit I've seen if you think the 13Ds are any better." My voice has a desperate edge that I can't tamp down entirely. "These girls I help… the ones the 13Ds are branding, selling… they're not willing. A few aren't even legal, but they're pretty good about hiding the shit like this that will bury them. At least the GBs are selling willing pussy and legal consensual sex, plus they're keeping it off the streets. They're not snatching runaways or girls in dire situations and selling some across the border, never to be seen or heard from again. Nor do they treat the girls under their care like dogs. Don't even get me started on the kids they're pullin' in to sell their product on the street."

"You know this for a fact?" Stone questions.

"Yeah, I've witnessed it firsthand." I look around the table, meeting certain men's gazes.

Mav leans back, jaw tight. He runs his hand down his face and scratches at his scruff-covered jaw. He looks taken aback and takes his time to consider this side of the coin, as I see it.

It's a no-win situation. I get it. Either way you dice it, we're fucked.

Cap interjects, "It's not something we need to decide now. But the times comin' when we're goin' to have to choose who we side with." When Cap realizes almost everyone is in agreement, he calls for a vote. When it's done, he nods. "The vote stands. For now, we hold 'em off. Buy us some time. Keep makin' payments to the 13Ds to keep Edge safe."

"Goose, Bodie, Grinder, and Stone will make the usual drop to the 13Ds on Monday night at ten. Mav, Dozer, Griz, and I will visit Edge this weekend and make sure before we hand over the money, they're keepin' up their end."

A few more items are discussed; most of it revolves around the businesses we all run for the club, the green we clean, the guns we sell, and upcoming runs we have to make to push product from the weed farms we partially own in Colorado. The meeting finally comes to an end, the sound of heavy footsteps, creaking chairs, and leather filling the space. Just as I make it to the door, I get called back by Cap.

Turning, I see him gliding his hand over the glossy surface of the wood table. The grain shines under the low light, reflecting the years of meetings, decisions, and history it's witnessed. He rocks back in his chair, plants his elbow on the table, and crosses his ankle over his knee.

"You sure you're good to keep making these payment runs?"

I nod. "Yeah, why wouldn't I be?"

"Heard tensions are thick between you and Veno."

Knowing this isn't going to be a quick conversation, I shut the door and take Griz's seat. The chair creaks under my weight, the leather cold and firm.

"Always been that way. We got history." I shrug. "Been amping up because he doesn't appreciate me stickin' my nose in his business. But the way I see it, if the girl's not there by choice and needs a way out, then I'm going to get her out."

"You know this could put our truce on shaky ground too?"

"It's one girl. One girl every few months. Either she'll come to me or the cops, or die trying to make a run for it. So, either way, they lose her. This way, the cops aren't all over them. And what the fuck do they care? They'll replace her in a week with someone new."

"Be real with me, how bad is it?"

"Veno kept his nose pretty clean for a while after he got out of the pen, but the more power El Jefe—fuck, I hate calling him that" I shake my head. Cap rolls his hand.

I continue, "Anyway, the more power *Antonio* hands off to Veno, the bolder Veno grows. It's gonna be a problem. No doubt in my mind. Antonio cares about his people, power, and money. He's scary fuckin' smart and ruthless."

"And Veno?"

"He only cares about power and money. It's an ego trip for him. And one day his greed is gonna turn brother against brother, and it'll be a shitstorm in our backyard. The girls Veno's trafficking and pimping out are kept under watch, taken to shady places, sold to scum of the earth, and force-fed drugs to keep them compliant and tied to him for their next fix. If they do want out or decide to get clean, it doesn't end well for them. They're here one day and gone the next. Not sure what's happening to them—either sold off or put in the ground."

As I watch Cap, his scowl deepens. He tries to mask his anger and disgust as he thinks through the problem logically. The way his hard eyes stare at nothing, the way his right fist curls, and how, like Dozer, his thick muscles bulge with tension. Then a look of utter disgust flashes across his face in the next second, and I wonder if his thoughts have turned to Taffy, his eighteen-year-old daughter.

"Is there more?" he asks.

"Veno's getting sloppy. Pushin' out a shit load of meth and it's bad shit. The crew he's building—they're heartless, scary fuckers. From the outside in, it looks like he's tryin' to make a name for himself and come out from Antonio's shadow. If I were Antonio, I'd start worrying about Veno making a power play. Because you can bet your ass sooner or later he will. He'll make a move and cut off the head that's been tying his hands."

The ice in Cap's eyes is glacial. "The last thing we want is Veno taking over. Let's keep an eye on him and his crew. Ideally, we keep him in line as much as we're able to and buy us time, make what moves we can until Edge isn't in the crosshairs. You and Taz put your heads together and come up with something."

I knock on the table and give him a stiff nod. "No problem."

"And keep doing what you can under their radar. Just don't let them catch up to you or tie it back to the club. Minimal waves. When Edge is free, we'll run their asses out of here."

Pride swells in my chest, and we clasp arms. The firm grip, warm and solid, is reassuring. A grin spreads across my face. "Was hoping you'd say that."

He gives me a grim smile in return. "Same page. Same book."

That's the thing about this club that sold me on becoming a member. Cap's not just looking after the members—he's looking after the community. Not just Los Lunas either. He cares deeply about the place we call home—local, state, and the country as a whole. And though he doesn't buy into the government's bullshit anymore, he still loves his fucking country to the depths of his soul. The kind of man who should and could lead a nation, but is content ruling over his small portion of the world.

"You just tell me what you need and when you need it. You don't have to do this on your own."

My chest inflates, fills fucking full to bursting. His words are exactly what I needed to hear. For a while now, I've been a lone man on a mission. But that's on me. Looking back at the insignia on the wall, I chuckle mirthlessly. The letters etched into the wood seem to glare back at me. UWL. UWR. UWF. United we live, ride, and fall.

Cap follows my gaze. "What?"

"Should've known better is all." I rake my hands through my hair. The strands slip through my fingers, coarse and damp with sweat. "To keep some of this bullshit to myself. To go at it alone. Not bringing you all in the know of what I've seen first-hand."

He chuckles, "Yeah, but it's just your way. Your daddy was the same. Always trying to play the lone hero until the problem was bigger than he could handle. I'm tellin' you, the apple never falls far." He spins in his chair and stands. Walking to the wall at the other end of church, he points to a picture full of soldiers, a few familiar faces in it, only these faces are forty years younger in the photo—at least the ones still living.

"Luckily, he came to us that day with some bad intel he'd been sworn to keep to himself, or this picture would've ended up much different. Without him in it, and maybe even without a few of us."

I join him and lean against the wall, getting a good view of the picture. The image is grainy, yellowed with age. My throat constricts as I swallow down the emotions rising at the picture of my dad, a time when he was healthy, whole, and from the looks of it, happy. Before he came back from war to a woman who didn't love him, before he saw the hell I'd lived through while he'd been serving, and before his disease stole so many days from us after that.

Cap studies the photo, a smile kicking up the side of his mouth. "These fuckers."

I laugh along with him.

"Some of the best men I've known. You're dad, one of the best of them."

I've heard it before, but I don't mind hearing it again. He could say it a thousand times, and I'd listen with rapt attention. Because you never get sick of hearing about the loved ones you lost. Maybe it's because you feel like you only truly lose them when you no longer speak their name and reminisce about the ways they impacted your life. But damn, does it bring back a flood of memories of my childhood with the man I thought hung the moon in spades. Memories that aren't riddled with potholes, and are crystal clear and easy to recall, like it all happened yesterday.

"Ha! Listen to me. Such a sad sap. But fuck I miss them. Pappy, too, though, I know a lot of you don't like to hear it."

"Not many know him like you do."

"Nah, and he'd prefer it that way, to tell ya the truth of it. The mask he wears was crafted out of necessity."

"How's that?"

"Being a scrawny immigrant kid from Ireland back then was no small feat. His daddy and his brothers were fighting to claim territory, and put food on the table, put a lot of heat on him and his brother, Griz, too. Surviving took everything they had and then some."

"And underneath it?"

"There's a good man. Loyal as the day is long. Someone you'd want standing next to you when you're facing down your worst end. Not only because they'd give the enemy a hell of a fight, but you know they'd step in front of you when a bullet with your name engraved on it came callin'."

"It's like that, huh?"

He nods and turns, his steely blue-gray eyes meet my gaze and hold firm. "It's like that."

"Your word is enough for me."

Closer now, he grips my shoulder, like my father was known to do. "Appreciate that. Now, if I could only get the rest of them"—he tilts his head toward the closed door— "to see it my way.

"They will. Probably not Taz, but definitely most." We both laugh at that.

"Hope so."

"So, you for the GBs comin'? Or you just don't see a way around it?" I ask.

"Definitely the second one. On the first, it depends on who's runnin' the ship here. Pappy will stay in Cali with Vaughn. I trust him, but I also know the loose boundaries he has, and all the ways he's willing to make green. He overvalues money, in my opinion. Always has because of his roots. Takes unnecessary risks to obtain it. It's the one sticking point we've always had. Nowhere near the top of my totem pole, but for him, it's second only to them. Vaughn and Deeds. Some of his methods, I'm okay with… some, I'm not. We understand each other and respect it. But who knows who he'll place to run the chapter here. A chapter President twice removed and outta his sight, might not run the club how Pappy or I would like. I'll have a say, but my input will only go so far, and no doubt they may try to get away with shit under our noses. Keep it clean for a few years, sure, but after Pappy's head turns the other way, no one can know what they'll do. Highly doubt they'll follow the outlaw letter of the law the way we do."

"So, a shitstorm for another day."

"Yeah, I expect it will be."

Exhaling, I grit out, "Well, fuck."

He grins. "Exactly. Nothin' we can't handle."

"You seem pretty confident about that."

Crossing his arms over his large chest, he rests against the table, half sitting on the edge. "I am. In you." He kicks his head towards the door. "In most of those knuckleheads out there. We got somethin' good here and we're doin' it for the right reasons. We believe in somethin' better than ourselves. At the end of the day, the other clubs and gangs fightin' for turf and money will lose because they're not willing to give their lives for what they're fightin' for. They got no heart behind their beliefs. We're different. And they're gonna figure that out eventually. Just a little too late to do anything about it. Mark my words."

I nod, but I get lost in thought. I start tapping my fingers against my pocket, touching the coin there. I remember the day this path here opened up for me. *A pack of Harleys came barreling down the street. One of the bike's engines roared louder as the front runner pulled a U-turn and circled back. I'd been working on renovations on the duplex I purchased when the big fella with long, grizzly gray-blonde hair, dark sunglasses, and a leather jacket with club colors pulled up and parked in my motherfucking driveway. I'd lost weight and muscle in the hospital and rehab. I'd been drenched in sweat from the heat and feeling weak and lethargic, struggling with life in general. At first, I didn't know what the fuck was going on. I figured I was about to have a throwdown with a gang member for doing nothing more than existing or giving him the eyeball. And yeah, maybe I had since I hadn't liked what I saw of Albuquerque since returning. And this was another thing on that list of fucked-up shit I'd have to deal with.*

The large biker dismounted and met me at the edge of the driveway. By then, his boys had turned to follow him and were closing in on us. I didn't think there was any chance of taking them on and winning, but then this big dude eyed me up and down and said, "Shit, you're still the spittin' image of your old man. Changed a bit since his funeral. For a minute there, I thought I was seein' a ghost. How you been, son?"

It was then that it clicked—who he was. His hair was long and unruly, and the beard also threw me off, but my mind finally connected the dots.

"Cap?" I met his strong handshake with one of my own.

"Yeah, you remember?" He smiled a big-ass smile and waved his group over to us as we got to catching up.

Before he left that day, he invited me to come check out the club. No commitment, just a beer and a good time. I'd been in a dark place during those days. Popping pills to cope with the migraines, because they numbered it all, the pain, the loneliness, the grief. I had shit all going for me at the time… a girl I couldn't find, memories I couldn't hold on to, a father buried and gone, and an abusive mother I hadn't seen since I was a child. The rope Cap presented pulled me out of my head and gave me a way to do something good with the extra time I'd been given. A reason to wake up the next day and care about the day after that. I'd nearly died. Nearly. But I didn't, and it had to be for a reason. Being around other vets had been good for me. There was an easy kinship there because, even though most had gone to war and returned in one piece, many of them understood what I was going through and had issues of their own.

It didn't take me long to join. Getting off the opioids had been challenging, but they helped me kick them. Prospecting had been a pain in the ass, downright humiliating at times, and yet I understood the importance of the initiating ritual. How it breaks down the ego and weeds out the men who wouldn't be able to hack it in the long run, while humbling a man at the same time.

I come back to myself when Cap slaps his hand on my bicep to get my attention. "You keep savin' who you can save. The club has your back if you need us. You don't have to do it alone unless you want to. Remember that." He gives it one last squeeze on my arm before he guides me out of church, and we join the rest of the boys at the bar in the main room.

I try to remind myself of Cap's words for many days to come—that I don't have to go through what I'm going through alone.

LILY

CHAPTER 20

*You may never know the depths of sacrifice
others have made on your behalf.*

The daggers laced with jealousy are impossible to miss but not hard to ignore. In fact, I take it as a compliment now. Something about me makes some women feel inferior. I've come to accept it.

Maybe it's the confidence I've clawed back, the armor I wear that's been reforged by decades of mistreatment and abuse, and how each blow that knocked me down made me fight to come back stronger.

Maybe they also recognize that my inner wolf is more dangerous than theirs. Let's face it—an animalistic hierarchy is constantly at play. We may not consciously recognize it, but like wolves in a pack, we always seek to establish our place within it.

Life has shaped me into something else—something they don't understand, something they can't relate to, something other women shrink in fear of but fight against by trying to knock me back down.

But I am who I am; either you like me, or you don't. It's empowering once you embrace it.

Few women see past this outer shell to the heart of me. They judge me based on all they see. It is what it is. I've learned to live with it. Simply put, those women who prejudge aren't worth my time or effort to befriend.

Only women who have experienced something similar seek to know more.

Over the last few months, I've let Raven and Bianca into my small bubble. They've been similarly forged by life's hard knocks, with their own tragic stories to tell.

Bianca is an exotic beauty with Brazilian heritage. She works weekend nights and hires a nurse to stay with her son during her shifts.

Right away, I could see that her desperation stemmed from something beyond her need to make as much money as possible each night. The "extras," the willingness to push boundaries, and OTCs or "outside the club" meet-ups, were a cry for help. When I learned she was doing all she could to pull herself out of a bad domestic abuse situation and put enough money aside to move away from her current boyfriend, I made it my mission to do all I could to help her achieve that goal. Raven jumped on board, and we'd all become close quickly. The fact that Raven and I were the only ones who saw Bianca's struggle for what it was solidified my opinion of some of the other women here.

The three of us quickly established our own little group, one in which I've found some solidarity.

At my locker, next to Bianca's, I smile at the gift bag I placed around the handle of her locker. Inside are a few little gifts for her son: a Ty duck plushie, a crossword puzzle book for kids, and a new box of crayons. It's not much, but I know it'll put a smile on her son's face all the same.

Then, I swap my everyday underwear for one made entirely of satin—baby-doll pink—and weave the ties through a matching corset that lifts my breasts just right. I pull on thigh-highs with a ribbon and bow at the top, followed by delicate heels with ribbons that I lace up my calves. The click of the sky-high pink stilettos echoes as I move through the dressing room.

At my assigned vanity, I pin my real hair down and put on a wig made with real human hair. After putting on my face—dramatic smoky eye makeup and winged eyeliner—I clip on the heart earrings—glittering crystals that catch the dressing room lights. I smooth my fingers through my long platinum hair and style the voluminous waves so the top half is plated into long twin pigtails. For the final touch, over the corset, I put on a fluffy layered skirt with buckle details and a pink leopard-print bodice top with feathery wrist cuffs. The fitted top is sheer enough to hint at what lies beneath, and the effect of the shirt and skirt draws attention to my small waist.

I take one last look at myself in the mirror and grin at my reflection. In this outfit, I'm a whole new person… a sultry Barbie doll. This dance is a strategic one. A step forward in the bigger game I'm playing.

The metal on the bottom of my heels clicks against the flooring as I walk through the dressing room on my way out. The whispers that follow me are nothing but white noise. They bounce off the shield I've erected to keep the negative opinions and chatty Cathys out of my sphere.

I head down the hall and turn the corner just in time to hear Finn's voice, deep and a bit strained. "I don't give a shit about the money. She says she needs time, and we'll give her as much as she needs."

His tone is like steel, and it stops me for a second. I blink as I take in the scene—Finn, tense and defensive, arms crossed tightly over his chest. Raven is a few feet in front of him. Her expression hard and determined, one hand on her hip as she argues back. I slow my stride. Their attention swings toward me. Raven's eyes dip immediately to my outfit, and she smirks. Finn? His focus stays fixed on my legs. Something flickers across his face.

I pretend not to notice. Bending down, I fix a ribbon on my calf, giving him a better view of my curves, before trailing my hand up my leg as I straighten.

"Too much?" I ask, with a hint of a tease.

Raven chokes on a laugh.

It takes Finn a moment to respond. When he finally speaks, his hoarse tone gives me a hint that the outfit choice is hitting its mark. "Not at all."

His eyes burn with irritation when they venture up my body. Something darker shades them when they get to my chest. I note he's also grinding his molars if the pulse jumping at his jaw is any indication. His body is rigid.

He rips his stare away from me and pins it back on Raven.

"We were just talking about you." Raven's enjoying watching him unravel.

Finn's scowl deepens. Unease and frustration roll off him.

"One of our regulars wants some private time with yo—" Raven starts.

Finn cuts her off. "I told her no. That we've talked about it, and you said you'd let me know when you were ready to do privates."

I nod in agreement, because yeah, I did. But it's time to step up and get the game moving in the direction I've chosen.

Raven adds quickly, "It's a semi-private dance, second-floor stage. It's up to you if you want it to go further into a lap dance. He's loaded and willing to lay down a good deal of green for time with you. But you won't be alone. I can send one of the bouncers up there to watch over things."

Finn growls caveman-style and holds up his hand. "It's got to be her decision."

"I know," she snaps. "I'm just relaying the information."

"Done. Now give her a second to think it over." They stare each other down for long enough that it becomes awkward.

Raven smiles and flutters her hand in his direction. "In case you didn't know, what's happening here is pretty obvious. The others will figure it out soon enough. My best advice… you two need to figure your shit out."

"Rave," he says.

"What? It's spilling over and throwing off the whole vibe in the club." She points at him. "Fix it, be together, or let it go is all I'm saying."

She turns and walks off as if she didn't just tell off her boss. Finn pinches the bridge of his nose and lets out a pent-up breath before facing me.

"You don't have to do this unless you want to." The way he's looking at me, it's like he's begging me not to do it. But I've already made my decision. I'm doing what's best for both of us in the long run, what will help keep him and his club safe.

"You'll be watching, right?" My voice lowers with an edge of seduction, my body angling slightly toward him as I close the space between us. His eyes dilate as they roam over me. The intensity there lures me in, making it hard to think clearly. His lips part. I stare at him and nearly sway forward as he bites his bottom lip. The urge to lean in and taste him is oh-so tempting.

It takes everything I have to deny myself.

"I'll protect you," he murmurs, his voice a rasp. "That's not ever anything you should have to question." His words hang in the air between us, thick with tension.

I give him a grim smile. "Then I'm ready. Lead the way, Captain." Do I let my hand rest on his chest and pat the Road Captain patch? Yes, I do. It's to remind myself why this step forward is the right one—what I risk if I don't put more distance between us.

CHAPTER 21

Don't let your dreams slip from your grasp and fall into the lap of someone unworthy.

The bass from "*Check On It*" by Beyoncé thrums as I runway-walk down the stage and drag a silver chair out behind me, every beat pulsing through my body as I work my hips.

We're on the second floor in a sectioned-off VIP area. The stage is about ten feet round, which means I'll have to adjust my routine to fit the space. The client chose to sit front and center instead of on the long, L-shaped couch against the wall, so I take that into account too.

The routine is one I choreographed myself. It has a ton of attitude and sass. It was meant for a wider audience, but adjusting it to deliver some focused, sweet seduction shouldn't be too hard. It drips sex: some parts are slow and deliberate, while others are fast—popping, twerking, and naughty movements that flash my best assets. I use the chair as a prop and place it as close to the edge of the stage as I can while still giving myself room to move around it.

Eye contact is key, and I make sure to reconnect my gaze with the suits often, playing around with different expressions while I bite my nail, play with the ends of my hair, and slowly rise from a bend where my ass is up and the main attraction—the enticement giving him a good glimpse beneath my skirt from his vantage point.

Midway through, he's so enthralled that he's lifted his drink to his mouth but has yet to take a sip of it, as if he's forgotten it's even in his hand.

He's an older gentleman with nice eyes—a big tipper—and he's become a regular over the last few months. He's good-looking, in his fifties maybe, well-dressed, with money practically spilling from his suit pocket, but I barely see him. He's a paycheck, a distraction, a golden ticket to Finn's torture—because if I have to suffer through this, he can too.

Near the end of the song, when my skirt has been discarded, I crawl toward the client and curl my finger repeatedly to entice him closer. His gaze is focused on my face, but as I kneel, spread my knees, and begin to thrust my hips to the rhythm, it quickly moves down my body until it rests between my thighs.

I arch my back and pump my hips as I draw my sheer top up and over my head. After licking my finger, I trail it down my neck and chest. I let my hand guide his gaze downward as I tease my stomach, then palm my sex, continuing to rock and roll my upper body to the rhythm of the song, mimicking the way I ride a man in the throes of passion. My head swings from side to side, whipping my hair back and forth. A light sheen of sweat coats my skin. My mouth is parted just slightly, and I peer down at him through half-closed eyes.

The only thing missing is the man underneath me.

This is the scene I paint for him, and by the lust I see covering his features, he's living out the fantasy in his head.

I ride out the song until the last few hard-hitting beats, then end in a sultry pose, with my chest pressed forward, one hand in my hair holding it off my neck, the other on my thigh.

A new song, a slower and mixed version of "Partition," begins. I use the buildup to catch my breath and swing my legs over the edge of the stage. I cross them in front of the suit. Using his tie, I pull him closer and whisper in his ear, letting my heavy breath tease his earlobe. I relay sinful words, ones I know will level him, while my mind is locked on the man who's been content so far to watch from the shadows.

I'm tempted to see how long Finn's control lasts—if watching me seduce another man has any effect on him whatsoever.

The suit eagerly accepts my offer for a lap dance.

He holds out his hand to help me off the stage, and I keep hold of it so I can lead him to the couch. Surprise flits over his features when I pull him to me and then push him down to sit in front of me. He scoots back and gets comfortable, then smiles cockily up at me.

The intentional seduction of two men at once begins. As I dance, my hands trail over my skin—they're an extension of the wave and current moving through my body as the music washes over me.

I infuse the grace of ballet and belly dancing, weaving them into my erotic movements. I give my brain permission to let go of the count and steps, and just feel, letting my hands roam where they may: brushing over the edge of my panties, fingers toying with the fabric, cupping my breasts, and playing with my hair. The client visibly hardens. His need to touch grows, his eyes darkening, his tongue darting out to sweep over his bottom lip as if he's craving a taste of what's being presented.

While straddling his lap, I pin his arms to the side and hold them there long enough that he understands to keep them there. Then I'm free to simply enjoy the moment and play. The song's beats guide me, and my body becomes another instrument, working in tandem with the rhythm. I work myself over the client's lap—graze his erection at first, then make more contact for longer strokes to build his cravings for more.

Leaning closer, I let my breath skate over the skin of his neck until he rewards my efforts with a full-body shiver. His words, when they come, are dirty and desperate. He begs to touch me. To let him take me home. Offers the world on a silver platter.

The effect I have over him sends elation through me, especially when the figure in the shadows moves and steps into the dim light.

The moment I meet the blue eyes from across the room, my movements slow. My gaze flirts on and off with his, saying, *"This could be you. You touching me. You inside me."* My body screams these words, though my lips stay silent.

Finn's expression is fierce—a tempest gathering strength. There's desire, but also a massive amount of tension in his body, a warning in his eyes, and his unbreakable control appears to be crumbling, which sends an intoxicating rush of adrenaline through me.

Everything else fades away. I get lost in the turbulent emotions rolling off him, his dark stare, and in the client's desperation. I absorb all of it and let them fuel the fantasies that run wild and take up primary residence in my mind.

FINN

I try my damndest to keep myself in check. I really do. But then she touches him, nearly puts her mouth on him, and all bets are off. My mind rebels. A rush of signals, like synapses firing, has my muscles coiling and moving on their own.

I don't give a fuck if he has money, if she needs it, or if this guy's a powerful man who could fuck with my business. Because none of that changes the fact that he's undeserving of even a fraction of her attention or time.

For that matter, neither am I, but these thoughts don't stop me from moving forward, or from my control over my emotions dwindling.

Something about her gets to me. Like this woman alone can tug and pull on the strings of my sanity and break me down to what I am at my very core. A man riding the edge of madness.

The need for her resonates so loudly inside of me that watching her with another man has my heart pounding like a fucking drum.

This undeniable connection tethering us demands to be known and felt, and trying to push it away has it doubling back twice as strong. When it began, I have no fucking idea. Maybe that sounds corny as hell. But it was there the first day she arrived, standing over me, shining like a fucking beacon of hope and light during a dark day.

I let her slip through my fingers, and this is the result.

This act. A dance. Something I pay her for. Fuck. Yes, fuck! I'm the dumb fuck who pays her for this. To perform for another and offer up her body, planting the seed in the client's head that he could have her.

The fucked-up-ness of it hits me like a giant goddamn demolition ball to the gut and keeps coming until it's impossible to stand here another moment and act indifferent to it all.

It should be simple. Un-fucking-complicated.

She's what I want.

To see more of. To get to know. All the big and little things. All of it. There's a vacant spot at the center of my goddamn world and inner circle, and instead of letting a ghost occupy it for the rest of my days, this woman—who's turned my life upside down—could fill it.

It's what I want, but I've been too cautious and haven't given voice to it.

As if she hears the emotions raging inside of me from where I stand, her soul-searing eyes lift, searching me out. I take another step forward and meet her gaze with my own. For a heartbeat, the connection we share flares to life. Her movements slow. Time seems to allow us space, as if paying this moment the respect it deserves, allowing us both time to recognize and feel it.

The truth of whatever the fuck this is vibrates in my chest. It digs in so deeply that it fucks with me a bit. It makes me think all kinds of irrational thoughts about a future we don't have because it's one I most likely won't live long enough to see.

But the way she's staring at me... I see that same truth mirrored.

And I know—God, I know—she feels it too. The way she looks at me tells me what her mouth denies.

Her gaze shifts back to the man in front of her. She smiles flirtatiously at him.

Our moment shatters. I swear to God, I hear glass breaking in my head at the same moment that a strike of pain spears through my temple. It blinds me momentarily.

The next few minutes are a tilt-a-whirl of hell to witness. She twists the knife deeper as she moves over him. Touches him. Tempts him with a near kiss. Whispers little secrets in his ear.

Secrets that I wish were mine and mine alone.

The vibrations, the fucking rattle that starts in my bones, the fever on my skin, is otherworldly.

Un-fucking-explainable.

The song ends, and a new one slowly begins. This one, pure sex.

Her hips rise and fall. Her nails sink into his shirt as she holds on to his shoulders and grinds down. Her head kicks back, causing her hair to sway down her back. Then her hand goes down to the tie on her corset, and she slowly starts to loosen the string holding it together.

Before it falls open, she clutches it with one hand, prolonging the reveal. But I can't. I can't… I can't watch one more damn moment of this. I already want to put my fist through this asshole's face. If he sees even another inch of her skin—or touches her in any way—I'm not sure he'll live to see tomorrow.

Before I can react, she peels the fucking corset away and drops it to the floor at her feet.

The snap is fucking audible in my head.

Iridescent pasties cover her nipples. Her breasts, heavy and free now, are a feast for the eyes. A sight this motherfucker has no right to.

The bark of words is loud enough to be heard over the music. "That's enough! Show's over."

They both startle at the sharp bite in my words. It's rude and unprofessional, but I couldn't give a fuck.

"You." I point at him. "Get the fuck out."

Lily does something I don't expect. She rises and smiles knowingly. She turns her head slightly, maybe trying to hide it from me, but I see it plain as fucking day and read her like a book.

Ohhhh-hooo… this fucking woman. That hint of a wicked smile right there at the corner of her lips.

Holy fuck.

She did this on purpose.

That knowledge heightens my instincts to the point that when the suit walks toward me, I step into his path and block his exit. Because I'm not the club owner anymore. What's riding me, the fucking beast stretching under my skin, is breathing smoke and pushing aggression and anger to the surface. In my head, I'm smashing this asshole's face against the goddamn wall, breaking his nose in the process, and pinning his arm behind him until his blessed bones break.

The suit must finally catch on to the present danger because a flicker of fear flashes over his features. He mumbles a thank-you to Lily and then dashes quickly around me.

I meet his gaze the entire time, silently telling him: *Don't come back.*

Lily plops onto the couch and relaxes. She doesn't get dressed. No, she lazily twirls the ends of her hair while biting her bottom lip. She's the vision of a babydoll vixen, and she's staring right back at me, while scissoring her legs, rubbing them against each other as if to fight off the ache between her thighs. Only, she doesn't stop there. She lets her hand rest across her panty line and teases the top edge.

When I arch my eyebrow, she very deliberately plants her feet on the floor and spreads her thighs. A *come-hither* dare if I ever saw one. It's naughty, dirty, and a seductive move done with sultry grace, and yeah, it draws me right the fuck in.

Her other hand trails down her chest. Those deft fingers play with her belly button. She's fiddling with a tiny diamond piercing. It's so small, I missed it until now.

It's slightly disturbing—her power over me, how she can level me with a look, cut to the heart of me, reel me in, and peel back layers of control to expose what's raw, hungry, and wanting underneath. The man I become in moments like this, the one who acts on impulse alone, is fucking *untethered* and dangerous. And he takes over completely when she goes one step further and lets her fingers play with her clit over her panties.

Her head tilts back, and those gorgeous blue eyes damn me— because I come fucking undone.

This isn't lust. It goes *beyond.*

She hasn't simply dragged me out of the numbness, the dark space inside my mind that I've been buried in for too long, she's woken me the fuck up. Has driven me fucking crazy with hunger. Has made me an obsessive, possessive motherfucker who craves any small piece of her she's willing to give. She's making me *feel* again with a fever I didn't even know existed.

I'd all but given up on there being an *us*. But by the way she's looking at me now? I was dead fucking wrong. She's not out of reach. She's just been waiting for me to be man enough to act on my feelings. Why else would she have orchestrated this moment, fucking *engineered* it to get a rise out of me?

Well, here I am, little minx. *Here. I. Fucking. Am.*

My logic's gone. Control? Out the window. All that's left is a feral man on the brink of madness, completely unsound, but if that's what she wants, then that's what she gets.

My stride eventually puts me toe to toe with her. Those fingers of hers continue to work and leave behind a damp spot. My knees damn near buckle at the sight.

Fuck. I need her taste on my tongue.

The moan... the *fucking moan* she releases has my cock jerking in response.

It's a distress signal if I ever heard one.

To the man in me—the starving bastard who needs to help others to feel whole—it's a call to action.

I take a step forward, and she instantly raises a foot, pressing it against my stomach, stopping me in my tracks. She tilts her head to the side and gives me an impish smirk.

I glare down at her foot and chuckle. Does she really think that'll stop me?

I latch my hand around her calf, giving it a warning squeeze, which has her raising an eyebrow in challenge. *Ohh...* she wants to play some more, huh?

Fine. Let's play.

I match her expression, raising my brow right back, and slide my hand up her leg. Goosebumps spread over her flesh at my touch. The silky smoothness of her leg is divine under my palm, and then her other foot comes up. Her fucking heels dig into my stomach. The threat is unmistakable. A bluff, or will she truly impale me if I don't back down?

Guess we'll find the fuck out, won't we?

Testing it, I lean over her and plant my hand on the back of the couch. Her legs bend. The fierce glare she gives is not a deterrent. If anything, it lights me fuck up.

"I like you down there. Under me. Seems like it's where you belong."

"That right?" She tries to sit up. But I refuse to let her go and tighten my hold on her leg.

"Thinkin' so, yeah."

Her breath catches. And I realize it's in these small tells that she reveals all.

It hurts like a motherfucker when her heels stab deeper. However, this is the kind of pain I could get addicted to. And thankfully, my tolerance levels are better than most. Only when I prove my point— that she can't break free of me, and I can keep her locked up as long as I wish—do I let my grip go and allow her legs to slip back to the floor.

I place my other hand on the couch and cage her in. Our breaths dance together as I stare down at her. The fire she's throwing in her eyes alone has me hard as fuck.

"Don't let me stop you. Open those fucking thighs and finish getting yourself off."

The defiance in her gaze speaks volumes.

"I said open them, woman."

"And if I don't?"

With a growl layering my tone, I repeat myself. "One. Last. Fucking. Time. Open. Them. Or you won't like what comes next, Lil'."

She twists so that her body is straightened. She flutters her lashes and smirks at me, which is going to earn her a smack to her ass if she's not careful. But then, like a good girl, she finally widens those pretty thighs of hers. Her hand runs up and down the inside of her thigh before it comes to rest over her pussy.

"Are you just going to watch?"

"Is that what you want?"

She eyes me critically for a moment and shrugs. "And if I want more?"

"You can have whatever your little wicked heart desires, and I think you know it. So what do you want, Lil'?"

The side of her mouth pulls into a broader smile.

"Anything?"

"Anything."

She considers me for a long time and then says something I didn't expect to leave her lips. "Lose the shirt and trade places with me." As I consider her words, she stands, places her hand on my chest, and backs me up a step. She takes a moment to place a kiss on my jaw and bites it, which sends a bolt of raw desire through me. And that's before she fucking nibbles her way to my ear and whispers, "Before you touch me, I want to learn what you taste like and hear you moan my name."

Jesus Christ.

She's a lit end to a trail of gasoline, and goddamn… I can't wait to see how long and hot she burns. There's so much fight in her that I know it'll be a war between sexes, a power play, and one I can't wait to win.

Within seconds, I'm exactly where she wants me—dressed down, shirt tossed, and on the couch in her place. Reaching out, I take her fingers into mine and pull her down over me. So it's my lap, my cock, my thighs she's sitting on.

Going from seeing it to experiencing it firsthand, taking in her sultry floral scent, watching how the lights shimmer over her features, and finally getting close enough to see the striations of gold in her irises, it's everything. The sweat on her skin, the golden highlights in her hair, the small details that make her feel more human and less doll-like—it all has my body igniting with need. Need for her. To touch, taste, and fuck this beautiful creature.

Her fingernails feel like heaven as they trace the ink of my chest tattoo. She trails her nail over it, learning the artistry put into the design. Her eyes flick up to mine repeatedly to check on my reaction. Me? I'm spinning. Her touch both grounds me and has me spiraling. My heart is fucking racing. Her beauty up close… any and all imperfections—scars, smeared mascara, a pimple she's tried to cover up, and a divot in her nose, possibly from an old piercing—add to her complexity. They are all pieces that make up this stunning creature I've captured for a moment in time.

"How long have you had this one?"

It takes me a moment to recall. "Seven years or so."

"Hurt?"

"On the ribs, yeah. And the parts on my upper chest. Those sessions were a real bitch."

She smirks and chuckles. "I bet."

I rub my thumb over the one on her collarbone. "How long?"

She looks down at the dandelion seedlings. "About the same. Maybe eight years."

"How many in total?"

"Ah, jeez." She shakes her head. "I don't know. You've no doubt seen the wings on my back. So with those, I'd say maybe a dozen. You?"

"Triple that." And I hold out my arms for her inspection. She takes a few moments to study each arm, my tattooed hands, and even the one of an infinity symbol held together with a feather and the words "life" and "love", which sits low near my belt, just above my pelvic bone. Her mouth pinches as she runs her thumb over it, but moves on quickly. She takes the most interest in my Ranger tattoos—especially the ones dedicated to the men on my team I lost. I watch as she silently says their names, and something about it hits me straight in the heart.

She meets my gaze. "I'm sorry. I'm sure they meant a lot to you."

"Thank you."

"Sorry, this is probably a mood killer."

I shrug and say, "Meaningful, though, at least to me. I'll never regret a moment I spend respecting the lives they lived, their dedication, or their sacrifice."

Her smile holds a melancholy quality to it, and understanding.

"I'm glad you made it back."

I don't feel the words, but say them anyway. "Yeah, me too."

Her hands move up to my shoulders, my neck, and then they tunnel into my hair. Her nails play with it, learning it too. They scratch gently against my scalp. The fucking feeling of them… my God… so fucking good. The groan it pulls out of me is guttural.

My eyes are closed, but I hear her chuckle, low and sultry.

The massage she delivers to my scalp, the way she explores my hair and body as if playing it like a musical instrument, is yet another art she must have mastered. She drains me of all tension. She pours bliss and heat from her touch straight into me. I'm incapable of escaping this feeling and not getting hooked on it.

I open my eyes lazily to watch her. Her breaths are shallow, her plump lips parted, and fuck, they look so soft, pliable.

I want a taste. But I don't think I can stop once I do. All the fantasies that have been running through my mind over the last few months hit me at once.

I want those. To experience them with her. Every. Single. One.

My fingers fucking her. My mouth on her while I lick her sweet cunt. Her lips wrapped around my cock. My fist in her hair while she's choking me down to the hilt. Fucking her and flipping her over on the bed so I can rut into her from behind while holding her down. In every way we can imagine. Every hole. All the things. Just get lost in it until neither of us has an ounce of energy left to spend and then pass the fuck out next to one another.

What would it be like to hold her then? Would she let me?

More than anything, I want to show her that no one else in the world could ever touch, need her, or love her the way I ache to.

Her lips twitch, and for a second, I think she'll kiss me as she leans in. But no. It's a taunt. It's a tease. My heart pounds in my chest. My pulse roars in my ears. My exhalations come out short and choppy.

"You gonna keep on with the teasin', or will you take what you want?"

Her lips move to my ear, and a shiver rolls through me as her lips brush my lobe. "What I want is for you to not touch… not move… and for this to be all on me. You're the one in the position of power and authority here, but I'm fully aware of this. So later, if this ever comes to light, you have the ability to say I seduced you. You sat back and didn't do a thing. I was the one who took advantage of you."

"No one's going to believe I wasn't a willing participant."

She smiles naughtily and laughs a little at this. "Yes, I know. But we're going to pretend. Because when you choose this again, it's all on you. This time. This time is on me. My choice. My willingness to put my job on the line. My sin. And I'm choosing to own it. Whether you blame me tomorrow or not."

"Blame you? Why would I blame you?"

Her eyes fill with something—an emotion I can't name. Shame, maybe. Like there's a memory or thought she's slipped into.

Instead of answering, she gets up. I sit up and reach out to grab her, but she holds up a finger. "I'm just turning the music down."

"Why?"

"Because I want to hear you."

"Hear me?"

"I want to hear how you say my name when I make you lose your mind."

"Lily," I breathe, rough and hoarse. "Come the fuck here, woman."

She comes back, her large breasts swaying and bobbing as she strolls toward me. It's fucking memorizing.

I hold out my hand to pull her back onto my lap.

She places her finger on my lips and shushes me. Then she's spreading my legs wider, dropping to her knees in front of me, and running her hands over my thighs. She wastes no time. She goes for the buttons on my jeans and deftly pops each one free, revealing my briefs underneath.

Leaning over me, she squishes her breasts to my chest and grips my hair. She stares into my eyes, and slowly, giving me a chance to change my mind, she finally, finally fucking kisses me. Since it's probably the only part of me I can use to place a claim on her, I do just that. I kiss her back for everything I'm worth. She moans first. Then I let my voice loose and do the same. Our teeth clank. Our tongues dance. She bites my lip first. I kiss the fuck out of her again, more aggressively this time. I don't hold back. I grip the back of her head and ravage her mouth, then suck her bottom lip and hold it with my teeth for a moment before letting it slowly slip away.

We're fucking. Just with our mouths, and it's both sensual and brutal.

We hardly breathe. What ragged breaths we do manage are ragged gasps. It's like a hit of an intoxicating drug, ecstasy straight to the bloodstream, and one taste is all it takes for me to think I'll be craving this for the rest of my days.

When her mouth leaves mine, I chase it, reclaim it, and draw her right back into me. She comes with a bit of a fight to her, but slowly gives in and falls into the kiss again.

Finally, she plants her hand on my chest and forces me back. My chest is expanding and heaving from the lack of air. Hers does the same. Her mouth is red with beard burn. Her lips, swollen and fucking indecent. But oh so damn beautiful.

"Now." She points at me. "Stay there and let me have my fun. I want to learn what the rest of you tastes like." I'm tempted to say fuck it and just grab her, toss her on the couch beside me and crawl over her, but for now, I obey. I'll play by her rules and let her take what she needs.

She lays a trail of kisses across my neck and chest first. She's the opposite of timid. Her kisses are as complex as she is. A soft kiss, a hard suck, a bite to leave behind an impression, and God, do they ratchet me up.

She leaves teeth marks across my chest.

A harsher bite to my tattoo pec has me shouting, "Fucking hell, Lily. Jesus, woman!" To which she laughs and grins devilishly. Then she's working over my nipples, bait and switching on me again, leaving them blazing red and aching. She's marking me the fuck up, and holy shit, does it feel good.

I never knew my body could be lit up this way. It's as if she's waking up every inch of my skin—bringing me back to life.

As she moves down my body, her nails scratch my chest. The lines she leaves behind are pink and pebbled. I shudder and moan. My body goes boneless. My head falls to the back of the couch as I sink further, opening my thighs to give her the room to kneel between them. I keep my eyes on her because I don't want to miss a moment of it.

Her nose travels the length of my treasure trail as she inhales my scent. Then she licks along the line of my briefs.

I quickly help her out by lifting so she can pull my jeans and my black briefs down and off.

The moment her cool breath hits the head of my cock is transcendent. She gives it a similar treatment but goes easy with the teeth. She noses it, breathes in the scent of me, and then blows hot breath across my tip. Her lush lips brush over the head—back and forth, back and forth. Then her mouth loves on it as she kisses, mouths, and licks one side, then the other. She ventures down it to the base, paying it the same homage as the rest. She sucks on the skin around my girth, comes back to the tip, and hints at teeth play. The threat is there. The danger, but she never fully sinks them deep.

Essentially, she plays me like a fucking fiddle. I can't breathe with the want of what I know is coming. I can't look away. And I'm higher than I've ever been and not for a fucking pill.

Her hand wraps around the base. Her tongue sweeps through the precum there, and she gives me a good glimpse before she takes it into her mouth and swallows it.

I reach forward and thread my fingers through her hair while groaning. The sound reverberates in my chest. "Oh fuck, woman. Are you tryin' to kill me?"

She licks up the side, blows a wicked breath over the wetness, the fucking menace. Then she works herself down my length. She takes it all. Takes me to the fucking hilt and swallows around me. I jackknife up. "Good God, that's it. All of it. Just like that."

The feel of her throat constricting around my dick is heady as fuck. I wrap my other hand lightly around her throat so I can feel it there. Feel her pulse beat under my fingertips.

She moans around me, and damn, it feels like heaven. It's all I can do to stop myself from taking over, forcing her to fuck that mouth up and down over and over again.

"Jes-sus, you wicked-fucking-vixen."

She's not concerned whatsoever about keeping it clean and pretty. She makes a fucking mess of the blowjob in the best of ways.

And dear God, when she hums, my body lights on fire.

Fuck. "Yeah, oh, fuck." I nearly lose it.

She takes my cock with legendary skill, uses her fist in tandem. When I'm shaking, at the very end of my rope, barely staving off the need to cum down her throat, she pops off. Her tongue swirls over my tip. She plays with my slit and teases me as she rubs the head back and forth over her pouty lips.

Then this she-devil restarts the torture session all over again. She doubles down, edging me to within an inch of my life.

"Christ, woman! I'm there. Stop playing with me."

"Ask."

"Ask what?"

"Ask me for it?"

"Lily."

She crawls up and over me, places a few kisses on my chest, before her face comes to be level with mine. Her face, her abused lips, all of it has me nearly crashing my lips to hers, because I want to taste myself on her.

"Do you want me to swallow everything you give me?"

Palming her jaw, I give it to her straight. "You're damn right I do."

She combs her fingers through my hair, pushes it behind my ear. "Then ask me."

"You said, the next time, it was up to me to choose this?"

By the look on her face, I can tell my question throws her off— disrupts her wicked little game. Her eyes narrow a bit, and her mouth twitches. Yeah, I'm reading her right. And knowing her like I'm learning to, and trusting my gut, I do what feels right. What my body screams for.

I take back the control she's stolen.

I lean forward, take her face between my hands, and kiss the fuck out of her. I don't stop there. When our lips part, I lace my tone with the need running through me. "You're gonna take me back into that sinful, wicked *fucking* mouth, aren't you, baby? And let me not only fuck it" —I squeeze her throat with my free hand so hard that I hope my fingerprints leave an impression on her skin— "but own it as I come down this throat. Because this—" I lift my chin and stare directly

230

into her eyes so she knows I'm no longer fucking around— "this is my fucking choice."

The smile—it's that goddamn smile, wide and stunning—does me in. Lost. I'm fucking lost for that smile.

I don't bluff. Using my grip on her hair, I bring her lips back to my cock, and she opens for me. I start slow, thrusting into her wet mouth again and again, taking my pleasure she so willingly offers. Placing my other hand on the couch, I use the leverage to rise and fuck into her mouth with forceful, punishing thrusts. Her eyes are on mine, and it's the green light to take everything I need. So I do.

Her nails sink into my thigh, and the pain doubles the pleasure.

I come in rapid, short bursts into her mouth. Grunting as I bow forward from the force of it. Her throat tightens around the head of my cock as I spill down her throat. She swallows as much as she can.

What spills out… she daintily licks up after. Swipes her finger over the last bit that escaped and licks her finger clean like it's a goddamn lollipop, making a show of it like she does everything else.

It's the closest thing to heaven a man like me could hope for.

For a few glorious moments, everything is right in my world. Her mouth still tastes like me when she lets me pull her in for one more kiss — slow, deep, hungry enough to make me want to drag her right back down to the couch. I feel her smile against my lips, feel the faint tremor in her hands as she runs them over my chest.

Then we gather and right our clothing. Neither of us says a word. There's no need—not with the way her eyes keep flicking back up to my mouth like she's starving for another taste but won't let herself ask.

Where it all goes wrong from there, I have no fucking idea. But the night doesn't end with her in my arms the way I pictured it. Instead, I'm left in the dark, replaying that kiss, that laugh, every promise I thought I heard in her voice—and wondering what the fuck I missed.

CHAPTER 22

Looking back, can't you see how the way you dance with your demons was both beautiful and tragic?

Beside me, Roxy adjusts her teal G-string with a snap. She's laughing at something Charlotte said as she pulls a matching bra from her locker and adds the layered pieces of her stewardess costume until everything is in its rightful place.

Her new lingerie is on the higher end, and the makeup littering her vanity has been replaced with some from top-name brands. Even her ash-blonde hair has fresh highlights, and her dull matte lipstick now holds a fresh coat of lip gloss that shimmers with tiny sparkles. Every bit of it gives me the impression that no cost has been spared in her attempt to maintain the top spot in this unspoken battle for hierarchy at the club, which is fine. I love a challenge.

Zora runs a brush through her long, golden hair and throws it over her shoulder, "Ya'll will never guess who I ran into the other night?"

"Who?" Eva takes a second to respond as she lines her lips with red lipliner.

Zora spins around to address the group. "Mateo. I was just at the grocery store pickin' up a couple of things for dinner, and little man, who's not so little anymore, was there buyin' big boy wrappers?"

"What? Candy?" Honey, the newest girl, asks with utter sincerity, and the entire group bursts into laughter.

Zora frowns at her. "Jesus, Honey, no. Condoms. The boy's all grown up now, and he was loading up on condoms."

Eva saucily adds, "Goose's boy is sure growin' up mighty fine. I can't wait 'til he's not jailbait anymore."

My ears perk up, and I look around. All I see is naked flesh—tits out, someone lotioning their legs bare ass in the air, bits on full display, because, in the dressing room, there is zero time and room for modesty. It's something new dancers, like Honey, the one to my left, cling to for a few months, but all modesty goes out the window eventually.

I toss my hair and bend further over as I continue pulling up my white fishnets, mainly to hide my expression. It may not look like it, but my ears have zeroed in on the gossip.

Purrs and "Mm-hmm's" follow. Then Eva fans herself. "I'd love to teach that boy a thing or two. If Goose isn't up to havin' the talk about the birds and bees with him, I sure am."

"Well, if he was buyin' condoms then he sure as shit already knows about the birds and bees, right?" This comes from Zora.

Eva smiles wickedly. "Yeah, but I'm talkin' about a lesson with show and tell, no words necessary." As a unit, the girls laugh and high-five each other.

Honey laughs along with them, but it's an uncomfortable laugh.

Remembering the kid who brought Finn's pills, I ask, "Who's Mateo?"

Roxy raises an eyebrow and turns away from me without answering.

It's Eva who does. "The dark-haired boy who stopped in a while back. You saw him, didn't ya? Good looking, kind of emo. That's Goose's son."

My heart stutters and tumbles over itself in shock. I snap my gaze to Eva. "He has a son?"

"Yeah, about what?" Eva glances around at the others.

"Seventeen," Charlotte chimes in, dousing herself in perfume. She's an older redhead with breasts so large they enter a room a full second before she does. "High-schooler. Goose used to let him hang around here a while back, but that stopped when one of the girls started flirting with him. Kid's never been back since, except the other night."

"Jeez, Charlotte! That's too much!" Eva waves her hand. "We don't all wanna smell like a burnt rose."

Roxy says, "Kid probably got his first chubby right here in this room."

Charlotte shakes her head. "Don't let the boss man hear you talkin' about his boy that way. He's protective as hell of that kid."

My mouth moves on its own. "He really has a son?" Nearly every woman stops and stares at me for a moment. I realize how that must sound. "Is he… or was he married, or is his son from a previous relationship or marriage or something?"

Raven appears in the doorway. By the scowl on her face, it's clear she caught some of the conversation. As the other girls sense her presence, an uncomfortable hush fills the room.

"We open in ten. Be ready and where you're supposed to be. And if you want to keep your jobs, I suggest you stay away from Mateo. Is that clear?" She points at a few of the dancers, her glare forcing nearly every woman to avoid eye contact. Then her gaze lands on me. Her frown deepens before she turns and disappears.

I move to my vanity to brush out my hair. I rip through any tangles with aggressive strokes.

Silence follows, except for a few hushed exchanges.

Eva stops behind my vanity before she goes out the door and lowers her tone so as not to be overheard. "Not married, but I think he was at one point. And he must still love her, 'cause he's never shown much interest in anyone here. He keeps his personal life pretty private, though, so it's hard to say. He never touches the dancers, and anyone who comes on strong with him doesn't stick around long. Just a word to the wise."

I meet her sympathetic look with a forced grin. "Thanks."

The fakeass smile stays plastered to my face as my mind reels. Internally, I try to shut off my emotions, but the switch isn't working because too many questions are tumbling through my brain.

Mateo is in high school, so around the same age I was when I met

Finn, which means he would have been a small boy back then.

If he's Finn's son, then why wouldn't he have told me about him? And married… that can't be right.

My world sort of tilts on its axis.

Pull yourself together, you have an act to perform.

But my head is a mess, and it bleeds through my performance. When I catch sight of Finn watching from where he's leaning against the wall, it only makes matters worse. He's in all black, wearing his cut, with half of his hair pulled back in a ponytail. The neon lights highlight every impressive, masculine feature.

The steps, the choreo, vacate my mind completely. I end up improvising the end of the routine. The clientele doesn't seem to notice my fucked up, but he appears to. If his furrowed brow and tilted head are any indication.

After exiting the stage, I find Raven and wait until I have a moment alone with her. Getting ready for my next routine will take some time, and she's busy assisting with props and a last-minute costume fix, but I pull her aside when I can, because there's no way I'm getting back up there until I know more. So yeah, I don't mince words—neither of us has time for that.

"Does Finn have a son?"

She stops cold, and a strained look blankets her face. My arms cross over my stomach as I wait for her response. She eyes me critically. "Why? Do you have a thing against guys with kids?"

"What? No."

She matches my pose and raises an eyebrow. "So, if I said yes, it wouldn't bother you?"

That answer is a straight punch to the chest. I suck in a breath as I try to speak. "I—"

She cuts me off before I can wrap my head around it and respond. "Never mind, I can tell by your face that it does."

It does. Fuck me, it does—but not for the reason she's thinking. She can't read my mind to know that what she's told me might rewrite our history. It has the potential to turn our tragic story into something else entirely—a story not worth telling, where Finn and I were nothing more than two people playing house, while he had a son and possibly another woman out there somewhere waiting for him.

That's insane, right? My mind instantly rejects the notion because I can't see it. Finn surely would have mentioned having a son.

Rationally, I know he could have had Mateo with a high school sweetheart, or maybe he's a stepson, or—fuck! A million different scenarios flitter through my brain. Perhaps he accidentally got a girl pregnant. There has to be a reason for it. It's him not saying a word about it that's bothering the hell out of me.

But what if the past I believe is what was a fevered dream?

I relive some of our moments together and view them in a darker light. The crisp pages of our story have cracked and yellowed with age, and now threaten to tear completely with this possible new version of it. But maybe I'm way off base, because none of this makes any sense. I'm too shaken to think clearly. Before I can gather my thoughts, Raven's pulled away by other dancers clamoring for her help.

As she backs away, she calls out. "I promise, we'll talk later, okay?"

I promise.

Those words gut me.

I nod numbly and turn for the dressing room.

I barely make it to the bathroom in time, before dropping to my knees to vomit into the toilet. The bile scorches my throat, rising again and again until there's nothing left. I tell myself that it doesn't matter. That this is a job, and precisely why I should have to stay away from him, like I'd planned to.

I let down my guard during the VIP performance because selfishly, I wanted one more memory with him. I'd told myself it would give me the perfect chance to get a closer look at his tattoos, to understand him better—but look how that turned out.

I cracked the door open a silver, and he barrelled right through.

It was a mistake—one that won't happen again. Letting him weave his way into my heart when he has the power to destroy what's left of it will only end one way—badly.

And not just for me. For both of us.

Not feeling up to my original routine, I change it up. I give Alexi my new music and slip into a costume I've been saving for a special night. It's a black-and-white ensemble: black slacks, a sleek silk matching shirt, a white tie, and suspenders. The outfit feels like armor—polished on the outside, but heavy with the weight of everything I'm about to shed. I darken my makeup, each brushstroke feeling like another layer of control. Large black smoky rings line my eyes, overly large lashes make them more prominent, and I add bright red lipstick to my overdrawn lips. My hands tremble as I pin my hair into a tight bun. I secure the top hat, letting the extended long brim cast shadows over my eyes, hiding the turmoil beneath.

Before stepping out, I grab two things—a sleek black cane with a silver handle and my split mask—half angelic, pure white and flawlessly beautiful on one side, ugly, ruined, dark, and demonic on the other. There's a jagged line separating the two sides, and the color is the exact shade of my heels and lipstick.

Grabbing one out of the vase of flowers I received from a client, I pin a white rose to my lapel, a symbol of purity and beauty.

Alex, our emcee, greets me before I take the stage. "Wow, okay. We're doing this. Just like we practiced?"

"Yeah."

"All right. Benny said no problem on the lights, we've got you covered."

"Thanks, Alex. You're a gem."

He rubs his hands together, and a wide smile spreads across his face. "I can't wait to see this for real. Break a leg, yeah?"

"Will do. And crank it, will ya?"

He smirks. "Anything you want, babe. We got you."

The club is pitch black a moment before the music starts. The neon has been turned off. The sea of patrons is nothing more than a murmur of voices filling the pitch black club. But the energy they exude is palpable, and their cheers when I'm announced are a bit overwhelming.

I zone them out and center myself.

The first note plays as a red spotlight flares above me, isolating me on the stage. I sit, back rigid, shoulders squared, in a black, high-back, antique chair.

My throne for the night.

I hold the cane between my knees, the silver-tipped end planted into the floor between my stilettos. My head bowed, so my face remains hidden.

My *mashed-up* version of "Policy of Truth" by Depeche Mode and "Angels" by Within Temptation begins with a haunting, hypnotic tone that echoes for ten counts. I use those ten counts to my advantage, swiveling my neck creepily, tilting my head up slightly so the crowd can see one side of the mask.

As I do this, the red spotlight spreads outward across the stage.

A low, lulling synth builds, creating an air of tension. I wait until the eerie, melodic layer hits to swivel my neck and reveal the other side of the mask to the audience. My shoulders begin to dip and rise in opposition to each other, a stilted and minute figure eight; the motion becomes slightly bigger each time.

Then comes a pulsing, electronic beat. It's heady, a steady countdown. My frame rises from the chair, coming to life like a marionette doll. My heart pounds in time with the thumping beat as I begin to dance, my movements becoming increasingly dramatic.

As I circle the throne, I caress it, worshiping the hard surface of the antique wood. My past love's throne. The pedestal I've put him on.

Leaving the throne, I start my floor routine and work my way down the stage.

My heels, the metal on the bottom, clack against the stage with each step I take. The bottom of the cane hitting the floor at the down beat does the same.

I spin and bend, and work my hips as I go, sweeping and spinning the cane and even catching it after giving it a small throw in the air while completing a split. I move in powerful bursts, followed by slow sweeping arcs, my hands brushing against my suit as if I can feel the truth clawing beneath the fabric, needing to break free. The beat hits hard, relentless, and I know it's coming—the unraveling.

The spotlight begins to pulse on and off, making each pose I take under the lights look like a still-life. Each one is deliberate, different, and synchronized with the beat. The red light flickers in perfect time, and another blinks on to mimic it. The placement of the second spotlight helps me cast long, distorted shadows on the black backdrop behind me.

When the chorus begins, I tug at the collar of my shirt, ripping it open and cutting away the pristine, polished facade. The black fabric feels suffocating, each piece a reminder of the lies I've built to polish up the ugly truth. The white lies and pretty excuses I've told myself to create the version of the story that was never real. The black layers underneath represent the dark deeds I've talked myself into committing in the name of "saving myself."

As I work the floor, I rip the layers away. With a sharp tug, I loosen the white tie around my neck, slipping it free and letting it fall to the ground. After plucking the fake white rose off my lapel, I twirl it between my fingers for a moment before dropping it. I crush it beneath my heel with relish.

For emphasis, I spear the end of the cane on the rose and send both across the stage.

Before taking hold of the pole, I yank the suspenders down and peel off my shirt, baring skin that glistens under the harsh spotlight. The satin black slacks follow, slipping down my hips and puddling at my feet, cast off on the stage like the false promises I once believed in.

My movements grow sharper, more violent. I twist and turn and pose. Each shred of fabric reflects another deception I've wrapped myself in to survive. What's left is barely there strips of black fabric—one band across my chest, just wide enough to hide my nipples, and a slender thong.

The routine is not for the faint of heart. It's a dangerous one, with death-defying holds and risky positions with rapid releases and jarring catches. The Iron X demands every ounce of my strength — I grip the pole with my hands, lock my core, and hold my body straight out sideways, hovering midair like a human cross defying gravity. The Spatchcock tests my flexibility, splitting me open in an impossible arch, my hips screaming against the stretch.

Before I come back down to earth, I steady my breath and lock into an Extended Butterfly — arms reaching back, legs split wide, my body trembling as I hold the position and give the impression of a winged bird suspended in flight. My last trick is a Phoenix: no hands, just momentum and muscle, until I let it all go and dismount.

Cool air hits my skin, but I don't feel relief. Only anger. I'm raging at Finn, at myself, at everything I didn't see and everything I built up in my head that has caused me pain and heartache for so long.

A battle I've waged inside my own mind for too many years, when the ugly truth was right there for me to discover. I hid from it, and wallowed in this misery, for what? To discover it was all a lie this whole time?

I pour everything inside me into the dance. Near the end, I walk off the stage, through the customers, and to the bar. The pulsing red light follows and spreads outward to envelope the crowd in stages, a victim count growing, a bleeding wound. My body feels like lead, weighed down by what I've learned and what I suspect.

My thoughts are riotous and chaotic, as I pull myself on top of the bar. For a few counts, I let the rhythm guide my movements as I stand and dance on top of it. Then I drop to my knees and slowly rock as the song winds down. I unpin the fedora and my bun. I toss the hat and let my long hair spill out around me. It's a relief and freeing.

The audience is going nuts, but I barely hear them.

Finn calls my name. No, Goose, because I don't know this man, and he definitely isn't who I thought he was. I tell myself this is the very last time I'll refer to him as the man I once thought I knew.

What a gullible fucking girl I was.

I wonder if that's what he told his buddies when he told them about me. Or did he even care enough to mention me at all? Is that why no one ever got word to me about his condition? Had he even mentioned me to them, or was I just some sad girl he saved? A dirty secret he kept buried?

Makes sense since no one had known who the fuck I was when I went around asking about him. I remember how pathetic I felt. How pathetic I looked. They treated me like some poor little girl who just got played, and was too stupid to realize it.

The recruiter's expression that day got burned into my memory, and still, when I think about it, it has my chest pinching with pain.

Without hesitation, I tear the mask from my face and drop it at his feet. It's always been hard to see clearly through the masks, through the lies, but here's his chance.

Then I reach behind the bar and snatch a three-quarters full bottle of whiskey. Bending backwards, I recline my body on the bar and tilt my head back, enough to meet his enraged stare. The chorus hits one last time, and each ending word feels profound.

You lying fucking bastard and your policy of truth.

Goose's dark eyes are nearly black. He growls and motions for me to "Get off the goddamn bar" and come to him. His hand is up, reaching for me. I wiggle the bottle as I raise it above me.

I feel broken, vulnerable, but at least it's real. I'm not hiding anymore. My true self has come out to play and show him who he's dealing with.

As I begin tipping the liquor bottle, he shouts my name.

But I pay it no mind as I upend the bottle and bathe in liquid as it spills down my frame.

The music comes to an abrupt end. For a long moment, I stay there, head tilted toward the ceiling, sucking in oxygen, filling my lungs. They expand and constrict, and it feels like for the first fucking time in my life, I can truly breathe without a weight hindering me.

When I eventually sit up, I spin and extend the bottle to Goose. Before his hand can close around it, I drop it. He doesn't catch it in time, and it shatters at his feet.

While he gapes at the mess, I take a client's offered hand and dismount gracefully from the bar.

I completely ignore the man shouting after me as I walk the fuck away, and I make a point to smear my eyeliner and lipstick down my face as I stride back toward the stage. Because I don't fucking care anymore. And I don't need to hide my truths from myself anymore.

I grab my cane on my way back, and in one final gesture, I collapse into the throne with legs crossed. The crowd is going insane, so I place my hand over my lips in a shushing gesture.

When they grant me the silence this moment deserves, I drop the cane on the floor and let it clatter with finality. And I swear to God, you can hear it echoing off the walls until the audience erupts.

For a long moment, I just breathe, in for three, hold for three, out for three. In. Hold. Out. And I let it all go. Let go of him and this idea of him that I planted in my head and have held on to. I let go of the childhood fantasy story I had of us that I've been subconsciously clinging to for way too long, and tell myself that version of us never truly existed.

From here forward, I'll view Goose with open eyes and from every angle before letting him ever take another small piece of my heart. He's a flawed man who's not my savior, and never was.

I walk off the stage, my back straight, head held high, my heart pounding, but finally free.

CHAPTER 23

Emotions can be tricky and deceiving when heightened or buried for too long.

The minute I sit down at my vanity and catch my reflection in the mirror, regret slams into me. Everything I just did plays on a loop, each moment a reminder of how I let my emotions take complete control and let myself unravel.

"Oh, God." I press my palms into my face. It does nothing to stop the panic from rising in my chest. I royally fucked this up. Let the old pain run wild, unchecked.

Goose's glare flashes through my mind, that furious look as I kneeled defiantly in front of him on the bar. I groan into my hands, pressing harder, trying to block out the memory, but it lingers stubbornly. My breathing is shallow and erratic. It takes a minute before I can calm it enough to pull myself together.

Grabbing some makeup remover, I get to work on my face. When I finish, I drop my hands and stare at my reflection, eyes searching the glass for something—anything—that makes sense. "What the hell are you doing? Are you trying to get yourself fired?"

The words sound foreign, hollow.

A soft voice pulls me back. "You okay?"

I jump at the sound, gasping as my heart kicks against my ribcage. Raven stands in the doorway, her presence as quiet as a shadow.

"Yeah." My voice cracks. "I don't know what came over me." I try for a casual shrug, but it falls flat. "I'll apologize to Goose. That went a bit far."

Raven steps inside, her heels a barely there click on the dressing room floor. She moves with a confidence that's both intimidating and calming, like she's never once had to fake being sure of herself. She pulls a chair over, spins it around, and sits facing me, her dark bangs hiding part of her face, but her eyes—sharp and knowing—miss nothing.

I swallow hard, avoiding her gaze. She crosses her legs, her skirt riding up slightly, revealing a tattoo of a starry night that stretches along her thigh. Her heel bounces lazily, like she's got all the time in the world to wait for me to spill my guts.

"Be real with me." Her voice is gentle but firm.

I let out a shaky breath, my eyes dropping to my hands, fingers clenching and unclenching in my lap. There's something about her that makes me want to be real. Maybe it's the way she sees through all the bullshit. She doesn't need to ask twice. She already knows I'm wearing a mask nearly every day I'm here, and that scares me more than anything.

"I don't know why I did it," I admit, the words brittle, breaking apart as they leave my mouth. "I fucked up." I shrug, a half-hearted motion. "You don't have to say it. I know I did."

Her gaze doesn't falter. "That—" She gestures with a thumb over her shoulder, pointing back toward the stage. "—that was raw, exceptional, and a glimpse of the real you."

A half-sob, half-laugh escapes me, and I shake my head. "The real me?"

She doesn't hesitate, her hand reaching out, fingertips grazing the ends of my hair before letting the strands fall back into place. "Everyone else might see this"—she motions to me in my pink fluffy robe, but meaning my carefully curated exterior—"but I don't think this is the version of you that matters."

Her hand falls over mine, a squeeze, gentle but reassuring. "But tonight, you're here, right on the surface. Whatever brought that kind

246

of emotion out… it's destructive." She smiles softly, eyes glinting with something close to approval. "But good. Because this is the person I want to get to know. This is who I think I could call a friend."

I swipe a tear from my cheek before it can fall, my throat tightening. "God, Raven. I danced on the fucking bar." It comes out as a half-laugh, half-sob.

She chuckles, a dark, quiet sound, the absurdity of the situation hitting us both at once.

She gets up, grabs a few tissues, and passes them to me. I wipe up my face.

When I'm done, I cover my face with my hands for a long minute, as I pull myself back together. "Earlier, in the dressing room… the girls were talking." She nods, as if she already knows, or maybe she suspects this to be the reason. "They said some things mainly about Mateo, and it made me think Finn—that Goose—isn't as unattached as I thought. It made me feel like…"

I trail off, my words failing me, but Raven's hand returns to cover mine.

"Like what you two shared in those small moments meant nothing," she finishes for me. "That it was all a lie. That it made everything wrong instead of something good."

I nod, swallowing hard against the lump in my throat.

"Mateo, well, that's Finn's story to tell, but him being in the picture shouldn't change how you feel about him."

"It wasn't just about him. It was the thought of his mother and the fact that he never told me about him."

"Oh."

"Yeah."

"I've seen how he looks at you, Lily. How you look at him. Do you think he'd do that if he had any interest in someone else?" Her words are soft but hit hard.

My throat feels tight. I clear it, my voice hoarse with emotion when I finally speak. "I… no. It's just…one of those things, you know? Something so strong you can't contain it, even if you try. Like the anger and jealousy just grabbed me by the throat and wouldn't let go.

I couldn't think clearly. Uhhhh... don't ask me to explain it, because I don't think I can."

"I'm not asking you to," she says. "And maybe it shouldn't be contained or explained."

I blink at her, confused. "No?"

"No." She leans back, eyes steady on mine. "I just want to know what you'll do about it. I can't tell you with absolute certainty that Goose is unattached, but I can tell you this... he doesn't react to anyone like he does with you. He's not attached to anyone or anything enough to be this pissed, this... affected. From the moment you showed up, he's been off-kilter. And he could use someone in his life who cares enough to shake him up. Make him take notice."

A sad smile tugs at my lips, unbidden. There's a weight in my chest, something heavy and melancholy, but at the same time, I feel lighter. Because someone finally noticed my pain. Someone saw it, and they're not judging me.

"You have my full permission, Lily," Raven says, her smile turning wry. "Shake that man's world. Wake him up. Make him earn you and prove he's worthy."

I let out a small, bitter laugh. "What about the club's fraternizing policy?"

She leans back, crossing her arms as she does. "Stupidest goddamn rule. Smash it to bits, Lil'. Smash it to fucking bits."

"And the mother?"

"You're not going to know until you ask."

I raise a brow at this.

She grins. "So ask him."

I should have expected it. I didn't, though, and that's on me. So when I exit the club through the back entrance and hear "What the fuck was that?" shouted at me, I nearly jump out of my skin.

Goose pushes off from the outer wall and rounds on me with so much fury that I take a cautious step back. His lips are pressed in a tight line, and his salt-and-pepper hair now hangs loose around his face, making him look darker, more dangerous. In a heartbeat, he's towering over me in a way that sends my pulse skittering.

I stumble over my response. "I'm sorry."

He rakes his hair back and holds it. His chest rises and falls in heavy breaths, his eyes staying locked on me. "You're sorry?"

I open my mouth, but he cuts me off.

Dropping his arm, he says, "Sorry, doesn't fucking cut it. I'd fire someone on the spot for that shit and not give a damn. So give me a good fucking reason why I shouldn't. Why the fuck would you do something like that?"

I swallow, trying to keep my voice steady, giving him as much honesty as possible. "I got some shitty news before I went on tonight."

"That's no—"

"I know!" I shout, cutting him off as my words tumble out in a rush. "I know it's a stupid excuse. You don't think I know that? I've been telling myself exactly that since I stepped off stage. I let my emotions take over. I tried not to. But…"

His glare sharpens. "That shit doesn't fly with me."

I shake my head, frustration creeping into my voice as I try to explain. "I'm not giving you an excuse. I'm telling you the truth. I've never told anyone this, so give me a minute."

He crosses his arms tight around his chest, his stance unyielding, but his gaze softens just a fraction, giving me room to continue.

"Even in my head, this sounds dumb," I mutter.

"Just say it."

I drop my bag to the ground and lean against the building, taking a deep breath before I open my mouth again. "You're probably gonna think I'm crazy, and honestly, telling you this is probably the last thing I should be doing, because it might just make it worse."

He steps closer, his heat radiating toward me. His presence pulls my focus away from the nervousness bubbling up inside. His gaze—sharp and intense—makes it harder to get the words out, but I push through.

"Music, dancing… it's not just performance for me. When I dance, it's like I'm pulled somewhere deep inside my head, and what comes out is all heart, muscle memory, and raw emotion. I'm there, but it's not me at the same time. Everything just… takes over."

His blue eyes bore into me, but they're no longer just angry. Something else lingers in them now—something I can't name.

"On stage, it's different. I'm usually in control while performing. But when I'm feeling too much, when the emotions get twisted up with the music… I lose control. It all comes out. I try, but sometimes I can't stop it."

His jaw tightens. He closes the distance between us, until we share a small, intimate space. My heart is racing, but I force myself to keep talking.

"An emotional cocktail like I had tonight?" I continue, my voice quieter now. "It's like a bomb going off. My heart and body take over, and no matter how hard I try, I can't reel it in."

I dip my head and fidget with the rings on my fingers. "I know how this sounds. It sounds like I'm unreliable and can't keep it together. I get that."

He doesn't say anything and the silence is heavy as I wait him out. When he finally speaks, his voice is quieter than I expected. "What was it, then? What made you lose your cool tonight?"

I lift my head, meeting his gaze head-on. "Have you ever had someone you care about lie to you? Tell you something you believed with everything you had, only to find out it was all a lie?"

His eyes flick away, his expression darkening for a beat, like my question dragged up something he'd rather not remember. When his gaze returns to mine, there's something raw in it. "Yeah," he says, his voice rougher than before.

My heart twists. "It makes you feel like an idiot, right? Because deep down, you knew it was too good to be true. You knew something was off."

He nods, his eyes tracing the lines of my face.

"That's the kind of news I got tonight," I say quietly.

He softly sweeps a few stray strands of my hair away from my forehead and tucks them behind my ear. A simple act that makes my breath hitch. "I'm sorry."

The words are gruff, but they land with surprising weight, like they carry more than just an apology for what happened tonight. His hand drops to his side, but his body remains close.

"It fucked me up," I admit, the words slipping out before I can stop them.

"Next time, come to me. Tell me what's going on. I won't put you up there if you're not in the right headspace."

"I will," I whisper, my voice barely audible over the pounding of my heart.

"Say it," he presses. His tone is firm but not unkind. "Say exactly what you'll do if this happens again."

I roll my eyes but give in, the corner of my mouth twitching. "Next time, I'll tell you or Raven what's going on."

"If I let you stay."

My jaw drops, but then I see it—the ghost of a grin tugging at the corner of his lips.

I shake my head, smiling despite my chaotic emotions. "Yeah, if you let me stay." I flutter my lashes dramatically, my voice sugary sweet. "Please, Goose. Please let me stay. I'm sooo sorry I danced on the bar and dropped the bottle at your feet."

His eyes blaze with heat as they rake over me. "Are you?" he murmurs, his voice rougher now. "Because it sounds like you're not sorry at all." He comes closer and props his hands on the wall behind me, caging me in. He lowers his face to mine.

I raise an eyebrow. "I mean… the tips were pretty amazing." I take a shaky breath, and my words come out softer, breathier. Internally, I'm screaming at myself to stop being foolish. This right here is what turned me into an emotional mess to begin with.

"And…" The words disappear because his face touches mine, his lips brush over my cheek.

"And?" He whispers the word in my ear. My entire body shudders. Butterflies do loopty loops in my stomach, as chills race down my arms.

Hoarsely, I say, "And your pissed-off face... I don't think I'll ever forget it."

The distance between our bodies disappears. He presses his lower body against mine. My body melts against his without permission. I place a hand on his chest, trying to hold him off, but he doesn't budge. His hot breath fans over my lips. The scent of whiskey and mint has my gaze zeroing in on his mouth.

"Lil'?"

"Yeah."

"You're staring?

"What?"

"You're staring at my mouth, like it has all the answers you're looking for."

"I'm not."

"Now, that's a lie, and we both know it."

My heart stutters. I'm torn between pushing him away and pulling him closer. I know what I should do. "I can't think when you're this close." It's the truth too. His nearness scrambles my goddamn brain.

His smile is dangerous and indecent. "I think today you've been more honest with me than ever before. Keep going, and I just might figure you out."

His words are light, but the intensity between us is anything but.

"I doubt that," I whisper. "I'm more complicated than you think."

"Maybe. But I fucking love your kind of complicated, woman."

My fingers curl into the leather of his cut. I grip it with both hands and do what I shouldn't. I pull him closer, raise onto my tippytoes, and kiss him.

It's a soft kiss, an exploration. He deepens it, but there's tenderness there too. Our tongues stroke and play for a moment before he lightly places a chokehold on my neck, sending a thrill through me.

I snake one hand into his long hair as he lifts me, pressing me against the wall, and grinds his lower body into mine.

Heat floods into my core as I ride the ridge of his cock.

Suddenly, he lets go. My feet drop back to the ground as he yanks back and hisses. "Fuck." His hand comes up to place a fist over his eye.

"Are you all right?" I ask and touch his shoulder with concern.

"Son of a bitch!" He shakes his head. "No, just give me a moment." The words are harsh. I let my hand drop from his arm. His jaw muscles clench, and he takes a couple of deep breaths.

"What's wrong?"

He stumbles slightly and plants one hand on the wall to steady himself. "Why the hell is it so much worse when I'm around you?"

Panic grips my chest. "What?"

He straightens, turns, and leans his back against the stucco. His eyes open, and his face twists with a grimace. "It's like this shit has been escalating ever since you showed up. Coincidence or is there something you're not telling me?"

"What do you mean?" is what I go with. The lie, my default. It's what I know. What comes easily.

He stares hard. It's not kind or anything like the look he was giving me before. It's probing. There's disbelief written all over his features.

"You have no idea what I'm talking about?"

"No."

"No?"

I shake my head.

"Ever since you showed up, my migraines have gotten worse. There are things, memories that come back to me at certain times that seem to connect."

My insides are rioting, but I do my best to keep my expression blank."Like what?"

"Like now, when you said my name, and that night with the cat. And sometimes… sometimes when you dance, it triggers a reaction. It's like seeing or hearing certain things unlocks something in my head, and suddenly I can see a past that's been out of reach for me until now. That has to mean something."

He stares at me for a long time.

Containing the whirlwind of thoughts and emotions his statement stirs up takes great effort on my part, because I'm warring with myself. My fight-or-flight instinct is running rampant. "I'm sorry. I don't know why it's happening."

"The thing is, Lily, there's something behind those eyes of yours. Something you're not telling me. Something you don't want me to know. I can see it when you look at me."

This has me floundering for a response. My mouth opens, but nothing comes out.

"Tell me it's nothing."

I push down the shock and try to keep it from showing on my face. "It is. Or at least I'm not aware of whatever it is you think I'm keeping from you."

His gaze analyzes me. He looks away for a beat, smooths his hair back, and asks, "So it's just me being mental?"

"I didn't say that."

"But you're also skirting around the fact that there is something you're not telling me, right?"

"Goose."

"What?"

"There are just some things I'm not ready to talk about. Can you just let it go?" He's way too close to the truth, and I'm terrified that he will figure it out. I'm too deep into this for that discovery to end well.

"No. I really can't."

"Then maybe this was a bad idea to begin with."

He stares and then huffs an incredulous chuckle that holds no humor whatsoever. "Jesus, woman, you're a mind fuck, you know that?" He says it in jest, but it hits home.

"And you're not?" The words just sort of fly out of my mouth. That's the only excuse I have for them.

Based on his glare, I might as well have slapped him. He steps away, and I latch onto his arm. "Where are you going?"

"Gonna call it a night and talk about this another time." His words slice through me, cold and final.

I throw my hands up in frustration. "Of course you'd say that. Why not just leave me the fuck alone if you're just going to push me away right after you reel me in?" I reach down and grab my bag and throw it over my shoulder. "I mean, fuck, I don't need this." I'm pushing these emotions forward, spoiling for a fight, doing anything I can to get him to back off, because I sense how easily this whole thing could unravel and fall apart now. How much I must have given away, and maybe he's piecing it together.

I start walking.

"Woman, wait—"

"No," I snap, turn, and walk backwards. "Goodnight, bossman. I'll see you on Tuesday." Then I spin again and let the distance I put between us speak for me.

"Lil'!"

Like what, is it going to take a lobotomy for me to get this man out of my system? Have I not already learned my lesson here?

Goddamn it, Lily.

With that thought in mind, I don't stop. I keep walking, knowing that distance is the answer. I need to get somewhere I can get my head straight and regroup. Stop this nonsense that I should have never let get started to begin with.

CHAPTER 24

*Beware of the mask you wear to play the part.
The longer you wear it, the harder it is to leave
behind.*

After the confrontation with Finn, sleep is hard to come by. I lie awake most nights, staring at the ceiling, replaying my decisions since arriving back in New Mexico, trying to figure out what I've revealed that could hint at my true identity, and what missteps I've taken.

The fact that Goose has a son leaves me with lingering questions I still want to get to the bottom of. But over the next few days, I try to keep my mind occupied so that thoughts of Goose and his son don't eat away at me.

At the club, I'm all smiles and playfulness—and more cautious than ever around Goose. If he speaks directly to me, I respond with pleasant replies, giving as little away as possible. I can tell he senses my forced indifference, but he doesn't say anything. Instead, his eyes flicker with some unspoken question, and he analyzes my every reaction. I, in turn, attempt to stay out of his way and am careful about meeting his gaze for too long.

On my next day off, I buy a second car—an old, nondescript sedan that won't attract attention—and contact a realtor to secure the home I want to purchase, which is a few doors down from Goose's place.

It's a small house that's recently been updated, tucked under a canopy of aspen and maple trees, with a front lawn that's overgrown and in need of tending. It'll work perfectly as an excuse to keep a stealthy eye on the neighbors, especially when spring begins.

My disguise for this role—an elderly widow with a green thumb—includes a few muumuu dresses, which are my go-to in this persona. The dresses shield my figure, and I use both sunglasses and wide-brimmed hats to not only block out the sun but also shield my face.

Some days, I simply sit in a wicker chair on the porch while indulging in sunflower seeds or sipping hot tea while reading a magazine. When it begins to warm up, I spend a few hours each day digging in the soil of the flowerbeds, replacing old plants with new, more vibrant, colorful flowers. I've found that the sharp scents of freshly cut grass, the earthy aroma of damp soil, and fresh flowers help to calm my nerves.

While I work, I watch and wait for Goose to show himself in any capacity.

When the devices arrive, I steal over in the dead of night and plant GPS trackers on Goose's bike and the remodeled '70 Roadrunner in his driveway. But for the most part, Goose is predictable and rarely leaves his home for anything other than simple errands, Wet Tips, visiting the clubhouse, or running club business.

At least twice a week, I visit Dozer's gym. The guys there gradually warm up to me. It's slow going, but every so often, one or two will chat me up.

Mostly, I dive into music and dance, which includes co-choreographing a few group routines with Raven. She thinks performing group numbers might be a great way to bring the girls at Wet Tips together and put an end to the cliques. It was an idea I shared when we went out to lunch together, and she wants to run with it.

Outside of the club, I find a local dance studio willing to let me rent space to practice. The time slots are during the day because the kids they teach come in the evenings. And I love it. Getting entirely away from the nightclub to practice helps me work through my emotions healthily. I get to stretch my skills and work in other genres of dance that center me, rather than rile me up.

The owner approaches me shortly after I start there and asks if I'd consider coaching a couple of the more experienced dancers on their senior teams, or be willing to teach a masterclass. To say I'm flattered is an understatement. I don't need or want the money; just sharing my love of dance is enough. So I accept and end up donating the money back to the studio to assist some of the families struggling to pay their monthly fees.

Staying busy helps keep my anxiety about what's ahead to a minimum. It's a coping mechanism—and for quite a while, it works.

When I first opened Goose's file, I was taken aback by one of the addresses of the rentals he owned—the old duplex he'd been renting when we met. The one he left me to stay in alone. Thankfully, it wasn't the one he lived in now, but it did make me wonder how that came about.

His buildings are in some of the poorer parts of town, and by all accounts, they're some of the nicest places to rent for how much he charges. I know this because I "accidentally" ran into a few of his tenants at the grocery store and initiated conversations with them. I mentioned being new in town and looking for a place, but I was worried about reaching out via the ads in the paper or online because I didn't want to get taken advantage of. They all had nothing but good things to say about Goose as a landlord. Some sang his praises like he was some kind of freaking saint.

Through them and my spying, I learn that Goose and Mateo live on the top floor of their current place, and Goose rents out the apartments below.

I'm not proud of it, but my curiosity about Mateo increases as the days progress. My need to know this side of Goose pushes me past caring about the sins I will no doubt pay for later, and I begin to follow Mateo to school, to his job at Bodie's autobody shop, and to a park he visits often, where he sits alone by a tree and writes in a notepad.

The image of him there immediately brings back memories of a younger Goose doing the same thing. He'd write in his journals nightly.

Mateo reminds me of Goose in a lot of ways. He's a lone wolf kind of guy—stoic most of the time.

He spends his free time riding his old Honda Shadow, and every so often, he'll do some death-defying stunts—pop wheelies, peel out, and take it over a hundred on a straightaway. Once, he stood up on it while I was following him, and I swear to God my heart jackrabbitted so fast with fear for him that I thought that damn thing would fly right out of my chest.

He skips classes quite a bit, smokes cigarettes and weed, and every so often, he'll sneak out of the house and not make it back until just before dawn. Sometimes on a school night.

This is what I witness on the nights I'm not at the nightclub.

Am I proud of my sleuthing on a teenage boy? No. Does it give me some insight into Goose's parental style? Yep.

In a way, it's like Goose isn't a big part of his life. They never go out together and are rarely in the same place at the same time. Again, the GPS tracker at work. Another sin to add to the list I'm amassing.

The more I watch Mateo, the more questions I have.

Is Goose clueless about his son, or just an awful parent?

Maybe both.

I mean, sure, the kid is obviously not a choir boy. But he's also not like the other immature and rowdy boys I see at his school. He's not a childish asshole. If anything, he seems to be just a kid who's mad at the world, and I'm curious as to why.

His loneliness and silent anger draw me in.

I try to keep my distance. I really do.

But he's an enigma and a big part of Goose's life, so in the end, I venture closer.

As I walk into the fast-food joint, the bell above the door jingles. For months, I've watched from a safe distance, keeping tabs, never getting too close; however, that decision to stay away changed today.

My footsteps carry me straight to the counter. After eyeing the menu momentarily, I order a Frito pie and a chicken quesadilla. My voice is steady, despite my racing pulse.

For this adventure, I've opted for a different disguise: a dark stain over my natural hair color, zero makeup, large prescription glasses that make my eyes appear bigger, and brown contacts. I found the department store polo at the local thrift store, and I've paired it with bland khaki pants and ballet flats. I look ordinary, forgettable.

When my order's ready, I scan the seating area. It doesn't take long to spot him. Mateo is in a booth to the right, his back is to me. There's a stunning middle-aged woman with him. She's facing me. I take note of her carefully constructed appearance. The two have similar features, which they should, seeing as it's his mother.

It's the moment I've waited for and the reason I braved this close encounter.

Her chestnut hair is silky smooth and rests in a subtle curl above her shoulders. She's polished, and her jewelry appears to be expensive.

I slip quietly into the booth directly behind them and set my purse down.

Mateo is more intense up close, especially with the glare he's sporting. His brown eyes are deep-set and surrounded by long lashes. With the mustache and the beginnings of stubble along his jawline, he could easily be mistaken for older than he is.

"How's the food?" she asks.

"Fine," he replies, his tone flat.

A few minutes later, she speaks up again. "How's soccer?"

"I quit the team," he says with a shrug, as if it doesn't matter, and lays down his fork.

"What? Why?"

"I don't see the point."

"But you love soccer!" Her voice rises, almost pleading.

"No, *you* loved watching me play soccer until something better came along."

"That's not fair, and you know it. This isn't about me loving him more than you."

"So what?" Mateo continues, his voice dripping with sarcasm. "If you hadn't met him, we'd be fine? I'd still be living at home?"

Her voice rises when she replies. "You needed a good male role model, Mattie. That's why I did what I did. We were fighting all the time."

Mateo lets out a bitter laugh. "Yeah, nothing says good role model like the man you dumped me for."

Her breath hitches. "That's not—"

He sits forward and places his arms on the table. "Isn't it telling…?"

"What?"

He raises a brow at her. "That, when I needed a male role model, your new husband isn't the first guy who came to mind?"

"Why do you always have to start a fight? I'm trying to spend time with you. Can we not argue about him every time?"

He mutters something under his breath.

I sit still, caught between feeling like I should leave and wanting to hear more. This is private, but the devil on my shoulder wins out because this has only given me yet more questions I need answers to.

"Look, I know you think I'm a bad mom for what I did, and maybe I am. But I was making the best decision I could at the time."

"Looking out for yourself, you mean," Mateo shoots back, his voice cold. "Moving me out so you could move your new life in."

"Dammit, Mattie," she hisses, frustration evident. She starts to slide out of the booth.

Mateo's tone shifts. "Okay, I'm sorry. Don't leave."

She huffs and exhales heavily. "Then tell me honestly," she says, sitting back in her seat. "Why are you so angry with me? Is it just him, or is this about your dad? And why did you quit the team?"

His answers are less aggressive this time. "I don't want to talk about him or dad. With soccer… it was just taking up so much of my time. It's not going anywhere, so I don't see the point anymore. I'd rather get a job. I'm done wasting my life on it."

She sighs, long and deep. "Okay. I guess that makes sense when you put it like that. How are your grades?" Her tone softens.

"Fine. I've got the credits I need to graduate."

"And college?"

His gaze flickers toward me, and I quickly avert my eyes.

"Mom, let's be real. I'm not signing up for four more years of school."

"If it's about money—"

"It's not about money!" His frustration boils over.

"I just don't want you to throw your twenties away. College is the best experience. I want you to have that. I don't want you to reject it and regret it later. Will you think about going for a year and then decide if it's right for you?"

Mateo's tone hardens. "You're still not listening. I'm not a college boy. I don't care about school, and I'm not wasting another second of my life on it. I'm going to work as a mechanic's assistant. Maybe open a bike shop of my own one day, making custom bikes. Work on art in my free time."

"I thought that was just a hobby."

"Not to me." His voice cracks, and I watch as he angrily swipes his fingers under one eye. He's speaking from his heart. That much is clear. And I get it.

It takes me back to when I tried to convince my mom to let me quit pageants and focus more on becoming a professional dancer and choreographer. The fights we'd get into about it were epic. She couldn't wrap her head around it. She told me I was dreaming Hollywood dreams, and warned me how many girls I'd be competing against if I tried to make it in LA. She all but said I wouldn't make it, like I didn't have the talent to get there, couldn't hack it in the big city.

Pretty girls are a dime a dozen in Hollywood. Like that's all I was, or what my worth amounted to, being pretty. She'd watched me dance my whole life and didn't believe in me. That fucking hurt.

Everything changed when she met my stepfather. He backed her up, but his reasons for not wanting me to leave town weren't as well-meaning. As the months slipped by, the danger he presented became apparent. He drank and got weird. Weird turned to flirty. Flirty turned to inappropriate. And it's escalated from there. When he entered my room one night and woke me from sleep, the writing was on the wall. I'd screamed and woke my mother, and that was the first time my mother believed his excuses and took his side.

Me? I was a liar.

The threats came next, and my life slowly started to fall apart.

And when the only person who could protect me, who knew me better than anyone else in the world, ended up being manipulated by my abuser to believe I was nothing but a lying, attention-seeking, spoiled brat who was just pissed off because I wasn't getting my own way... well... it changes you. It pushes you to desperate measures, which is why I ended up running away.

Another life disrupted by a new man. One not worthy of her. Another child cast aside for someone else's fresh start, making the ability to work out issues fucking impossible, and escaping the situation, at least in my case, seemed like the only possible answer.

So does my heart ache at witnessing Goose's son go through something similar? Damn right it does.

His mother's tone becomes consoling. "He'd want you to go to college. To give it a try at least."

Mateo freezes. "Don't do that," he snaps. "Don't use him to get what you want." He shoves out of the booth, standing abruptly. "You know what? Forget it. I fucking knew this was a bad idea."

"Mattie, wait—"

But he's already halfway to the door. She tries to stop him from leaving, but he throws off her hand when she grabs him. "Go live your happy life with your new family. And don't have more kids if you're just going to kick them out when they don't fit your grand plans."

His mother stands frozen for a long moment. When she turns, she takes in the room. A flush covers her cheeks. She's flustered as she returns to the booth, grabs her purse, pays for their food, and then hurries out the door.

I hear Mateo's bike rev up and the ferocity as he peels out of the parking lot.

I sit there, my mind racing. I don't understand all of it, but one thing is clear—Goose's son feels the same way I did. Abandoned by someone he trusted to love him. It frays a person, leaving them with lasting scars.

This kind of betrayal is life-altering. I know this better than most. It makes me wonder how Goose fits into it all. Is he aware of the emotional turmoil his son is battling? What is he doing to help Mateo through it? And if he doesn't know, what will Mateo do to cope with the pain?

Do I listen to the reasonable part of my brain that throws up caution and warning roadblocks on these thoughts? Nope. Instead, I let them fan the flames of my need for answers.

I spend the better part of the day planning my next steps, even though deep down, I know I'm entering more dangerous territory by inserting myself into Goose's private life.

CHAPTER 25

*Our actions in the dark can be full of light and
fueled by love.*

A week later, I'm on the porch enjoying a cup of coffee. The
smell of damp earth after a heavy rain fills my lungs as I
curl up with a warm blanket and listen to the thunder rumble
overhead and the crickets sing their song.

Every so often, I shoo a small bug away from my reading light.
Yeah, I could go inside to avoid them, but I'm enjoying the tranquility
the night brings and the bright sparks of lightning that flash across the
sky while I read an article about Anglomania, the mix of tradition and
anarchy in English style.

One of the things I missed the most about New Mexico was the
beautiful storms and the never-ending sky. The entire city seems to go
quiet on nights like this, and I find it peaceful.

It's a simple joy that's interrupted when Goose exits his front door.
He's dressed for stealth—a black hoodie and tactical pants. There's a
large duffle bag in his hand. His wariness is apparent as he scans his
surroundings before getting into his Roadrunner, which now appears
black at night, but is actually painted a charcoal gray color with white
pinstripes.

After flipping my blanket off my legs, I head inside to throw on a
quick disguise, grab a few supplies, and my keys.

I have a link to access the GPS tracker I placed on his vehicle, so I'm not too worried. But my shitty sedan isn't as fast as my beamer, which is currently in storage. I do my best to catch up without breaking too many traffic laws.

Worry fills me ten or so minutes later when his movements stop. I'm about two miles out, so I curse every red light on my way, and slam the pedal down when they eventually turn green.

I hit the empty parking garage, and search for his car. I find it on the second level. The garage is near the mall and theater, so for a moment I tell myself there's a good chance he's indulging in a late-night movie. He's an action flicks junkie, and particularly loved the ones with convoluted plots and surprise endings, the kind you'd have to watch twice to catch all the clues.

Way back when, I remember how blown away he'd been when I told him I'd never seen *Indiana Jones*. He went out that night and rented every single one in the series, a shitload of candy, and we spent an entire night watching them back to back.

So I settle in, preparing for a long, boring wait. As I sit there, something about the duffle nags at me. Pulling out my phone, I call the theater and check the current show listings. When nothing fits the kind of movie he'd be down for, a restless feeling begins to creep along my spine.

I'm missing something.

I can sense it, and this puts me on high alert.

A few minutes pass before I reverse out of the parking spot. I go up one level and continue to scan the garage. An older Jeep Cherokee comes toward me. It's dark green, and at first, I nearly dismiss it, but the man behind the wheel, the one wearing a beanie, has visible silver hair beneath, and his hands are littered with tattoos. Goose.

When he turns the corner, I quickly do a U-turn. I let him gain some distance and tail him.

My fingers clench around the steering wheel as we enter the more derelict parts of town. Unease fills me. Being here brings back many unpleasant memories.

I barely survived these streets. At seventeen, I'd been desperate for help, dying for a way out. It was a cage I thought I'd never escape. Every day was a spin of the roulette wheel. The chance of being killed by a John I had the rotten luck of getting into a car with, or from one of the punishments Veno delivered when I didn't pull in enough cash or perform to his standards—was a real possibility.

The day the police raided the hotel where Veno kept me and the other girls still haunts me. I'd been beaten black and blue for defying him that day, and that very hotel sits at the end of this street.

In a way, it was also the first day of this new life I'm living. Not just because I made it out, but because it was the day Goose found me hiding in the closet under a blanket.

Based on what he'd told me, he'd had a personal vendetta against the 13Ds. They'd broken into his home while he'd been on his last tour of duty. They'd used it as a temporary meth lab. When he'd come home to say his goodbyes to his father, who lay dying in a care facility, Goose discovered two men cooking this shit in his house and had made it his personal mission to send the people responsible to prison. Joey, his best friend on the force, helped him. Goose surveilled the 13Ds for weeks and turned all the evidence he'd gathered on them over to his friend, who then organized the raid and brought a SWAT team to clean out the building that night and arrest Veno.

I'd managed to hide. The last thing I wanted to do was be sent back home and be at my stepfather's mercy again, not after what I'd already gone through.

Goose found me. When that closet door opened, he was there, crouched down and peering in at me from the other side.

The days leading up to that night were some of the most harrowing moments of my life. The memories hit me like a Mack truck barreling through a barricade, and the wall I've put up surrounding that part of my past breaks apart as if made of dust. My breathing gets difficult. The air feels thick and becomes harder to pull into my lungs.

Reaching over, I search through my purse for my inhaler. When I come up empty, I yank the bag into my lap and look again. I switch on the overhead light as I search for that chunk of plastic that always

269

takes up a good portion of space in my purse. I upend the contents onto my passenger seat and scour through them, but the sinking pit in my stomach tells me what my subconscious already knows.

It's not here.

"Shit! Motherfuck." I slam my palm repeatedly onto the steering wheel and bite my lip. *Fuck. Fuck. Fuck.*

I used it earlier today when I got stung. Scorpions are no joke in New Mexico. I had antivenom on hand, but it still caught me off guard and freaked me out. So even though I had my preventative inhaler in the bathroom cupboard, I used my emergency inhaler from my purse to fight off the panic attack I felt coming on.

And it's now sitting on my kitchen counter.

It's fine. Just focus on your breathing. In for three. Hold. Out for three.

A therapist in California I used to see believed my panic attacks, or "anxiety disorder" as she liked to call it, stemmed from a fear of not being able to breathe and from childhood trauma. She reasoned that suffering from asthma attacks without the proper care or medication for so long as a child, and the physical demands I'd been under during that time—the rigorous training for competitions and pageants—combined with not only the abuse, but with such high expectations placed on me, could all be a factor.

Which was something I'd already reasoned out myself.

But she did give me some valuable advice. She'd been the first doctor to recommend I learn some natural breathing techniques, coping skills, and preventative measures. That I needed to learn how to recover from an episode and not always rely on my inhaler.

With her help and some extra research, I learned various breathing and relaxation techniques. Yoga, multi-vitamins, and minimizing my caffeine intake also helped.

I essentially learned enough to fight off some attacks without medication. But try convincing my brain of that—when it knows that if I lose my shit, my quick fix, my fucking pacifier, is nowhere to be found. That kind of panic? It doesn't listen to logic.

My anxiety is still sky-high, but I work through it, and slowly but surely, my breathing begins to ease.

Goose pulls to the curb two blocks down the road. Even though the lighting here is sparse, I check my wig and smooth some bangs over my forehead. I keep driving and take the next left, then rapidly turn once I'm out of his sight and circle back until the Jeeps in view.

I turn off my lights and creep forward along the curb. After shutting off the car, I grab my binoculars.

The next hour is spent watching Goose sit idly in the Jeep.

Movement in an alleyway is what draws my attention away from him. A girl with short curly brown hair stands there in a gold mini dress and a black raincoat. She's looking up and down the street. One arm is tucked close to her body, and it's held in a sling. Her gaze pauses on the Jeep. She ducks back into the alley, and a couple of minutes go by before she peeks out again. After a quick look around, she takes off with a burst of speed towards the Jeep. She opens the back door and slips quickly inside and out of sight.

The light inside the vehicle doesn't illuminate as she gets in, and this sends flutters through my stomach.

I recognize this. Not the girl. Not the Jeep. But the scenario. The pick-up. The shady arrangement.

My heart fucking plummets.

I've been that girl. Back then, Veno trusted me to do as I was told. The threat of his retaliation kept me in line. This was before I'd learned that certain Johns could be just as brutal as Veno. When I tried to escape and failed, any freedom I had was taken away. From then on, I wasn't allowed to go anywhere outside the hotel without an escort.

Goose pulls away from the curb. I throw the binoculars into the passenger seat and quickly follow. They get on the freeway heading north. I do my best to keep a reasonable distance behind. All the while, my mind is racing, trying to make sense of this.

He drives on and on. My gas gauge gets dangerously close to the E. Thankfully, Goose pulls off the freeway and stops at a gas station before I run completely out. The woman stays inside the vehicle. She doesn't even pop her head up, which seems odd. Where he's taking her is anyone's guess, but you can bet your ass I'm going to keep an eye on him until I find out.

I spy older cars in the parking lot of a strip mall across the street. I pull in. I can't tail him in the same vehicle. Not without blowing my cover. I contemplate which will be easiest to hotwire. Popping the glovebox open, I pull out my Hellcat. A gift from Deeds on my last birthday. It's a beautiful silver handgun with the name "Gypsy" inscribed on the handle, and an arrow engraved along the right side of the barrel. I slide it, along with the rest of the shit I dumped out, into my purse.

Grabbing my phone, I take a deep breath before pulling up the contact name and number I need and hitting the call button.

"Who this?" A familiar drawl greets me after a few rings.

"Is that how you greet your favorite drinkin' buddy?" I ask, voice low and urgent.

A gasp. "Gypsy, holy fuck! Is that you?"

"Yeah, it's me. Look, I'm in a situation here and need your expertise."

"Name it."

"I need a refresher on how to hotwire a car. And fast."

"What kind of car?"

"Hmmm. There's a couple here to choose from." I relay the older models here because I know those are going to be the best to choose from.

With Bones walking me through it, I go through the motions, and when the older sedan roars to life, I let out a whoop of joy. "Bones, you're a genius!"

"You gonna wear my name on your ass as a thank you?"

I smirk, despite the tension coursing through me. "You wish."

He chuckles. "Can't blame a man for trying. Take care, Gypsy Girl. Don't be a stranger. Sure nice to hear that sweet voice of yours."

"You got it."

With that, I hang up and drive north. I have to play catch-up and hope against hope that Goose stays on the same route.

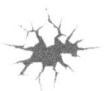

FINN

After opening the motel room door, I let Larissa enter first. Then I follow her inside and drop my duffle on the bed, before walking to the windows and closing the curtains.

I've been on high alert, but you can never be too careful where the 13Ds are concerned. It's one of the reasons why I now drive so far out of the city to reconnect girls like Larissa with their families.

Turning, I ask, "So Veno had one of his guys watching you? That's why you were late?"

Her eyes are red-rimmed and dilated. They dart around the room. She's rubbing her hands up and down her too-thin arms, and she seems jittery as hell. I note the multiple fresh track marks on her inner elbows and how, in just two weeks, she appears to have lost more weight. The handprint bruise around her neck has also faded from green to yellow.

"He's watching all the girls extra close now."

Shame and guilt have my stomach bottoming out. Their freedom is getting restricted because of me. Veno's tightening the noose, which means he feels threatened. Not a good sign. Dogs backed into a corner—especially rabid ones like him—get vicious and unpredictable. It's a precarious tightrope I'm walking here with people's lives, and though I've been trying to navigate it with care, there's going to be fallout no matter what.

I rub my jaw and shake my head. "I'm sorry."

"Don't be. You can't save us all, and it's not you who should be sorry." She attempts a false smile, exhales, and sits on the bed. I don't miss the slight wince that flashes over her face.

I pull off my hoodie and remove the beanie from my head, tossing both into my bag. Then I pull out the supplies I have for her: something to eat and a few bottles of water. I hand them over, along with a backpack that contains spare clothes, hair dye, and emergency hygiene necessities. Then I walk around, grab one of the chairs, and take a seat in front of her. My hands funnel through my hair to push it back before I lace them together and lean forward.

She immediately takes out one of the sandwiches and begins to eat. "Are my parents coming?"

"Yes, they'll be here in a few hours."

She nods, and a grim smile graces her face as she brushes crumbs away from her mouth.

Even though she probably can't wait to be reunited with her parents, I imagine sharing what she's been through is going to be hard on them all. No doubt her absence from their lives for the last nine months has been torture. Not as much torture as what she's been through, but still.

It doesn't take long before her tears begin to fall. I do what I can to support her while also giving her space. In my experience, physical touch is the last thing she wants. So I pass her tissues, and promise that now and in the future, if she needs me to, I'll stand between her and the monsters she never wants to see again.

I wait until she calms before gesturing towards her newly marred cheek—the fresh bruise and a small cut. "How'd you get that?"

She shakes her head, "You don't wanna know."

I nod and let the subject drop, replacing it with another. "So what did you find out? Anything?" My own shame at having ulterior motives eats away at me, but like always, I fight past it, because if I can save two birds with one action and do right by them both, then I need to take this chance. Even if it makes me feel like a bastard, I'm praying for at least one more feather. One more piece of the puzzle I can use to tie the past together.

She takes a long draw on a bottle of water before answering. "A little from Kandy. I caught her on a good night. Girl was so high on H, she probably doesn't remember a thing."

"What'd she say?"

"You were right. There was a girl. Someone Veno had a huge hard-on for, I guess. Kandy called her Baby Girl, but she said Veno called her Angel. Guess Kandy trained her. But she said she didn't work on the streets for long. Was kept in the hotel mainly after she tried to make a run for it. She said some John tried to buy her out once, but Veno wasn't havin' it. Then one day, poof, she was just gone." She shrugs. "That's all I could get out of her." She fidgets with the cap. "The rest was just gibberish as her eyes rolled back in her head."

"Gibberish? Like what?"

"It didn't make much sense."

I reach over, grab my bag, and drag it towards me. I pull out a pen and a notebook. "Try to remember her exact words if you can. I wouldn't ask if it wasn't important."

Her face scrunches up in concentration, and her eyes dart to the side. "Something like, 'Sex on legs. Men like that… they aren't for us.' Then she laughed and said, 'Fairy tales… fuckin' fairies, horse shit, girlfriend. They may rescue you when you be crawlin', crawlin', crawlin' out of the gutter, but they're all too good to be true. You'll see. You'll go poof, too. There's no flying the coop.'" She shakes her head. "See, nuts."

I make her repeat it twice and jot it all down, then rub my hand over my face as I try to make sense of the parts I don't understand.

"Thank you. I know it doesn't sound like much, but I need to know all I can about her." At the same time, dread fills me because Larissa's probing could mean trouble for the club and ramifications for Edge if they tie this back to me. Edge is only safe on the inside if the truce holds and the 13Ds on the inside protect him from the enemies he's facing while in lockup.

The guilt I feel at putting him at risk makes me, quite frankly, sick to my stomach, but it's another thing I'm going to have to live with if I stay this course.

I nod toward the bathroom. "Why don't you take a shower and get changed? Then we'll get started on your hair."

She stands and rubs her arm. "Thank you. I can't thank you enough…" She shakes her head as more tears spill down her cheeks.

I never know how to take their gratitude. I feel it, but it doesn't feel like something I can or should accept. "Let me know when you start feeling like you need something. What I can give ya won't curb the cravings, but it'll take the edge off."

It's subtle, but her eyes venture for a moment to my bag. She swallows thickly and nods. "I'm okay for now."

"How long it takes to get clean is up to you. It's a battle every goddamn day, but it is one you have to start at some point if you want to really live." She keeps nodding and sweeps her fingers under her eyes. "I've been there, so I know how hard it is. It'll take time, but you'll get there."

When she shuts the bathroom door and locks it, I massage the back of my neck, trying to relieve some of the pain ricocheting through my head, and stare down at the notes I've made.

A tidal wave of regret washes over me. For the life of me, I can't figure out why I would have left Elle here in Albuquerque. Why didn't I send her away? This place was obviously not a safe environment for her. Why would I have thought she'd be okay?

Kandy's tirade makes little sense, but a few words spark hope in my chest.

Poof. Disappear. Fly the coop. Is it possible she found a way out?

I pray she did and is living a good life wherever she is now. If I can't find her, then I hope she's at least happy and safe.

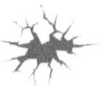

LILY

My stomach grumbles with hunger, but I don't dare leave. Several hours have passed as I sit and wait for any movement in the motel room Goose and the girl entered. It's not until a Tahoe pulls up near three in the morning and parks next to Goose's Jeep that anything noteworthy happens.

I perk up at this new arrival and grab my binoculars in time to spy a woman jump out of the vehicle. She beelines it for Goose's room and knocks aggressively. Soon after, the male driver of the Tahoe steps up behind her. Both are thin and tall and dressed casually.

When the motel room door opens, the girl practically flies out of it. She crashes into the woman with such force that they nearly topple over. They hug fiercely. The man's arms surround them both. Goose steps out of the room. He leans against the building beside his open motel room door and watches the group. Every so often, he scans the parking lot and the surrounding area.

When the family heads inside the room, Goose stays outside. He looks up towards the sky. Out of nowhere, he holds his hand up and points towards the stars.

My shoulders, which were locked in place, drop in relief. I pry my bone-white fingers off the steering wheel and cover my mouth, breathing into my hands to fight the tears building.

Because I know what this is. Not some seedy affair. This is Goose doing what he's done before. Saving a girl who probably had no hope of saving herself.

Lily

CHAPTER 26

*Pieces made from wood hold great meaning
and a lifetime of memories.*

Through the front window, I watch Goose and Bodie load a new rocking chair into Bodie's old beater truck. Even though it's the crack of dawn, they're full of energy. They work together with ease and efficiency. It's as if the two have their own language. There are hand signals and barking laughter from Bodie. Goose flips him the bird at one point before they both jump into the cab and drive off.

Curious and determined now, I tail them.

I spend most of the drive lost in nostalgia as I take in the Albuquerque skyline and the variety of different hues—blush to magenta, layered with sparse cloud cover. There's an old sailor proverb claiming pink or red skies are a delight at night, but to take warning if they appear in the morning.

I'm pretty superstitious, but this is one I don't give any credence to.

To me, they're one of life's natural phenomena that showcase how beautiful nature can be with its adaptation to shifting weather and the ever-changing lunar phase cycle. But I'm often captivated by things like this—tornadoes, dust storms, and the flash monsoons we get here quite often. I'm also a sucker for sunrises and sunsets, thunder and lightning storms. I love taking in the view from great heights or sitting in a dense forest to hear the birds chattering with one another. These things hold my whole heart, and I've only shared them with one other person in the whole world—a person who might no longer hold those memories.

But I guess it is what it is.

The city's traffic nearly swallows me up, but I eventually find Bodie's truck and weave through the congestion until I'm just a half-dozen cars behind. It's not until they travel down a certain street that I realize where they're headed, and my heart sinks.

Bodie parks his truck in front of the building—the one Goose and I lived in for a time before he went off to play hero and left me behind. They pull the rocking chair from the truck bed and set it gently on the sidewalk. Goose takes out a rag and wipes it down, treating it as if it holds great value.

Then, as if time hadn't stolen so much already from us, he walks up the old, cracked path toward the building, and I'm hit with a moment of déjà vu when he reappears with a familiar older man walking with a cane. His hand is on Goose's arm. He's using Goose and his cane to steady himself as he lumbers forward.

My chest tightens at the sight of Goose's old landlord.

Fifteen years have gone by, and those years haven't been kind to him. This bastard. He's thinner now, hunched over, with a pathetic comb-over that barely conceals his balding head. My throat tightens as the past ploughs through my mind like a freight train.

The incessant banging on the front door comes at 9:30 a.m. and again at 4:00 p.m. When it returns a little later that night, it doesn't stop.

"Listen, girl. I know you're in there. Open up!"

His shouts have anxiety running rampant in my chest. I've ignored the landlord's demands in the hopes that if I put him off long enough, I'd hear from Finn. Then he could resolve this issue, but day after day goes by with no word from him, and I know I've ignored the landlord's demand for entry for as long as I can.

But I still can't get off the couch to answer the door because the fear of getting kicked out and having nowhere to go is paralyzing. Although I know at some point, he'll use his key to get in if I don't answer.

"Last warning, girl. Don't make me call the police to escort you from the building."

I bite my nails to the quick as I debate what to do. Instead of answering, I search the phonebook and look up the local recruitment office. After finding the address and phone number, I jot down the info and stuff it in my pocket.

When I open the door a crack, just enough to see the landlord on the other side, I find his face level with mine and his small beady eyes set into a scowl under his bushy gray eyebrows.

"Rent was due three and a half weeks ago," he snaps. "If you can't pay up, you and your boyfriend need to go."

"There must be some mistake. Finn said he'd paid ahead for four months."

"He did no such thing." The landlord pushes the door open another inch with his foot, and a heavy rock settles in my stomach.

"You got my money, or are you packing up?"

"Can you just give me another week or two. He's overseas, and I haven't been able to reach him. Finn has the money, and he'll pay it. I think there's just been some kind of mix-up."

"No, I can't afford to wait. My mortgage payment was due on the first, and that's why rent is due on the first. If you can't afford the place, then I suggest you start gathering your things."

"But I don't have anywhere to go."

"Family?"

I'm nervous about answering honestly. I shake my head, though, taking a chance and hoping he'll be more lenient if he knows I'll be homeless if he kicks me out today.

He shakes his head in return. The strands of his thinning hair shift to reveal the bald spot beneath. "Not my problem. I'm running a business here, not a charity."

"Did his check bounce?"

The landlord scoffs. "He never paid me. If he told you that, then he lied. Now, are you going to get me the money or not?"

"How much is the rent?"

"Seven fifty."

Panic surges through me. My eyes dart around the nearly barren apartment, searching for something—anything—I can sell to come up with the cash. But the place is as empty as my options, except for the few personal items Finn salvaged from his father's house, which I wouldn't sell. Those items mean the world to him. They're all that's left after his dad's passing and the incident with the Thirteen Devils using it as a meth lab.

He cherishes every piece of what he's kept.

"I'll try, but I might need more time." Maybe Finn really didn't pay him, but it's hard to imagine. Finn has his shit together. He's responsible. So unless this is simply his way of cutting ties and letting me down gently, I don't see it being true. Weeks ago, I would have never believed he'd leave me to fend for myself, but now, with no word from him at all, my doubts are growing daily.

The scowl doesn't leave the old man's face. At my plea, his expression hardens and turns to resolve. He hikes his thumb up and over his shoulder. "Girl, I can't just wait around forever. Not when I can find someone else tomorrow to move in and pay up."

"I'll go to the recruit—"

"There's no point waiting if you can't get me the money." He pushes open the door and steps inside.

"Hey!" I try to stop him, but he manhandles me out of the way.

"Sorry, but you gotta go. Just clear out, and I won't call the cops."

He marches over to Finn's boxes in the corner and opens the top one—the one with Finn's journals. I run over and slam my hand down on the top, preventing him from digging through Finn's things, seeing his private thoughts.

I have two choices: Leave and go back to the streets, or come up with the money. The landlord fucking pushes me back and reopens the box. After pulling a journal free, he flips through the pages. Without thinking, I rip it from his hands and clutch it to my chest. I swallow hard past the lump in my throat.

"Look, I'll get it," I say, my voice brittle even though conviction begins to build inside me. "By the end of the week. I swear."

"How?"

"I don't know, but I will."

He pauses, and he eyes me up and down. His gaze fills with a predatory gleam. "All of it?"

I nod and try to portray a confidence I don't feel.

"You're a pretty girl."

My stomach twists as his gaze travels down my body. I'm not dressed in anything special, but his gaze has me wanting to cover up.

In response, I force a half-smile onto my face and push a "Thank you" past my lips. "Maybe…"

"What?"

"Maybe we can work out some kind of arrangement."

I know this look. Finn is one of the only men I've come across who doesn't look at me like this. But I've been isolated here. Away from Veno and his men, away from most people to tell the truth of it. I've sort of been a hermit since Finn left, and I hate feeling like this again—like I'm at the mercy of a man with power over me—I'm not prepared for it.

I should be, though. This is, after all, how the opposite sex has always seen me, as a possession or someone to take advantage of. They see the shell I wear and nothing else.

Back in the present, I watch Goose help his old landlord sit in the rocking chair. Goose's looking down at him, granting him one of his rare smiles. The sight of it has something vile stirring inside me. Something dark and twisted.

The relationship between them shocks the hell out of me. I try to reason it out. The Goose I knew would never care for a man like this.

It pisses me off—how can Goose be so blind to the danger lurking in and around him? Is his head stuck in the fucking sand? Are his migraines hindering his ability to think clearly?

Maybe like me, he's just another flawed, complex human being who doesn't have his shit together. This I get. But it also makes me worry that Goose is wholly unprepared for the war coming his way.

CHAPTER 27

The most attractive quality a person can have is a damn good sense of humor.

My reservations about joining Raven for drinks sit heavy at the forefront of my mind as I pull into the parking lot. Passing nearly two dozen motorcycles lined up in front of the bar doesn't help. It's not that I don't know what I'm walking into—I do. Monday nights are something of a ritual for the HOCs, after all. It's more the idea of *who* might be among them that has me planning for the best and preparing for the worst.

Will Goose being here deter me from moving forward with the next part of my plan?

No.

Just like his proximity hasn't stopped me from dancing my ass off at Wet Tips night after night, agreeing to lap dances, or flirting with a few of his brothers whenever the opportunity presents itself.

If anything, knowing it gets under his skin only spurs me on. And there's something about my flirting with Stone in particular that riles his blood. It's something he can't mask.

So I make a point to focus my attention on him. Call it a small slice of vindication—for the hell I lived through because of him, and the chaos he's stirred up in my head lately.

Everything I've discovered about him recently has thrown me for a loop. I'm honestly not sure how to deal with any of it.

In some ways, I don't feel as if I know him at all.

So is it smart to be in his orbit with a good dose of alcohol in my system? No. Absolutely not. This would add a whole new layer of risk to an already complicated situation. Add to the fact that certain types of alcohol hit me differently and trigger all kinds of reactions, which means I must make a conscious effort to keep myself in check tonight.

After finally finding a spot in the packed lot, I take a moment to pull myself together. Using the sun visor mirror, I reapply my lipstick and work on slipping into character, practicing my expressions, whispering lines under my breath. When I'm ready, I pocket the lipstick, cash, and ID, and step out of the car. After locking my purse in the trunk, I head for the front door.

My stone-washed jeans, like my shirt, are tight as sin, and the black leather boots I'm wearing hit mid-knee with five-inch heels. They're hell on my feet, but worth it for the attention they draw. My shirt's the real showstopper, though. It's black, sleeveless, with a plunging neckline and a shamelessly low back that shows off my ink.

It's the perfect outfit to help me blend in at a biker bar, while also standing out.

I've paired it with my jewelry, my armor—the one part of me that's real. Two layered silver necklaces, bracelets that jingle when I move, and all my favorite rings, which also happen to be my good luck charms—rings that I spin now and then, when I'm stressed, which tonight are a necessity.

Dressing for effect is something I learned through my lifelong addiction to fashion and lifestyle magazines. Back when I couldn't get an education, they were my window into the worlds I wanted to know more about. The rings came later and help to ground me to my true identity whenever I'm emotionally overwhelmed.

Music also helps, which is the case as I get closer and hear Creedence Clearwater Revival's "Run Through the Jungle" filtering out from inside the bar. I hum the tune as I approach.

A younger prospect, one of the bikers going through the MC's initiation process, guards the bikes, and near him are a few other guys who are smoking. One of them whistles when he sees me, but I just smile, wave, and keep walking.

My steps slow when I spy the dark-green Harley with the heart-shaped seat. Before I can get too deep in my feels about it, my attention is pulled away by a voice filled with pure grit. "Jesus, sweetheart! Where you been all my life?"

He's a thick-chested biker with long, wild, red hair and an equally unruly beard. His cut is aged to perfection and riddled with patches that speak of a lifetime not only in the MC but on the open road. He's standing against the building, wearing jeans and a black and white plaid shirt, with his sleeves rolled up to his forearms, which are covered in faded tattoos. He's sporting a black bandana and large chunky rings, and a smoke hangs precariously from his lips.

I've run into him a time or two at the strip club, and so far, I've gotten away with my ruse. He's given me questioning looks now and again, as if he's trying to place where we've met before, but hasn't yet pieced it together.

I give Griz a warm grin as I approach. "Looking for you. But you're a hard man to find."

His chuckle is both deep and sexy.

Deeds' uncle is seven years older than Pappy, and has more silver running through his hair and beard than he did when I first met him, which was the night Goose popped back into my life like a resurrected ghost.

He's the kind of person you fall instantly in love with. Down to earth, rock-steady, and funny as hell. Which is how this second meeting of souls pretty much goes.

He sidles up to me and places his hand on my lower back. "You gonna allow a man to escort your pretty ass inside? Make all these young fuckers jealous because I saw you first?" He jerks his chin toward the front door. "I'm not sure it's smart to let you go in there lookin' like that. Gonna break some necks when the boys catch sight of ya. Maybe even a few hearts."

I chuckle heartily. "Yeah? Am I breakin' yours?"

His gaze ventures down my front. "Darlin', you've got no damn idea how smokin' you are, do ya?"

"Maybe a little," I confess.

"Damn. That's even sexier. Confident, smokin', and smart enough to know it. From what I've seen, talented too. You married?"

"Not yet? You applying for the job?"

"Let's see where tonight goes, and I just might be."

We share a laugh as he opens one side of the large wooden front doors. Then he extends his elbow to me and I give him a genuine smile as I wrap my arm around his.

"Surely, if seeing me dance at the club didn't kill 'em, then I doubt my ass in a pair of jeans will."

He shakes his head. "A great ass in denim is like kryptonite to these fuckers. Watch and learn, young Padawan." He pats my hand.

"Well, I've worked pretty damn hard to keep it in shape. Let's hope you're right."

It's my persona talking, one that wears confidence like a second skin. And there lies the secret. I have to become this version of myself to pull it off with any success. To really and truly feel it down to my bones.

Griz's gruff words bring me out of my head and back into the moment. "Ya gonna save me a dance, darlin'?"

"Oh, do they have a dance floor?"

"Sure do. You know how to swing?"

"Wouldn't be a very good dancer if I didn't."

"True that." He nods. "How about I come find you after you've settled in and found your people?"

"I'd love that. Do you happen to know where Raven is?"

Music reverberates around the bar. There's a heavy scent of weed, and it's packed with people. We get a few odd looks as people check us out, but I ignore them in favor of finding the woman with ebony hair who talked me into this adventure.

Framed pictures and beer signage cover the walls, pictures from a time long past—MC clubs from the sixties and seventies, and some of the Hollywood icons from that era, too. Plus, Woodstock memorabilia, old concert posters, and record covers.

I take it all in as I enter and search the crowd for Raven.

A large group is gathered in front of a massive dartboard to my right, and further back are three pool tables. A good many HOCs are in that area. Stone is currently circling a table, preparing to take his shot.

In the middle of it all is a sectioned-off dance floor, which is surrounded by hefty wooden tables and chairs. The place has a more saloon-like vibe than a bar, and reminds me of a place I once visited in San Antonio.

"Raven's at the bar chattin' up Beth," Griz answers and proceeds to steer me through the crowd. He pushes a big guy wearing a cowboy hat out of the way. The guy spins with a harsh look on his face and opens his mouth, but the second he gets a look at who shoved him, he backs up and shuts his mouth.

More of the same happens until we arrive at the bar. At which point, I see Raven on a stool doing exactly what Griz said. She's got her elbows on the bar top and is talking animatedly over the music to the stunning blonde woman working behind the counter.

"Look who I found outside," Griz announces as we approach.

Raven turns. The bartender's gaze falls on me, and I put two and two together, realizing Beth is Bethany Hodge, Old Lady to Travis Hodge, owner of the bar and the man serving drinks at the other end of it.

"Hey! I was wondering if you were going to show," Raven calls out. She taps the guy on the seat next to her and whispers something. The guy looks at her, looks back at me, but it's not until his eyes land on Griz that he jumps off his seat and gestures for me to take it.

As I sit, Griz places a few bills on the bar and tells Bethany, "Get her whatever she wants. Make her feel welcome."

Bethany nods. "That I can do."

Griz pats my back. "Don't forget about that dance, darlin'."

"You're number one on my dance card," I joke back, and he chuckles before he strides off.

Bethany sweeps up the money. "What can I get ya?"

I look over to see Raven drinking a beer, and say, "I'll have what she's having."

Bethany sets the bottle in front of me in no time. Raven quickly introduces us. "Beth, Lily. Lily, Beth or Bethany. She goes by either. Lily's the new girl at Tips. No doubt you've heard about her by now."

Bethany smirks. Her striking light-green eyes trail over my attire. "Love the top. Daring and dangerous. I don't have the guts to pull something like that off, but love a woman who can."

"Thank you. Not too much?"

"Hell no," they say at the exact same time.

Raven points and beats Bethany to the punch. "Jinx, motherfucker."

"Goddamnit!" Bethany sighs and walks down the bar. She comes back with a bottle of Naked Diablo and pours a shot. She glares at Raven for a moment before she throws it back. She coughs and hisses in a quick breath. "Fuck. That shit hits like getting bitch-slapped by your ex." She flips Raven off and snaps, "You suck."

The girl crush sinks in at Bethany's unruly behavior and effortless beauty. She comes across as a no-frills kind of woman—short nails, nude lip gloss, golden eye shadow. Her wheat-colored hair rests in barely there waves just above her shoulders, and sparse freckles cover the bridge of her small nose. They're adorably sexy.

She studies me for a moment and says, "The new girl, huh? You likin' it there?"

I shrug. "Yeah, it's not a bad gig. The other girls are hit or miss, but I'm adjusting."

Bethany crosses her arms and leans forward onto the bar. "Yeah, and I don't suppose you'd tell me if you've seen my old man dragging girls into the back room for some one-on-one time and stuffing dollar bills in G-strings?" She pokes her thumb over her shoulder at Hodge. Red flags immediately wave all around me. Hodge turns. He eyes the three of us suspiciously. His gaze jumps from Bethany to Raven to me. His eyes flare with recognition. Bethany looks over at him and glares. When she centers her gaze back on me, Hodge is motioning with his hand in a cut motion across his neck.

"Oh, uh-mmm." I bite the inside of my cheek.

Raven laughs. "Oh, you two, stop. That's so mean." She points two fingers at Hodge. He bursts out laughing. Bethany's expression breaks into a devious smile. "Yes, he does shove money into G-strings, but that's it and you know it." Darting a glance at me, Raven says, "She knows everything. She's just testing where your loyalty lies. Think of it as initiation into the cool female side of the HOC family." To Bethany, she chides, "God, yours and Hodge's sick sense of humor scares me sometimes."

Bethany chuckles. "I'm sorry. I don't get out much, so I have to find humor where I can."

"Stay-at-home mom. Most of the time," Raven explains. "Has the cutest damn baby on the planet. Axel, her son, is a cute little shit, too, although he's not so little anymore."

Bethany's grin is sweet when she replies, "If they'd only stay little forever. I don't know about this whole growing-up thing. It's like you lose all control over them at eleven, and it's all downhill from there."

Hodge comes over, throws his arm around Bethany's waist, and grins. "You're welcome." She nudges her hip into his; he bumps hers right back. "Don't be takin' all the credit for our cute kids."

"I wouldn't dream of it. But Medda does have my eyes and chin," she jokes. A guy down at the end of the bar waves to get Hodge's attention. He holds up a finger and turns back to us.

"Hey, Lily, right? Welcome to our little humble bar in the middle of BFE." The way he says the last part has Bethany rolling her eyes.

"Thanks. Appreciate the warm welcome."

When Hodge turns to help the customer, Bethany rests her hands on the bar and leans forward. She lowers her voice. "That's not all Medda got from his DNA. He also gave her a little pig nose."

Somehow he manages to hear her or read her lips, because he whips a towel at her ass. She shrieks and swats at the weapon. "Woman!" He growls. "How many times do I got to set you straight? It's not a fuckin' pig nose. Just because it tilts up doesn't mean it's the snout of a goddamn hog." He scowls, but the corner of his mouth is lifted as he saunters away. "Be-fuckin'-have yourself."

"I never said I didn't like it," she yells after him.

He waves her off and starts talking with the guy down the bar.

Raven elbows me. "They're strange. It takes some getting used to.

But honestly, she's one of the only old ladies I can stand. Her and Spice—err Kendra. Septic's old lady." She turns on her stool and looks around for a bit before pointing to the back where most of the HOCs are gathered around the pool tables. "She's the short, hot Latina with the kickin' curves and dark, curly hair."

I spot Kendra right away and nod. I already knew what she looked like, but putting a face to the name and picture helps too. She's precisely as Raven described her, and I note that her smile is wide and beautiful, something a photograph just doesn't capture completely. I can't hear her laugh over the music, but can see it's boisterous.

"That's not much of a compliment," Bethany retorts. The disgust on her face at the mention of other old ladies speaks volumes. "I still hate you for switching teams on me. I was hoping you'd let a brother claim you and be one of the few old ladies at the club gigs I can stand to hang out with." She looks at me. A cunning grin builds on her face. "Speaking of…"

"Don't even think about it," Raven admonishes. "You're not coaxing her to the dark side. Not yet."

Bethany's gaze swings to me. "Oh, no, no, no. Please tell me you don't bat for her team, too? Fuck!"

Raven mock glares at her. She turns to me. A twinkle sparks in her eyes. "Baby, should I tell her or just let her enjoy the show?" I read her intentions as if they are words floating up on a teleprompter. I grin and follow her lead. Time to give Bethany a taste of her own medicine.

Raven's hand sweeps my hair away from my shoulder and cradles my cheek. She brings my face close to hers. Her other hand slides up my thigh, and she yanks me forward, nearly pulling me off my stool.

Chaos explodes behind us, and cheers drown out The Black Keys song playing overhead as Raven's mouth descends. Our lips are a breath away from connecting when she stops. Our eyes open, meet, and laughter bubbles up between us as we break apart.

Bethany slaps the bar top. "Ya'll suck!"

The boos behind us drown out the song.

Then a voice I've come to know well shouts, "Holy Fuck! What is happening here? Why'd you stop? Thought I'd died and gone to heaven. Resume please, or rewind or what-the-fuck-ever, because that was hot as fuck." Bodie comes up behind us, and his gaze bounces back and forth between me and Raven. His black ball cap is turned backwards, and his blond curls stick out the sides above his ears. His sinful grin and dimples are on full display. A white T-shirt with black graffiti art sits under his cut, and he's sporting faded, dark-gray jeans that hang low on his hips.

"Sorry, no can do," Raven fires back.

"Come on! One more time, but this time there needs to be actual lip lockin' and a hell lotta tongue action."

Raven turns and pushes him. "Get outta here. You sick bastard. It was a joke." He comes close again and tries to put his arm over her shoulder. She facepalms him out of her space. Bodie knocks away her hand, unaffected, and stands behind our stools, his arms over the top of both.

The pleading look he levels on me is full of promised misery if I don't give in. "Lil', you're my girl. Surely you wouldn't leave a man hangin' like that."

"Actually." Raven points at me. "That's kind of her specialty."

"True." We laugh and tap the tops of our beers together.

A sour expression fills his face. He shouts out to Hodge. "You see this shit? They get a brother all charged up and then nothin'."

Hodge lets out a chuckle and says, "Climbin' the wrong tree with those three, man. Doesn't take more than two brain cells to see that."

Bodie hollers at him, "Maybe you should cut 'em off, then. New rule. No tongue action, no alcohol."

Bethany interjects, "My bar. My rules. And I say they can drink whatever they like."

"Hodge! Talk to you fuckin' woman. She's talkin' back."

Striding toward us, Hodge says, "Brother, you ain't had it good in the sack until you got a sassy bitch in your bed."

"Amen!" someone hollers behind us.

"How about we welcome Lily to our place properly and get this night off to a good start? What do ya say?" Bethany grins and passes him the Naked Diablo.

He picks it up, and his features scrunch with distaste. "Fuck, really?"

She nods at him. "Double dog dare you, baby."

He smirks and shakes his head. He grabs a couple of shot glasses and pours shots for everyone. Then Hodge holds up his shot, and we do the same. "To new hot-as-fuck friends who know how to keep a secret. May you never have enough of them."

We all repeat the mantra and clink our glasses together before throwing them back.

"Jesus." Hodge wipes the back of his hand across his mouth.

"Motherfucker," Bodie groans. "What the fuck did I just drink?"

Which is pretty much how the next hour goes as we tell stories and banter with one another. One story brings to mind another, and all too soon, my own inner red flags start waving. Because not only have I drank way too fucking much, laughed to the point my sides hurt, but I begin to spill details about myself. Like how I got started dancing—as a small child in all the many pageants my mother entered me into. Where I'm originally from—Georgia. And that I have only been back once since I was a teen, which tells them a whole fucking lot about my early life.

Somewhere in the middle of it all, I have a moment where I take stock of the people, the feeling of kinship, and the fact that I have a genuine smile on my face. At some point, I dropped the act without even realizing it. I've been participating in the conversations around me with natural enjoyment and interest in their lives. I stopped playing a role and have completely stepped out of character. Sure, my head plays tennis as I watch these people bicker and joke around, which eventually makes me a little dizzy, but I also kind of love it.

Like a stamp on that statement, Bethany grabs the nozzle connected to the soda and aims it at her husband. "Keep tellin' the bar about our sex life and you'll be wet the rest of the night, and not in a good way."

He holds up his hands and walks away to help more customers while smiling like a fiend.

A throat clears behind me. I nearly slip from my stool when I look back to see a whole lot of muscle packed into a tight navy shirt.

Looking up, I read the rank patch on his cut and then peer into light blue-gray eyes, which are so sharp they could cut glass.

He's not looking at me, though. He's looking straight ahead.

Bethany turns back to us. Her face pales, and she slowly lowers the nozzle from view.

Dozer clears his throat. "Didn't mean to interrupt."

Bethany visibly swallows, and she grabs a hand towel on the counter. Her fingers clench around it. "What can I get you?"

"Another round of beers for everyone."

"Sure."

An uncomfortable silence settles around our little group as Bethany walks away to grab the beers and pop the tops off. It sticks for a few long seconds after she hands them off to Dozer, and he leaves. Hodge watches the interaction. A scowl quickly replaces his joyful expression. His gaze swings from his wife to his HOC brother and back again. Bethany shakes her head and grants us a fake smile.

"What just happened?" Because you know, my filter has vanished at this point.

There's complete silence until Raven muffles a cough and says, "Bulldozed."

"Yep, pretty much," is Bethany's reply.

The jovial mood sobers, but there's still plenty of good conversation, and I learn a little about the people I'll be spending the next few months of my life getting to know better.

FINN

I'm half-perched on my stool, waiting for Dozer to take his shot, when I spy the last woman I expected to see tonight sitting at the bar. The sight stirs my blood, and has my thoughts spill out of my mouth. "What's she doing here?"

"Who?" Bodie asks, and his gaze follows mine when I lift my chin toward the bar.

Meanwhile, I'm eyeing Lily's ass in those jeans, and the tattooed wings covering her back, revealed by her top. She's sitting next to Raven, and the two are chatting up Bethany.

It suddenly makes sense why the men around this side of the room started migrating one by one toward the bar, because Bethany, Raven, and Lily together make quite a sight, like damn Charlie's Angels.

"God almighty! Would you look at that!" Bodie jumps off his chair. "I need another drink. You comin'?"

I give him an annoyed stare. He shrugs it off and makes his way through the bar. Halfway to his goal, he's waylaid by a busty brunette. He doesn't miss a beat and pulls her into him. As if he knows we're watching, he turns to us, and smiles cockily. When he eventually breaks away, he hollers, "Wish me luck!"

"With any other group of women, he'd be golden. But those three…" Cap, our president, shakes his head. "Got a twenty that says they'll eat him alive."

"I'll bet you a hundi that he doesn't walk away alone," says Kendra, Septic's loca little old lady. She's sitting on my other side, and has been watching her old man kick all of our asses at pool the entire night.

Catching on to her words, everyone in our group cranes their necks to watch the spectacle play out.

Taz is leaning against the wall and flipping a knife end over end. He chuckles darkly under his breath. "That brunette is who he'll be beddin' tonight. She's easy. He may look for a challenge, but he'll settle for what he can have with the least amount of effort."

Griz eyes Taz skeptically for a moment and then nods in agreement. "True that."

"Shit," Kendra grumbles, and begins to play with her lip ring as she watches the group at the bar. "Now that I think about it… you might be right, Taz."

"Always am," he deadpans.

"So what you're sayin' is, you've got nothin' better to do than analyze Bodie's love life. Just say the word, man, and if the tattoo

shop's that slow, we can all come get some new ink to keep you busy."
Dozer throws this out and shakes his head at Taz.

Taz catches his knife, sharp end in his hand. He squeezes his fist.
His face shows nothing. He merely stares at Dozer. And their running
rivalry continues. We thought it would die down with time, but it
doesn't look like that's happening anytime soon.

Septic arrives at the table and steps up to his wife. She wraps her
arms around his neck before planting a peck on his lips when he leans
in for a kiss.

Cap, our president, knocks his knuckles on the table. He delivers a
harsh look to his son before giving the same to Taz, but it's not until
Mav, who's lurking in the corner, says, "Knock it off, T," that Taz lets
it go. The two seem to somehow understand each other. Or maybe
it's that Taz is the only one who can stand to put up with Mav's mood
swings and vice versa.

Mav watches us all with disinterest as he lights up another smoke,
not giving a fuck if he's supposed to smoke indoors or not. Then he
upends his beer bottle and finishes it. It dangles between his fingers as
he takes a long pull on his cigarette.

"Oh shit! Did you see that?" Kendra goes up on her tippytoes. She
moves her head around to peer through the crowd. "Raven just laid
one on that chick sitting next to her. What's her name... that new girl
you hired?" She looks over at me with wonder and excitement.

"Lily?"

"Yeah."

"Laid one on her?" Looking over, I have to wait for a few people to
move out of the way before Lily comes back into view.

"Yep, on the lips. Did you know she swung that way?" she asks me
as she retakes her seat.

I think of the way Lily reacted to my touch and the small glances
we've shared. The way she plays people like fiddles and can read a
room within minutes and adjust to fit in. That's all it takes to reject
any notion that she's interested in Raven. Plus, Raven isn't one to
fuck around on her partner. Her goal above anything would be to get
Bodie to back off. She'd kiss anyone to make that happen. Lily, or a

frog. Wouldn't matter as long as it got the brother to leave her the hell alone for the night.

"I don't go around asking my employees who they like to fuck."

My declaration pretty much shuts down the conversation on that matter, and thankfully, it moves on to Cap and Griz telling stories of the "old days," which has Kendra and the honey on Stone's lap enthralled. That is, until Dozer gets up and makes his way to the bar.

"Maybe he'll have better luck with the new chick," Kendra says.

"He's got more interest in what's behind the bar," Taz mutters.

The balls on this one. I shake my head. The fact he says that shit out loud, his caustic mouth, and the careless way he airs the club's dirty laundry is what puts him at odds with half the club. Not that he gives a rat's ass about any of that, though. He couldn't care less who he pisses off, as long as he has his say.

Changing the subject, Griz asks, "You ready for me, Spice?" Kendra smiles warmly and nods. Septic lets her go after he plants another kiss on her mouth. When they break apart, Kendra jumps up from her chair and latches onto Griz's offered arm.

Swear to fuck, the man has more game than the rest of us combined because he spends most of his Monday nights spinning women around the dance floor.

After I finish my beer, I stand and drop some money on the table. "If the waitress comes by, order another round," I mutter before heading to the men's room.

Stone calls out, "What? You gettin' in on the action?"

"Is it a crime to take a piss?"

He glares up at me from where he sits, but I couldn't give a fuck. There's something about him that rubs me the wrong way. Yes, part of it is the way he puts his hands on Lily and the way he talks to her. But there's something else. His stance on club issues often differs from mine. It's hard to trust a brother whose decisions seem swayed more by money than on what's good for the club long-term.

Truth be told, I want nothing more than to buy Lily a drink and sit in her company. Maybe spend the entire night talking to her and putting my hands on her. But it's a fucking fantasy—something that haunts me daily and no matter how much I want it otherwise. Guess I've made my fucking bed.

I may never know exactly what I'd said that set her off, and that's the part that fucks with me. Because now my only choice is to live with the consequences.

It takes a lot of willpower to look away from Lily once I see her up close. It was just a glimpse of her laughing. That's it.

Her fucking smile, her laugh… and it does shit to me that I have no words for.

Before leaving the men's room, I stare at this version of myself that doesn't feel real.

The mirror doesn't show the truths hidden under the surface, the mess underneath, the missing pieces that make me feel like a fucking spinning compass. Nor does it show the dark thoughts of death when the pain becomes all I see, or these new cravings for things with Lily that I can't voice or give in to.

There's also the madman chasing a ghost, constantly searching for feathers and breadcrumbs, and clinging to the hope that if I can find enough of them, they'll put my world right. When a link ties to Lily in some way, my mind grabs it with both hands, because it's the only way I can cope with my shitty fractured existence, and I start believing something I shouldn't.

That Lily could be Elle.

Fucking crazy, right?

Does anyone else know what that's like? To feel like your mind is the most fucked-up part of who you are? That you can't trust your own thoughts? That what you believe may not be real because your brain has the power to rearrange all the pieces to fit whatever scenario will help you get by for another day?

What I want is her. And doing nothing about it is eating a hole inside of me bigger than the ones already inside my head.

What I see looking back at me is a pretender who acts like he's got his shit together, when in reality, I'm losing my goddamn mind. Camouflaging myself so no one sees how fucked-up things are in my head.

Bodie sees through it. Soon, others will too.

CHAPTER 28

Facing the consequences of our actions, that's the hard part, even when we know we've done the right thing.

When I first see Lily walking toward me after I leave the restroom, I think it's a dream. Surely, I can't be this lucky. But yeah, it's her, and when she spots me, her footsteps falter.

"Oh, hey," she says with a hesitant, nervous expression.

"Hey, yourself." I take a few more steps and move to the right so she can walk right by, only she doesn't.

She strides forward and stops right in front of me. Her head is cocked to the side, her gaze following my hand as I rub it over my chest, which constricts at how fucking beautiful she looks tonight.

Her hair has loose waves, and her makeup isn't performance makeup or overdone. It's still done with an artistic eye to highlight her best features, sure, but more naturally. It lets her beauty stand on its own without the glitter, shimmer, and dramatic coloring she uses on stage.

"You're here. I wasn't sure you would be," she says. "Was kinda hoping you wouldn't be, to be honest." This last part is muttered under her breath.

"Why's that?"

"It's a school night."

I lean my shoulder against the wall, and she does the same. I peer down at her, wondering what in the fuck a school night has to do with anything. Then it dawns on me. Someone probably told her about Mateo, and she's wondering why I'm not home, making sure he's tucked into bed. Little does she know, he doesn't listen to a word I say. Actually, he goes out of his way to do the opposite most of the time. Contrary little shit that he is. If I told him to be home by ten or even to go to bed at a reasonable hour, he'd stay out all night to spite me.

Our relationship is precarious. If I tug too much, he pulls back. Since he's nearly eighteen, there's only so much rope left on my end of the line. Come May, I won't have any say about where he goes and what he does.

"Do you mean because of Mateo?"

She runs her fingers through her hair and then fidgets with the ends. "His name might have been brought up in the dressing room in passing."

Passing, my ass.

"Uh-huh. I'm sure that's not all they said." Sure enough, her mouth purses. "Well, he's fine. He's not about to let me stay home to wipe his ass. Prefers it, actually, if I stay out of his business." I raise an eyebrow. *A lot like how I'd prefer my employees to stay out of mine.*

"Right." She nods a little, opens her mouth to ask something else, but quickly shuts it. She takes a step to the side, as if to walk away. But that frown is like a hook in my chest. I raise my hand and softly wrap it around her waist. I use my hold to turn her towards me.

"Ask me."

Flustered, she blinks up at me. "What?"

"Whatever it was you were gonna ask me, ask me."

She searches my gaze with those gorgeous eyes of hers. The earnest emotion vanishes soon after, like she intentionally shuts it down.

"Ask me," I repeat in a softer, pleading tone. "Please."

"It doesn't matter."

I don't know why—it's unexpected and comes so swiftly I'm not prepared for it—but anger and annoyance slam into me with such force, because yes, it fucking matters. Whatever it was, I can tell it matters a whole hell of a lot to her. She's hiding her feelings, lying straight to my face, and she knows I hate it. If it was anyone else, I'd say fuck off. Have a nice life. I don't need people who can't be real with me in my life. But this isn't anyone. This is Lily.

"Goddamn it, woman. I said fuckin' ask me."

This is one of those moments Dozer mentioned, and this time I'm not going to let it slip through my fingers.

Seeing my resolve, something sparks in her eyes. She comes back just as fierce and tries to push me away. I force her back and brace my arms against the wall beside her head.

"We're not leaving this spot until you do," I growl at her. Her eyes blaze with fury, but I couldn't give a fuck, until she looks away and won't look me directly in the eye. I grab her chin and force her to.

"Open that pretty mouth and ask what's on your mind."

"It's not my business," she says through gritted teeth.

"Make it your business. Come on, you've got me. Right here. Right now. My full attention and my permission, even."

"Fine." It takes a moment for the words to spill from her pretty, petal-pink lips. "Is his mom… what was… what is she to you? You know, with what we've done together, I guess I wanted to know if I took advantage of the situation and put you in a difficult position." It's spit with some venom. The heat in her gaze spreads warmth through my chest.

"You think I'd cheat on my woman if I had one?"

She shrugs. Fucking shrugs.

"What do the words say on my body, Lily? The ones you can see?" I hold my arm out and twist it so she can easily read the words inked there.

Her eyes trail over my biceps and forearms. I can feel it as if it's a physical touch.

"Could mean shit."

Ohhh, ho, ho. This fucking woman. The gravel coating my tone leaves nothing to the imagination. "Not to me. These are the fucking words I live by. That I'll die by." I brush my hand through her hair and push some strands away from her eyes, then cup her cheek. "You'd know more about that if you didn't avoid me every fucking day."

"How long were you with her?" The tone she uses, the clipped words, finally give me some insight. She's jealous. The green monster that has been ever-present inside me since she showed up is right there, shining out of the glare she's leveling on me.

My cock likes this very much.

I lean closer. "We were never together. Not like that."

"Was she some past fling or something—a one-night stand?"

I shake my head. *Wrong again.*

I think of Mateo's mom and feel so much regret for not doing more when I could have. Joey's wife, or widow now, has been through a lot. My best friend's death was hard on her, on them both. He was killed in the line of duty, but I've suspected for a long time that Veno had something to do with it. Joey arrested him all those years ago, and Veno promised he would make him pay.

I have no proof. It's just a gut instinct.

I took over being the father figure in Mateo's life when Joey died, and I've never disputed being his father when people ask. So yeah, I can see how she'd get the wrong idea from the women at the club.

"No. She's a friend's wife." My thumb rubs over her jaw. I'm taken in by the beauty mixed with pain that I see in her irises. She glares up at me as she tries to understand. Even the ridge above her lip leading to her nose is cute—all the small things about her get to me. I swear I could stare at this woman for hours on end and never get enough. Which makes me want to punch myself for not telling her the day I hired her that I'd find her something else, another job, so we could figure out this attraction. "He's not my son, Lily."

Her eyes widen. "What?"

"Exactly what I said."

The warmth of her body seeps into mine. I don't miss how fucking phenomenal it feels to have her warm body and curves pressed against me. "He's not mine. But for all intents and purposes, I'm the father figure in his life. When his dad, Joey, my best friend, died, I stepped up to help his wife and Mateo, his son. When she met her new man, and

Mateo and the guy weren't getting along, he moved in as a temporary fix. He needed a place to stay, and I had the room." I shrug. "I owed it to his dad to step up, because he did the same for me many times over when I needed it the most."

She studies my face. "You're serious?"

"Yeah, Joey was a cop. He died in the line of duty. Mateo's been pretty messed up since. It got worse when his mom met this guy. Things kind of blew up."

"Do you do that often?"

Not understanding, I furrow my brow.

"Help desperate souls? People in distress?" she asks.

"I wouldn't necessarily call it that," I say a bit harshly, because if she only knew the stories of the people I've helped, she wouldn't add insult to injury by talking about them like this. They're more than victims and definitely not to blame for the shitty cards life dealt them.

"I didn't mean for it to sound judgmental or callous."

"Good, because the people I help matter to me…" I shake my head. "They're so much more than what's been done to them or their circumstances."

Some of the best moments of my life have been when I've made a difference in someone else's life. At the end of the day, it's why I made it through the shit I have. This is what gives my existence meaning and has me pressing forward beyond trying to find the ghost of my past.

She furrows her brow as she stares up at me. "You really care about them?" I open my mouth, but she hurries to say. "That came out wrong. I mean, this means a lot to you, doesn't it?"

"Yeah, it does."

She searches my face. "Will you tell me why?"

She may not realize it, but her hand that was once pushing me away is now resting on my chest over my heart. It's a point of comfort that I cling to as I tell her something I've never really shared with anyone.

"Rivers and I and one other guy, Lars, are the only ones who survived that roadside bomb. I barely made it. For whatever reason, I was given more time. I want that to mean something. Maybe that's because I can't do my part with the army anymore, or because I want to make the most of the time I have, tally up points for the man upstairs. Either way, I just can't stand by and not help people who need it most, or protect those who can't protect themselves."

"That…"

"What?"

"Reminds me of someone."

Her expression has softened. Her sultry scent surrounds me, and it's intoxicating. I breathe it in as my gaze travels over her face.

Her hand begins to roam up, and without warning, it curls around my neck. A shiver of sensation rushes down my spine.

I'm all too aware of the distance from her mouth to mine. It seems like nothing. Infinitesimal. Like bridging that space and connecting my mouth to hers could be so simple.

I ask the only thing on my mind. "If I kissed you, would you welcome it? Or are you gonna keep running and giving every excuse in the book for not giving in to this thing going on between us?"

"I'm not running or mak—"

"Yeah, you are."

"Is that what you think?"

"Yeah, it is. The why of it is what I don't know."

She huffs.

"Am I wrong?"

She says nothing, and that right there is my answer, isn't it?

"If you don't want me, or don't want me to kiss you, please tell me and walk the fuck away. Right now. Walk and know that I won't chase you down. I won't try anything again. I let this lie, and we can go on being nothing to each other."

I rub her cheekbone again and lean so I can say these next words against the shell of her ear. "If you want me, tell me, woman. Just say it. Say yes." Arousal floods my body when her head kicks back and her body relaxes. Swear to God, a whimper escapes her lips.

I pull back and look at her. "You're so fired up over the possibility I could have been with someone else, but you also keep treating this like it's nothing. It ain't nothing to me. So, which is it? Either walk away, or give us a chance, because God's honest truth, Lil', I can't keep doin' this back and forth with you. It's drivin' me fuckin' crazy."

She bites her bottom lip. Her other hand is now on my waist, under my cut. The hold she has on me is strong. But so is whatever hold she has over her emotions.

"Walk or say yes."

Then finally, thank fuck, her grip tightens on me and she pulls me forward. A breath away I pause for only a moment to prepare my heart to give in and fall fully, because yes, this is fucking happening. Our mouths connect and my body lights right the fuck up. It's slow. Slow and filled with meaning, and tenderness. A brushing of lips. Breathes shared. Soft licks. Tongues that dance in concert. A groan from me that has her deepening the kiss and grasping me tighter.

She makes a husky noise in the back of her throat. The sound sends a shock wave through every part of me. Her fingers thread into my hair, and she grabs a handful. I do the same and devour her just as fiercely. I let my desperation leak through, and she responds in kind.

Pressing forward with my hips, I grind my body into hers. Her thighs part, and she welcomes me in, wastes no time, and begins to rock against me.

When she sucks on my bottom lip, the action goes straight to my dick.

I pick her up and wrap her legs around my waist. Her curves under my hands feel like heaven. She tilts her head up and sucks in a quick breath. I take full advantage, placing harsh kisses along her jaw and neck. I savor her scent and the taste of her skin, wanting nothing more than to take as much of her in as I can, and at the same time leave my mark behind.

The ferocity of my need for this woman rivals anything I've ever known.

The heady and smoky way she gasps my name is music to my fucking ears. "Christ, I missed the way you kiss. Missed this," she mumbles.

"What?"

"No-nothing. Shut up and keep kissing me."

I do just that, and palm her breast as we both get worked up into a frenzy. She places her hand over mine and squeezes, so I give it to her harder. Do I despise the layers of fabric separating us? Yes, I curse their existence. If I could wish them away, I would in a heartbeat.

Fucking her in all the ways I've dreamed about is at the forefront of my mind.

The sounds she makes… the inhales, exhales, breathy pleas, gasps, and pants… they undo me. They egg me on and tell me everything I've been dying to know. That she aches for me just as much as I ache for her.

She may try to deny it later, but there's no denying this. Her body language says it all.

"If I fucked you, Lil', would you call out my fucking name? Let me hear it in full volume as you lost your mind for me?"

"Jesus!"

"Yeah, you would. Wouldn't you? What else, Lil'? Would you tell me all of those little fantasies locked inside that gorgeous mind of yours? And give me a chance to play them out with you?"

Shouts are what break us apart. A flood of people run into the hallway. Lily slaps my cut until I set her down. Panic covers the faces of the people running toward us.

Someone shouts, "They have guns!"

I point at Lily and snap, "Stay here!" But I quickly change my mind and drag her by the arm to the back door. After pushing it open, I funnel people out. Lily stays by my side. Grabbing her harshly, I look her dead in the eye and tell her, "I don't know what the fuck's happening, but get somewhere safe and stay there. I'll find you." I push her in the direction of the door.

She stands there holding on to the door for a moment and tries to resist. "No, I'm not—"

"Go, Lil'. I'll be fine. I promise." I don't back down. The concern filling her features means everything to me. But neither of us has time to indulge in these feelings.

The fear doesn't leave her eyes, but her hand drops from the door, and it closes with her on the other side of it.

A rush of relief floods over me at knowing she's safe. Spinning around, I yell for the rest of the people coming down the hall to get out using the back door. Then I quickly stride toward where the chaos and shouts are coming from.

What I find waiting for me in the bar stops me cold. The Thirteen Devils, firearms in hand, with barrels pointed at my brothers. One motherfucker has his aimed at Hodge's face. Hodge isn't empty-handed. He has a shotgun leveled at him from behind the bar.

Rage has my blood pounding in my ears. *Veno.*

Somewhere in the back of my mind, I know this isn't my house. But it's as if these fuckers are doing exactly that, busting into my fucking home, invading something sacred that triggers all my protective instincts, and firing the first shot in an act of war. By the look on my brothers' faces, they feel the same, and they're ready for shit to go down here and now.

Some of the smarter people, the ones not involved, flee.

Veno is at the bar, shots lined up in front of him. He's wearing a royal blue plaid shirt and dark jeans with white sneakers. Teardrop tattoos trail down the side of his face. He's eyeing Bethany as he throws back a shot. The Devil behind the bar has his golden Glock at Bethany's temple, and she's visibly shaking.

Veno throws back two more shots in quick succession, gives a haughty laugh, and wipes his mouth with the back of his hand.

"What, ese? You gringos don't know how to show a little fuckin' hospitality?" he says, spreading his arms. "Figured if I came down in person to deliver this warning, you'd at least pretend to be happy to see me." He lets out a low laugh, all teeth and no warmth. "No?" He shrugs and scans the room in a slow once-over.

When he sees me, he stops cold. His grin flatlines.

His happy mask slips. His smugness is replaced by a sharper, cold calculation.

Not a second later, his gaze cuts past me to the right, and his expression shifts again. One brow arches, and he mutters under his breath, "La puta madre…"

I turn. My fucking heart shoots up into my throat. Lily's standing just off to my side, stone still, eyes locked on Veno.

Fuck.

Her eyes lift to mine.

I expect to see fear, guilt, maybe even regret.

But what I get instead is pure fire—fierce determination written across every inch of her face.

"I told you to get out."

"I know. I couldn't walk away."

Veno says, "Well, look who it is… bienvenida a casa, ángel."

I step in front of Lily and push her behind me, while cutting Veno off with a snarl, "What the fuck do you think you're doin' here?"

Cap's already front and center, Dozer flanking his right, Griz on the left. My brothers form a wall in front of the civvies behind them. Taz is all twitchy violence—knife in one hand, pistol in the other—taunting the devil he's staring down. Mav's got a gun barrel pressed into his forehead, and he's still glaring like he's daring the fucker to pull the trigger.

We're not outnumbered, but one wrong move and this will get ugly, because we were un-fucking-prepared. In this tight space, it'll be a bloodbath if someone starts shooting.

Veno reaches behind him and takes a gun from behind his waist, casual but deliberate, and proceeds to wave it in the air like it's punctuation. "Quería dejarlo bien claro, cabrón."

I wanted to make it perfectly clear, asshole.

He lifts his chin. "You fuck with my business, fuck with *me*, I fuck with you and yours."

"If you're gonna—"

Veno glares Cap down. "Not speakin' to you. Speakin' to this motherfucker right here." He raises his gun sideways and levels it on me. "No hay línea que no cruce pa' devolver el favor. Eye for an eye, hijo de tu puta madre." *There's no line I won't cross to return the favor. Eye for an eye, son of a bitch.*

I clock it, the gun. The theatrics. The posturing. The men. Their positions. How many firearms they have, and who Veno brought with him.

This ain't about bullets. It's about the *message*.

"Message delivered. Now get the fuck out."

"Nah, Cabrón."

I stride forward to keep him focused on me. "You gonna shoot, shoot."

The force he brought… the bullshit conversation… it's not a bloodbath he wants. So I call him on it. I know what he wants, but it's not something I'm prepared to back down on. "You gonna shoot. Shoot."

"Goose!" The panic in Lily's tone jacks up my adrenaline. I wave for her to stay behind me. She does. Her fingers wrap around the back of my cut, and her body presses against my back. Whether it's to keep herself on her feet or to keep me close, I don't know, but it brings me some comfort.

Taz echoes my statement. "Don't fuck around and talk about shit. Get the party started, if that's what you came here to do."

Veno's gaze circles the room and then snaps back to me. He jerks his chin toward a group of his Thirteen Devils, and suddenly they're flipping tables and trashing the place like it's routine.

"Like I said. You fuck with what's mine… I fuck with what's yours. Cabrón. That's how this is gonna work from now on, ¿comprendes?"

Grinder and Stone move to stop them. Cap calls them off, shouting, "Let them."

Another Devil moves behind the bar, and using his gun, he sweeps bottles off the shelves and onto the floor.

Hodge tries to intervene, but Bethany grabs hold of him and yanks him back. The fire burning in Hodge's eyes says it all. His body is locked up, and he's ready to unleash hell if given the go-ahead.

Veno leisurely walks around the room. His gaze travels over Raven. "Such pretty little things you have." He reaches out and touches her hair. She jerks back so his hand drops from her. This has him smiling wickedly and he gives another humorless laugh. "At least now I know when another one of my girls goes missing, where to find a replacement."

My muscles jump with the need to act. It's all I can do to stay still.

Then his gaze moves from me over each HOC he passes. He trades a long, loaded look with Cap before finally squaring up in front of me.

"No te creas que me olvidé de ti. Nos veremos pronto…"

Don't think I forgot about you. We'll see each other soon…

"Don't understand a fuckin' word you said. If you're gonna threaten me, better be man enough to say the fuckin' words so I can hear 'um."

He let's loose and unhinged laugh at this, and a cocky smile splits across his face. He raises a gun and presses it to my temple.

"This clear enough for you, motherfucker?" he says, voice low and the words spit out from his gritted teeth. "Touch what's mine again, Cabrón, and I *will* fucking end you."

Lily's grip tightens on the back of my cut. A soft, pained sound— half-whimper, half warning—slips from her.

He spins the gun, and it digs into my skin. Then moves it not so gently down my face.

I feel it before I see Lily move. She lets go of my cut, comes around me, and before I can push her behind me, Veno grabs her and yanks her forward.

He holds the gun under her chin and pushes her face up. His fingers are sinched around her arm so tightly that she cries out.

At the terror in her eyes, I freeze. Blackness clouds my vision. My heart fucking threatens to burst from my chest. Flashbacks from hundreds of dreams stand front and center like street signs in my mind, linking the past with the present.

Only it was Elle he'd been holding and do this exact same fucked up dance with.

My voice drops, as a warm, calm fills me. I punch him in his goddamn throat and disarm him before he can get his bearings. I flip the gun and shove it into his forehead. The men around me use this window of time in the same way. A few rounds pop off. By whom and where, I can't tell.

The only thoughts I have are for the Devil in front of me and the woman I'm pushing to the side so she's free of the fallout.

"Lay one more fuckin' hand on her, on any woman here, and I'll put so many bullets in you they'll be little left for your mama to weep over. And I won't stop comin' until every one of you fuckers are six feet under. I will personally bury every goddamn Devil. I swear it." I'll kill him, and lay waste to his pitiful gang if need be.

A hand plants itself on my shoulder. Bodie stands to my right, cautioning me with a look.

Cap speaks up from the other side of the room. "This is done. Message received. You've had your fun. Now, get the fuck out of our bar. Tell Antonio, he'll be hearin' from me, because as far as I'm concerned, this truce is over. No business dealings until this is sorted."

Veno lifts his chin at me. His jaw muscles twitch. He tries to hide the fear he has of his brother, but these small tells give him away.

Hodge fires his shotgun. Veno's head snaps to the side to see one of his men go down. Slammin' the hand with the gun into Veno's temple is fucking satisfying. It takes two hits for his legs to go out from under him. When he's out cold, he falls like a rock to the floor. Stepping over him, I point the weapon at his forehead and tell the rest of his crew, "He's dead right here and now if you don't drop the guns and get the fuck out."

Most are disarmed by now, but the few remaining pause to consider me.

Cautiously, they begin to raise their hands and drop their guns. Hodge is standing behind the bar and has his shotgun aimed down. Whoever the fuck he shot is hollering and groaning in pain.

He growls, "This is what happens when you lay your hands on another man's woman."

Cap's voice cuts through the room, sharp as a blade. He gestures toward Veno and barks at the closest Devil, "Get this piece of shit outta here. You got ten seconds or none of y'all are walkin' out."

Veno moans as his men haul him up. His eyes snap open, and that lethal glare on his bloodied face promises retribution. He spits more Spanish at me, fast and low, but I'm done with him. I turn and scan the bar, assessing the damage.

A few of the Thirteen Devils are dragging out their injured, stumbling and bleeding, while the rest clear a path.

At the door, Veno stops. His eyes land on me, hold for a beat, then flick to Lily beside me. He fucking smiles again, showing a mouth full of bloody teeth.

"Like I said. Such pretty things you have. Best keep an eye on 'em… or you might just wake up one day and find them gone. You know how it is—girls just up and vanishin' lately."

The fear that hits me is a tidal wave; it crashes in with such force that my knees weaken.

He laughs again. "And I'll make sure your guy, the one you all are payin' us to keep nice and cozy, has got some good friends keepin' him company. He's so pretty, it shouldn't be hard to do."

Dread settles over the room, thick enough to choke on. It wraps around us all as we start putting the bar back together, piece by broken piece.

I keep Lily close the rest of the night, closer than a shadow. My eyes track her every move. She's calm on the surface, but I know her. She's shaken. She's trying to hold it together for everyone else.

When it's over, I offer to drive her home. Hell, I *beg* her to come back to mine with me—to the clubhouse, anywhere but alone. I don't care if it makes me look weak. I'm past pride. I just need her safe.

Tonight wasn't a fucking wake-up call. I didn't realize the danger being with me could put her in.

Lily's stubborn. She says she can handle herself, that she needs to sleep in her own bed, and she's dealt with guys like Veno before. She won't let his threats make her run in fear. She tells me she has a gun and knows how to protect herself.

When I still won't let it go, she gets angry. She tells me that if anything, being with me puts her in more danger.

That shock of her words and the truth of that statement is what has me backing off.

Because, yeah—she's right and tonight wasn't a fucking reality check. Anyone close to me will be on Veno's radar.

I try to follow her home by hanging back a few cars. But she drives like she's trying to lose me. Maybe she is. I push my bike harder, but she takes some wildass turns and disappears into the night. Gone. I punch the gas and search for a while, but she's nowhere to be found.

Thankfully, she sends a text when she makes it home, telling me she's home and safe.

But even after that, I spend the rest of the night wide awake, pacing my room and raking my hands through my hair, thinking of all the ways Veno could get revenge on me by hurting her.

Just because she's okay now doesn't mean she will be tomorrow. Or the day after that.

Because being close to me?

It painted a big, red target on her back.

And there's nothing I can do to change that now, no matter how much I want to.

CHAPTER 29

*We're often our own dealer in the hands of fate,
playing with half the deck.*

A hand moves down my abs. The movement wakes me and has
my cock perking up as well.

"You gonna grab that?" A husky, feminine voice asks, and
the body partially above mine shifts.

Groggy from the drugs and alcohol still swimming in my system,
her words don't register, but when I peer down through sleep-crusted
eyes, my heart soars at the sight of her dark hair. The curves of her
body are visible beneath the thin white sheet, and seeing them has me
wanting more than just a feast for my eyes.

Reaching down, I find her hand and guide her palm up and down
my cock. She chuckles and gives in, closes her fist around me, and
begins to pump my dick.

"Strócáil mé mar sin féin," I groan out as pleasure rockets through
me.

Stroke me just like that.

Fuck yeah, I'm on board with starting this day off right. I run my
hand down her back and lean up a little to discard the sheet and grab
her thigh, drawing it closer.

It's not until my eyes catch on the tattoo there that I realize it's not
Lily. Where unmarked skin should be, a massive panther tattoo sits.

Kat.

Shit.

But then again, it makes sense.

Seeing as the woman I thought it was is where I sent her—two states away, giving her attention to another club, to another man. A man I've longed wished had stayed dead.

"You ready for me, baby?" Kat moans and begins to descend, placing lingering kisses on my abs as she moves down my body.

I notice the contrasts the most when she looks up to give me a sleepy smile. Smoky makeup she didn't wash off before bed like Lily does, brown eyes not blue, and a black lace tattoo above her fake tits, where Lily is naturally blessed. Kat's still damn beautiful, but there's a hardness to her. She's jaded and dark, where Lily is light and full of a soulfulness you just can't replicate.

However, when Kat tongues my slit, and sweeps said tongue over every inch of my cock, all thoughts of Lily vacate my mind. Kat may not be the one I want, but until my girl comes back to me, she'll do just fine.

Then I hear it, and go still. A vibration that has the hairs on my neck prickling. Popping up on my elbow, I look over. *Fuck*, my phone. It's lit up and dancing on the end table. I have no fucking idea why it's on silent and not ringing. When I spy the name on the screen, I immediately move to snatch it up.

Kat cries out in protest because I've all but yanked my cock from her mouth to sit up on the side of the bed.

The fact that it's just past 8:00 a.m. and she's calling zaps me fully awake as my mind whirls with all the ways shit could've gone south.

After answering, I lift the phone to my ear. "I'm here. What's wrong?"

Silence. Fucking silence.

I throw my arm out trying to cut off the bitching going off behind me, because fuck Kat right now and her jealous-crazy-girl bullshit. My actions only escalate the situation, though, because the bitch starts fucking slapping me. I hold the phone away and shout, "Knock that the fuck off."

"It's her, isn't it?"

I stand and point towards the door. "Shut the fuck up or get out!"

Then I march into the bathroom and slam the door closed behind me.

Breathing hard, I plant my hand on the door and lower my voice to a whisper. "Gypsy, talk to me."

"Where were you?"

"I'm here." I squeeze my eyes closed.

"You weren't, though, and that's the point. You said you would be, but you weren't."

Fuck. I punch the door. "I'm sorry. Won't happen again." The truth of that vow bleeds through my tone.

"What if I was in trouble?"

I'd burn the fucking world down to get to you. "My fucking phone. I think Kat fucked with it—put it on silent."

"You said you'd have my back if I did this."

My chest pinches with pain at her words. "And I fucking do. You know that. Look, I'll sleep with it in my hand if I have to." When she doesn't immediately respond, I press my knuckles into the wood and grind them against the solid surface until pain spreads through my arm. "Goddamnit, Gypsy. I fucked her. That's it. I didn't realize she jacked with my phone. Don't question shit just because I made one fuck up."

Fucking nothing. Dead goddamn air.

"Please, talk to me."

"I don't think we have as much time as we thought."

Stepping back, I grasp my neck and squeeze. "What? Why do you say that?"

She exhales a long breath. The sound of it sends fucking shivers over my skin. "Because the truce with the Thirteen Devils is over. Finn—Goose... he's done something. There was talk of girls going missing. He's been helping girls get away from Veno and Veno knows. Shit blew up in a big way last night."

"What?"

"Nothing. That's not the important part. The point is that things between the HOCs and the 13Ds are falling apart sooner than we thought. So you should be ready for that. Goose and Veno Chavez are ready to kill each other."

"So, nothing's changed."

She chuckles darkly. "Nope."

A sharp bang hits the door from the other side. I clench my fist and pound back three times. A tirade of curses fly as Kat screams at me. Lily is silent on the other end of the line as if she's listening to every word.

Lily grumbles, "For either of us, apparently."

I give a humorless laugh. "Touché."

When Kat doesn't let up, I contemplate opening the door so I can take her by the arm and kick her the fuck out of my bedroom, but burning that bridge will leave me stuck with the loose pussy around the club until I can work my way back into her good graces. I need her to get my mind off Lily until she comes home. Kat fills the void better than anyone else. So, I'll put up with her being a bitch until I don't have to anymore.

"Something else you should know," she says. "This puts Edge at risk, too. That truce—even if it was duct tape on a bullet hole—was keeping him alive inside. You got someone you trust enough to send in with him? 'Cause if you don't, he's not gonna last long."

I don't answer right away—not because I'm debating whether to help my old friend. I am. I will. But the logistics… they're a bitch. I'd need someone I trust, someone willing to get locked in and ride hell with Edge, and then somehow get out clean when the job's done. Legally, preferably. But I've never been picky.

"I'll figure it out," I say finally. "Might take some time. But I'll make it happen."

Lily starts talking about her night at Hodge's. Her voice is in my ear, soft and steady, but I'm not hearing the words. Not really. Not over the fucking *cinema of carnage* running behind my eyes. I see her— dressed like sin, dipped in moonlight, surrounded by men sniffing around her like starving carnivores hunting meat. I'm clenching my jaw so tight my molars might crack. The images filling my mind have hot fury building behind my ribcage.

I see dead men. Not metaphorically—*literally*. I'm standing over them, blade slick, breath heaving from the effort it took to carve them up. I don't fantasize about it. I *plan* it. I trace pressure points in my mind like a sculptor running hands over marble, picture the way flesh splits when metal kisses it. I think about the gasping. The twitching. The last, panicked breath.

I've been court-ordered through a circus of headshrinks—quacks in cheap suits who scribble notes like they've got me pegged. They love their labels. Impulse control issues. Anger management. Antisocial Personality Disorder with borderline sociopathic tendencies.

Cute.

They only know the shit I got caught for. Not the stuff I *got away with*.

What they don't get is—I *do* manage it. Every fucking day. I leash it. Choke it down. Keep it coiled like a rattler under my skin. But when I *do* let it out? I make sure it's on people who have no damn right to breathe in the first place.

A few minutes into the call, I hear my bedroom door creak open. I step out of the bathroom and spot Kat, fully dressed and fuming, standing at the threshold between my room and the hallway. She's carrying a bag, a few of her things. This isn't just her giving me space. This is her saying goodbye. *Again.*

I lift a finger and mouth the word, "Wait."

She flips me the bird, then slams the door on her way out.

Son of a fucking bitch.

I grip the doorframe and slam my forehead against the wood. Once. Twice. Three times. Why is it the second one fucking thing goes right, the rest of my life decides to fall apart?

Lily's still talking, her voice a lifeline and a torment all at once. I collapse onto the edge of my bed, light up a smoke, and try to breathe the rage back into its cage. But when she gets to the part about the Thirteen Devils—guns drawn, Veno calling her *Angel* like he's branding her with it, and threatening to see her again, all while Goose stands beside her—I fist a hand in my hair and *yank* until my scalp burns.

It feels like someone buried a ten-inch serrated blade in my gut, and with every word she says, it twists deeper.

I knew she was walking into a shitstorm. I knew Veno would rear his head eventually. But I thought I'd be there when he did. Or when she finishes the jobs with the HOCs and finally delivers the payback he's had coming.

Sending her there... it's all in the name of saving my club and giving her the justice and closure she was owed. She's more capable than anyone I know. She knows the life, the area, and can blend in like a chameleon for whatever job is required of her. She can slip through cracks most men don't even see.

But it's killing me every day knowing I could lose her to *him*, to Goose. Her bird man.

Now, not only is he stirring up shit with the 13Ds and speeding up the timeline of events, he's putting a bright-red bullseye on her—making her presence known to the scum who branded her, ran her like a mule, tried to crush her before she even turned eighteen. They could come for her now before she's ready. Before she gets to *end* it on her terms.

She should have a chance to face down Veno and put him to ground for what he did to her, but I hoped to be by her side when that day came.

I need her more than her bird man does. I need the peace she brings to my mind. I'd be dead without her, either from pulling the trigger myself, or because I'd gone off the rails.

Without her, I know what kind of man I'll become. *My father.* The seed is there, planted and watered with three decades of his fucked-up gospel of truth. Mayhem. Green. Power. That's his holy trinity. Everything he does in life is to achieve those three things, and he expects me to carry those values forward—to take the patch, and turn the tables on the cartel after he's opened the door wide for them to lay waste to our MC. The fucking pressure he puts on me mounts daily—to be worthy of taking his patch and walking in his footsteps.

Without Lily holding that spiritual window of happiness that she shines into my life open and reminding me of what matters, I'll lose sight of what's important. I know I will. Reality already feels half out of my grasp as it is.

Yes, I'm playing fucking roulette with my heart, my life, and many others, and betting on green. But I've run out of options. My father's running this club into the ground, and the war we're facing—it has the potential to erase our MC from the fucking map. The HOCs are a big part of that, whether they know it or not. Every chapter and club we're tied to is. And I need to know who I can count on to stand with us when the pieces on the board start making their strategic moves.

If her bird man keeps sticking his nose where it doesn't belong and stirring up shit with the Thirteen Devils, the war will come to a head sooner rather than later.

Which fucks with my entire plan and throws everything into chaos.

In a different way, it works in my favor. Because if my girl seeks anything in this life, it's a path with solid ground. Goose's future, more than ever now, leads to an early grave. Mine, with her by my side, leads to a kingdom. One, we could rule together.

One day, maybe sooner than intended, my Gypsy Girl will weigh the risks and finally fucking see what she has right here waiting for her. Not only am I more capable of providing for and protecting her, but I have years ahead of me. He doesn't.

She just has to face her demons first. Then she'll make her choice and fly back where she belongs.

Good things come to those who wait, right?

Lucky for me, I'm a patient motherfucker.

CHAPTER 30

There's no negotiating with the Devil. He's never satisfied.

The atmosphere is tense as we prepare to leave the clubhouse. No one talks, but the silence is far from peaceful. There's the *click, click, click* of bullets being loaded, plus the clang of metal hitting metal as magazines slide into place and our heavy artillery is piled into duffles we're taking with us. My brothers and I have done this enough; it's like clockwork.

Bodie's standing across from me, shirtless. He reaches forward and grabs a Kevlar vest from the pile on the pool table and straps it on, before yanking his tee on over the top. He's one of the last to don one.

They're a precautionary measure—in case this meeting is a trap, and the weight of that possibility sits heavy in the room. It's the reason for the silence. We're mentally preparing ourselves for whatever's waiting for us in the desert.

Maybe it'll go smoothly, like Cap hopes. Maybe it won't.

Either way, whatever outcome we face is on me. That truth gnaws like sharp teeth at my conscience. Cause and effect. Saving these girls has repercussions. This is it. It's a fact, and it's fucking with my head, because how can it be the right thing if I'm just trading a life for a life?

If I lose a brother today because I save Larissa, is it worth it?

I don't have the answer.

All I have is the unease sitting like a dead weight in my gut and the mother of all migraines pulsing in a constant beat behind my eyes.

This is what has me digging through my supply of pills before we leave and popping one. I need to be able to see straight and have a clear mind going into this. The pain and guilt make it damn near impossible to do so, and I won't be the weak fucking link today if the 13Ds come to the meeting with ill intentions.

When we exit the clubhouse, I immediately put on my shades to block out the bright-orange ball sitting high in the sky, casting long shadows across the cracked lot. Heat radiates off the asphalt, penetrating through the soles of my boots. The dry, arid scent of earth on the breeze is of little comfort.

I latch my gear to my bike first. After pulling on my gloves, I roll my shoulders and try to relieve some of the tension in my upper back. It's caused by bracing against the pain and has only gotten worse as the day progressed.

Before I can straddle my ride, Cap comes over. His large hand grips my shoulder. He squeezes once.

"You good?"

Cap's always been like that—able to read people like they're an open third-grade textbook. He's a mountain of a man, with lines carved into his face from years of sporting wide smiles and deep frowns. Guess it comes part and parcel with leading an MC and a bunch of misfits who, at times, don't act like fucking grown-ups.

The pain is hard to hide, but with him, there's little need to. He knows. The concern covering his features says as much.

I shake my head once. "Would you be?"

"Nothin' to it." Cap's tone is steady, grounding, the kind of voice that could talk a man off a ledge. "We knew this was comin'. Was fully aware of what you were doing, and you had my blessing. Just because we have blowback doesn't mean you gotta let that rest on your shoulders alone. Anything worth doin' comes with consequences, right?"

I let his words sink in, but the guilt doesn't release its hold on me. I still hear the news about Edge, still imagine him in the prison infirmary, stabbed and beaten half to death.

I didn't stab the knife or dish out the beating, but I might as well have.

Cap pats the Road Captain patch on my cut and nods once. "This means you look out for others. Doesn't mean just for the club."

I nod and the tight band constricting my chest relaxes a little at his words.

"But Edge, man. Fuck."

"We're gonna get Edge the help he needs on the inside. We'll make it right in the end, yeah?"

"Yeah," I murmur. It's a promise, and one I plan to keep.

Cap makes his way to his bike. He thumps Dozer on the back of the head as he passes. Dozer grumbles and tries to swipe at his old man, but Cap evades him. The usual banter between the guys feels forced today, like we're all just trying to keep the nerves at bay.

Bodie catches my eye. He lifts his chin in acknowledgement. I do the same. My gaze travels over the group assembled. I take a mental picture of this moment and store it away before throwing my leg over my bike and turning the ignition.

The familiar rumble that used to be a balm to my soul has my head pounding, but I fight through it as I yank my neck gaiter up to cover the lower half of my face. It's black and white, faded, half stars and stripes, half skeleton with sharp canines on the top. I strap on my helmet and then gun the throttle a few times before pulling up behind Cap and Dozer, ready to lead the way for the others.

We jump onto Highway 85 and head south. It's a long, empty stretch of road. No signs of life except the occasional car and a few tumbleweeds blowing across the asphalt. The horizon is a wavering line, distorted by heat, and in the distance are red jagged plains.

The sun burns hotter as we go. I sweat like mad under the layers, and the Kevlar makes it ten times worse. It's the kind of heat that feels insufficient to your lungs, leaves you with cracked lips, and makes you desperate for a tall glass of water.

The landscape changes as we take a narrow one-lane road toward our destination. The ground beneath us turns rougher, more uneven, cracked from years of neglect. The air is thick with dust, like a suffocating blanket, and I can feel the grit collecting on my skin and coating my mouth despite the neck gaiter.

When we finally reach the wide, open stretch of desert, there's nothing except endless sun-scorched earth. Which is a blessing and a curse—few places to hide if things go south, but few places for our enemies to run as well.

I stay on high alert, scanning the area for any sign of movement. Every shadow feels like a threat, every ripple in the heat a warning. The closer we get to the meet-up point, the tighter my chest feels, the sense of wrongness coiling.

We have one goal in this meetup, and that's to put the truce back in place long enough to get Edge out. Making temporary peace is not what we want to do, but it's the only way we can buy the time we need to make that happen.

Antonio and his people arrive ten minutes late. Their rides consist of two trucks, and two souped-up SUV's. They gleam with fancy paint jobs and chrome rims that catch in the sunlight.

I clock fifteen 13Ds, including two that stay in the SUV. There's a vast difference between Antonio's men and Veno's, mainly in dress and posture. Antonio's are dressed in designer labels, nice button shirts, and slacks, where Veno's are in T-shirts, plaid, jeans, and one big motherfucker has no shirt at all. He's covered in dark tattoos. They cover his chest, face, and bald head. It's not the sight of him that has us moving with caution as we get closer; it's the amount of hardware the 13Ds are flaunting, ARs and handguns.

I analyze everything I can through the fog of dulled pain. Their stances, where their trigger fingers are, how they hold the weapons, and where each man stands. I need to know who the primary threats are going to be if bullets start flying.

Antonio is standing cool and collected in front of a midnight

Escalade, radiating arrogance, chin lifted, like he already knows how this is going to play out. He exudes wealth and power—navy suit, crisp white shirt, a few pieces of gold jewelry, and shiny shoes. Visible tattoos everywhere except for the left side of his face.

Taz, always the loose cannon, is the first to break the silence. "What? No welcome wagon and hellos?" he says, his voice dripping with sarcasm. He's grinning like a madman, like he's hoping shit goes sideways.

"Lock it up, T," Mav growls.

Taz just laughs, that manic sound that lets everyone know exactly where his head's at. "Just saying… these fuckers don't quite look ready to kiss and make up."

Dozer is shaking his head. "This already looks like it's gonna go to hell in a handbasket, no need to send it downriver."

Cap throws Taz a look that could cut steel as he swings off his bike. "Don't start something I'll have to finish."

Using the gun in his hand, Taz salutes him with it like an asshole, a grin still firmly in place.

Cap turns to Antonio, his voice low and calm. "Thought this was to be a peaceful meetup to discuss new terms."

Cap follows Veno's glare to me, and our gazes connect. I nod at him because I know he's got to do or say whatever he needs to make peace.

I have no problem towing the line today, but the way Veno is eyeing me gives me the impression that's the opposite of what he wants. He's wearing a white T-shirt and dark jeans, and a blue bandana is tied around his head. His Glock is currently pointed down and resting next to his thigh.

He may be letting his brother do the talking, but by the looks of it, he has plenty to say.

Dozer moves with Cap as he strolls forward, standing at his right side in case he needs to become his shield. The rest of the HOCs spread out.

Antonio calls out, "Thought it necessary to show you we mean business since from what I'd heard, you're not keepin' up your end of the deal."

Cap huffs. "Neither are you, though, if we're splittin' hairs."

Antonio's mouth pulls into a taunting smile. His dark eyes crinkling at the sides. "Looks like we have things to work out then, boundaries to reset."

Cap's never one for small talk, nods. "That we do."

Antonio chuckles and glances at his men. He says something in Spanish, and whatever it is sparks a round of humor from his men. Stone translates. It's just taunts to rile us up. Septic raises an eyebrow and fires back in rapid Spanish, his words sharp and cutting.

Antonio saunters forward. His men raise their guns. But he motions for them to lower them with a wave of his hand. His gaze lands squarely on me. "You like taking what belongs to us, *cabrón*."

I give Cap a quick glance to see if I should respond. He nods.

"That's not the way I see it."

"No? How do you see it, then? Please enlighten me."

I shrug, because the question is fucking rhetorical. "They're not yours, plain and simple."

Antonio rubs his knuckles. His dark eyes travel over me. His mouth quirks. "Says who? You?"

I don't justify that with a response.

"I don't like people fuckin' with my business. You're takin' what doesn't belong to you, is exactly that. So let me be clear. It happens again, I not only take my anger out on your man on the inside, but I begin to fuck with your people. That clear enough for you?"

I go stone-still so I don't do something stupid and shoot him. He studies my reaction and smiles.

"Do we understand each other?"

Heat creeps up the back of my neck, but I keep my face blank.

For a moment, the desert is deathly quiet. Everyone's tense, hands twitching near their guns, waiting for the first move. It wouldn't take much to set this off.

Cap steps in, voice steady as a rock. "The only reason we're goin' to tow the line on this now is because of our man on the inside. But let *me* be clear. We don't see eye to eye on this. We'll continue to clean your money; you'll pay us for this service. We're payin' you to protect our man. But the minute that stops—if harm comes to him in any way again—that's when this deal between us ends and we reevaluate what we'll allow to be runnin' through our territory and who we do business with."

Antonio's smile returns. "That, right, *cabrón?*"

"Yeah, that's right." Cap turns and reaches to take the large duffle bag from Grinder. He drops it at Antonio's feet.

"For Edge's protection. Plus, enough for your losses to smooth shit over."

The fact that we have to eat shit right now, hollows out my stomach. I want nothing more than to see every one of these motherfuckers in the ground. They don't know it, but their time is coming. For now though, we're going to let them think they have the upper hand.

Because massive carnage would have its drawbacks too. The Feds. Prison. We have to be patient. We have to be smart. We have a plan. This is what keeps me and all of my brothers from slaughtering the 13Ds right here and now.

Antonio waves over two men. One of them lifts the bag and unzips it. He shows Antonio the contents, which Antonio appears pleased by, but there's no fucking knowing with this guy.

Veno continues to stare me the fuck down, and for just a blink of time, I mentally picture how I'd bury this piece of shit. First, I'd pump him full of all the drugs he's so fond of, then I'd let the girls fuck him up to their hearts' content. A slow death would follow. There are so many bones you can break in the human body. Hearing his snap would bring me immense pleasure. I'd draw it out as long as possible until he's begging with his last breath for death.

It would end with his brain matter splattered across the floor and his dead eyes staring back at me. I'd take a picture of it too, because that's a memory I'd never want to part with.

Antonio says, "This'll do for now, but the price goes up from here on out. If you want your boy whole when he gets out, you pay us double."

"That's bullshit," Taz spits. "After you rocked his shit, you expect us to pay double and believe you'll keep your word."

Guns come up as Taz charges at Antonio. Mav grabs hold of Taz at the last minute and wrestles him back as Taz runs his mouth. Dozer jumps in to help. They force Taz back until he's a safe distance away, then talk him down in low, harsh whispers.

It takes a while before everyone settles down. When they do, Antonio calls out to Cap as he walks back towards his SUV, "If you can't keep your dog on a leash, don't bring him next time."

Taz growls and rushes forward. More brothers grab him.

Antonio gives us all one last parting look before he slides on his shades and gets inside the SUV.

Veno walks towards me. Every muscle in my body locks up. I can't react, no matter the shit he'll spew, I have to keep myself under control. He places his face to the left of mine and says under his breath. "This isn't over," his voice drips with menace. "Better keep that Angel of yours close. Wouldn't want her to go *poof* and disappear on you, would you?"

His words chill me to the bone. Then he walks away. Bodie, thank fuck, holds on to my arm, because I've stepped forward to go after him.

As soon as they're out of earshot, Septic spits on the ground, shaking his head. "This is temporary. Remember that."

"Should've shot him," Taz mutters under his breath.

Bodie grins, rubbing his hands together. "Still could."

Dozer cracks his knuckles, eyes still on the horizon where Antonio disappeared. "Cap?"

Cap shakes his head, his voice level but tight. "Another day. We ride this out until it comes to a head. Because this sure as shit isn't over."

I stay silent, my mind racing, trying to understand the meaning of Veno's threat. It nags at me for a long time, and later that night, I dip back into my journals for anything I can find relating to the word or name, Angel. I know there's something, but, at the moment, I can't grasp it. My head's too fucked to think clearly.

LOST LYREBIRD

CHAPTER 31

Grief is a journey we must all eventually walk through. Thankfully, we don't have to walk it alone.

NOVEMBER 2007

I arrive at the cemetery at midday. The sky is overcast with gray clouds, and it is as if the world feels the weight of this loss. I stand with Raven, watching on as Bethany exits the limo. Her hair is pinned in a simple French twist with a few strands having come loose. Her black dress and pumps are modest and simple. The dress itself hugs her tall and lithe figure and comes to rest just under her knees. Her face is red, splotchy, and devoid of makeup, but exquisite even like this, heartbroken, and completely devastated.

Her tears are small rivers that trail down her cheeks and drip like raindrops from her chin. She's clutching a handful of tissues in one hand, but it's as if she's given up using them.

Axel, her teenage son, exits after her and immediately goes to her side. His long blonde hair is in a low ponytail, and he's wearing a slim-fit black suit sans tie. Bethany walks with her arm around his shoulders, the sides of their heads pressed together as they hold onto each other and make their way down the road to the hearse. Bethany's mother follows, an older and shorter version of her daughter. She's carrying Bethany's daughter, Medda, a small blonde child, and the little one is asleep, her head full of curls resting on her grandma's shoulder.

It takes a while for the HOC members and other bikers who followed the hearse procession through the city to arrive and park in a long line down the cemetery street. The roar of what must be over two hundred bikes is like a sorrowful song on blast to the town, letting everyone who hears it know that a man who lived his life with love for the open road has passed on.

Dozer and Goose, as one, pull the black and silver casket from inside the hearse. Cap, Griz, Mav, and Septic step forward to grab on. They hoist it until it rests on their shoulders. Bodie keeps a white-gloved hand on the back and follows them as they carry the casket to the gravesite.

Goose's face is stoic. His hair is loose and hangs a bit over his eyes, which are red-rimmed and puffy. Dozer, who is unable to wipe his tears, grinds his jaw as if to fight against his inner turmoil. Cap's face holds more anger. His gray-blue eyes blaze with it. The others fare no better, all caught up in the emotions riding them at losing their HOC brother.

Bethany, Axel, and the rest of the family follow the pallbearers carrying Hodge. The procession is slow and sober. Eventually, Raven and I are able to fall in and join the long line of people attending the funeral. We walk arm in arm.

We take seats opposite the family. Most of the HOCs stand off to the side. The vast number of civilians and bikers surround them and the casket. Many support clubs have also come to pay their respects. Pappy, Smoke, Deeds, and at least another two dozen Greenbacks among them.

It's an emotional ceremony. A pastor delivers Calvin Hodge's last rites. He reads passages from the bible about death and loss, but afterwards it's his words of wisdom that bring as much relief as grief. Sentiments about a cut lifespan, unexpected loss, and finding ways to focus on the life Hodge lived, the happiness his years blessed many with, instead of dwelling in the darkness of why and time lost.

It's unreal that he's gone. Here one day and gone the next. That a senior citizen blasting through a red light could cut his life short in a blink.

Bethany sobs into her son's shoulder. He tries to comfort her as best he can, but he's falling apart as well. It's heartbreaking to witness. When certain moments get to be too much for me, Raven squeezes my hand and vice versa.

What wrecks me the most is seeing Goose pinch his eyes repeatedly to remove his tears. A dam ruptures, and it's as if his tears are contagious because mine flow more freely behind my glasses and spill down my face. I feel his grief somehow, as if it's my own.

I dab and wipe the tears that come, but it's no use. The tissues are drenched and pointless.

I let myself feel it. I let my heart ache for him and everyone here. I let their pain sink in, and for the first time, as I watch them experience this loss, I see them as a family. Not an MC. Not like the Greenbacks. But a close-knit unit of individuals who care deeply and hold the well-being of the club, its members, and their families above that of greed or power or money.

Over the past few months, their actions, their investment in this town, and their care for one another has shown me that *this* is the value to be found in a motorcycle club, in a brotherhood. At the core of what they believe in is each other, meaningful pursuits, and that, united in this, they can prosper. This is what a good MC looks like when a man with a good heart leads it and believes that the club and their families come first.

I think back to the last and only funeral I attended. A memory I haven't thought of for many years.

I was only a child when my father passed, and most of my memories of him are nothing but wisps in the ether. But I remember his smile. What his blue eyes looked like when they lit up. I remember those God-awful corduroy short-shorts he wore with polos, and how he'd chip and putt golf balls on our front lawn, always itching for the next day he could be on the green, his favorite pastime. I remember the joy he took in lawnwork, and how immaculately he kept our lawn and flowerbeds. He actually swore there was a method to his madness, his diagonal mowing that crisscrossed. What it was, I'll never know.

He valued things he didn't have when he was younger, like a beautiful home, large yard, and our vehicles. Everything we had, material things, he treated with the utmost care.

It took me years to understand this wasn't him being materialistic, it was that he was a simple man who loved all life could offer, and he took care of everything he was ever blessed with, because he knew what it was like to go without.

He, too, was taken too soon. And like with Bethany, the loss tore my mother up. She'd been a mess the day of the funeral, and for many months following it. At the time, I had no idea how much losing my father would change her or change my own path in life.

It makes you wonder how any choice at any given moment can lead you down different pathways. How it's a never-ending maze until we can one day find our own rest in death. When and where you stop along the way and what sections you choose to explore further, the people and material things you pick up to take with you, are to be determined by each person, I guess, as they make their choices to go left or right or straight on through in those moments.

It's fucking crazy when you think about it.

Because who would I be if I'd taken a different Greyhound bus to escape my stepfather after my mom's utter denial?

How might it have changed my life?

I sit with this question for a while. I let my mind run wild with the possibilities and what-ifs, until the subconscious little devil in my head scolds me. Because ultimately… It doesn't matter.

I am who I am. Flaws and choices and all.

What choices I make going forward are the only ones that matter.

Bethany curls forward and screams, then sobs. Axel folds over her back and holds her as he does the same. Bethany's mother throws her free right arm around the two and tries to comfort them both. But the ripple effect is felt by everyone witnessing it, and together in this space, there is shared grief for her, them, and the loss we are all experiencing all over again.

Nick, Dozer's mother and Cap's wife, comes forward and offers to take Medda from Bethany's mother so she can hold her daughter. Dozer brushes away a steady flow of tears. Cap stands beside him, his hand on his son's neck. Bodie has his hand on Goose's shoulder as Goose's shoulders shake.

It's not a loss or a day that will easily, if ever, be forgotten.

CHAPTER 32

When life drags you back, let it stretch the bowstring. Then release with the force of an arrow destined to pierce through anything in its way.

Hodge's death investigation is ruled an accident. As the days continue to pass, I can't let go of the notion that it seems too convenient, too perfectly normal, like the accident was all but wrapped up in a pretty pink bow.

Maybe because Hodge shot one of Veno's men, it's not something Veno would just let go. There would be payback for that, and my gut instinct told me Veno had something to do with it.

So I reach out to Bones and ask him to double-check the details, dig into the investigation, and research the driver of the vehicle.

Bones doesn't find anything in the elderly man's bank records. Nothing on his credit cards either. And I've nearly given up this crazy idea, because surely, if Veno played a part and was somehow responsible, something of value would have been exchanged.

It's Bones' idea to do a reverse search. To dig through Veno's and Antonio's records for the connection, which to me seems like a needle in a haystack situation, but Bones, being Bones, finds it.

No influx of cash changed hands, but something valuable was

erased: a massive amount of gambling debt. The casino ownership is in the name of an LLC, which is owned by a shell company, which is owned by another cloaked business. It all ties back to Antonio Chavez, whom Bones compliments as a wickedly smart businessman, because he's hidden a lot of his shady dealings through layers of shell companies and a great many aliases.

I don't share this information with anyone else. I use it to arm myself with the knowledge of how ruthless and connected the Thirteen Devils have become if they can pull something like this off with no one catching on.

There's also the fact that Veno was able to get an appeal, and his case overturned. He was right back to his old ways, and yet, there's little heat from the cops, which makes me believe that Antonio is greasing hands and pulling strings. My guess is he's blackmailing influential figures to keep his business running smoothly. It's what I have done for the Greenbacks, and it's one of the most powerful methods to get people to comply with your demands.

The more I learn about them, the more I worry that the HOCs don't see the true beast they've gotten into bed with. It confirms everything Deeds told me and more. Which has me shifting my focus from trailing Goose, Mateo, and the HOCs to spending some of my time digging deeper into Veno, Antonio, and their operation.

I tell myself it has nothing to do with the fact that Veno is gunning for Goose and the HOCs—that taking Veno out was always part of the plan.

The suitcase Deeds hands to me a couple of hours later is proof of that. The cost of it put a massive dent in my savings. Still, in my opinion, it's worth every penny, because it contains everything I need to end Veno and his crew—a combination of deadly arsenal.

As I enter the code and flip the suitcase open to inspect the contents, Deeds watches from a few feet away. He backs up and plants his hands and ass on the edge of a massive headstone. "When are you planning to go through with it?"

I shrug as my fingers trail over the syringes, pill bottles, and poison. "I'm going to build up to it. First things first, I need to select a few women who aren't cowed by Veno and are willing to take the risk. I'll need to earn their trust, and then they'll need to earn mine in return. They'll need to be trained too, so Veno and his men don't suspect anything."

"Do you have a few women in mind?"

I nod. "I've been scoping out the building Veno now runs things out of for some time. There are two, I think, that have potential. But who knows? The drugs and their addiction will need to be factored in, and I won't know how far gone they are, or how committed they might be to this cause, until I get to know them. I'm just hoping the thought of getting back to their families and taking back some of the power Veno stole for them will be enough of a motivation factor that they'll do the work and take the risk." I caress the weapons lying in the form inserts for a moment before shutting the case and relocking it. I leave the large case at my feet when I stand. "I'll offer them freedom from the cage he keeps them in, but they have to be willing to do what it will take to open the door and walk out of it."

He nods and takes another look around the empty cemetery to make sure we are, in fact, alone. "And Veno?"

"I'm going to save him for last."

"You'll wait for me to get here? I wanna help."

The smile I give is fake. The lie, an act. One, I rarely use with Deeds, because out of all the humans on this earth, he's the one I trust the most. And it does warm my heart that he wants to help. But taking care of Veno, has always been something I want to do alone.

It'll be a day I relive all the trauma I've gone to therapy to work through, and I know when that day comes, every bit of darkness I've beaten back will rise to the surface to combat it. A day where I'm hoping I'll finally lay my demons to rest when I put Veno in the ground, but a traumatic one because of the emotions involved in closing this chapter of my life.

It's too personal to share with him or any other living soul. So I continue to feed him the lie, knowing I'll have to apologize and make it up to him down the road.

He chuckles under his breath. "How's it going with the little buggers."

I make a face, a sour one. Breeding scorpions and taking care of them without getting stung is a whole hell of a lot harder than the instructions I read online, and than the expert I'd asked at the university led me to believe. "Let's just say, I'm surviving. Some days it's more of a pain of the ass than it's worth."

"It won't be in the end."

"No, I expect not."

Deeds shifts and smirks. "And hows the bird man, treating you?"

I roll my eyes and look away. "Like another regular employee."

Deeds knows nothing about the incidents where I momentarily lost my mind and kissed Goose, or where we did more than kiss. I've actually shared very little about Goose with him, because he's completely clean, and the only information I relay has been purely about who I suspect might be a rat for a third party, like the cartel or the Thirteen Devils. Also, who sides with the Greenbacks coming into New Mexico versus who opposes or dislikes them, on a notable level. But I'm still working my way into the club, so there's not a ton of information to be exchanged.

"Still doesn't realize who you are?"

"No, I told you. He can't remember certain parts of his life. For whatever reason, that time period slipped into a black hole."

"Fucking crazy."

"You're telling me. I mean, he has recollections sometimes, but nothing solid."

"So you've settled on Stone, then?"

I flip my hair and shrug. "He's the best option." I raise a finger for each point. "He's easy to manipulate. Believes I'm as dumb as I seem. And he's the HOC most likely to be one of the rats for the Thirteens, based on what I've gathered so far."

He hurrumphs at that and looks off to the side. He seems lost in thought, so I check in.

"How's your mom doing?"

He shakes his head for a long time and folds his arms over his chest. "Not good. She's miserable. Angry. And fed up with the chemo treatments." He rubs his hand over his mouth and holds it there a moment before dropping it to his side. "They just seem to make her sicker. She's been talking about quitting them altogether so she can just live the rest of her life not feeling like complete shit."

"What does your dad think?"

"That she should keep doing them. They fight about it constantly."

"And you're what? For it, against it?"

He tilts his head this way and that. "It's not really up to me, but if it'll work, then yeah, for it, I guess. Although, I'm the one mostly taking care of her, so I also see what they're doing to her. It's like they're killing her or pushing her close to death. Maybe that's what needs to happen to kill the cancer, but it's fuckin' tears me up to watch it day by day. That's my fuckin' mom, you know?"

"Yeah, I know. I'm sorry. And I know that doesn't really mean shit, but I don't really know what else to say or how to help."

He sweeps his hand through his red hair as he stands.

"The stuff you've been sending her has helped. She loved that spiced tea shit, and the gummies. The blanket is like her daily comfort buddy, and she's wrapped up in it nearly every day."

"Did she like the mug?"

He laughs. "Fuck yeah, she did. She can't wait to smash it once she's in remission. It's like a little reminder each day as she drinks her coffee that she's gonna beat it and then be back to raising hell."

I smile widely at this. "I love that."

"Thanks for caring enough to think about her."

I nod and say, "Of course." I don't tell him that it's not just for her, it's for him too.

He walks up to me and pulls me into his arms. The hug I give him is intended to convey friendship and comfort. But after a few minutes of holding one another, he lifts my chin and kisses me.

I go through the motions, do all the right things to make it appear as if I'm into it.

But Deeds must sense something's off because he pulls back and stares down at me. "What's up with you?"

"Nothing. My head's just on the job, you know."

He studies me for a moment longer and steps back. "All right. If you say so." Which is said sarcastically and with a raised eyebrow.

"I just… got a lot on my mind."

He exhales and fishes his keys out of his jeans. "Guess, I'll get back on the road then."

He's fishing, feeling me out, wondering or maybe hoping if I'll invite him to spend the night, which is a bad idea on so many levels, but that's not why I don't.

Honestly, it's that my body felt absolutely nothing this time when he kissed me. If anything, it rebelled. Which is disturbing, because I've always been attracted to Deeds.

Fucking Finn.

My head's all messed up over him, and this weird distance between us that developed after the incident at the bar.

We'd fought about him trying to be my protector that night, and since then, he'd backed off.

Which is what I wanted, or at least what I told myself I wanted, because my focus needed to be elsewhere now that Veno was aware I was back in town.

I guess what's thrown me for a loop is that he's been content to keep the distance this time, even though he also seems to be watching me from afar, and still throws those intense looks my way. It's possible he's grieving the loss of his friend, or it could be that Veno's threats had him reevaluating things, but either way, it's another unanswered question mark in our non-relationship.

Deeds jingles his keys, waiting.

I force another smile I don't feel. "Raincheck?"

The corner of his mouth kicks to the side. He nods. "Raincheck."

"Be careful," I say.

"You too, babe." He closes the distance, places a kiss on my forehead, and walks away without looking back.

I remain in the empty graveyard long after he's gone. I use the suitcase as a chair while I plan my next movements and listen to the sounds of silence.

LOST LYREBIRD

Lily

CHAPTER 33

Acting like prey in a dangerous environment
may be the very reason you become prey.

Stone texts me an invite to a party at the clubhouse. His text comes as I'm leaving Bethany's house after checking in on her. I debate for a while as I drive back to my place.

I know what I need to do. I have for months. But stepping on this path is going to be the most difficult part of my plan to get closer to the HOCs.

After heading home, I shower and dry my hair, and text Stone my yes. Then, I painstakingly decide what to wear while I repaint my nails a dark red color. Not wanting to set the standards too high to begin with, I chose sexy, lacy black lingerie. For my outfit, I go with a distressed black-and-white crop tank top with Motley Crue written in red lettering across the chest, pairing it with ripped cutoffs and strappy heels.

When I arrive at 9:00 p.m., Stone is waiting for me in the parking lot and escorts me inside the clubhouse.

The second we're over the threshold, I'm greeted by a haze of smoke that lingers in the main lounge area, along with the faint hint of motor oil and the varying scenes of the men who, for the most part, live here, so their scents, too, are interwoven into the walls and furniture.

Van Morrison croons a soulful tune, audible underneath the rough timbre of male voices and the more playful voices of the women keeping them company. I receive a few thorough once-overs, but I pretend not to notice their scrutiny or interest.

Stone's hand stays pressed to my back as he guides me forward. My gaze travels around the room, and I make confident eye contact so I don't appear to be easy prey.

Like at the Greenbacks clubhouse, the club's history is scattered throughout the interior, in every framed photo and memorabilia they've chosen to display. However, there's an added patriotic theme here.

The long bar we stop at is on the right side of the room and spans nearly the length of it. The liquor shelves sit in front of a massive mirror and are stocked to the gills with a large variety of liquor.

Stone immediately orders us a round of beers. I run my hand over the worn bartop and think of all the memories it holds, the years of use and abuse it's seen. If it could talk, I bet it would have some fucking fantastic stories to tell.

A group of men huddle near the pool table on the far side of the room. The clack of pool balls occasionally cuts through the noise.

As the party kicks into gear and after a few rounds of beers, Stone pulls me toward a group of bikers in the far corner. I play the part, smiling and hamming it up. Griz, with his cocky grin, winks at me, and Bodie gives me a confused look.

It's the first time he hasn't flirted with me on sight, and for some reason, it throws me off for a second. When his gaze jumps across the room, I follow it.

Goose looks to have just walked in, and he stops cold a few feet inside the door, frozen there by the sight of me. He's scowling, his look murderous.

I hate how vulnerable I feel under his gaze, so I focus my attention elsewhere.

I haven't spoken to him about anything besides inconsequential work details since before Hodge's funeral, weeks ago. He's absent from Wet Tips more and more often lately, supposedly due to the headaches, or at least that's what's being spread by the gossip mill, aka dressing room chatter.

We're ships passing by each other, more often than not, passing with barely any acknowledgement. It's as if we've finally gotten pretty skilled at ignoring the connection that seems to tie us together. Sure, at times, we trade half-hearted pleasantries, but we also go out of our way to avoid each other more often than not.

I should be grateful he's granted me some space. I'm going to need it to do what I need to do here. Because, quite frankly, it will be a whole hell of a lot easier without his presence, but it doesn't look like I'm going to be able to infiltrate his club without him bearing witness to my methods.

Fucking fantastic.

A layer of torture to add on to what I'm about to put myself through. *Awesome.*

Stone manhandles me most of the night. I'm treated like nothing more than a lap-trophy and plaything. His hands roam freely and often. I let it all happen, and outwardly it may appear like I even enjoy myself. On the inside, I'm cringing, and it feels like my skin is crawling.

Things escalate as he pulls me to the dance floor. His large hands squeeze my ass to the point of pain as he forces my body against his and attempts to dirty dance with me. His kisses taste like licking an ashtray. He laps at my mouth, but not in a good way, since I have to subtly wipe my face afterwards to get rid of the excess moisture.

I hear a muffled curse and turn my head in time to see Goose walk by. He goes to the bar and not too long after, downs a full glass of brown liquor.

When I look back over at him a few moments later, his dark-blue gaze is colder than I've ever seen it. There's something else there, too, like confusion and frustration.

As the night progresses, more women arrive—hangarounds, there for the sole purpose of entertaining the HOCs in whatever way demanded of them.

The music changes to a more sultry, headier, ominous beat, and things turn from playful fun to sexual, as if the song itself sends a sensual pulse through the room, putting all the wayward souls under its spell.

Thankfully, Stone doesn't start stripping my clothes off until we're behind closed doors. Sure, there is plenty of petting, kissing, and foreplay, but the down-and-dirty stuff, which I have to battle with myself internally to perform, takes place inside his room, against a wall.

It's over within ten minutes, so the torture doesn't last for long, and I give the excuse of an early morning dance lesson, so I don't have to stay the night. Instead, I dress and high-tail it out of there as fast as I can without it appearing as if I'm running.

Halfway home, I have to pull over to throw up.

The image of Goose's face when I descended the stairs and returned to the main lounge area is at the forefront of my mind. He was sitting at a card table with Bodie and a few others, playing a late-night game of poker, as he bore witness to my walk of shame.

The judgment and righteous anger practically leaked off him, making every step I took toward the exit monumental.

CHAPTER 34

Oh, the beautiful lies we tell ourselves to make all our wrongs feel right.

JANUARY 2008

Time passes as I sink deeper into the role of a hangaround. It starts slow, just dropping in some nights to visit the clubhouse for drinks and what most there would consider a good time. Eventually, I'm deemed trustworthy enough to come around whenever I feel like it, and as I slowly become friends with some of the women at *Wet Tips,* I bring them along with me. Mainly, so I don't stand out as the only *new girl.*

We become the main attraction, dancing for the guys at parties, and pleasuring anyone we decide to latch on to for the night, while reveling in the highs that come with alcohol, Mary Jane, and wild nights filled with music and sex.

I push my conscience to the very back of my mind and keep it there.

Goose becomes a constant figure in my periphery. Always watching from afar as if he loves nothing more than to torture himself, and me by extension. He doesn't say a word, stop me, or intervene. He's my shadow, my watcher from the sidelines. He drinks or smokes the night away, and delivers condemnation by his expression alone, not saying a word but punishing me for my choices, and making every walk of shame a two-party occasion, because he's somehow always there to see it.

I know what I do here is for the right reasons, but it doesn't make it any less difficult.

The night terrors return, and I often wake to dreams of Goose. Either he dies like Hodge, and I play Bethany, the grieving widow sitting by the casket, or I claw at the dirt, trying to save him from the grave he's buried in.

These vivid dreams haunt me long after waking. Keeping my mind and body busy seems to be the only way to shake them from my thoughts.

Living off little rest and stressed to the max due to all the burdens I'm trying to juggle has me on a knife's edge. My mask, control, and patience are paper-thin and in danger of breaking.

So the next time Stone's hand begins creeping under my skirt while he kisses my neck, I glare right back at Goose, scolding him with a look that says *look the fuck away if you don't like it.*

He never does.

He watches it all and this creates an endless cycle of misery we both must endure.

Stone talks me into joining him and some of the other HOCs at a bike rally in Reno. It's been a while since I've ridden on the back of a bike for long periods, so at first, I'm a little nervous, but the trip goes off without a hitch. Getting away from the clubhouse and out on the open road does wonders to improve my mood.

He may not be the man I want to ride with, but I take pleasure where I can find it these days, which on the drive there, consists of the wind in my hair and the scenery as we pass through the desert.

We stop for one night at a KOA. As Stone and the other guys set up camp, I stretch my limbs and work to untangle my hair before rebraiding it. A couple of the old ladies and other clubpieces do the same. Then we pull together a meal out of the supplies we brought with us. I hand out waters and beers to those who want them.

A couple of people have followed in their vehicles, and when they unload the chairs and firewood, I take a seat and claim a spot around the fire pit. After the fire gets going, we spend the better part of the night listening to stories of times past from the storytellers in the group.

Goose chooses a seat on the opposite side of the fire from me. For the most part, he's just as intrigued by the tales being vividly painted for us as I am. He's drinking and even taking part in the conversation, corroborating events and even adding details that have been left out.

Seeing him so carefree is kind of devastating to the emotional wall I'm trying to maintain. So is his smile and laugh when they make an appearance.

"So, this jackass not only flips me off, he swerves like he's gonna run me the fuck over. The guy's towing a fucking fifth-wheel. He's got his wife and kids in the truck, and the fifth-wheel's like thirty fucking feet long, and he pulls into my lane any time I speed up to get close enough to yell at him to pull the fuck over." Bodie is waving his arms around while he speaks, and his full beer sloshes over the rim every now and then.

Septic is enthralled and smiling. Kendra is on his lap, and she asks, "So what'd you do?"

Bodie shrugs. "I was tempted to shoot his tires out."

Kendra gasps, "Tell me you didn't."

"No, I fuckin' didn't. What the fuck, Spice? I just told you there were kids in the fuckin' truck." Bodie gives Septic a look that says, *is she really that dense*? But to be fair, he did kind of lead us all there.

Then he says, "I followed his redneck ass until he pulled off the freeway and then chased him around the motherfuckin' gas station until I got a hold of him. I beat him senseless where the kids couldn't see their dad whining like a pansy-ass."

"And it took him three fuckin' laps around that building to catch him," Goose supplies and Dozer confirms by holding up three fingers.

"What?" Bodie exclaims. "That fucker was fast as hell, and it had been a minute since I've had to run my ass off like that. Had enough of that shit in the Army to last a lifetime. And like who the fuck does cardio willingly? Dumb fucks that's who."

Dozer, Kendra, and a few others raise their hands.

Bodie's drink spills as he points it at each person who raised their hand. "Dumb fucks. The lot of ya." He intentionally shakes his bottle at them and lets drops sprinkle on a few of them.

"What the fuck, man?" Dozer swipes off the beer now on his jeans.

"You've been baptized in the name of… I don't know… humanity."

"Humanity?"

"Yeah, like the regular people of this world who don't have time for shit like cardio and meal prep. Now, as long as you don't do that shit again, we can be friends."

"Hey, now," Kendra says. "I love runn—"

Septic places his hand over her mouth, and when her gaze snaps to his, he shakes his head. "Don't argue with him or he'll go on and on all night." To Bodie, he says, "Finish the story. So you beat his ass?"

"But you should've heard him," Dozer cuts in. He looks at Goose. "Do you remember what he was yelling as he chased that asshole down?" Dozer can barely get the words out. He wipes tears of laughter from his eyes. "'Slow down, you dopey hillbilly fuck, so I can send your ass back to bumfuckville.' And I think he said something like, 'I'm gonna put my boot so far up your ass, your roosters gonna crow.'"

The entire group loses their shit.

"Bumfuckville," Goose laughs and shakes his head. "Fuck, I forgot about that part. Jesus."

"And what was the wife screaming the entire time?" Dozer asks Goose.

"Hooligans. She called us fuckin' hooligans. It's like we were in a time warp or we'd been dropped in a bad episode of Pleasantville."

"So what happened after you beat his ass?" Septic asks.

Bodie opens his mouth, but Goose holds his hand up and replies. "He made the guy kiss the toe of his boot before he'd let him leave."

"No shit?" Septic says.

"No shit," Goose replies. "He had to apologize, beg for forgiveness on his goddamn knees, promise to never fuck with another biker again, and then kiss the toe of his boot."

Bodie shrugs. "Funny what a gun to the face can do to a man, am I right?"

"Bodie!" Kendra scolds.

"What? You can bet your ass he's gonna think twice about driving like an asshole and starting fights with another motorist."

"That's a thing for you, isn't it?" Stone enters the conversation.

Bodie smiles. "Yep, number one fuckin' pet peeve. People who drive like douche nozzles."

"Swear to fuck, he must have worked at the DMV or been a meter maid in another life," Dozer adds.

"Or maybe he was a pi—" Septic starts.

Bodie cuts him off. "Don't you fuckin' dare say a pig or I'm throwing this fuckin' beer at your head."

When I laugh, Goose's deep blue gaze immediately connects with mine.

Breaking the connection is the hard part. I do, eventually, but not before my mind runs a little wild with fantasies of what this moment would look like in a different light. With me sitting on his lap versus Stone's. What would it have been like today if I'd ridden on the back of his bike?

Though yes, that's not possible, but still the visual does pop into my mind for a split second.

Goose's fierce gaze seems to imply he's thinking similar thoughts because the emotion in his eyes is telling.

So, yeah, I force myself to refocus my attention on Stone. I click off my emotions as much as I'm able to and act the part, while trying to ignore the stare I can feel directed at me from across the party as the night wears on.

After some heavy petting with Stone later that night in the privacy of his tent, I beg off and tell him I'm on my period. I encourage him to rejoin the party and get what he needs from one of the other girls. I've dosed him with sleeping pills a few times to get a reprieve, but I try not to do that too often so he doesn't catch on. It takes some major convincing to get him to go, but he finally leaves me and rejoins the party.

I spend the next hour praying he doesn't return any time soon and listening to the voices from the party. Goose's is low and hard to hear, but when I focus on it, the cadence of it eventually lulls me to sleep.

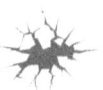

FINN

Cajun, Pike, and other members of our El Paso chapter rolled in later than expected. Griz, Bodie, Mav, and I help them set up camp alongside ours with nothing but the firelight to guide us. Having just finished, we're standing around shooting the shit when Star strolls up with a few cold beers and passes them out. She's one of the clubpieces that came along for the ride. A pretty blonde thing with a nice figure, but a mouth that leaves a lot to be desired. Taz often refers to her as the club's tank skank. Mainly, because she's not particular. She chases after any biker with a hog, particularly those with a higher-ranking patch.

Tonight, for whatever reason, I'm the unlucky bastard she's set her sights on.

I take the beer graciously, but frown at her when she runs her hand up my chest. Without invitation, she wraps her hand around the back of my neck, presses her body into mine, and huskily whispers, "Can I do anything else for you?"

A weighty pause follows, like the others have stopped talking to listen in.

What I suspect is that Bodie—the one whose bike she rode in on—put her up to it. She's been vying for my attention most of the night—giving me sultry looks, staying close, touching me on occasion, clinging to me like a wet leaf, and no matter how gently I try to let her down, the girl won't take a hint.

Bodie's smirk, and the knowing fucking gleam in his eyes tell me I'm right.

I've been with her in the past, usually on wild-as-fuck nights when I've gotten too wasted to know better. And with how hard up I am, yeah, it's fucking tempting.

But she's not what I need. Not what I want.

Not going to lie, the thought did cross my mind earlier of using her as a way to not only distract me from Stone's meaty paws all over Lily, but to see if the roles were reversed, and Lily had to witness someone all over me, would she feel what I feel? Would she give a fuck?

I never got the chance to test that theory. Stone dragged Lily off to his tent before I could fully consider it, and they've been in there for a while.

Sure, I could use Star as payback. It would give me something else to think about other than the awful thoughts running through my mind of what the fuck is happening inside that tent at this moment. But I'm just not that guy. I want what I want, and Star may be able to get me off in the end, but the hollow feeling I'll be left with afterwards just isn't worth it.

I'd rather suffer in silence.

"Nah, sweetheart. I'm good."

"Really?"

She looks aghast at this, like I'm fucking crazy. Maybe I am. Because isn't that what a masochist is, someone who loves the pain of his own self-inflicted torment?

Instead of enjoying myself and finding someone who can love on me now, I'm filling my head with thoughts that make me sick to my stomach, staying on the peripheral of the party to catch any hint of lovemaking coming from this side of the camp, and turning myself inside out over a woman who runs from me at every opportunity.

I came on this trip to spend more time with her.

Sick, right? When I knew from the onset that she'd be accompanying Stone.

It was a guarantee that I'd see shit I didn't like, that I'd be filled with jealousy to the brim, and hate every moment of it. And yet, here the fuck I am.

Watching. Waiting. Listening.

Hopelessly hoping for an outcome to this trip that ends with Lily somehow in my arms instead of the ones probably wrapped around her.

I emphasize this last part by removing Star's hand and nodding toward the group partying closer to the fire pit. "Go enjoy yourself."

"If you're sure?

I nod, "More than."

She nods but fuck if her advances don't get more daring as the night wears on.

I'm almost at my limit of patience when—color me surprised as fuck—Stone reemerges at the party in nothing but his jeans, his massively tatted up chest on full display, and takes her off my hands.

When they're both distracted, I take the opportunity to slip into the dark and out of sight.

I'm sitting in a lawn chair behind Stone's tent at the far end of the camp. For the most part, the laughter and hollering of our group drown out all sound. But every so often, when it quiets, I hear Lily's soft snores.

They're fucking cute.

Yeah, I know it's ridiculous. Not just that I find the way she breathes when she sleeps adorable, but that I'm sitting alone in the dead of night, propped on my elbow with my chin on my fist, head tilted to the side so I can catch any small sound she makes, like a desperate fool.

The moon is a large crescent, and it's bright tonight. It someone were to come upon me, they'd surely ask what the fuck I'm doing. So I'm grateful that no one has, because there would be no hiding it.

I tell myself it's not just to listen to her sleep. It's to make sure no one fucks with her. That's how I justify it to myself. That I'm protecting her from any drunk bastard who might stumble into the tent thinking it's theirs and find her inside.

Time moves slowly forward, and little by little, the party dies off.

Stone, thank fuck, doesn't return to the tent.

I'm so dialed in to any sounds she makes that my own breaths sync with hers, and her breathy exhales soon pull me into a peaceful doze. I'm not sure how much time passes this way, but at some point, my eyes close.

A small, helpless cry is what wakes me, nearly causing me to fall out of the chair.

Her "No, no, no," causes a chain reaction in me, and my body jerks to full wakefulness.

The pills have worn off, and the pain is a crushing presence throbbing in my skull. But I couldn't give a fuck. I push it to the side and stumble to the front of the tent.

Lily's distress escalates. I unzip the front flap quickly and peer inside. My exhale is made entirely of relief. The window on the side of the tent is open, letting in just enough moonlight to see by. She's alone and wrapped up like a burrito in a green sleeping bag with her head on a pillow at the other end of the tent.

I take a moment to pull myself together, letting my heart rate resettle.

It's my name escaping her lips in a small whimper that draws me forward. Not Goose. *Finn.* And the way she says it. It isn't just spoken softly; there was a wealth of feeling behind it, like a plea or a prayer.

With all the stealth I can muster, I crawl inside the tent, not yet sure if I intend to wake her or comfort her from the bad dream. She's facing me, her fingers clasped around the end of the pillow. Her lashes flutter, and there's movement behind her eyelids.

Another distressed whine leaves her. She shakes her head slightly as if to say *no*, and her hand squeezes tightly, releases, again and again. This time, when she cries out, her lips part afterwards, and she speaks. "You pro-o-mised me-e."

Promise.

And it's this that levels me where I sit crouched before her.

Because this word… it has the power to shift my world completely.

To send my heart soaring to the fucking clouds and beyond. But when I grasp what this could possibly mean... the scale of how much it means to me, my heart falls like a fucking anvil.

For years, I've questioned my recollections, my logical reasoning, and my own sanity. That's been magnified a hundredfold since Lily arrived. I've hoarded every memory and sifted through them a million times to sort truth from fiction. I've but given up hope that any of it would make sense. But those words spilling from her lips...

You promised me.

This may very well be the truth behind why she's pushing me away.

The same truth I've been searching for for nearly ten fucking years.

The grandest of feathers, and something I've never forgotten, no matter how many other memories I've lost. Because it's written in bold black letters all over my bedroom walls.

YOU PROMISED HER.

KEEP YOUR PROMISE.

They have been guiding my path and pushing me forward when I lose hope, because it was never a promise I meant to break.

The fact that I did and left Elle behind, and not only behind, but vulnerable, helpless, and alone, has gutted me to my core, made me feel like the one person in this life I was meant to protect, I failed. Little by little, it has eaten at my soul and crippled my mind.

I've been telling myself for months that I'm losing it. That I've gone mad when I make a correlation to something Lily does or says to a memory from my past.

But what if these links aren't false connections?

What if I wasn't getting it wrong but just being led astray?

Fuck.

The riotous anger comes then. Because Jesus. It makes sense.

I suspected when my notes about the name Angel and Veno's words about her pointed to this, but I talked myself out of it.

And I get that this isn't solid proof, but it's enough to have me questioning everything: the legitimacy of Lily's stories, background, and information that she's been spoon-feeding me from day one.

Has she been lying this entire time? Lying to keep me at a distance?

Because that's the one thing that's never added up. Why am I the only one she stays away from?

Why push me away and seek attention from every HOC brother but shun me when the attraction we share is undeniable?

Suspicion and anger drive me away. I've never been good at hiding my emotions, and I already know the answers I'll get if I approach this directly—more of the same.

When I make it back to my tent, my head's fucked—a mess of puzzle pieces, feathers, and breadcrumbs that whirl around like a janky merry-go-round inside my brain.

How many other things did I dismiss about her because I thought they were trivial?

Fuck. Fuck. *Fuck.*

Sharp pain spreads to the back of my skull and down my spine. It gets more intense the longer I try to reason it all out.

I push through it only to be rewarded with another bloody nose. I need to stop. Stop thinking. This riddle has taken more than ten years off my life, no, triple that, and if I don't quit, it'll take even more. My brain feels like it's tearing itself apart the more I try to remember.

I pop a few pills, and they inevitably pull me under and grant me mercy. The numbness sinks in and slows down the spinning in my mind.

I don't know how long I sleep, but Bodie shakes me awake sometime later. "Hey, man. Everyone's getting ready to head out."

I try to get up. I really do. But he's a blur, and my body feels like a heavy bag when I attempt to sit up. I finally manage it, and I rub my eyes as I try to shake off the exhaustion weighing me down. It doesn't help that my head is screaming this morning,

"What happened?" Bodie is holding up the bloody shirt I used last night to stop the nosebleed. His face is filled with concern.

"Just another nose bleed. Not a big deal."

I avoid his gaze as I run my hand over the blankets searching for the pill bottle. He finds it before I do and passes it over to me.

"Grab me some water, will ya?"

He nods and leaves to do just that. While he's gone, I swallow two pills dry. When he returns, I take another two under his watchful gaze and chase them down with water.

"I told the guys to take off without us. I'll stay behind with you until you're up to riding, and we'll meet up with them when we get to Reno. Which means, you're gonna lay your ass back down and get a few more hours of shuteye."

I'm already shaking my head before he finishes speaking. "No. Go. I'll be fine."

But after a small argument with him, that's precisely what happens.

I give in, lie back down, and pass the fuck out.

Three thoughts keep circling in my head as Bodie and I ride toward Reno. One: I need to figure out how to go about getting answers from Lily in ways she can't deny. Two: That this is the first time I've been negligent in my duties as Road Captain, and with the way my life is going, I need to do the honorable thing and step down and hand in my patch. There's a chance, though a slim one, that Cap will cut me out of the club because of the pills, but I need to come clean about them. Three: the sobriety coin in my pocket feels like it's burning a hole through my jeans. I don't deserve to carry it anymore, and doing so feels like a sin in itself. It's another broken promise that wrecks me. This one to my father.

But I can't function without the pills. And I'm also no good to anyone if I can't think clearly.

So I'm damned either way.

It sinks home with each mile I drive that there's no winning this battle. There's only surviving it long enough to do what I'm here to do. If Lily's who I think she is, confirming that and explaining myself, seeking her forgiveness before I go… that's all I can hope for.

LOST LYREBIRD

CHAPTER 35

It's a rare person who can carry a wealth of secrets and keep them close to the vest.

It's not until we enter the local bar that I realize the Greenbacks are attending the same bike rally. Deeds, ever one to stir up trouble, keeps making eyes at me from across the bar, until I motion for him to cut that shit out.

Lowering his face, he tucks his long auburn hair behind his ear and laughs to himself. When I again catch his hazel gaze, he raises a brow at me, and smirks like this is a game and he's amused. For a while, he toes the line. But this only lasts long enough for him to navigate the crowded room and work his way towards me. Under his cut, he's sporting a red flannel, and his black ripped jeans hug the muscles in his legs. When he brushes by me, he leans in close, and his hot breath brushes over my ear. "Meet me out back."

I don't react in any way.

I do, however, keep him in my peripheral vision, and when he exits the bar, I tell Stone I need to use the ladies' room. He nods distractedly and says, "All right, babe." Then pats my ass as he turns back to continue the conversation he's having with Septic.

I enter the bathroom and come back out to tell Stone how disgusting it is and that I'm going to try the one in the restaurant next door.

"I said, all right, babe." He stares hard at me for a moment, like me interrupting his conversation to tell him where I'm going is getting on his last nerve. As I walk away, I internally smile at this.

I'm mad as hell when I turn the corner of the building to find Deeds smoking a cigarette and leaning against the brick wall. One boot is planted behind him, and when he sees me, a wide-as-fuck grin splits his face.

He tries to hug me and plant a kiss on my cheek in welcome, but I push him back because if even one HOC sees us together, we're both fucked.

He's bothered by my rejection but quickly moves on to more important matters. He pushes me for the details I've collected since we talked.

I share everything except the new information I discovered the day before I left for this trip. I don't tell him about Mateo or how I spotted a man in an Aston Martin pulling up to Finn's place when Finn wasn't home. Or how Mateo answered the door, and instead of letting the man inside, he quickly stepped out and shut the door behind him. He'd pushed the man back and had the fiercest scowl I've seen to date covered his features.

I paused in my gardening. Something about his reaction raised some massive red flags.

The visitor was Hispanic, with short, slick, dark hair, and dressed sharply in a charcoal-tailored suit.

The tension between them escalated rapidly—clipped words, and then the suit slammed Mateo against the exterior wall, pinning him there, and jabbed his finger inches from Mateo's face. Mateo struggled, tried to fight him off, but the man doubled him over with a punch to the gut, and the boy fell to the ground and started coughing. The suit crouched, said something, then stood and walked off. He peered around the neighborhood, and I quickly got back to my gardening like I hadn't seen a thing.

He was in his car within seconds and speeding down the street.

I couldn't do a thing about any of it, except memorize the license plates.

But I had a feeling I knew who the man was, and instead of relying on Bones to confirm it, I planned to do my own digging when we returned to Albuquerque, because this wasn't information I wanted Deeds to have. It would put Mateo in danger with the Greenbacks if the man was who I suspected him to be, or if I found out Mateo was involved in any way with the Thirteen Devils.

Deeds asks about my progress with the girls in Veno's circle next. I relay my most recent clandestine meet-up from the other night. But midway through, his hazel gaze veers away from mine and focuses on something behind me.

The low, "Oh, fuck" under his breath tells me all I need to know.

Doom grabs a tight hold of my stomach and twists as I spin around to see who it is.

It's Griz.

He's turned the corner, and he's frozen as his gaze rakes over the two of us. I see it in his eyes, the moment it all clicks into place.

His red-and-grey eyebrows are pulled together, and the wrinkles on his forehead from the glower he's leveling on us doesn't bode well.

The alleyway is deathly quiet as he takes his time walking towards us.

He bypasses me. Then he pushes Deeds with such force that he crashes back into the wall. With his forearm to Deeds' throat, he pins his nephew there, and growls into his face, "I may love you, you little son of a bitch, but like I've told your father... fuck with my club, and it'll be the last fuckin' thing you ever do. Blood ties aren't everything in this life. And I'll cut them without a second thought if you fuck us over."

"What the fuck you talkin' about, old man?"

"You tell me. What the fuck is this?"

Deeds' response is to lie, "Nothin'. Just gettin' to know each other." This earns him a solid punch to the face and sends him stumbling down the alley. He stands and massages his jaw, working it back and forth, and rubs it with his palm. "Fuck, Uncle G."

"Talk now, and no bullshit. What the fuck is this?" Griz motions to me.

Deeds reevaluates his uncle, and he nods while holding his hands up in a peace gesture. "Just calm down, and I'll explain everything."

I don't stay for the whole conversation. I have to get back or risk Stone finding me with them. But later, Griz takes me aside and makes me repeat the entire story. He's honest and tells me he's one lie away from taking the entire situation to Cap and letting the chips fall where they may. So if he senses even one untruth spill from my mouth, he'll do just that. He wants to compare my story to Deeds'.

Griz steals me from Stone for the night and doesn't make excuses about it. Just tells Stone that I'll be spending the night with him. Stone's reaction is to puff up and throw around a pissed off demeanor. But that's it, because honestly, what can he do? Nothing.

So I spend the better part of the night convincing Griz to help us carry out our plans, that the more people we have working towards the same goals, the sooner we can stop this whole charade and turn the tables on the men who would see the end of both clubs.

Thankfully, my story and Deeds' add up, and Griz doesn't turn me in to Cap. It's a near miss, and it rattles me because I realize that I'm so far deep into this now that one more mistake like the one today, and this entire plan could unravel.

I can't afford to fuck this up.

My survival is now wrapped up in Deeds' plan, and seeing it out to the end is the only option.

Griz becomes my safe haven. His room becomes a place I can crash on the nights I spend at the clubhouse. He essentially becomes my beard so I can do what I need to while still being considered a clubpiece.

Something about seeing me with Griz sends Stone and Goose completely over the edge. Stone gets angry. He practically stomps around the clubhouse, and whenever I'm there, he goes out of his way to try to make me jealous with any girl he can get his hands on. He even gets into a drunken brawl with a local at Hodge's Bar.

Goose almost entirely disappears.

His presence at the clubhouse and Wet Tips is sporadic.

When he does show up, he's a mess: unkempt, hair out of place, clothes wrinkled to hell, and he starts drinking heavily. The intense desire for me is replaced with cold, detached stares, as if I've crossed some invisible line and he wants nothing to do with the woman I've become.

I'm in the middle of unloading the groceries I purchased for the club, a job I've taken on as a clubpiece to help out, when, without warning, the door bursts open behind me. Bodie enters the kitchen like a hurricane, takes hold of my arm, and spins me.

"Ow! What the hell, Bodie?"

The righteous anger catches me entirely off guard. "You tell me. What the hell are you doing, Lily?" He cages me against the counter and spits his response so venomously that I reel back from him.

"Uh-mmm… restocking the pantry and fridge. What the fuck does it look like I'm doing?"

"You're fucking him up and, from what I can tell, you're doing it on purpose." His steely gaze analyzes my face. "What I want to know is, why?"

His accusation is a straight punch to the chest, but I keep my expression as neutral as possible while considering how to reply.

Before I can, he shakes his head and backs away. His eyes travel up and down my body. His glare is glacial when his gaze reconnects with mine. "Don't fuckin' act like you don't know what I'm talkin' about."

"Bodie, I'm just living my fucking life. If he chooses to watch me and obsess over what I'm doing, then that's his business, not mine."

He gives me a repulsed look, like I'm shit on the bottom of his shoe, and stalks out the kitchen, letting the door slam behind him.

Lily

CHAPTER 36

Is the lie worth telling? If so, then is it truly wrong to lie?

FEBRUARY 2008

I t's dawn when I slip out of Griz's room and head to the first floor. The sun hasn't fully risen yet, and what light there is casts a pale glow over the remnants of last night's party.

Griz and I bailed from it early and spent most of the night in his room talking, trading secrets, slow dancing, and smoking the night away, which is what we've been doing for weeks now. Occasionally, we hold one another, providing basic physical comfort. It's all either of us wants or needs: companionship that has nothing to do with sex. Even though we portray something else entirely to the club. All in the name of protecting those we care about.

I even spilled my heart out to him about Goose and our past, which helped lessen the sting of it. Seeing things from Griz's perspective gave me a better understanding of who this new version of Goose is and what he went through.

Which does make it harder to stay away. But Griz agrees, in the end, it will be Goose's saving grace. The less he knows about all of it, the better off he'll be.

I wade as quietly as possible through the mess from the party. The only sounds are the faint snoring of the remaining occupants and the steady hum of the fan in the corner. Otherwise, the clubhouse is eerily still, waiting for these men to rise, meet another day, and cause more chaos.

Griz's thick socks, which are pulled up to my knees, protect my feet from the cold floor. His vintage Grateful Dead T-shirt smells like Old Spice and cloves, and hits me mid-thigh. It's something I found in the back of his closet that no longer fits him, and I've claimed it for my own.

When I finally locate my phone, which I lost somewhere in between Jager shots, I carefully pry it from the crack in the couch, being mindful of the couple asleep there.

A loud clatter has me nearly coming out of my skin, and I whirl around to see a glass bottle roll across the floor. My pulse quickens not only from the scare, but at finding Goose standing behind me. His eyes are glazed. He's holding a joint and lazily brings it to his lips as he scrutinizes me.

His hair now reaches past his shoulders, and he looks worse for wear. There's a hardened edge to him lately. He's lost weight, has dark circles under his eyes, and his brows are constantly pinched together when he looks at me. Whether it's the headaches or my perceived indifference triggering the scowl is anyone's guess, but either way, it's taking a toll on him.

Griz thinks it's due in part to Hodge's death and Goose's belief that he played a part in it. The loss has hit some of the HOCs worse than others, and it's obvious that many of them are still grieving.

After taking a pull on the joint, he asks, "So this is you now, huh?" His tone holds a shitload of condemnation, and it's hard not to become immediately defensive.

I force a caustic smile, trying to brush it off. "Yeah, I guess it is."

He shakes his head, his expression darkening. "You seem real fuckin' happy about it."

I don't notice how far gone he is until he walks to the bar and stumbles into a stool. "Motherfucker." He looks at the stool like he's wondering how the fuck it got there, and puts a hand out to catch himself on the bar.

Warning alarms blare in my mind, and my instinct kicks in. Before I know it, I'm moving toward him. "Goose—" I reach out, my hand landing on his arm, but he raises his arm to push mine away, his movements slow.

"Don't. Don't fuckin' show you care now."

The words hit harder than I expect, as does the hurt that covers his features. Seeing his usually calm demeanor slip has me taking a step back. "Of course I care."

He doesn't answer, just leans forward onto the bar and then over it to grab a bottle of whiskey. He drags it across the counter to him and thumps it on the bar. It's clumsy and stuttered, like he's completely stoned out of his goddamn mind.

He pats his front pocket before he slips his hand inside and pulls out a pill bottle. He shakes it first, then lifts it up to examine the label closer and mutters something under his breath.

The rattle of pills is loud in the silence of the room.

My anxiety spikes as I watch him struggle to read the label. "What are those?"

He ignores me, his hands fumbling with the cap, frustration building on his face as he tries unsuccessfully to open it. The cap finally pops off and falls to the floor. Then he drops the bottle on the counter, and it tips over. Pills scatter everywhere. For a moment, he just stares at them. Then he shrugs—fucking shrugs—swipes his hand over the counter, and tosses a bunch of them into his mouth. He grabs the liquor bottle and chases them down.

I latch onto his arm. "What are you doing?" It comes out more like a screech, as my concern for him skyrockets. I pry the whiskey bottle from his grip and set it on the counter, then snatch up the pill bottle and glance at the label. The knot in my stomach tightens. "Oxy? You're not supposed to mix them with alcohol. And it says to take one every eight hours, not a handful!"

He turns to me, blinks a few times, and smirks. His blue eyes—a sea I could get lost in, but can't afford to—darken. A slow, bitter curve builds on his lips. Before I can react, he grabs the whiskey again and starts chugging it, the liquid sliding down his throat in long, reckless gulps.

"Stop it!" I lunge for it again and pry the bottle from his hand. I'm successful, but the tussle causes a shit-ton of it to spill over his shirt and cut.

He rounds on me and delivers a deadly glare. "What the fuck?"

"Why are you doing this?"

He gets right up in my face. "Why do you think? Because I'm done. Done giving a shit. Done trying. Done with all of it. And I'm fucking dying, Lil', so what the fuck does it matter how I go?"

The air around us crackles with the bleakness of his words. My breath hitches, and I shake my head, refusing to believe it. "You're not dying. Don't say that."

He laughs, a sound so hollow and humorless it sends a chill down my spine. "Yeah, I am. You can lie to yourself all you want, but it's a fuckin' fact. These migraines are fucking eating at my brain, and it's only a matter of time before they put me down for good. I thought…" His words trail off. "I thought I could figure shit out, but I can't think… I can't. It's just too much to sift through."

"You're not making any sense."

He chuckles darkly and nods. "Story of my fuckin' life."

His hair has fallen forward over his face. He glares at me through the strands. The vulnerability in his eyes is a stab straight to the chest. His pain is visible—if I had only cared to look deeper. It's raw and open, like an unstitched wound he's letting me see. I remind myself that he's not like me. He doesn't lie or omit things to get what he wants. His words are always the complete truth, and that's what I need to take these as.

But oh, how they twist the knife. He genuinely believes he's not going to make it through this.

"So what?" My voice trembles. "You're just gonna give up? Just swallow a bunch of pills until one day you don't wake up?"

He shrugs, a nonchalant motion that breaks me. "Maybe."

"Goddamn it, Goose! Why?" The frustration boils over, my voice cracking as I step toward him. "This doesn't make any goddamn sense, why?"

He turns on me, eyes blazing, filled with a fury I don't recognize. "You know exactly why. I can't watch this shit. I can't watch this night after night and do fuckin' nothing about it. You want to fuck around. You want to be with men who don't see you. Who treats you like nothin' more than a great piece of ass. Fine! But I don't want to see it. I fuckin' can't! Don't you get that?"

"What I do has nothing to do with you."

"Doesn't it, though? Because it sure as fuck feels to me like it does." He steps closer, towering over me, his breath hot against my skin. "Like there's a reason behind it all and I'm just too fuckin' dumb to figure it all out. That or I'm losing my goddamn mind. Which is it? Huh, Lil'? Can you at least tell me that?"

I try to turn away, but he grabs my wrist, yanking me back, pulling me closer until I can feel the heat radiating off him, his chest barely brushing against mine. My heart slams against my ribs, and I'm breathing hard, trying to stay calm.

His voice drops to a whisper, rough and ragged as his lips hover near my ear. "You think I don't know what you're doing? You think I don't see how much you hate being with them? Stone? Grinder? Mav? You try to hide it, but I see how much you don't want it. You hate it, but you keep forcing both of us to endure this shit." His tone is laced with jealousy and something darker. "You think I don't... don't see?"

"See what?"

"See why you're really here."

Panic flitters through my nervous system. "I'm just living my life. It has nothing to do with you."

"Is that right?"

"Yes!"

"Then tell me why you can't keep yourself from looking my way. Why you're so adamant about stayin' away when you've nearly fucked every brother here?" His voice lowers. "Why can't I get you outta my head? And why, when I dream, do I see a woman who looks an awful lot like you?"

I shiver at his words, a full fucking body tremor. "I don't know."

"Bullshit."

"I don't know!"

"Jesus, man!" Taz hollers. "Can y'all take this shit somewhere else? Somewhere fuckin' private, and let us sleep? It's seven fuckin' a.m."

Goose grabs my hand and drags me down the hallway. I try to pry myself from his grip so I can get the fuck out of here, but his hold on me is unrelenting. He walks into the Chapel, their meeting room, and I fight yet again to free myself, slapping at his chest. Because going in there is a death sentence. I know this. He knows this. But he's dragging me in anyway.

He slams the door once we're inside, and he uses his body to force mine back. I stumble over a chair and push it to the side when he keeps coming. "You're here to fuck, right? Then let's fuck. You wanna be a clubpiece, then I'll treat you like a clubpiece." Brows pinched and eyes hard, he shoves my shoulder until I fall back, ass on the church table.

With quick, harsh movements, he shrugs off his cut and throws it onto a chair. Then his hands go to his belt, and he starts unlatching it. I get up to move past him, but he pushes me again. I swear to God, I nearly punch him, because what the actual fuck is happening? How did it come to this?

When he tries to grab my hands, I scream in his face. "Knock it the fuck off! I'm not fucking you." I shove him. He retaliates by caging my hands.

Leaning closer, he snarls down at me. "Why the fuck not. Isn't this why you're here? For a good-fuckin'-time? Well, I'm ready for that, Lil'. Show me what I've been missing out on."

He manhandles me, goes for my T-shirt, attempting to lift it. I fight to keep it in place. Eventually, he wins and yanks it off me. With his lower body, he pushes into mine and forces me back against the table. The second his hand goes for my panties, I slap him, hard.

He stops, but only for a heartbeat. Then he tunnels his fingers harshly into my hair and crashes his mouth over mine. It's the whiskey, I tell myself. The motherfucking whiskey on his breath that has me stilling. His mouth claims mine. His teeth bite my bottom lip, and his kiss softens, transforms into something altogether different. That's when I start kissing him back.

The kiss builds like a storm gathering force.

He gives me his tenderness, his untamed desire, and his fucking soul in that kiss. It's consuming, raw, pent-up, primal, and shreds any control of the situation I had.

When he interweaves tender, sweet caresses with his tongue, I let go completely and just feel.

His grip, which was unforgiving, becomes an exploration as his hands begin to travel over my skin.

His kisses are devastatingly deep, and he moves my head so he can worship my mouth. It's like nothing I've ever experienced and feels as if it could go on forever. It fucking shifts my world. The arousal flooding through my body has me moaning. "Jesus, Goose." I breathe those words against his lips when we come up for air.

I weave my hands under his cut and black Henley and let them trail up his chest. My fingers study the sparse chest hair there, and the prominent muscles.

My heartbeat jackrabbits out of control. And the taste of him, of his skin as I nip and nibble my way to his jaw, as I place hard kisses over his neck, spins us both out of control.

He lets out a half-growl half-groan. "Woman, you have no goddamn idea what you do to me."

He retakes my mouth in a savage kiss. It doesn't stop there. His mouth trails over my jaw and neck, while his fingers knead my breast. Using his other hand, he grips the space between my thigh and ass so he can grind his cock against my pussy.

The jean fabric is abrasive and unpleasant, but feeling him through the material is thrilling.

The confession spills from his lips. "You've got no idea how hard it's been to stay away. Knew it would be just fuckin' like this."

When his kisses journey to my neck, he sucks on my skin there until it stings, until there's no doubt in my mind, he's left a bruise behind. He does the same to the other side, only this time he doubles down, leaving what I imagine are two hickies branded on my skin.

I go boneless and lie down on the church table, as fucking sacrilegious as it is. He follows me down and latches onto my breast with a growl. His tongue swirls around the peak, and his blue-eyed gaze meets mine as he plays there. Like a traveling prophet, he spills his truth, his absolute desire for me into the devotion he shows to every inch of my skin.

He spends a good deal of time working me over before his mouth travels down between the valley of my breasts.

It's the beginning of the end for me. Because what follows is delicious, decadent torture.

He spreads my thighs wider and hikes one over his shoulder. Seeing him between my legs is a vision I won't soon forget. The intensity in the depths of his eyes says what I've tried to deny—that he won't stop coming for me until he claims me in every way.

My fingers pull at his hair because I can't help myself now. I can't deny this is what I've wanted for so long—to ride his face and feel his mouth on me.

He feasts like a man possessed, takes my pussy with so much pressure and force that it steals a cry from my lips and has my back bowing off the table. It's a fucking out-of-body experience that takes over as he makes a meal of me.

A long groan rips from me, followed by a breathy, "Oh my fucking God, Goose."

"Sing for me, Lil' Bird. That's it, sing, baby."

The skill he uses on my clit to tease it and bring me to the brink is insane. His teeth nip, his tongue flutters over clit in rhythmic and repetitive movements that send my mind reeling. The action has my orgasm cresting and my core clenching around nothing, and dying to be filled.

"Fuck, I may never stop, woman. You taste too fuckin' good. Honey and like a sweet fuckin' lemondrop on my tongue. "

He begins to fuck me with his tongue, using his grip on my thighs to rock my hips against his mouth, fucking his tongue into me as deep as possible, while he thumb strums my clit. In and out. In. And. Out. I moan and gasp out his name, while swinging my head back and forth as I battle to hold off my orgasm because I don't want it to end.

"Jesus fucking Christ, Goose!"

"That's it. Cry for me. Show me how much you love it and let me give you what you need, baby." He punctuates those words with sinking two fingers into me and begins to pump them, stretching me open. Then he hooks them inside until he hits the spot. A spot that has me crying out, "Oh-oh-oh fuck. I'm going to cum."

He growls against my clit, and it sends vibrations through me.

That's all it takes for the storm he conjured inside of me to break, and my orgasm to come crashing forward. My head kicks back as I shout from the force of it. The sound echoes around the room. "Goose. Uh-uh, God… Goose," I mutter his name over and over again. I soar so fucking high and ride the waves of the peak as my thoughts scramble. My core clenches and releases, and his fingers work me through the shock waves of my release as they crest and recede.

Then I'm gasping for oxygen and sucking in quick breaths to fill my lungs.

"Yeah, baby. Love you watching you cum all over my fucking mouth, Lil'."

"Jesus, Goose." I hear the crack in my voice as I moan his name one last time in a long, breathless syllable. The gravity of the orgasm shakes me. It's like before today, I'd forgotten what this could feel like when it's honest and true, and not a forced act I'm doing to play a part.

He grunts in approval and hums as he laps at my pussy. Blissful pleasure rolls through me again, and I float as I come down.

His tongue softens its ministrations by the time I return to reality.

"I know this body in a way I shouldn't. Like a memory I can't reach. My hands somehow know the feel of you. Do you know what that's like? To know, but not know? It's killin' me, Lil'."

His words yank me back into the present, and both send my heart soaring and wreck me at the same time.

I see how it would play out if I don't do what I should and push him away. I see how easily we could fall back in love and get lost in him. Because fuck, I'm more than halfway there, I've just been lying and denying it to the best of my ability. To myself and him.

I push him back as I stand. "No, I don't know. And how could you?"

His eyes narrow, and for a second, I see it—the hurt buried beneath the anger, beneath the haze of whatever he's taken to dull the pain. The muscle pulses in his jaw, and he clenches his teeth. The tension from earlier returns, so does the scowl.

"You do it so well, I almost missed it."

"Missed what?" I ask.

"I think you know."

"I don't."

Taking my hand into his, he smiles sadly, his thumb brushes over my knuckles. "Tell me, Lil'." His voice is quieter now, a dangerous edge still lurking beneath the surface. "Why do you care what happens to me?" The rawness there makes my chest tighten. "What the fuck do you care what I take? Or what I do? Why push me away when you don't do it with anyone else?"

I just stare at him, as I think about everything he's witnessed. I should walk away. I should deliver a retort so cold that it will keep him at a safe distance. But I can't. Not when I know what he's doing to himself. Not when I know he's so close to breaking and that he thinks he's knocking on death's door.

"Look. It's not about you," I say as earnestly as possible. "I just want to live a little, and I'm not ready to get tied down to any man. So don't torture yourself over my decisions, even if you don't understand them."

His gaze studies my face for a long time, then his grip loosens, and he drops my arm. For a moment, I think maybe—just maybe—he'll listen. But he exhales in a huff and shakes his head. Then he fixes his belt. He grabs his shirt and cut, and turns, strides out of the room, leaving me shocked as hell in his wake.

I quickly dress and follow him, making it into the lounge room in time to see him pocket the pills.

He gives me one long last look. "Don't let what I do stop you from having a good time."

It feels like a swift kick to the gut, those words, and the sickness in my stomach mounts as I watch him leave the clubhouse. My chest aches fiercely with the need to go after him. The shame, anger, and guilt are paralyzing. It all blurs together. I want to scream at him and tell him he does matter, that he's always mattered. In all the years, it's only ever been him. That the knowing without knowing is real. But those words will be his demise, not his salvation.

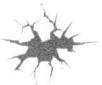

LILY

A few days after the incident with Goose, I meet up with Raven for lunch. We order appetizers and drinks—iced tea for her and pink lemonade for me—before Raven gets straight to the point.

"He's not okay, Lily." Raven has leaned forward so as to keep this conversation private from the other patrons of the restaurant. She looks impeccable in a short nude dress with matching pumps, but her expression is pinched, and there are dark circles under her eyes. Her fingers are cinched so tightly around her biceps that they dig into her skin.

"I know," I reply, doing my best to brush it off like it isn't tearing me apart to watch from afar.

I feel guilt as if it's a toxic layer to my skin, and I can't shake it or wash it off. Guilt as if I wrote him the prescription, poured the drink, or lit up the joint and passed it over to him. Sure, I can talk my way around it because these are his choices to make after all, but it doesn't negate the fact that in some way, I feel directly responsible.

"He's fading. I don't know what he's on, but it's bad. I'm worried about him. Some days he doesn't even call to let me know he's not coming in. Others, he doesn't pick up his phone when I call to check on him. That's not like him."

"What do you want me to do? I'm not sure how I can help." The act is extremely difficult to pull off because inside, I'm shaking.

The way she stares me down with no words, only silence, speaks volumes. Finally, she takes a long inhale and asks, "Do you care for him?"

This has my hackles rising. "Of course I do." More than she could ever know.

She grabs my hand, pulls me closer, and squeezes her fingers around mine. "I know you do, and that's why I'm asking you this. Because if there is anyone who can get through to him, I think it's you. It doesn't make sense, and it doesn't have to. Not to me or anyone else. But there's something there between you. The more you push him away, the worse it gets, and the less I see of the real you. It's like the fact that you both are denying it is only making it stronger and making you both act out in strange and, quite frankly, stupid ways. So yeah, I see it and I don't give a fuck what it is as long as you try for me to see if you can help him."

I fight the bile rising up behind my throat and the rock in the pit of my stomach. "What do you want me to do?"

"Just talk to him. Try to see if he'll see a doctor. I know it's a big ask. But I'm asking anyway. If not for Goose, do it for me, please. I love that damn man as if he's my big brother. I don't want to live in a world where he's not showing up to prove to us all that there are still good men left on this planet. Because make no mistake, Lily, that's what he is underneath all of this, this addiction that's grabbed hold of him, and the pain that he has to live with daily. He's a damn good fucking man. The best. Please see through it and find a way to reach him."

She stares at me, fucking through me, and with her whole heart pouring right there through her eyes, I can't deny her."

Nodding, I say, "Okay, I'll talk to him. I'm not sure if it will do any good, but I will at least try."

Another squeeze. "Thank you."

When I get back to my hotel, I sink down to the floor against the closed door and stay there for a long time as I fight the dread mounting inside of me.

Fuck. This man is going to be the death of me because my heart can't stand to watch him fall. I can't deny the love I still have for him. Through all the years. The hurt. The anger and frustration, it's the love that overrides everything.

Ten fucking years and he's still my everything.

So why the fuck am I putting everything before him?

Good fucking questions, Lily. You need to figure your shit out.

My mind drifts back to the day this all started and the first moment I laid eyes on Finn.

"You sure you want to do this, baby girl?" Destiny asks. There's doubt and compassion in her eyes. "I got no choice. I leave, they'll hurt my boy. But you, you could make a run for it." She's taken me under her wing, given me a crash course of how to make it on the streets, and though a part of me wants to do what she says, run like hell, the other part of me knows I have nowhere to run to. And that most likely I'll end up dead if I try.

I don't really have a choice anymore. The skin between my thumb and pointer finger is burned, and raised with blisters. A brand that tells me I'm no longer free to do as I please. From what I've heard, it's nearly impossible to escape the Thirteen Devils once they've branded you as their property.

If I run, they'll hunt me down. If I don't deliver cash at the end of the night, I won't just receive a backhand to the face this time, I'll be beaten within an inch of my life. And I can already feel my skin itching. The ache for another hit is getting stronger with each second. If I leave now, the withdrawals will hit, and I know it will only be a matter of time before my body overrides my brain and demands I go back to the one man who'll make it all stop.

Kandy spins around from where she's standing by the curb. "Don't be puttin' crazy-ass thoughts in her head. Veno hears you been flappin' your lips like that he'll cut your fuckin' tits off, mama. She's his new money train now, whether she likes it or not."

"Mind your own, puta. She's sixteen. The girl's got no fuckin' business doin' what we do."

"Seventeen, actually," I say, but Destiny and Kandy ignore me.

"Ah bullshit, Des. Age means nothin'. A girl that bleeds, can breed.

And it's not like she's a virgin."

Destiny turns her back on Kandy, but that doesn't keep Kandy from saying what's on her mind. "She's branded now. There ain't no way out no more. You fillin' her head with thoughts of runnin' is only gonna get her killed, 'ight? What she needs is to be told it ain't nothin'. That she'll get used to it just like we have." Kandy's chocolate eyes swing to lock with mine. "It's all about the green, baby girl. Suck 'em, fuck 'em, but get the dough up front. That's your world now. You do that— your life is gonna be cherries. You don't... well... it's gonna be nothin' but pain." Her gaze hardens and moves to Destiny's. "That's what the girl needs to hear."

For the next thirty minutes or so, the tension between Destiny and Kandy slowly dissolves. All too soon, they're back to gossiping about the other girls and telling trick stories that have even a smile forming on my face.

Before I hear the car coming, both women go quiet. Like a switch has been flipped, Kandy and Destiny straighten, suck in, and become all smiles. They saunter towards the approaching car and peacock, flaunting their best attributes. Under their breath, they categorize the curb crawler before the vehicle comes to a stop.

From what Kandy can remember, he likes to deliver a little pain, slaps on the ass, pinching, a little choking, but nothing that crosses the border into brutal.

For all her blustering, Kandy moves directly in front of me, swinging her hips from side to side when the John tries to look around her. Filling up the space in his open window, she cuts me out of his view completely. It could be purely selfish, so she ensures she clears her quota for the night, but for some reason, I don't think that's her only motivation for steering his attention away from me.

Quick words are exchanged, and before getting into the car, she turns and winks at me.

Coming back to stand beside me, Destiny sighs, "Here's to hopin' the next one is a harmless suit with a fat wallet."

While we wait, Destiny talks about her little boy. She's worried because he won't stop coughing, and Pedro, the father and one of

Veno's right-hand men, won't let her take him to see a doctor.

As the minutes tick by, I become calmed by her soothing voice and the distant hum of traffic on the freeway. When the next person approaches us, it isn't by car. Popping off the wall, Destiny looks down the street. "Oh, look who it is."

I lean forward and cock my head to the side to see a man running in our direction. Not in an aggressive way. But a little more than a leisurely jog.

"We call him Sex-On-Legs, honey."

It's not until he runs under the glow of the nearest street light that I get a good look. Tall, broad, dark from head to toe, and rippling with muscles. Precisely what the nickname proclaims him to be. And there's something about the way he holds himself that has my stomach cartwheeling. Maybe it's the fact that he's in total control of his body. Everything muscle, every limb, and he races through the hot night like nothing out here in the darkest and seediest part of town could touch him.

"Flaunt what you got, baby girl. If anyone can finally tempt him into a night of fun, it's you."

At the sight of him, I seem to be unable to move. I'm too struck by his masculine beauty and the intensity covering his features.

Then his head turns. His fierce eyes lock with mine. His steps falter as my chest seizes.

Mother of God… he's even more gorgeous than I thought.

Hair black as oil. Jaw cut sharply like it's made from stone. And the muscles on this guy…

His eyes drift down my body, taking in all the ways I've tried to make myself look older. It takes a few seconds for him to look his fill, and when he's finished, his brows draw together in disapproval. He shakes his head and resumes his run. Just jogs right the hell by.

Leaving me behind like I'm nothing.

Maybe I am to a guy like him.

Destiny calls after him. "Oh, sexy, where you goin'? We'd give you two for the price of one."

Yeah, no. Maybe Destiny could handle a man like that. But I'm not so sure.

He looks like the kind of man who could make me question everything about myself and wish I'd made better choices. Thoughts that a girl like me can't afford to dwell on.

This is my life now, no matter how much I wish otherwise.

LOST LYREBIRD

CHAPTER 37

Grief is a lake we visit and wade into. Don't stay too long or you may get pulled under.

The dead can't talk back, but they sure as hell are good listeners. I truly believe that. I've seen enough evidence of it in my life to the point it's indisputable.

Since my father's passing, he's been here somehow, watching over me. Helping when he can. Guiding me in some way. But I'm no longer able to feel his lingering presence. Whether that's from the shit coursing through my veins drowning him out, or it's his way of showing his disapproval—I don't know.

After crouching down, I reach out and feel the headstone by touch to center myself. It's blurry, and the words engraved on the front blend together.

I don't know what he wants me to do. All I want is some freedom from the pain, for a day, for an hour, for a fucking moment. That's not achievable without the pills anymore. I've tried everything Alister recommended—more sleep, changing my diet, limiting my caffeine intake, cognitive and physical therapy. I took time away from the club to avoid the loud music and lights.

Nothing works.

I've gone under the knife twice in the past with no improvement, and the recovery was a nightmare. I can't go through that again.

It's gotten to the point that everything's a trigger. Pushing my brain to work through a simple puzzle brings pain. Working with my saw or any loud equipment in my shop does the same. Using my muscles to chisel and sand, or overexerting myself in any way, is rewarded by a migraine. Being on the road alone and surrounded by silence is my only escape from it all. But I have to wear earplugs. The roar of my bike has to be muted to even enjoy the one thing that I used to enjoy most in the world, and that's no way to live.

Time makes it worse, and it's the one thing I can't run from or avoid.

There's no fixing this. Agony or functionality are my only two options.

The number of people getting hurt in my wake is growing by the day. Hodge. Bethany and her kids, Axel and Medda. The girls who are being retaliated against because I got Larissa out. Not being able to put a stop to Veno and letting him profit from these girls weighs on me, too, but my hands are tied.

And what I did to Lily is inexcusable.

It replays over and over again in my mind, the look on her face when she slapped me.

Yeah, she'd been into it in the end, but what if she hadn't been? Would I have stopped? I want to say yes, but the truth is… I'd been at the end of my rope, so fucking furious and jealous. Fed the fuck up with watching another man put his hands on her. She'd been laughing and rubbing up against Griz all night, and then disappeared upstairs with him, and I just knew I couldn't fucking do it anymore.

These are the regrets I'll take to the grave with me.

That and the fact I can't take Veno down on my way out because it would blow back on the club and my brothers.

Taking my sobriety coin from my pocket, I lay it over my father's headstone. When I first got sober, I came here and promised him I'd stay clean, that I'd use my time here wisely, and help those I could. That I'd do no harm, only good.

More broken promises to add to the list.

I pull out the small black and silver compass from my cut. It belonged to my father's friend Ben. He'd passed not even a year after my father, and gifted it to me in his will. They'd been in a long-term care facility together, and though my father was in the Army and Ben was in the Navy, they hit it off like they'd known each other for years. Just two old Vets giving the nurses a run for their money, or so Anita, the head nurse, used to say when I'd call to check in on my dad.

Now, I could throw a stone and hit Ben's grave with how close it is. And even though I know that neither of them truly rests at peace here, it comforts me, in case I'm wrong.

The compass has a surprising weight to it. Flipping it over, I run my thumb over the inscription. *I am the master of my fate. I am the captain of my soul.*

If only that were true.

I lay it beside the coin on the headstone. Then I run my fingers over the letters and numbers that tell the world very little about the man this grave marker stands in place of.

TRENT MATTHEW MCCOWN
BELOVED FATHER AND FRIEND
1946-1997

He was the kind of man who knew how to fix everything and turned every conversation into a lesson about life. If I asked for money so I could go on a date, it was a sit-down session where he'd impart wisdom on me about how to treat a woman. If I came home late after a night out with my friends, or got pissed off after one of my games, nothing slid. They were opportunities to share what he'd learned about life, and looking back, I'm thankful for those moments. Though at the time, I hated them immensely.

God, what I wouldn't fucking give to have one of those sit-downs now. Pour my heart out to him and let him tell me what to do, how to fix my life, how to get rid of the holes and fight this fucking abyss I've fallen into, maybe be my guide me back to the light.

If only I could go back. There's so much I'd change. I'd sit and listen with rapt attention to the wisdom he'd impart. Perhaps not to gripe so much about what I saw as meaningless babble. It's funny how we can only see that shit looking back. We just fly right past these monumental moments that are the best parts of our life and don't see them for what they are until they're in our rearview.

I look up and stare at the bright stars overhead, and get lost in the night sky as I talk about it all with him. I talk about Elle. About all I've done to find her and how all of the notes I have led me to believe that the woman in my life, the only one I've come to care about in all my years on this earth, seems to be one and the same. But I don't trust my own mind, because well, it can't be trusted.

I talk about my dreams, Veno, the woman I've helped, my brothers, the club, and the people there, and lastly, the things in life that used to make me happy.

When I've spilled my guts and confessed to it all, I pull the gun from my waistband and hold it in my right hand. It's a choice. A last resort. A way out of this madness. I came here to pour my heart out and seek answers, but if that doesn't happen, then I guess that's answer enough, right?

I'm hoping for a sign, something, to tell me to hold on.

I just don't know what else to do at this point. But this endless cycle of pain needs to come to an end, either way, because I don't want anyone else to get hurt due to my actions.

It's my soul at risk. Dad taught me that much. We weren't religious in the same sense that other people are, but believed the basics of heaven and hell, and in the man upstairs and one below. My dad taught me that you choose your path by your deeds. You end up where you deserve to be based on how you live your life, and at the end of the day, you either pave your way to heaven or hell.

If I go through with it, it will be my one-way ticket to a place where my dad won't be waiting for me. Yet, there's been no sign to help find a different path.

When I fall on my ass because my balance is fucked, I stay there. Staring down at the gun, I let the best and worst moments of what I can remember play through my mind, wondering if this will be all there is for me.

If it ends here.

LOST LYREBIRD

No matter how long the journey or
how harsh the weather, birds will brave
many dangers to find their way home

HARBINGERS OF CHAOS

REVEL IN CHAOS

REGRET NOTHING

NEW MEXICO

Part two

CHAPTER 38

*Shadows of the past never disappear entirely.
They linger, haunt our present and future if
we don't shine enough light on them.*

JULY 1997 – 10 Years earlier

Had I known the last time I visited during my last leave would be the last time we'd speak, or the last time he would assess me with his knowing gaze, I would have stayed longer. I'd have found a way to stretch time, make the most of our moments, maybe even talked about more deep and meaningful things. As I grip his pale, frail, and weightless hand in mine, I can't stop thinking about all the things I don't know about my own father, and how now, I'll never know.

My inability to face the severity of his illness has caught up with me. The lies I'd told myself. We'd work out our shit another time. That he'd recover. He'd bounce back. He always did.

But this is different.

This is the end.

The lies I'd told myself had been born out of necessity. At the time, they'd helped me compartmentalize.

His denials about being sick, his disappearances at odd times—the fact that he looked me in the eye for years and lied straight to my face.

The memory of finding him sprawled on our kitchen floor, lips blue, chest barely moving, and me not knowing what the fuck to do—this all drove a solid wedge a mile wide between us. When the truth unraveled later in the emergency room, my despair over the possibility of losing the only family member I gave a fuck about, sent me into a tailspin and I'd been scrambling for something else to hold onto.

I knew I had to find something to anchor me to this world; otherwise, I might just choose one day to follow right after him. Watching him die day by day would break me into a thousand pieces. And I just couldn't fucking do it.

My enlistment in the Army, was my out. My excuse. I didn't want a front-row seat to him withering away, and I told myself strangers could better provide the care he needed.

And with the belief in the lie, I could pretend his duplicity didn't shatter our relationship. I could pretend to be the perfect son while hiding a wealth of dark thoughts living inside my mind. The Army granted me distance from it all, which in turn gave me the ability to keep the wrath that existed under my skin from showing itself.

I'd been young and in denial. It wasn't the only path I could have taken. How ironic that as my time in the service winds down, his time here ends, giving me no time to make it right and recover what we've lost.

He's not waking, and there's not a goddamn thing I can do to change it.

Carefully, I shift his wrinkled hand and place it to rest over his chest. Every joint in my body rebels as I stand. Sitting here for hours on end after doing the same on the flight home has me stiff all over. My body isn't used to being stationary.

I place my palm gently over his for a moment and listen to him take his stuttering breaths. Spittle coats his mouth under the breathing mask, and though I've wiped it away a few times, it quickly returns. Each breath is labored and accompanied by a sucking gurgle, and out with a whoosh through his lips.

His failing lungs don't have the capacity to hold the oxygen he needs to live. The doctor estimates they're at thirty percent now. Air is flowing into the mask covering his nose, but he can't hold it in his lungs long enough to do much good. There's not enough oxygen getting to his head, heart, and other organs, so everything is shutting down.

He's slipped into a coma, and he's not going to wake up. I found that out from his doctor upon arrival.

It had nearly knocked me to my knees. Beating back the tsunami of emotion took everything I had. I just thank fuck I waited until the doctor left my dad's room before I lost my shit. Because it hit me then. The lies, along with an inferno of anger at my father, at myself, and it all became un-fucking-bearable. It took every bit of my self-control to keep myself from tearing the place apart.

When I managed to get myself under control, grief struck like a vicious bitch. I cried like a goddamn kid and not like a twenty-nine-year-old Army Ranger.

Fortunately, my dad, in his comatose state, saw none of it.

I take solace in the fact that he's being given morphine to dull his pain. I don't know if he's aware of my presence. I want to believe he is, but who the fuck knows.

I fill my own lungs with his teakwood and clove scent as I finger-comb some of his wiry gray hair away from his weathered brow. I close my eyes for a moment to commit that smell to memory. It's hard to see him this way. He's so thin. His cheeks sunken in.

I place a kiss on top of his head. "Love you, Pop. I'll be back. Going to head to the house, check on things, maybe take a shower, because damn." I give myself a quick sniff and yep, I'm ripe. "I'll be back." The words tumble out in a hoarse whisper, emotion clogging my throat. "Hang in there, alright." Before I can get overwhelmed, I turn to leave.

Mr. Nava is wheeling himself down the hallway towards me. The faded navy tats covering his hands blur as he propels himself forward. He's heavier, a broad chest and torso with a slimmer lower half. When he stops in front of me, I squeeze his shoulder, not sure what to say.

"Shit, son. This just came out of nowhere." He shakes his head. "Started wheezing and later that night he was complaining that he couldn't breathe. I thought he'd be right as rain like always after a rest or at least hold on until you got here, but he just couldn't hold off any longer, I guess. Still no change?"

"Nah, and the doctor doesn't think he has long. A few days at most."

"I'm sorry, Finn. He'd fight to stay with you if he could."

I squeeze his shoulder again and nod. "I know." Then I change the subject to him and how he's doing, so I can keep my shit together. He fills me in on what his kids have been up to since the last time I was stateside, but he keeps it brief, probably because I look like shit, and he knows my mind is on my dad.

"I'm glad he's had you here with him, this last year." I'm earnest about it too. The last few times I did reach out, it was "Ben this" and "Ben that." Had they been any younger and healthier, I have no doubt I would have been bailing their asses out of jail.

The thought makes me almost smile.

When I finally make my way to the exit, I note the changes I missed upon arrival: a new TV in the dining area, some unfamiliar faces, and new furniture. Pauline, as always, has the TV cranked all the way up as she watches the evening news and crochets while sitting in a rocking chair. A couple of the doors I pass in the hallway are decorated with red, white, and blue; some with flags, giving voice to the holiday I missed while on the flight here.

The last door I pass before the nurse's station has a hand-drawn picture of stick figures underneath a cloud filled with fireworks. It's a kid's drawing and cute as shit.

When I reach the front desk, I lean on the elevated granite surface as I wait for Anita, my favorite nurse here, to pause in her form-filling and acknowledge me. She's been my saving grace these last few years, always keeping me up to date on Dad's treatments and moods, going above and beyond to help me find ways to save money or apply for assistance where I can. Things I never would have known about without her help.

Still filling out forms, she tilts her head and spares me a quick glance.

"Just wanted to let you know, I'm going to swing home for a bit, shower, maybe get a few hours of shuteye."

"About time. Can't be any use to anyone as tired as you are."

There's no denying it, so I don't.

"How long was the flight?" she asks.

I rub my face, feeling every one of the hours I've spent awake and especially the hours I had to travel to get here, while riddled with worry that I wouldn't make it in time. "Fourteen or so hours in total with layovers."

"You driving?"

Hitching my thumb over my shoulder, I mutter, "Got the bike. My friend had it stored in his garage for me, and he and his wife met me with it at the airport so I could have some wheels as soon as I touched down."

She stops doing paperwork and raises her head. Her dark-brown eyes throw daggers as she pierces me with a fierce expression. Stabbing her pen in my direction for emphasis, she says, "Go get some rest and a good dinner. But so help me, Sergeant McCown, if you crash on that damn bike, I will hunt you down, you hear me!"

I knock on the counter. The corner of my mouth lifts in a half-grin. "I'll be careful."

She mutters, "You better. Don't you dare make this old woman live with that kind of guilt."

"I've got my pager. Page me if there's any change."

"I promise. I'll keep an eye on him."

Turning, I head towards the automatic double doors, but shout over my shoulder, "You're an angel, Anita."

She laughs and points towards the ceiling, "From your mouth to God's ears."

I chuckle as I leave the facility. When the fresh air hits me, I draw the recent scent of rain mixed with desert musk into my lungs. The scent is grounding and brings back many memories. There's nothing like it. The desert in Iraq is nothing like it is here in New Mexico.

A few minutes later, I'm accelerating through a turn on autopilot, my thoughts circling. I've been thinking about the past, back to when it all started, when the doctor first explained Dad's disease.

At the time, I couldn't for the life of me wrap my head around it. Any of it. My dad dying. The fact his disease, COPD, wasn't curable. The fact that even with a lung transplant, the mortality rate was still astronomically high.

The doctor said the highways in his lungs were shutting down, one by one, as if it were some fucking motorway somewhere with exits and onramps, toll roads and roadblocks due to construction. He finished by explaining it would eventually be fatal. Fucking fatal. They could only work to sustain his health as best as they could and give him as many years as possible, but in the best case, he would have eight to ten years with me if we were lucky.

God, I'd been so angry.

So fucking angry.

I could have set the world on fire and burned it down. Because not only was he sick, but he'd hidden it from me for almost three years, until he'd been too sick to hide it anymore.

The fury I lived with after finding out about his diagnosis and deceit boiled inside every cell of my body. It lived and breathed as if a separate entity. It filled every vein. I'd been a silent supernova throughout the rest of my junior year in high school. Walking down the hallways, silent as a ghost, ready to explode at any moment. Some nights, I imagined myself standing on a cliff in some far-off place and raging at the storm coming in from the sea, screaming with every ounce of breath. Rain and a strong wind would pelt me, and I would just rage right back at it with everything I had.

I battled it for months, the silent sea storm. Sometimes I had the strength to stand. Sometimes I didn't and crashed to my knees. When I did fall, head bent, I would push my fists as deep into the sand as I could, and then punch it for all I was worth.

This is what lived in my head. Because outside of it, I was a shell of indifference.

I tried to hide this battle from my dad. But of course, he saw through it. He had a unique gift that way, of reading people. He bought me a journal and a set of expensive felt-tip pens. He sat me down and told me that the anger was like a cancer. He was already sick, there was nothing to be done about it, but he'd be damned if I ruined myself over my feelings about it too. He said it would eat me up from the inside out if I didn't get it out somehow, that regret and anger were funny like that. That sometimes mental illness manifests as a real condition in the body, because the mind, body, and soul are connected in ways we can't fathom. He truly believed the mind could condemn or save you depending on your mindset.

He swore he would never read the journal or invade my privacy.

I think he knew how dark my thoughts were and that they were getting darker day by day. Hell, maybe his own troubled past gave him insight into how I'd turn out if I kept feeding the "wrong wolf".

I ignored the journal for months until one day, I didn't.

It turned out that writing it on paper hadn't been the worst idea. But yeah, I guess part of the reason I had been holding it in was because I didn't want anyone to see it, the vilest, worst parts of me. Him most of all. It wasn't his fault he was sick. Lying about it was, but in some small way, I understood that he didn't want his sickness impacting the choices I made at that point in my life. That had been his reasoning and in a way, I hated it, but I'd also got it.

I was going somewhere with baseball, or so the future prospects at the time hinted at. I had a natural talent and high hopes. We'd been anticipating a scholarship at a good school, which would most likely mean I'd be leaving New Mexico after graduating from high school.

His illness changed that.

It was exactly what he didn't want, but fuck him. He was my dad. I wasn't going to play another game if he was too sick to come and watch me.

So we both lost in the end. I lost my love for the game, and he hated that he was the cause of it.

I'd gone through two journals in a little over a month, and there had been no signs of stopping once I started pouring all the emotions out. A few months after I started journaling my thoughts, there was a noticeable difference in how I felt.

It had worked. I didn't tell him that. But my dad knew.

It took me a long time to come to terms with everything. Years in fact. And then I'd been approached by an Army recruiter, and the rest is history. I saw my out and a way to pay for the care he was going to need as the situation worsened.

I'd enlisted and convinced myself it was the right path to take.

I regret that the most. The lost time. The time he had remaining, which I essentially threw away and ran from.

I know I should be thankful he made it this long. Thirteen years is much longer than his doctor gave him, but also, it's my dad, and I'm too young to watch the man who raised me die.

These thoughts circle as I make my way home, where I'll no doubt need to take some time to write some of them out, or at the very least grab one of my journals to take back to the nursing home with me when I return.

I'm pretty confident, I'm going to need an outlet for when he gets to the end and after. Only God knows how in the hell I'm going to live the rest of my life without him.

It's funny how a large period of time away from a place can give you fresh eyes. Those are my thoughts as I gun my Fatboy down the familiar yet also unrecognizable street. It's been a while, but I don't remember the paint on the homes here being so faded, or the yards looking this worse for wear. It's as if no one throws away shit anymore; they just repurpose it because they can't be bothered to take it to the dump.

I'm light on the throttle. Not wanting to wake the neighborhood at this ungodly hour, but another block down, I pass a house with a party in full bloom, their music bumping loud enough to drown out the growl from my Harley.

At the next turn, I eye the group of kids standing there and take note of the broken streetlight. I gun the throttle just enough at the last turn to get me the rest of the way home, then slowly pull up to the curb. Gravel slides under my boots, sending tiny vibrations up my legs.

It doesn't take long for unease to skate across my skin as I take in our two-bedroom rambler.

"Fuuuuck. Come the fuck on. Are you kidding me? Fuck."

Apparently, I'd been lied to. There's an overturned trash can in the driveway, debris scattered everywhere, some of it even stuck in the chain link, and caught in the overgrown grass. But what really has me pissed is the fact that the garage has been tagged with spray paint.

"Son of a bitch." I've been paying a property management company to take care of this place, keep it up. By the looks of it, they haven't done shit in the last few months. I thrust the kickstand down and, after biting the tip of my glove, peel one off, then the other.

The gang symbol on the garage is a black devil's head with curled horns. The numbers one and three are scrawled in the eye sockets in blue paint.

A rock drops into the pit of my stomach as I take it all in.

I rub my face, try to shake the sleep and tension out of it, but my anger is building fast. There's nothing I can do about this right now, but goddamn it, this is the last thing I needed.

After taking off my chin strap, I rip off my helmet and fight not to throw the damn thing. This is going to cost me. Guess getting ahead of the bills and keeping extra money in savings wasn't in the cards for me. Not when life keeps throwing buckets of shit at me every time I get close to even.

I'm dead on my feet, and I need to get back to my dad. I can't leave the driveway like this, and obviously, I can't trust strangers to do shit for me. So, with curses spilling from my lips, I start grabbing piece after piece of trash. I flip the garbage can back to its feet, toss what I've collected inside. It's enough for now, but it's far from done.

As I turn to head back, I freeze. My peripheral catches movement, and I slowly spin around to find a face staring at me from behind the curtains of the front bay window.

What the actual fuck?

The hairs on my neck prickle as I stride forward. I don't bother with the gate; I just plant my hands on the top of the chain-link and vault over it.

The thought of some stranger squatting here makes my vision go red. Did they go through my dad's things? Steal shit?

I hear shouting coming from inside. I can't make out the words, but it sounds like someone's yelling in Spanish. My heart races as I kick at the front door. It doesn't budge. Feels like something more than just a deadbolt is keeping it shut.

Oh, some fucker is gonna die today.

I kick and kick until the frame splinters. Using my shoulder, I wedge it the rest of the way open, forcing my way through until it finally gives. When it does, I stumble inside and grab the couch to steady myself. The smell hits me like a fucking wall—overpowering, burning my nostrils in seconds.

Training kicks in, and I yank my shirt up to cover the lower half of my face, but it's useless. The air stinks like rotten eggs mixed with paint thinner, the stench so sharp it makes my eyes water. My throat tightens, and I gag.

I don't have a second to get my bearings before the sound of a gunshot splits the air. I drop to the floor, fast, like a stone falling through water, my heart racing in an instant.

Motherfucker.

More shots ring out, clunking and pinging against the walls and furniture—way too fucking close. Thankfully, the couch gives me some cover, and I'm close enough to grab the coffee table. Using every bit of my strength, I tip it over and shove it in front of me, adding another layer of protection from the person firing from the direction of the kitchen.

I curse myself for leaving my sidearm locked in the small safe inside my bag, which is still on my bike. I let personal attachment and emotion override my training. That's the part that surprises the hell out of me. I should've assessed the situation, not rushed in blind, but it's too late to dwell on it now.

A crash echoes, then the unmistakable sound of a fuck ton of glass shattering.

Which could be a window or the back sliding door.

I catch a few Spanish words shouted in a panicked tone—"Vámonos" and "Mijo"—the rest is lost on me. But it's clear whoever's in my house speaks it fluently, and they're fleeing into the backyard.

Tempting fate, I peek around the table. When I don't see anyone, I crawl forward. The air is thick, heavy with poison, making it hard to breathe, but I fight through it. I pull myself into a crouch, double-checking the area to be sure they're gone, before slowly rising to my feet.

I move carefully, making sure there's cover in case someone's waiting for me.

At the threshold of the kitchen, the destruction hits me like a punch to the gut. For a moment, I freeze, stunned. Plastic jugs are scattered across the floor, along with tubes, plastic barrels, beakers, measuring cups, and some large silver cooking pots—some standing, others tipped over in chaos. Smoke rises from the far corner, a small fire starting to take hold.

The setup is crude but distinguishable. A goddamn meth lab.

So… motherfucking dead.

I yank open a drawer and grab the largest knife I can find. It's not much, but I'm damn good with blades. Speed has always been my advantage. I was good at baseball for the same reason, and it's saved my ass more times than I can count during hand-to-hand training. With a knife, I can do some serious damage.

My heart's hammering, adrenaline coursing through me. I force out steady breaths, then turn and head toward the dining room.

I almost throw the knife when I see them. Thank God I don't. I freeze just in time—a kid, no older than fourteen or fifteen, stuck at the shattered glass door. He's tugging at a bag that's caught on the glass at the bottom, grunting in frustration as it refuses to budge.

At the sight of me, he crouches, then yells something behind him. My grip tightens on the knife as I move closer. His eyes widen with fear, and he slowly rises, letting go of the bag. His hands shake visibly.

He looks like a scared fucking deer caught in headlights. His dark brown eyes are locked on the knife in my hand, and I know in that moment: he's not the threat.

A shadow moves behind him, and instinct kicks in. I duck back behind the wall just as another shot rings out. The bullet slams into the wall near my head, plaster exploding around me.

I sneak another look around the corner. The bag is gone, and I see two figures—one large, one small—darting into the night.

God, he was just a kid.

I'm fucking thankful I didn't throw the knife. Because that's the last thing I need, to add another shadow to the ones that already haunt me.

Uncertainty and anger war within me. Part of me wants to chase them down, but another part of me wants to be smarter about this. What drives me forward is the kid.

Rivers' mantra flashes through my mind. "Always go with option C." His reckless, kamikaze attitude keeps our team on edge, and sometimes it means we have to pull his crazy ass out of dangerous situations because he won't hold back. A mix of options A and B— that's option C. The best of both.

The first thing I do is grab the fire extinguisher and put out the flames. Then I grab my dad's old firearm from the safe in the garage, slipping it into the waistband at my back. I'm not planning to shoot anyone unless it comes down to me or them. Along with the gun, I grab a tire iron, a hunting knife, and duct tape.

As I dart through the backyard, I clear every shadow, using what little I can for cover. Every step is taken with care.

When I reach the back fence, I hear an engine rev, the RPMs higher than normal. My footsteps quicken. After scaling the fence, I head toward the noise, east and a half block up the road. Each car becomes my shield. Not foolproof, but it's all I've got.

There's music blaring from a vehicle, tires screeching, and more words shouted in Spanish. This time, I do my best to pick out the words so I can figure out their meaning later.

"¡Levántalo! ¡Levántalo! ¡Rápido!"

Lift it up! Lift it up! Quick!

A younger voice responds, "Estoy tratando, papá."

I'm trying, Dad.

I shrug out of my leather jacket, needing to move freely. Fortunately,

I'd worn an old, threadbare grey t-shirt underneath.

"No puedo. Es muy pesado."

I can't. It's too heavy.

I hear a sob, followed by a cry of pain, then more cursing.

The engine revs again, echoing through the neighborhood. I peek around the front of the car I'm crouched behind and measure the distance from where I stand to their car, judging by the light spilling on the pavement. I sprint in a crouch from one car to the next. If I get close enough, I might catch some identifying info for Joey when I call this in.

What I see next is a boxy, blue Chevy with fresh paint and chromed-out wheels. It's riding low, and I can just make out the driver, mostly in shadow.

"Vamos, mueve el culo. ¿Qué carajo pasó? Explicar. ¿Alguien rompió la puerta? ¿Policías?

Come on, move your ass. What the hell happened? Explain. Did someone break the door down? Was it the cops?

Multiple voices come in rapid-fire succession.

The driver, one hand on the wheel, the other hanging out the open window, looks back at the people in the backseat. I focus on the bigger guy next to him—buzzed short hair, thick rings on his fingers, and a horrible scar running from his mouth to his ear. When the driver turns back to face the front, I take him in. He's bald with a thick, dark mustache. A black and white bandana is folded and sits low on his forehead. There's a massive tattoo covering his forearm—a large black scorpion is on top of another with its tail poised to strike the scorpion below. He also has three small teardrops tattooed beneath the corner of his eye, and the same image on my garage is tattooed on his neck as well as his hand that's on the steering wheel.

It's got to be enough.

I duck back behind the car and wait until they speed off down the road.

Back inside through the smashed door, I grab a notebook and write down everything I can remember. Then I grab the wall phone and call Joey. He sounds groggy but promises he'll be here in twenty minutes.

My gaze zeroes in on a metal pot lying on its side on the floor. Brownish-yellow liquid is leaking out. There's a massive puddle on the kitchen floor, spreading, now even creeping toward the carpet. I don't know why I focus on it—it's just that it makes everything worse.

Looking around the house, I realize there's no fixing this, and even if I could, it'll never be the same.

Anger burns through me, a violent itch under my skin, demanding action. More action than just reporting it to the cops. The hell if I'm going to wait for them to figure out who these assholes are and eventually catch them. I trust Joey—he's a damn good detective—but this is personal. The need to exact my own revenge is riding me hard.

LOST LYREBIRD

CHAPTER 39

Time for a last goodbye is a gift, make the most of it.

JULY 1997

I run through the automatic front doors as soon as they open, and the fact that Anita isn't there waiting causes panic to flare inside my chest. There's another nurse. She waves me forward in a hurried manner. Together, we run down the illuminated hallway. The closer we get, the more I hear—Anita's voice, calling out orders.

When I enter, I see Rhonda, the head RN, working over my father. She's doing CPR while Anita squeezes a plastic bubble to push air into his lungs.

I freeze in the doorway. Anita's eyes fly up to mine. She doesn't stop squeezing and never loses count, but she shakes her head.

Though my feet weigh me down with what feels like a hundred pounds per step, I move forward. "How long?" Because I refuse to let him go without at least getting a chance to say goodbye.

Anita flicks a glance at her watch. "A little over four minutes."

The blaring sound of the monitor has been turned off at some point, but I see the flat, blue line sliding across the screen.

Rhonda's black hair has come out of her clip, and a few strands stick to her lips. It's obvious she's tried her best, but I fucking refuse to give up on him.

She's not strong enough, and though I know I'm about to get security called on my ass, I bodily move her out of the way so I can take over.

She screeches, "What are you doing?" And she attempts to pry my hands away. But I push her back and start again.

"Your arms aren't strong enough to force enough air in."

"You can't—"

"It's okay." Anita holds up a hand. "He's a medic in the Army. He knows what he's doing."

Rhonda snaps, "Anita, think rationally here—"

"I am." The two women stare each other down. "You're tired, and your compressions were only getting weaker. What we've been doing hasn't worked. It's his father. Let him try."

Anita glares at me, fear in her eyes. "Don't crack his chest."

I nod once in understanding, get on the bed, knees on each side of him, and lean over his chest. Counting in my head as I go. I want to detach to do this right, but I can't. I keep telling myself I know how to do this. I've done it so many times. But also the words . . . *This can't be how things end* pops into my mind.

"Adrenaline?" I ask.

"Already injected," Anita replies.

"How much?"

"One cc."

"Let's do one more. Shock pads?"

"They're on."

"How many times has he been hit?"

"Two."

"Level?"

"150"

"Turn it up and hit him again. 200."

Thankfully, Anita and a nurse move around the room rapidly to help me. Rhonda throws up her hands. After watching for a few seconds, she grabs the defibrillator and takes over. "Check the pads, Nancy. Make sure he's thoroughly connected."

After the next set of compressions, I back off as they shock him.

Nothing. I recenter myself over him and start a new round of compressions.

Rhonda calls out, "Anita, slow down the ventilation."

The other nurse, Nancy, reconnects a pad that came loose from my dad's chest. She smooths it over before stepping back. When I get close to the end of my count, Anita lifts the ventilation mask and backs up. I leave him again and watch and pray under my breath.

"Clear!"

The jolt rolls over his prone body.

"Anything?" At the same time, I move forward and press my fingers to his neck.

"I feel something, confirm." Then my dad gasps and sucks in a gurgling breath, his chest rises and falls in a stutter.

Rhonda shouts behind me, "He's back. Record the time."

I grab my dad's hand and squeeze it. "Just hold on, Pop." Anita puts the regular oxygen mask over his face, and his jagged breaths return.

Movement out of the corner of my eye draws my attention. Mr. Nava has wheeled himself into the room and is watching us all from just inside the doorway. He's leaning on one of the arms of his wheelchair, and his hand covers his mouth. We nod at each other. "You did the right thing," he says. "He'd want more time with you. Would want you to have a chance to say goodbye."

Anita, Rhonda, and Nancy move around me. They read his vitals and trade information about his stats back and forth. It's white noise to me. The only thing I can focus on is each rattling breath my father takes. They're gifts and somehow fill me with shame at the same time.

Moving close to my old man, I sit beside him on the edge of his bed. I watch him struggle for air while I grip his hand firmly in mine, holding on to him and stealing some time back from fate. I'm thinking only of myself, and my selfishness doesn't escape me. The guilt is simply lower on the totem of emotions filling me to the brim.

I'll pay for what I've done here, no doubt in my mind.

It's my heart in charge at the moment, and the rest I'll deal with later.

The minutes slide into hours, and then another day dawns.

I use the time to talk to him. I stay by his side and tell him everything I can think of about me and my life. I may not be able to know everything about him, but I can sure as hell tell him everything I've held back, details I've never shared with another soul, so before he goes, he knows all of me.

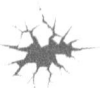

The moment comes. I feel it creeping up on me, like a fading connection, the strength of the bond we share withering. On the opposite end, within me, there's a ball of anxiety, a knot stuck in my throat, a barrier between me and my ability to speak.

The last bit of control I have on my emotions is snapping taut. I know he needs to know I'm okay, and he can go now. I've said what I need to tell him, and I'm just waiting for him.

I want to be able to say *it's okay to go. I love you, and I know it's time.* But those words just won't come. Maybe because years ago, we swore to never lie to each other again. Not after I found him on the floor that day and had to watch as the paramedics performed CPR before they carried him out of our house on a stretcher to the ambulance.

Instead of voicing the lie, I do what I promised and give him the truth.

"Still upset you didn't tell me. I can't tell you what that did to me that day. Coming home from school to find you on the floor. It sent me spinning. I grew up thinking you were untouchable, unshakeable, and that day shook my world to the point it was no longer recognizable."

His eyes flutter behind his eyelids, giving me the sense that maybe he can hear me.

"I don't know if I'll honestly ever forgive you for that."

I sit on the edge of the bed and fix his blanket.

"There were things I'd always meant to ask you. Yeah, I know I should have done it before now, but it was just never the right time, you know? Like what was it about my mom that made her worthy of your love, and yet not mom material? I never understood that."

This next one is a little harder to voice. "Did she ever… you know… reach out again… try to make contact?" *Ask about me? Try to see me?*

"Not something you can answer, but I need to get this out. I think it's why I'm holding on. Still some things left unsaid and bottled up. I keep thinking, as I look at you this way, that I don't want this for you. I don't want you in pain, and I don't want you to suffer anymore. You've suffered enough. I know you need to rest and move on. I know part of what is holding you back is me." I give a humorless laugh and choke up. I stand and grasp the back of my head.

"Holy fuck, this is hard." Tears are welling in my eyes, and I'm fighting them back, but they keep brimming.

I pace a few steps and speak. "I'm sorry. I feel like a little fucking kid suddenly, and I'm clinging to your leg for dear life because I'm afraid to face the world without you right here." I shake my head. Turning, I place my hands on the bed beside his thigh and lean over, letting my head hang between my shoulders. The tears come. I wipe them away rapidly, but more fill those same spaces.

Rolling my shoulders and sucking in a long breath, I go on. "I thought I could do this…" And then a sob tears out of me. I crouch down and cover my face. *Oh God. Oh God.* "Fuck!"

This is it. But I can't. I can't say goodbye. *I can't.* Those words repeat over and over inside my head as tears flood my face, fill my hands, and fall past them. The emotion pours out, my shoulders shaking. I lose my balance and sit on the floor. I sit there, my head between my knees, my hands over my head.

I don't know how long it goes on, but for a good long while, I let the turbulent grief roll through me in a way I never have before. God knows what the patients and nurses think.

When I eventually pull myself together, I use my shirt to wipe my face. I scrape myself off the floor and sit beside him again, my hand resting on his arm.

"I guess I wasn't as ready as I thought." My tone is gruff but steady. "I don't know how to do this. I mean… I knew… of course I knew this day was coming… dreaded it. But I thought I'd be okay. I mean… not okay… but better about handling it. I'm not, in case you missed that." I chuckle through a few tears. They come slower now, but steadily. I wipe roughly at my jaw. Honestly, it's pointless. The river running down my face is endless.

"I know it's your time, Pop. You've done your best to prepare me for this. Even though nothing you or I could have done could have prepared me for this. But I'm… I'm gonna be okay." I cover my mouth to cage in the sob that tries to escape. When I get control of myself, I clear my throat. "I'm not that same angry kid. There's gonna be a lot of grief. There's gonna be days I'm not okay. There's gonna be tough times, I'm sure. But you go on up and watch over me so I can't get through those times, okay. Because knowing you're there and looking out will help. Knowing I'm not totally alone will help." I cover my eyes, pinch the bridge of my nose, then quickly rub away the wetness.

"I'll miss you." I nod and swallow the thick knot in my throat. "I'll miss you so goddamn much. But, I'll be okay." A hand on my back. I jolt for a moment, but then I see Anita and she's got a box of tissues and one held out to me.

"Thank you," I whisper, and she wraps her arm more firmly around me.

We sit in silence together for a few minutes, watching him.

Finally, I ask her, "How do I tell him it's okay to go—that he can let go now?" Her kind brown eyes meet mine.

"Just like that, sweetie." She takes my hand, places it over his. "He knows. He's just waiting for the right moment."

Less than an hour later, he takes his last breath. His heartbeat on the monitor flattens to a line. Instead of jumping into action, Anita, Mr. Nava, Rhonda, and Nancy keep me company as we all watch that line continue to move across the screen endlessly. Anita disconnects it a few minutes later when I'm ready for her to do so. Then she asks if she can say a prayer for him. I nod and bow my head to listen.

"May God keep you and hold you dear. May you never once again fear, because though our time on earth with you is no more, we will find solace that you're safe and loved with those who've gone before. May your journeys never end until we meet again, my love and friend."

Afterwards, I sit beside him, holding his hand even though I know he's gone. I stay until his body heat slowly loses its warmth.

One day, hopefully in the far future, I'll see him again. For now, though, we've said our last goodbye. I'm at least thankful I got the opportunity to do so, even if I'll pay for it later.

CHAPTER 40

One should never fuck with what another holds sacred, because it's not a slight we can allow to go unpunished.

JULY 1997

The bar smells like stale beer and fried food. A few rough-edged men sitting at the bar top look to be regulars. They're watching sports highlights on the television mounted behind the bar.

Joey's sitting way back in the corner in a booth. When he catches sight of me, he flags me down. As I weave through the dim interior, I notice a group of street cops scarfing down lunch a few tables away from where Joey sits. We're only a few blocks away from the precinct, so I figure this must be a local hangout for the men in blue, probably the reason Joey wanted to meet here.

I raise an eyebrow when I take in my oldest friend's spiffed-up attire, a pressed light-blue collared shirt underneath what looks to be a tailored navy coat. His short black hair is styled, not a hair out of place, and there's even a silver pin on his tie. A far cry from the man I saw on Sunday, who showed up in a ratty New Mexico State T-shirt, basketball shorts, and sneakers, and an even farther cry from the kid who'd just throw on any old thing off his bedroom floor back in the day. He never cared what he looked like back then. His priority had been to get the fuck out of his house. End of.

But, *my, my, my*, how time has changed him.

There's a hint of his badge and gun under his jacket, and when I slide into the booth across from him, I can't help but take the piss. "Damn, Mr. America, you clean up *real* nice. You got a talent too, or is it the way you can strut in a swimsuit that wins you the title?"

He plays the part and gives me a cheeky grin and princess wave that quickly turns into a middle finger. Then he smooths his hand down his shirt and tie. "Don't I, though. Ehh…" He shrugs. "Part of the new gig. Not my favorite thing about it. But gotta dress the part though, you know?"

"How's work?" I ask.

"Hella busy right now. Had a double homicide in Rio Rancho two nights ago, and it was a doozy. Thankfully, they let us public service workers have a lunch break now and again."

"Everyone's gotta eat, right?" I say.

"Right." He tosses the menu over to me. "It's on me. Order whatever you like."

"How's the beer?" I eye his glass of water and consider ordering the same, but fuck if I don't deserve a beer or two after the month I've had.

"Better than decent, I'd say."

"That's good enough for me." I eye the menu until I make my decision. When I lift my gaze, Joey's face is pinched with a troubling expression. He fixes his suit coat and shifts forward, resting his elbows on the table, and lowering his voice. "How's the rest of the cleanup going?"

"It's going. The crew I hired has gotten most of the heavy shit out. When they're finished, I'll tear out the carpet and flooring and go shopping for some decent replacements."

"I wish I could've done more to help, but, fuck, my time off is pretty limited with our little one in and out of the hospital and these cases piling up on my desk."

"They still can't figure out why he's in so much pain?"

"Nope. A couple of ideas but nothing definitive."

"Fuck, that's messed up."

He shakes his head, and I can tell by the dour expression on his face and by the way his fingers tap on the table that he's worried about it. From what he told me Sunday, he's also pissed that his son, Mateo, is not getting the help he needs, or at least some answers as to why his back hurts all the time.

"I'm sorry, man, that's gotta be hard."

"It is. But he's being a champ about it and pushing through, and Tavia is researching the internet daily. She found information last night about something called Juvenile Ankylosing Spondylitis. It's arthritis in the spine and joints. Turns out it's something her uncle had when he was in high school and it's hereditary, and she thinks that might be what's wrong with him."

"No shit?"

"Yeah, swear to God she'll have it figured out before the doctors we're paying boatloads to do."

"I don't doubt it." Tavia loves that kid more than life itself, and she was our school valedictorian. She's wicked smart and a good mom. "Is she still a paralegal at that same firm?"

"Only part-time now while we work through this."

The bartender arrives, and we order. As soon as he leaves our table, Joey says, "I can swing by next Sunday, too, if you're still at it."

I wave him off. "You did enough, and this is what's important to me." He already came to the small funeral I had for my father and gave up time with his wife and kid all day on Sunday to help me clean out some of my dad's house. We salvaged what we could, a few boxes of things I didn't want to part with, which wasn't much. Most everything had to be thrown out. It's still a damn mess, but I've been granted more leave to allow me time to grieve and deal with it all, so I'm not worried about not getting it done in time. It'll get done when it's done, and then I'll put the place up for sale.

"You find out what was up with the property management company?"

"Went out of business three months ago."

"And they didn't notify you?"

"Nope."

"Shit."

"That about sums it up."

"You know, you could file a suit. Want me to have Tavia check into it for you?"

Fuck, that's the last thing I have time for, but ultimately, yeah, someone needs to be held accountable, and I'm just pissed enough about it all to see it through. We discuss the process, and he tells me he'll have Tavia get me more information and set up an appointment with the attorney she works for.

Our meals come quickly. It's not until we're done with our burgers, and I'm on my second beer, that I approach the other reason for meeting him for lunch.

"Appreciate you digging into this for me. I know it's not your thing."

This time, he waves me off. "Honestly, I don't mind. Beats looking at pictures of dead bodies all day, and it gave me a chance to catch up with a friend in narcotics."

"Not too much trouble then?"

"I may have tripped some wires and asked too many questions."

When I scowl, he returns the look and says, "Calm down."

"I did it on purpose. I wanted to see who's holding back and covering for these guys. I was smart about it, just wanted to tip my hand a little and get a feel for who might be getting paid under the table by them to look the other way."

"And did you find anything?"

"I think so, yeah. The Thirteen Devils are already on a watch list. The guy you gave a description of sounds like the boss man, Antonio Chavez's little brother, Julio Chavez. He goes by the name Veno, short for Veneno. The fucker's nickname literally means poison." He huffs, draws back while shaking his head. "Dude's bad news."

"I could have told you that."

His smile is grim. "Yeah, well. Seeing is believing, right? His rap sheet is ridiculous. Domestic violence, a few drug charges, and there's been some allegations of rape, but his brother's lawyer got him off scot-free from those."

My already tense muscles lock up further.

"I'll tell you the rest, but first I need you to promise me something."

"And that is?"

"That you won't do anything stupid."

I nod in agreement. Delivering some payback to those motherfuckers is forefront in my mind, but I'll be smart about it. I'm not going to run off half-cocked.

He nods, scanning my face before he reaches into his breast pocket and pulls out some papers. He lays them face up on the table. I see a better image of the man driving the vehicle that night. It's a mug shot.

"Yep, that's the driver."

"Veno." Then he moves the paper to the side and shows me the next one. It's a picture of another Hispanic man, one who's older with sharper facial features, but the resemblance is there. "This is Antonio. This is why you gotta be smart. He's not someone you want to fuck with. He's not a thug. He's street smart and a savvy businessman—keeps his hands clean for the most part. We don't have anything solid on him. We've pinned him for a few crimes, but nothing ever sticks."

He shakes his head. "My gut tells me they've gotten away with the shit they have so far because Antonio's putting money into the pockets of someone or more than one someone at the precinct."

I open my mouth to warn him to be careful again because the last fucking thing I want is something happening to him or his family because of this mess, but he holds up his hand.

"I know, and I'll be more careful. I've been around long enough to know who to trust and when to hold my cards close to my chest."

Reaching behind me, I pull out the pictures I've acquired over the last few nights.

While leaning over, he whispers, "What's…" He snatches them up and quickly goes through them, the evidence I've amassed while watching the hotel.

"That one there, girl can't be older than sixteen, seventeen."

"And these are what John's coming in and out of the hotel?"

"Looks like, yeah."

"Jesus, Finn…" he mutters, shaking his head. "I guess I should've known you'd do something like this."

"They trashed my fucking home. Nearly made me miss my opportunity to say goodbye to my dad. The last thing I was going to do was sit on my ass and let them get away with it."

He's shaking his head. Then he sighs heavily and slides the papers back to me. "Send me a digital copy."

I nod once, and we stare at each other.

"My guess is either narcotics is looking to take down the bigger fish, as in Antonio, or the Feds are involved and are working the case on their side, in which case, they'd limit how much local detectives can get involved."

"Makes sense. But still bureaucratic bullshit."

"Yeah, at its finest. I'll see what I can find out, though."

"Only if it's safe to do so."

"I'll take precautions." He exhales heavily and slumps back in the booth.

The weight of our discussion sits heavy on both of our shoulders as Joey pays and we exit the bar.

Before we part ways, he levels me with a look and says, "Number one thing, man. Stay off their radar."

"I will. You don't need to worry about me."

He shakes his head, concern etched deep in his face. "I'll take this to my chief if I have to, but I promise, somehow, some way, we'll get the needle moving on these guys. In the meantime, keep your distance. Okay? Give me time to work this the right way."

My time on leave is limited. I don't want to waste it sitting around when I could use it to gather intel on the Thirteen Devils, and that's exactly what I plan to do.

With utter sincerity, I tell him, "We'll try it your way first. But if your people don't pull through, I'm gonna handle it my way. This is personal. They made it fucking personal, and I'm gonna deliver payback before I have to head back to my team. That kid and those girls need somebody to step up and make sure these guys get taken down. If it's not your people, then it's going to me and mine."

I go back night after night and watch from the shadows. The more I watch, the more I feel the need to do something. The hotel is a hot spot for the vilest of men. When I see the way the Thirteen Devils handle the girls and the fear in their eyes, or the ones with vacant faces, my rage boils over. One of them looks to be underage and not only that, she's sporting new bruises every time I see her.

It's all I can do to stand aside and not go on a rampage. I know I'm not the only one who sees what's going on here, yet I'm the only one trying to do something about it.

I honestly can't take it anymore, and if the police aren't on board soon, I'm going to have to take matters into my own hands.

If no one's coming to save them, I will. I'll find a way to make it happen.

The 13D's may have their claws deep in this city, but they're not invincible. I've taken down worse. And I'm not above doing this alone if I have to.

I'm with Joey as the raid goes down. It's almost midnight, and nearly every room of the hotel is lit from the inside, showing full occupancy, although it's mostly the east side of the hotel where Veno and his crew do business.

We're parked a block away, close enough to see everything unfold, but far enough that we won't be spotted. Joey made it clear: I'm not part of this. I'm just here to watch. But staying on the sidelines feels wrong. Every muscle in my body is coiled, waiting for the raid to pop off.

When the SWAT team members move in, guns raised, they move like clockwork, something I know all too well. Doors are kicked in, flashbangs go off, and the chaos erupts. Cop cars flood into the parking lot next and provide backup.

13Ds start exiting the hotel. Most are armed, and instead of dropping their weapons to surrender when told to, they immediately begin firing back.

Two of Veno's men go down before they can get shots off, bullets ripping through their chests.

All hell breaks loose from there.

The aftermath is brutal, and it ends with casualties on both sides, but Veno and his surviving men in custody. Some SWAT members and officers are escorting girls from the hotel. Some are crying, others are too far gone to even react. They're dirty and dazed, some sporting bruises, and watching girl after girl come down the stairs has my chest constricting.

I know I did the right thing, pushing and pushing until the cops took action, but there's a whole hell of a lot of frustration and anger inside me, too. Pain for what they've been through, for the days wasted in bureaucratic bullshit, while we waited for the judge to sign off on this raid.

This is why I'm here. This moment makes me feel like my father's death had a purpose. It was to bring me home, to catch these fuckers, and to save these women.

It's why I'll never stop fighting for what I believe in. It fucking matters.

When those who are capable stop fighting, the lives of the innocent pay the price.

Joey's talking to me, something about the investigation, but my thoughts are on these girls and not on whatever he's saying.

When my time with the Army is up, this is the fight I want to dive headfirst into.

This feeling fucking resonates and my bones to the point I practically vibrate with it. And now that it's there, it's going to be damn near impossible to stay clear-headed during the next few months of service.

When the cops finish clearing the building, I ask Joey if I can see inside. I need to see it with my own eyes, to make sure this sticks with me.

The rooms are worse than I imagined—filthy mattresses, dirty walls, stained carpet. It feels haunted, as if the forced sex, violence, and fear linger in the fucking air and walls of it now.

I make myself go through each room, cataloguing every detail, wanting to know what these women went through so I can work to prevent it from happening to others.

It's in the second-to-last room, when something odd happens. I hear a faint shuffling. The hairs on my arms stand on end, and a shiver races down my spine.

"Hello, is someone here?"

There's another muffled sound, and then all goes quiet.

It reminds me of when, as a kid, every spring, we'd have birds that would break through the mesh on our dryer vent and get stuck in the little tubing. My dad had to disassemble the ventilation system and rescue the bird every single time. Sometimes it would injure itself trying to break free, and my dad would try to nurse it back to health. It didn't always work, but he tried.

I sit on the bed and wait to see if I can hear it again, but ten minutes go by and nothing.

I sigh as if defeated and walk towards the door. I open and shut it, and then remain absolutely still, and wait.

Minutes go by before the shuffling resumes. A sound just like the bird made: a fluttering.

With silent steps, I close in on the closet. The sound quiets as I arrive at the door, as if whatever or whoever's there has picked up on my presence.

I palm my gun and aim it in front of me. After placing my fingers on the edge of the closet door, I slowly draw it open.

Huddled in the corner, hidden beneath a blanket, is the girl. The underage one I've been concerned about. She's in her late teens, maybe, but it's hard to tell because her face is a mass of bruises, and she's got a puffy eye and busted lip. She's small, thin, and so scared she's trembling, but fuck, the look she's giving me. It's a glare that could cut stone.

Her eyes are blue, and her hair has been dyed blonde, evident by her dark roots. She has olive skin and strong, exaggerated features.

It's her eyes, though, that keep me somewhat paralyzed in place, because she has the eyes of someone who's seen too much. Too much pain, too much horror. They're soul-searing. They level me on the spot.

I immediately take my finger off the trigger and hold up my gun, then tuck it away and out of sight. I crouch down and, using the softest voice I can manage, I say, "Hey. It's okay. I'm not gonna hurt you." When she remains frozen, I go on, "I'm not a cop, but I can go grab one if you want. They're taking all the other girls to the hospital and then to the precinct so they can call their families."

I won't ever forget the terror that floods into her eyes at that moment. She shakes her head vigorously. "No cops," she says.

"Uh… okay. Can you tell me why?"

She doesn't respond for the longest time. I wait her out.

"They'll send me back home. I can't go back there."

It takes over an hour to coax her out of the closet. It's only after demanding a favor of Joey, and begging him not to say a word about her to anyone else, and both of us promising her that we won't turn her over to the cops, that she comes out. Joey doesn't like it, but I fight him on it. There's a reason she's hiding out from the cops who would send her home. And until I find out what it is, I can't in good conscience hand her over to them.

My gut tells me to believe her and give her a chance to choose her own path forward. She's had enough choices taken away from her; I'm not about to do the same.

So yeah, that's how I find her. The little bird who later tells me her name is Elle.

LOST LYREBIRD

CHAPTER 41

Open your mind to the possibility that a helping hand is always there, being offered by a friend, a loved one, and sometimes even from the universe itself.

FEBRUARY 2008

We're at the airport and my flight leaves in an hour. It's time to say goodbye and head through TSA security, but I don't want to leave her. I'm sick to my stomach at the thought of having to do so, but I'm due back on base by tomorrow, and I've put off leaving for as long as I dare.

The only thought that helps calm the anxiety I'm feeling is that I only have four more months left in the Army, and I've done all I can to set her up until my enlistment period ends.

I cradle her face in my hand, tilting her chin until her eyes meet mine. They're a piercing blue—the exact shade of forget-me-nots—but right now they're wide, swimming with fear.

She swats my hand away and darts a glance over her shoulder at the people weaving around us, their footsteps and muttered conversations a blur in the background. Then she leans in so close, her voice sharp and a bit shaking. "I'm serious. Don't worry about me. Worry about yourself. Don't do something stupid like get yourself killed."

I can't help it—I smile down at her, soft and amused. It's too damn cute, watching her trip over her own panic just for me. "I won't."

She snaps, "You don't know that!"

I laugh. "And yet, I do. I promise."

Her mouth pinches tight, the corners trembling with all the words she's biting back. "Promises are useless."

"Not mine," I say, voice low but certain.

"So you say."

God, I want to kiss her right then—kiss that bratty defiance off her mouth and make her believe me. But I hold myself back.

"I guess we'll see when I get back," I murmur, as I raise my hand again and rub my thumb over her cheekbone. I study her face one last time, hoping this memory and all the ones we shared will hold me over until I can come back to her.

The dream breaks into wisps of smoke. Pain floods in with its absence, and I wake in the graveyard to something tickling my nose. The sun is high above me, and the ground is wet beneath. The dew has soaked into my jeans.

I groan as I try to brush the offending feather tickling my nose away.

A bird squawking startles me, and I tilt my head up to see a crow perched on my father's headstone. It takes a couple of steps across the top, turns, and looks at me. When I sit up, it squawks angrily again and takes flight. It soars higher and higher into the clear blue and bright sky.

I hiss from the pain the brightness causes, and hold up my hand to shield my eyes.

It's not until I set my hand back down that I notice the black feather on the ground next to me. I pick it up, dumbfounded, and stare at it for a moment. I raise it to my face and spin it between my fingers by the quill tip.

Under the direct sunlight and at different angles, the feather's dull gray-black color changes. It shimmers with a rainbow of iridescent colors—bronze, deep blue, purple, and green. Colors you'd never see unless you add light.

My mind latches onto those colors and immediately goes to Lily dancing under a variety of spotlights. The acts, the music, the costumes.

My colorful and talented girl, so much like an exotic bird. She shows me what she wants me to see. Not just me. Everyone only sees what she wants them to see.

Because she's a performer. Not just a dancer, but an actress putting on a show.

I sit with that thought for a moment.

Maybe studying the past isn't the answer. Maybe studying who she is now, is.

The face from my dream comes back to me when I reach for it. It's nothing but a flash of memory, but it's enough. Although her features have changed slightly with maturity, her eyes remain the same. The same forget-me-not blue with a honey yellow hue around her irises.

It's the one thing I'm certain of, and for now, it's enough.

My gun is lying beside me, and as I stand, I pick it up. I lift the back of my shirt and tuck the weapon back into my waistband.

I take a moment to rub the sleep from my eyes. The pressure and piercing pain bouncing around inside my skull are back.

I'm about to turn and walk away when a gleam catches my eye. The sun hits the sobriety coin at just the right angle, so that it momentarily blinds me. Under the bright sunlight, it appears new and shiny, a brilliant gold. Like the day it was first given to me. I stare at it and the compass for a long time. The arrow of the compass is pointing toward the coin. Then I look down at the colorful feather in my left hand.

I asked for a fucking sign. If this isn't it, I don't know what is.

Something about that hits me hard, and the breakdown I've held at bay crashes over me. It's an emotional floodgate that bursts, and with it, I lose all composure. Tears brim in my eyes and spill down my cheeks. Using the headstone to steady myself, the grief, despair, and frustration pour freely out of me.

I'm a mess when the floodgates finally close, or at least my shirt is since I've used it to dry my face.

I stare at the items on the gravestone and my father's name for a few moments before I knock on the headstone in acknowledgement and to cement my new vow to my father to try again. To give sobriety another shot.

I gently pick up the coin and the compass, and slide both into my pants pocket. And even though it makes me feel like a sentimental fool, I tuck the feather behind my ear and leave with this innate feeling that it's not just my father watching over me anymore. That maybe Ben is too, and with them both on my side, looking out for me, I might just have a better chance of figuring out how to survive this.

To myself, I make a separate promise: not to come back here and do what I did last night.

Lose hope.

LOST LYREBIRD

CHAPTER 42

Her burden heavy, her wings broken, it was no mystery why she never learned to fly.

MARCH 2008

I exit *Wet Tips* into the warm, sticky night. A thin sheen of sweat instantly forms on my overheated skin. I stayed late to get some private time on the stage. There's a new routine I've been dying to practice, but with it being the beginning of spring, the local studio is in comp season, and dance rooms are harder to come by.

In the parking lot, the streetlights cast long shadows. I pause, taking a cautious look around before quietly shutting the door behind me.

The low hum of crickets sing their creepy little song as my pulse thrums in my ears and my heels click on the cracked asphalt.

I stayed longer than I meant to. My muscles ache, and my feet are screaming from the abuse I put them through. Getting home to soak in the tub is the only thing on my mind. Well, that and maybe a glass of wine and some light reading before I crash for the night.

As I round the back of a large truck, a man comes into view. The shock of seeing him leaning against my car has my hand flying up to my throat. I swiftly back up and prepare to run. But then his head lifts, and it's not until I take in his familiar features that my nerves settle.

It's Goose.

He looks better than the last time I saw him. His shoulders are relaxed, and his long hair has been cut so it rests against his collar. Both sides are currently tucked behind his ears. When he sees me, his weight shifts, and he lifts both hands in a calming gesture. His voice is low and raspy as he says, "I'm sorry, I didn't mean to scare you. I just wanted to make sure you got to your car okay and apologize for what happened at the clubhouse last week."

"It's like four in the morning. How long have you been waiting here?"

"Since we closed for the night. Wasn't tired and thought I'd stick around."

"Why?"

"Just wanted to see you, and maybe chat.

My skin prickles with unease. I manage a nod. "Oookayy." Internally, I'm freaking out.

His eyes dart over my face, searching for something. "You good?" he asks, his voice softer, as if he's afraid I'll flee from him.

"Yeah," I lie, my throat tight. "I just didn't expect to run into anyone."

He looks around the parking lot. "I'm going to get more lights installed soon, so it's not so dark out here. Don't like the idea of you ladies walking out and not being able to see clearly."

"That would be nice."

He nods. "I'll get it done then."

The silence that falls between us feels suffocating, heavy with everything unsaid. My footsteps crunch against the gravel as I walk towards my car, and he turns to face me as I unlock my door.

He slides his thumbs into the pockets of his jeans. The rhythmic tapping begins. He's staring at me in that way he does, where it feels like he's taking in every detail. "That was one hell of a routine you did tonight."

"Yeah? You liked it?" I attempt to sound casual, though praise coming from his mouth has my nerves going haywire.

"Pretty sure there wasn't a guy, or woman, for that matter, in the house who didn't," he says, an eyebrow raised and his mouth holding a crooked smile. "It was nothing like I've ever seen before. Different because it had that element of danger. The group number was a big hit too."

The warmth of his compliment spreads through me, loosening the tightness in my chest. I smile. I was proud of the girls tonight— how we came together, every move in sync. It wasn't our first group number, but it was the biggest performance yet, and the routine had taken weeks to nail down. Practicing together and having a joint goal seemed to help me bond with them and build friendships, which in turn helped my social circle grow.

Tonight's success had been special because I'd choreographed the dance, and seeing the crowd eat it up, and the girls celebrate afterward, meant a lot to me. It had felt like a mountain peak reached, a successful culmination of all the hard work I'd put in, finally paying off.

"Not something you see in places like this anymore," Goose adds, his tone thoughtful.

Opening my door, I set my purse on my seat, then shut the door and lean against it. "Do you mind? I mean, Raven said you wouldn't care and that she had carte blanche to do whatever. But I wasn't sure."

He shakes his head. Strands of his hair fall forward, but he quickly retucks them behind his ear. His goatee is trimmed, and his jaw is shaved. He looks a lot more like he did back when I first auditioned, more put together. He's wearing his cut tonight and a gray Henley with weathered jeans. I take a moment to eye his masculine jewelry and appreciate how good he looks tonight.

He's back to being sinfully good-looking, which is hell on my heart.

"Not my area of expertise," he admits, the edge of a grin remains on his lips. "But by the reaction of the crowd, I'd say they're going to want more."

We share a moment, a fragile smile passing between us. It's nice to just, you know, talk, like normal people do.

The tension is ever-present, which is evident when his gaze drops to take in my outfit, booty shorts, and a sports bra. But being able to co-exist in the same space without it being this overwhelming is new. There's still chemistry, still desire, but not the combustible energy firing back and forth. Maybe because he's not glaring at me. He's softer tonight, and it's like my body immediately feels his energy and has adapted to match it.

I motion toward my car. "It's pretty late. I bet you're tire—"

My words trail off as I spot a flower on my windshield, held there by my windshield wiper. It's a dark-pink peony, my favorite. And there is only one person in the world who knows this fact about me.

I slowly peel it from the wiper and face Goose.

Looking down and away, he scuffs his boot against the gravel, the sound grating against the silence. "I saw it and thought, why not. Think of it as both an apology for the other night and a thank you for helping Raven with the other girls. She told me you've been helping her a lot, and I wanted to let you know I truly appreciate it."

"I love doing it."

He clears his throat. "That's good. I've heard things have improved between you and the other girls."

"As much as they can, I guess. But yeah, it's better."

"Good. Glad they're not giving you hell anymore. You don't deserve that. You never did."

Does my body zing with pleasure? Yes, it sure the fuck does. Am I going to let it show how much his words are getting to me?

Hell no.

When he looks back up, his eyes meet and hold mine. A flicker of something passes between us—hope, regret, both maybe.

I bring the flower up to my nose. The scent triggers memories—good ones. It reminds me of my little sister, Lacy, and our aunt, Lisa. She loved gardening and planting flowers. She often put Lacy and me to work in her garden when we spent the weekend. I savor the memories because good ones like this of my family are hard to come by. Lacy is the only one I still speak to, and that hurts sometimes when I let myself think about it too long.

"It's beautiful. Thank you."

"You're welcome."

The moment stretches on. I open my mouth to see how he's doing with the pills, to see if he needs help, but I also don't want to ruin this night. Instead, I opt to be a coward.

My "Goodnight" comes out soft. I've always disliked the word 'goodnight' because it feels so final. Never more so than in this moment.

His smile is thin. "Night, Lil'."

He nods once and ambles to his bike. After it fires up, he motions for me to go first. As I drive away from the lot, his headlights follow me for two miles. This time, when I check the review mirror, it's to appreciate the view behind me.

When he eventually turns left and heads down another road, I'm left with this odd sensation. If I had to name it, it would be a sudden lack of comfort. As if having him following me gave me a sense of safety, and I want it back.

I find a new flower on my windshield every night, different kinds, and in varying shades. Each night, Goose's there waiting, leaning against the building, to greet me and walk me to my car. He's back part-time at the club and doesn't usually stay for long if he does show up, and it's ridiculous how my body reacts to just the knowledge that he's there, and how, when he's not, the entire energy of the club seems dimmed somehow.

He's been doing oddly wonderful things, too. Updating stuff around the club, hiring a new cleaning crew, buying the waitstaff all new uniforms, and taking on two new waitresses, so the girls on the floor aren't so overwhelmed. The increase in patrons had been stressing them out. They love the tips, but leave every night exhausted and overworked.

He also left a massive basket of sweets and baked goods in the dressing room. Raven had immediately grabbed the Ding Dongs and shoved one into her mouth with gusto. The dainty way she wiped her mouth afterwards had me laughing. She flipped me off and started in on the second one. I stole the rainbow-colored macarons and sunflower seeds and hid them in my vanity to snack on throughout the night.

A few days after, I made an appearance at the HOC Clubhouse and found out that the guys are planning to do a charity run to raise money for a battered women's shelter. Griz told me it had been Goose's idea and that he'd gotten all the brothers on board. When I mentioned it at practice the next day to Raven and the girls, they jumped on the bandwagon and we began brainstorming ways we could help raise money too.

The funds will provide clothing, hygiene products for the women and children, plus small comfort items for the kids who get displaced for a period of time when child services are called in.

Ultimately, we plan to hold two events to raise money due to the excitement and varying opinions about what we should do. The idea of dancing for charity lifts everyone's spirits, and with Easter just around the corner, we combine the holiday with a special event theme night. There's an increased charge at the door, items clients can purchase, and additional dancer perks. Extras cost extra. *Naughty Bunny Night* is the name Raven decides on, and she takes on the marketing and promotion with a focus on pulling in a higher-end crowd.

Our outfits—Playboy bunny costumes, vary in color, come with a bunny half mask that has long ears, and sparkle with crystals. Mine is lavender, and I pair it with a matching bow tie, dangly earrings, and sky-high platform shoes that are encrusted with iridescent rhinestones on the heel and wedge, and feature a clear upper toe and ankle strap.

Raven even dresses up for the event in an entirely black Playboy bunny suit with more modest heels.

The most memorable moment is when Goose walks out of his office and nearly collides with me in the hallway. He opens his mouth twice to say something and ends up rubbing his hand over his mouth, shaking his head, and raking his hand through his hair.

"Good talk." I pat his shoulder twice and then move past him to saunter down the hallway.

His response, "God help us all."

I put a little extra swing in my steps and grin like a lunatic because I can feel his gaze follow me until I'm out of sight.

There's some flirting and some heated looks from him throughout the night, but we keep it mostly professional, a lot like when we did when I started working at the club.

The only time he seems bothered is when other men touch me, like when Griz throws his arm around my shoulder and kisses my cheek, or when Stone tries to get me to go home with him at closing time.

Goose tries to hide his reaction, but it's obvious he's irritated by it. However, like before, he doesn't voice his feelings.

The other highlight of the night is the high level of excitement and participation from the audience. They join in to dance alongside us when Alex, our emcee, announces The Bunny Hop. We start a conga line through the club, getting everyone to dance and hop to the beat. The rabbit-themed music goes all night, and Alex continues to liven up the crowd with his enthusiasm, mixing his skills and song choices.

We rake in an obscene amount of money, more than double our goal, and the fact that we were able to connect with the audience in a way we hadn't thought of before leaves us all energized for days.

Raven takes note of it and says she's going to schedule more events like it throughout the year and see what other charities we might donate the money to.

I note that Goose stays, although he did disappear a number of times. I don't think anyone else sees the changes in him, but I do. Being at the club takes a toll on him. His features pinch together as the night wears on. He squints against the harsh lighting and even massages his temple on occasion, as if in pain.

When I lightly ask him about it, he brushes off my concern and puts up a mask of his own to act like he's fine when he's clearly not.

The second event we hold is in late April. It's a joint charity run and car wash we do with the HOCs, which is a sponsored bike ride followed by a raunchy bikini car wash that very nearly gets us all arrested. The HOCS go all out for it. They plaster posters all over town, invite local businesses, and chapters from other areas.

A Washing at *Wets* is what we end up calling the car wash part of the event, and it takes place after the guys get back from their drive to Santa Fe.

It gets a little wild, and there's backlash from the city, which means we have to put on tops to cover our assets. So the whole thing turns into a wet T-shirt affair.

But in the middle of all the chaos, Goose approaches me.

His head is down, and for a moment, he appears almost shy. "Hey."

Having just sprayed Zora for throwing a soaped-up sponge at me, I continue to smile as I greet him. "Hey, yourself."

"Would you do me the honor of washing my bike?" He's reaching behind him for his wallet on its chain. He opens it and leafs through a few hundred-dollar bills and grabs a number of them.

"Of course." He hands them to me. I'm not just taken aback by the amount of cash he places in my palm, but by the way his facial expression changes when I say yes. His eyebrow quirks and a sexy grin spreads across his mouth.

"Just you, if that's all right."

I bite my lip as I consider his request. The moment I do, his gaze locks on my mouth.

Then his gaze slowly rolls down from there, over my white, wet crop top, and jeans. The top itself is wet enough that the red bikini is obvious underneath. He palms the back of his neck and makes an unintelligible sound. "Damn, woman. Have some mercy on us poor mortal men, would ya."

A full smile breaks across my face, and I sweep my wet hair back. "What would be the fun in that?"

He chuckles. "Too right. Well, in that case. I'll just sit back and watch the show, yeah?"

I cock an eyebrow and pocket the cash. "And I'll make sure you get your money's worth."

He nearly chokes at that and has to pound his chest. He laughs, though, and shakes his head as he walks away. There's also a muttered, "Jesus, she's gonna kill me." Then he looks over his shoulder and says, "Give me a sec, and I'll bring it to ya."

He means the bike. But... I am currently eating up the sight of his ass in his worn jeans, and the cut that he fills out quite nicely.

While he's gone, I fight to suppress the flood of arousal coursing through me, but it's a losing battle.

Goose is not so subtle after he delivers his bike into my capable hands.

He watches from the sidelines as I take my time, thoroughly and with overly exaggerated movements, cleaning his bike. The entire time, I'm surrounded by music, laughter, and catcalls, but my world narrows in on this moment and the connection firing between us as I perform this service for him.

He leans against the corner of a buddy's car with his arms propped behind him on the hood, his ankles crossed, and his intense stare follows my every move.

It feels intimate, dirty, and meaningful.

Even though I'm completely wet, my insides are on fire. The heat he's throwing in his gaze is working wonders on my body, burning me up from the inside out.

We share some wicked smiles, and the gruff "thank you" he gives me after I finish includes a long, intense stare off, which sends my lady bits into a frenzy.

I spend hours that night trying and failing to relieve the ache with the toys in my bedside drawer. Nothing really satisfies the emptiness I feel or sates the desire for him that won't abate.

The good news is that the money we raise is beyond anything we could have anticipated, and the shelter is both shocked and overjoyed by the donation. The paper even picked up the story and did a piece about it, which shed some positive light on the club.

Helping the families at the shelter, especially the ones who primarily focus on women, women like us who have experienced similar trauma to what girls like me and some of the other dancers have gone through, makes us all feel like we have the power in our own way to make a difference.

On a personal level, it gives me a rush I've never experienced before, and one I don't want to come down from. I begin to imagine what I might do in the future with my life that will make a difference when all my grand schemes finally come to an end and I'm able to move on from the Greenbacks, the 13Ds, and the HOCs.

The thought is both welcome and one that, for the first time, doesn't feel like freedom, because the idea of leaving some of the friends behind that I made here doesn't sit well with me.

LOST LYREBIRD

CHAPTER 43

*Delicate beauty can be found in the simplest
things if we let it.
Like a rare flower, thorns and all.*

The day finally comes when I'm determined to talk to Goose about the pills. He's been looking better. Addiction, though, is tricky, and I know there are good days and bad. It's not something that can be kicked overnight. It's a constant struggle, but one I want him to know that he doesn't have to go through alone.

My mind is screaming at me to stay strong, have courage, but my heart… my damn stupid fucking heart can't help but stumble when I see him standing there outside the back door of the club, holding a flower this time.

It's purple. The rarest and hardest peony to find, and it's stunning. It symbolizes royalty, wisdom, and admiration. And it's not something you can find at just any old flower shop.

I love pink. To me, it's always been the equivalent of a feminine grey. A grey sky can easily bleed to pink with a bit of sunlight, turning what could have been a dreary day full of cloud cover into a sky stretched with splendor and serenity. But purple holds a special place in my heart. It represents spirituality and loving the mystical, darker side of myself, which senses otherness in the world and is open to the energy around me.

But it's not the only thing about this moment that hits me like an arrow to the chest. It's the perfection of it.

"Hey." He twirls the flower in his fingers and smooths his other hand down over his button-up shirt, which is black and nicely pressed. His jeans look new, and so do his combat boots. His hair is tied partially back away from his face in a half ponytail, although there are strands still tucked behind his ear.

"Hey, yourself."

When I close the distance, he holds the flower out to me. My heart lights up because I've always felt that a bouquet diminishes the power and brilliance found in a single flower.

I don't see the box until he pulls it out of his pocket and holds it out to me. It's small, tiny really, and baby blue.

I blush, like honest-to-God blush, as I take the flower and thank him, and then the box. I open it, and pull out a small keychain. It's a wooden dreamcatcher with three feathers in varying shades of purple and pink attached to it.

"I had a little extra wood sitting around the shop and thought I'd try my hand at carving some smaller pieces. This was my first attempt, so hopefully it's all right."

I rub my thumb over it and smile. "It's beautiful."

How can he get this so right? Does he know the profound impact these little symbols have on me? How my heart both soars and wants to curl up to protect itself? Because this hints at something. A past he's claimed to have no memory of. Is it coming back to him, or is this a coincidence?

I thank him again, close my eyes, and smell the peony. I take in the sultry, subtle scent while telling my inner girly girl to chill the fuck out. When I blink open and peer up at him, he's smiling.

"You like it?"

Holding it up, I say, "I like them all, but this one. It's my favorite."

"Yeah?

My grin is genuine.

"What's the occasion?"

He shrugs, and he kicks his chin toward the lot. When I move closer, his hand goes to the small of my back. I put the key chain back in the box and tuck it into my purse. Together, we make the short walk to my car.

"What else do you like?"

"Oh, are we doing the get-to-know-you thing?"

He shrugs. "If you want. Or you could reveal the more important stuff. Favorite position. Pet names you love. How a man might convince you to go for a ride with him on his bike?"

I stall at this and look up at him. He shifts in place, goes to run his hand through his hair, but stops before he can ruin its perfect placement and drops his hand.

The air vacates my lungs. "Are you asking me out?"

The corner of his lip pulls to the side. His fingers press more firmly into my back. "I thought it was obvious that that's what I've been working up to."

"What about everything else, the rules or whatever?"

He squints and scratches his jaw. He peers at me with kind eyes. It's a soft, sweet look, and the walls around my heart crumble to dust. "There's not a damn person working here that isn't aware of my attraction to you. The rules have been followed for as long as physically possible. Now, I'm getting shit for not manning the fuck up."

It shocks me at first, but then causes a laugh to bubble out of me. "Are you serious?"

"As a fuckin' heart attack."

"So is this you manning up?"

He takes the flower from me and tucks the stem into my purse, then he grabs my hand, pulls me into him, and pinches my chin. "No, babe. This is." The kiss is a feather-light brush of lips at first, followed by a soft exploration. I fucking melt and give myself over to it. I run my hands up his chest and then lace them behind his neck and pour myself into the kiss.

When we finally break apart, he takes my hand and intertwines his fingers with mine. He tugs me after him toward my car. "So tomorrow, are you free?"

The club is closed tomorrow, and I did have plans—a hike with Raven, and a girls' night with her and Bethany, but nothing that I can't change. It's not smart. In fact, it's completely and utterly stupid. It's the opposite of what I should be doing, which is to put him at a distance.

But I'm weak for this man. Weak for him in a way that can never be explained. It's just something that is.

"What might I be doing if I said I was free?"

"Taking a ride with me somewhere. You'll want to bring a swimsuit and something to change into. There's a special place I want to take you to. Raven says you like to hike, and there's this hidden gem I think you'll like. If we make good time, I'll take you out to dinner on the drive back."

"But your bike's not made for two people."

He raises a brow and smirks. "True, that's why I've asked to borrow a friend's."

Fuck. Him. Fuck this man. His smile is devastating and knowing. Like he knows I won't be able to say no.

He invades my space. "Say yes."

So, in somewhat of a daze, I do. He leads me the rest of the way to my car. Opens the motherfucking door for me and holds it as I get in. Instead of closing it, he takes a moment and simply looks at me. And I realize something when he does.

It's the silences.

The way we can look at one another and enjoy the silences. The way we know, without it ever being spoken, what's here–energy, attraction, and something magnetic that pulls, and it's irresistible.

He tells me goodnight and turns to head back to his bike. I exhale and suck in air, place my hand over my chest, and try to breathe. Because fuck it's hard, another panic attack in reverse.

I can't help but ridicule myself later that night for being a coward and selfish. I'm ignoring the problems in favor of finding some personal joy in the present.

CHAPTER 44

*Cherish the people that you would take with
you on any adventure.*

Having the woman of your dreams wrapped around you as you navigate the open highway is a feeling unlike any other. With Lily's hands laced on my stomach, I feel as if there's nothing I can't conquer. Her warmth bleeds into me. Anchors me. For the first time in a long time, I feel almost whole.

I'm tempted to keep driving, to keep pushing for days, where it's just us and the open road. It's something I could get used to, exploring the hidden gems of the world with her. A new day, a new adventure. Fuck, it sounds sublime. Like a dream I had once and lost, lost along with the rest.

Would she be up for it if our past and present weren't tying us down?

The way she readily agreed makes me think she would, and I long for a day when my little bird would navigate any challenge with me if we somehow reached a point where our ghosts could be laid to rest and our future stretched before us.

She meets me at the club, and we set out at dawn.

Honestly, when I asked for the date, I expected her to put up more of a fight or batter me with questions. But it's as if she's finally letting down her guard, because she readily accepted, which floored the fuck out of me.

It's progress, a step forward, and there's something monumental about that. Getting the opportunity to earn the trust of a woman who's been through a rough life and protects her heart—reaching a point where she brings down her walls to not only let you see past them, but to also give you a chance to prove yourself worthy and earn possibly more than her trust, maybe even her heart—is everything.

Through the straightaways, twists and turns, as wind whips past us, and the sunshine bears down on us, I tell myself to revel in the moment and be grateful for it. For one day at least, things are going in my favor. So I won't fuck it up. For now, I'll let the past go and enjoy the present with the woman I've chosen to make mine.

When I can, I place my hand over hers, or I palm her thigh to try to convey, through feeling alone, how much having this time with her means to me.

Hours later, I slow as I pull off into a gravel lot. The sole of my boots skates across the dirt as I come to a stop. Lily moves to get off the bike, but I hold firm to her hands on my chest, stealing just a few more seconds of her grounding effect on me.

Then she's using my shoulders for leverage as she dismounts the bike. She removes the helmet I loaned her and brushes some of the escaped strands from her ponytail back from her face. She huffs a second later, pulls the tie out. After finger-combing it back into submission, she quickly weaves it into a loose braid that hangs over one shoulder.

Tipping the front of her sunglasses down, she peers at me over the top of them. The impact of those forget-me-nots is devastating to my ability to remain calm and collected, and yeah, to my goddamn dick because hello, the sassy look sends a rush of heat straight to my cock.

"Are we stopping to stretch our legs, or is this the place?"

"We're here."

I lift my chin towards the east ridges and the path revealed between the pines. After putting the kickstand down, I remove my helmet and gloves while Lily walks around and loosens up her limbs. As soon as I'm off the bike, I do the same.

It's a good ache—one I know well. Doing it side by side with a woman is new, though, and watching her bend and stretch as she takes in the view and our surroundings sends my thoughts into unsafe territory.

I imagine all the ways I want to get lost with her in those woods. Kissing her against a tree. Picking her up and having a wild-as-fuck romp in the wilderness. A dozen different scenarios fly through my head.

So I turn, adjust my stiff dick, trying to put distance between me and my depraved mind. When I'm somewhat more clear-headed, I face her and crack my neck, then twist to do the same to my back. When I'm rewarded with audible pops, Lily makes a face—an adorable one where her features pinch together. Then she turns and motions to me. She wraps her arms around her chest.

"Help me pop mine. I can never do it by myself."

Well, fuck.

Cautiously, I wrap my arms around her. Lily's gaze darts up to mine, and she gives me a knowing smile. Because yeah, I'm stiff and the matter's only getting worse as I press more firmly into her. Partly her fault, because she's wearing skin-tight jeans and a see-through red crop top.

We're not perfectly aligned—but the subtle difference of her smaller frame against my larger one—appeals to me.

Looking down, I meet her eyes. "You sure?"

Her grin turns wicked.

"Course. Wouldn't ask if I wasn't. Now stop being a baby, and do me." She laughs at this.

It's quite possible I'm not the only one with sex on the brain.

I lift her easily and jar her enough that her back does indeed pop. She lets out a relieved sigh, and her grin stays firmly in place when I release her. She bends over one hip and then the other. She even plays it up, fucking taunting me with her body, and it takes everything in me not to reward her behavior with a smack to her gorgeous ass.

After facing the mountains, she crosses one arm in front of her, holds on to it, and turns. Then repeats it in reverse.

463

"It's beautiful here. What's this place called?" She lifts her sunglasses to the top of her head, and her gaze travels over the meadow before us and up the mountainside. The sunlight plays over the tops of the trees, lending deeper contrast to the places it doesn't penetrate.

"Sunrise Valley."

"Never heard of it."

"Because the people who know of it don't share it. It's the only way it stays this way. Otherwise, it'll become something else."

She thinks about this for a moment and nods. "I can see why."

"The trails are amazing here. Full of wildlife too, so be careful and pay attention to your surroundings."

"Sir, yes, sir." She salutes me, and it's at this point that I'm certain I'll be leaving my handprint on her ass by the end of the day because it looks as if her attitude is out in full force.

Chuckling and shaking my head, I go to my saddlebag and get our supplies. The backpack is stuffed to the gills, and it'll be heavy, but I didn't anticipate all the shit she'd want to bring. Buying a bigger bag for our next date is at the top of my to-do list.

When I'm ready, I don't ask. I take her hand in mine and pull her after me as I start the trek to our destination.

As we walk, I ask all the safe questions. They might seem to be insignificant details about her, where she's traveled before, where she'd like to go, what she does in her free time, but they're not. She tells me about the girls she teaches at the studio. I take note of anything she reveals that makes her light up. I stay away from any topics that would get her guard up and shut down the steady flow of conversation between us.

There's over an hour of hiking, some bird-watching, and moments where we pause our journey to observe deer and a few critters making their way across the forest.

At one point, Lily asks me to stop and digs through the bag I'm carrying so she can use her inhaler. She tells me about her asthma, and it checks out with everything I researched about it online, with a few added details.

It must help, because her breaths, compared to before, are quieter.

My fingers itch for a pen. My hands ache to hold the notebook hidden at the bottom of my bag. The need to jot down everything I learn about her rides me hard. However, that would only reveal what I'm doing. I'm learning. Analyzing. Tying threads. Gathering breadcrumbs and piecing a puzzle together, what's been left unfinished too long.

LILY

The lake and waterfall, when we eventually get to them, are breathtaking. It's not as big as I imagined, but still majestic. Moss-covered rocks surround it on three sides. The water is a dark green in the deeper parts and more teal in the shallower areas, where sand-colored rocks can be seen under the surface. The air is fresh and clean up here, and the temperature is somewhere in the mid-70s.

A perfect day for a hike with a slight breeze, which has helped to keep my sweating to a minimum.

"Wow. It truly is gorgeous here."

Goose nods as he sets down the backpack. Then he rolls his shoulders and stretches his back again. Black sunglasses cover his eyes, but I can see that his face is a little pinched.

"You all right?"

"Yeah, a bit of a headache. But it's not bad. I'll take something for it in a minute."

"I've noticed that you're doing better with them lately."

He gives a grim smile. "New medication. I finally visited the doctor and checked into my options."

"You did?"

He shrugs. "Yeah. Bodie's been hounding me for a while. And the headaches had gotten to a point that I just couldn't take anymore. So, in a way, it was the only thing I could do."

"You don't seem happy about it."

He shakes his head. "It's a stop-gap, is all. The meds help, but they're not a cure, and my body is going to adapt to them sooner or later, and I'll be back to searching for a new way to cope with the pain."

"So it's just a pause button on the pain?"

"Yeah, which is all I can hope for at this point."

"Isn't there anything else they can do? Like…" I take a moment and gather my thoughts, and even though I'm nervous as hell, I spill the rest of what I'm thinking. "Okay, I'll be honest. I did some research and found out some things. I don't know your medical history, so I was shooting in the dark, but I found a ton of information when I dug deeper on migraine remedies. There are some medications in testing with good results, some natural remedies, massage, acupuncture, and there are a few surgeons who are worth their weight in gold, according to the reviews."

He stares at me for what feels like an eternity. Like, way too fucking long. The corner of his mouth pulls to the side.

"Oh, shut up." I slap his arm, but he ends up grabbing my hand and using it to yank me close.

"Damn, woman. You have no fucking idea what that means to me that you did that."

"What, that I'd take time out of my day to help you if I can?"

He nods. "That and you didn't just look for a quick fix. You cared enough to do more, learn more."

"Well, I kind of like you. Sometimes. Not always." I emphasize by trying to push away, but he holds on tight and even wraps his arms around me. He takes off his glasses and tucks them into the collar of his shirt. When he hits me with that soft look again, my muscles instantly relax, because those deep pools of blue put me in a sort of trance, and I'm suddenly putty in his arms.

Fuck. This man. This time, my inner voice doesn't snap at me harshly. She whispers it like an exhaltation.

His voice is husky when he says, "Thank you. Maybe over dinner, you could tell me everything you found out."

I tuck a wayward strand of hair behind his ear, and his eyes close momentarily. "I'd like that."

It's me who initiates the kiss. Because his skin is gorgeous in the sunlight, his half-smile is too much of a temptation, and I mean, he's right there. It would be criminal not to, right? Right. Or at least that's what I tell myself.

I join my mouth to his, and he grips the sides of my face, taking full advantage of the kiss.

We get a bit carried away, tongues stroking softly and languidly over each other, small nips, and stifled moans. When we break apart, he coughs and adjusts himself. Then he steps away, removes his sunglasses from his shirt, peels off said shirt, and drops both into his bag.

If I thought I was a mess over him before, it's nothing compared to the intense simmering heat that lights inside my body. Because holy hell, this man. His chest is glorious. The definition in his chest and arms. The dark treasure trail. The sun on his olive skin. The tattoos. They just do it for me.

He starts on his belt next, and my attention is absorbed in the sight and sound it makes as he opens it and then unbuttons his jeans.

Am I frozen in place and staring?

Yes, yes, I am.

He takes off his hiking boots and socks and then pushes down his jeans, revealing dark gray boxer briefs. It's at this point that he laughs, smiles a full smile. "Are we swimming to cool off or are you just going to eye fuck me all day?"

"I'm not—"

"You are. I'm not complaining. You wanna eye fuck me, you can go right ahead. Do it as long as you like." He spreads his arms wide and wades into the water, and I watch the muscles dance over his back as he moves. The massive tattoo of his colors is incredibly sexy.

Doubly so when he turns, sinks into the water, and rises out of it dripping wet. He rakes his hair back and swipes water from his face.

Mary, Mother of God. Is he doing this on purpose?

Then he splashes me. Fucking splashes me. "You getting in or what?"

I fling the droplets off my arm and glare at him. He keeps walking backward, getting farther and farther away with each step.

"What if I said I couldn't swim?"

"Can you?"

"Maybe."

"That's a yes."

"Okay, yes."

He eyes me critically. "Then what is it?"

I know. And maybe he does, too, and that's why he picked this place, this adventure, this perfect day. If I get in that water, this relationship changes. Because there is no fucking way I walk away from it without touching him and vice versa.

So what does he do?

He fucking bawks. Like a chicken. It starts low and soft, but gradually increases in volume.

Motherfucker. Nervous energy spirals through me as I fumble to take off my top. Shuck my shorts. Step out of my shoes. I'm tempted to ball up my stinky socks and throw them at him, but I refrain, barely.

He doesn't look away. Instead, he stands chest deep in the water and watches me enter the lake

in nothing but a baby-blue string bikini. I take the band out of my hair and run my fingers through it until it falls in loose waves.

He mutters a curse under his breath and rubs his hand over his chest.

I smirk and cautiously make my way around the rocks and into the lake.

When I'm in deep enough, I disappear under the water and swim to him. I don't stop swimming until I reach him, then I rise and stand before him. Not as the girl he used to know, but in his eyes, I can see that who I am now is who he wants. He consumes me with his gaze, in a way that tells me he loves what he sees.

As if to put an exclamation point on that, he cups my cheek and rubs his thumb over my cheekbone. The desire in his gaze makes it impossible to look away.

And I know that this… this is it. The moment I either give in to him and embrace this fully, or make excuses and spend the rest of the day trying to fight this gravitational pull.

It's *the* most pivotal fucking moment of my life. And what do I do besides meet his intense blue-eyed gaze with my own, and study those features that I have loved for too damn long?

I say fuck it, because I can't keep denying this feeling anymore. Doing so puts me at odds with myself, my own mind, my own sanity. It's a constant battle of wills that I lose every damn time, because the ache for him is all I've ever known. And I don't want to keep struggling in vain. Not for one more day, one more minute, one more second.

I want to fucking live and find happiness. Every path I take leads me back to him as if trying to show me where I need to go to find it. I'm finally ready to listen and see where this road leads.

And in a way, I've always known that running from this feeling is a lost cause. Whatever we have is stronger than any force I've ever come in contact with. It's like Fate just won't let us be anything but this—together and in love, or the whole fucking world falls apart for the both of us.

So yeah, I give in and take what I've craved for so long. I palm the back of his neck at the same time he wraps his hand around my waist. I'm yanked into his body, and I tug his mouth down to mine. We eliminate every inch of space between us, and the moment we make contact is akin to two weather systems colliding. A life-altering force affecting time and space.

Water splashes from the waterfall, a bird cries, and the world rights itself.

Separately, the sexual tension is weatherable and bearable, but together and connected, it dominates everything and bows to nothing. Finn and I—we are just pawns to this intense connection we share.

Which also seems dialed up to the highest level, as if we both know it's our one last shot to get it right.

I give him all of me in that kiss, and if the way he greedily devours my mouth and boldly explores my curves is any indication, he gives me all of him in return.

We cling to each other like our lives depend on this moment. Hell, maybe it does.

When I jump, he catches me. My arms wind behind his neck, and my legs easily wrap around his waist.

Another bird cries out nearby. We both peer up to see a flock of them take off as one into the sky. When I look back down, I search his eyes. He cradles my face and stares up at me.

"Are we doing this?"

I nod. "We're doing this."

"Thank fuck." And then he pulls me in for another kiss. I hum in pleasure against his mouth, and he sucks on my tongue a moment before deepening the kiss. His fingers knead my back, then venture down, and he grips my ass. I grind down hard against the hard ridge of his cock. The half-growl, half-groan he releases has my belly fluttering with excitement, and chills breaking out across my fevered skin.

On our next breath, he shakes his head. "Woman, you've got no damn idea what you do to me."

I grin slyly. "Tell me."

"Rock my fuckin' world in the best goddamn way."

"Yeah?"

"Fuck yes, you do."

I suck on his bottom lip. I'm rewarded with his fingers sinking into my flesh more deeply. After lightly scraping my teeth across his lip, I let it go. Our tongues dance, and he tilts my head to change up the angle of our kiss.

Sinking my fingers into his hair, I lightly scratch his scalp. His fingers deftly untie the string at my back. I only leave his mouth for a split second to let him rip the offending bikini top away, and he tosses it aside without care, before crashing his lips back to mine.

When my breasts press against his chest, his sparse chest hair brushes over my nipples. With my left hand, I reach down and palm his cock. Then I sneak my hand under his briefs and moan at the velvety feel of him as I wrap my fingers around him. The water helps ease the glide as I stroke my hand up and down a few times, and then caress his sack. His growl is one hundred percent primal and all need.

I try to push his briefs out of the way, but I don't manage it entirely.

He helps, and then his hand comes back to me. His fingers delve under my swimsuit at my core. He finds my clint instantly and rubs the aching nub with skilled fingers, using a swift and harsh circular motion.

The kiss turns scorching, and we both moan at the same time.

The desperate need riding us is maddening and all-consuming.

When the heat between us builds to the point that I can't take it anymore, I beg for more.

"Please, please, get inside me."

"You sure?"

"Nope, but we're doing this anyway."

Then he says two words that make my fucking day. My year. "I'm clean."

"Me too."

He doesn't mess with getting rid of my swimsuit. He simply pushes the material aside. And oh, my fucking god. When he starts pulling me down on his blessed cock, and entering me, I gasp because Jesus Christ, I'd forgotten how endowed he was. It's a stretch, but the very best kind.

His groan is long and drawn out and sends a shiver down my spine. I break from the kiss to suck in a sharp breath. "Jesus."

"Oh fuck, the feel of you opening up for me. Does it feel good, baby?"

"So fucking good."

He slowly begins to thrust, and I grip his shoulders and move in a rhythm I know so well.

But everything is different this time, though. Because it's not just sex, it's all the emotions of love wrapped up together into one—desire, hunger, ecstasy, obsession, passion, and even a little vulnerability.

"You riding my cock is sexy as hell, you know that? Can't wait to see it. Can't wait to lay you out on my bed and fucking punish this pussy from the hell you've put me through."

"You say such sweet things," I scold in jest.

"Just wait until I get you beneath me, woman. You'll see how absolutely not-sweet I can be."

"Is that a promise?" Saying the words has my heart fluttering, but I can't not give voice to them.

"You bet your ass it is."

"Good. I'm gonna hold you to it."

"Go right ahead."

I kiss him hard instead of answering. It's a relief to at least know with utter certainty that I'm not alone in this. The thought of that ignites my very soul.

The water laps at our bodies, and we create our own current. The surface of the small lake ripples with the waves we make together.

As the force behind his thrusts grows harsher, and our movements become more unsteady as we lose ourselves to the pleasure, curses fly from our mouths whenever we part. Goose, for his part, speaks in non-intelligible grunts, and groans, and it's a melody that says so much more than spoken words do. We're satisfying a longing and a craving for each other that's been a long time coming, and it's so mind-altering that reality bends to a pinpoint and nothing outside this little bubble of pleasure matters.

I hold on tight as he drives into me. I work my body over his and revel in the sensations of pleasure. I've learned that my breath on his ear drives him wild. So I keep my face near his and whisper in his ear how fucking good he feels inside me. Then I nibble on his earlobe and bite down.

"Fucking, hell. Get there. Fuck, I'm going to come. Wanna feel you gripping me baby and cumming all over my cock. Yeah, baby. Cum, Lily. Come on, my sweet little vixen."

His hand comes up to cradle my face. I pull his thumb into my mouth and suck on it. He, in turn, tunnels his other hand behind my head and grabs a handful of my hair, and just that slight pinch of pain rockets me straight into my orgasm. My pussy pulses around his cock.

"Fuck. I feel you. I fuckin' feel you squeezing me so goddamn tight." He drives into me one, two, three, more times. Each time punctuated by the sharp snap of his hips. He takes my mouth in a rough kiss and groans against my lips as his release barrels into him.

As the kiss turns more tender, and as his body starts to relax, I can't help but think, *fuck reality.* I just want him and I never want to leave this moment or forget this feeling. Not having this and knowing it existed has been pure torture. Something I never want to let slip through my hands again.

Even if it's just fucking. We're damn good at it. And I don't care what tomorrow brings as long as I can count on more of this with him.

CHAPTER 45

Exploring each other that's the best part.

I wake slowly from a blissful sleep instead of a nightmare or vivid dream. Judging by the amount of light filtering into the room through the blinds, it's the early hours. The air holds that morning chill, made more noticeable by the fact that the sweet creature lying next to me has stolen a good deal of the sheets sometime in the night.

I carefully turn so I can lean on my elbow and take her in like this.

She's a stomach sleeper. Her face is pressed to the sheet. Her pillow is nowhere in sight. The tips of her fingers are a breath away from her thick bottom lip, and her other hand is hidden under the messy waves of her brown and caramel mane of hair.

As I revel in her beauty, flashes of the best day of my life come back to me. Our morning ride yesterday. Making love in the lake next to the waterfall. Our dinner conversation at the family-owned restaurant. And laying her out for the first time on my bed, and taking her apart piece by piece until she begged for me to put an end to the torment and get inside of her.

I'm so fucking thankful I'm able to recall those moments with clarity. I wrote them down in my journal just in case, but I can't express how much it means to hold them in my mind's eye, too.

I remember the feel of her body hugging mine on our rides. I remember the way her skin glowed in the sunlight. The sassy, playful way she bantered with me on the hike, and the wonder on her face when we arrived at the waterfall. The desperate whimpers and moans I drew from her as we came together that first time, and the slow way we came down from that combustible heat last night. She didn't retreat like I'd thought she might. She didn't get dressed and try to make an escape. She loved on me, ran her fingers through my hair, pecked my lips, and was the softest version of her that I'd ever experienced.

Maybe yesterday was as transformative for her as it was for me.

At the lake, we'd played around in the water for about an hour, and after I'd pulled the blanket from my backpack, we'd lain out to dry in the sun afterward. I unpacked the supplies, and we snacked for a while. I went back to my detail collecting, but not in the way I had before. I wasn't digging for more information, I was letting her unravel for me and appreciating every single thing her choices and words told me.

And last night, I took my time learning every inch of her skin, every curve of her body, listening to each breathy plea, gasp, and desperate moan.

I let myself relive the best moments and a few memories in particular, take up billboard space inside my head. Her lying spread on my bed and writhing as she fucked herself on her fingers. The way she pulled them out and fed them to me—the fierce, earnest desire in her eyes as she did.

Her level of greed for the forbidden and lurid aspects of sex is pure intoxication. I swear to God it puts me in a haze where the feeling, touch, taste, sounds, and the sight of her are all that matter.

The way her back bowed as I took her without mercy and fucked her with abandon. The way her breath exited her lungs in one solid punch when I lifted her legs onto my shoulders, bent over her, and slid back inside her. How she scraped her nails so deeply into my skin that they left their mark on the man underneath the skin.

Fuck she did. Maybe she doesn't realize it, but she did.

The image of her pussy stretched around my cock. The way her body moved, skin dewy with sweat, and rolling to a rhythm that resembled waves cresting and receding. Then she pushed me back and turned, and I took her from behind while gripping her small hips.

I got my wish and finally spanked her ass, and her response encouraged me to let go and fulfill that desire to my heart's content.

Hearing her scratchy voice hoarsely shout my name to the ceiling when she hit her peak brought mine forward like a siren's call, and we came apart together.

As we lay together afterward, catching our breath, I thought of only one thing—that I could do this for a lifetime, and it wouldn't be enough.

This moment is different than all the others, though. This is solace. Her at peace. A wild thing at rest. Even though my bodily functions scream at me to piss, brush my teeth, and get coffee loaded into my veins, I deny every impulse because this is what I want most—to see this beautiful creature lying right beside me.

When I can no longer put off my bodily needs, I move as slowly as possible and do my best not to wake her. I'm successful. Within a dozen minutes or so, I'm back. Coffee in hand and bad breath banished.

After gently placing a cup on the end table beside her side of the bed, I retreat to mine and crawl back under the covers with her.

It's a while before she stirs. Then her legs scissor under the sheets. A small moan escapes her before her husky voice says, "I can feel you watching me."

Chuckling under my breath, I retort, "Is that right?"

She sweeps her hair out of her face. "Yes. Mr. Creepy Creeperton." She sits up and has no qualms about her naked body. The flesh on display is delicious and enticing. I lick my bottom lip, and I let my gaze roam over her.

She smirks knowingly.

"What? I can't watch the woman I fucked into the mattress last night, sleep?"

She shrugs. "It's your bed, your room, so I guess you can do whatever you like."

Damn right it is. And if it were up to me, it's where she'd stay.

I say none of it.

Instead, I take a sip from my coffee. Before I can lower it back to my lap, she reaches for it. I motion to the other side of the bed. "I made you one too, but I wasn't sure how you take it."

"Coffee is coffee. I dress it up and make it as sugary sweet as possible, but that's me. When I'm desperate, I'll take it any way I can get it. Caffeine is life, and without it, well, let's just say, I'd be the zombiest zombie who ever was. So yeah, hand it over or I'll attack." She waves her hand.

When I still don't pass it over, she lifts an eyebrow. I motion to her cup. She ignores me.

Finally, she says, "I want to taste yours. You can judge a lot about a person by the way they take their coffee."

"Is that right?"

"Why the defiance, Mr. Road Captain? Are you not an agreeable morning person? Because this feels like something I need to know. Yesterday, you gave me whatever I asked for. Today, a sip of your coffee is off-limits. Hmmm… maybe I need to rethink a few things."

I grunt out a laugh when she raises her brow at me.

She looks around after taking in my room, mainly the bookshelves filled with books, and says, "I know you have the right words, but you choose to go silent a lot of the time. Why is that?"

"I just don't see the need to talk like I know more than I do, or talk about shit that doesn't matter."

Her eyes narrow on me. "Are you going to share or not?"

I give up my cup. While taking it, she spills a bit over the rim and onto her hand. She clutches the cup with one hand while hissing and shaking out the other. "Shit, that's hot."

"Did you burn yourself?"

"Yeah, but it's my fault. I didn't expect it to be near boiling."

It's my turn to lift a brow. "So what does that say about me?"

Eyeing me, she carefully brings the brim of the mug to her mouth. Her eyes close as she takes a small sip. Then her head sways side to side. A small, impish smile graces her lips. "You like your coffee. It's probably one of the simple pleasures you invest money in. Because this isn't something you get off the shelf in a regular grocery store."

Impressed, I confirm. "I special ordered it from a company in Utah, of all places. I had to shop around a bit to find it. There are a few I order from, but this one's my favorite. I'm good with spending money on the things that are important to me."

She hums and eyes me over the rim as she takes another sip.

"What else?" I ask.

Her gaze drops to the mug. "The temperature of it. You drink a lot of coffee. You've probably burned your mouth enough times that you're not as susceptible to the heat like a normal person might be."

"What's normal?"

"The statistical average human being occupying the planet's opinion."

I chuckle at that and try to take the mug back. She pulls it away. "I'm not done."

"More knowledge to share?"

"Yes. You probably feel the same about morning coffee as I do, or it's the caffeine high you need. I'm going to go with the taste, though, that's the part you love."

I nod and hold out my hand.

"The heat also says you're not afraid to get burned, or you're a masochist. Maybe both." She studies me for a moment. "Yep, both. You like to punish yourself, don't you?"

I chuckle darkly because she's not wrong.

When she finishes the first cup, she passes it over and then immediately reaches for the other cup on the bedside table. This time, she shares it. Then she sinks back into the sheets and moans as she gets comfortable. "Your bed is so soft. And these sheets, what the hell are they?"

"Bamboo. Cooling sheets."

"Just a warning… I may never leave."

"I've got no problem with that."

Her laugh brings a smile to my face. I stare at her long enough that the moment becomes weighted with feeling. Because, fuck, she's a stunning creature. She shies away from it by turning her face. For a split second, she inhales the scent of her pillow, then faces the opposite way towards the window and the sunshine streaming in.

"Do you ever wish time had a pause button?" she asks in a breathy whisper.

I join her and curl up against her back. "I haven't ever thought about it. But if there was such a thing, I'd want a rewind one."

She inches back so I help and pull her more fully against me. She fits up snug, her curves filling all the space my body doesn't. I sweep her hair away from her neck and lightly run my mouth over her shoulder and then up her neck. A pleased whimper escapes her, which eggs me on. I release a hot breath over her ear. Her entire body shudders and she presses her ass into me.

I take her lobe between my teeth. An exhale leaves her in a rush. Her body also jerks as if the jolt of pleasure hit her all at once. I trail my fingers down her arm, first tickling the skin there, then moving my hand to her hip, then her stomach. I use my strength to force her back as I rut into her from behind, and she reciprocates, riding my cock with her ass, and in doing so, it wedges itself between her cheeks.

The fantasy of taking her ass rushes into my mind. By the way she's responding, by the way she loses herself in those heady moments of pleasure, by the way she loves my dirty mouth, I'm confident that with time, she'll let me take her there.

The idea of it has my cock aching, and my mind sifting through all my dirtiest fantasies, wondering which one we can explore next.

My fingers find her entrance. Her hand covers mine, pushing me to fill her with my fingers. So I do, I fill her with two fingers and pump them into her as she begins to move.

"Damn it! I hate that you can do this. That I'm such a slut for you sometimes. Like you just have to turn on a switch, look at me a certain way, touch me, and all my good intentions go out the window."

"Yeah?"

"Yes, the part of me with a rational mind goes poof. Fucking runs and hides. Let's this version of me take over."

"And which one is that?"

"The stupid one. The weak one."

"Not stupid. Just honest with what you want." Then I bite into her neck as punishment. "And not weak."

"Not true."

"Well, if it is, it's the same for me, Lil'. You have the same fucking power over me."

Looking back over her shoulder, her blue eyes meet mine. I palm her cheek and press my forehead to hers. "The same fucking power. It's not one-sided, so don't think you're the only one who loses control when we're like this. And there's nothing wrong with how we feel."

She turns and faces me fully. The kiss she takes is demanding and desperate. Her small hands push me until I fall onto my back. She quickly straddles me and begins rubbing her pussy over my cock as she looks down from above.

"Then be weak for me," she says in a husky tone as if pleading with me to prove I'm not full of shit.

So I relent. I force my muscles to relax, and I lie back. Bending one arm behind my head, I let her take over. I run my hand down over her thigh, then back up her hip until I can cup her breast in my hand and work my thumb over her pebbled nipple.

"Condom."

I motion to the drawers on my right. "Top drawer."

She leaves me only for a sparse few seconds to find them, and then she's working a condom over my length. We started using them as soon as we had access to them. I resent them because they're a barrier between us, but I get why it's important and why she'd want to switch back to using them. She's on the pill, but still, there's always the risk, and this is new.

She covers me with the condom and works her fist up and down my cock, as I strum her clit until she's primed for me.

She doesn't waste time. And she's not shy about taking what she needs. She lifts up and sits on my cock without needing to be told to. After sitting up, I palm her face and eat her lips, sucking her bottom one into my mouth and nipping at it, before letting it go.

Then I trail my lips over inch after pretty inch of her skin. Her clavicle, neck, collarbone, and her beautiful breasts. I tease her nipples until they're both tortured and a rose-pink from the abuse.

"Before you come, I want my mouth on you. Want you holdin' the

481

headboard as you ride my tongue. Then you can sink back over my dick and get yourself off.

"Is that an order, Captain?"

"You're goddamn right it is."

"Topping from the bottom, are we?"

I grin. "Don't act like you don't like it, when we both know you do."

"Oh, yeah? And what if I want to be the boss in the bedroom?"

"Woman, if you want control, take it. Don't run your mouth about it. You want to ride this cock, it's right fuckin' here for you any time you want it. But I guaran-fuckin'-tee it's not what's going to make your sweet pussy weep. You forget. I've studied your reactions. It's not control that gets you hot. Maybe it's enough to get you off, but what makes this body come undone is when you can let go and lose all of it."

"So you say."

"It's my mouth, my orders, and my praise that sets you off. It's the way I can flip you around and take what I want without asking for permission. It's the way this loss of control lets you enjoy every moment and stop thinking. That's what makes your body sing for me. And it's such a sweet fucking song, Lil'. One, I'll never get enough of."

I slap her ass and watch the way her body jerks from the contact. Her eyes flare. There's anger there, but so much fucking heat too. "Oh, woman, don't play me for a second. I fucking know what this body is begging for. Maybe even better than you do."

She begins rolling her hips slowly over me. Teasing me. Based on her devilish smile, she believes she's getting the upper hand. When, in actuality, it's the opposite. She's simply showing me her tells, and I'm eating up every single one of them to use on her later, when she's done playing around.

"I don't know. From where I'm sitting… the view looks awfully good. I just might get used to it. Think maybe I'll stay up here a while. Have my fun. You just sit back and relax, old man."

"Oh, old man now, is it?"

She grins coyly. "Yep."

"Woman, keep it up and I'll show you how fast this old man can move."

Her arched eyebrow just adds to the punishment I'm planning to deliver later.

She's playing because she still thinks this is something casual. Something fun. Maybe even something she thinks she'll be walking away from.

It isn't. This woman is my present and my future. I know this to my very core when I look in her eyes.

Her eyes say, *it's all in good fun.*

Mine, or at least what I hope mine say is, *this is inevitable, baby. You and me. It always has been. Whether you want to accept it or not.*

I chut my chin out at her. "Come up here and let me put my mouth on you."

"No."

"Yes."

She slows even more and comes to a stop above me. She places a hand beside my head, and a curtain of her hair shields us from the sunlight pouring into the room. A sly smile graces her lips. "You know, I'm suddenly not horny. Do you care if I take a shower before I go?" She lifts off me and starts crawling on her hands and knees toward the end of the bed. I grab her by her fucking ankle.

"Why are you crawlin' away from me? Stop fighting something we both know you want."

Looking back at me over her shoulder, she bites her lip. No fucking shit, she tests a man's willpower and patience. Then she doubles down on the sass and wiggles her fine bare ass at me, poking the bear on purpose as if she's begging for whatever punishment is coming her way.

"Get back here."

"Make me."

I laugh, "Why do you have to be so fucking naughty, Lil'? You want the brand of my hand on your ass, is that it?" Every time she gets a foot away, I drag her ass back towards me. "Woman, quit it."

"I want a shower."

"You can have a shower after I dirty you up some more." The wicked smile she throws me does it.

With one last pull from me, her arms go out from under her, and I'm over her in a heartbeat. My body caging hers beneath me as she struggles to get free. She wanted a fight, well, she's got it.

Her breathing begins to labor. Her ass presses up against me, her body demanding what her mouth and mind won't let her voice—the need to be dominated and praised to high heaven. Those are her kinks, and they just happen to be what I excel at in bed.

Mouth next to her ear, I growl. "You're at my mercy now, Lil'. Are you gonna keep fighting it or give in?"

She tests for wiggle room, and I bear down on her, grab both her wrists and hold them in a tight grip against the mattress. "Tell you what, if you lie here, like the slut you claim to be for my cock, and take this hard fucking I'm about to give you, I'll reward you."

She shudders. The whimper she makes is audible enough that I need no more words. I part her thighs with one of mine and with one hand remaining on her wrists, I use the other to guide my cock back to her slick-as-hell wet pussy.

I drive roughly into her, one quick, harsh thrust, until my balls rest against her cunt. I withdraw and slam back inside her a second later.

"Got any words for me now—any more of that sass?"

I drive into her harder, faster, and begin punching my hips forward at a brutal pace. "Come on, baby. Let me hear how much attitude can pour from that sweet fucking mouth of yours with my cock buried so damn deep inside you."

She groans and shakes her head. A weak whimper escapes her.

"Yeah, that's what I thought." I move my mouth over her neck and run the coarse hairs of my goatee over her skin. Gooseflesh breaks out on her arms, the hair standing on end. At the sight, a grin spreads across my face.

Her pussy grips me so fucking good. Every time I pull out of her, her hips try to follow my retreat. She's physically seeking out my cock to get more of it.

"You're not trying to fuck me from the bottom, are you?"

The little vixen nods this time.

"I was going to fuck you with my mouth, make love to your tits, and let you ride my dick. But that's not what you crave, is it?"

The shake of her head is small. She buries her face into the mattress and makes unintelligible sounds, and I change to long, languid strokes that end with me buried as far inside her body as I can go.

I spread her legs wider and wedge myself deeper. My next thrusts have her crying out.

Yeah, this is what my woman wants.

I begin speeding them up, until I'm rutting and pistoning my hips, fucking her so thoroughly that she turns her face and gasps, crying out my name on an exhale.

We also move up the bed to the point we near the end of the mattress. I curl my arms under hers and cage her there, pinning her down and essentially taking away her ability to move.

Lily goes mindless when I do. Her words are utter nonsense, but full of pleasure.

"What fantasy is going through that little mind of yours, Lil'? What is it that you imagine happening but won't put voice to? Hmmm…"

She again hides her face into the mattress.

"There's nothin' you could say that I wouldn't give you. Except another man. So what is it? Do you imagine getting strapped down? Ravaged? Being utterly powerless? What if I hunted you in the dark? Ran you down into a pile of dirt and muddy leaves—is the danger or the force you like?"

The moan is full on this time. She's muffling it, but oh, how it sounds like a rock ballad to my fuckin' ears. I hit on whatever it is she fantasizes about, and I intend to do every one of those things until I know which ones she loves the most.

"Can you picture it, Lil? You're running for your life and being caught and fucked?"

Her pussy grips my cock in a stranglehold and coats my dick with how wet she is. The more I flame this fantasy, the wetter she gets.

"What if I threw you down and ripped the clothes from your body.

Would you fight me? Or would you let me rut into this tight cunt and claim this pussy for my own?"

Her head snaps to the side. The hitched inhale proceeds, her breathy, "Oh my fucking God, Finn!"

I check in with her.

"You good, baby?

She whispers back. "Oh fuck, don't stop."

"I won't. I've got you. We're gonna ride out this fantasy together, aren't we, baby?"

"Yes."

"That's it, woman. Let me see what lives inside that head of yours. There isn't anything you could say or show me that I wouldn't welcome with open arms. I want to know this mind and this body in every way I can. So if it's to be a naughty fucking filthy girl, you're gonna let down those walls and let me explore, aren't you?"

Another moan.

"Is that a yes?"

"Jesus! Yes."

"Good." I pound into her and revel in her cries for more.

"Oh my fucking Godddd. Don't stop. Don't stop. Uh… Finn."

Her responses aren't calculated or an act. This is Lily, out of her mind and indulging in her physical desires. Her brain has finally turned off.

"You'd hear me unbuckling my belt, wouldn't you, baby?" I withdraw and ram myself back inside and swivel my hips.

"Jesus! Yes, yes, I hear it."

"Yeah, you do. And then just like this. I'd force your legs apart and make your pussy accept me whether you wanted it or not. Isn't that right?"

"Holy fuck, Finn!"

I use every bit of my strength to give her what she needs, using my knees and the mattress to force my cock so deeply that her pussy won't be the same tomorrow. Because that's what I want. To rut, and mark, and fuck her so thoroughly, she'll never forget this moment or me.

She's crying out now, actual fucking tears are on her cheeks, but it's purely an emotional release, and letting go of something she's probably held in for years. Showing me a part of herself she most likely never showed another soul.

The harder I fuck her, the louder she gets. She's so close. I can feel the grip she's got on me. The walls of her sweet cunt tightening and squeezing me in a death grip.

"I'm gonna come. Can you feel me about to spill inside you? Going to breed this pussy and mark you as mine."

The words work like a trigger on a gun being pulled. Her orgasm hits like a shockwave, her cunt clamps around my cock, and a shudder rolls through her. Her walls grip me for all they're worth. The sensation goes straight to my balls, and I follow her down the rabbit hole and let the fantasy take me over the edge. "Lil', Lil', Lil'. Goddamn, woman. Yeah, so fucking good." Her name is like a prayer, falling over and over from my lips as I ride out the ripples of pleasure pulsing through my body.

It's dark and heady, and fucking perfect because we just tore down walls and got to the heart of something. And she trusted me enough to take us there. A hunter and prey kink that gives me a wealth of future fantasies to explore. And even though my cock is fucking spent, I can't wait to dive into another one with her.

I move off to the side, but also turn her and pull her onto my chest. She hides her face at first in the crook of my neck. Letting my hand roam over her back, I let her feel as much of my skin as she can to ground herself.

"Fuck. I don't know where that came from," she whispers.

"Same place our dreams do. Nothing to be ashamed of."

"Says you."

"Lily, I'd be more than happy to explore the fantasies going on up here." I point to my own head. "Don't for a minute think they're not as dark or as dirty, because they are. Maybe even more so. And you know what? I don't give a fuck. They are what they are. I am who I am. You are who you are. The more we try to hide it and deny it, the less true we are to ourselves, to each other."

"The things you say, Goose."

"What?"

"They, just, you know…? Kind of wreck me sometimes."

"Just sometimes."

"Yeah." She's quiet for a moment. Then she looks up at me with a devastating expression, and her blue eyes hold mine. The words she voices next spill from her as if they're a confession. "Sometimes they also make me feel completely normal and whole."

LOST LYREBIRD

CHAPTER 46

Don't wait for the right moment to have the
meaningful conversations with those you love.

For the next week, Goose watches my performances from the shadows of the club. He's my specter, and my routine is elevated to another level when I know he's there.

Some nights he only stays long enough to see me dance, others, he stays for the entire shift, but disappears into his office after I'm done. Raven even adjusts our schedule to push our group routine and my solo closer together to accommodate this.

Whether or not he stays, he's always there at the end of the night to greet me at the back door to hold my hand, and walk me to my car.

He ensures I'm safely on my way before jumping on his bike and following me down the road, and it's a feeling I could get addicted to—the kissing me senseless before I get into my car, and the comfort of seeing his headlight in my rearview.

As the days progress, my feelings for him start to scare me because I know that what I'm doing here will eventually drive a wedge between us.

Since I never got a chance to discuss his migraines or head injury with him the night after the waterfall, I decide to print out everything I researched online and leave the papers for him on his desk.

He's fighting this struggle alone, or trying to, and hiding it from the rest of the world. What I don't understand is why he thinks he needs to do so. While I stand at my locker and change into street clothes, I build up enough courage to approach the subject with him, and find out why.

The flower tonight is a white rose in full bloom. When I take it from his hand, I prick my finger on one of the thorns and drop it as I reel back. Instead of picking up the flower, Goose grabs my hand and inspects the wound. A drop of blood wells up, and he wipes it away, only for another to rise up in its place.

"Hold on a sec." He goes to his bike and comes back with a bandana and wraps up my finger, which is ridiculous because it's bulky as all hell, but the gesture is sweet. He ties the end with a simple knot.

"It's not going to win you any beauty pageants, but it'll do for now."

"Can you imagine? My mother would have a field…" The words just fly right the fuck out of my mouth, and when I register them, my entire body goes cold.

Goose, at least at first, doesn't act like anything is out of the ordinary about my answer. He bends down, picks up the flower, and gently hands it to me.

Needing to change the subject and fast, I ask, "Did you see the papers I left on your desk?"

He pulls the folded papers from his back pocket. "Yeah, I'll look them over tomorrow. Not in the right headspace for it tonight."

"Did you get another migraine?"

He nods. "Yeah, just one of those days when it's unrelenting."

I let the question rip from me before I can second-guess myself. "Are you still taking the pain pills? I know you said the doctor gave you new medication, but does that mean you don't need those anymore, or do you take those too?"

Tension instantly coils in his shoulders. "Does it change things if I am? How you feel about me?"

I clench my fist around the strap of my purse, using it as an anchor. I also want to make sure my inhaler's close by in case this goes south. "Just humor me."

He stops, huffs, and tilts his head down. His hands go to his hips as he shakes his head. "Humor you?"

"Yeah."

His gaze, when it rises, is suddenly sharp and unreadable. The muscle in his jaw ticks. There's an edge to him—a side he rarely shows, one that appears when he's angry or his control is about to unravel. "I was taking them before because it was better to be numb and half-dead than watch you ruin yourself," he says with conviction.

My head jerks back, "Ruin myself?"

"Yeah."

The judgment in his tone instantly has my back up. Turning fully to face him, I cross my arms. "Excuse me? We may be doing"—I motion to him and then back to myself—"whatever this is. But that doesn't give you the right to shame me for what I did when we weren't together."

His lips set in a firm line. "Ditto, babe."

"No. It's not the same. I wasn't filling my body with garbage. Sleeping with men who aren't you, that's my prerogative because, guess what, it's my fucking body."

He throws up his hands and half-turns before facing me again. "Do you even hear yourself? How hypocritical is that?"

I cross my arms over my chest. "Sex and drugs are not the same."

"Yeah," he huffs. "Keep telling yourself that." His mouth twists in a sardonic grin.

"What? They're not!"

He exhales and then groans, his frustration evidently boiling over. His hand comes up and rubs at his forehead. He breathes for a moment and tries to calm down. Then his hand drops, and his features are pinched together as he stares at me. In a gentler tone, he says, "Was it all to get back at me? Tell me that much at least? To punish me because, if so, you were fantastic at it."

My stomach twists into a knot. "What?"

"You heard me."

My hands drop to my side. "I wasn't trying to hurt you."

He runs his hand over his mouth and he eyes me critically. His brow hitches up. "Are you sure about that?" His voice is dark, mocking.

"Because it sure as hell feels like you wanted me to suffer. And I did. I suffered through it for as long as I could. More than you'll ever know. But it became too much, okay? The pain in here"—he palms his chest, and puts two fingers to his temple—"and here."

My fingernails dig into the skin of my palms. When I don't say anything because I don't know what to say, he lets out a long breath.

"Tell me this, Lil'. Why them and not me?"

"Just… I don't know, and I don't have to justify it to you."

"That's your answer?"

"What else do you want me to say?"

He grinds his molars and his jaw flexes. "If I was no one and nothing to you, then why do you care so goddamn much what I do, huh? Why the fuck do I care so much about what you do? What the fuck does any of it matter, Lily? I think you know, but it's not like you'll finally come clean."

The tension pulls taut in the air between us. "What do you mean?"

He scoffs. "You know exactly what I'm talking about."

"No, I don't. Why don't you spell it the fuck out for me?"

He throws his arms out as if baring his soul to me. "You make me *remember*, and remembering *fucking hurts*." He hurls those words at me. "That's why I was getting more and more flashbacks, all because of you. I don't remember all of it, but I remember enough, and the rest I've figured out on my own."

I freeze in place. "Remember what?"

His studies my features. "I remember the girl I met before my tour of duty. The one standing right the fuck in front of me. Yeah, it feels like another lifetime. I don't know all the details, but I see it, Lil'. When I close my eyes." He palms his forehead. "When I dream, when the fuckin' migraines work overtime to split my brain in half. There's another life there that I had with you, where we meant a whole hell of a lot to each other."

"I-I don't. . ." Panic. Absolute panic overtakes me. The easy lies won't come and taper off. I try again, and it comes out the same. My body is going haywire, my nerves jumping, and my heart racing like it's on steroids.

I take a few measured breaths and pull the lie from somewhere deep inside of myself. They're not the words I want to say, but the ones he needs to hear. "That girl, whoever she was, isn't me."

Without warning, he strides closer, grabs my arm, pulls me closer, and the heat of his body melts into mine. My body reacts to his proximity, softening, giving my head no time to catch up.

"No?" he challenges. He palms my cheek and leans forward. For a long time, he just stares me down with his penetrating blue gaze as he analyzes my face.

"No."

His face touches mine, and his lips brush against my ear. Dropping his voice to a dangerous whisper, which sends a shiver down my spine, he says, "You can keep telling them, but I'm not buying these pretty little lies anymore, Lil'. I can read your tells. I see beyond what you're trying to hide."

I push at his chest, try to pry myself away, but his hold tightens.

"I see you," he says. "The real you. I see the act. The unhappiness. The way you force yourself to do things you hate. I see the parts you play when other people are around. The mask you let slip when they're not. I see it all and I know there's a version of you that knows who the fuck I am to you. That you've known me for a long damn time."

He lets me go, and I stumble back. He lifts his hand. "Go ahead, make me feel like I'm the crazy one here. Like it's all in my head."

A rock lodges itself in my throat, and fireflies take flight in my stomach. "I'm not saying that."

"Tell me you didn't already know who I was the minute you arrived here. Go ahead. Fucking nuts, right?"

"I didn't say you're crazy!" I snap at him. "I said, I'm not that fucking girl!" *Not anymore.*

He points at my face. "That right fucking there. That split second when your mouth moves but your eyes tell a different story. They don't match, babe." He comes forward, but I push him off me. He proceeds to eliminate the space and tries again. "I want the truth."

I stare up at him. *I can't.* He's not ready to hear it, and I'm not ready to relive it. Shaking my head, I glare right back at him. He reaches out to grab my hand. I slap it away and snap, "Don't fucking touch me."

I turn my back on him and march to my car. His footsteps follow.

"Why is that so hard to do?" His laugh comes out bitter and sharp. "Huh?"

I wave a hand behind me. "Believe what you want."

"Everything in me tells me *that's* who you are. That all those fucking pieces, all those feathers, they're you. It's the only thing that makes what you did, what you're still doing to me, make sense, Little Bird."

Fury rips through me. Spinning, I shout, "*Don't* call me that!"

His eyes spark to life at my anger. "What? *Little Bird*?"

I stab a finger towards him. "Don't."

"Why not?"

I practically spit the words at him. "Because, first of all, I'm no one's. Least of all yours. And I'm sure as hell not some little bird in need of saving, or some girl who didn't mean shit to you."

I unlock my car and open the door.

With a few quick strides, he grabs the car door, then my elbow, and pulls me away from it. When he spins me around, I slap him.

He growls, grabs both of my hands, and presses them down at my sides. He forcibly plants me against the side of my car and slams the door shut.

Then he's discarding his cut, tossing it onto the hood. In one swift motion, he rips his shirt over his head and throws it on top of his jacket. His chest heaves as he glares at me, slapping a hand against his bare skin over his hard pecs and the massive tattoo taking up residence on his skin.

"Look at me! Look at my fucking chest and tell me you didn't mean shit to me! Christ, Little Bird. Can't you see you meant everything to me?"

My laugh is low and haunted. "Not enough."

"Don't say that. God, don't fucking say that. Because it feels like I've spent half my life searching for you." He cups my face in both his hands, his thumbs wiping the tears from my cheeks. His guttural tone is pleading. "You're a glorious mindfuck, Lily, but I know who you are. I don't know how I lost you, but I'll be damned if I let you walk away from me without telling me why."

When I stay silent, he demands, "Tell me why."

"I didn't walk the fuck away. You *disappeared!* I had no way to reach you. No word from you. And I stayed as long as I fucking could, waiting around for you. Do you have any idea of the situation you left me in—with Veno—with that creepy-as-fuck Chester-the-Molester landlord of yours."

He snaps, "I didn't disappear on you. I got blown the fuck up!"

I shout right back, "I know that now!"

"So why come here and lie about who you are? Why not tell me and help me remember?"

I lock up at this and search my mind for a lie he'll believe. It's more of a half-truth than a full-out lie. "The shit I've done... the things I've had to do to survive..." *after you left. "Y*ou have no goddamn idea."

"Then tell me."

"I can't. I won't. Not when you're so quick to judge, and I'm not going to relive all of that shit just so you can get your answers."

His mouth sets in a firm line. He presses his forehead to mine. "I've murdered people. I've got so much blood on my hands, you could drown in it. I abandoned my own father when he needed me the most. I've slept with countless women. Done every drug imaginable. There's not one damn thing you could say to me that would make it impossible for me not to love you."

"Yeah, there is, you just don't realize it."

He rasps, "God, woman. Don't you see?"

"See what?"

"I already fucking do! I fucking do. I have and I do and it's the only goddamn thing in this life that makes any sense to me."

Tears blur my vision, and I can't hold it together anymore. "Finn..."

"Please, baby," he whispers. "Please." He backs up and stares directly into my eyes.

A fist squeezes the heart in my chest. "Please, just let it go. There are things I can't say, reasons I kept my distance, and you're only making me realize I was right to."

"You can tell me. Whatever it is."

I push him back and remove myself from his temporary cage. I reopen my door and use it as a barrier between us. "See that's the thing, Goose. I can't. I honestly can't. Because you might think it will fix this, but I promise you, it will be the end of us."

He places his hand over my cheek, then gently pecks my lips, trying to get me to soften for him. I'm shaking as I fight not to give in to him. His lips brush back and forth over mine. "I love you. I loved you then, I fucking know it, and I love you now, lies and all. I just need you to trust me and let me in."

I pry his hand away. The hope on his face fades. "I can't. Not yet. Maybe someday, but until then, I need you to back off."

"Lily."

"No, I'm sorry, just... I can't. I think maybe we rushed into this and should... I didn't think this through."

"What?" When I stay silent, he shouts, "What... just say it?"

"This isn't a good idea."

"What the fuck. You've got to be kidding me. How the fuck can you say that*!*" He cradles the back of his head and paces a few steps away, looking toward the sky. When he faces me again, he's breathing heavily and his face is riddled with anger. "Please tell me you're not serious."

I clench my fingers around the door, ready to shut him out before I change my mind. I tell myself it's for him. It's what I have to do to keep him safe and away from the mess I've weaved. "I am. Let's just cool it for a while, okay?"

"Lil'. Don't do this, baby. Please don't fucking do this."

"I'm sorry. This is my fault. I shouldn't have started this with you, knowing I couldn't let you in."

"It doesn't have to be like this."

I look down for a moment. Images come to mind of how wrong this could all go if I don't walk away. If I come clean as a rat, as a spy, it will implicate him. I've seen the Greenback kill their own men for less countless times. He's only safe if he knows nothing. When my gaze meets his again, I hope my eyes convey how fucking sorry I am, and how torn. "That's the thing... it does. I wish it didn't, but it does."

I see him swing his fist and kick the dirt, and hear his yelled, "God-fucking-damnit," as I get into my car, and shut the door. He closes the distance and puts his hand on the car as if to stop me. I slowly pull forward. As I move through the parking lot, I watch him in the rearview mirror. I see him grip his head with both hands in frustration. He sinks to his knees on the blacktop, his hands go to the ground, and he bows his head.

For the next few days, he's absent from the club. No longer there when I leave. No one has heard from him. Raven says he won't answer her calls, and his HOC brothers can't find him.

He's simply a ghost.

CHAPTER 47

*The darkest parts of ourselves know things
that the light version can only touch the
surface of.*

I've lost track of time. Days have passed since I locked myself in
this room, surrounded by all the remnants of my little bird. With
the blackout curtains drawn tight, it suits me just fine.

I've gone off the meds cold turkey, welcomed the migraines with
open arms.

Am I punishing myself?

Fuck yes, I am.

Because I knew better—I knew not to push her for answers yet, and
I did it anyway.

The fact that she'd triggered me by leaving those papers on my
desk is no excuse.

It was meant to be a kind gesture. At first, when she mentioned it,
I was floored at all the work she'd done to get me help. However, the
more I thought it over, the more bothered I became. I fucking hated
that she felt she needed to take care of me, and not the other way
around. I didn't want to be the weak link in this relationship.

But no matter which way you slice it, I was, and always would be.

I was a thing to be fixed, worried over, a motherfucking bomb
waiting to detonate. I wasn't getting any better, and eventually my

brain would give up the fight. I wasn't a safe bet or a good one for her or anyone, for that matter. And that was without even considering the danger Veno posed to her if she became mine.

I'd tried to push those thoughts to the back of my mind. I really did. But then she'd brought up the pills and my addiction, and everything I'd been holding back rushed forward and straight out of my mouth.

I'd ruined every bit of the progress I'd made. All of it. And her walls came right back up, probably stronger than ever, and I only had myself to blame.

I throw the empty whiskey bottle in my frustration. It hits the wall and shatters on impact. Glass shards fall in all directions and land on top of the papers on the ground, along with the empty pizza box.

When I pull the joint from my lips, I miss the ashtray entirely and burn a few holes in my comforter. In my haste to grab it before it lights on fire, I jar the entire thing, and the ashtray spills over the side of the bed to the floor. The joint duplicates the holes there.

Story of my fucking life.

I end up just stepping on the joint to put it out.

The light is dim, but enough to see the clouds of smoke swirling throughout the room from the weed I've been smoking, which, along with the whiskey, is the only small mercies I've granted myself from the pain.

The mess doesn't escape my notice. What once was an organized collection of journals and notes is now an explosion of paper. They cover my walls and the floor. The important ones are pinned up, while the non-important ones are discarded and lie in layers on the floor. They're a collage of old memories and rainbow highlights.

From where I sit on the end of my bed, I reach forward, trembling fingers and all, and pull one more journal from the large pile. I flip through the pages searching for pink highlights. The words swim in front of my eyes, and every time I try to focus harder, the letters blur, running together in a mess of ink and bad handwriting. I gave up cutting them out yesterday. Now, I just rip the entire page out and set it in a pile beside me, until I have a chance to pin it to the wall along with the others.

Pulling my shirt away from my body, I fan myself. For whatever reason, I'm sweating more than normal. I can't tell if it's from the fever under my skin or the lack of air conditioning. I'd crank it up and get some air ventilation in here, except that would require me to leave this room and pay a visit to the sunlight, which holds no appeal.

Instead, I read a few of the pink passages out loud under my breath. My voice is thick and slurred. My body also feels heavy, like I'm sinking into the mattress, and when I move my arm, it's numb and slow to respond, sluggish.

The next page is a sketch I once tried to do of her face—a half-finished disaster—I discard it. It looks nothing like her at all. In fact, it's a mockery of her beauty.

I glance up and let my gaze travel over the walls. I've taken a few sneaky pictures of her with my camera, but they're not great. Their shit, if I'm being honest, and don't do her justice. But they, too, are pinned up there, sitting beside my notes about her, her likes and dislikes, descriptions of *her* tattoos, her song choices, any and every detail she's revealed is plastered up there.

It was her all along, and I didn't see it. She was right fucking here.

Lily. Elle. Only it was never Elle, was it? It was *L* for *Lily*. Lilian Bennett. Her full name claws its way through my chest, twisting tighter with every utterance. She's been on the missing persons list since 1996. She's originally from Georgia. Never graduated from high school. Her father passed away when she was a child, but she has a mother named Suzanna and one little sister, Lacy. Or at least that's what Dozer's computer genius friend was able to track down for me, a guy he calls Whiz Kid, once I sent him more valuable information about her and a few pictures.

The information he sent helped me tie a few strings together from the past to the present. Other breadcrumbs I discovered by dubious means, either from info Raven divulged about her, or from my observing her day to day. Like her obsession with fashion magazines, fear of cats, flower preference, drink of choice—tea or lemonade, her asthma, her favorite colors, tattoos, particularly the wings on her back. Rainbow macaroons and sunflower seeds— the snacks Raven told me she took from the basket I had delivered. The ever-present and colorful nail polish on her toes. Her skills on stage. Not just an exotic dancer, but a performer. A beauty pageant queen multiple times over.

There's a new spiritual side to her that doesn't tie in, but I believe it's who she's become over the years. Hints to this are the dreamcatcher that now hangs from her rearview mirror. The palm reading she's done for the other girls at the club as a parlor trick.

She loves the outdoors, a contrast with how she portrays herself. She begs Raven to hike to the peak of Sandia with her at least once a month. When I had Raven take me to the exact spot, my mind fucking exploded. I had been there before with her. I felt it down to my bones. There were small flashes of a memory, but nothing I could fully grasp.

Even her fucking phone case, which speaks for her love to wander, is a map of the parts of Europe. I have memories of a map with pins like these, and I believe they marked the places she wanted to see.

These are the most prominent feathers and crumbs.

However, the thing that gives her away more than anything else is the rhythm in her soul, the music that lives inside of her. She hums with energy. It vibrates outward from her, this inner song only she can hear.

She reveals who she is under her skin every time she takes the stage. Yes, it's sexy as hell, but it's so much more than that. She cuts herself open up there and tells every single person in the audience something about herself on a deeper level. She loves music and is always somehow able to find the best songs for each routine. But the kicker is, she doesn't sing. She hums the music. Even when there's no music, she'll sometimes hum a tune under her breath.

My hummingbird. I'm certain that's why there's a hummingbird tattoo on my hand, and I suspect there's still a pink one on hers under the makeup.

I stand and make my way to the wall. I trip over something on the floor and barely stay upright. My balance is off, and the migraine has me closing my eyes for a spare second as I bear the pain and pressure it delivers in a throbbing, steady pace. The more I try to make sense of it all, the worse it gets.

The heat is also getting to me, and in this closed-off room, all I can hear is my heartbeat thumping like a bass drum in my ears.

The coppery taste should be my first clue that something's wrong, only it's not. Nor is it the warm liquid that spills over my lips. It's nothing but a nuisance I wipe away.

It's not until I touch a few of the notes and leave behind a blood handprint that I realize what's happening, that I'm bleeding.

The stains left behind are a bit macabre.

Fuck.

It *doesn't matter*.

My temple pulses its song of torment, and I slap my hand onto the wall, using it to remain standing.

I pinch my eyes closed and brace against it, but it's no use. There's no escape from it.

When I open my eyes and turn away from the wall, the room spins and goes black. I blink to clear my vision and look at the blurring colors littering the floor. The drum in my head gets louder.

I stumble as I take steps towards the bed. Somehow, I land on my knees. When I look down and see pink, I rifle through the papers and see that I've discarded notes about her in haste. I try to read the words, but can't read my own goddamn handwriting.

Some papers have what looks to be red leaves on them.

"Ughhh. Fuuccck." A nail drives home inside my head, and I growl as it tunnels deeper. I press the heels of my hands into my eyes as it throbs and pulses in time with my slow heartbeat.

"Motherfucker. Why the fuck does it hurt so fucking much?" I slur.

My head is being pried apart. There's no escaping it. It's pure agony and un-fucking-relenting.

Even the pain-filled groan I let loose does a number on my head.

Tears born of frustration well up in my eyes and spill over.

"Make it stop," I whisper as more tears begin to spill down my face. "Just… fucking make it stop. Please. Please. Please." I sink my fingers into my hair and cradle my head. "I… I can't do this anymore." I let the tears drip from my chin to the floor.

I'm done. Done. I just can't fucking take it anymore.

Shouting to the ceiling, I ask, "Why the fuck is this happening to me? Answer me that! What the fuck did I do to deserve this, huh? Haven't I suffered enough? What the fuck do you want from me?" I beg with everything that I am for some fucking mercy, for some fucking help, for some one up there to see me, fucking see me, and give me some goddamn mercy for once from this fucking endless torture.

Because I can't get her out of my head, and I don't want to. But thoughts of her are literally killing me.

When no response comes, no goddamn sign, I search out the pills, crawl to them until I'm able to find a bottle on the floor. I don't give a fuck what pills they are as long as they make it stop. It's harder than it should be to open the lid. When I do, I tip the bottle up and take a few and swallow them dry. Seeing as this is more pain than I've ever experienced before, I don't wait for those to work their magic. I take a few more to make sure I'll have enough in my system to quiet the raging storm in my mind.

I sit against my bed and cover my eyes with my hands as I wait for them to take effect. The only sound I hear is my heart gonging a deafening and ominous toll inside my head. I breathe heavily through the agony until it begins to quiet.

A door slams.

"Finn?" Mateo's voice is shrill and loud as fuck. He knocks on my door. "Finn!"

"What?"

"Everyone's been calling and says you're not picking up your phone."

His voice comes again sometime later, and it's echoey. "Finn."

"What?"

"Did you hear me?"

I clear the lump in my throat. "Yeah."

"Can I come in?"

I'm not sure how much time passes, but he shouts my name again and again.

It's so loud. I can't take it. "P-p-please stop." But I don't say it loud enough for him to hear, because words are fucking hard to come by now.

The door opens. Mateo mutters, "What the hell? What did you do?"

I pry my hands away to see him kneeling in front of me. He grabs my shoulders and turns me so I'm looking him in the eye. He slaps my cheek lightly, "Hey, hey, look at me. What's going on?"

I grab his arm, and my hand leaves a bloody print on his sleeve.

"Lily…" I rasp, my voice is hoarse, hardly audible. "It's… *Lily*."

Mateo looks at me, frowning, his eyes darting around the wreckage and madness that is my bedroom. He scans the walls, and his eyes widen. "The girl?"

I nod and grip his shoulder tightly. The world is going dark and tilting sideways. "Don't… don't let me forget. It's her. It's *Lily*."

"Okay, okay," Mateo says. "Just calm down. I promise, I won't let you forget."

But that's not enough. I grip him harder, desperate, the fear clawing at me and pulling me under. "*Say it*. Say her name."

"Lily," his voice steady and sure. "I won't forget."

I nod, my chest heaving as I try to hold on. ""L-l-lily…" I whisper, as the blackness invades my vision. "M-my b-b-bird."

I slump against Mateo and feel his arms come around me. A flat surface rises up underneath me. *I can't forget.*

LILY

My phone buzzes on the counter. The name flashing on the screen is the last one I want to see.

Goose.

I tighten my grip on the kitchen sink, staring out the window, trying to focus on anything but the ache in my chest. I'm torn on whether to answer it. He's been MIA, and this is proof at least that he's okay.

I want to verify it for myself, but I also can't open that door again because once open, it's so hard to shut out.

The phone stops vibrating for a second, but then it starts up again.

"Damn him," I mutter under my breath. My hand shakes as I reach for the phone, and on the fifth ring, I finally swipe to answer, snapping the phone to my ear.

"Goose, I said all—"

"Lily?"

It's not Goose. The voice on the other end is panicked, hurried, and not that of a man, but younger.

"This is Mateo," he says in a rush. "You don't know me. But I live with Goose. And he's… he passed out. I think he took something. Pain meds or something, and there's alcohol everywhere. He's bleeding too. I called 911, but I don't know when the ambulance will get here, and I don't know what to do. I don't know his insurance or how to give CPR. I tried to reach Bodie and Raven, but no one's picking up."

My hand flies to my mouth, and the other I use to brace myself against the counter. "Wait, slow down. You said Finn's passed out? Is he breathing?"

"Yeah, but he's out cold. The ambulance should be here soon, but I… I don't know how to handle any of this."

My breath hitches, and the floor suddenly feels like it's sliding out from under me. "I'm coming. I'll be right there."

I don't even think about it. I hang up and *run*.

I fly out my front door and race down my front steps. My legs pump beneath me, feet pounding the pavement as I race toward Goose's place. My pulse thrums in my ears. The warm evening air is balmy against my skin as I cut through it and push my body to its limits. My muscles burn, and my breathing comes in short, sharp bursts.

My plan had been to keep as far away from him as possible, but now… *none of that matters*.

When I finally reach Finn's place, I practically fall through the front door.

"Mateo?"

My eyes fly around the spacious studio apartment with a huge open area, and then to the door on the right that's Finn's bedroom.

"In here!" he calls out and appears in the doorway of another room on my left.

He waves for me to follow him. When I enter the room, I very nearly trip over a liquor bottle. The room is in total chaos, papers strewn all over the floor, pill bottles, piles of journals scattered around, and yeah, more liquor bottles.

But it's the sight of Finn lying on the floor with blood on his face that sends a wave of nausea through me and nearly takes the strength from my knees.

I rush forward and fall to his side. Resting my hand over his chest, I confirm for myself that he is still breathing. The sigh that leaves me is full of relief. I check his pulse, which is slow and weak.

"Is he going to be okay?" Mateo's standing. He has one arm wrapped around his stomach, the other crossed over his chest as he bites his thumb. His face is pale, and his eyes appear haunted.

"I think he's just lost consciousness, but we'll get him to the hospital just in case."

He nods "I didn't expect you to get here so fast. Thank you," he says, sounding surprised but grateful.

I peer back down at Finn. His nose is still bleeding. His shirt and jeans are stained with blood, and some of it's dried on his face. My hands tremble as I shake him gently. "Finn. Finn, wake up. What did you take?" Though I try to stay calm for Mateo's sake, fear coats every syllable I utter.

Finn groans, his head lolls to the side. His lips move, but it's a jumble of sounds, nothing coherent.

"Help me get him up," I say with confidence, despite the adrenaline and anxiety pumping through my veins. "We need to get him to the bathroom."

Mateo doesn't hesitate. He moves to Finn's other side, and together, we haul him up and drag him into the bathroom. Finn's dead weight has us using every bit of our strength to manage it. We get him to the toilet and prop him up. My hands are visibly shaking as I grab his face, turning it toward me. "Finn, you need to wake up. You have to *puke* this shit up. Do you hear me? Finn."

His head rolls forward. I go dizzy as the shortness of my breath tries to pull me under, my chest burns as the panic attack tries to take hold, but I fight through it. I don't have time to get lost in my own head.

Before I can think too much about it, I pry his mouth open and shove my fingers down his throat, hoping it'll trigger his gag reflex. He gags, his body jerking forward, and finally, he vomits into the toilet. I hold him steady and try again. When he's vomited up most of what's in his system, Mateo helps me move him, and I sit back against the tub with him in my arms. While combing my fingers through his hair, I whisper, "Stay with me, okay. Please, baby. Stay with me." The words keep spilling from my lips over and over again.

Finally, the high-pitched screech of a siren cuts through the air. Mateo leaves the room. Not too long after, he comes back with the EMTs, and we start answering their questions as best we can.

They take over Finn's care, and I step back to let them work. "He has dissociative amnesia and often gets really bad migraines. He's been on meds for it, but I think he's been taking more than he should or mixing them with pain pills and alcohol."

"Are you his wife?"

"Yes," I say, my voice firm. Because fuck them or anyone who would keep me away on that technicality.

One of the paramedics nods, checking Finn's vitals, and the other places oxygen over his face. When he's stabilized, they work to load him onto the stretcher.

I ask which hospital they're taking him to and let them know I'll follow in my own car. Mateo steps up beside me, his face a mix of worry and guilt. "Can I ride with you?" he asks.

"Of course. I just need to grab my keys."

As the paramedics wheel Finn out, Mateo and I follow and watch them load him into the ambulance. When they take off, I pull out my phone, my hands trembling so badly that I misdial and have to start over. When I manage to get it to work, I call Raven. It goes straight to voicemail. So I dial Roxy and tell her what's going on and that I need

Bodie's number. She gives it to me and tells me she'll keep trying to reach Raven. It rings three times before he picks up.

"Yeah?" Bodie's voice is thick with sleep.

No time for pleasantries, I say, "Bodie, it's Lily. Finn... he's in bad shape. Mateo found him passed out, and the EMTs just took him to the hospital. We're heading there now... to Presbyterian. Can you get there?"

His voice sharpens and quickly becomes alert. "Yeah, of course. Is he... okay?"

"I don't know. I think so, but... it was... he was bleeding pretty badly."

"I'll be right there."

I hang up and immediately call Raven, but it goes straight to voicemail again, so I leave her a message. "Raven, it's Lily. Finn is being taken to Presbyterian Hospital. I'm heading there now with Mateo. Call me as soon as you get this."

The memory of what I saw earlier—his body sprawled out, I can't shake it from my mind. *Focus.*

Needing to do something more than stand here before the panic completely takes over, I tell myself I need to pack a bag for him. He'll need clothes, toiletries... anything that'll make him comfortable once he's conscious. If he *wakes up.* No, fuck that. He's going to wake up. He has to. I swallow hard, pushing the negative thoughts away.

We reenter the apartment and go back into Finn's room. This time it's the walls that stop me cold.

Papers are plastered everywhere, from the floor to the ceiling. Words are written in the areas of the wall I can see, and strings are tying one thing to the next like a web. There are images, drawings, messy handwriting, fragments of thoughts, journal pages, magazine cuttings, and newspaper clippings.

I scan the walls in a state of disbelief. My hand covers my lower face as I move around and take it all in.

These are things I recognize: memories, conversations, places, people, or moments of my life. To anyone else, they would be seemingly random, but they're all pieces of me.

The highlighted words… they're what gut me the most. Little fragments of another time and place, snippets of conversations we had all those years ago. Pieces of that shared history he's found and held on to. It's pretty damn obvious he's been desperate to keep track of everything, even the most minor details. But some of this is also new, like he's been collecting tidbits about me and adding them to the wall.

Finn's handwriting is messy but recognizable. I read a few of the notes. *Where'd you go just now? Get back, you're too close to the edge. I thought you'd like something to read to pass the time. It's just a cat. I promise. I promise. I promise*

Each one brings up a brutally painful memory because these are also things and conversations I haven't been able to let go of.

It's chaotic, overwhelming, and obsessive. A little mad and insane. And it breaks my fucking heart, because this was Finn trying to find me.

Tears fall. I swipe them away, but more take their place.

"Is… is it you?" Mateo's voice is soft, hesitant. He comes forward and stands next to me, his expression laced with worry.

I don't have it in me to deny it anymore. Not after seeing this. I nod stiffly, my throat all but closed up. "Yeah," I whisper.

The emotions bubbling to the surface are overwhelming. I surrender fully to them because there's no other option when I see the utter devastation I've wrought. *God, Finn.* I wipe at my face over and over.

When I can pull myself together, I ask Mateo, "Why does he highlight them in different colors?"

"He color codes them. Best I can tell, green for his Army days, blue for stuff with his dad, and pink for you."

I nod in understanding.

"And purple?"

"He says it's Puff the Magic Dragon shit. Like stuff he doesn't think it real."

A half-sob, half-laugh bursts out of me because that, too, is a memory. A movie I forced him to watch because, as a child, it had been my favorite.

In a way, it's as if I'm invading Finn's private thoughts, but at the same time, these are all our moments. He always shared his journals with me, never hiding anything, never lying or keeping secrets. He was an open book, and it looks like he still is.

When we eventually get a bag packed and leave the apartment, I tell Mateo I only live a few houses away. He gives me an odd look. I don't respond to or acknowledge it.

I'm not in the headspace to explain the fuckedupness of me or my life.

As we drive to the hospital, Mateo stares out the window, his shoulders tense. His jaw muscle keeps flexing as if he's fighting his own mental battles. The hand, fisted on his thigh, is bone-white.

I glance over at him, worry gnawing at me. I want to say something, anything, to comfort him. But I don't know what to say. How do I explain what he saw? How do I tell him that the man he thought he knew is still there underneath the pain, just flawed, like us all?

I reach over and gently squeeze his hand. His only response is to not pull away. And it's enough.

LILY

CHAPTER 48

The kindest souls offer forgiveness before it's earned.

We sit in the waiting room, Mateo and I, side by side. Time seems to stretch on endlessly. From where we sit, we hear someone alert the staff to a code blue, and it nearly gives me heart failure. The idea that Finn's heart could flatline has emotions bursting out of me that I cannot contain.

As tears spill down my face, I pray. Pray to a God I don't believe in, and like I never have before. I used to think that if God existed, he'd sure as fuck written me off ages ago.

Now, though, I need him to hear every word echoing out from the deepest parts of my soul.

Please. Please. Please. Not him. Not him. Give us more time. Please. I'll do anything for more time.

I pray harder, gripping the chair beneath me as if holding on will keep him here. The yearning for this wish to be granted has me holding my stomach, which is twisted with worry, and rocking forward. When a sob tears from me, arms encircle me. Mateo's. His arms are so much slimmer than Finn's, but it's a comfort as he holds me while I break down.

I brush and brush the tears away, but more take their place. A never-ending torrent. All for him. Only ever for him.

And still we wait.

The sound of boots pounding down the hallway eventually shakes me out of the anxious grief. I look up, blinking through the blur of tears. An army of HOCs marches into the room—Bodie, Dozer, Cap, Griz, Maverick, and Taz. Their dark presence fills the small space, a stark contrast to the sterile waiting room.

Mateo and I stand abruptly, stepping forward as they approach. The sight of them is a comfort until Bodie's face crumples in an instant, misunderstanding my expression and tears. He shakes his head, grabs his stomach like he's been punched. "No," he practically shouts, his voice strangled. He bends over, clutching himself like he's bracing for the worst.

"We don't know. He's not gone, or at least we're not sure. We're still waiting to hear."

Bodie exhales, long and shaky, his hands moving to the back of his head as he straightens up, relief crashing through him like a wave. "Oh, thank fuck." He starts pacing, once, twice, then stops, his boots heavy on the linoleum as he tries to steady himself, sucking in deep breaths.

Dozer moves to stand beside him, his large hand resting on Bodie's shoulder, murmuring something low enough that I can't catch what he says. I focus on the way Bodie's face tightens, eyebrows drawn together, and the emotional storm he's struggling to contain.

Cap approaches Mateo and me. His massive body dwarfs mine. His face is pinched with concern, and his mouth is set into a hard line. "What do you know?" His gruff and no-nonsense demeanor is something I've become accustomed to.

"The ambulance brought him in around two fifteen. I was at his house because Mateo called me, and we had just enough time to get him to puke up most of what he'd taken." I glance at Mateo, standing stoically and silently next to me.

His voice betrays how shaken he is. "He collapsed, and he wasn't making much sense. He's been bad for a while, but this..." Mateo shakes his head. "This is the worst I've ever seen him. He was high, drunk—I don't fucking know—but he was slurring his words and

516

murmuring about Lily. That's why I called her. He told me…" His voice falters as his eyes dart to mine.

"It's okay," I reassure him, soft but firm. "I know."

Mateo's shoulders roll forward before he continues. "He said, 'It's Lily'. The girl, the one he's been looking for. He made me say her name. Made me promise not to let him forget."

Bodie freezes. His eyes narrow on me, searching my face as if it will reveal the truth.

I don't really care what he sees. This is me—messy bun, tear-streaked face, the oversized shirt, and black stretch pants. His gaze falls to my shirt—*Finn's shirt*—the one I changed into when I realized mine had puke on it.

Reaching behind me, I grab Finn's cut that's draped over the back of my chair, and I walk it over to him. He takes it from me when I pass it to him.

His piercing gaze stays locked with mine. I'm not sure if the others know what this means, but by the look in Bodie's eyes, he sure the hell does.

The room feels like it's holding its breath as the other HOC members exchange glances, their gazes ping-ponging between me and Bodie.

I expect him to yell at me, to lay into me with all the blame I deserve. The thundering beat in my chest picks up rhythm as I brace myself for a fight. It never comes. Instead, he motions me to follow him down the hallway until we're out of sight and earshot of the others. There he shakes his head and grumbles, "Fuckin' forget-me-nots." He chuckles sardonically. "When he first told me about you, he said. "They're goddamn beautiful, but fuck… sad too… like they've seen some shit, you know?'" He gets choked up and places a fist over his mouth, then clears his throat and drops his hand after he's gathered himself together.

It tears me the fuck apart to see tears brim in his eyes, and my tears make a reappearance. I swipe at each one, but still they fall. Bodie tilts his head toward the ceiling as if to will his tears away. "He knew," he whispers huskily. "From the moment he saw you again… something in him *knew*. I all but told him he was crazy."

"I didn't want him to know," I say, shakily. "I tried so hard to hide it from him. I lied every time he got close to the truth."

"Why?" His question is gentle.

"Because the past hurt too fucking much to revisit. And I lost him once… I couldn't let him in and go through that all over again."

Bodie laughs, but there's no humor in it. "How's that working out for ya?"

More tears tumble down my face. "Fuck you. It's not, okay."

He nods, says, "Fuck you, too. Now let's stop fighting and get him the help he needs, yeah?" His smile builds and, without warning, pulls me into a fierce hug. The smell of him—a mixture of weed, smoke, grease, and leather—fills my senses. Somewhat similar to Finn's, and it sort of wrecks me, because what if I never again get to experience Finn's hugs, his arms around me, and take in his scent.

I bury my face in his chest, and the tears come faster, sobs wracking my body as I cling to him. He holds me through every second of it and murmurs that it'll be okay, that *he'll* be okay. The other bikers are speaking in low whispers behind us. But I can't focus on what they're discussing. It's just me and Bodie in a sterile hallway. The world is spinning around us as he tries to fill me with hope instead of dread.

It feels like hours pass, though it's likely no more than another hour before the doctor comes to inform us of Finn's condition. "McCown Family?"

I'm sitting in an uncomfortable waiting chair between Mateo and Raven, who just barely arrived. We all stand and move toward him— me, Mateo, Raven, Bodie, and the rest of the HOC crew behind us. Every one of us responds because, yeah, *we're his family*. He has no living blood relatives except his mother, and he doesn't consider her family. This is the family he would claim if he was well enough to do so.

We solemnly listen to every word the doctor says. My knees go weak at one point. Raven links arms with mine to hold me steady.

Six times over the legal limit repeats over and over in my head. They had to pump his stomach and give him Naloxone. The doctor is concerned about the nosebleeds and wants to run additional tests. Bodie explains his head injury and the surgeries he's already undergone. They discuss the next steps, tests, and possible options.

All the while, the idea that this happened because he pushed himself, his brain, to its limit, replays in my mind.

The guilt I feel is insurmountable. The pressure sets in, and without warning, I step away as I struggle to suck air into my lungs. I press a hand to my chest and fight it, but the burn builds behind my ribcage, and my breaths shorten, my gasps for oxygen come quicker and quicker. I rest my back against the wall and tilt my head up as my vision swims. It feels as if my lungs aren't expanding. Like they're paralyzed or frozen in place.

Raven helps me to the floor and coaches me to breathe through it. I gasp out the word "inhaler" and point towards my purse. Mateo grabs it and searches through it. He finds the inhaler and rushes it over to me.

I take two quick puffs from it, and then I continue to fight for air as I wait.

When the attack finally tapers off, I explain to the men standing over us with stricken faces that I have asthma and get panic attacks sometimes, mostly due to shock or stress, and that they started when I was young.

Raven sweeps my hair from my face. "My father gets panic attacks, too. But he doesn't have asthma. I wondered about it because I've noticed some of the signs, and I've seen you use your inhaler a few times."

"The two don't always go hand in hand, asthma and panic attacks. I'm just one of the unlucky ones plagued by both."

Afterwards, as we sit and wait while Bodie and Cap check on Finn. In the silence, my thoughts tunnel down a darker road, to all Finn went through over the years. How hard he's searched for answers, and fought through so much pain to do so, to the point it was fucking killing him. But he kept doing it because he couldn't let me go.

Look at me! Look at my fucking chest and tell me you didn't mean shit to me! Christ, Little Bird. Can't you see you meant everything to me?

God, Finn.

The tattoo on his chest is a black silhouette of a woman standing by a tree, and parts of her are transforming into dozens of birds that take flight up and over the other side of his chest and neck. I've been in denial. Altering the meaning to fit my version of our story.

It feels like I've spent half my life searching for you.

He had, and I won't let him hurt himself searching for answers anymore. I'll give him whatever answers he needs, anything I have in my power to give.

It's a promise I intended to keep. To myself and him. I'll fight for him, with him, and I won't tell him one more fucking lie to save myself from the fallout. I'll help him through this in any way I can. Take care of him, like he once took care of me.

CHAPTER 49

*The flipside of what sustains us is that it can
also drain us of life when absent.*

I feel a feather-light touch on my arm, then my face. My body is impossibly heavy, every muscle thick with exhaustion, and my eyelids refuse to cooperate. But that touch, so soft and delicate, drifts down my arm, and then unexpectedly, gives warmth when a hand grips mine.

"Finn." Her angelic and soothing voice pierces through the fog clouding my head. "Can you open your eyes, baby?"

It's a lifeline, pulling me closer to the surface.

"Finn."

My head hurts, a dull ache radiating through my skull, but muted, somewhat distant, which I'm thankful for. When I blink open my eyes, her form slowly sharpens. She sits beside me. Lily. Even in my hazy state, I'd know those features anywhere.

She rises slightly from her seat, and for a second, fear that she's going to disappear and that this dream is ending fills me. My hand tightens around hers instinctively, desperate to keep her here, with me. But the image doesn't disappear. Instead, she leans over me. Her fingers brush through my hair, smoothing it back from my face with the gentlest touch.

"Hey, baby," she whispers, her voice soft, but a touch of sadness lingering beneath the surface.

"Lil'," I murmur, my voice hoarse.

"I'm here," she says, her swollen and red-rimmed eyes locking onto mine, and I can't look away.

"What happened?"

She frowns and her brows bunch together. It tugs at my chest, pulling at the ache that's been there for so long. "Too many pills, baby. We nearly lost you."

I close my eyes, the weight of it all pressing down on me.

"Hey, hey. Look at me," she says.

She's beautiful—so fucking beautiful—even without the makeup, without the armor she usually wears, and she's never looked more real to me than in this moment. Puffy eyes and all. There's a messy bun piled on top of her head, and she's wearing an oversized hoodie.

I study her tender expression. The warmth in my chest spreads, a combination of relief and regret. "You called me, baby," I murmur, the words slipping out before I can stop them.

She chuckles softly, and the sound wraps around me like a blanket, comforting and familiar.

"Am I dreaming?" This feels too good to be anything but a dream.

"No, baby. This is real." Her fingers trail over my forehead and temple, then through my hair again, and it's feels so fucking good. I never want it to stop. "Stay with me, Finn," she whispers the gentle plea. A feather-light touch brushes across my lips.

I blink, trying to fight the pull that's dragging at the edges of my consciousness. When my eyes open again, she's still there, leaning over me.

"Not uh," I tease weakly, my lips curling into a faint smile. "Call me baby."

I open my eyes, fighting the heaviness, and see her—*really* see her. She's right there, and I realize that the kiss wasn't a dream. "Do that again," I beg.

She does. Her lips meet mine again. This time, I let go of her hand so I can cup her face, but the weight of my arm feels strange, like it's not my own. My strength returns slowly, and finally, I cup her cheek, my thumb trails over her smooth skin as I hold her face. She's close enough that I can feel her breath on my lips.

I've missed this so fucking much.

"Fuck hell, Lil'. I missed you," I breathe, pulling back to my lips, just a peck. It's all I need, this small connection to her. "But I don't remember." I groan, "That doesn't make sense, does it?"

She laughs softly, that low, sexy sound that sends warmth through me. "Your mind and body know, baby. I get it."

"Yeah," I murmur, my voice trailing off. "That."

The moment feels too perfect to be real, and I want to stay lost in it. But then there's a clatter, a burst of chatter from the doorway, and reality crashes in.

"Oh, fuck. He's awake. Hey, love birds," Bodie's boisterous shout has Lily pulling away just enough to glance toward the door.

My hand falls back to hers, and she laces her fingers through mine. I shift in the bed, angling my head enough to see him.

Bodie, with a large bag in his hands, grins as he takes in the scene. That's when I realize Mateo's in the room, sitting quietly in the corner. Dozer and Raven follow Bodie in, their arms full of takeout bags and coffee. The delicious scent, when it reaches me, makes my stomach respond with interest.

Bodie sets his bag down on the table beside me. When his gaze connects with mine, his smile dims.

"How're you feeling?"

"Like shit. Drained," I admit, but it's not just the physical pain—it's the weight of everything. The mess I've made and dragged everyone through.

"I bet."

Lily squeezes my hand and says, "I'll give you two a second to chat." She flashes me a slight grin that tugs at my heart, then lets go of my hand.

I want to cling to her, keep her close, but I know better. Clinging to her like a desperate man isn't a turn-on. Going against my instincts, I let her go, for now.

"You gave us a scare, man," Bodie says, claiming my full attention.

"Guess I'm getting pretty good at that," I mumble, the fog in my brain lifting a little more. I try to swallow, but my throat is dry, and I wince as I shift further up on the bed. I search for the remote. He finds it and hands it over to me. I raise the top of the bed so I can sit up fully.

Bodie chuckles, though there's no humor in it. "Yeah, well, I could do without the practice. Nearly gave me a heart attack, man. I'm too young for that shit." He takes a seat in the chair Lily vacated and leans back in it while running a hand through his messy waves.

I glance over at Lily, who's standing off to the side, watching us quietly, her arms crossed like she's holding herself together.

Bodie follows my gaze, then leans in, lowering his voice. "You found her."

I shake my head, because that doesn't feel quite right.

"What?" he asks.

"Nothin', man. Can't really voice the shit going on in my head at the moment."

He nods. "Yeah, I get it. Don't push yourself to either. Just relax and know you're a lucky son of a bitch." He leans forward and places his hand on my arm. "She loves you, man. Wouldn't leave your side."

I close my eyes for a second, letting his words sink in. *Lucky*. Yeah, maybe I am. Because if this is reality and not a dream, if she's here and calling me baby, then fuck yeah, I'd say I'm lucky. But only in this.

There's still the massive issue of how I got here in the first place, and what I'll do when whatever they have pumping into my IV to numb the pain wears off.

"And for what it's worth, I'm glad you're finally together, no matter how it came about."

"Will you watch over her…? You know, with Veno still out for blood."

His hand squeezes my arm. "Don't even ask. We'll watch everything—*her*, especially, and Mateo. We got you."

Turning my arm, I grip his. It's a promise, a vow. Once made, I relax back, the tension leaving my frame. If there is anyone in this world I trust to have my back, it's him. He stands. Hesitates. After letting out a pent-up breath, he mutters, "I'm sorry I forced the pills on you. I thought it would buy you time. I realize now, after talking to the doctor, that you're going to know your own body better than anyone else, and if the other pills were fucking you up in a way you didn't like, then I should have taken you at your word and listened, looked for another option."

Guilt fills his expression. Closing my eyes, I shake my head and say, "No, don't do that. Don't put this on yourself. My problem. My choices. If I'd taken them like I should have, I wouldn't be here. I wanted it to end, so I popped 'em like Tic Tacs to make that happen. Just got sick of the constant pain, you know. And without her, none of it made sense. Didn't see the point of just prolonging the inevitable."

He nods. "I get it. But we'll find a way to fix it. I swear we will. And you have a reason to live now, brother. So, keep pushing through."

I open my eyes, staring up at the ceiling. The faint hum of the hospital machinery fills the silence. "No more pills. That's not the answer. There's got to be another way."

"No more pills," Bodie replies, his tone saying he'll make sure of it. "I'll call that surgeon in Cali—when you're ready. I think it's time you see what your options are on that route or with some of the stuff Lily told me about. No more quick fixes. Someone somewhere will know how to help. And maybe a little rehab."

Fuck.

The word *rehab* hangs between us, heavy and suffocating. I glance over at Lily again, and she meets my gaze. There's no judgment, just quiet understanding. I imagine they've talked quite a bit while I've been out, and the fear and concern in her blue eyes nearly undoes me. She's here. Finally, here with me. And she's waiting to see what comes next.

Bodie waits patiently, watching me closely. The rest of the room sits in utter silence, like they're all waiting to see what I'll choose.

I scan the room and see the stark fear and hope on all their faces. I pause on Mateo's, seeing how much emotion he's holding back—the storm brewing in his eyes. When I glance at Lily, she's worrying her lip and shifting in place.

There she is. *My little bird*. Afraid to hope for more than this, but wanting it just the same.

Her eyes are soft, shimmering with unshed tears, but she stands strong, like she's been through hell and back and is still standing. My heart aches, the weight of everything crashing down on me as I look at her, and for a long time, I say nothing. Just look at her.

"What should I do, Lil'?" I ask quietly, my voice barely more than a rasp.

Her breath catches, and I see her lips tremble before she presses them together. She steps forward, her gaze never leaving mine, and comes to stand beside me again. Gently, she reaches for my hand, her fingers slipping into mine. The warmth of her touch sends a shudder through me.

"I want more time," she whispers, her voice thick with emotion but steady, determined. "Any time we can steal, Finn. I want it. So whatever we have to do to help you and buy more of it, then we do it."

That hits me hard. *Any time we can steal*. I swallow past the lump in my throat, push through the haze in my head, trying to find the right words. Her hand squeezes mine, and somehow that simple touch gives me the strength.

I meet and hold her stare. "Bodie might be right about rehab. I don't want to do it, but getting clean might be for the best before I figure out what comes next."

She nods and squeezes my fingers.

"Will you wait for me?"

Lily smiles, tears slipping down her cheeks. She leans down and presses her lips to mine. She gives me a lingering kiss. It's like a promise—a silent one we both understand.

"As long as it takes. Wild horses and all that shit couldn't keep me away." Tears trail down her face now. She cups my cheek, her eyes never leaving mine. "I promise, baby."

I promise.

It's everything I need to hear. We share a kiss, and then she sits beside me, our hands clasped together. We hold on to one another tight, as if we're both afraid to let go. And for the first time in a long time, the weight of my addiction and pain feels a little lighter. Everything in my life feels fragile, like I'm standing on the edge of something that could go either way. But this—*her*—the dream of a life with this beautiful, crazy woman is a solid one I want with everything I am. Something I would die to hold on to.

Bodie watches us, his expression softening with relief, and when Lily steps back, he nods, standing up. "You're making the right choice, man," he says, his voice full of emotion. "I can feel it in my nether regions."

Shaking my head, a gruff laugh escapes me, but it turns into a groan as a sharp pain slices through my head.

Dozer smacks the back of Bodie's head.

"Shit," Bodie says. "What was that for?"

"For making him laugh."

Bodie rolls his eyes, but I love seeing the way Lily smiles at their antics. Raven looks less amused, probably because Bodie constantly tries her patience.

Bodie grumbles, "Fuck. I didn't realize this was a funeral."

"Oh my God!" Lily laughs, covering her mouth with her hand.

Raven gasps and screeches, "Bodie!"

Flashing his dimples, Bodie asks, "What, too soon?"

Dozer yanks him into a headlock—not a serious one, but just enough to shut him up. Bodie manages to get free and gives him the finger as he curses and moves to the other side of the room. He digs through the to-go bags. He comes back and passes me over what looks to be a breakfast burrito from my favorite fast-food joint. I open the wrapping to see the burrito covered in green chili, just how I like it.

Once finished, and while the others are occupied in conversation, I motion Mateo forward.

He comes to my side, and I ask, "You okay?"

There's a shadow in his gaze. He plays it off, trying to show he's unaffected.

"I'm sorry," I tell him. "It won't happen again."

With a grim nod, he says, "Yeah, okay."

"You were supposed to see any of that. It's not right, what I put you through." When he doesn't say anything, I sigh and say, "I'll get right, get clean, and I be there for you. I know this isn't what you need—you needed someone stable to depend on, and I'm sorry, I've fucked this up."

"You don't have to apologize to me. I'm not your problem."

"No, you're not, but it doesn't mean I don't want you to be. I like having you at my place. I like being there for you when you need someone, and I want to continue to be if you'll let me."

He wraps his arms around his stomach and nods. Emotionally, he's shut down, and I know it'll take time. But I can only move forward and make this up to him, prove to him and everyone here what I'm made of. If I have to go away for a bit to sort myself out, then it's what I need to do.

But before I do, I'll make sure he's solid, watched out for. He may not be my son, but I care for him like he's my own flesh and blood. Right now, my head can't wrap around the details, but I know Raven and Bodie will help. Lily and the club will too.

Glancing around the room, I take in the faces of the people who've stood by me, who haven't given up on me, and I know I've got no other choice but to turn this around. I've got to get some help and keep fighting through the pain.

As Lily and I lock eyes one more time, my heart gives a heavy, hopeful thud.

It's a promise I mean to keep.

I gave up heaven for this girl. There is nothing on earth I wouldn't do for her.

LOST LYREBIRD

CHAPTER 50

We all need a partner in crime who will help us murder, maim, and bury a body.

The thrum of soulful music and low murmur of voices is a balm to my nerves as I pull open the clubhouse door. My Chanel boots thud against the concrete floor as I stride confidently across the room. A few men and women are huddled in small groups. My gaze sweeps over them until it lands abruptly on the couple in the corner and the man with a throaty, sexy laugh.

Bodie is lounging in one of the worn leather chairs with a girl draped across his lap. He's wearing only jeans and a black ball cap that's somewhat shielding his eyes. The girl's arms are wrapped around his neck. Her head is tilted, and the two are currently liplocked. She's moaning as she rocks her hips over him, her hands running over his ripped, sparsely tattooed chest.

Thankfully, she's fully clothed.

The moment he hears my footsteps, Bodie breaks from the kiss and turns his head. His expression falls when he sees me. In one smooth motion, he nudges the girl off his lap. "Go on," he mutters, voice low and clipped. She huffs, rolling her eyes dramatically as she struts away.

He grabs his shirt from the arm of the chair, throws it on, then adjusts his cap back over his blond waves. When he's close enough, his voice cuts through the air, low and tight. "Lily, what the hell are you doing here? You shouldn't be here without Goose."

I wave him off. "Relax. I'm not here to cause trouble or hang out. I'm here for you. I need a favor."

His mouth kicks up on one side. He crosses his arms over his broad chest, stretching the ash-white T-shirt over his large biceps. "A favor, huh?" His tone is skeptical. "What kind of favor would that be?" He waggles his eyebrows at me in jest. "Want a shopping buddy? Need to try on some lingerie, and I'll be your thumbs up or thumbs down guy?"

I step closer, lowering my voice so only he can hear. "No, not that kind of help, you dope. The kind where I need someone I can trust to do some shady shit with me."

"How shady?"

"Like level eleven, on a scale of one to ten."

He laughs. "Which is?"

"Let's just say today I'm Karma—since the bitch doesn't know how to do her job right."

He rubs his hands together in excitement. "Tell me more."

"Murder, maiming, and mayhem."

His eyes light up. "Oh, ho, ho! Now we're tal—"

I place my fingers over his loud-ass mouth. "Shhh!" His eyes go wide... like, how dare I shush him. "It's not something we want to shout to the rafters."

He sweeps my hand away. "Why the fuck not? You think they care?" Looking around, he says, "They don't fucking care. They'd have your back, too, if you let them."

My gaze roams over the main room and lands on Dozer and Griz at the bar. Griz throws me a sexy smile before taking a drag from his cigarette. Dozer gives me a chin nod and a wave. Taz's gaze is locked on us from the couch where a girl is kneeling before him and presently kissing her way down his chest. He's sucking on a toothpick. But yeah, girl or not, he looks ready to jump up and do just that. Come to my aid if asked.

Cap walks in from the hallway at that exact moment and says,

"Hello, Sweetheart. How's Goose this morning?"

"He's doing good."

"Tell him we'll be up to see him the minute he's up for visitors, yeah?"

I give him a soft grin. "I will."

Cap heads to the bar, where Lita—one of the clubpieces, a pretty Latina—is standing behind. She hurries to grab him a beer when he asks for one.

I acknowledge that Bodie has a point. "Okay, yes. That may be. But I just need you. You'll get why when we get there."

"Me?" He raises a brow, his mouth lifting into a cocky grin. "You're choosing me over one of the other guys? Really? Color me intrigued."

"I'm serious, Bodie," I say, voice steady, though my heart hammers beneath the surface. "I'm about to do something… that could send me away for a very long time. And I need the help of someone I can trust with my life. So, it's you. Or no one."

His brows lift, and he steps back slightly, appraising me like I'm a puzzle he's just beginning to figure out. He recrosses his arms and bobs his head. "Then lay it out for me, Lil'. What do ya need?"

After exhaling, I say, "First, I need you to call off my babysitting detail. Grinder's great. A real teddy bear, but he can't follow me today. Tell him you'll take over. Then I need your assistance taking care of a problem. Can you do that for me?"

His gaze narrows. "That's givin' me shit all to go off of."

"Well, I need to know I can trust you to be on board with my plan before I fill you in on the details."

He studies me for a beat longer, as if weighing my words. The hard edges soften, replaced by the Bodie I know—charming, teasing, always ready to have some fun. A slow, lazy grin spreads across his face. "I've gotta admit, Lil', I'm liking this version of you. You don't have a twin by chance?"

I roll my eyes, but a small smile tugs at my lips. "Not a twin, but I have a sister. A young, very innocent sister who knows absolutely nothing about the kind of life I lead."

"Oh shit. That's my crack. Where is she, and when do I get to meet her?"

I pat his chest. "Hahaha. The answer to that is never, Bodie. Never."

"I thought you liked me. That's fuckin' mean, Lil'."

"Unless you want a bullet hole in your dick, it's a rule you'll abide by."

"Jesus! Woman. Who the fuck are you right now?"

It only takes me a second to think through my answer, and what I give him is the absolute truth. "This is me. Someone who knows how to handle herself. Someone you don't want to fuck with. You get me?"

"Yeah, yeah. Fuck. But tell me—is it weird that my cock jumped in my pants at that statement?" He holds up his hands when I open my mouth to scold him. "Calm down. I mean that in a totally platonic way."

"Aww, Bodie." I pat his chest again. "I love you."

He throws his arm around my shoulder. Looking down at me, he says, "I love you, too. You know we're gonna be tight, right? Like a throuple, me, you, and Goose."

He cuts me off before I can say a word, placing his fingers over my lips this time. "Platonic throuple. I mean… you two are going to fuck like bunnies, but I'll be that third wheel to your love fest that's clinging on to you both like a motherfucker."

I wrap my arm around his waist. "I have absolutely no doubt."

"Good. Just wanted to make that clear." Reaching up, he twists his ball cap backwards. "Alright, I'm in. Whatever it is, I'm your guy." His grin turns mischievous, that gleam returning to his eyes. "But you better make it worth my while. You know how boring it is around here without Goose. I have shit all to do. Apparently, babysitting his ass was the highlight of my day."

"Trust me, this isn't gonna be boring." I let a grin slip, matching his energy. "And if you play your cards right, I might even take you out for ice cream afterward. Like a good boy." My voice dips low, teasing.

Bodie's eyes light up with amusement. "Oh ho! You had me at ice cream, but asking me to be a good boy? Now you've gone too far."

I laugh, and he flashes a broad smile, his dimples cutting deep into his cheeks.

"So give me the deets," Bodie says, his smile fading like he's ready for whatever chaos comes next.

Taz seems to be reading my lips with how hard he's focused on my face. "Not here."

Bodie grabs my hand and begins leading me out of the clubhouse. I trail after him, trying to keep up with his quick pace.

"I'm gonna need your real name so I can—" He covers his mouth, coughs, and mumbles under his breath, "Track down this sister just to make sure she's, you know, not in any danger. Like, a distant bodyguard situation, if needed."

"Oh God. I created a monster."

He nods. "Yes, you sure in the fuck did."

"It's Lilian Bennett, by the way."

"Lilian. I like that. Like a lioness, which suits you. So, Lilian, where are you from?"

I point at him. "That's for me to know and you to find out. If you're good and I can trust that you won't go looking for my little sister."

He laughs and waves me off. His carefree charm is back in full force, but beneath the easy smiles and jokes, I can sense the seriousness lurking there. He might play around, but I know when it counts, he's got my back. And for what I'm about to do, that's exactly what I need.

In the parking lot next to my car, I fill him in. The laughter drains from his face so fast it's like watching a switch flipping. Gonc is the comedian, and in his place is the Army Ranger I've only heard stories about—the man who saved Finn's life when their Humvee hit a roadside bomb. His face has morphed into one with determination. His eyes blaze with fury, and every muscle on his body is taut. It's a side of Bodie people rarely see—the lethal side. The protective motherfucker underneath all the womanizing is a good man.

His movements are sharp and deliberate as he mounts his dark purple motorcycle. The comic book character painted on the tank is what gave me the idea for tonight, and I can't wait to see what he makes of my plans once he hears them.

The engine growls to life beneath him like a beast ready to be unleashed.

Knowing Finn is doing his part—slogging through detox and rehab—I need to do mine. He'll be ready for answers soon, and I'm going to make damn sure I have them, no matter what.

The apartment building is so much nicer than I remember it. The fact that Finn owns it makes me feel protective of not only the place but the occupants. So setting fire to it is not an option, not when a half dozen of his tenants call it home and Finn himself has updated it from the derelict relic it used to be.

From where I parked down the street, I can't help but wonder how his old landlord stayed under Finn's radar for so long, and how many women the creep has taken advantage of in that time.

I flip down the visor and start pinning my hair back. My hands move with purpose. Bodie roars up behind me and jumps into the passenger seat of my car just as I start adjusting the wig over my hair. I take out a brush from my bag and comb through the pigtails, then tuck away any remaining strands of my own hair.

I glance at him to see what he makes of this. His face is set in a bewildered expression—until he sees me pull out the clown makeup. His eyes light up with pure glee.

"Well, fuck. This is not what I was expecting." He lets out a low whistle. "You sure as hell make life interesting, Lil."

I force a smile, feeling my nerves buzzing under my skin, but Bodie's infectious grin makes it easier.

"I brought stuff for you too, if you're up for it?" I gesture to the bag in the back, and his eyes practically sparkle.

"Really?" He grabs it and sets it on his lap, pulling out the items like a kid on Christmas morning. His laugh echoes through the car, pure and uninhibited. "Oh my god, how did you know? The clown makeup makes so much more sense now."

"See, I remember Finn talking about his Army buddy who was obsessed with *Batman*. Movies, comics, you name it. He said the guy was constantly throwing out one-liners, and at the time, he swore it was annoying as hell." I pause, a fond smile tugging at my lips. "But it stuck with me over the years. How Finn would grumble about you, but it was that kind of grumbling that meant he actually liked it, sort of… in an it drives me up the fucking wall… but it's also entertaining because he keeps life interesting."

Bodie's grin grows even brighter, if that's possible. "He talked about me?" He says it like he didn't hear another word I said.

"Yeah, you crazy nutjob. He did. And I want you to remember something, alright?" I continue, my voice softening. "Finn loves you, Bodie. He's irritable and messed up right now, but that's just the addiction talking. He's going to get through it, and when he does, he'll thank you for everything you've done for him, for being the friend he needed, even when life got dark, and he didn't want anyone telling him how to fix his shitty circumstances. It means a lot to him, though he might never say it. You're always watching his back, caring enough to see him through his dark days, and for saving his life…" I hold up a finger. "More than once. That shit means the world to him."

The weight of my words hang in the air thick with emotion. I focus on my makeup, not looking at him, because I know how men are with "feelings". But I had to tell him. Finn's not the only one struggling here.

Bodie clears his throat, his voice a little rough. "Where's my wig and my gun?"

"No gun," I say, keeping my tone light. "Too loud. But there's green hair spray for you in the bottom of the bag. And I'll do your makeup."

He grins widely. "Do I get the bat or the stabby poker thing?"

I raise an eyebrow.

"Alright. Stabby thing, it is."

"There's a knife too—with a purple handle."

"Oh, hell yes." He practically bounces in his seat, like he's filled with pure joy.

"One more question. Do I actually get to use said stabby thing?"

"Yes, Bodie. We're burying this guy today."

"Seriously?"

Done with my face, I turn to him fully. "Seriously." I pull the stapled papers from the bag and hand them over. "This is what lives on this guy's computer. What he's into." It's a summary, not the actual photos or search results that Bones found under the landlord's IP address. The bastard had moved on from sick and twisted pornography to child pornography, confirming for me that I couldn't wait for life to take its natural course. He needed to be put down.

Bodie reads it all and gives me a determined nod. He rubs his hands over his jean-clad thighs. "Alright. Let's do this shit."

"Okay, hold still." I set the makeup on the front console and roll down the windows. Tearing off a square, I use a paper towel to shield his face and start spraying his hair green. Then I grab the white paint and spread it over his face.

As I work on his makeup, he shifts repeatedly. "I'm so fuckin' excited right now." I can't help but laugh. He does too, and I feel like a little kid who has suddenly found another friend who loves playing dress-up. The only issue is, he's too hyped to sit still, constantly wanting to check my progress in the mirror.

"Hold still or it'll be midnight before we get in there."

"Will you do the smiley face on my hand too? And the neck tattoos? Not exact, but something quick and badass. Can you do that?"

Smiling, I say, "Yeah, No problem. But only if you hold the fuck still."

"Okay, okay. Sheesh, woman."

It takes another half an hour to finish. Once I'm done, I step out of the car, peeling off the top layer of my clothes to reveal what's underneath. Bodie follows, sliding on the colorful suit jacket I bought him.

We're going to look like a couple of crazies walking down the street, but that can't be helped. Hopefully, people think it's a gig for a birthday party.

Bodie drops the bag on the hood and pulls out the fire poker. The knife he slides into his breast pocket after testing its sharpness. When I meet him on his side of the car, he hands me the bat.

I take it with a wicked grin. "You ready?"

He nods, grinning like a maniac. "And I just want to say, Lil'—you're my new favorite person. Like, ride or fuckin' die. I got you."

"Yeah?"

"Fuck yes."

I smirk and start skipping down the street, twirling the bat in my hand. "Why so serious?" I call back.

"Hey!" he hollers, jogging to catch up. "That's my line!"

I laugh, my heart lighter than it's been in a long while. "Are you smiling?" I call over my shoulder.

"You bet your ass I am," he replies.

"Good," I say. "You're breaking character if you're not."

"Wait… wait… wait!" Bodie suddenly yells, running to catch up. "Where's my machine gun? I just realized you forgot my fuckin' machine gun!"

I laugh so hard it's almost painful. "No machine guns were available for this venture, sorry."

"Well, why the fuck not?"

"I promise, next adventure, there will be machine guns."

"Now we're talkin'."

I shake my head, grinning. "I love you, you know that?"

"Yeah, Lil'. Samesies."

Just as we're about to enter the building, he hits me with, "I just figured out our ship name."

Spinning around, taken me off guard, I ask, "Our what?"

"Third wheel to your love fest, remember? Our throuple. I just came up with our ship name."

I take a few deep breaths, preparing for how this is going to go down. "Do I even wanna know?"

He grins. "Of course you do."

I roll my shoulders back, trying to rid them of the tension mounting there. Once it's gone, I say, "Okay, lay it on me."

He lays the crowbar on his shoulder and gets a firmer grip on our supply bag. But he's smiling like his namesake. "Loose, Boose."

I stare at him and give absolutely nothing away. "That's an awful name."

He glares. "No it the fuck isn't. It's gold."

"Can we argue about our ship name when we're not about to, " I whisper the last part, "murder a pedophile."

He huffs, "Okay, fine. But we're comin' back to it later. This is important shit."

"Alright. We will. I promise." I pin him with a serious stare. "Now, one more time. Do you have my back? No matter what?"

"Fuck yes, I do. You got mine?"

"No question." I hold out a fist to him with that same wild grin. He stares at it for a long time and opens his mouth. I tut and snap, "No fisting jokes. We have shit to do."

"Why do you have to steal my thunder? It was going to be a good one."

"Because the longer we stay out here, the more suspicious we look. Neighbors are going to realize we're up to no good."

He exhales, nods, and bumps his fist to mine. He follows me into the building and points down the hallway.

My gaze locks on the door with the silver number one above the keyhole. I let the memories of the landlord's threats of eviction if I didn't perform sexual acts for him fuel my steps.

Bodie whispers, "You know they say that friends who kill together, stay together."

"Oh, is that what they say?"

"Yep."

At the door, I stand to the side and arch an eyebrow. "Care to do the honors, friend?" I nod my chin towards it.

"I'd love to." He pulls his leg up like he's winding up for a pitch, then kicks the door with so much force it bursts open. "Like ridin' a fuckin' bike." His smile has never been wider.

Honestly, I'm pretty sure mine hasn't either. I let him enter first, following behind with a spring in my step as his wicked, demented laugh echoes down the hallway. He slips right into his role as if he were made for it. And I have to say, it's a laugh even Jack Nicholson would be proud of.

Hours later, we call it a night. The tarped body is stashed in my trunk, and a box full of Finn's old journals is placed on my back seat.

I've done what I can to scrub the blood from my body and the residue of it from under my fingernails, but the need for a shower grows by the minute.

It took longer than we anticipated to take care of the body, but now that it's behind us, I feel lighter—my heart, less heavy.

Bodie is still riding high from playing a deranged psycho. I eye him and try to gauge how long it's going to be before he comes down. Maybe a day or two. Honestly, I think I really have created a monster.

Seeing this side of Bodie taught me one thing—fucking with kids is a hard line for him, and God help any man who ever reveals they've crossed it. A demon lives in that man, and he'll come out to play if that trigger gets flipped.

Reaching into my car, I pull out my bag. When I find the makeup wipes, I grab a few. I try to pass some to Bodie, but he waves me off. I squat down next to my side mirror and begin cleaning off my face. When I'm done, I face him. "So, any regrets?"

"None. You?"

"Not a one."

I pull the pins from my hair and remove the wig. After storing it along with the rest of the evidence of our little venture in my bag, I toss the bag back into the car. Bodie holds up the knife he used earlier. "Can I keep it?"

"It's all yours."

He grins and tucks it through his belt loop.

I lean back against the car, taking a moment to relax and take in the peaceful night. He joins me.

"Are we tellin' Goose about this?"

With a heavy exhale, I say, "Yep. No more secrets or lies. That's what we agreed to. We're waiting until we can talk face-to-face to dig into the past, but we've agreed we're done keeping things from each other."

He dips his chin. "Good for you. Sounds like you guys finally figured things out."

I shrug, staring out at the dark road ahead. "We're working on it."

"Yeah, the couple thing is hard. Fuck, adulting is hard."

I chuckle. "It's the worst, isn't it?"

He palms his face, smearing what's left of his makeup. Not that it wasn't already wrecked from the night's chaos, but now he really looks like the mad clown. "Shit," he laughs when he sees all the makeup on his hands. He wipes it on his pants. Then his smile fades, and his voice drops. "Wish I could figure my own shit out too… but I think that ship has sailed."

That catches me off guard. I turn fully toward him, my brows pinching together. "How so?"

He glances at me, then quickly looks away. "You don't want to hear this."

"Come on, we're BFs now, aren't we? Hit me with it. You never know, maybe getting a woman's perspective will help."

He snorts at that, running a hand through his hair. "You haven't met her yet—my wife. Blaire. Not because I don't want you to—generally, we avoid mixing the clubpieces with the old ladies. Because of you know, all the catfights that break out when the two collide. No offense. I know that's not you anymore."

"None taken."

"Yeah, it's just a thing. Otherwise, shit gets real. You know how it is."

I laugh. "I've seen and heard a thing or two."

"Anyway, we've been together since she got pregnant, but it's always been rocky." He pauses, almost hesitant.

I can see it coming. "That's why you sleep around? Because it's not love. Not the real kind." It's blunt, but there's no point in dancing around it. Not with him.

He sighs, shrugging. "Yeah. No. It's never really been that. I find her sexy as hell. But she knows it and uses it against me. Swear to fuck, she tries to guide me around by my dick. She's either wantin' to fuck me or bitch me out. There's no in between with her. The other women… that's because she gets off on being jealous, or sometimes I do it when she freezes me out." He shrugs.

"It sounds like it's a game to both of you."

He huffs. "Yeah, maybe it is."

"Does she know everything about what goes on in the clubhouse?"

"Depends on the day. Some days, she wants to know every dirty detail, and she gets off on it. Other days, she acts like I'm the worst piece of shit on the planet. It's a fucking mindfuck. One moment, she's hot and heavy. The next, she's an ice queen and ready to cut my dick off."

"Is she worth it, if you found a way to work through your issues? Is that even possible, you think?"

He stiffens. "Fuck, you don't pull any punches, do you?"

I shrug. "It's two simple questions. Is it fixable, or is she worth the time and mindfuckery? Or are you just putting off the inevitable?"

He doesn't answer right away. The silence that follows is telling. He stares off into the distance, then finally admits, "I don't know how to answer either of those."

He does. His hesitation says more than any words could. I don't push him, though. Telling someone to end a relationship never works unless they're ready to hear it, and most of the time, it only pushes them back into the situation because they want to be the one who makes the decision. They want you to be wrong.

Bodie's not there yet. One day, but today's not that day.

"I'm no relationship expert," I say instead, trying to soften the blow. "I've got my own stuff to sort out. I was fucked up over Finn for years, lied about everything and pushed him away because I couldn't face my past or face him long enough to learn his truths, and look where that got us."

He grins, a wicked gleam in his eyes. "Murderers standing on the side of the road dressed as clowns?"

I laugh, backhanding his chest. "No, dummy. Him in rehab, nearly killing himself to win me back."

"Oh… yeah. That."

"Yeah. That."

Bodie's smile fades again, the weight of his situation settling back in. "What about my kids? If I leave her, I know she'll try to take them, and there's no doubt in my mind, she'll keep them from me."

"She can try," I say firmly. "But we're not going to let her. We'll hire the best lawyers, dig up whatever dirt we need to. And if push comes to shove…" I give him a dark smile. "We'll bury another body together."

He snorts, but there's a glint of hope in his eyes. "Yeah?"

"Yeah. That's what BFs are for, right?" I hold up my fist, and he laughs, bumping it with his own. "Now there's fisting. That's what I'm talkin' about." His dimples are back, and it's a welcome sight.

"No fisting, but you're definitely in ride or die status."

He nods. "Ride or motherfucking die. I'll take it."

LOST LYREBIRD

CHAPTER 51

The most profound love may come with trigger warnings, but the hell you fight through could be worth it in the end.

I had to wait months to see Finn again after he'd admitted himself into a medical rehab program. We'd found him one in Colorado that could not only help him with his addiction, but also his PTSD, migraines, and depression—which he'd also been diagnosed with.

He could have visitors every week after the first month, but he'd asked me to give him some time to work through some of it first. They were going to try some different medications to help with the migraines, and the side effects could alter his moods. He also didn't want me to witness him go through what he called some of the uglier parts of addiction, which were the first he'd have to face: denial and withdrawals.

But today's the day, and my nerves are in fucking shambles. Each step closer feels like a battle against myself. My chest flutters with the threat of a panic attack. My hands tremble as I fidget with the rings on my fingers, which are loaded down with all my favorites, and all my tattoos are on full display.

I've never felt so self-conscious, so unsure. Every detail matters—from the tone of my lip gloss, my jewelry, to the way my hair curls just right over my shoulder—because he's going to see me. See the real me without a disguise for one purpose or another.

It's stupid, really, this back and forth in my head. But the weight of today—of what this visit means—has me second-guessing everything. I've changed my outfit a dozen times, put my hair up, taken it down, wiped off my lipstick and reapplied a few different shades, trying to find one that fit just right, like I'm some lovesick teenager.

I finally settled on an Anne Taylor leopard-print top and designer leather pants, paired with black Dolce & Gabbana heels. Because I'm no longer hiding my wealth, or my addiction to high fashion. This is me. The outfit feels like a second skin.

I wonder if he's doing the same—worrying about what I'll think of this version of him. Probably not, but the thought settles some of my nerves.

I flip down the visor in my Beamer, checking my reflection one last time. The gloss shines perfectly, but there's a smudge under my eyes, a leftover trace of the tears I shed earlier, and I swipe it away with a tissue, trying to make myself look presentable, though it feels futile. Because inside, I'm a mess.

I take a hit from my inhaler and do a few deep breathing techniques. My heart's still racing, a flutter of panic at the back of my throat, but really, it's now or never.

You've never been a coward, and you're not about to start now.

I grab the box from the backseat, hip-check the car door shut, and start toward the facility. I force myself to breathe slow and steady. God help me, only this man has the power to send my emotions spiraling like this—turning me inside out.

When I finally make it inside, the facility feels colder and emptier than I expected. The nurse at the reception desk directs me down the hallway and to the right, but when I get there, the room is empty.

For a split second, fear grips me, it appears as if no one occupies the room. The bed's made, everything is sparse and impersonal or tucked away. The fear that maybe he didn't make it through this after all and left is there, but then I turn and see his shirts hanging in the open closet.

I breathe out a sigh of relief. He's still here—still fighting.

After depositing the box on the bed, I walk back to the front. The nurse looks confused at first, but then personally guides me to the courtyard. She points him out from afar, and the moment I see him, the world tilts and resets itself.

I'm drawn forward by the mere sight of him.

His back is to me, but even from here, I can see he's different. He's standing facing the sunset, his posture stronger than I've seen in months. He's wearing simple clothes—just jeans and a dark gray Henley, his hands tucked into his back pockets.

His hair hangs down over his shoulders, catching the soft golden light of the setting sun. There's something quietly powerful about him, like the roughness of him has been sanded down just enough to reveal his quiet strength.

As I get closer, I realize he's put some muscle on. It shows in the broader set of his shoulders, the definition of his arms, and his lean waist. He's filled out again and has been working on his body, something I knew from our phone calls, but not something I've seen. He looks good. Like he's in between the man I met and the man he was when I came back to him.

A man who, despite all the scars and darkness, is still standing.

The trees behind him are a blend of maples, cherry blossoms, and aspens, and the colors stretch out in front of him in hues of maroon, pink, and varying shades of green. The scene is so vivid, so starkly beautiful, that I imprint it in my mind, wanting to remember him like this—strong, alive, standing against this backdrop, no longer a ghost but real and here and waiting for me to find him.

My heart aches, my soul recognizing how special this day is, how monumental. It's as if no matter how many twists and turns we took to get here, this was always where we'd end up. Together.

If I didn't think it sounded like some hopeless romantic bullshit, I'd swear he's my soulmate. My twin flame. Because how else do I explain the way my heart reacts when I see him? The way my whole body hums with awareness when he's near? This undeniable response makes me wonder and believe that there's more to us than biological chemistry.

The crunch of leaves underfoot must give me away, because he turns slightly. The sunset cast golden highlights over his rugged face. The moment his gaze lands on me, his face lights up, and everything inside me stirs.

He wreaks havoc on my heart with just that one look.

His gaze is warm and piercing, brighter, but still holding that same depth, the weight of everything he's been through.

And God, he looks fucking incredible.

He turns fully toward me, a full smile splitting across his face, and that's it. A tear escapes. My throat tightens. My voice is hoarse with emotion as I call out, "Hey, baby."

He opens his tattooed arms, and I walk straight into them. He hugs me fiercely, and I bury my face in his chest, soaking in the comfort found within his arms. It's like the warmest blanket in front of a fire on a rainy day. They are solace and peace, and everything my body has been aching for.

I hug him just as fiercely, listening to the steady beat of his heart.

His scent is a heady mix of cedar and mint and all him. It settles my nervous energy somehow, and I could breathe it in forever.

After a long moment, he draws back and cups my face, his thumb gently traces my jaw. His eyes stay locked on mine, the intensity of his gaze makes my heart flutter.

That smile, the one he lost for so long, is there. Seeing it has butterflies tap-dancing in my chest. Like's he's saved it for me, for this moment. And fuck, I'm undone by it.

I go to speak, but he places a single finger over my lips. "Let me just look at you, Lil'. It feels like I've waited forever to see you look at me this way again." His voice is gravelly and low and does all sorts of things to my body.

I'm crying now, damn him. Smiling through my tears, but crying nonetheless. My own personal fucking wrecking ball, ladies and gentlemen. That's what this man is.

"Okay, I'm ready. But first, you gotta say it again." He grins wickedly.

I shake my head, confused. "Say what?"

He jerks his chin towards the direction I came from. "What you said when you saw me."

I laugh and nearly roll my eyes. I palm the side of his face and stare straight into his eyes. "Hey, baby."

"Fuck. Yeah, just like that. Best thing I've heard in my life."

"You're crazy."

"For you. Yes. You had your doubts?"

His gray-blue eyes stay locked on my face with such focus it's like he's seeing right into my soul, laying everything bare between us without a word. He pulls me forward and hugs me again. His arms wrap tightly around me, and the fabric of his shirt is soft under my fingers as I slide my hand over his chest and hold him close.

"I guess not."

He tilts his head down, lifting my chin with his knuckle. "You're fucking beautiful, Lil'. In a take-my-fucking-breath-away kind of way." His thumb traces the line of my jaw.

"Oh, stop." I lightly slap his chest.

"I don't know how else to say it. I just feel it here, you know?" He presses his palm to his chest and holds it there over mine.

I swipe away more tears. "You're making me ruin my makeup."

He shrugs. "I like you like this. Real. Honest. Just you. Wild and stunning."

"Am I gonna have to kiss you so you stop with the compliments?"

He laughs. And Jesus, the sound is amazing. Husky and hoarse. Rough. Like him. "Now, that's a grand fuckin' idea."

My gaze travels over his face. "Yeah." My voice is low and quiet, like a whisper. I run my fingers through his hair, and it feels like silk. It's healthy and gorgeous, and I absolutely love the shade that the black and grey make together.

Palming my neck, he tilts my face, and our breath skates over one another's. His other hand travels down resting lower on my back, nearly palming my ass.

"Should we be doing this? Aren't there rules or something we're breaking?" I ask.

"I could give a fuck at this moment."

"Me too."

"Then how about you break the rules with me, baby?"

I close the distance and kiss him. It's deep and passionate, to the point he dips me back and takes more and more from me, exploring my mouth. The groan he makes rumbles through me. I moan in return. Heat floods my body, and the ache between my legs grows unbearable. I've never wanted to have my way with a man as badly as I do him. If we were anywhere else…

I kiss him harder, deeper, until the world fades away and all that's left is him—his taste, his touch, the way his body moves against mine. His hand cups the back of my head, tilting my face so he can devour me from a new angle. I melt into him, lost in the heat of his mouth, the slide of his tongue, the press of his body. The hardness I feel pressing into me.

It's not just a kiss—it's a claim, a promise, a brand.

"Fuck," he growls, his voice rough with need as he pulls back just enough to meet my gaze. His dark blue eyes are nearly black with desire, and there's something wild in them, something untamed and dangerous. "We're gonna get my ass kicked out of here, but I could care less."

I smile, breathless, flushed, my hands still tangled in his hair. "No conjugal visits for inmates?"

He gives that half-growl, half-groan of his. An animalistic, possessive sound that goes straight to my pussy and has me aching.

Placing his forehead on mine, he shakes his head. "You have no idea how much that makes me want to walk right the fuck outta here." His hand slides down to my ass, gripping me tightly as he pulls me against him, grinding against me. I gasp, the heat between us building to an unbearable level. I feel like I'm standing on the edge of a cliff, one more touch, one more kiss, could send me over the edge. And God, I want to fall. But tempting him further will only make it harder for both of us to stop.

Patting his chest, I take one small step back and smile, trying to ease the tension. "Soon," I promise, my voice a low whisper. The weight of that word hangs between us—it's filled with everything we want but can't have just yet. "As soon as you get out of here."

He closes his eyes, breathing deeply, like he's trying to rein in the urge swirling between us. His hand slides between us so he can adjust himself, as his brow furrows in frustration.

"Four more weeks sounds like an eternity all of a sudden," he mutters, a wry grin tugging at his lips despite the heat in his voice.

"You can do it," I say, softer now, with more certainty. I'm trying to be the strong one, but it's hard. I'm just as wound up, just as desperate for him. But we have to hold out. There's too much at stake.

He nods, exhaling a long breath. The heat in his gaze simmers just beneath the surface, but it also holds something softer now, too. Gratitude. Resolve.

I grab his hand and brush my thumb over the back of it, grounding both of us in the quiet that's settled around us. "Come on," I whisper, tugging his hand, guiding him over to the bench a few feet away. The cool fall air helps to soothe some of the heat we stirred up, as does the distracting view of the sunset, which is still painted in shades of azure, amber, and orange.

"I brought you something," I tell him as I make him take a seat.

He tries to pull me down beside him, but I say, "You'll see. I have to go get it. I left it in your room. I'll be right back." I sense his gaze, the weight of it like an anchor, grounding me, even when I step inside the building.

I grab the box from his bed and carry it back out. It's a little worn now, the edges fraying from the years it's seen, but it's sturdy enough to hold the collection of his old journals and the letters I've written him, the ones I could never send. It holds pieces of both of us—our pasts, our memories, everything that's brought us together to begin with.

When I return, curiosity flickers in his eyes as I place the box in front of him on the ground. He immediately runs his hand over the barely sealed top, fingers tracing the edges of the cardboard as if he knows what it contains.

"What's in here?"

I sit beside him, close enough that our arms rest against one another.

"Your old journals," I say softly. "And… some letters I wrote you." I feel my cheeks warm as I say it. The vulnerability in that admission hangs in the air, a confession of everything I've held back for so long.

He looks at the box for a long moment, as if it's heavier than it really is. When he finally opens it, his hands tremble just a little, the emotion already building before he's even seen what's inside.

"If you're not ready to do this now, you can wait," I tell him. "And I don't mean that in the way it sounds. I just mean, this is heavy. I understand if now's not the time, especially with the surgery looming."

He palms my thigh and squeezes it. "I'm okay, Lil'. This is what I've wanted for so long. I'm not gonna shy away from it now."

I move in closer and lean over a bit to point to the journals. "They are in chronological order if you want to start with the earliest one. I also labeled and dated them so you have a bit of a trigger warning in case you need it."

He chuckles low, throws his arm around me, pulls me close to his side, and places a kiss on my head.

"Thanks, baby. It means a lot that you're doin' this."

Drawing his arm back, he pulls out the first journal. It's old, the leather worn from years of use. He runs his thumb over the cover, his eyes distant for a moment, as if just touching it pulls him back to another time.

"I used to write in these every night," he murmurs, voice hoarse, like he's remembering things that hurt to say out loud.

"I know," I lean into him, offering him the comfort of my presence as he begins to flip through the pages. The words are his, but the weight of them feels shared. He reads in silence for a while, his brow furrowing as he skims old entries about his dad, about the moments that shaped him into the man he is today. The rawness of his past lay bare on the page between us.

He lays his hand on my leg and squeezes. "I'll take more time and go through these later, but I can't tell you what these mean to me. Thank you."

"You're welcome."

He leans down, plucks one of the letters from the box. One of my letters. His hand lovingly caresses the paper. He looks over at me, his eyes glassy. For the first time, I see the cracks beneath his strength. He unfolds the letter, fingers tracing the ink like he's trying to understand the weight of the words written there.

He starts reading, his voice low and rough as he recites my words. I slide my hand onto his back and run my palm back and forth. There's a tremor in his voice, revealing how much this moment is costing him. His eyes flick over the lines, taking in every word, his breath catching as he reads my thoughts from years ago—my confusion, my pain, my longing for him.

It's all there. Everything I never had the courage to say.

The ending is what kind of guts us both.

I trusted you. When you promised me the world, I believed you. I fell so hard and so fast and thought you were going to be the one man in my life who wouldn't let me down.

That all feels like wishful thinking now.

Like the dreams of a naïve girl.

A promise is a promise, though, right?

When he reaches the end of the letter, he lets out a shaky breath, and for a moment, there's only the sound of the wind rustling through the trees. He pinches the tears from his eyes. Then he closes the letter and leans forward, elbows resting on his knees as he places his hand over his mouth. His shoulders shaking slightly, his breath uneven.

My heart clenches in my chest as I watch him cry and struggle with his emotions, emotions he rarely lets himself feel. He's never let this vulnerable side of himself show, and it both breaks something inside of me and gives me courage to be just as brave and vulnerable.

"It's okay," I tell him.

He leans back and palms my face, his thumb tracing my cheekbone. His eyes lock on mine. "No, it's not, but it will be."

I smile through my tears.

"A promise is a promise, right?" His gaze is soft and full of love.

My heart soars. "Yeah, it is. At least to me."

He nods, then pulls me in for a hug and kisses my temple. "To me, too."

"Thank you for trusting me again with your heart," he chokes out. Pulling back, he presses his forehead against mine. The words are simple, but the weight of them is everything. "I'll handle it with care. As much as I'm able, for as long as I have."

We stay like that for a long moment, breathing in sync, our foreheads pressed together, our hands clutching each other like we're trying to hold on to the only thing that makes sense in the world.

And in this moment, nothing else matters.

I spend the rest of the night, before visiting hours end, telling him our story. My version of it, at least. I don't sugar coat it. Because what he needs is the honest-to-God truth, and that's exactly what I give him.

Over the next few days, I tell him the rest—the past he didn't see coming, the one I was trying to protect him from. We talk about Deeds, the Greenbacks, why I came here to begin with, the years he missed, like the ones where I danced in Vegas, and we even talk about Veno, and my plans for him and the girls. I retell him about my past, about my mother's philandering ways after my father passed away, and my stepfather's abuse once he moved in. I even share my most well-kept secret, which is that of my baby sister, who's a college student at Berkeley and the only member of my family I still keep in touch with.

The only secret I hold close to my chest is Mateo's, because it will hit Finn hard, and I want to be certain before delivering that emotional blow. It's also Mateo's story to tell, but I'm not sure he has enough faith in anyone, including Finn, to come clean about it.

LOST LYREBIRD

CHAPTER 52

She danced, and at the same time, opened a window into her soul.

I step through the front door of *Wet Tips* tonight as a patron. The familiar hum of bass rattles through my chest the moment I hit the main floor and it's there, I stop for a moment, to take it all in and pat the sobriety coin in my pocket.

Partly, in remembrance of the road I've traveled. A reminder that I don't ever want to go back to the man I was before rehab. But also in thanks for this second chance. A chance to spend the rest of my life proving to the woman I love that I'm worthy of her.

It's been three months, a week, and a day since I was last here, and yet it feels like a whole hell of a lot longer.

Everything feels different. Music hits differently. The wind and sun on my skin, the rumble of my bike beneath me, even colors, scents, and food, they just all hit me more intensely, as if they were dulled by the pain or the poison in my veins. Even the way the lights on the stage seem to hold more color. Probably because I'm no longer lost to the grey fog of pain I was in, which is thanks to my new medication and pain management regimen.

My name is shouted from the left, and turning, I find my brothers in their usual spots waiting for me, smirks plastered on their faces.

Bodie stands to greet me with a wide, mischievous as hell grin.

"Whew wee! Lookin' good, old man!" he hollers. He grips my arm, and I grip his. Then he's bringing me in for a bone-crushing hug and claps me on the back.

Dozer is next up. "How's life on the straight and narrow, brother?"

I shrug, a smile pulling at my lips. "Feels like trying to walk a tightrope every damn day, but I'm good. Damn good. My reason is solid as fuck, and it's nice to be outta there." Dozer's hug puts Bodie's to shame. Cap's right behind him, and looking him in the eye is something I've been dreading. But maybe I shouldn't have, because he just claps me on the shoulder and murmurs, "I'm proud of you." It stirs up a wealth of warm feelings in my chest and has the tension that built instantly upon seeing him disintegrating into nothing.

To tell the truth, I'm proud of myself, too.

Their greeting sets off a chain reaction. Every HOC takes their turn welcoming me back to the fold.

There are quite a few members I haven't seen in months. Bodie and Dozer, though, visited a number of times. They kept my spirits up, encouraging me to keep going. Bodie had even charmed the nurses into letting him visit outside of normal hours and brought in treats, shit regular patients weren't allowed to have. The downside was being buggered by the nurses for the next few days to see when he might stop back by, as if the man lived off some kind of schedule or something. *Hah!*

Dozer's gifts were more practical. He brought me some free weights and a pull-up bar so I could focus on something helpful like getting back into shape.

With all the time I had on my hands, having that outlet had been a life raft. The free time you have to think can drive you fucking crazy if you focus on all you have to regret and atone for.

Stone is the only one who doesn't get up to greet me. He gives me a chin lift as a hello, which speaks volumes.

Now that I know what I know about him, the signs are easier to spot.

As a unit, we make our way toward the bar, and Cap orders a round of drinks. Bryan, my bartender, greets me and shakes my hand. He looks a little uncomfortable when he asks me what I'll have, and I get it. It's weird as fuck for me too, but I put him at ease and order a water. It's the first time I've had the choice, but it's an easy one, seeing as alcohol wasn't my vice, but it contributed to my problem.

"So, Bodie said your surgery is just around the corner and you'll want a few of us going to Cali with you?" Dozer asks after things settle down.

"Yeah. You, Bodie, and Griz, if that's alright."

He looks at me a little odd, but nods. "Alright. Then, we'll be there."

I slap his back. "I appreciate it."

Griz meets my gaze for a moment, and we share a quiet conversation in that look, a worry about how shit is going to go down when I fill Dozer and the others in on what's going on.

I catch sight of Raven moving through the table towards me, and just as I stand from my stool, she throws her arms around me, giving me a tight hug.

"Hey, you," I say with real affection.

She draws back and slaps my bicep. "It's so damn good to see you."

"You too."

"Was wondering when you were going to show. Lily said you'd be here sooner."

"Turns out getting out of rehab is somehow more of a pain in the ass than getting in."

She chuckles. "Lily would come out, but they don't have much time before they go on. Plus, she didn't want to give away any hints about tonight's show. Glad you're here, though, because she was having a meltdown thinking you were going to miss it."

"Does she know I'm here?"

She laughs. "Are you kidding? She's been watching the door all night from backstage. She knows."

A big grin splits across my face at this. "Good."

"Yeah, make sure you wrangle yourself a good seat. This number tonight is one she's been quite the drill sergeant about. It means a lot to her. She's been fucking relentless at practice."

"That bad?"

"Two girls quit." I raise a brow, but Raven waves me off. "A loss, but not a big one. It's fine. I've already found someone to replace one of them, and I'll hold auditions soon."

"You did good, Raven. I appreciate you taking over things for me. I've heard nothing but high praise."

She sidles up closer and nudges my shoulder. "So about that raise…"

I laugh and nudge her back. "You got it."

Her eyes light up. "Really?"

"Yeah. You've earned it. I was also thinking we'd make it official and change your title to manager."

"Oh my God. If I'd known the way to your heart was a long vacation, I would have made you take one ages ago." We both laugh at her ribbing and word usage. *Vacation.* If only. "Well, we're about to start, so I'd better get back there."

"Tell her to break a leg or whatever it is you're supposed to say."

Raven nods and turns. She runs smack into Bodie, whose gaze is down as if he'd been checking out her ass. As she glares at him, he runs his thumb over his lip. Raven rolls her eyes. "Bodie," She says in a low, smoky voice.

"Yeah, babe?"

"For the love of God, I'm a lesbian and I have a girlfriend. We've been together for two years. You have no chance. Like, none whatsoever. Not only am I not attracted to you, I plan to ask her to marry me." He opens his mouth to respond, and she holds her hand up. "No, you can't be our third. Because again, you don't have the necessary equipment for what gets us off, and in case you haven't figured it out yet, I'm the top… as in, I'm the one that does the fuckin', so unless you'd like your ass pegged, no. You know what? Not even then."

"You've had a girlfriend for two years?" We all bust a gut when that's the question he responds with. But then he follows it up with, "Wait, wait, wait. You're the man in this relationship?"

"Top."

"Yeah, top or whatever."

564

She laughs and shoots me a look. Bodie's eyes track her gaze and lock with mine.

Oh shit.

His gaze pings from her to me, and back again. His incredulous look finally settles on me when Raven walks away with her hands in the air. "Just sayin'," she calls out. "Dick and balls are not my cup of tea unless they're the ones I'm strapping on myself. So find a new obsession, or I'm going to kick your ass."

"Ohhhh, Goosie, you have some es'plainin' to do," He singsongs, and I run a hand through my hair, groaning. I already know the shit I'm about to receive from him.

"It's been pretty obvious, man. You've even met her before," Dozer adds. Bodie looks around at all the other HOCs. "You all knew about this girlfriend? And that Raven's a top?"

A few of them shrug and nod.

"You fuckers. And you kept me in the dark on purpose."

"We just wanted to see how long it would take you to figure it out," Dozer tells him, chuckling under his breath.

Bodie points at Griz, who's smirking; at Taz, who is spinning a toothpick in his mouth around a manic grin; and at Cap, who's shaking his head in disapproval of us all.

"Asshole's, the lot of ya." He pouts and plops onto a stool at the bar. He shoots a glare at each of us and then says something that totally throws me off. "Well, I have a secret too. And it's about your girl."

"What?"

"I'm not sayin' shit.'"

He shrugs as the corner of his mouth hikes up. *Fucker.*

Then it dawns on me. I sidle closer. "Oh, do you mean about your little Harley and Joker adventure?"

He shushes me before asking, "She told you?"

"Of course she did."

"And?"

"And what? It's not like I can do anything about it now."

"Right. Yeah. No. That's, uh-mmm" he coughs "kind of a done deal. No takebacks."

"From what I hear, he deserved it and then some."

"So we're good. You're not pissed?"

I shake my head and cross my arms as I lean against the bar. "Nah, we're good. Just thankful you had her back. Means a lot to me that you did."

His gaze stays level on me for a minute, and then he slowly nods.

"What?"

He shakes his head once. "Just good to have you back, man. Like, back back."

I grin, understanding what he means. "It's nice to be back. It's been a hell of a wild ride."

"That it has."

"And I'm glad you've been right there beside me through it. Not sure I'd have made it otherwise."

I slap his back and cure him of the emotional moment when I see his eyes tear up.

Then the lights dim, and the entire mood in the club shifts. You can feel it like a physical force charging the air, and it sends anticipation crawling up my spine.

Bodie shoulder checks me. "Brace yourself, brother."

A wave of silence ripples through the room. A single spotlight flares to life, illuminating a lone woman standing center stage. A woman with curves I'd recognize anywhere. Her head's bowed, and her hands are held as if in prayer.

It's the costume, though, that takes the cake. It's not anything I could have predicted—a white nun's habit, a black and white sultry dress underneath with wide slits, revealing the very tip of her thighs down to her black heeled boots.

Then the music hits and sends a pitching sound around the room, her head slowly lifts. The song is *Personal Jesus* by Depeche Mode, and the minute the opening lyrics sound off, the audience goes fucking wild.

Because damn, this is going to be insane.

The crowd is feeling it too.

Rapid thumping beats fill the room, quickly followed by the

strumming of an electric guitar. Lily strides forward in a saucy runway walk, heels stomping on the floor to the beat in a calculated, sensual march.

A white headpiece drapes over her shoulders, framing her face that's pure perfection. But it's the sultry, defiant look in her eyes that kills me. They're sharp and piercing as they land on me and carry a world of holy rebellion. The effect is sacred and profane in equal measure. A thick white collar circles her throat, unattached to her dress, which is cut low and covers little. A large black cross just under her cleavage above a black belt.

It's deliciously sinful. My cock agrees based on the way it tries to jump to attention.

This woman… she fucking knows precisely what's been on my mind. Knows she's putting me in quite the state, and by the look on her face, she's just as hungry for what's coming her way. Which God's honest truth, must be the point.

The sin I plan to commit with her is going to be downright sacrilegious. Where time loses meaning and boundaries disappear along with our sanity.

Because yeah, fuck, I plan to devour her and not come up for air anytime soon.

The other dancers are lined up behind her. It's hard to tell how many there are, they walk forward as one, moving with eerie synchronicity.

From the front, at first, all you can see are their boots tapping against the floor, their arms extended, the line of their legs as they kick out in perfect unison. Then they spread out across the floor in a pattern, some in similarly sensual nun habits, others in short black or white dresses that barely graze their thighs, the hem swaying as they step forward. They wear the same high-heeled black boots that click with authority against the stage floor. Their red lips are curved into the faintest of smirks. Dark eyeliner and smoky makeup gives them an edge of danger.

Large silver crosses swing from their necks with each movement. Pausing for effect, they drop to their knees, pressing their hands against their thighs, and spread their legs open, revealing white panties along with acres of skin. The choreography is sharp and sultry, bodies undulating in perfect harmony.

The lights flicker, casting shadows and beams across their bodies, highlighting every curve. The group flows as one as they rise to their feet, circling one another, their movements now more suggestive, more fluid. The high-heeled boots clack in unison, sharp staccato sounds cut through the pulsing beat of the music.

Lily leads the dance, her movements powerful, her body commanding the stage. The other girls fan out beside her.

When the dancers drop again, their bodies slide across the stage, pushing off with one foot as their hips thrust up to the beat.

They move like soldiers and fuck yeah, she's trained them well. Their skills are unlike anything I've seen, and their sharp lines hold the precision of military-like training. But it's Lily—always Lily— that sets my blood on fire. Every flick of her wrist, every turn of her hips is flawless.

She owns each movement, her body more sensual, and her talent shining above the rest. Her gaze keeps coming back to mine. I feel it deep in my chest, like a jolt straight to the heart. It's a silent communication between two people who crave one another in a way no one here could possibly understand. The audience and other dancers practically fade into the background. It feels as if she's performing for me alone. And I'm pinned under a stare full of promise and a fuck ton of heat.

She's mine. That's what she's saying. That and *soon.*

Then, mid-song, the stage transforms. Water begins trickling down from above. It grows into a downpour, soon every girl on stage is wet as the dancers spin seduction and work up the crowd into a frenzy. They stomp and slap the water, creating waves of splashes that look more dramatic under the spotlights. They swipe and kick at it, sending it flying which adds to the visual effect. Their white dresses become translucent, turning what was already hot into something outrageously sexy.

It's fucking mesmerizing.

Lily's soaked—her legs, her curves—all of it magnified by the slickness of her olive skin under the neon. She's not just dancing anymore; she's commanding respect and showing who the queen of this show is, and I can't tear my eyes away. My fingers dig into my jean-clad thighs likeI'm holding myself back from yanking her off the stage.

She struts toward the center of the stage, hips swaying, the dress clinging to her, until she grabs the long ends of her skirt and rips them away. Then comes the top. The other girls do the same. What remains is the embodiment of a fantasy every man here will never be able to forget. Sheer white triangle panties with a cross over their mounds and nipples, everything mostly sheer, because they are soaked.

Sexiest motherfucking thing I've ever seen.

Lily strolls to center stage as the music winds down. On the final note, she raises her arms, and the rest of the dancers follow, striking a pose so sharp and powerful it feels like a declaration. A prayer to the heavens, hands clasped above their heads, then they drop to their knees in perfect unison.

The expansion of their chests as they fill their lungs with air is the only sound, the only movement in the entire club, until the crowd goes absolutely insane and in a wave of exhilaration.

Lily's forget-me-not eyes stay locked on me. They burn straight into me as the lights dim. Daring me, taunting me, promising me. Telling me that this is for me.

Her last dance on stage is dedicated to me.

Because with Lily… there's always a message for me in each song, I just have to pay attention to discover the underlying meaning. If I'd known this from the beginning, could I have realized who she was to me sooner? I have no goddamn idea, but I know now, and I know she declared her devotion and love for me in that song.

The question is… what the fuck am I going to do about it?

Raven wasn't kidding. Lily's going out with a bang.

The crowd roars, but I can't tear my eyes off her. Everyone's standing and hollering as Bodie leans in, muttering, "I'd sell my soul to see that every fucking night."

You and me both, but only to see her. The other girls could take the night off.

I shoot him a look in total agreement. I'm hard as fuck right now and dying to get my woman alone, to finally touch all that skin she just displayed. To say there might be a minor punishment involved isn't an exaggeration. I'm jealous as fuck that anyone else got to see this, her like this. Knowing it's the last time is the only thing that eases the burn.

I stand, and the guys give me shit—Bodie hollering something about never seeing me get a boner in public—but I don't care. I make my way toward the hallway, towards my office, where I'll wait for her. Because I have plans… big plans, and I'm dying to see them through.

LOST LYREBIRD

CHAPTER 53

A balance of power is always at play.

Raven's compliments don't compute. Her mouth is moving, saying something about tonight's dance. They're words spoken in plain English. However, they make no sense when they're not the ones I want to hear. Because I only have one burning question that needs to be answered, and she's deliberately dancing around it, fucking torturing me.

As soon as I finish zipping up my dress, I turn and give her a glare that promises bodily harm if she doesn't tell me what I need to know.

"Where's Finn?"

She grins knowingly, glances at her nails, and frowns. "What'll you give me for this information?"

I huff, grab my heels from my bag, and step into them. When I'm fully ready, I fan myself. Yes, I'm sweating. I've been brimming with nervous excitement all day, but this is next level. My body is buzzing, like it's plugged into an outlet—fried and overheated. The thrill of finally getting to see him has been building to the point I'm about to snap. And I will if Raven doesn't stop teasing me.

"He's waiting for you in his office," she says at last. "Try not to scare the clients with all the screaming you're about to do. They might think someone's being murdered back there."

"See? Was that so hard?" I sigh.

"No, but seeing you all flustered is bringing me and the girls great joy after all of those insane practice sessions you put us through."

"Hope you're not in too much trouble," Olivia chimes in.

I couldn't care less if anyone hears us.

And trouble? God, I *want* trouble. The worst kind there is—with him. I want him with a force capable of tearing down every wall between us. This is a secret to no one, which is clear from the slew of raunchy taunts they throw my way as I exit the dressing room.

"Get it, girl!"

"Ride that stick shift like you stole it!"

"No dismounting before eight seconds!"

"Oh, Captain, my Captain!"

Alone in the hallway, I finally voice my answer. "I plan to. And yes, he's my Captain."

Halfway there, my steps falter. I could blame it on the sky-high, rocker-chic stilettos, but the truth is, anticipation is getting the best of me.

Wearing leather probably wasn't the smartest choice—but the black, strappy dress felt right. Simple. Sexy. A little daring, since it barely covers my ass and clings to every curve—plus, it's easy to slip out of and shows off my ink, most of which is on full display.

I took the time to freshen up a bit and dabbed perfume on my neck and wrists. My makeup is natural—just a smoky eye and a bit of shimmer on my lips. The jewelry I usually wear for luck and mental strength is absent.

There's only one piece I chose to wear, and my hope is he'll take the gesture as intended and understand its meaning.

That I'm coming to him bare of all my armor, my masks, and as a woman who no longer has anything to hide. One who accepted the role I played in our destructive journey.

While Finn was in rehab, I spent some time in therapy, reliving what I had to do to survive. Revisiting the past wasn't pretty. It was downright brutal at times—like walking through hell, landmines at every step—but I realized something while doing it. I'd bottled a lot of the past up and refused to face it. I'd denied that it had any bearing on my present or future, but that wasn't true.

I had to dive in, relive it, bleed it out so I could heal. And, somehow, find my most authentic self on the other side.

Because the blame for our separation didn't rest on Finn's shoulders, and it didn't rest on mine.

Life happened.

Fucking life, in all its messy, brutal chaos, threw roadblocks in our way. It forced us to navigate around so many detours and obstacles before we could find each other again.

And therapy helped me see how my own actions changed us, changed me.

I spent weeks alone in nature, self-reflecting. I've been trying to forgive myself for the poor choices I made that led me to do what I've done to Finn. I forgave Finn when he was in the hospital. But forgiving myself has been much harder to do.

Am I there yet? No. Not fully. But it's a journey I'll keep walking until I do.

I've made peace with all the versions of myself I used to survive, and laid some to rest. The ones I need, the essential parts, I've fused into who I'll be going forward—who I want to be for him. The woman who's strong enough to stand beside him, soft enough to take care of him when he lets me. Honest and whole, or at least, I will be for him.

The dog tags around my neck are a piece of our history—a symbol of what didn't break us, and proof I'm his as much as he's mine.

His door is wide open when I get to it.

I take a fortifying breath before sliding my hand up the frame and striking a pose so he can take in the view. I cover the dog tags with my fist and tease them along the chain. "Hey, Boss Man. I heard you wanted to see me. Hope I'm not in too much trouble."

He's sitting on the edge of his desk, hands gripping it beside his thighs, ankles crossed as he waits. His hair is down, tucked behind one ear. The black jeans and black Henley look sexy as fuck on him, and I eat up the vision that is my man.

His gaze snaps up, eyes raking over me. "Woman, you are trouble wrapped in one delicious package."

"Is that right?"

He chuckles. "Yeah, and you damn well know it."

Maybe I do. But Finn? He's everything that weakens me. His sleeves are pushed up, revealing his metalcore jewelry and tattoos. The veins in his thick forearms? Sinfully delicious. He's masculine to the core—silent, broody, possessive. And there's a wicked complex mind behind it all. The extra muscle he's packed on is a bonus. But honestly? I'd take him any way I could get him.

He's stitched himself onto my heart, and there's no coming back from it. Like before, his love is this all-consuming thing that I can't get enough of—unforgettable, irreversible.

But it's not just the love he gives—it's who he is. I'm in awe of the way he's faced the darkest parts of himself and fought to survive. I'm inspired by the way he lives by his own code, cares for those who need a savior, and sees through all of life's bullshit.

That's what sends my attraction into overdrive.

Because he's one of the good ones. A good man—flawed, but selfless. Intelligent, but humble. An addict and a lethal killer, but honorable. The kind of man who'd go above and beyond for someone in need—and who I know, without question, would lay down his life for mine.

He's everything I always knew I wanted, but never had the courage to claim, until now.

He's it. My person. And tonight, I plan to take what's rightfully mine.

Trailing a finger down my thigh, I let my dress ride up, revealing the barest hint of the garter beneath.

He stands slowly. "Come the fuck here, Lil' Bird." His voice is pure gravel. That hunger? It tells me I've misjudged who the hunter is in this scenario, which threatens to turn my fantasy on its head.

"Nuh-uh. You need to appreciate all the effort I put in before you rip this dress off me."

"Is that right?" He licks his bottom lip, his gaze dragging over me slowly, pausing on the curve of my thighs.

"I did go to a lot of effort." I lean against the door frame, crossing my legs.

He groans—low, guttural, barely contained—and bites down on his thumb, eyes locked on the lace of my thigh-highs. He eyes me with pure hunger, like he's fighting the urge to pounce. "Jesus! Look at you."

I smirk, but I can feel the tension rising. My bones tremble under my skin, vibrating like a tuning fork at his nearness.

"What's wrong, baby?" I ask, my voice coming out sweet and sugary. "You seem a little…" I shrug, "on edge."

"You have no fucking idea," he rasps. Getting up slowly, he takes his time striding toward me, his eyes never leaving mine. He leans over me, plants his arm bent above my head. "You don't know what you do to me, Lil'."

Smirking, I say saucily, "Maybe I do." Every inch of me is pulled tight, coiled, waiting. My heart is racing like I just ran a few laps, and there's a good possibility I might go off like a Roman candle the moment he touches me.

When he entered rehab, I agreed to his "no sex" rule—no sex with anyone else ever again, and none with each other until he finished the program. He said not until he felt like himself again.

So the last few weeks have been a lesson in patience.

That doesn't mean we kept our hands to ourselves. No. If his time in rehab taught me anything, it was how intoxicating and thrilling restraint can be—and it gave me a thorough education on what those muscles are capable of. I also relearned a few things about foreplay and found all the ways you could bend the rules without actually breaking them.

Thankfully, the "no sex" rule has flown out the window. We're finally free to do what we want.

No more rules.

No more barriers.

I reveal the dog tags, drag them down, and slip one between my breasts. The other hangs beside it, there for his viewing pleasure.

At the sight of them, the heat in his eyes turns molten. The tension builds until the air hums—crackling between us. I let the moment stretch. Let it simmer.

Then I reach out and toy with the buttons of his shirt. He visibly shudders beneath my touch. Not stopping there, I drag my nails down his chest, skimming over those newly defined abs. I take a second to appreciate the work he's put in, then hook a finger into his belt, give it a quick, deliberate yank—and unlatch it.

He raises an eyebrow. "It's like that, huh?"

"Yes. I was under the impression that the no sex rule is ancient history. Was I wrong?"

"If it weren't, it would have been obliterated the second you walked in wearing this outfit."

"Then what are you waiting for?"

The corner of his mouth hikes up as he fishes the dog tag free from my cleavage. His grip slides up the chain until it tightens around my neck, giving him the leverage he needs to draw me closer. His blue eyes burn with need as they travel over my face.

"Just wanted to get a good, long look first before I make a mess out of you."

"Yeah?"

"Yeah," he says, voice husky.

I smile wickedly. "Go right ahead."

"Give me those goddamn lips, Woman," he growls. Using the chain, he tugs me forward. His lips crash against mine, leaving me no other option than to surrender to him. I melt against his body and let myself get lost for a moment in the way he makes me feel.

The kiss is filthy—raw, unrestrained need. His tongue tangles with mine, coaxing, dominating, devouring. I moan and let my hands explore his chest like they're learning a second language. He bites my bottom lip, then sucks it into his mouth, groaning when I whimper.

When he finally breaks away, we're both breathless. He rests his forehead against mine, one hand still on the chain, the other cradling my face.

"You fuckin' wreck me, baby. And god, I missed you."

My hand slides down, cupping his dick through his jeans. His eyes close, jaw clenched as a tortured sound escapes him. The sound is music to my ears.

"How much?" I ask, as I begin jacking him.

"Lil' Bird." He shakes his head.

Drawing back, he asks, "Are you gonna be my dirty little vixen today? Is that what this is about?" He dips his chin, indicating my dress, and then lays his hand over mine, adding pressure.

"I was leaning that way." I flash him a sly grin.

"Tell me then what you want—what you need, Lil'. I wanna know exactly how you want it."

"How do I want you?" I tease, my tone soft and sensual, but also curious as to what he means. "I think you know the answer to that."

His grip on my neck tightens, making my breath hitch. It also sends a zing of pleasure rippling through me.

"I wanna know how this plays out in that wicked little mind of yours. How you've always wanted it, but never trusted anyone enough to say it out loud."

I caress his face with my gaze, memorizing every contour. His straight brows, deep-set eyes, and his beautiful lips, half hidden behind his goatee. Seeing strands of hair about to fall into his eyes, I sweep them back and run my nails lovingly through the hair by his temple. He grants me one of his rare, precious smiles.

"The God's honest truth?"

"Yeah, the God's honest truth."

So I let the words spill from me—no lies, no pretty omissions. "I want a man who's not afraid to fuck me. And I mean fuck me—raw, real, and sinfully dirty. Someone who has no trouble taking control without abusing it. He can throw me around as long as it's for pleasure. And I love all surfaces—it doesn't have to be in a bed."

I run my thumb over his bottom lip, and he nips at it. "Go on."

"I want to be taken without being taken advantage of. I want a man who will be a man—but still let the softer parts of me shine. Who makes room for those darker, naughtier parts, too. Someone who loves them all equally. Mostly, I want someone who'll treat my body like it's his own personal toy made for his pleasure, but give me the same in return on those rare days when I need to be the one in charge."

Saying it out loud makes me nervous about his response, but I push through and give him everything I've felt but never given voice to. "Control is something I've always had in situations like this, but more often than not, I want to let go and just feel—without having to think. I want to be so overwhelmed by it that I *can't* think."

"You want it taken from you? Not handed over—*taken*? Control?"

"Yes. Not all the time, but… yeah, that's what I've fantasized about."

"That kind of dynamic requires a level of trust. Safety. A way to stop things—so you know you can always stop me if you're not feeling it."

I open my mouth, ready to make a smartass comment to lighten the moment, and he must know it's coming, because he presses his thumb over my lips.

"We don't need safe words," he says. "What I need you to promise me is that if you ever want to stop, or get triggered, or things change, or whatever the case may be, you speak up. That's it. Just be honest with me about how you're feeling. Can you do that?"

When he removes his hand, I let a slow grin stretch across my lips. "Yeah, baby. I can do that."

A relationship with Finn isn't like anything I've ever had before. There's nothing fake, nothing unclear. It's a baring of our souls—leaving no room for ambiguity.

Not able to help myself, I go on. "I'm not done." He chuckles, and the smile that spreads across his face steals my heart.

"I want a man who will sate himself with me. Edge me. Make me beg for it—damn near torture me in the process. I want to be so far gone with wanting that I lose my mind. So close to breaking that I don't know which way is up."

He takes my hand and sucks on my thumb, which makes it hard to concentrate, but somehow I do, though the steadiness in my voice wavers. "I want to see that primal side of you. Hear it in your voice. I don't want a man who holds back or is too afraid to ask for what he wants. I want someone depraved enough to say fuck it and take it— who craves the taste of me on his fingers and face. Then—after we've exhausted ourselves—I want to find the other sides of that man. The one who holds me like I mean more to him than his ego will admit."

He releases my thumb and brings my knuckles to his lips. "I can do that." His irises are dark with promise, pupils blown wide. He opens his mouth to say more, but I raise a brow because I'm still not done.

"I've been taken like this by one man." I hold up my finger for emphasis. "One man in my life. And honestly, I used to wish it hadn't happened. I really fucking did. But it was that fucking good with him every time, so I couldn't. Every goddamn woman should know what that feels like—at least once. So I'm not willing to part with those memories, no matter how much they cost me."

"Oh, yeah?" By his deepening grin, I can tell he's catching on now. "If he was that good in bed… and gentle and caring afterwards… where is he?"

"Standing right in front of me. Alive and well. And thank-fucking-you for making the rest of my sexual experiences utterly unsatisfying. I went ten fucking years without it—and then I only had a few days to re-experience it before it was taken away from me again." I draw out the last word.

His sends a flutter through my stomach.

"Well, what do you say we try for a never-ending trilogy? Third time's a charm and all that."

"Yeah, but sometimes the sequels aren't better than the originals."

His smile widens. "I'm thinking this one just might be."

He lets go of the chain, and his hands trail down my body. When they get to my thighs, he circles them and says, "Up."

I lace my fingers behind his neck, and when I jump, he catches me—my legs instantly locking around his waist. The slam of his office door is loud and aggressive, but it's the best sound I've heard all night. Because finally, he's all mine and I don't plan to come up for air anytime soon.

He walks me across the room and swipes his hand across the desk, sending everything clattering to the floor. Lying me out on top of it, he follows me down, covering me with his weight. His fingers bury themselves in my hair as he pulls me in—his mouth capturing mine in a kiss that short-circuits my brain.

He teases me with playful nips on my lower lip before pulling back to study my face.

"It was that good, huh?"

"Yes, you bastard." I slap his arm.

Our breaths mingle as he caresses my cheekbone. "Because I gave you that kind of experience in the first place, or because it was only for a limited time?"

"It's like being given the most delicious chocolate bar and having it cut out of your diet entirely! You tell me what that could do to a person."

He chuckles. "Well, no more diets. You can have anything your little heart desires, Lil' Bird, anything." I love that he's playing along, joking about our messed-up past and giving me these lighthearted moments. "I wish I could remember every single second of those moments with you, but some of them I may never get back."

"I know. It's okay."

"I'm not sure how sex with me now is going to compare to the hot stud you had in your bed all those years ago? Hope I don't fall short of those expectations." His forehead meets mine. He lifts my hand and laces our fingers together. The gesture and sincerity in his expression warms my heart, and abso-fucking-lutely melts me.

"First of all, there was no bed. It was a new mattress on the floor because you hadn't bought a bedframe yet. And it wasn't mine. It was yours."

He tilts his head, squinting his eyes as if in deep thought. "There's something. Laughing. Candy and a little box TV on the floor."

I grin, warmth bubbling in my chest. "Our movie marathons while I was healing. You rented every action flick and bought a shitload of candy. Then lost your mind when I told you I didn't know who Indiana Jones was. You ran out, rented every one of those movies, and made me watch them."

"I did?"

"Yes, you were adamant that I be properly educated about those movies in particular."

His smile softens. "They were my dad's favorite."

"Yeah, I know, baby."

He closes his eyes for a beat, and when they reopen, he says, "I can hear your laugh in my head."

Which pulls a laugh from me.

He smiles as he gazes down at me. "That one."

It's in these moments that I feel something I've hardly ever felt before—pure joy and love. God, I fucking love him so much it's like my heart can't be contained inside my chest. I can't escape it. And I don't want to. But it also scares the shit out of me, because having it—and losing it again—is terrifying.

It might just be my biggest fear.

"So about this first time. Are you going to tell me all about it?"

"Someday," I tease. I pull his face closer to mine and nip at his lip.

"Not sure I can deliver, Lil' Bird, if I don't know the details."

"That's too bad. Honestly, it was one of the top reasons I was so keen to come back here." I steal another kiss from him, and for a second or two, we lose ourselves in it.

"I didn't say I wasn't going to try like hell to make it even better."

"You think you have it in you, old man?" I smirk.

"The way I see it, I've got some time to make up for, seeing as I could have spent the last ten years loving you, making you happy, starting a family… getting you pregnant and fat with my babies." I swat at him, and he laughs, catching my hand.

He takes a moment and eyes the tattoo on my hand, the pink hummingbird. His lips tenderly kiss my skin there. When his gaze meets mine again, he says, "You're the reason, though. The reason I'm still here. This unfinished business between us—this story we haven't finished—is now ours to write. It's why I kept fighting. Because I somehow knew this was waiting for me, if I could find you. Deep down, I think I always knew. And we'll have our story, Lil'. It might've started early, and come a little late, but it's finally our time to live it. I'm not going anywhere. And this sap is so fucking in love with you that he can't see straight. Honestly, my life makes no damn sense without you."

I'm a complete mess for him. But that's not what I say. What I say is a little mean. "You are a sap."

He laughs and nods. "I am. But just for you."

I tap his chest three times over his heart. "Just for me. And I fucking love you too."

He lays his hand over mine.

"Now, can we move this along?" I ask softly and with total sincerity. "Because I think I've waited long enough to be yours."

"Ditto, woman."

His mouth claims mine, fierce and possessive. There's little need for oxygen when my desire to be as close to him as possible overrides everything else. It's a carnality I've never experienced before. A high that both devastates me and sets my world right.

But yes, breathing is essential, and we finally break the kiss. Only, Finn's not done. His mouth slides along my jaw, runs up and down my neck, branding his way across my skin there, and then down to my collarbone. They're rough kisses, meant to mark and leave an impression. The coarse brush of his goatee, too, has my skin tingling in its wake.

He attempts to lower the top of my dress for better access. It doesn't have much give, but it's enough for him to find the tattoo in a copy of his handwriting. His words. Etched into me.

There is beauty in her movements,
    pain in her eyes,
and a storm in her soul.

~ My dreamweaver and little bird.

It was a note he'd made in his journal. I saw it one day while visiting him in rehab. To say I was touched is an understatement. I burst into tears. I also sat on the floor by his bed until I could pull myself together. Because how can one goddamn man have this kind of power over me? He slayed me with those words, broke my heart, and mended it fully at the same time.

After snapping a photo of it, I made an appointment with Taz so he could permanently ink them into my skin. I didn't just want those words with me always; I wanted to see them every day when I looked in the mirror, so I could maybe start to see myself the way he saw me.

He pauses and pulls back. Those dark irises of his flick up to mine. "This is new."

"I got it a few days ago."

He huffs under his breath, "Somebody was snooping."

"No secrets, right?"

He nods. "No secrets."

His thumb traces the ink. A second later, his mouth replaces it. His lips tickle, and I fucking giggle because, wow, I didn't think I had a tickle spot on my entire body. I was so very wrong.

Just like he did when he explored my body without the makeup for the first time, he pays homage to each tattoo as if they're a map to my soul. Spends a torturous amount of time lovingly touching and kissing each one. He starts on my torso, moves to my arms, then my legs. Especially the ones I painstakingly hid from him and sometimes the world before he went to rehab.

His mouth on my inner thigh has me groaning his name. The next kiss is higher up, and he adds more pressure from his hands as he grips my thighs so I can't shy away from him.

"You have no idea how maddening it's been to wait. There's drug withdrawals, and there's you. Getting another taste of you is all that's been on my damn mind since the last time I had my mouth on you." His fingers dance over the garter belt, playing with it. Moving inward, he strums my clit above my panties. It's deliberately slow, ratcheting up my need for more.

"Finn," I moan, more out of desperation than anything else.

He continues rubbing my clit, slow and relentless, torturing me for endless moments. It's a performance—his own private show. Even as he hooks his fingers into the sides of my panties and peels them down my legs, he takes his sweet time. Then he playfully twirls them around his finger once before flinging them across the room.

I shake my head and curl my finger, beckoning him back closer.

Dropping to his knees, he spreads my thighs wide to accommodate his large frame. One hand slips behind my ass so that the second his breath brushes over my clit, he can pull me to his mouth. The long, slow, languid lick up my center has my core tightening.

I lie back, close my eyes, and enjoy everything he makes me feel. The pressure of his hands on my skin. The heat of his breath against my pussy. The wet glide of his tongue. The rapid flicks over my clit. Even the scrape of his goatee on my sensitive flesh. All of it drives me wild, threatening to pull me under.

"Jesus, woman. You're like a decadent dessert I've been denied for too damn long. Think I'm gonna be here a while takin' my feel."

He's a man possessed as he devours me. I tug out his hair tie, threading my fingers into his hair, and use it to hold on. Rocking my hips, I attempt fuck him right back, but he growls and tightens his hold on me. The growl is fierce and possessive, and I swear the vibration of it ripples through my entire body.

He drives his tongue inside me. Two fingers soon follow. He curls them and begins to fuck them in rapid succession. I begin to shake. In mere moments, a haze settles over me as all other thoughts melt away.

"Oh, God. Finn! Fuck. That… that feels so fucking good. Don't stop, baby. Don't stop."

His calloused palm roughly abuses my breast. That talented tongue of his returns to my clit. Looking down, I meet his dark gaze, and it's the predatory stare along with his ministrations, and the fact that his fingers know what they fuck they are doing to my body—all of it shoves me completely over the edge and into a land of euphoria, my head snapping back, and a cry spilling from my lips as I cum around his fingers.

"Fuck. Uh. Jesus, Finn. I'm…fuck."

"Yeah. Say it just like that. Like it's a mercy plea, because that's what you are, Lil'. You're at my fucking mercy."

He doesn't ease up for even a second. He sucks my clit into his mouth, and I ride out the orgasm as his fingers pump into me.

I'm breathless and spent, too sensitive to take any more, and when I try to pull away—he finally lets me. After dragging a hand over his face, he brings his fingers to his mouth, like he's savoring every last trace.

Tilt sideways, I pull the zipper of my dress down. He brushes my hand away and takes over. That too lands on the floor.

His mouth moves to my stomach, where his tongue circles the petite diamond stud nestled there.

I pull on his hair, raise his head, and tangle our tongues together—consuming him the way he consumes me, tasting myself on his mouth.

"You taste good, don't you, baby?"

I nod and lick at his bottom lip.

He groans, and I feel it everywhere. His need—his desperation to be closer—matches mine. I pull at the hem of his shirt. He grabs it by the collar and peels it off. Every movement has those delicious muscles of his flexing.

The second his shirt hits the floor, his hungry eyes locked on mine.

I lightly run my nails over the ink of his chest piece—the one that speaks to me now in a way it didn't before. It makes me feel like the missing piece of his soul—the woman he couldn't let go of. The one he had inked here as a daily reminder of me, so he would never forget, and so we could find each other again. His reason for living and pushing through the pain.

It's art. It's love in its truest form.

And in a way, this version of him is more real: scars, tattoos, all of it. Not perfection, but rough edges. A body that tells a story, and it's a story I'll hold in my heart for as long as I live.

He pulls my thigh around his hip. "I can't wait anymore, Lil'. The thought of being back inside you has been consuming my mind and driving me fucking mad. Wanna feel you, baby, all around me. Been waiting, but not sure I can wait another second to feel you again."

I grin. "Right there with you."

"Good. Then we're done fuckin' waiting."

After picking me up, he sits me on the arm of the couch. I fumble with his belt and the button on his jeans, needing him so fuckin badly that my hands are trembling. He helps. Eventually, his jeans and briefs litter the floor along with the other articles of clothing we've discarded.

We've both been tested, and I have an IUD, so there's no question about him taking me bare.

The thought of it has my core tightening with want. I widen my legs to let him in, and he groans at the sight before him. Then he closes the distance and grabs the chain around my neck, while his other hand dips between my legs, his fingers sliding back inside me.

"You ready for me, Lil'?"

I nod.

"Let me hear it, then."

"Yes. More than."

"You sure? Because I'm about to deliver on what you ask for."

With all the sass I can muster, I tease, "Promises, promises."

He chuckles darkly and twists the chain around his fist. His other hand grabs his cock. For a moment, he watches the tip of his cock as he runs it up and down over my slick pussy. Raising the chain, he lifts my chin and takes my mouth in a long, drawn-out kiss. He notches the head of his cock inside me, and so painfully slowly, pushes forward.

The feel of him is better than I remembered. Memory doesn't do it justice. His cock is thick and veiny, wide at the tip, with a girth that leaves little to the imagination and guarantees a lasting impression, one I'll absolutely feel tomorrow.

With one hand guiding my hip to meet his, he slides out and back in. Out and back in. Each glide hits a different depth until he's seated fully inside me.

It begins as a gradual, torturous seduction—more about savoring the feel of our connection than the need to reach an orgasm.

Long steady strokes.

Kisses along my neck and shoulders.

His fingertips brand my skin as they cup my breasts and play with my nipples.

His scent surrounds me, and I breathe it in as I begin to let go.

Then he's gently laying me back until my shoulder blades rest against the cushions, though my ass stays on the arm of the couch. The angle gives him better access to my body, which he takes full advantage of.

Grasping my hip in a deadly grip, his pace increases. The harsh snap of his hips has me huskily crying out his name.

"Fuck, you feel so fuckin' good, baby. So goddamn right," he mutters breathlessly as he begins to pound into me.

"Same. Fuck. So good." My back bows on the next rut he delivers.

"Wrap those pretty legs around me, woman."

I do—and his shaft drives forward to the moment my ankles cross at the small of his back.

He slides his hand up the chain. The constriction to my airway does something to me— sends me spiralling.

He pulls out, only to slam back into me with a punishing thrust that rocks my entire body. There's nothing I can do but lie there and take it. I nearly bite down on my hand to muffle the cries threatening to break free as the sensation turns over-fucking-whelming.

"Finn—Jesus," I gasp, clutching onto him like a lifeline, digging my nails into his skin, marking him like he's no doubt marked me with his harsh kisses.

"It's all right, baby. You can take it. I know you can."

His gaze locks onto my tits as they bounce from the force of his thrusts. "Fucking hell. This body was made to take me. This pussy? Made for me. Wasn't it?"

"Yes."

"That's right. And you take it so damn good, Lil'. Like the perfect naughty little vixen you are. My good fucking girl, huh?"

"God, yes. Yours."

"Yeah, you are."

And I swear to God, it becomes a fucking religious experience as he fucks me with so much power and at an angle that hits just right.

My whole body shakes as my orgasm rushes forward. I whisper his name along with God's, giving voice to pleasure and the reverence it deserves, because the coming together, the reconnection of us in this way, has been years in the making, and it's the best fucking thing I've ever felt.

He withdraws and manhandles me, flips me like it's nothing. He lays me over the end of the couch, spreads my thighs with his, and rams back inside me.

"Fuck, Finn."

"Like this, baby? Is this how you want it?" he asks.

"Fuck, yes."

"Any way you want it. That's what I'll give you. As filthy or as sweet as you need it."

He slaps my ass. Once. Twice. And a third time. His thrust roughly into me, over and over again. I plant my hands on the couch to keep upright. He grabs my shoulder and forces me onto his cock.

He slams home again and again. "So fuckin' good, baby. How the fuck I could… forget… this… is beyond me. Because, fuck. This… this is what Heaven's like, baby."

He withdraws and rams back into me, nailing my cervix and causing an explosion of air to escape my lungs. My breath hitches now with each drive forward.

But it's the moment he sinks his teeth into my shoulder that does it. They dig in deep, and it's the pain, mixed with the pleasure, that sends me over the edge and fucking destroys me. I cry out my release as I fucking fly. My pussy begins to pulse around him. Reality leaves me, and the rising waves of pleasure rip me apart.

"Yeah, that's it, let me feel it. Like a fuckin' vice around me, Lil'."

Finn pounds into me like an untamed beast, grunting and groaning as the pleasure also becomes too much for him, all the while prolonging the agony and the bliss of my orgasm.

"Fuck. Oh, Fuck. That's it. Keep comin' for me, baby. Grippin' my cock so damn good."

I'm drifting through the aftershocks when his fingers sink deeply into my shoulder and hip, and his body goes rigid. "Fuccckkk. Jesus Christ." I feel his seed pump into me, accompanied by his deep groan that is so very loud in this small office. "God fuckin' damn." His pleasure is so primal that gravel coats each word.

Then his chest connects with my back as he lays his sated body over mine. His breaths sync with mine. His hand lay on top of mine, and he weaves our fingers together. We both suck in air, pulling in as much of it into our lungs as we can with quick, unsteady breaths.

"You wreck me, baby, but I love it. Swear to fuck it's like being reborn cumming inside you."

Then he's kissing me. My shoulder, my neck, under my hairline.

His lips trail up my spine, which fucking tickles. I swat at him and tell him to knock that shit off, but he only laughs and holds me down so he can continue his sweet torture.

Once he has his strength back, he's back on his knees, spreading my legs open.

"Gonna clean you up, baby. Clean up the mess I made of this pretty pussy."

His tongue trails down my crack, causing my body to jackknife. "Jesus, Finn!" His name falls like a desperate prayer from my lips.

His hands take a firm grip of my hips so I can't shy away from him. "Hold still. I'm not done." He slaps my ass and chuckles darkly. He then proceeds to clean me up with his mouth. I'm so sensitive that my body jerks. I whimper and moan because once again I'm at his mercy.

When he's finished the job and abused my ass with his rough handling, he relents and stands. He picks me up and carries me the short distance to the far side of the couch, laying me down. Before I can blink, his solid body is stretched over mine, and his mouth takes mine. The kiss is hot and deep—musk and sweet honey—it's us, combined, desperate and whole. Eventually, the intensity shifts, the kiss softening into something slower, something achingly tender. I bring my hand to his face, rubbing my palm against his stubble and goatee, letting the sensation ground me. I pour every ounce of the love I feel for him into it, letting it bleed from my lips into his.

The moment is filled with the kind of love that only comes from years of history. It's so intimate, so overflowing with affection, that tears well in my eyes.

I'm not sure how much time passes, but sometime later, after he switches places with me and holds me in his arms, I say, "That was…" I shake my head, words failing me.

"What?" he asks, grinning down at me like the bastard he is—because he already knows. It was the best sex of my life.

"Just absolutely insane."

"Insanely good, you mean."

I give him a blissed-out, lazy smile and nod. "Yes. So insanely good."

"So I haven't lost my touch?"

I laugh. "Nope. Not even a little bit. You still got it, old man."

He smirks, takes my hand, and kisses each of my fingers, slow and deliberate, like he's memorizing them. And all I can think is: *Fuck this man.* Fuck this man who can steal my heart with such ease, who makes me feel like his whole world with nothing more than a look. Who owns my body and my goddamn soul. I'm done for. Completely in love. So in love, I can't even see straight.

And I hate him for it.

But I love him for it even more.

LILY

CHAPTER 54

*What are the puzzle pieces that make up one's
life story? What are yours?*

I step out of the dressing room, and Finn's right there, leaning
against the wall, his arms crossed. His head is tipped back slightly
as he waits for me. The second his eyes meet mine, he lets out a
low, throaty groan that sends a ripple of heat through me.

"Woman," he mutters, his eyes scanning me from head to toe. "I
told you not to come out here lookin' like that."

I raise an eyebrow, giving him a teasing smile. "Like what?"

He pushes off the wall and comes toward me with purpose, his
hands finding my hips immediately. His fingers flex, like he's already
fighting the urge to pull me into him. "Like sin, Lily. It gives a man
ideas." His gaze drops to my lower half. "Those jeans aren't helping."

I laugh softly, loving the way his possessive streak makes him
frown like he's frustrated. "You said the leather dress was too short,"
I remind him, smirking.

"Yeah, and now I'm regretting it. These ripped jeans are just giving
everyone a damn roadmap to check out your ass. Rips in all the wrong
places."

I laugh again, the sound bubbling up from deep inside as I roll my
eyes at him. "Finn," I say, as I slip on my new leather jacket. "You
know you don't have to worry about anyone else, right?"

He tugs me closer, his forehead resting against mine. His breath is warm on my lips. His eyes lock onto mine with that fierce look that always makes my heart flutter. "I know, but it doesn't mean I like them looking."

I grin and lean up to kiss him quickly, nipping at his lower lip just enough to feel him tense. "Yours," I whisper, and the way his body reacts makes me feel powerful, cherished.

Hand in hand, we make our way out into the main room of Wet Tips, and the second we step in, I feel the energy shift. The HOCs are still here, drinking, partying, and enjoying the dancers, but the second they spot us, a ripple happens.

"The just fucked look looks good on you, G," Bodie pipes up, grinning like the devil himself. He points a lazy finger at us, and I can already see the teasing glint in his eyes.

The rest of the crew erupts into laughter, their voices rising above the thumping music. Finn tenses beside me, his arm slipping around my waist, pulling me into his side. I can feel the heat of his body seeping into me, and despite the teasing, it's grounding. It's Finn silently telling them, *Yeah, she's mine*.

Griz adds his two cents, a grin spreading wide across his face. "About goddamn time. I thought I was gonna need to lock you both in a cell until you finally had your way with one another. Glad, it didn't come to that."

"As if I'd let that happen," Finn mutters.

"Glad you two worked things out. Congrats." Dozer tips his beer bottle toward us. His voice is thick with drunken approval.

Stone is sitting off to the side, nursing a beer, but I catch the way he looks at us, the way his jaw clenches. The resentment and jealousy pour off him.

"Alright, alright," Finn grumbles, leading me toward the exit. "Enough. Got a woman to take home to my bed and a life to live. You fuckers have a good night, yeah?"

A few of the guys, including Bodie and Dozer, follow us out of the club. When we step outside, I glance around, confusion knitting my brow when we walk down the row of bikes and I don't spot Finn's among them.

"Finn," I say, glancing at him. "Where's your bike?"

"Right here," he murmurs, grabbing my hand and pulling to the right.

The bike he brings me to is a new Harley, sleek and black, with a paint job that makes my breath catch in my throat. The tank is adorned with an arrow and a beautiful dreamcatcher, feathers trailing down the tank. It's in masculine shades, with a few feminine details, like the small soft-pink feathers. The seat extends and is large enough for two with a backrest.

"Finn…" My voice cracks, emotion hitting me hard as I take it all in. "Is this yours? You traded in your freaking bike?"

"Wanted to mark the occasion by doing something special, and I figured since you'd be riding with me quite a bit, I want you comfortable. Plus, new bike, new memories," he says, his voice soft. "You're not just along for the ride anymore. You're a part of this life now."

Without thinking, I jump up and he catches me effortlessly. My lips crash against his. I give him a heated, grateful kiss. He groans into my mouth, his hands gripping my ass and the back of my head and he stumbles one step before he rights us.

The guys erupt into wolf whistles and jeers behind us, but I don't care. Finn deepens the kiss. My legs wrap tightly around his waist, and for a moment, it's just us. Just me and him, tangled up in the kiss, the world disappearing around us.

"Get a room, for fuck's sake!" Bodie shouts with mock disgust, but there's clear affection in his tone.

Finn pulls back just enough to smirk against my lips. "I plan on it," he mutters, his voice low. "Right after I take you for a ride."

We go for a long ass ride and it's glorious. I cling to him the entire time, and he shows me affection in small gestures—his hand over mine on his stomach, running his palm up and down my thigh. When we finally make it to his house, clothing starts coming off before we make it past the threshold.

Finn performs like the man is making up for lost time. He's

insatiable, which suits me just fine. His desire for me is the sweetest compliment, although it's not just my body he wants. He's also constantly asking me things about myself, and no one listens quite like Finn. He doesn't zone out. He pays attention to all the tiny details, like he's still cataloguing everything about me and committing it to memory.

We essentially fuck for three days straight. It's only the need for food that drives us to leave his room.

On day four, we complete a puzzle together and venture out to his workshop, where he shows me a whole new side to him that I never knew existed. A soulful and artistic side. I immediately fall in love with his creations, and know that watching him create is going to be my new favorite pastime.

Mateo is the only person we let into our little bubble. He hangs around one night when we order takeout, and it's the first time the three of us relax on the couch to watch a movie together. It feels surprisingly easy, even with Mateo's walls still firmly in place. I learn small things about him in these quiet moments, but he never lets much slip—his expression stays guarded, his thoughts hidden behind eyes that say so much and yet give nothing away.

Still, I'm determined to crack the code that makes him tick, to earn my way inside his world and, at the very least, become his friend. I know it'll take time, but it feels worth it.

Because whether he realizes it or not, we're a family now. And families don't give up on each other.

LOST LYREBIRD

CHAPTER 55

Karma is tricky in that the venom you spew will one day come back on you, and the good you do will too.

JUNE 2008

The sharp clatter of the closet door rattles through the dingy hotel room as Veno thrashes inside. His muffled curses and cries of pain, which are hindered by a large strip of duct tape, fill me with wicked satisfaction. Every kick, every futile attempt to break free, is power I'm taking back bit by bit from the man who stole so much of it from me.

I slide the closet door open a couple of inches, enough to see his face peeking out of the body bag we've tied him up inside. We made a perfect hole in it for his face to peek out and sealed the sides, so we can watch his agony unfold, with the insects inside getting out.

When the light from the room illuminates his face, he screams and twists, which no doubt delivers another round of vicious stings; any movement is bound to do so. His pupils are blown wide. The look on his face—pure, helpless fury—pulls a grin from me.

He screeches behind the tape and his back bows. Seconds later, his eyes roll back in his head, and he blacks out.

"How much longer you wanna play with him, Lil' Bird?" Finn's voice comes from behind me, tinged with amusement. He's lounging on the bed, his back resting casually against the headboard, legs crossed, remote in hand as he channel-surfs.

After closing the door, I go to him and kneel on the bed. The plastic covering crinkles under my weight, a nasty reminder of the nightmare I lived through in this very room. I shoot a glance at the blanket in disgust. The degree of filth committed here still lingers.

The time will soon come when I burn it to the ground, but not yet. Not today.

"Another hour, at least," I say, grinning as Veno slams his shoulder into the door again, letting me know he's resumed consciousness. The violent rattling and pain-filled screams carry on.

Finn chuckles low, half focused on the TV but splitting his attention long enough to give me a half-smile. "You're call. I'm just here in case you need me, you know, to do anything… anything at all."

I crawl closer, straddle his lap, and snake my arms around his neck. He smells like leather and sandalwood today. His new soap smells amazing, and it's something that's distinctly Finn. I grind down on him, making him moan under his breath, his half-grin disappears as desire fills his features. He sits up as hands find my waist, and his fingers dig roughly into my flesh.

"Thought you might be upset about the lack of disguises," I tease.

His eyebrows twitch as if I've hit a nerve. Lips pursed, he leans back, barely restraining a frown now.

I arch an eyebrow at him and shift my weight. Knowing just how to tempt him back into a good mood, I fist his shirt and brush my lips over his neck. I place playful bites there and suck deeply on his skin.

He moans my name and his cock jerks beneath me, hardening further.

In one quick movement, Finn flips me onto my back, pinning my wrists above my head. The bed creaks under us, the dirty mattress sinking with our combined weight. Heat radiating from him.

I shriek and wiggle to break free, because *ew…* this bed is disgusting, but Finn doesn't budge.

"Woman." His voice is a low growl, eyes blazing with hunger.

"Yes." I smile sweetly at him. He pries my legs open with his knee and forces them apart to make room for himself. I undulate against his cock, causing him to curse under his breath.

"There is a man locked in the closet."

"I know," I whisper. "I put him there."

He studies my face and says, "Something about this makes you horny, doesn't it?"

I open my mouth to protest, but he cuts me off. "Don't lie."

I sigh, deflating against the mattress. "Okay, fine. Yes, it's… I don't know. I love the power of it. Making him pay for what he did—to me, to the other girls—it's… freeing. Like I'm conquering something."

Finn's lips part, his breath coming a little faster. His eyes flicker with something primal, and his hips thrust a few times against my pussy. "Well, when you put it that way…" He trails off, his grip tightening.

"See."

He freezes. His grip tightens on my wrists. "Wait… did this happen with the landlord too?"

"Oh my god, Finn!" I struggle, and he lets me up. I slap both hands on his solid chest. "Are you seriously jealous right now?"

"I'm just asking because of the way you're reacting. I'm wondering if this happened when you and Bodie were having your little medieval villain moment."

"No, okay. That was different. That guy, I don't know. It was different because I was with Bodie. He's, like, friend material, not you."

"Well, you can't blame a guy for askin'. I just wanted to make sure."

I shake my head incredulously. I grip both sides of his face. "Yes, I can. I can't believe you were jealous. You don't ever have to worry about that. I thought you knew that."

He stares down at me, "For the most part, I do."

"You don't ever have to worry," I whisper, my voice serious now. "It's you, Finn. It. This feeling. It's only something I feel when I'm with you. It always has been."

"I'm older than you, Lil'. What about when I'm so old I need to use a cane because I have bad hips or some shit." He's playing now and being sarcastic, but I know the age difference has always been an issue. It was the reason it took him so long when we first met to even kiss me. So yeah, I catch on to the underlying concern he probably doesn't even realize is there behind his words.

"Especially then," I say, my lips brushing his. "I've got a thing for older men, remember? A big thing for one in particular."

"That right?"

I peck his lips and latch on to the bottom one with my teeth before letting it go.

A loud thud echoes from the closet. We both look over and listen. For a few seconds, I revel in the sounds Veno's making.

"You seemed pretty disappointed when it turned out Veno was such an easy grab. Admit it—you wanted to see me in that old lady costume."

Finn's laugh sends warmth flooding into my chest. He catches my jaw in his hand, tilting my head so his teeth can graze the sensitive spot just under my ear. "Nope," he murmurs. "Definitely not that. Now, if you were to put on the pink skirt, corset, and those ridiculous shoes with the ribbons… I'd be… well, let's just say, a man could be motivated to do a great many things if you were wearing those."

"What kind of things?"

He pulls my legs up and forces them around his waist. "Bend you over the edge of the bed, for one. Spank this ass, another." Without warning, he does just that. Swats said ass.

I wiggle to get free, but he holds me down. Pumps his hips repeatedly into me. It lights me up.

"I'd also remove the ribbons with my teeth and taste you from head to toe."

"Is that right?"

He pinches my chin and takes my mouth. "And take your ass again, because I know how much you secretly love it when I do."

I trail a fingernail down the side of his face. Grip his hair with my other hand, and use it to tilt his head down. I kiss him like my life depends on it. It's a greedy, obsession-for-each-other-fueled kind of kiss.

When we come up for air, I ask, "What, pray tell, gave me away?"

He chuckles. "How about the way not one intelligible word could be spoken from these lips." He rubs his thumb over my mouth. "It was all, uh-oh-ah-shhhh or some muffled cry into the pillow. Even the curse words you tried to say weren't actual words you could finish."

"You made sure of that by fucking them out of me."

He smiles full on now. "Damn right I did. Nothing is better than watching you clutch that pillow for dear life, bury your face inside it, lose yourself to the point you forget all the pretty little words inside your head."

"Or un-pretty words in this case."

"Oh, they were pretty. There was also the way you reached around and sank your nails into my ass, and left marks for a week."

Fuck. Okay, he has a point.

It's like this now between us. He can read me so easily, or maybe it's just that I'm no longer trying to hide myself away from him. He's pulling out a side of me I didn't even know existed. And there's freedom to be found in it, because I don't feel I have to act a certain way for him. I can feel any way I want to, say anything I want to, and do, for the most part, anything I want. He lets me run wild and lets the pieces fall where they may.

I pull back to meet his eyes. "Tell you what. As soon as we bury him, you can lay me out over the hood of your car, anyway you like. Think of it as how we'll celebrate this chapter in our life finally coming to an end."

His blue irises brighten. Surprise and enthusiasm fill them. "Close the book on it with a bang. I like that." He chuckles, and I grin wickedly back at him.

Yes, it's romantic, even with the piece of shit crying out and banging against the closet door. I'm twisted enough to get off on imagining how much pain Veno's experiencing and what his pleas for mercy sound like underneath the duct tape, while I'm over here attempting to sex up my man.

Grinning like fiends, we get off the bed and check on our captive.

We stare down at Veno, and sick satisfaction bubbles inside of me to see that there's foam running out of the sides of his mouth.

"I just wish he'd put up more of a fight, you know? It was too easy," Finn says.

"It's called preparation, baby." I pat Finn's chest. At his scowl, I go on. "It's okay, I'll teach you." He simply shakes his head.

I crouch down and reach in to shake the body bag, which has Veno thrashing again. His face is red, his breathing is labored, and there's snot running out of his nose.

Finn sighs, "Can we please get this over with. He's giving me a headache."

I laugh softly, nodding. "Yeah, let's get him out to the car."

Together, we grab onto the bag and pull Veno out of the closet. He squirms like the worm he is, trying to get free. It's no use, though.

I bend down, but Finn hauls me back up. "Don't get so close, Lil'."

I roll my eyes at him. "It's fine. He honestly can't hurt me anymore." Finn watches me closely, but at my words, he relaxes a bit.

I crouch down beside Veno, stare into his eyes as he writhes in pain. "This," I say, my voice cold. "This is how I wanted to remember you. Helpless. Desperate. Full of poison. Getting exactly what you deserve. Eye for an eye. I nearly paid some other lowlife to make you his bitch but I didn't want you to get even a measure of satisfaction out of it. Plus, there are just some lines I'm not willing to cross."

Veno tries to glare at me, but his eyes flutter as if he's going to lose consciousness again. So I slap his face to get his attention. "That closet. That's where I hid from the cops when they came to shut down your operation. That's how Goose found me."

His eyes flicker to Finn and then back to me.

"If I hadn't been hiding when they raided the place, then we would have never met. I'm thankful for that. Not any of the shit you put me through. But I'm fucking thankful that I get to come back here and know that I survived it. That you won't survive me. And that there was some grand reason why it all had to happen the way it did. It sucks, but it's my life. My story." I stand and move away from him.

I wasn't sure if he would, but Finn speaks next. He pulls out a knife and squats down. He covers Veno's mouth and uses his grip to keep his head steady. He trails the tip of the blade down and cuts the teardrops from Veno's face near his eye, while Veno squeals like a pig. "You put a fuckin' meth lab in my dad's house. He was dying, and your boys were cooking your poison in his house. My last fuckin' piece of him. That house, all of our memories. You took that from me. So, I made it my mission to take you and your operation down. As soon as Edge is out of prison, the HOCs will hunt down every member of your little gang and your brothers. Rest assured, they'll be joining you in hell real soon."

Veno is pleading now, but his pleas fall on deaf ears.

Finn adds, "Let's see what the real Devil thinks of you, shall we?"

I make the sign of the cross and say, "Amen."

Finn smirks at me, and I grin right back. When every single tear drop is removed from Veno's face, Finn sets down the knife and holds his hand out to me. "Hand me the syringe."

I go to my bag and pull out the small box. I open it. In the foam inlay is a syringe with enough PCP and Adrenaline to deliver a near-deadly dose. It'll have Veno hyped up and hallucinating, filled with paranoia. The Adrenaline will spike his heart rate, blood pressure, and make him feel like he's dying. He will lose complete touch with reality. It'll induce so much fear in him that he may just die of fright before the other poison now filling his veins from the little critters in the bag with him kills him.

For the next few hours, if he lives that long, he'll be experiencing a waking nightmare, and there will be absolutely nothing he can do to escape it.

I place the syringe in Finn's hand, and he wastes no time in finding a vein on Veno's neck and pumping him full of the drug.

Veno writhes, bucking against the unyielding fabric of the bag. Within seconds, he'll be seeing things that aren't there, and panic will devour logic. The drugs, poison, and Adrenaline will have him racing on an endless road toward madness until the moment his heart finally stops.

We watch and wait until it takes hold, then, together, and under the cover of night, we carry him out to the car and stuff him into the trunk.

I jump into the passenger seat of Finn's Roadrunner as he slides behind the wheel. As we pull away, I let my gaze drift back to the hotel, picturing how it'll look once we're done with it. We'll tear it down piece by piece and rebuild something that saves lives instead of destroying them—a halfway house where people battling addiction can detox, get therapy, and find a fresh start. First, though, we have to stick to the plan, take down the Thirteens, and free Albuquerque from scum like them. After that, we'll make this place a haven for people like us, and find the right specialists to help us run it right. It's a long-term goal—but it's one we're both ready for.

Raven will run the strip club, and Finn has promised to up her salary again when that happens.

As we drive through some of the most desolate plains of New Mexico, the night lights up as lightning streaks across the sky. It comes in waves, and the storm looks like it's gathering force. It only grows closer as we drive west.

Finn rolls down the windows and smirks at me knowingly. I grin right back and put my hand outside the window to let it surf in the wind rushing by. Every so often, thunder rumbles and drowns out the low tunes playing on the car stereo. It's a frightening and yet beautiful sound. It's as if the world knows how important this night is and is celebrating this victory with us.

When we arrive at the place we've chosen for this special occasion, Finn parks his car as close as he can to the hole. Together, we lug Veno to the spot. The bucket we brought out here earlier is beside the pit.

Thunder rolls above us, and lightning pulses sporadically through the night sky filled with gray clouds.

Finn drops Veno like a sack of potatoes, and it's music to my ears when I hear he's still alive and kicking. Veno thrashes inside the body bag, the nylon shuddering with every convulsion. The scorpions trapped in there with him are probably no doubt attacking his bare skin, their stings punching hot needles of venom through his veins. He tries to scream, but the duct tape over his mouth turns every howl into a strangled, wet gasp.

Finn crouches down. He looks up at me to make sure I'm ready. I am.

I couldn't remove the wicked grin covering my lips, even if I wanted to, as I open the small four-inch cap on the top of the bucket that we rigged, and funnel the thick hose inside. Finn does the same and cuts a hole into the body bag, and inserts the other end of the hose before adding a few layers of duct tape so nothing can escape. Then I tip the bucket on its side and watch all the scorpions travel through the clear tubing to their new home.

Veno's breaths tear through his nose in ragged bursts, each inhale too shallow, each exhale a muffled whimper against the tape. Veins stand out like ropes across his temples, pulsing under skin slick with sweat and venom. His eyes, wide and glassy, dart wildly around, and his head shakes from side to side as he tries to scream behind the tape— as if he's fighting invisible horrors only he can see. It's a symphony to my ears. Something I have waited ages to hear. It fucking soothes my soul.

And I have to admit. The absolute agony covering his face is a sight that will bring me great joy for years and years to come.

My smile builds as I listen to the sweet music he makes. It closes an old wound. I imagine it does the same for Finn. Facing this demon from our past and ensuring he never ventured back into the light of day, was something we both needed to do before we could move forward and start planning our future.

Using my foot, I roll Veno closer to the hole. Finn helps. Then Finn passes me his spare flashlight. We let Veno's head hang over the edge so he can peer inside the black pit, which almost looks like an abyss.

I shine the light directly in his face as I crouch beside him. "We measured it. The drop is nearly twenty-seven feet. So you're likely to survive it as long as you don't, you know, land on your head. You will, however, probably have some severe injuries from that kind of a fall. My hope is at least a few broken bones. A leg, an arm, maybe both. I'm sure that alone will be agony. But nothing you don't deserve, right?"

Then I shine the light into the hole and let him see the pile of bones at the very bottom, Finn threw in days ago. Where he dug them up, I have no idea, and I didn't ask.

As my light moves, the dark ground moves too. The multitude of scorpions I'd been breeding for months have been relocated here. The snakes were an added bonus from Finn.

We just wanted to make sure there was no way Veno would walk away from his fate. He'll die in this cavern, filled with poison, and no matter how loud he screams for help, no one will hear his pleas or come to save him.

Veno must catch on because his struggles renew.

Finn stands beside me at the edge of the hole. He kicks some dust into it, and with the light shining down, it almost looks like glittered fog in a spotlight, like when I'm on stage.

I glance up and see Finn is mesmerized by it, too. His gaze finds mine, and he grins.

"You ready to end this chapter, Lil' Bird?"

"So fuckin' ready. You?"

"More than. You want to do the honors?" he asks.

I stand and dust off my hands. "Together?"

He nods, "Together." So we do just that. We make sweet music together as we push Veno over the edge. Finn holds me through the concerts of sound after he hits the bottom.

I hold off on my final plans for Antonio and the rest of the Veno inner circle. Finn and I agreed to let the HOCs take care of the remaining Thirteen Devils—they've earned the right to dish out their payback for what they did to Edge. Edge deserves his own shot at poetic justice, too. Once he's freed from prison, all bets are off, and the poor excuse of a truce between the HOCs and the Thirteen Devils will come to an end.

I'm counting down the days.

Finn arranges for the HOCs he trusts most—and the ones I'm

confident in—to come out to California under the guise of protecting me while he goes under the knife. We're going to use the opportunity to bring a few of the brothers in on the bigger picture—the scale of the war that may be coming.

I promise the women I'm working with in Veno's circle that, for now, this is for the best. Having the HOCs on their side won't just improve our chances of surviving—it'll make them more likely to help long-term, to offer real protection when it counts.

To give the women something now, a taste of justice, we take out one of the Thirteen Devils' major warehouses—one stocked with product that puts them deep in cartel debt. I let two of the girls play lookout while I fire at the propane tanks outside. They're sensitive enough to blow from heat alone, and they do just that—the first one goes when my bullet hits, then the other.

We wait.

We watch.

From the roof of a nearby building, we grin as half a dozen Thirteens scramble to escape the flames. Just when they think they've made it out, the bomb we planted the night before goes off. They try to run, but the blast is massive, and few, if any, survive.

It's the cherry on top of a slice of revenge that has me grinning on the inside for days—and leaves behind a deep, unshakable satisfaction.

I also hand over part of the contents of the suitcase Deeds gave me to the women. Over the next few days, they distribute it to the others on the street and in Veno's warehouse, where he ran his sex trafficking operation. The men who visit at night start getting sicker and sicker. When the poison kicks in, sex is the last thing on their minds.

The visits dry up.

The girls get a sliver of peace.

And the end finally comes into view.

My plan—no matter how ugly or soaked in darkness—is being carried out for the right reasons. The tattoo I've been planning for my right ribcage will mark the occasion. It says it all:

Be the hand of fate, if fate needs an angel to fly the Devil back

to hell.

It's not a beautiful bird. It's a vengeful angel with black wings, surrounded by sparks of pink sky, gray clouds, and lightning. It's the only kind of angel I'd ever consider myself to be. One that shouldn't be fucked with anymore.

It'll take a long time to complete, but time is one thing I have in abundance. And it gives me an excuse to get closer to the best tattoo artist in New Mexico—Taz.

Who also happens to be the most unhinged HOC and the last man I need to test to see where his real loyalties lie.

LOST LYREBIRD

CHAPTER 56

Don't let go of the memories that changed you, even if they hurt to revisit.

Today we're reliving one of the memories that has fallen into a black hole, lost somewhere in the tangled mess of Finn's mind. It saddens me that so many pieces of our past are scattered, like fragments of a life we once had. But I hold on to the fact that he's here, now, and at least we have this—this chance to recreate those memories.

The tram rises slowly up the mountainside, and Finn stands behind me, his strong arms wrapped around me, his chin resting on my shoulder. My hands clutch onto his forearms, feeling the familiar warmth of his skin through the soft cotton of his t-shirt. His scent, a blend of leather, sandalwood, and the faintest trace of cologne, fills my senses, grounding me in this moment.

I turn my head to take in the view. The sprawling world below looks so small from up here, like a toy town, everything miniature and colorful. I'd forgotten about that, how small everything looks from this height.

The little boy next to us tugs on his dad's hand and points to where he thinks his house is. I smile and feel Finn pull back and look down at me. His breath is warm against my ear as he speaks. "Do you want that, baby?"

I half-turn in his arms, meeting his gaze. His blue eyes search mine, gentle and filled with curiosity.

"What?"

He jerks his chin toward the family, his eyes flicking back to the little boy and his father. I follow his gaze, watching the scene unfold—the child's giddy excitement, the father's patient smile. It's a beautiful picture, one that used to feel distant to me, like some foreign and unknown thing.

I've never felt like motherhood was in the cards for me. For a long time, it was because I could barely keep myself on solid ground, so there was no way I could provide for another or feel qualified to keep them safe. Nor did I lead the kind of life that had space for a child. Way back when Finn and I had first been an item, I'd been too young to consider it. My life, for the most part, has been a selfish one, purely about my wants, needs, and my own survival. But like before, Finn changes things. Him being in my life shifts the future, along with my feelings on the matter, and there are definitely little secret hopes budding to life. So yeah, the possibility lingers.

I give him honesty, what I'll always give him. "I don't know." He analyzes my features and nods.

"Do you?"

He thinks a moment. His gaze veers to some far-off place as if he's lost to the same thoughts. "Same. I don't know. Feels like things are too heavy right now to even think about it."

"Yeah," I nod, "But maybe someday."

He tightens his hold on me, swaying us gently as the tram continues its ascent. "Maybe someday sounds good, baby. We've got time to figure it out."

When the tram reaches the top of Sandia Peak, we exit last and walk around and through the visitor center. We take our time, and I guide him down onto a familiar hiking trail. Hands laced together, I lead him down an off-shoot path, one he took me to so many years ago. We come to a large clearing, a meadow, and I continue on, pulling him to the center.

It feels like stepping back into a forgotten dream.

He laughs when I move his hands and stick them into his pockets. He balked earlier when I told him he had to wear khaki cargo pants and a white T-shirt to help me recreate the exact memory. I didn't laugh, I just stared him down. When that didn't work, I got down on my knees and showed him how very much I would appreciate it if he did this for me. Needless to say, he grumbled about it, but I got my wish.

Now, standing in the same spot, wearing the same clothes, I grin up at him. "Now... ask me if I could have any superpower, what would it be?"

His brow quirks, and for a moment, he looks around like he's searching for something to say, just like he did back then. I can see the wheels turning in his head, and it's almost eerie how similar this is to that day. He had asked me question after question, eager to know everything about me.

Finally, he sighs and says, "If you could have any superpower, Lily, what would it be?"

I pick up a dandelion from the ground, twirling it between my fingers before blowing its tiny seeds into the wind. I shrug and say, "I'd choose to fly."

I glance over at Finn. He's still, and his eyes flutter and close. He tilts his head like he's trying to pull the memory from the depths of his mind. For a few moments, we stand there in silence, the breeze gently lifting the dandelion seeds higher into the air. I watch them take off to places unknown and give him the time he needs.

When his eyes open again, they're softer, tinged with something fragile but real. I eliminate the distance between us and place my hands on his chest, feeling the steady beat of his heart. "Hey, you okay?"

"Yeah," he grants me with a sad smile. "Vague images, but it's there. A few pieces of it, at least."

My heart swells. "Really?" I ask, my voice filled with hope.

He nods, his soft grin spreading wider. "The feather this time..." He lifts his chin toward the dandelions floating through the air. I grab another. After taking a steadying breath, I blow, and one by one, the seeds part from the base and float up.

"Exactly that," he says quietly, his gaze following the delicate movement of the tiny seeds. They drift away with the breeze, some float higher and higher until they're out of sight, and a rare few land on the ground. "It's there, Lily. Not the whole day, but this moment."

Tears prick at the corners of my eyes. I fight them back, a smile breaking through.

"Show me the rest," he whispers.

I move back to my original spot, slipping into the memory like it's a second skin. "I say, 'I'd like to fly', and then I ask you what you'd choose. You say invisibility, which, honestly, wasn't that surprising."

His laugh is abrupt and gruff. "Really?"

"Yeah, Mr. Invisible," I tease. "With my superpower, I could do more than just steal from the rich or spy on the neighbors. I'd be a bird and use my wings to fly away. Travel. See the world. I'd go as far as my wings could take me." I pause, my voice softening as I look up at him. "And then you said…'Wait. I changed my mind. I choose flying. I want to be a bird.'"

Finn's eyes close again, the same hint of vulnerability crossing his face as he whispers, "Yeah… I wanted to be with you. See the world with you."

I smile, my heart swelling with the beauty packed in that memory. "And later that night, you wrote it down. 'If she's a bird… I am too.'"

"You asked me the next day, 'What kind of birds, though?' Did we decide?"

He pulls me into his arms, holding me close as the fresh mountain air dances around us and picks up enough to have some dandelion seeds taking off on their own and soaring away like weightless feathers.

"I told you to guess and spent the day humming tunes. And you still didn't get it. You were dead set on swallows."

"Well, yeah, for obvious reasons." I smack his chest, and when I do, he catches my hand and holds it against him.

"Hummingbirds, dummy. Because they hum, like to music."

He says, "Which is something you always did because you can't sing to save your life."

I point at him and he nips at my finger. I pull it away just in time. "You, sir. Are ruining this moment."

He shakes his head and pulls me in for a tight hug. "Nah, nothing could ruin this moment." I reluctantly agree and wrap my arms around him. Burning my face in his chest, I take in his comforting scent and the sense of safety his arms hold.

The memory of that day—the laughter, the questions, the quiet moments between us—it all comes flooding back. And now, more than ever, I realize this is what I've always wanted. What I longed for. Nothing else qualified as a beautiful life. Because everything else would fall short if I didn't have this and him to share it with. The man whose pieces fit with mine in a way that locked us together and made us whole.

Someone who will hold me through the darkness, hold my hand through the chaos, through every up and down, and love me fiercely through it all.

CHAPTER 57

*Birds of a feather because flying through the
winds of this world alone is no way to fly.*

Lily stops short as she steps into the clubhouse and takes in the
changes. The usual rowdy energy is dialed down, replaced by
a more subdued crowd. For one, it's clean—probably cleaner
than she's ever seen it. Two, it's been aired out. A faint citrusy scent
and the aroma of barbecue fill the lounge room.

After greeting those inside the clubhouse, we make our way out
back. We're immediately assaulted by the sound of boisterous voices,
laughter, as well as the high-pitched squeals from kids chasing one
another. Multiple conversations are happening throughout the area.
Groups are congregated around the picnic tables, fire pits, and the old
timers are keeping Cap company as he mans the grill.

"Are you sure my skirt's not too short?" she asks, like there's time
to change into something else at this point.

My "Fuck, no," earns me a scowl.

Her eyes dart from person to person. Probably too many unfamiliar
faces to feel at home in a place she knows so well. Not the wild,
reckless, free-for-all she's used to. This is the side of the HOCs she's
not been privy to. The members and their families, children, and
friends of the club.

On the drive here, Lily flipped her hair several times, checked her
makeup twice, a clear giveaway that she's nervous about how this

will go. Still is. So I hold up my hand and offer it to her. She squeezes it tightly, and I return the gesture, letting her know that she can steal some of my strength to get through this if she needs it. I'm here to keep her grounded, guide her through this new version of this world she's only ever seen the darkest sides of. She's been through hell and back with me, but this, this is one of the reasons I pressed on, and I want her to be part of it.

Some of the old ladies are already eyeing her. Their expressions range from curiosity to subtle judgment. I hate it. But I have to let it play out. Or at least that was Cap's advice.

Beyond the label of "clubpiece," she has the added "stripper" title attached to her, and the women here who are threatened by her beauty and talent will use those to try to knock her down.

It's not right, but nothing short of threatening those who fuck with her, will fix it.

These women aren't for the faint of heart. They can be cruel and kind in equal measure, and they sure as shit have long-ass memories. She'll have to fight for her place among them, but I'm confident she will with time.

Bethany comes to the rescue, her usual bluntness cutting through the tension as she exits the back door and approaches us. "Ugh, I hate these things," she mutters. She's carrying a casserole dish, a plastic-wrapped plate of cookies on top of it, and Medda, her baby girl, is propped on her hip. "I swear, it's like a damn competition every time," Bethany continues, her voice lowering conspiratorially. "What dish to bring, whether it's good enough. What to wear. I can't stand it. But if I opt out, then I'm in deep shit. Or highly depressed and in need of medication, according to Nick. Like I can't fuckin' win, you know?"

She dips her chin towards the cookies, "Those are for you. I figured I'd bring a backup dessert just in case Goose didn't tell you how it works at these things. God forbid you don't bring something."

Lily gives her a hesitant smile and picks them up, her shoulders relaxing. "You're a lifesaver. Thank you."

"You were there when I needed it." She gives Lily a meaningful, sad smile. "I'm just repaying the favor." Bethany nudges her lightly with her elbow and whispers. "Nick'll give you hell, but she does it to everyone new. So prepare yourself. It's like some kind of hazing. Just keep your chin up, okay. Don't let any of the shit they sling get to you."

I glance over at Nick, Dozer's mom, holding court near the fire pit. As if she's aware we're talking about her, her gaze comes up and scans the yard. When it lands on us, she gives Bethany a grim smile and then Lily a long, appraising once-over. When her gaze moves to me, she raises an eyebrow. I meet it unflinchingly, letting her know without words how firm I stand on this decision. That yes, this is it. She's it for me. This is who I choose.

Nick watches Lily and Bethany. The corner of her mouth lifts. She nods back once in understanding as if to say, *okay then, let the games begin.*

She'll test her and push her. Ultimately, she's preparing Lily for the life she will lead and helping her establish her place here. She'll give her a good dose of tough love and then protect the hell out of her. Nick just wants to make sure she's worthy of this club, and that's love in her own twisted way.

"Come on," Bethany says, motioning toward the long tables set up where the food's being placed. "Let's set these down and then I'll introduce you around."

They weave through people to drop off the dishes. They head to the picnic tables where Dozer's bubbly blonde sister, Taffy, is sitting with Kendra and Blair, Septic and Bodie's old ladies. Taffy is talking a mile a minute with wild hand gestures. There's a massive smile on her face. She beams further when Bethany and Lily arrive and immediately jumps up to snatch Medda from Bethany so she can tickle and coo at her.

Dozer steps up beside me and slaps my back. His large frame casts a huge shadow on the overgrown grass. "You ready for this?"

I rub my hand over my mouth and shake my head. "No, but yeah. Ready to ask the question, but not ready for, well, you know."

Dozer chuckles heartily and smirks. "I bet. Well, I for one can't fuckin' wait to see it." His gaze travels over the yard. When it lands on the women at the picnic table, the jovial expression drops from his face. His gaze flicks to mine.

The only thing I can think to say is, "Give it time."

He clears his throat and looks away, "Yeah. Trying to. Not as easy as it sounds." He rubs the back of his neck. "Wish there was some kind of button I could hit to fast forward time."

"If you find one, let me know. I'd like to go back a decade and get a do-over."

"Actually, yeah, that sounds better. Then we could find a way to never let go in the first place."

I nod solemnly. Sadly, in life, there are no do-overs, only the present and future to look forward to. Which reminds me to appreciate the time I do have, however little of it that may be.

As the evening wears on and the sun and moon trade places in the sky, Lily's ability to make connections one-on-one becomes more apparent. It's not the same in a group. In those instances, she'll pull the actress out. It's almost as if she thinks she has a better chance of winning people over if she doesn't let them see her true self. Then she watches them long enough to know who she wants to get to know. I think she's taking the time to gauge who won't take advantage of her vulnerability and kindness, and based on this, she chooses who to spend her time with.

There's a story there, and I make a mental note that I hope will stay put, so I can ask her about it later. I'd like to know why and what this part of her personality stems from. Why the "masks" as she likes to call them? When did it start, and why does she still think she needs them in certain circumstances?

When I make it back to Lily, she's sitting in a lawn chair beside Bodie. He's talking animatedly, and she's laughing at something he said. I pass her a water bottle, having just grabbed one for each of us. She takes it with a pleased smile and pats the chair beside her. Before

I take my seat, I throw a few more logs into the fire pit, then move my chair closer to her so I can curl my arm around her shoulder to ward off the chill creeping into the night air.

"So then," Bodie picks up his story. "This guy tries to cut me off, right, because he's a dick, right? He's driving like an asshole, weaving in and out of traffic, and he's honking at people, like this motherfucker is the most important guy on the fuckin' planet and it's somehow our fucking fault he's late for his nine to five or some shit."

"Oh no, what did you do?"

He grins wickedly, and Lily half-covers her eyes.

"What do you think I did?"

She shakes her head.

"I got in front of him and slowed my ass down to a crawl. If he moved left, I moved left. If he moved right, then yeah, whatever I could do to make his day as fucked as he was making everyone else's."

"I'm surprised he didn't run you over."

"Probably wanted to, but that's the thing about the cut, Lil'. It demands respect or at least a good dose of fear, and that is power in and of itself."

"So what ended up happening?"

"Well, eventually he got off the freeway, so I followed him to his office. You know, just to let him know I knew where he worked. And that's when the idea came to me. I just thought if he's gonna drive like a douchebag, he's gonna own that shit. I had Taz design me a sticker, and his was the first car I tagged."

Lily's face lights up. "You got one on you? I wanna see it."

His brows pull together, and he shifts in his chair. He searches his pockets. When he doesn't find one, he says, "I have some up in my room. One sec. I'll be right back."

He takes off, and Lily turns to me. "Did you know about this? This side hustle he has going on?" She seems delighted by Bodie's antics, like he's not a grown-ass man who's going to get arrested eventually for harassing civilians.

"Yeah, I've been DB'd."

"DB'd?"

"That's what he calls it. The Douche Bag of the Day Award. Park outside the lines or over them, speed through a school zone, use your cell phone, cut someone off, don't let someone merge, forget to signal, hog the fast lane. He becomes a *fucking* menace. Thinks he's some kind of traffic vigilante. Looks for any damn reason to tag someone now. Follows them, slaps his stickers on their car. Never mind that douchebag is one fucking word, the bastard has made it two and made a fucking trend out of it. The green flowing in from it is insane."

"You're kidding?"

Shaking my head, I take a sip from my beer, then mutter, "Not even a little bit."

"What'd he tag you for?"

"Fucking tailgating him."

She laughs, which has me scowling. "I'm sorry. It's just. That's hilarious."

Bodie's out of breath by the time he gets back. He doesn't just give her a sticker. He hands her a bunch of the swag from his new business venture: a box of stickers, vinyl signs, a red T-shirt, and a white hat.

"Holy shit! I freaking love this!" She unfolds the shirt and checks out the design. I have to admit, Taz did a phenomenal job on it. It's a blend of new school but also a bit comic. There's a douchie-looking guy with a fuchsia polo tucked into high-waisted jeans, which are rolled up over white sneakers. His bald head is light blue, and an actual bag. There's a white douche nozzle rising out of the top of his head. The small nuances, tribal tattoos, white earbuds, speckled scruff on his jaw, and trophy he's holding up speak to Taz's skills and creativity. The detail is amazing, and the guy's smarmy smile tops the cake.

It's too bad Taz is dead set on the darker shit, because he's got killer skills in this area too.

"Pretty sweet, right? I've hired some college kids to pimp it out and even have a little warehouse. The brand is growing crazy fast. We can barely keep up."

"So you're not working full-time at the shop?" she asks.

He shakes his head and takes his seat, picks up his beer, and sets it on his thigh. "I do. And doin' both is gettin' to be too much. Might sell the rights to this biz after it's grown a bit. It was just an idea I had and mainly, I just wanted to fuck with people. Turns out that other people love fuckin' with other people too. Now anyone who wants to has a way to call the asshole drivers of the world out. Somethin' that's been a long time comin', in my opinion."

"Do I get to keep these?" she asks as she holds the red T-shirt to her torso.

Bodie beams. "Yeah, woman. They're yours. You can have as much shit as you want."

They go on chatting about his tagging adventures. He tells her story after story. Every so often, he pulls me in on the ones I've taken part in to back up his ass because, at times, he still goes off the rails and needs to be reeled in.

Observing these two, seeing their bond, tells me that not only did I bring Lily into my world to make me whole, but I gave Bodie someone who gets him at a level not many people do. There's a genuine friendship there. The chaos they could create together sorta scares the hell out of me, but it also brings me a measure of relief. Bodie is the brother I trust most. He's more than that, though; he's a brother to me in every way that matters.

Having him here, my own fucking savior to watch over her, if God forbid, I'm taken from this world, relieves me of the fear that she'd be alone, and if there is any rest to be found in death, it would be in this. Should the time come, they'll watch out for each other. God willing, that will be a long time from now. But who's to say?

CHAPTER 58

Navigate the perils of a danger zone if a glimpse of heaven is waiting on the other side.

Darkness settles, and most of the old ladies say their goodbyes, ushering kids home to bed. A few linger, embracing the rowdier side of MC nightlife. The party's moved into the clubhouse now, and the shift is unmistakable—especially when a few dancers from the club show up. What surprises me most is that Raven is among them for the first time. A few more girls trail in behind her, all tight dresses and ready smiles, making it clear what kind of night they're chasing. It's like the two worlds I've been straddling—the wild chaos of club life and this newer, calmer, more familial one—are crashing together right in front of me.

My stomach flips. Something feels off.

Maybe Finn just wanted to celebrate bringing me into the fold. When I think about it like that, it's actually kind of sweet.

He's telling me I belong by his side, whether we're with his HOC family or the crazier side of the MC life.

Some of the members send their wives away while they play. Finn isn't going to be one of them. That's what this means, and it puts my soul at ease.

I lean on the bar, elbows against the cool wood. The faint scent of weed lingers in the air. A heavy bass beat thumps through the room. I tap my fingers against the side of my drink and take a slow sip. The whiskey burns going down, but does little to settle the buzz crawling beneath my skin.

Kendra slides onto the stool beside me. The wood creaks under her weight. She's one of the few old ladies who's gone out of her way to make me feel welcome, and right now, I'm grateful for the distraction. Her soft, powdery perfume cuts through the haze of sweat, smoke, and liquor. She nudges me with her shoulder, lifting a fresh drink, condensation trailing down the glass.

"You doing okay?" she asks, as if she can sense the tension creeping into my muscles. She tilts her head, her dark eyes scanning the crowd.

"Nothing I haven't seen before," I say, forcing a laugh. I nod toward the growing crowd of clubpieces and HOC members on the far side of the room, where things are getting loud and a little wild. "It's just... a lot. One minute it's a family barbecue, and the next..." My voice trails off, and I gesture to the scene in front of me, where the mood has shifted into something else entirely.

Kendra chuckles, taking a sip of her drink. The ice clinks in her glass as she swirls it lazily. "Yeah, that's the club for you. There's never just one speed. You get used to it."

Her words settle over me, and I smile, but my mind is still racing. My eyes drift toward the door, searching for Finn. He said he'd be right back, that he needed to take care of something, but time feels stretched without him by my side.

That's addiction for you. Whether it's a pill, a drug, or a person. Once you're hooked, the absence of it forever gnaws at you.

And yes, I hate how needy that makes me feel.

"Here," Kendra says, reaching over the counter and grabbing a bottle. She pours two shots and hands one to me. "Loosen up a bit. Might as well enjoy yourself. You're the star tonight, after all."

I don't know what she means by that, but I take the shot to help settle me down. After clinking it against hers, we shoot them back. The cold liquid burns as it trickles down my throat, spreading heat through my veins.

Bodie appears out of nowhere, his usual flirty grin plastered on his face. He slides into the stool next to me, leaning in with that lazy, confident charm he's got down to an art.

"Lookin' a little tense there, Lil'. That's not like you. What's up?" he asks, his voice smooth, if not a little teasing.

"I'm fine," I say, shooting him a look that's both amused and exasperated. "It's just... you know, something's different about tonight, and I can't put my finger on it. That and I'm still reeling about earlier today. I've never done that before."

"Done what?" Bodie frowns, leaning closer, his voice lowering like he's ready to uncover some hidden truth.

"Been on the family side of things." I glance down, feeling the weight of the admission. "Even with the..." I hesitate, not wanting to name the Greenbacks here. "Well, you know. It was always the wild parties. Not barbeques and babies." And yes, Bodie is well-informed about everything. So far, he's the only one. Finn thought it best to test out our discussion on him first and see how Dozer might take the same news.

He frowns, "But it's time, Lil. You're not going anywhere, and you love him. This is his family, and by bringing you tonight, he's telling us all that you're his. For a HOC to do something like that... It's significant. A game changer. He wants you here in every way you can be, and he just declared that to the whole fuckin' club.

Kendra snorts into her drink, rolling her eyes. "Subtle as ever, Bodie."

"Hey, I didn't ruin the surprise," he quips, not missing a beat.

"What surprise?" I perk up.

His smile falls. "Oh shit."

"Bodie!" Kendra screeches.

My gaze bounces between them. "What surprise?" Does my voice pitch at the end? Yes, it does, because I knew it. I knew something more had to be going on here.

Kendra moves to stand behind Bodie and covers his mouth with her hand. He tries to pry it away. I laugh as they struggle.

Bodie finally breaks free and yells, "Septic, come get your woman! She's manhandling me! She tried to touch my penis!"

"I did not! You fat-faced liar." She punctuates this statement by giving him a titty twister.

He slaps her hand away. "Ouch, Ken. That fuckin' hurt." He clutches his hand over his nipple and massages it.

"Oh, stop being a crybaby." She has no sympathy and smacks his arm. "If I tell Goose you ruined the surprise, a titty twister is the least of your worries."

"God, you're so fuckin' mean, woman. Go pick on someone else for a change."

I laugh at their antics, the sound bubbling up unexpectedly and loosening something inside me. Then I spot Finn out of the corner of my eye, returning from wherever he disappeared to. He heads toward the bar, stuffing something behind it. The moment his eyes land on me, a slow smile spreads across his face.

He strides over, not bothering with pleasantries, as he pulls me off the stool and into his arms. I let out a soft laugh, but my heart pounds as his lips brush against my ear. "Miss me?"

"Maybe," I tease, my hands sliding over his broad shoulders. I feel the firm muscle beneath his cut as I pull him closer. His familiar scent—leather, soap, and the leftover scent from the bonfire—fills my senses, wrapping me in a comforting haze.

Bodie watches us with a knowing smirk. "Don't get too comfortable, Goose. I was just about to steal her away from you."

Finn doesn't even spare him a glance. "That right?" His gaze is locked on mine. His hand weaves into my hair. In the next heartbeat, he's kissing me possessively. It's a claim, a reminder that I belong to him and no other. The world around us blurs as he dips me back slightly, the cheers and wolf whistles fading into the background as I lose myself in him.

"Fuck, I found my new addiction," Finn says while licking his bottom lip."

"What?"

"Whiskey, on your lips, baby. Nothin' like the taste of it from your mouth."

His hands settle on my waist, the heat in his stare is doing crazy things to my body, lighting me up from the inside out. "Now tell this

632

fool once and for all who you belong to, Lil'.'"

"You. Just you."

The corner of his mouth kicks up. "You sure?"

Going up to my tippy toes, I place a peck on his lips. "Never more sure. Why? You change your mind about me?"

He palms my face and combs my hair back away from it, tucking strands behind my ear. "Never."

"Well, you two are just too disgustingly sweet for me. Please tone it down," Kendra jokes.

Finn pulls me into his side and puts his arm around my shoulder. We bullshit with Bodie and Kendra for a bit before Griz joins our little group and gives Finn shit for "stealing his girl." It's only because we're flush against each other that I feel Finn's body tense, but soon after, he jokes it off all in good fun.

The moment passes, and after a while, I feel lighter than I ever have. The music cranks up around us, the beat thrumming through the floor beneath my boots, and the crowd grows louder.

"Come on," Finn says, tugging me toward the dance floor. "Dance with me." My heart flutters like there's an excited bird caged inside with happy wings. His demand takes me off guard, but before I can question it, he pulls me toward the dance floor, weaving us through the crowd, and pulling me into his arms once we reach the center.

The weight of the night lifts, and my world zeros in on him alone. My arms circle his neck, his hands slide to my ass. After pulling our hips together, he grinds his lower body against mine. I softly comb my nails through his hair and lovingly caress his scar. His piercing gaze holds mine as we get lost in each other and the rhythm of the music.

There's a slight crinkle beside the corner of his eyes, and a slight smile on his mouth. Brushing my fingers over his bottom lip, I say, "You could let that smile loose; you know? It wouldn't kill you." I tilt my head this way and that. "Come on, I know it's there somewhere."

He fights it briefly, but then it breaks free—an unguarded smile builds. It's beautiful, and I can't help but grin back at him.

"There it is," I whisper, my heart swelling at the sight.

"Just for you, baby." He pulls me closer, so our bodies move as one in a slow figure eight. His warmth floods into me, and the gravity of this, at finally having all I've ached for for so long, hits me all at once. It takes everything in me not to let the emotions spill over.

"Finn?"

He draws back, and our breaths mingle in this tiny space between us. "Yeah, baby?"

"I kinda love you. Not sure if you've picked up on it, but I thought you should know."

His smile is blinding now, extended fully. It's devastating to my heart, in a way, Cupid probably takes out unsuspecting victims with this arrow. I haven't said it like this. So stark and naked. My whole heart thrown into those words. It's always been in the middle of our hard times, or the heat of passion, or said in the height of fear when I thought I was going to lose him.

However, this is simply because I can no longer contain it and no longer want to. I also want to give voice to it in the good times, in our steady moments of certainty.

He's my home. My peace. My future. That place I always wanted to find to land, but never could, because I did everything in my power to avoid him when he was precisely the very thing I needed. I may not always be able to say it with pretty words, but I plan to always show him by loving him so damn thoroughly he'll never doubt it.

"I know, baby. Love doesn't even seem like the right word, though, does it? You're my damn heart. That's the truth of it. You make every struggle I had to face to get here worth it. And I'd do it again if I knew this would be the outcome."

"You probably shouldn't say things like that."

He chuckles and looks down at me. "Why?"

"Because it makes me feel weak. Like I may need to hear it every day, and that sounds way too needy."

He studies me for a moment, and our movements slow. "Needing me doesn't have to be a bad thing, Lil'. Not when it's the same for me."

"No, but it is scary sometimes. The thought of losing it again."

He wraps his arms around my shoulders and holds me tight. Rocks me back and forth. "I get it. Having this and losing it, don't think I'd survive it a second time. God willing, we'll never have to."

A confession spills from my lips. "You know, I used to dream about you, too."

Drawing back, he lifts my chin. "You did?"

"Yeah, I ended up going to a hypnotist. Crazy thing is, it worked, well mostly, or at least for a while. Would you maybe want me to check into it for you?"

He shakes his head immediately. "I like the dreams, Lil'. I mean… yeah, they may suck and sometimes there's demons I have to face when I close my eyes, but there's also you, parts of you, and I don't want to miss out on any pieces still waiting for me to find them."

I finger away a stray tear that dares escape. "Damn it, Finn."

"God forbid I go first." He gets choked up at this. "Know that I'll be there waiting for you to find me." He pinches my chin and places a sweet kiss on my lips. "Just promise me, you'll find me too when the time comes."

"God, Finn. You wreck me. You know that?"

"You wreck me, too, baby. You save me and wreck me in equal measure."

His arms wrap around me again, and I bury my face in the curve between his neck and chest. We slow dance time and place blur around us. In this space, it's just us.

He holds me so tightly that I doubt death could pry us apart.

FINN

We sway together in the dim light, and my heart feels full, to the point it might gallop right out of my fucking chest. Lily, in my arms, soft and warm against me, is everything. It's what I've ached for nearly my entire life. Like I knew, I just knew this was the kind of happiness—

completeness, I'd been missing out on.

I've fought wars, faced death, and lost so much, but nothing—nothing—compares to the fear I have of losing her again. She's my tether to this life, my anchor, the point of the compass that tells me where home is. She came back to me, bared every scar, told every truth, and fought like hell for me when I couldn't fight for myself. I can never repay her for that, but tonight… tonight, I'll try.

She's always been my world, even when I was too blind or too broken to see it. I feel it in every beat of my heart and breath. My body knows hers, my soul recognizes this. We're bound, not just by time and circumstance, but by something deeper. She's the only woman who's ever made me feel this way—like I have a purpose and there's genuine hope for the future.

As we move together to the slow, heady beat, I'm lost in her. Underneath all that love, there's a nervousness bubbling up. I'm about to do something so wildly out of character, but damn it, she deserves it. She deserves a grand gesture. Something that shows her, in front of everyone, how much she means to me. For every moment she stayed by my side, for all the ways she fought for us, for me, for being brave enough to love me through the darkest hours.

She came here, and her actions have not only saved my club, but they will eventually save so many lives. We can now see what's coming, rather than being blindsided.

So yeah, this woman deserves everything, and I'm going to give it to her.

I meet Raven's gaze from across the room and nod. She grins a little maniacally and rushes off to do my bidding. She also holds her finger high in the air and circles it to signal to everyone that the time has indeed come.

Before Lily can catch on to the mood change around us, I guide her to the bar and order Lita to pour us a few shots. I'm gonna need a bit of liquid courage to get through it, and a shot or two isn't going to send me down river when I have so much to live for now.

Lily holds her shot up to mine and raises a brow. "You sure?"

I grin, "Positive."

636

"Okay, then cheers to . . ."

"To us. To our beginning and all the days ahead."

Her eyes light up. She repeats my words and clinks her glass against mine before we both sling them back.

Bodie comes up and lays his hand on my shoulder. "Hey, you ah... got a sec? I need you for that thing. Uh-mmm. You know?"

Lita coughs and tries to contain her laugh. I see Griz shake his head in my peripheral vision. Taz grumbles unintelligible words under his breath and palms his face. I give Bodie a look that promises death if he ruins this for me. Then I turn back to Lily.

"What's going on?" She asks, and her gaze darting around the clubhouse. Her brows knit together, a spark of curiosity spilling into her features.

I shake my head, give her waist a quick squeeze, and lean in to whisper in her ear. "Just got something I've got to do real quick. Wait for me?"

"Sure."

I pull away from her slightly, a grin tugging at my lips as I stare down at her confused, beautiful face. "I promise, I won't be long."

After leaving her, I slip into the crowd. Raven emerges, carrying a chair, to place it in the middle of the dance floor, a few feet away from where Lily stands. I hear Bodie's loud mouth yelling something, and the laughter that follows. I stride quickly to grab what I stashed behind the bar for this moment and slip into Cap's office.

It takes me a few minutes to change into the outfit Raven provided. Oh, she had many ideas. I shut down all but three to her chagrin. Ultimately, I had to go with the obvious choice and something that would leave a lasting impression. Then I spent nearly two weeks working with Raven when I could to learn some moves I could actually pull off.

From past accounts by new hires, I'd gotten the idea that Raven was a patient teacher. Maybe she was with the women, but all bets were off when the tables were turned, and I suddenly became her subordinate. It's like she got off on and giving me shit, found a bit of glee in reducing me to a piss poor student, who apparently, didn't have any rhythm, and she went as far as to tell me that my dance skills were a few decades out of date.

I'd show her. And fuck what anyone thought. This was for one woman and one woman only. I'd dance my ass off if it meant she'd say yes.

I finished buttoning up my shirt, threaded my belt into my pants, and slipped my shoes on. Then, I grabbed my cap and tucked it under my arm.

As a rule, I didn't wear much white—fuck knows why, maybe maybe it offends my dark soul. But everything but the bill of the cap was just that: stark white, except the buckles. I'd never live down this moment. Me, an Army guy in a Navy uniform, which was the point, to look like a certain pilot.

But this wasn't about me. It was about Lily, and this piece of our history tucked away in one of those journals. A string that tied her to my road name in a way she may not even remember.

I watched birds. Sometimes, I craned my neck to do so while on the road. Griz tried to settle me with one species of bird name or another, Crane, Buzzard, and fucking Sparrow. He'd thrown out name after name and even tried to tell me I didn't have a choice in the matter. Then he'd thrown out Goose, and something about it hit home, and just felt right.

I'd had no idea why at the time. It wasn't until I'd gone through the journals Lily had given me while in rehab that I realized why.

We'd watched Top Gun, and Lily had bawled her eyes out when Goose died. It reminded her of her dad, and she'd broken down, or so my notes said. It sparked a worry in her that I wouldn't return, and it's what had her demanding that promise from me.

The promise that kept me tethered to her all this time and searching for a ghost.

So I'd bring the memory full circle and show her that this Goose had at least made it home and planned to spend the rest of my remaining days by her side.

Before stepping out, I put on the cap. Bodie is standing right outside Cap's door, ready to signal Raven to start the music, but the moment he sees me, he loses his shit. A laugh explodes out of him, and even when he tries to cover his mouth to contain it, he can't. The fucker ends up taking his phone from his back pocket and snapping a picture.

Did I steal his phone and toss it down the hallway? I sure as fuck do. Then, head held high, I walked into the main room just as the opening notes of Danger Zone by Kenny Loggins starts crackling through the speakers.

I'd make a damn fool of myself if that's what it'd take to convince her to be my old lady and wear my property patch, which is exactly what I do.

The hollering and catcalls are distant echoes. I'm so in my own head, focused on Lily and my steps, that the crowd sort of fades into the background. It's like Lily said. Sometimes the music and the moment take over, and it's an out-of-body experience; the emotions take hold, and everything else, right or wrong, disappears.

Embarrassing myself doesn't matter.

Her smiles.

Her laughs.

Her tears.

Her nod of "yes".

The way she accepted the property vest and ran her fingers over Lil' Bird.

The way she practically tackled me to jump into my arms.

And the way she kissed me like she'd never been so happy in her entire life until this moment.

Those were the things that mattered.

I held her, knowing she was mine and that she always would be. A dream I never wanted to wake from. Each day will be a blessing. She could roam wherever she wished as long as she took me with her. That's what this meant to me. That no matter what came our way, we'd face it together, no matter the weather.

CHAPTER 59

What is it about you that makes your partner crave your time and attention? These are things you should know and wield with care.

I'm rinsing the conditioner from my hair in the shower when a breeze wafts over me. I spin around to see Finn standing there at the shower door naked. A flutter of excitement builds in my stomach at the sight of him in all his glory. His cock is hardening as his eyes trail over my body. He palms his base and runs his hand up and down its length.

"You're letting the cold air in."

"I just wanna look my fill first. You're quite somethin' to see, Lil' bird."

"Yeah?" I run the soap over my breasts and lather them under his heated gaze.

Finn doesn't have the ability to tell me no, and I often use his weaknesses for my body against him. In the end, I use this power to please the fuck out of him, and give him all the pleasure he's missed out on, so it's not necessarily a bad thing. It's just my part in the power play in our dynamic.

"Yeah, woman. I mean, look at you. It's a sight I could wake up to every day, and it would never be enough."

I grin and reach forward to grab his hand. "Shut up and get in here with me." The words are soft and sultry. He enters and closes the door behind him. His hands immediately go to my hips, but they quickly travel up my torso until he's caressing my breasts and teasing my nipple. The slight pinch as he rolls them tightly between his fingers sends a straight shot of heat to my pussy.

"Did you already wash yourself clean, or do you want me to do that for you. Because I'm all for doing this act of service to show my gratitude for last night?" His hand skates down my body slowly, and when his fingers find my wet folds, they slide smoothly through the wetness there. He doesn't wait or ask for permission; he merely slides two fingers slowly inside of me. Curling them, he so easily finds the spot that makes my breath hitch, and once he does, he hits it on repeat with insane accuracy. I clutch his shoulders and go up on tippy toes as I let out a reactionary moan from the pleasure.

He latches his other hand around my neck and guides my face to his so he can take my mouth.

He walks me back and we make out under the spray until he picks me up and forces my back against the tiled wall. I wrap my legs around him as his cock breaches my entrance and drives home.

In between our consuming kisses, he tries to speak. "Fuck, I can't... can't get enough. Best kind of drug there is, baby... you and the feel of you riding my cock like a fiend. Always willin' to take it. Isn't that right?"

"Yes."

"Doesn't matter when or where, does it?"

"Fuck no."

"Because you love it, don't you?"

"Finn."

"Don't you?"

"Yes."

I do. I love the smell of it. Love the high it gives me. I love the scent of him. His body, his cum. I love feeling it on my fingers, and I especially love what the sight of it dripping out of me does to him. To tell the truth, he's created a sex craved monster. I can't get enough of him either, and we often disappear from the world to get lost in each other like two nymphomaniacs drunk on love and ecstasy. He's my drug of choice, and I'm his. When we're together, time holds little meaning, maybe because we have so much of it to make up for, so we revel in the time we've been given.

The water raining down, accompanied by steam and music playing in the background, forms a soundtrack that mixes with our inhales and exhales, our gasps and moans. A song all of its own, and one I'll never get tired of hearing.

He reaches around and grabs my ass. His fingers dig into the skin as he uses his grip to pound into me. I swivel my hips and meet him thrust for thrust. My cries rise higher and higher. I cling to him as it gets to be too much.

"That's it. Take it, baby. Take what you need, like my very own little sex craved demon. My little nympho. That's what you are, isn't it?"

He grips my hips tightly and slams inside with three powerful thrusts.

"Oh, fuck. There. Yes. Jesus! Yes. I'm gonna… fuck, I'm gonna come!" I agree to it all and drag my nails down the muscles of his back as my orgasm hits with such a crippling intensity that my back bows, and I kick my head back to suck air into my lungs as I fall apart.

The heat in the shower water pales in comparison to the amount of heat radiating between us. Even as he continues to fuck me through it, my pussy clenching around him. His release comes fast and hard, and as his cum coats my inner walls, he lets out a long groan against my lips.

It's chaos and madness when we come together. Our kisses are a spark to a match that sets off a chain reaction of events, and what follows is an explosion of passion neither of us can contain. Shower. Floor. Bed. Countertop. Where and what we end up fucking on is anyone's guess.

He gently sets me back on my feet. I hold on to him until my knees aren't as weak anymore, which he gets a kick out of. Then we proceed to wash each other and every so often share a kiss that threatens to spin us into another fevered state.

"Still can't believe this is real sometimes." He says as he runs his hand over my hair.

"Believe it, baby," I say with a smirk. He wraps his arms full around me and holds me. Then he rocks me back and forth. I can't tell him what that does to me because then I'd be revealing my own weakness. The way he holds me. The comfort I find in his arms is the absolute best fucking thing I've felt in my life. It is my Holy Grail, and I never want a day to go by where I'm not exactly right here, where I want to be most.

When I finally pull back, I palm his scruffy cheek and ask, "You ready for this, the surgery, I mean?"

He shakes his head and his mouth pinches into a frown.

"Not really, but I want to get it over with."

"What worries you the most?"

He places his forehead on mine and closes his eyes. "I don't want to lose this, Lil'. I don't want them to fuck with my head and make it worse. Because, fuck. What if they make it worse?"

I'm terrified too. So fucking terrified that I haven't been sleeping as well. Goose bought me a dreamcatcher to hang above our bed, and coincidentally or not, the night terrors have lessened.

"Hey," I whisper, and he opens his eyes and pulls back to stare down at me. "You're forgetting something." His lips twitch as if to smile, but he keeps his frown in place. "You're forgetting about hope, baby. We have to hope for the best, and living in pain every day is no way to live. We just need to pray our damndest and have hope that everything will work out. Because we fucking deserve this break, don't we?"

He places a peck on my lips. "Yeah, we sure the fuck do."

"Then, good thoughts, okay. Don't fear the worst. Pray for the best. And no matter what, you have to promise to come back to me."

He pulls me in tight again and vows, "I promise. I fucking promise."

"I'll be waiting for you."

It's later, as he's getting dressed, that I voice my own fears. "What if you forget who I am?"

He comes to stand in front of where I'm sitting on the edge of the bed. He studies my face for a while and then hooks my hair behind my ear. "You gonna be right here by my side, no matter what?"

"Of course."

"Then make me remember, Lil'. Show me the journals. We'll both keep track of our days every day, and if I ever lose time, we'll backtrack or rewind or whatever. I'll relearn about those special moments we've had. Because I can't promise they won't happen. But I can promise that I'll never get enough of learning about our story and how each of those pieces fits together."

He brings me up to standing and wraps his arms around me. I cry a few silent tears into his shirt. I dread the day that happens. I know it will, and I cry for the future me that we will face that day, and how hard it will be for that version of me to show him through my point of view what he's missing from his. It's sad and it hurts, but it's the only path left for us.

It's our story, and it's riddled with holes, but it's also a perfectly pieced-together puzzle of beautiful feathers and breadcrumbs, full of dreams, music, and memories.

The story of us, and I'll forever be its storyteller for as long as we both shall live and maybe beyond that.

LILY

CHAPTER 60

Betrayal is one of the acts that cuts the deepest and leaves a lasting impression we never quite get over.

I paced the small space of the hotel room, my fingers shaking as I dialed Deeds' number on the burning phone I picked up. My heart pounds in my chest, and the words I'm about to say tumble through my mind. I've got one shot at this. One chance to pull this off and get him so worked up that he doesn't stop to think.

He answers on the second ring. "Gypsy?" His voice is sharp, immediately suspicious.

I swallow hard, injecting my voice with just the right amount of panic and fear. "Thank fuck you picked up. I'm in trouble. I— I don't know what to do."

"Wait, wait. Slow down. What's going on?"

"I don't know how, but they're on to me. They've figured it out. I had to run, Deeds, and I don't know how far behind me they are. I think I've lost them, but who the fuck knows." My voice cracks on the last part.

"Where are you?" Deeds' voice spikes, panic lacing every word.

I let out a shaky breath, pacing faster now, like I'm a caged animal trying to figure out an escape. "Finn! He figured it out and had them dig deeper into me. Fuck, Deeds, I don't know what to do. It's all fucked now. I barely got out of there in time."

"Are you hurt?" A door slams. He growls, "Did they fuckin' hurt you?"

"No, thankfully, I'm okay. Just freaking out."

I let out a broken sob, clutching the phone tighter as if that could somehow convey the desperation I need him to feel. "I slipped up, okay? I— I didn't mean to, but when Finn was in the hospital… God, it doesn't matter. All that matters is they know now. I need to run, Deeds. Or hide away for a while."

Deeds is silent for a moment, and I can practically hear the gears turning in his head. His voice drops low, deadly serious. "Tell me where you are and I'll come to you."

"I'm in Arizona," I whisper, letting the words tremble on my lips. "I'm hiding out, but I don't know how long I have. I need you, Deeds. I need you to come get me and help me disappear."

"Fuck!" His voice is raw, torn between anger and panic. "Why the hell didn't you call me sooner? You should have called me as soon as shit went down."

"I'm sorry. I was a mess, and I wanted to get somewhere safe before I reached out."

"Where are you exactly?"

"There's this diner," I say, my voice still shaky. "JJ's Diner. It's a few hours west of Tucson. I don't know if I can stay here long, Deeds."

"I'll be there as fast as I can. Don't fucking move, alright? Stay put."

I let out a breath of relief, though it's laced with just enough fear to keep him hooked. "Thank you. Please, hurry."

I hang up the phone and take a deep breath, my hands shaking less now that the call is over.

For a moment, I stand there, trying to shake off the tension that clings to my skin. And then, like a curtain lifting on a stage, the room around me comes back into focus. The heavy presence of the HOC brothers looms nearby, watching from different corners.

Dozer is the first to move, stepping forward with a smirk tugging at the corner of his lips. "You think he bought it?" he asks, crossing his arms over his chest, his massive frame looking even bigger in the small hotel room.

I nod, tucking the phone into my back pocket, still feeling the adrenaline thrumming through my veins. "Yeah, he's coming."

Bodie lets out a low whistle from where he's perched on the edge of the bed, twirling a pack of smokes between his fingers. "Damn, that gave me fuckin' chills! You're scary good at that. Like, I almost believed we were after you."

I let out a shaky laugh, but there's still a heaviness pressing on my chest. This is just the beginning. Everything we've discussed and have been planning since I shared my story with them leads to this moment, and I need to keep my head clear. All the payback I had planned on is now a plan I share with the HOCs, the few Finn and I trust to see them through.

Finn is leaning against the window, watching me, his arms crossed over his chest, the soft glow of the setting sun casting shadows across his face. His hair, now buzzed short on the sides and about an inch long on top, is something I'm still getting used to. He opted to cut it all off before his surgery, instead of having them shave a portion on the side. He runs a hand through it absentmindedly and winces as his fingers brush the side of his head where the stitches are still healing.

"You don't have to come with me," I say softly, not for the first time.

He huffs out a breath, the sound low and gruff. "We've been over this, Lil'. I'm not letting you go in there alone. I don't give a shit if I just had surgery or not."

He comes to me and wraps me up in his arms.

I pull back and palm his cheek. My heart aches at the scar peeking out from his messy spikes. The tiny fragment of metal they'd pulled from his skull was the catalyst for so many years of pain and damage, and while the surgery has helped, he's still recovering, still vulnerable. But that doesn't stop him from wanting to protect me. That's Finn, always pushing himself harder than he should.

I reach up and brush my fingers along the edge of his hairline, careful not to touch too close to the stitches. "You need to take it easy, okay? I can handle this."

He grabs my wrist gently, his blue eyes locking onto mine, full of that protective fierceness that makes my heart skip a beat. "I know you can. But we handle it together, or not at all."

I let out a soft sigh, knowing there's no winning this battle. "Fine. Together."

Finn pulls me closer, pressing a soft kiss to my forehead, his lips lingering there for a moment as if he's grounding himself. "Good."

Dozer steps up beside us, clapping Finn on the shoulder with a grin. "Either way, we'll keep her safe."

Taz, lounging on the bed, flicks his knife in the air and catches it with a wild grin. "This is gonna be fun. I can't wait to see the look on his face when he sees us stroll in."

I glance around the room, taking in the sight of these men, my family, standing behind me, ready to take on whatever comes our way. I know Deeds won't go down easily, and I know this confrontation will be ugly. But with Finn and the HOCs by my side, I'm ready for whatever happens next.

When Deeds calls me back to say he's close, I relay the information to the HOCs, and we prepare to head out. Finn grabs his cut, slipping it on as he meets my gaze. "You ready?"

I nod, feeling a surge of determination as I grab my purse. "As ready as I can be."

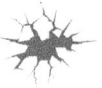

Sitting still and calm in the booth at JJ's is impossible. My hands are wrapped around a steaming cup of coffee in an attempt to still my nerves. The diner is quiet, with a few patrons scattered across the mom-and-pop place, a few people occupying the booths and barstools. Every once in a while, I glance out the large windows, watching the occasional car pass by, praying that no one here gets hurt today. The thought has a knot twisting in my gut.

My gaze drifts to the clock. Time is ticking away. Although I'm fully aware of how little of it I have left before my two worlds collide.

It needs to happen, but that thought doesn't make it any easier.

The coffee tastes bitter on my tongue. I force myself to take another sip. Minutes trudge on like molasses until I hear the familiar rumble of a motorcycle pulling into the lot. I don't need to turn to know it's Deeds—the sound his throaty hog gives him away.

The diner door jingles as it swings open. Deeds strides in like a man on a mission and heads straight for me. He's wearing his cut over a loose tan tank, multiple necklaces with beads on display. His black jeans are faded and fashionably ripped, the bottoms tucked inside his black combat boots.

He moves with that same coiled energy, intense and focused. His red-brown hair is cut short and faded on the sides in a stylishly messy fohawk. His sharp hazel eyes zero in on me immediately. The heat of his gaze burns into me as he approaches, and despite everything, my chest aches when a smile of relief graces his familiar face.

"Gypsy," he says softly, his voice laced with worry. "What the hell happened?"

An ache burrows in my chest when his eyes show true concern. I click off my emotions as best as I can, although I'm a bit out of practice.

Finn and Dozer emerge from the bathroom before I possibly begin to answer, explain, or apologize. They approach quietly, like predators circling their prey. My heart pounds loud enough that Deeds must hear it.

The diner door jingles, and noise slices through the quiet. It's followed by more boots solidly hitting the floor to eat up the distance between us. Deeds swivels in his seat and stiffens when he sees the men approaching us. Bodie and Taz quickly fall into position, their presence a wall of menace and purpose.

Dozer stops at our table and backs up to lean against the counter across from our booth. He crosses his arms over his massive chest. Turning quickly to the waitress, he says, "Get everyone out of here," his voice calm and authoritative. "And no cops or we're going to have problems. You all got that?" He looks around at the patrons, and everyone nods hastily as they rush to leave the diner.

Bodie and Taz usher patrons out the door, even going so far as to lock the place down, flipping the sign to "closed" and hitting the lights. With the sunlight as the only source of light, the tension between all the men heightens.

Deeds lets out a slow exhale, trying to cover his shock nonchalantly. He drapes one arm over the back of the booth, his body settling into a posture that's a little too casual. However, his hazel eyes are sharp and calculating as they flick between me and the men.

"Ethan." Deeds throws Dozer's real name out like an insult. "Appreciate the welcome wagon, but you boys didn't have to come all this way for little old me. Especially under false pretenses. Couldn't write me an email, or fuck." Deeds reaches into his pocket, produces his phone, and drops it on the table. "Could've fuckin' called."

"Decker." Dozer returns the insult. "Wanted to keep this meeting between us, have a sit down. I didn't know if you'd come alone, and the less people who know about this, the better."

Deeds' fierce gaze snaps to me. He motions to Dozer and then to Finn next to him. "So, this is your choice?" he asks in a cutting and harsh tone.

I swallow hard and force myself to hold his gaze and give him an honest answer. "You had your plans, and I had mine. They aligned once, but things changed with time."

"What changed?"

"I..." I look toward Finn, and he comes forward. He takes the seat beside me and puts his arm around my shoulder. I find strength in the blue depths of his irises. "I did, and..." Looking back across the table, I say, "My loyalties lie elsewhere now. I'm sorry."

"It's like that?" His features are pinched. There's anger, but hurt too. I think he's going to do something stupid, because Deeds' emotions tend to get the best of him. Being cornered was the only way to get him here alone, but it's also fired him up.

"Well, isn't that cute. The two little love birds finally figured their shit out."

"Deck."

"Nah, Gypsy. I can be pissed. My God given right to be. This fucker disappeared for how fuckin' long and left you to escape that place. Didn't lift a finger to help after he'd gotten the worst kind of target pinned on your back. Does he know all that shit? Know Veno stabbed you, and he let the Thirteens beat you so bad you were in the hospital for a week? That that shitty landlord of his made you trade favors for rent? That you still have nightmares and panic attacks all the fucking time because of that shit."

Finn raises his arm, rests his elbows on the table, and leans forward. "I know all of it. And I'm . . ."

"What?" Deeds spits out and matches his posturing.

"Fuckin' grateful you were there to see her through the worst of it."

Deeds looks at him for a long time. "Not what I thought you were gonna say."

Finn shrugs his shoulders. "Doesn't make it any less true. I care for her more than you know. It fuckin' rips me up that I wasn't there to protect her when she went through that shit. I would've done anything to save her from it."

Deeds' gaze bounces from Finn to me and back. "So it's for real for you then?"

"Always was. I'd been looking for her but didn't know how to track her down. There's a reason for that, which I think you're privy to."

"The injury, when you did your last tour?"

Finn nods. "Head injury. Shrapnel in the brain. Amnesia and the whole nine yards. Couldn't remember enough of the past to use it to find her."

Again, Deeds takes the time to answer. But his question this time isn't for Finn. It's for me. "So you finally made your choice."

"Lily and I, one of the deals we made was no more secrets. No more lies." His tone is calm but firm. That's why she came clean about what you sent her here to do. You were a big secret. One I wasn't fuckin' expecting."

"I'll bet, but I wanna hear it from her."

I give him the words I couldn't say when we were messing around. At the time, I told myself it was because I couldn't have Finn, so I couldn't give voice to them or own them like I do now. "It's always been him. I just didn't know what I do now, and that truth… it changed everything."

The silence that follows is heavy.

Deeds breaks it by asking, "So what all did you tell them?" He takes in the men present, like he's weighing every possible option and measuring their worth. His eyes dart to Dozer, the largest unspoken threat. "How much do you know?"

I hesitate, swallowing the lump in my throat. "Everything," I say quietly.

Dozer's glaring and hasn't taken his gaze off Deeds. "I'll get straight to the point, man—we need to know what you know. We got history, and I came here out of respect for that. Woulda hoped you'd do the same, but here we are."

Deeds lets out a slow breath, and that cocky, unbothered smirk creeps back onto his face. He stretches out and gets comfortable. "You gonna believe me?"

Finn fires back, "Can you back it up?"

"Some of it. But not everything, that's why I sent her." He motions to me. "I know the basics and what's happening on the cartel side of things from our point of view, but Lily's gonna have a better sense of who's on the inside that you can't trust."

Every eye in the room turns to me. Finn knows everything, but he's going to let me be the one to share all the details.

"You've got at least three Thirteen Devils in your club."

"Who?" This comes from Taz, and his face is a mask of disbelief.

Deed's cocks raises a brow and looks directly at me.

Dozer's head snaps to the side, and a surprised look crosses his features. "Three, you only told me of two."

"I'm certain of two, and the third I'm seventy percent sure of."

"Who?" Dozer snaps.

"Stone for sure, and Croc. Grinder is the one I'm not a hundred percent sure of, and he's a hard man to get close to, so that's why I'm not certain."

"Are you sure?"

I face all the HOCs and tell them exactly what I did, the full extent of it, the stuff they don't yet know about.

"I've followed you all for months and months. I bugged rooms, phone, and cars. Even a few of the businesses. Not to send the details to GBs but… well, think of it like a breach test and yes, I was gathering intel, but more to see where you all needed to beef up security and cover your asses. I also needed to know what rats you had inside your club and see if their ties ran deep or not."

"Holy shit, I feel completely violated," Bodie quips. Taz slaps him upside the head. "What? Don't you?"

Taz snaps, "Who the fuck are you?"

"She's what we call a fixer." Deeds taps his fingers on the table. "She is essentially a chess piece in a bigger game." He throws a devious smile at me. "One we use to blackmail high rollers or dirty politicians. She can blend in or stand out in any environment. Her job is not to judge the target, but find out how to take them down physically, financially, mentally, whatever way we need to go about it."

Finn knows this part, so it comes as no surprise to him; however, the others are reeling. Finn and I shared just enough to get them to this meeting and let them know that the Greenbacks aren't the enemy. Not really. So they know some of it, but not the full scope of what I've done to get this information.

We thought it best for them, the men we trust the most in the club, to see if we faced any fallout after revealing what we shared. Having Deeds back it up and admit he's the one who paid me to do this job, well, we hoped it would shift the weight of my actions onto him and hopefully give him some credit for doing it for the right reasons— maybe even create a small circle of trust between these men, Dozer and Deeds, who are also next in line to take up the president patch. If they are to become the next leaders of their separate clubs, and they're fighting one common enemy united, there's a better chance of us all making it out of this alive.

Finn's part of the plan, not mine.

See, this meeting wasn't just about gathering information and passing it on to the HOCs; it was also about me coming clean to the HOCs in a safe environment, with Deeds essentially owning up to it as the puppet master pulling my strings.

"Jesus, Lil' Bird, Bodie groans and covers his face. "You're like Mrs. Smith, and you never fucking told me?"

"Would you have believed me?"

He rubs his jaw. "Good point. Maybe. Probably. But I would have had a million questions."

I smirk at this. "No doubt."

"Seriously, bad ass though. Props." He smiles wickedly at me.

Taz smacks him again.

"Fuck, cut that shit out!" Bodie grumbles.

"Then be serious for a second so we can figure this shit out." Taz growls.

Dozer is scowling. "How much of our business did you leak to Deeds, and who has access to it is what I want to know."

"Just me and Bones, my tech guy. And Griz knows everything. He's been in the loop since he figured her out months ago."

"What?" Dozer's gaze snaps to me.

"I met him years ago when you all visited the Greenbacks. Which is when I first realized Finn wasn't dead like I'd thought he was. I'd met Griz then, and when he saw me talking with Deeds at the rally in Reno, he figured it out."

"And you knew all this?" Dozer asks Finn.

"She came clean to me while I was in rehab. This is me, protecting her while also keeping you all informed. We didn't want this falling into the wrong hands or her ass on the line because Deeds wasn't there to back up her story."

Dozer takes his time responding. His gaze travels from Finn to me. Finally, he asks, "What else don't I know?"

I exhale heavily and turn to Finn so he can see the regret on my face. "They got to Mateo. We've taken care of it, but he's pretty messed up over it."

"How?"

"His mom's boyfriend. That lawyer who was always getting the

Thirteen Devils off on technicalities. That was her boyfriend. He was using Mateo's mom as leverage over him, pushing Mateo to prospect into the club, and relay details about when Finn did runs or left the house. They pushed him into selling drugs at school."

"Are you serious?" Bodie's voice is full of fury.

"Yes, we got that info straight from the lawyer," I confirm.

"Right before I shot him and buried his ass." Finn tacks on.

Bodie's hand rubs against his mouth. "Fuck. Right under our fucking noses."

Dozer shares a grim expression with Finn. "Is it possible the others are being manipulated into giving them intel?"

"Grinder, I think so. Stone and Croc, could be, but I don't think so."

Dozer then turns to Deeds. "Tell us the rest."

"The cartel is behind it. They've infiltrated your club by using the Thirteens, and they've infiltrated mine. They're plans are to cut out the middlemen, you could say. Pappy's aware of it, but he thinks we have more time before they make their move. I don't. I'd like to clean house now and face the fallout, but he's not willing to risk it. Thinks it'll set off a chain of events that we're not yet ready for. He'll push it until the last moment, and who knows what that will look like.

Mainly, he wants to keep doing business. Profit as much as possible before all-out war breaks out.

So yeah, we need to know who we can trust, strengthen the club by recruiting the right men, and build alliances before it comes to a head.

If we can hit them with enough force before they're ready, we'll have a better chance of putting the balance of power back in our favor. They don't know we know, and that's our advantage."

"How did you figure this out?" Dozer asks.

"Little things at first and Gypsy." He motions to me. "She's how I knew for sure."

"Lily," Finn says sternly. I roll my eyes at him and grab his thigh. He lays his hand over his mind and grasps it tightly.

Deeds smirks at him. "Sorry, man. Just habit. Lily."

"She was able to confirm some things after working different angles and then shits just been off with the cartel, so we took a page out of their book and got some people on the inside on their side of the border. Once they made their way up the ranks, we were able to confirm that they are planning to eliminate any crews like ours by infiltrating their personnel into our clubs, much like sleeper agents. Like the Thirteens, they are forming crews on this side of the border and pushing their product, running their activities through them. The money all goes south, though, and they want a larger part of the take, so they're cutting out anyone they have to pay to get their shit in and out of the U.S."

"Holy fuck, are you for real, man?" This comes from Bodie. He looks shaken by the news.

Dozer thinks about it all for a long time before he speaks again. "When were you going to share this information with us?"

Deeds purses his lips and shadows flicker over his eyes, because he and I both know what he's about to say isn't going to land well.

"When we had to. When we knew who we could trust."

Dozer stands and lays his hands on the table. "Which was going to be when, never?"

"I don't know, okay! We were still working that part out."

Dozer shakes his head. His icy gaze is leveled on Deeds with deadly intent.

Deeds is completely unaffected by it. If anything, it boils his blood too and fires up that demon that lives under his skin. "Look, asshole. This isn't something you can go sayin' at church. This is who needs to know bullshit, and so far, your club hasn't seen any ill effects. I was making inroads and was gonna come to you when the time was right. This is exactly why I sent, Lily. I needed to know who to trust and who wasn't a rat posing as a HOC."

"Well, you sure and the fuck knew I wasn't."

"Look, man, the point was I didn't know who you would trust with it and didn't have solid information until recently. You can throw shade at me, but I was doing my level best to figure this shit out."

"Why didn't Pappy come to Cap with this. Why you?"

Deeds is silent for way too long.

Dozer reads him, though. "He doesn't want out of business with them, trying to find a way around it."

Deeds just stares back at him, his face blank.

Dozer chuckles humorlessly. "My dad has always said that Pappy valued green more than people's lives, and that was one line the HOCs would never cross. I get it now. Why he left."

"You done?"

Dozer pushes off the table. "Yeah, I'm fuckin' done."

Deeds takes a deep breath. "Don't let this come back to bite me in the ass. Because I'm warning you now, I'll come for you if word of this reaches Pappy."

Finn answers for Dozer because the man is seconds away from throwing a punch. "Understood. We've got as much invested in this as you. All I want to do his protect her and my club."

"I get that, just don't drag my name through the mud if shit goes down, or hell will come callin'."

Finn taps his hand on the table. "Same for us."

Deeds meets Dozer's gaze. "And we agree here and now to keep this between us. Cap and Pappy aren't to know."

Dozer nods, and with that, Deeds stands. He gives me one last lingering look before he turns to leave.

Taz is reluctant to step out of his way, and it's then that Deeds' temper flares to life. "Get the fuck out of my way, before I put you down."

"You could try," Taz grins.

"T, let him go," Dozer snaps.

Taz gives an exaggerated bow as he moves aside.

Deeds only looks back once more. The emotion in his gaze speaks volumes. An ache builds in my chest at the betrayal on his face. Yes, it makes me feel like absolute shit, and I know I'll never forget this moment. But it was the right thing to do. I hope, in time, he'll see that.

Finn's arm comes around me then. I tilt my head and look up at him. "Are you pissed?"

He shakes his head adamantly and places a kiss on my forehead. "No, babe. I'm not pissed."

"Comin' here like you did," Dozer says as he takes Deeds' seat, "was fuckin' dangerous, Lil' Bird. But fuck, you might have just saved all our fuckin' lives by doin' what you did. Thank you."

"What?"

"I'm fuckin' grateful, Lil'. What you did here was fuckin' brave, and if this meeting hadn't happened, who knows what the future would look like for us. Just wanted to say thank you and let you know, we're good."

The emotion trickles in and then rushes in a wave over me. A tear trails down my cheek, and another soon follows. Finn puts his arm around me and pulls me close. He holds me and runs his hand over my back.

I lost my oldest friend today, and it fucking hurts. Yes, I gained the loyalty of men who will be in my life, hopefully for quite a while. I hope the tradeoff is worth it and that, in time, Deeds will eventually forgive me.

"So what the fuck are we gonna do?" I hear Bodie ask.

Dozer's the one who responds. "First things first. We need to get rid of the rats, then we'll figure out the rest."

Taz chuckles, "Let's not sit around all day then. Let's get back and do some hunting."

"Stealthily." Dozer growls. "Which means that no one finds out what we're up to, and when they do disappear, we do it right so no one's the wiser."

"It'll take time and patience," Finn adds, and the others nod in agreement.

"What about Mateo. How do we make sure they don't get to him again?" Bodie asks.

Dozer thinks about it for a moment.

But Finn cuts in. "We bring him in. Let him prospect. Watch over him. He can be Lily's bodyguard because she's also going to need to be watched over. I'll sponsor him, and it'll be his main task. All of us, though, need to keep an eye on him and make sure they can't get to him. We'll send his mom somewhere safe, if we have to."

"Yeah, that's a good idea. Is he up for it, though?"

"He is," Bodie nods. "He's asked me how he would go about joinin' the club. Maybe it was because they were forcin' him to, but nah… I think he was lookin' for a way out. Now that I think about it."

Dozer checks in with the others and meets each of their gazes. "So we let him prospect, and he'll become Lily's shadow."

Finn drums his fingers on the table. "Yeah, I think it's for the best."

Bodie adds. "Me too."

"The kid acts like he's at death's door. But sure. I'm not opposed," Taz voices his opinion. "Just gonna be a mood killer is all."

Dozer shakes his head. "Like you're not?"

"What?"

Dozer waves his hand. "That's neither here nor there. My point is, if we agree, I'll get Cap on board and his blessing when we get back."

The men all nod their assent.

Dozer gets up from the table, and we all follow him out of the Diner.

As I ride on the back of Finn's bike on our way back to New Mexico, I can't help but wonder at how Mateo is going to take the news. We're going to be very close, real soon. I'm not upset about that. It'll give me a chance to get to know him on another level. Maybe then I can figure out how to fix what's broken between him and Finn, and Mateo not being alone might just be what he needs.

It's twenty-one days later, while in a local grocery store shopping for condoms and a few other essential items for the HOCs, when I come across a woman who is the female version of Deeds. She looks so much like him that when I enter the aisle where she's standing, I come to an abrupt halt.

Her hair color is the same shade of auburn, and she also has tan skin for a ginger, which is something you rarely see.

As I tentatively close the distance, I notice the items in her hands, and she raises one and then the other as if she's trying to decide between the two. Condoms, or a pumpkin necklace. When I strike up a conversation with her, what I notice immediately is the look in her eyes. They scream *help me*. I don't know how else to explain it.

So I do.

I offer her a quick escape from the cop following her around the store—a safe haven from whatever else she's running from. Little did I know at the time that she'd become not just a friend, but a sister in every way except by blood. She became the girl with many names, a pumpkin that transformed from a house mouse into one of the strongest females I know.

LOST LYREBIRD

EPILOGUE

Our stories will exist beyond the time we remain on this earth. Make it worthy of being retold.

JUNE 2017

It's a warm summer day, and the sun is reaching its apex in the sky. A breeze picks up strands of my hair and blows a few of them across my face, so I'm constantly tucking those wayward pieces behind my ear. A couple of the hairs are now gray, not a lot, but a few, and I quite like them. I refuse to dye it because I see them more as a badge of honor than anything else.

The tattoos on my body, the gray hairs, the wrinkles around my eyes and mouth speak of a life well-lived, and tell a story. Mine. And that's not something I would ever change. Not a chapter, page, any line, or any single word written in it.

Every so often, a bird or two draws nearer to keep me company while I sit on the blanket and read to him. I know you're not supposed to feed the bird, but I do. I bring dried bread every time I come here and break off little pieces and sprinkle the breadcrumbs in the grass for any bird brave enough to venture closer.

Finn used to give me hell about. He doesn't anymore. So I do what I want, and anyone who has the balls enough to tell me otherwise, I pretty much tell to fuck right the hell off.

I flip to the next page of the book, and tell him about the day we revisited the waterfall and how that too fell into what Finn liked to call the abyss in his mind, where memories would sometimes disappear into. I skim the naughty bits because I imagine hearing about that would be torture, considering the circumstances. Still, I tell him how during our little picnic by the lake, and how we got into a grape fight and how I ended up pelting Finn in the cheek so hard it left a mark, and how he tackled me down to the blanket and tickled me until I damn near peed my pants. Then he'd kissed me for a solid ten minutes straight, and when he pulled back, he told me there was something he'd been thinking about for a while and wanted to talk to me about it.

It was when he told me he was ready. Ready to have kids with me, or at least try. Maybe just the one, and he wanted to know if that was something I was open to.

Through my tears that bubbled up out of nowhere, I had nodded rapidly and yanked him down for another long kiss. It had been on my mind for months.

I'd often study little kids and mothers in particular. At first, I didn't understand the feelings it had stirred up inside of me, but as time passed, I realized that the warm feeling, the flutter in my stomach, the swelling of my heart as I saw the two interact, was something I began to ache for and want for my own.

But I was scared. I hadn't had the best mother, and although I had many friends with their children. I had even helped them out a bunch. I'd become the best aunt any kid could hope for. Being a mother, though, that was a dance and a role I didn't exactly know how to fill.

I'd seen it everywhere I looked. With Ember and Willow, and her other two little ones. With Bethany and her brood. Bodie and his crazy duo.

But yeah, I just wasn't sure if I'd be any good at it, but I wanted to try. I wanted to see where that road led, and just like I put my heart and soul into everything I did, I planned to do that with motherhood too.

As I tell him this part of the story, tears begin to fall from my face as I read the words out loud. They're happy tears. I keep reading and flipping through the pages. I tell him about the pregnancy. The god awful pregnancy that had me rethinking motherhood. I tell him how I got as big as a house and how Finn made sure to tell me each day how fantastic and sexy I was, even though I clearly wasn't.

I tell him the miserable ten hours of labor, and then about her birth, and how Finn had picked out the name Madison. He chose it because it was a play on both his dad's middle name and Mateo's name. Frankly, Finn thought it was hilarious. We'd have two mad kids, and it sort of fit us.

I pause at the end of the chapter, and speak freely so I can relay the truth and explain how the one thing Finn didn't count on with naming our daughter Madison, or Maddie for short, was how freaking confusing it was, because no one knows who we were talking about— our older son or our little girl.

It's at that point that I hear footsteps and look behind me to see Lacy, my little sister, walking towards me. She's more wiry than I am, and taller, with honey blonde hair that rests just below her shoulders. She's wearing ripped jeans, flip-flops, and a hippie-themed graphic T-shirt.

"Hey," she says as she takes a seat on the blanket beside me.

"Hey, yourself". I pull her immediately into a hug. When we pull away, I smooth some hair away from her cheek and smile. "How'd you find me?"

"Stopped by the new house. Finn said I'd find you here."

"I thought you weren't getting into town until tomorrow." I eye her nude makeup and the slight sunburn on her skin, which is probably from her driving here in her Jeep with the top down.

"I decided to take a sick day so I could get here a day earlier and spend a four-day weekend with my favorite niece."

"She's a handful, isn't she?"

She laughs and nods. "Yeah, she's like a mini you. When I pulled away from the house, she was doing cartwheels on the lawn in her Tinker Bell wings and a purple tutu. She did so many she fell right back down the minute she stood up."

I shake my head and laugh along with her.

"And Finn?"

"He was on the porch step, drinking coffee and watching her. Are you kidding? She wouldn't let him out of her sight. She was all 'Daddy, watch this. Daddy, look what I can do.'"

A grin overtakes my face, and I huff out a laugh. Because, yes, she has him completely wrapped around her finger, and if that girl loves anything, it's playing dressup and performing for not just Finn, but anyone who comes to our house to visit.

I indulge her, and sometimes, I even put on a costume of my own, and we play make-believe. Whether we're fairies, pirates, or superheroes, we go all in, and every so often, we wrangle Finn into participating in our adventures.

"So whatcha doin'?" Lacy eyes the open book on my lap and Finn's dad's headstone.

"Just reading to him. It's something Finn and I do." I close the book on my lap and shrug.

Lacy tilts her head and gives me a warm smile. "Do I ever get to hear this story of yours. Well, I guess yours and Finn's."

"You can buy it and read it, you know. It's online."

"Yeah, I know, but I want you to tell it to me."

Moisture builds behind my eyes, and I shake my head and look up for a moment as I try to fight the tears back.

"Fuck. I hate getting older. The hormones are the freaking worst. It's like being pregnant all over again."

"It's called being in touch with your emotions. You'll get used to it."

"Yeah, no thanks. I'd rather not," I say as I get to my feet.

"Yeah, I'm not sure I'm going to like that part either." She bites her bottom lip and looks down at the ground, and then back up at me. Her eyes dart away.

"What?"

For the first time, I fully take her in. When she rests her hand over the small bump showing from under her shirt, my brain nearly explodes.

"No…"

She takes a long inhale and nods. "Don't be mad. It just sort of happened the last time I came to visit. It was that night you and Finn left early from Hodge's. Bodie and I started talking and dancing, and one thing led to another. That's the other reason I'm here. Bodie wants to give things a go and wants to take care of me while I go through this part."

"Bodie's the father?"

She pauses and bites her nail, then nods slowly.

"Son of a…"

Fear and concern flood into her features. Ohhh… she should be concerned because I'm going to fucking kill him.

I snatch up the blanket. When I stand, I tuck the blanket and book into the crook of my arm and start marching toward the parking lot.

"Where are you going?"

"To murder him. I warned him if he touched you, I'd shoot him in his dick."

She chases after me. She even jumps into the passenger side of my Range Rover so she can try to talk me down from killing my husband's best friend. My best friend. But between the out-of-control hormones I've been experiencing, the hot sun, and the fact that he broke the one rule of our friendship, he'll be lucky if he has a dick tomorrow, or sees another day.

THE END

AUTHOR NOTE

A story that took ten years to write and spans ten years.
Fate or a coincidence.
I know which one I'll believe.
Lost Lyrebird has been beautifully reimagined into what it has become today,
and I'm thankful for all the pieces I found to add to it along the way.
This one was definitely a journey I'll never forget.

ACKNOWLEDGEMENTS

Wow… this somehow seems more daunting than writing a new chapter, because ten years is a long freaking time to summarize all of the Thank You's I owe so many people. First, I would like to thank my mother and sister. They are the pillars of our family and of my strength. They truly hold me up when I need it the most, and always make me laugh, sometimes at the most inappropriate things. They don't let me disappear from reality for too long, check on me constantly, and bring me back to the real world when I get too far down my fictional rabbit hole.

Thank you to the rest of my family for the constant positivity and support. The love you give is unconditional, and I appreciate that more than you know. I wouldn't be this creative without all the stories I grew up hearing from family members, or the good times we've shared. Uncle John…*cough*, you might just be the funniest person I know. My family is epic, and they are the reason I am the way I am. As we say, the crazy trickles down through our DNA.

Thank you to all my loved ones for your support, for always being a listening ear, and encouraging me to keep writing.

Thank you to my not-so-little minions for your patience and never letting me get a big head about literally anything, because you know, I'm just your mom. You three have grown alongside me on this journey, and I know what was sacrificed to make this possible. I love you so much for letting me do this and being okay with crappy meals when I'm in my editing phase. Thanks for rolling with the punches life has thrown at us and sticking by my side through it all.

Thank you to all the people who encouraged and supported me throughout this journey. This includes so many things: author social media support, edits, beta reading, proofreading, marketing graphics, shares, and comments.

Eliza has been a true lifesaver, and I can never repay you for jumping in to help me when I needed it most. Thank you for everything!

Thank you to my fabulous, patient, kind, and supportive HOC Honey's, which has become my Briar Patch Team/Street Team. I am so freakin' grateful for every single one of you. You have been vocal, positive, and helpful. Thank you a hundred times over for all you do, have done, and for your continued support. These wonderful people include my Hype Team, Streat Team, beta readers, and proofreaders. Thank you to Paula, Alesha, Angi, Andrea, Josh, Wendy, Heather, Ash, Mel, Alyssa, Heidi, Katherine, Yondette, Kelli, Kate, Jonesy, Brenna, Precious, JennyT, Rachel, Kellie, Katherine, Sarah, Linda, and Melissa. I'm so sorry if I forgot anyone.

Thank you to Heather Firth, Joe Arden, The Real Joe Arden Team, and Blue Nose Audio. I'm writing this pre-audiobook record, but I know it will be a fantastic work of art, and I trust you all to do my words justice and bring this book to life in the best way possible. I realize it's a big ask because it's a massive book, with heavy emotional scenes, and a plethora of characters, but I'm confident that I've found the right voice actors for this project. I appreciate you taking this on, and I look forward to hearing the finished audiobook.

Thank you to all my Audio Attic and Romance Book World friends. You provided a wealth of positivity and creative inspiration, which helped bring this book baby to life.

Thank you to every supportive reader who created graphics, edits, shared a book review or post, liked or commented, or supported me in any way. As an indie author, I'm deeply appreciative of all you do to help spread the word about my book and the support you give. Please know everything you do doesn't go unnoticed or unappreciated. Thank you!

Thank you to all the Booktokers who also use your platform to promote or review romance books. We love you and appreciate you!

Thank you to all the third parties who helped make this possible: Roz & Taylor, Grey's Promotions, Pretty Little Images, Dream Echo

Designs, Hunter at BB Editing, and the artists who continue to make creative works that help bring my books and characters to life in a whole new way.

Thank you, Dad. You may not be here to read this, but I know you're watching over me and holding my hand through every single journey I take. This one's for you.

My Free Bird

ABOUT THE AUTHOR

Darby Briar is an American author who loves writing stories about men with broken souls and women who don't know their own strength. She's a lover of fiction and epic stories, but prefers stories with hard-won romance and ones that include an ending worthy of their struggle. She grew up in Utah and still lives in the northern part of the state. She has three adorable mini adults, whom Darby refers to as her minions.

She credits her grandma as a big influence on her love of romance dramas. She grew up sitting next to her as she watched soap operas, and Darby distinctly remembers the "scandelicous" books sitting out in the open on her coffee table.

Darby took a few years off writing to raise her kids and is finishing up her degree in Creative Writing.

For special editions, book swag, to join her newsletter, and for more information
visit Darby's pages below.
Website: **www.darbybriar.com**
Special editions are available on her Website for
Burning Ember
A Perfect Christmas with Chaos
Follow on Amazon
Tiktok: @darbybriarauthor
Instagram
Pinterest: **PinterestInstagram: @darbybriarauthor**
FB: Author Darby Briar
Goodreads

I love to hear from readers.

Let me know which HOC is your favorite and whose story you want to see next.

TRIGGER WARNINGS

Use of Nicknames & Terminology: Some characters in this book use nicknames or language that may be considered derogatory. These choices are meant to reflect the mindset of certain characters and create an authentic, immersive setting. One example is the name *Gypsy*, which is used by the Greenbacks as a nickname for Lily.

Abuse and Trauma
Addiction
Age Gap
Anxiety and Fear
Death of a Loved One
Death of a Parent
Drug Use
Emotional Manipulation
Emotional Trauma
Gaslighting
Graphic Language
Human Trafficking
Mental Illness
Military Combat-related Incident, Injury, Death, and PTSD
Murder
Obsessive Behavior
Past Sexual Exploitation
Psychological Trauma
Self-Destructive Behavior
Self-Harm

LOST LYREBIRD

Sex between Non-MMC
Sexually Explicit Scenes
Sexual Abuse
Stalking
Suicidal Thoughts
Torture